# Praise for the Marq'ssan Cycle

...SF on a broader scale...its metaphors apply to a very human tangle of loyalty and betrayal, politics and idealism—Wells and Orwell updated....

—*Locus*, June 2005

The third volume of the Marq'ssan cycle, *Tsunami*, confirms what the second volume, *Renegade*, made clear: the narrative drive and sheer invention of the work is more than up to the size, scope, and ambition of this extraordinary project. What a grand job! What a great read! It's been a long time since I've read science fiction with such a dramatic grip on the political complexities of our slow progress toward the better world we all wish for.

—Samuel R. Delany, author of *Dhalgren* and *Trouble on Triton*

"[Duchamp] overwhelmingly rises to the challenges she sets herself through the nuanced development of strong characters over the course of these first three volumes of the Marq'ssan Cycle..."

—Amy J. Ransom, *NYRSF*, April 2007

"...easily one of the best science fiction series I've read in years. It strips bare the arbitrary structures of our world (sexuality, gender, government) and rebuilds them in complex, new structures that are strikingly at odds with our experience...."

—Sean Melican, *Ideomancer*, March 2007

"...the closest comparison one might give is to some of Le Guin's later work—no small recommendation. Worth looking for."

—*Asimov's*, June 2006

"[T]hose with a serious interest in dystopias and particularly the feminist version thereof should find L. Timmel Duchamp's Marq'ssan Cycle a rewarding experience."

—*NYRSF*, December 2005

"Politically savvy and philosophically relevant, this title puts a human face on today's problems."

—*Library Journal*, June 15, 2005

# Blood in the Fruit

# Books by L. Timmel Duchamp

*Love's Body, Dancing in Time*

*The Grand Conversation*

*Red Rose Rages (Bleeding)*


The Marq'ssan Cycle

*Alanya to Alanya*

*Renegade*

*Tsunami*


Edited by L. Timmel Duchamp

*Talking Back*

*WisCon Chronicles, Vol 1*

# Blood in the Fruit

*Book Four of the Marq'ssan Cycle*

by L. Timmel Duchamp

Aqueduct Press, PO Box 95787
Seattle, WA 98145-2787
www.aqueductpress.com

Library of Congress Control Number: 2007907251

ISBN: 978-1-933500-15-7
ISBN-10: 1-933500-15-8
First Edition, First Printing, January 2008


16 15 14 13 12 11 10 09 08     1 2 3 4 5


COVER ACKNOWLEDGMENTS
Cover Design by Lynne Jensen Lampe
Cover photos Ocotillo, Sunset, Prisoner: © Royalty-Free/CORBIS
Cover photo of Emma Goldman speaking in Union Square, © Bettmann/ CORBIS collection
Cover photo of Red Square, Courtesy University of Washington Libraries Special Collections, UWC0121
Book Design by Kathryn Wilham

Fingers Touching by Lori Hillard



This book was set in a digital version of Monotype Walbaum, available through AGFA Monotype. The original typeface was designed by Justus Erich Walbaum.



Printed in the USA by Thomson-Shore, Inc, Dexter, MI

For Kathryn Wilham and Elizabeth Walter

## ACKNOWLEDGMENTS

During the months in which I composed the third and fourth books of the Marq'ssan Cycle I read widely in the human rights literature. The works that stand out in my mind today are Jacobo Timerman, *Prisoner without a Name, Cell without a Number*, Elaine Scarry, *The Body in Pain*, the American Association for the Advancement of Science volume, *The Breaking of Bodies and Minds: Torture, Psychiatric Abuse, and the Health Professions* (eds. Eric Stover and Elena O. Nightingale, MD), *Mission to South Africa: The Commonwealth Report*, and *Psychological Operations in Guerrilla Warfare: The CIA's Nicaragua Manual* (published in a single volume with essays by Washington Post reporter Joanne Omang and NYU law professor and Vice Chairman of America's Watch and Helsinki Watch Aryeh Neier). Glancing through the shelves in my library groaning with these and other books, I could not help shivering when my eye lighted on the illustrated pamphlet put out by the CIA titled *The Freedom Fighter's Manual*, which provides simple instructions in Spanish for carrying out numerous tactics of sabotage that would be invaluable for any would-be terrorist today; as I recall, this manual for sabotage simply confirmed what I had been reading about CIA tactics and ideas about civil order. As I've noted previously, although everything about Security Services, a fictional government agency of the equally fictitious Executive, is a product of my imagination, I found three books of great assistance in structuring my creation of this fictional institution: Philip Agee's *Inside the Company: CIA Diary*; Victor Marchetti's *The CIA and the Cult of Intelligence*; and John Stockwell's *In Search of Enemies: A CIA Story*.

It gives me great pleasure to thank the numerous individuals who, over the course of the two decades since I first drafted *Blood in the Fruit*, read the novel in ms and offered me usefully frank comments on it. Among these I especially appreciate the efforts and support of Tom Duchamp, Dr. Joan Haran, Professor Ann Hibner Koblitz, and Elizabeth Walter. The critiques they offered were a labor of love; I will always be grateful to them for their engagement with my work. Kathryn Wilham, who edited *Blood in the Fruit*, was absolutely key from the beginning; her confidence in my vision for the Marq'ssan Cycle was vital to my completing and then deciding to publish it.

Since woman's greatest misfortune has been that she was looked upon as either angel or devil, her true salvation lies in being placed on earth; namely, in being considered human, and therefore subject to all human follies and mistakes.

—Emma Goldman

The individual is the heart of society, conserving the essence of social life; society is the lungs which are distributing the element to keep the life essence—that is, the individual— pure and strong.

—Emma Goldman

There is not a single penal institution or reformatory in the United States where men are not tortured "to be made good," by means of the black-jack, the club, the strait-jacket, the water-cure, the "humming bird" (an electrical contrivance run along the human body), the solitary, the bull-ring, and starvation diet. In these institutions his will is broken, his soul degraded, his spirit subdued by the deadly monotony and routine of prison life. In Ohio, Illinois, Pennsylvania, Missouri, and in the South, these horrors have become so flagrant as to reach the outside world, while in most other prisons the same Christian methods still prevail. But prison walls rarely allow the agonized shrieks of the victims to escape—prison walls are thick, they dull the sound. Society might with greater immunity abolish all prisons at once, than to hope for protection from these twentieth-century chambers of horrors.

—Emma Goldman (1910)

# Chapter One

Speeding away from the island, the boat bumped over the surface of the sea as though it were a washboard. The violent jolts and loud slaps, steady and rhythmical, drove the Mozart out of her head and stilled her fingers' movement on the imaginary keyboard she had made of the railing. She loved the wild violence of the wind tearing through her hair, whipping into her eyes. It helped her forget that stifling house, clearing her head of its suffocating opulence, its demand that all speech be muffled, all laughter be smothered. As far as she could tell only her music ever pierced its hush. The staff crept about so silently, their voices so discreetly lowered, that she could not imagine that any of them had the faintest breath of life in them. How different from her grandmother's house, where people sang and laughed and joked—outside her grandmother's presence, of course, but perceptibly, all over the house—and where there had been those who would tease her, making her giggle and shriek until her throat was too full of phlegm to talk. There were none like that here. But then, except for one woman, the entire staff consisted of men. What else could you expect from a house full of males?

Gray and heavy, the horizon stretched endlessly, looming low over the waves spuming sick green-gray and brown foam. She would ask him to replace the worst of her tutors. It was worth a try. He had said, after all, that if she "gave them a chance" a while longer and she still could not stand them, he'd consent to their being replaced. Of course he didn't want to bother. That was the real reason behind his reluctance to change them. She had given up on persuading him to any larger concessions. He certainly wouldn't let her return to Barbados; nor would he let her return to Crowder's, which though horrible was not quite as bad as exile here. She saw now that she could have gotten used to Crowder's, could have gotten used to all the nonsense enforced at schools—for then, at least, she wouldn't have been so alone, so swallowed up by silence as she was here.

Alexandra blinked and held her face tight to keep the threatened tears at bay. "Don't feel sorry for yourself, it does no good," she imagined Mama saying to her. And she reminded herself: You're a woman now, Alexandra. You're sixteen. Self-pity is childish. And it could be worse.

Could it? Alexandra found that hard to believe. Even her mother admitted it was bad. But then the very thought of being around him turned Mama's stomach. He wasn't as bad as he'd first seemed, though. Once you understood how sad and lonely he was, it was easy to see why he got so nasty at times. He needed someone to take care of him.

But not me, Alexandra protested under her breath. Not me, I hardly know him. If Elizabeth hadn't left him like that, everything would have been all right. He claimed Elizabeth owed him an infinite amount of loyalty and gratitude. Elizabeth's letter, though, put it differently. Alexandra's heart lifted at the thought that Elizabeth had cared enough about her to risk sending it. Elizabeth had been worried that she might feel abandoned by her, had wanted her to know that things were more complicated—and uglier—than she, Alexandra, would ever know. Surely Elizabeth had been right to go like that if there were no other way for her to have gotten free of a burden she could no longer bear? Mama had been so evasive, so cagey when talking about Elizabeth. And then had suddenly given her that shivery serious look and said, "It will be up to you now, Alexandra. Without Elizabeth to manage him you'll have to learn how to do it. You know how he feels about me. There's only you, now." And then all that talk about Daniel, about how Papa had "given up on him." Mama always talked in that vague, hard-to-understand way whenever the subject was something important, as though she didn't really want her to understand.

Alexandra realized that some of the wet was not sea spray, but rain. In this climate she always felt chilled to the bone—except, of course, when sitting in the bath or sauna or before a wood fire. Even during the summer she'd found her fingers cold and stiff enough to make playing difficult. But no one else up here seemed to notice the cold. They said that sometimes it snowed here. What would it be like, snow on the ocean and on the beach? Would ice cover the rocks even with the surf crashing over them? Alexandra stared down into the water and thought of how cold it must be. Hypothermia in ten or fifteen minutes, Peters often mumbled at her to try to get her to stay inside the cabin. "Don't want to fall in, Ms. Sedgewick, do you. Hypothermia in ten or fifteen minutes for someone with *your* build." Of course he just wanted to make her uncomfortable. Mama had explained about how Papa's Higgins-run staff would regard her as a nuisance and possible threat.

Everything was so complicated, so *dark*. Not like Barbados where everything was light, simple, open, *warm*. Most of the people on Papa's staff were just plain creepy. *Whatever you do, darling, don't ask questions about anything you don't understand. Security people don't like questions.* So she followed Mama's advice and tried figuring things out for herself. *Security people*, Mama said: even though he was "on leave," probably for good. And when explaining about why everyone was after Elizabeth, Mama had said that as far as Security people were concerned, once a Security person always a Security person: retirement or leave only referred to stopping work, not stopping being that kind of person, anymore than someone could stop being an executive. Elizabeth, for instance, would always be an executive, no matter that she had gone renegade. Certain things were immutable.

Alexandra spotted land. Finally! The cold had been close to driving her into the cabin, but she knew she could hold out the few minutes more. These Wednesday afternoon runs to the mainland were always the same, of course, but they broke the dullness and silence and sameness of the house. What if she went the other two afternoons a week, too? Would she still feel that way? For Peters the run was probably boring, maybe even irksome. How many times had he done it in his life? But of course being sub-exec and male he might stop in at that tavern down the block from the post office, which would give him an interest. Did Peters do those sorts of things? According to Nicole, all Papa's gorillas sat around gambling and drinking all the time they weren't on duty. And went to the mainland once a week to visit the town's only prostitute. Shivering, Alexandra pulled her cape more tightly around her body. A cup of hot cider would be perfect now. She'd have Peters make her something hot on the way back. Tea, probably, would be all they'd have available. Mama, of course, would know how to go about stocking up this boat if she knew she'd be riding in it once a week. Well, she'd just have to make herself learn to do those things, too. No one was going to do them for her.

The motor cut out. The rush of silence roared in Alexandra's ears as the boat drifted toward the dock and the now-operating magnetic field in the prow drew the boat into the berth. Smoothly, with the usual audible snick and whine, the boat's lock engaged. Alexandra disembarked, walked the few steps to the autos parked only yards from the dock, and snugged down into the little one-seater. She drove to town, aware that as usual the buses leaving from the fish processing plant were about half a minute's drive to the east. Had Peters (or whoever else had been coming in for the mail and supplies all these years) always timed it so that one came to the intersection of the town's main street with that road going out to the factory just before all those buses did? *She'd* never know, because she'd never want to make as much conversation with Peters as would be necessary to elicit such information. Those buses going to and from the factory must be the most stir—apart from the islanders' visits—the town ever experienced. Nicole said there was no longer any vid reception this far out in the wilds, so that left only the radio, a slow version of the internet, and DVDs. How did the people living here stand it? No wonder they never smiled at her when she smiled at them. They'd probably forgotten how. Like everyone (except on rare occasions, Nicole) in that house. No wonder Papa said he was "in exile." No one could possibly *choose* to live in such a place.

She parked outside the post office, within three yards of its door in case the call included parcels, as often happened. She hopped out of the auto and glanced up and down the street. Not a soul, of course: only a mangy, one-eyed, marmalade tom watching her from the window of the hardware store. Sighing, Alexandra pulled open the heavy glass door. Vernier, seated on her stool behind the counter and listening (as usual) to a soap on the radio, watched her come in. Alexandra wondered if Vernier had ever in her life cracked even one smile—even as a kid, which Alexandra found hard to believe someone as spare and gray and sere as the postmaster had ever been...

"Good afternoon," Alexandra said, approaching the counter.

"Afternoon, Ms. Sedgewick."

Alexandra handed her the large leather bag. "It's a pretty chilly day," she said.

Vernier grunted, then turned away from the counter and shuffled into the back room. Alexandra leaned against the counter and stared at the pictures of vid-stars plastering the walls of Vernier's domain. In one picture a man and a woman—dressed like executives—gazed into one another's eyes as they held glasses of champagne in toasting position. Did the people who wrote or designed such things realize the preposterousness of it? If they did, they must be terribly cynical, laughing up their sleeves at the millions who were addicted to such images. If they didn't, they were pretty out of it. Either way, the picture made Alexandra queasy.

Vernier returned with the leather bag hooked over her shoulder. "Here's all the flat stuff," she said, dumping the bag onto the counter. "But there're some packages, too."

She couldn't recapture last week's excitement over all the parcels that had come for her birthday, but there might still be other things for her. The scores and compact discs she'd ordered in September, for one thing. Or clothing. Mama and Grandmother were always sending her clothing, though it was doubtful she'd be getting anything from them so soon after her birthday.

After a long, boring five minutes Vernier finally appeared with a dolly-load of parcels. Flipping a section of the counter up to let herself out, she wheeled the dolly out into the customers' side. When Alexandra reached for the leather bag, Vernier said sharply, "I'll get that as long as I'm taking all this stuff out to your vehicle. You can hold the door open for me."

Alexandra moved ahead of Vernier, pushed open the door, and stood outside with her back against it while Vernier trundled past. Alexandra then unlocked the carrier set into the roof of the auto and watched as Vernier unloaded the dolly into it. "See you next week," Alexandra said when Vernier had finished.

"Good-bye, Ms. Sedgewick." Vernier turned and went back into the post office. Alexandra looked up and down the deserted street, got into the auto, and started the motor. Vernier was the only woman other than Nicole she had seen in the last two months. But she was so aloof she might as well not even be there.

Alexandra spent the return crossing inside the cabin with Peters, sipping tea and sorting the mail. Her haul was above average—letters from Grandfather Raines, Sarah, and Mama, and two packages. She would wait until she got home to open anything. Having Peters there would ruin everything. Except for a letter for Professor Hands, the rest of the mail was for Papa, of course.

As they docked, Alexandra observed the small jet parked next to her father's at one end of the landing strip. No one ever came to the island—not even Mama. In fact, Mama sent her letters to the Georgetown house, from which they were forwarded, precisely because Papa insisted that the tightest secrecy of his whereabouts be maintained. She stared hard at the plane, and her pulse quickened. Could he have changed his mind and allowed a visit here? As a special— late—birthday present? He was always giving her things for no reason at all. Maybe he had finally figured out that visits from Grandmother or Mama would be better presents than things like jewelry.

Alexandra went in as usual through the northeast door. Higgins was waiting for her. "Your father asked me to tell you that tea with him is canceled today and that he won't be able to see you until dinner." He spoke stiffly and kept his eyes fixed on a spot on the wall behind her. But then he never made eye-contact with her. The only person Higgins ever seemed to actually look at was her father.

"That plane outside…?"

Higgins's pasty face gave nothing away. "A visitor who's with your father right now."

"Oh," Alexandra said. "I see." She moved past him and slowly ascended the staircase. At the landing she paused for a moment to listen to the silence before heading to the east wing. She would light the fire in the Music Room and read her letters and have tea there. It would be fun skipping those long two-plus hours with him.

In the east wing the wind howled and the waves seemed almost to be thumping the house. Alexandra went into the Music Room and dumped her mail and parcels on the sofa. Before even taking off her cape she went to the fireplace, grabbed one of the long matches from the basket on the mantelshelf, and crouched to light the ready-laid

fire. But she froze when she heard the word "Weatherall" eerily pro-
jected within the cavernous hollow of the fireplace. "Hill wants to
know whether it's possible she could still get into Security's system
if she tried to," the same voice went on. It must, Alexandra thought,
be coming from the Small Study, which was directly below the Music
Room, somehow carried up by the shared chimney. They must be
standing right by the fireplace, or maybe sitting in the padded leather
chairs flanking it.

Her father's rumble was much lower, much less audible. Alexandra
strained to hear. "...likely. If you want to be sure, you'll have to...the
whole damned system." Alexandra could barely make out her father's words.

"Would it be possible for her to dip into files and then destroy
them afterwards?" the other man said, *his* voice clear and distinct.

"If she can get in at all, yes," her father said, his voice appreciably
louder. "Why, has a file disappeared?"

"Several recon satellite picture and analysis files, all of them to
do with those training camps the Free Zone bitches are operating.
Whoever broke in wiped every damned file, right after which the
aliens zapped every fucking one of our recon sats."

After a few very long seconds, during which Alexandra remembered her mother's warning that she not under any circumstances listen to anything to do with Security business, not even if her father
wished her to—*The less you know, the safer you are. You never know,
Alexandra, you never know what to expect. You mustn't eavesdrop, you
mustn't let him talk to you about any of it. Clear?* —her father's voice,
unusually loud and distinct, floated up the chimney: "I suggest you
take it that there's a serious likelihood she's gone to work for the aliens,
Wedgewood. That kind of coincidence can't be accidental."

"There's more, sir," the other voice said.

"Go on."

"The aliens have been making one strike a month against corporate
targets. For four consecutive months they've hit in descending order
of importance companies Booth has major holdings in. Nobody knows
for sure how much he's lost, but it has to be considerable. Probably
between twenty-five and thirty-five percent of his entire holdings."

Her father made a barking sound Alexandra identified as a laugh. "That cinches it, Wedgewood. There's no other way the aliens could know his portfolio. She kept tabs on it, I know that for a fact. And if there's anyone that bitch would be after—besides myself—it would be Booth...Booth first, and then me."

After a long pause the other man said, "Hill is pressuring me to divulge your whereabouts. He's damned anxious about you."

"Hill can fuck himself."

"He's been breathing down my neck on this. And considering his shake-up—which is still on-going—it's not clear I won't be canned, too, if I don't give him *some*thing."

"Balls. He's purged everyone who's demonstrated long-term loyalty to Weatherall. You weren't one of them. He knows he can't run the Company without the help of old-timers. He'll keep you on at least until he thinks he's figured out how to run Security Services. Not that he'll ever be able to, not Hill. After all, *we* told *him* how to run the Justice Department. And Booth knows squat about Security."

"It's a godawful mess, I have to say that."

"Damned straight it is."

There was a silence. Alexandra, noticing that her thighs had cramped, scratched the tip of the match over a brick, watched the match flare into flame, and touched the flame to the screws of paper nestled among the kindling. She stood up and stepped back from the fireplace. She shouldn't have listened, she thought. If he were to find out... Pushing aside the ugly memory of the scene they'd had over Elizabeth, Alexandra backed away from the fireplace and glanced over her shoulder at the closed, though not locked, door. Someone could have come into the room and caught her eavesdropping. She had been stupid, terribly stupid. She picked up the remote to the compact disc player and cued up the recording of Avison concerti. Then she took her handset from her pocket and ordered tea. Finally, she turned to the parcels. The largest one held scores. She glanced through them and laid them aside. If the visitor continued to occupy Papa, she could sight-read through some of them after dinner. The other parcel, she saw as she stared at the address label, had originally been sent to Crowder's, and had then been forwarded to Georgetown, and from there to here. Odd. Surely everyone who knew she had gone to Crowder's knew she had left there not long after she'd arrived. It must have been a mistake by a service-tech who'd been given the old address through careless-ness. That kind of thing sometimes happened.

Pulling the plastifoam away she found four elegant, leather-bound books. She opened one of them and saw that it had been specially done with thick vellum pages and old-fashioned type. She'd seen such books in the library downstairs and also in the Georgetown house, but had never owned one. As she leafed through the one titled *The Oppoponax*, a slip of flimsy fell out. Curious, Alexandra unfolded and read it.

9 October, 2086

Alexandra,

I didn't forget your birthday, love. This should reach you by the thirteenth, though I can't be sure. I'm sorry I won't be there to sponsor you at the Diana. But of course Felice will see to that for you.

I think of you often and wish I could be there to see you come into your womanhood. You have wonderful experiences ahead of you, for however the fixed males want us to envy their lack, the fact is that we, not they, have the joy of incomparable pleasure, and this is something it is impossible to regret, however much they would like us to.

You must immediately destroy the wrappings the books came in (and don't even look at the data markings on the label if you haven't already done so), as well as this flimsy—unless, of course, you choose to betray me, but I don't believe for a minute that you would.

I hope, love, that your exile from Barbados is growing less painful with time. You must keep remembering that when you come legally of age you will have the right to choose. And in the meantime, seize whatever pleasure comes your way, in whatever form. And don't forget your

Elizabeth, who cares for you.

Alexandra held the flimsy to her cheek. She wished she could keep it, but she knew it would be too dangerous for Elizabeth if she did. After reading it over one more time she wadded it up and gathered the wrappings and mailing label. These she carried to the fireplace.

She hesitated. Before consigning them to flames, she pulled out the mailing label and stared at it. Regina, Saskatchewan, the label named the parcel's point of origin. Alexandra threw everything into the fire, seized the poker, and moved the papers around until they had all burned. Then she set the firescreen in place and returned to the sofa. How could she explain such lovely books to Papa? But he never went into her bedroom suite. And besides, he would probably assume Grandmother or Grandfather had given them to her. It would never occur to him that Elizabeth might contact her.

Saskatchewan…Elizabeth was in Saskatchewan now. That earlier letter had been from Ontario. But how dangerous, her sending things to Crowder's: if Alexandra had not been the one to get the mail today, her father might have seen the parcel and expressed curiosity. Or someone at the Georgetown house might have opened it. Tears came into Alexandra's eyes. Elizabeth must care a great deal for her to take that kind of risk.

She picked up the books without even looking at the other three titles and carried them to her room. She would not risk the chance of someone's seeing them in the Music Room.

When she returned, wearing a shawl instead of the cape and with her hair freshly brushed, she found that the tea tray had been left on the coffee table. Brioche and jam, of course. Nicole always made brioche for Wednesday tea, poppy-seed cake for Thursday, and custard tart on Mondays. The other days were "free days," as Nicole called them. When Alexandra had asked her why on Mondays, Wednesdays, and Thursdays she invariably baked the same things for tea, Nicole had said, "How should I know what's going through your father's head? Maybe it's the only way he can keep track of the days of the week. You think of a better answer than that, tell me. Or better yet, ask him why yourself. I'm just the cook here. I do what I'm told to do."

"Just the cook," though, apparently carried clout within the household power structure, for Alexandra had noticed how careful her father's gorillas were to stay out of her way—though their inclination, as unfixed males, was otherwise. Probably it was difficult to get a cook as good as Nicole to live in this godforsaken place. Since Alexandra had taken over the household accounts from Higgins, she knew that Nicole got paid three times as much as any other service-tech in the household. That kind of salary told its own tale.

Alexandra set the tray down on the rug in front of the fire and settled against a pile of cushions to munch the buttery brioche, sip the tangy herb tea, and read her letters. If it were always like this she might not mind being here. But tomorrow they'd be back to the same old dreary routine, lessons in the morning, piano practice in the afternoon, and her father in the evenings. How nice it would be to snuggle up beside Mama or Grandmother right now, with Mama laughing at something droll her latest girl had been saying, while the girl winked at her, Alexandra, as though to laugh at all of them—herself, Mama, and Alexandra. Would those days ever return? Probably not. Everything would be different when she came of age. She would be a fully grown woman then, and Mama would probably act toward her the way Grandmother acted toward Mama.

Alexandra pressed back her tears—stupid self-pity! she scolded herself—and opened Grandfather's letter first. She would save Mama's for last. They were so silly they invariably made her laugh.

[ii]

Before going down to dinner, Alexandra phoned Higgins for possible instructions, but Higgins said only that she'd be dining with her father and that she was to go down to the Small Study just before eight as usual. From her dressing-room window Alexandra could see the plane down on the landing strip, so she knew the visitor hadn't left. It had been months since dinner on weeknights had included anyone other than herself and her father. It felt like years, though, when she thought of it. She'd dined with her father every night since that single week with Mama in Montreal in July. The addition on Saturday nights of whomever of her tutors happened to have stayed on the island for the weekend made little difference, for they were all subdued around him. It had been three months since that week with Mama. It felt like an eternity: time passed excruciatingly slowly here.

At three minutes to eight by the jeweled watch her father had given her for her birthday, Alexandra tapped on the closed door of the Small Study, turned the ornate glass and brass doorknob, pushed the door open, and stepped in. They had the gas lit in here instead of the electric lights, imbuing the room with its full gothic flavor. Alexandra glanced at her father's face first, to gauge certain things: his mood, his level of inebriation, his attitude toward the man seated in the other padded leather chair. Given the conversation about Elizabeth she had overheard, Alexandra expected to find his mood horrible. But when he saw her the corners of his mouth contorted in the grimace Alexandra had come to accept as a smile, so she knew that against all odds his mood was *good*—and that for some reason he was pleased to see her.

"Alexandra, I'd like you to meet Philip Wedgewood. He's Director of the Division of Security Central in Security Services."

Wedgewood rose to his feet. Conscious of her duty, Alexandra stared into the chilly blue eyes and offered her hand. He gave off creepy vibes as only Security people did, and his handshake was limp and clammy. Alexandra covertly wiped her hand on her thick Shetland and angora tunic and returned the empty formula demanded by his saying he was pleased to meet her. She tried to remember an occasion on which she had seen a male executive shaking hands with her mother, but none occurred to her.

Papa moved toward her, explaining that they would dine in the Informal Dining Room. Grimacing with another of his grotesque smiles, he put his hand on her shoulder. Her shoulder stiffened; and it took her great effort to push back the automatic surge of adrenalin any male's touch inevitably provoked in her. Although—since Mama had explained about the conditioning her years of self-defense courses had set in place—she understood why she had this response, still she found it difficult to control. She always had to rein herself in to keep from making a physical defense response. As for Papa, he didn't understand, he only thought her shy or—sometimes—willful. And she didn't know how to explain to him without aggravating what Mama said was his most sensitive spot: his lack of knowledge about executive ways. Anyone raised as an executive would understand and would not need to be told about conditioning. It was precisely because of misunderstandings like this that they were doomed always to be uncomfortable together.

They had the gas lit in the dining room, too, as well as the candelabra on the table. In such light her father's face looked almost attractive, for it softened the severity of its bone structure, the harshness of the way he held his jaw, and the tightness around his eyes. The other man looked uneasy when Penderel appeared with the soup: perhaps he, too, found the butler's Victorian get-up strange? Alexandra knew for a fact that the professors found the extreme Victorianism weird, but naturally their experience would be limited. If Wedgewood found it strange…perhaps it *was* strange? She tried to imagine her mother in this setting, but failed. Mama would clash, jarringly—making either the Victorianism absurd or her own style ridiculous, depending on whether the gothic ambiance was stronger than that her mother carried around with her. But of course such a showdown would never take place.

"So," he said when they'd started their soup. "My daughter and I have been following the account in the *Executive Times* of the trials and tribulations of restoring the Ballanchine. What's DC gossip got to say on the matter?"

Alexandra stared at him. Since when did her father care about ballet? And then it occurred to her: this must be his social persona. It couldn't be for Wedgewood's sake, not considering everything she'd overheard earlier. So did that mean it was for hers? She grew confused as she tried to understand what was going on.

Between spoonfuls, Wedgewood said, "Then you know the last EMP just about wiped out all plans to revive it—as well as all the other pre-Blanket performing institutions. But the story is that Ferguson's son is really hot on ballet—he is in fact on the Ballanchine board—and is pushing Ferguson to giving them preferential treatment on the basis of the importance of keeping up morale and tone in DC."

Ferguson, Alexandra guessed, must refer to Jason Ferguson, the Secretary of Energy and Technology.

"But will that be enough to rescue any of the season?" Papa asked skeptically.

Wedgewood smiled. "Perhaps not, but our dear darling Lennox is involved, too."

Papa scowled. Alexandra braced for a storm: obviously Wedgewood was not to be counted on to maintain the status quo. "What does that traitorous bitch have to do with it, and what would it matter if she were involved, anyway?"

Before answering, Wedgewood dabbed his napkin to his lips and drank from his water glass. "A great deal. She has some bee in her bonnet about ballet, too, and is also on the board. But as for her pull, well it's considerable, especially now that she's served Booth so well."

Her father glared down the table at her. "Stop dallying, Alexandra, and get this stuff cleared. I think we've all finished?"

Alexandra pushed the call button and glanced over at Wedgewood. No one had finished, certainly not Wedgewood or herself. Mama had told her she changed courses too fast, that people liked a little lag, especially after the soup. But they hadn't even finished their soup. Penderel came in and cleared their plates. Alexandra gestured to him to pour out more wine.

When Penderel had gone, her father said, "It's a wonder Booth didn't try to foist her off on Hill."

Hill, Alexandra thought, must refer to the Acting Chief of Security, formerly the Attorney General. She coughed, trying to call attention to her presence so that they wouldn't say things they didn't want her to hear. Apparently she succeeded, for Wedgewood looked pointedly at her and then back at her father.

But— "I have full confidence in my daughter's discretion, Wedgewood," Papa said, staring down the table at her. He said it as though it were an important revelation, as though it signified a great deal. And the look he was giving her... He turned his stare onto Wedgewood, whose austere lips had pursued into even meaner thinness. "One wonders why Booth would find it necessary to reward her. After all, she *did* very little—and precisely because Weatherall was wary of her connection with Booth."

"Bull*shit*," Wedgewood said. "Who the hell do you think did all the fingering for Booth before Hill was brought in? No one with any Company feeling would have betrayed it to an outsider the way she did. That bitch started with Baldridge and worked her way down. None of us are happy to see the kind of chaos we have to deal with now, believe me. I wasn't a fan of Weatherall and her people, but I sure as hell wouldn't have fingered them the way that bitch did."

It was as though she weren't there, Alexandra thought. Not that she had any idea what they were talking about: maybe that's why he had decided they could talk about such things in front of her?

"Booth will learn his mistake eventually," Papa said in his sneering voice. "He thinks he can gut Security without damaging his own interests. But consider, Wedgewood: since the Blanket we alone have kept control over the masses. Com & Tran won't be able to work their magic, not without a functioning national vid system. That's been made abundantly clear. As for his control over the Executive—Military will surprise them all, I've no doubt. We both know what happens when Military is left unbridled by Security's countervailing weight."

With Penderel's return, they fell silent. To Alexandra's uneasy surprise, Penderel set the usual bouquet of parsley by her plate as he did every night when he served the entrée. Would her idiosyncrasy be tolerated with a guest present?

"So Lennox, you say, is adding her push to getting the Ballanchine going." Papa resumed the previous subject as he conveyed meat from the serving dish Penderel held out to him to his plate. "When is it thought there will be a first performance?"

"They're trying for New Year's, I gather," Wedgewood said.

Penderel moved around the table to serve Wedgewood. "Then we must look into getting tickets for opening night, don't you think, Alexandra?" Her father floated an eerie smile down the table at her.

What *was* it that was going on? He'd never shown any interest in such things before. And now they might be going to DC to watch a dance performance? "I'd love to go," Alexandra said. "I have only the foggiest memories of seeing the Ballanchine before the Blanket." It had been Marie who had taken her to some matinee performances, Alexandra remembered. Marie…Marie who had been so nice to her when everyone else had been so nasty. Marie hadn't liked Daniel at all.

Penderel came around to her and held out the serving dish. Alexandra took the fork in her fingers and said, very low, "Don't forget to change the wine before you leave, Penderel." Penderel wasn't used to serving more than two people at once. And Papa usually took charge of the wine himself. She sighed as she watched Penderel taking away her used wine glass. What would Mama say about her drinking wine? Nothing good, that was certain. Two glasses with dinner every night. Papa considered abstinence from alcohol nonsense and somehow personally inconvenient to himself. *With the kind of life you're going to be*

*leading, Alexandra, a knowledge of and taste for wine will be essential.*
What did that *mean?* How little she understood of life with her father.
Without anyone to explain it to her would she ever lose her confusion?
Or was this what it was like being grown up? Everything had been so
simple before. And now daily everything grew more complicated.

When Penderel left the room and the men lapsed back into their
"shop talk," Alexandra munched her parsley, confident they'd never
notice. They were off in another world, one wholly foreign to her.
Which was as she preferred it.

# Chapter Two

Hazel slipped her thumb and index finger into the space between two cedar slats in the closed blind and nudged them apart; leaning forward, her nose and forehead grazing the blind, she peered down at the street and swept her gaze as far in either direction as she could. She saw nothing of significance. Only Shirl's van, parked halfway down the block, keeping its usual lonely vigil.

The sight did not ease her anxiety.

Hazel walked back to her chair and stood motionless. Staring down at the book lying on the seat, abandoned, she rubbed her arms and sighed. Reading was hopeless. She'd been over the same page four or five times already. A cup of tea, maybe? Making it would at least give her something to do.

On her way downstairs the thought came to her that she could not go on living this way. Bad enough that they spent so much of their existence taking security precautions, which had the effect of fostering the most obsessive and paranoid mind-set imaginable. But Liz's new habit of staying out past midnight two or three times a week frayed Hazel's nerves as security routines did not. The first time Liz had done it, Hazel had called her, to make sure she was all right, and Liz had taken that tone of exaggerated patience that hinted that Hazel's concern smacked more of jealousy than actual worry. And so Hazel had resolved never to call to check on Liz's safety again. But each time, as the hours crawled by, Hazel worried that something *had* "happened." And each time she realized her powerlessness: realized that she would have no way of knowing for certain until it was too late, to help Liz—or herself. For presumably if they caught Liz, Hazel's own safety would be compromised, too. And each time Hazel told herself that such speculations and worries were nonsense, that she should simply go to sleep in her own bed and stop fussing over a woman who knew well how to take care of herself.

Not that she'd ever been able to fall asleep before Liz had finally come home.

Hazel filled the kettle and switched it on. And she thought again about moving out. Liz claimed that she, Hazel, was as much a quarry as she herself. But then Liz felt acutely responsible for having "dragged" her (as she insisted on putting it) into peril, and her sense of responsibility tended to make her over-protective. Hazel knew that if she were to tell Liz she was moving out, Liz would instantly object that her, Hazel's, safety would thereby be compromised. But surely there must be a way of taking care of her own safety without living with Liz?

Hazel looked through the selection of teas and settled on an herbal orange blend. She had to admit that the house tended to spook her and that that probably fed her unease about Liz's staying out late. Although she was the occupant most often present in it, this house had never felt like "home." Its style and size struck her as foreign, as belonging to someone she was only visiting. And Gillian—their "inside security"—in her room at the back seemed more a member of the household than Liz, who mostly came home only to sleep. Surely hotel accommodations would be more appropriate to Liz's habits than any house.

Yeah, but a hotel would be too risky.

The kettle's whistle startled Hazel. Jumpy mouse, she scoffed at herself, switching it off. She poured the boiling water over the tea bag and paced the kitchen, waiting for the tea to steep. After only three minutes, she fished the tea bag out of the cup. She hated strong tea, while Liz insisted on it. But then Liz liked straight lime juice, while she, Hazel, loathed undiluted fruit juices of any sort. And Liz was decidedly sexually promiscuous, while she, Hazel—

*That's enough, Hazel.*

Hazel turned off the kitchen light and moved slowly through the first floor of the house, checking. Checking for what? she asked herself. Shying away from the question, she halted her prowl and drove herself back upstairs. *Drink your tea and go to bed, Hazel. This is nonsense.*

Hazel was still wide awake—thinking that lying in the dark made her anxiety worse—when Liz arrived home sometime after 1:30. Hazel listened to her go into her own room first before crossing the hall to Hazel's. Seeing Liz silhouetted in the doorway, Hazel sat up. "It's okay, Liz, I'm awake," she said.

"But darling, why are you in here? It's silly, you know, when you always end up in my bed."

Liz was right, of course: except during that one monster of a quarrel that had gone on for two days. But lying in that big empty bed would have made the waiting worse. "I feel swallowed up when I'm in your bed by myself," Hazel said. She swung her feet onto the floor and grabbed her robe to protect her naked body from the chilly air, then followed Liz back across the hall.

Hazel climbed into the massive, extra long bed and watched Liz undress. "Just a quick run under the shower, darling, and I'll be finished," she said. Probably, Hazel reflected, to get the smell of the other woman off her. Liz wouldn't have cared for herself. Her thoughtfulness about such things never failed to impress Hazel, and all the more since Liz had never before engaged in the kind of stable relationship they now shared.

When Liz came out of the bathroom she stood for a few seconds near the foot of the bed fluffing her short thick mop of golden hair, then stretched from toes to ceiling, momentarily goddessesque in the display of her proportions and visible physical strength. "So! To bed!" She laughed. "Lord what a long day it's been!"

Hazel grinned. "You look as though you could go on for hours more."

Liz threw back the covers on her side of the bed, sat down on the edge, slung her long legs up into the bed, and pulled the covers over her body. "So have you figured out what I'm going to do about Simon's proposal?" she asked, rolling onto her side to face Hazel. She touched Hazel's cheek in a caress and combed her fingers through Hazel's hair.

"You're asking my opinion?"

Liz wrinkled her nose. "Now don't tell me you're just a secretary, darling. Of course I'm asking your opinion! That's not so odd, is it?"

No, not so odd, not when they were in bed. It would have been odd, though, if Liz had asked her in another context. "I don't think it's a good idea for us to get mixed up with Simon in any way," Hazel said, watching Liz's lively aquamarine eyes for signs of agreement or disagreement. "Security is after her as much as they're after us. Maybe even more. By forming a tie with her we increase our vulnerability to being found." Hazel hesitated. "And there are other reasons, too, but I doubt they'd appeal much to you."

Liz's lips thinned. "Moral reasons, you mean."

Hazel did not deny it.

"But what about the possible benefits?"

"It's too risky," Hazel said. "Besides, if the Co-op people found out we were doing business with Simon, we could lose their goodwill. And I don't think we want to do that, do we." Hazel hated always having to put things in terms of practical advantages versus disadvantages, but she got nowhere in discussions like these unless she did.

"You're probably right," Liz said, drawing her palm down Hazel's back and cupping her buttock. "Better that I sleep on it and tackle it in the morning. Turn out the light, darling, and scoot over here so we can cuddle."

Hazel hesitated. If she didn't bring up the subject of moving now, she might not get another chance for a while, for most nights Liz had too much on her mind to be easily approached about anything other than work-related matters. "There's something we need to talk about," she said—and bit her lip when she saw the familiar smooth mask slide over Liz's face. She probably didn't even realize that she was wearing it, Hazel thought. A sort of *what now?* expression of forced patience and forbearance. Though it wasn't as though she ever made scenes, Hazel thought.

"You're sure it has to be now, darling? It's so late."

"Please, Liz. It's important. You see, I think it would be best if I moved out. I've been thinking, and I realized that it wouldn't change things very much, it would just mean—"

"Wait a minute," Liz interrupted, sitting up. Her voice acquired an edge. "Before you go any further, tell me *exactly* what this is all about."

Hazel sat up, too. The way Liz's eyes had narrowed and her nostrils were flaring suggested anger. It was sometimes hard to tell with her—especially at the beginning of quarrels—when anger seethed below the smoothly veiled surface. "It's just what I said, Liz. I think it would be best if I moved out."

"Why? Is there some problem between us you've been hiding from me?"

"Not that *I* know of," Hazel said, irritated at Liz's assumption that if there were a problem it would be up to her, Hazel, to identify and reveal it.

"Then why are you threatening to move out?"

"Why are you talking about threatening?"

"Answer my question."

That was a typical executive order if she'd ever heard one, Hazel thought. Why did Liz always have to lapse into that attitude whenever she felt she'd lost control over her? "Is that an order, Madam?" Hazel inquired ironically. But at the fleeting expression of hurt that flitted across that beautiful face just before it shuttered itself, Hazel regretted having indulged her angry impulse. "I'm sorry, Liz," she whispered, putting her hand on Liz's hard-muscled forearm. "I didn't mean that. But I hate it when you take that tone with me."

"Tell me why." Liz's face had turned to stone, and her arm rock-like in its rigidity.

Hazel drew a deep breath. "Tonight, like all the other nights you've stayed out late, I worried about you. Maybe it's the lack of any time-frame, or something like that. But whatever it is, it upsets me. If we lived apart I wouldn't have that problem. We could spend most nights together and then, on the other nights, since I wouldn't be lying awake listening for you, it wouldn't matter." But even as Hazel expounded this plan a niggling doubt crept in: would she instead lie awake the entire night instead of a few hours, since she wouldn't know until the next day whether Liz had gotten home safely?

Liz's eyes flashed in blue fury. "You know how much I hate being manipulated, Hazel. You think I don't see through your ploy? I told you, didn't I, that if my trysting upset you I'd give it up. Why can't you just come right out and say that you're jealous? I've already told you I'd understand if you were. It's not as though I can't live without trysting. I went almost ten years living in near-celibacy because of the damned job. But we've already been through this. What's the point? Are you trying to punish me for even having the desire to tryst?"

Hazel shook her head. "No, no, you've got it all wrong, Liz. Maybe I don't understand your desire for it, but I don't find it threatening, either. You're very considerate about the way you do it. And besides, you've made your feelings for me clear."

"Then what is this threat about moving out for if not to get me to stop?"

"I don't want you to stop," Hazel said, trying to keep her voice steady. "I think that would be a mistake. Eventually you'd resent me for imposing that kind of restriction on you. I don't think of my idea as a threat, but as a solution. We'll still see one another as much as we always do. It's not as though we spend that much time here together. You're hardly ever home, you know. Instead of coming here, you could come to my place."

Liz's hands, lying on top of the covers, clenched into fists. "I've told you how important it is to me that we live together."

"But Liz." Hazel spoke in a murmur, making her voice as reassuring as she could. "We *will* be living together, almost exactly the same as we always have. With only that one difference."

"Bullshit. Let's at least be clear about the fact that our relationship would undergo a major change if we began living apart. So you win. I'll give up the trysting. And now can we turn off the light and go to sleep?"

"That's not what I want, Liz," Hazel said, determined to make Liz see that she was not proposing this out of jealousy, that she was not attempting a covert manipulative strategy. "I—"

The light went out.

A split-second later the phone chirped. Hazel heard Liz groping on her night table for her handset. "Weatherall here," Liz said, her voice cold, crisp, efficient. After a few seconds her voice went on, "All right, here's how we'll handle it. You call Gillian and have her take the rear first floor. I'll take the front. You'll circle around outside, examining every bush, every square foot of sod surrounding the house. How many do you think there are?" In the pause, Hazel, her heart galloping in fear, gasped for breath. Liz spoke again: "All right. So we'll play it cautious. Stun weapons only, Shirl. And now, let's do it." Hazel heard Liz replacing the handset. "You'll have to carry a stungun, Hazel," Liz whispered. "We have no choice since we don't know how many of the bastards there are."

So the moment they'd always feared had arrived. Just like that, without warning, in the middle of the night. Her teeth chattering, her knees shaking, Hazel got up, put on her robe, and took the stun-gun Liz pressed into her hands. "It's set and ready to go, darling. Promise me you won't hesitate to use it?"

"I promise."

"That's my Hazel," Liz said softly, bumping her nose into Hazel's face then quickly brushing her lips over Hazel's cheek. "I'll go downstairs first, darling. You'll position yourself at the top of the stairs and listen as hard as you can. Listen for anyone getting in through the second-story windows. And listen to my movements. Clear?"

"Understood," Hazel whispered, but Liz had already begun moving away. Hazel crept after her, groping carefully to avoid crashing into the furniture. The pounding of her heart seemed to shake her entire body. The time they'd planned and hoped against had finally arrived: anything could happen. *Anything*. And she, Hazel, was worse than useless. What if this had happened an hour earlier, before Liz had returned home? Probably she'd have been used as a hostage. That was how those people operated.

*Those people*: intruders in their house, at that very moment. Hazel, slipping down the hall, strained to hear; but Liz moved soundlessly, in spite of her size. Remembering Liz's skill, speed, and sheer physical power, Hazel's confidence in Liz's ability resurged. Between Liz, Shirl, and Gillian, surely one intruder, no matter how invincible, could be handled.

Her knees strangely wobbly, her arms and legs weak and trembling, Hazel steadied herself against the banister, waiting for Liz's orders. Except for her mediocre ability to aim and fire a stun-gun, she was useless. But it was conceivable that that one little thing might be required as back-up.

Hazel jumped when she heard a crash. What should she do? What *could* she do besides stand motionless, listen, and wait? There followed a thud, a clang of heavy glass or pottery breaking, a sharp cry—not Liz's, Hazel thought. Then: "Hazel!" *That* was Liz's voice. "Come into the study."

Hazel sped down the stairs, her heart beating faster, faster—sweat lathering her body, trickling down her ribs. She burst into the study and Liz's voice—Hazel could see nothing of her location—said quietly, "There's a flashlight in the top right-hand drawer of the desk, Hazel. Get it out, would you."

Groping her way through the dark to the desk, she cried out in startlement.

"What is it?"

"I've stepped in glass, I think."

"Damn," Liz said. "And of course you're barefoot."

Hazel reached the desk, opened the drawer, and felt around in it until her hands encountered a plastic tube that could only be a flashlight. "I've got it, Liz."

"Good. Turn it on and find us. We're in the corner farthest away from the door."

*Us?*

Hazel felt for the button and switched on the light; she played its beam around that corner until it fell on Liz's face. Liz squinted, and Hazel lowered the beam. Liz, she saw, was straddling a man lying prone, her feet gripping his knees, her hands pressing both of his into the small of his back. "What I want you to do now, Hazel, is come here, put your stun-gun a few inches from the back of his head, and fire."

Hazel's throat closed. "My god, Liz," she started to protest. "Can't you just handcuff him?"

"It's the only way we can be sure of handling him safely, Hazel. Do it quickly, before I wear out. I can't maintain this hold forever."

Hazel's stomach pitched, and her hands shook; she played the light on the floor, glittering with shards of glass, to guide her way. With each step she took she imagined slivers of glass being driven further and further into her feet. Certainly there were enough discrete points of pain for that image to represent a possible reality. When she reached Liz, she first knelt, then fell back on her heels, for her knees were shaking.

"Do it, darling," Liz urged.

Hazel sucked in a deep, shaky breath, moved her right hand until the stun-gun was only inches from the man's left ear, and pulled the trigger. She looked away as he started flopping about in a stun fit.

"Keep the light steady," Liz said sharply.

Hazel pocketed the stun-gun and shifted the flashlight into her right hand. As Liz cuffed their intruder, Hazel noticed that she hadn't a stitch on her body.

"Okay, darling," Liz said when she had finished. "Give me the flashlight. I want you to stay here with him while I check out the rest of the house. Don't hesitate to fire if you think you see another intruder. Though getting stunned is an unpleasant experience, it's not ultimately harmful." That, Hazel thought as she heard Liz moving away, must refer to the possibility of her shooting Shirl or Gillian by mistake.

When the man stopped flopping and flailing, Hazel reminded herself that he was cuffed, and she had the stun-gun, and that he must be terribly disoriented and probably didn't even know where he was. His breath came in gasps. After about a minute he started moving around, presumably because he had become aware that his hands were bound. Hazel felt sick as she imagined the sorts of things that must be going through his mind. How long would it take before he remembered what he had been doing and where he must be? Lying in the dark with a fractured short-term memory would be scary for anyone, even an SIC officer.

Into the silence marked only by the man's gasping and flailing and her own harsh breathing and loud heartbeat came a distant splintering of glass, a loud crash, the pounding of feet running through the house, and then, long seconds later, Gillian's voice bellowing "I've got the bastard!"

Perhaps half a minute later—though it seemed an eternity—Liz returned. "The Women's Patrol have just arrived, Hazel. They're scouring the area looking for possible back-ups to the three we've caught."

"Three?" Hazel said faintly.

"Three." Liz's voice was grim. The beam of the flashlight played over the debris of glass and pottery littering the floor. "What a mess!" She picked her way toward Hazel and the intruder. "Has he recovered from the charge yet?"

"I think so," Hazel said, wondering what he was making of their conversation.

When Liz reached her she handed the flashlight to Hazel. "I want you to shine it on him so I can see what I'm doing."

Hazel focused the beam on the intruder. He lay still now, his head turned away from her. Suddenly, Liz swung her leg forward—away from the man's body—and then drove her heel backwards, into his flank, with tremendous force. He yelped at about the same time Hazel cried out, "Liz!"

"Roll over," Liz ordered him.

The man lay still. "More of the same?" Liz said, her voice harder than Hazel had ever heard it.

"No, Liz, don't!"

"Hold the light steady, Hazel. It's all we've got since these animals cut the power line into the house." Without warning, she kicked him in the same place, with even greater force. This time the man screamed, and his breath came in sobs.

"For godsake, Liz!"

"Broken ribs are painful. And he knows that punctured lungs are even worse," Liz said in that same hateful voice. "Roll over, boy, or there'll be more."

"Can't move," the man gasped. "Need medical attention."

"As soon as you're cooperative," Liz said.

Hazel, shivering, decided that if Liz moved to kick him again she'd interpose her own body between them. It was obvious she'd seriously hurt him.

The man turned his head toward Hazel, then slowly rolled over, away from them, so that the unhurt side of his body absorbed the pressure of the roll. Each groan and gasp the man made inscribed Hazel's body with traces of excruciating sympathetic pain. At last he lay on his back, his arms and hands under his body, his face rigid. Liz bent over him; Hazel braced herself to make Liz stop, but Liz only rifled his pockets. "Shine the light on my hands," she said. Hazel obeyed and saw that Liz held a thin leather wallet. Liz opened the wallet and whistled. "Pretty confident, weren't you, carrying your ID around like this. Navy, is it. I'm actually quite surprised." In addition to the photocard Liz was examining, Hazel also saw his yellow plastic. He was a professional, then, whoever he was. "Unless of course this is a dummy photocard made up by the Company," Liz said. "I'm sure a short interrogation will settle it. But first you're going to tell us what the set-up is outside. What your back-up is and who and how many people are working on this little operation."

"Just the three of us," the man gasped.

"Shine the light on his face, Hazel."

Hazel obeyed, but said, "Liz, you mustn't hurt him any more. Promise me you won't."

"Let me handle this, Hazel. Just hold the damned light, that's all I ask."

The man's face suddenly clenched, and he screamed.

"Stop it, Liz!" Hazel shrieked the words, raising her voice above the horrible sound coming out of the man. She leaned forward and grabbed at Liz's arm.

"Damn it, Hazel, hold the light on his face!"

"Stop hurting him, Liz!"

"If you can't do that one simple thing I'm asking of you, leave the room," Liz said coldly.

The horrible sound still hadn't stopped. "I swear to you, Liz, if you don't stop it, we're through," Hazel burst out. "I swear it!" She knew she couldn't physically stop Liz from doing whatever it was that was making the man scream. Their relationship was all she had to bargain with.

"Is that an ultimatum?"

Hazel swallowed. "I wouldn't be able to live with you or myself if—"

"For the birthing fuck, girl, this man is our enemy. Do you know what they'd be doing to us if we hadn't stopped them?"

"That's irrelevant," Hazel said. "I mean it, Liz. I'm deadly serious."

Hazel heard movement and sensed that Liz had stood up. "All right, Hazel." The anger was raw in her voice. "We'll talk outside."

Hazel lit their way over the glass-strewn floor, her heart pounding as violently as it had when she'd been waiting upstairs in the dark. As soon as they stepped into the hall, Liz closed the study door. Liz took the flashlight from Hazel and held both of Hazel's wrists in her other hand. "Now listen to me, Hazel." Her voice was low and even. "We could still be in quite a lot of danger if these naval intelligence boys are part of a larger team ready to close in on us when they don't

hear from the first three by a certain time. Do you understand what
I'm saying?"

"Yes, Liz, I understand. I'm not the fool you seem to think me."

"Then you must also see that I have no choice but to get information out of this one."

Hazel wished they could see one another's faces. "I won't stand by
while you torture him, Liz."

"That's melodramatic exaggeration, Hazel. You don't understand
a thing about any of this. I suggest you go out to the kitchen and sit
with Gillian and leave this to me."

Hazel leaned against the wall for support. Her knees shook so, she
thought they might buckle. "I meant what I said, Liz. I'm not going
to close my eyes to it."

"Didn't I just explain to you our situation, Hazel? Let me put
it plainer: it's us or them. Would you rather be the one screaming
in pain? Because believe me, that's what would happen to us—and
worse—if they manage to capture us."

Hazel swallowed. "I understand all that," she whispered. "But
that doesn't mean we have to be like them. What does it make us if
you carry out and I stand by as an accessory to torture—"

"Stop saying that," Liz hissed at her.

Hazel's voice trembled. "I'm just calling it what it is."

The words hung in the air, almost palpable between them. Finally,
Liz said, "What am I to do instead, Hazel? Tell me that."

"Set a trap for the others. You said the Women's Patrol had arrived. And I'm sure Shirl has called in reinforcements, too. Or else we
could just leave this place." Hazel inhaled shakily. "My god, Liz, you
don't know that he's going to tell you anything. He'll probably hold
out as long as he can. And even if he does tell you something, how will
you be able to believe anything he says?"

"I just don't see any other way," Liz said wearily.

"I can't accept that. It's wrong, Liz. And I think a part of you knows
that, too. Everything between us will be spoiled if you go through
with what you've started. I can *feel* it. Whatever kind of rationalizing
you do, there's no getting around what I'm feeling."

Another long silence fell between them, and Hazel knew Liz was
thinking. She became aware of the murmur of voices somewhere in

the back of the house, of Liz's breathing, and of the smell of Liz's sweat mixed with the elusive perfume she always wore.

After a long time, Liz lifted Hazel's wrists and brushed her lips over Hazel's fingers. "You win, Hazel," she whispered. "You win. But I hope we don't regret it." Liz drew Hazel close in a tight hug, and again Hazel realized that Liz was stark naked. When Liz stepped back, she said, "Go out to the kitchen and tell the Women's Patrol we need a mobile med-unit."

A stream of tears gushed from Hazel's eyes. She snatched at Liz's hand. "I love you, Liz," she whispered.

Liz squeezed her hand, then released it. "Go now, darling. I'll return to our prisoner and try to think what to do next." Doubt snaked into Hazel's mind, but she realized there'd be so little time for Liz to do anything much that such suspicion was unfair.

She groped her way to the kitchen, moving painfully on her cut soles, trying to compose herself before facing the others. They didn't know Liz as she did. The best thing, she thought, would be to wipe what had just passed between her and Liz out of her mind, out of her memory.

# Chapter Three

## [i]

They'd been at it for only twenty minutes when he threw down his racquet and said, "Enough, Alexandra, I can't concentrate today." Without waiting for her reply, he stalked off to the shower room. His game had been worse than usual, but Alexandra had assumed it was more a matter of his being hung-over than being unable to concentrate. Still…she thought of Higgins' cryptic comment to her yesterday that she should "be as supportive as possible" this weekend, that "tomorrow and the day after would probably be very difficult," and that "the danger of his starting a binge will be high." As if that weren't bad enough, he'd gotten really embarrassing, talking about how well she had done "helping" her father through "rough times" and "helping him control his drinking."

Alexandra sat down in the middle of the court. She knew he'd take at least fifteen minutes to shower and dress. She checked her watch. If she'd been thinking, she wouldn't have left her outdoor clothing in the shower room. The wind had turned bitter; it was too cold outside to run back to the house in her racquet-ball togs. According to Nicole, the grounds staff was predicting snow. "Being locals," Nicole had said, "they should know."

To Alexandra's surprise, her father emerged from the shower room in under ten minutes. "Don't dawdle, Alexandra," he said. "There's something I want to show you when you've showered and dressed."

Another political science lesson? Or was there something on the island he had a sudden urge to show off? Surely there was nothing else inside the house he could inflict upon her: during her first few months here they'd gone through the house room by room so that he could favor her with a lecture on every painting, every piece of sculpture, and every architectural feature the house boasted.

Standing under the hot, needle-sharp shower, Alexandra fleetingly wished for another long weekend in DC. If only he'd let her go on the weekends as the professors were allowed to do. Or to see her mother. (Mama was in Rio now, "escaping winter.") But at least she had something to look forward to: tomorrow, at long last, Clarice would be arriving. It had taken weeks to get the security clearance. Alexandra felt certain her father disliked the whole idea of Clarice, but apart from the security stipulation, he hadn't been able to give a reason for stopping her from coming. How, after all, could he argue against Mama's insistence that she should have a female valet to take care of her clothes and grooming? "Why a foreigner?" Papa had grumbled. Of course that's why the clearance had taken so long. "Mama says it will be a painless way for me to learn Italian," Alexandra had replied.

Quickly she toweled dry and dressed: in his current mood his impatience would probably make him cutting and hypercritical. Perhaps whatever it was he wanted to show her wouldn't take long and then he'd let her go practice or read or listen to music. The usual Saturday dinner and movie was canceled because all the professors were away for the weekend. It would be a very long Saturday indeed if he decided they had to talk all day and into the evening. Their "talks" mostly consisted of his lecturing at her and brushing aside her questions as irrelevant or stupid. And when he started talking about the Company, as he had recently begun doing…that was the worst. It felt…dangerous. And Mama had said he shouldn't. But *he* kept saying that she needed to understand the organizational structure of Security Services and its relation to the Executive…

Alexandra returned to the court and found her father leaning against the wall with his arms folded over his chest. He took her arm and walked her to the gymnasium door. When he opened it, a sharp blast of cold air assaulted them, and Alexandra shivered under her fur. The leaden sky loomed low. "They're saying it's going to snow," she said as they half-jogged to the house. Alexandra listened to the waves slamming against the rocks and—as she often did—wondered what would happen to the sea when it snowed. She found the very notion difficult to visualize, as though it were a paradox that snow could drop onto tossing, white-foamed waves.

When they neared the house, instead of going in by the side door, Papa steered her east. As they rounded the corner of the east wing, Alexandra thought he meant them to go in through the French windows of the Small Study. But when he veered them sharply away from the house, she knew it could not be that. And then her father halted. Before them stood the statue she had often noticed from the windows of the Small Study and the Music Room; the statue had always given her the creeps because the many thin red veins running through the white marble reminded her of blood vessels. Near the statue a holly tree raged out of control, the only non-cropped shrub or tree Alexandra had ever noticed on the island outside of the woods. She looked at her father. Did he mean to deliver a lecture on the statue, perhaps? His gaze seemed fixed on it, but after a while moved to the nearby growth of holly.

At last he spoke, his voice so low she had to strain against the roar of the surf and wind to hear it. "Under that holly bush is buried the woman represented by this statue, Alexandra." Alexandra started; a shiver ran over her. Someone had been buried *here*? It sounded crazy. "Tomorrow is the anniversary of her death," he said. "She died nine years ago. I had her buried here because she was the single most important person in my life." Alexandra stared at his face, wondering if this were delusion or truth. If truth... His gaze pulled away from the holly and drilled into hers. "Unfortunately, she was a traitor. She died because of her treachery against me and our country. She singlehandedly started the Civil War."

Alexandra tried to think of something to say, but though she searched frantically for a comment or question that would be appropriate, her mind remained stubbornly blank. "And you had her body brought here after her death?" she finally thought to ask.

He hesitated, then said, faintly, "Yes. And then I commissioned the statue to be made." He could not seem to take his eyes off the statue. As the wind, gusting, lifted the hair on the crown of his head, Alexandra was struck by the poignancy of his loneliness. So her father had loved a woman...and obviously long after he'd been fixed: offering the final proof of his incompatibility with the executive world. "You met her once, you know," he said. "Just after the Blanket, when she was staying in the Georgetown house." Without warning, he put his arm around her shoulders. "I want to tell you about her, Alexandra. She was quite extraordinary. But you're shivering. Let's go in now."

They circled the house and went in through the northeast door. Hot chocolate, Alexandra thought, and a roaring fire: that's what she wanted.

[ii]

"It's a long, long story," her father said, pouring out his first glass of the day. "But one I would very much like to tell you."

He wanted her to understand him, Alexandra realized. Because he was so lonely. "I'd like to hear it, Papa," she said.

He sank down into one of the big padded leather armchairs. "It's a terrible story with an unhappy ending. But you're sixteen now..." He held his glass to his nose and breathed in the bouquet of the dark ruby wine, then lowered the rim to his lips and took a sip. "It all began thirty-five years ago. I never told her the very beginning of it, I don't quite know why..." He shrugged. "I first saw her in a cafe, in Bonn. She was at the next table, talking to a man. They were both professionals, you understand. They were drinking wine. She spoke passionately about a play she had seen the week before. She had one of those lilting yet powerful voices. Her face was filled with excitement and light; her eyes, a deep glowing blue, sparkled, radiating warmth. I could see that the man with her was entirely captivated. During the course of the conversation I felt something building between them. To be explicit, sexual excitement. Suddenly they clasped hands, got up, and left. I had no doubt they intended to have sex within the hour."

How strange, Alexandra thought, how strange to think of men and women being like that, though of course that's how Hollywood portrayed executives... Her father looked into his glass, then back at Alexandra. "I was indulging in a sort of voyeurism, I suppose." He shrugged. "I carried that impression of her around with me for weeks. I'd wake up thinking about her, wanting her. And I didn't even know her name." He laughed. "I looked for her everywhere I went, even outside of Bonn. I began going to the theater two or three times a week in the wild hope that I might see her at a play, because I knew she liked plays. But I saw her nowhere."

He took a long pull at his wine. "Until one day I discovered that she was on the Company payroll, as a contract employee. Every six months as Chief Controller of the Western Europe territory I reviewed the on-going projects and caseloads of officers at each Western European station and base. It was usually a matter of glancing through summary reports, giving my personal attention only to long-term or big-budget projects. One of our long-term projects at that time involved the infiltration of GFI, Green Forces International, an anti-US subversive group. Kay, as it turned out, was our agent inside the group. An image of her photocard was included in the project dossier. Needless to say, when I saw that photo I at once accessed her file. I learned she was a historian doing research at the state archives. She was working for us in order to finance her research. My first thought was to arrange a meeting with her. But two objections occurred to me. First, it was against all the rules of tradecraft for me to meet her personally, much less get involved with her. And second, it might not be her. A photo isn't much to go on."

An almost sheepish expression flickered across his face. "Since I was already a fair way toward being obsessed with her, I concentrated on the second objection and put the first out of my mind. I suggested that a way be found to bring her into the station—which at that time was located on a US military base—so that she could be thoroughly debriefed to help determine the current status of the project. When the time came for her debriefing, I put in an appearance so that I could see her for myself. I immediately recognized her. And so the agony began."

He rose from his chair and began to pace. "You see, I knew very well I couldn't have her. That it would expose not only her and the project but myself as well, since at that time I had a diplomatic cover that I preferred to keep intact." He drank the rest of the wine in his glass and set the glass down on the table by his chair. "But the longer I resisted, the more I wanted her." His mouth twisted wryly in what Alexandra interpreted as a smile; more disquieting, his eyes had acquired an excited gleam. "It's the matter of forbidden fruit. Eventually, inevitably, the temptation becomes impossible to withstand. Within two months I had sunk so low that I arranged to meet her for one of her debriefings. You understand, we usually sent a cut-out only marginally connected with the station, someone who could pass for a social acquaintance of hers. A professional, of course."

He closed his eyes and rocked back and forth on his heels. "From then on—once I'd met her and taken her to bed—I fought a constant battle for control over myself." He opened his eyes and looked at Alexandra. "I would try to stop seeing her, but would always break down after two or three weeks, unable to control my desire for her." His mouth twisted again. "Until you've experienced the fierceness of sexual desire, you won't really be able to understand what I'm talking about. Not that it was only sex, for I craved her company, her conversation—you can't imagine what it's like talking to someone so brilliant, so *engaged. Everything* interested her, and she always had something fresh to say." He frowned. "*Usually* had something fresh to say. Certain subjects she was foolish on, but they were avoidable."

Alexandra set her empty cup down. How extraordinary, his talking to her like this. No one had ever talked to her about such things before. And as far as executive males went, none would ever talk about sexual feelings in this way. Or would they? *Until you've experienced the fierceness of sexual desire…* If Mama or Elizabeth had said something like that to her, she would have been avid to hear more, for she had been so curious about sex for a long time. But coming from *him*, it made her uncomfortable. It felt *wrong*, maybe…improper? No, that wasn't the word for it. She couldn't, in fact, find the word for it. And the expression on his face—his eyes were glittering, and even his posture was different, more alive, somehow.

He moved to the table and poured more wine into his glass. "Of course, I had other women at the time. But they all bored me by comparison. I'd always had a lot of variety in sexual partners—not as much as say somebody like Weatherall, but a reasonably high turnover."

Did that mean Elizabeth had a lot of lovers?

He sipped the wine, set the glass down, and resumed pacing. "Of course, my first impulse was to get her off that project and working more closely with the station. When her multiplicity of talents became apparent, I knew she would make a superb officer. The only catch with that idea, however, was that recruiting her into permanent employment would entail her going back to the States for an extended period of training. So I tried to think up ways of incorporating her into the station's workload without necessarily having to do that. Again breaking all the rules, I did that while she was still working on the GFI project. When she finally got enough on them and we shut them down—every operating cell across Europe, thanks to her cleverness and skill—I was able to involve her more directly in the projects I personally oversaw. But that meant a lot of traveling, which interfered with her research...I could see she was beginning to feel tugged in both directions. Still, the more pressure I exerted, the more she involved herself." Frowning, he picked up his wine glass. "It was at that time, Alexandra, that I was told I'd have to go through with the surgery without further delay." He looked straight at her, as though to make sure she understood he was referring to being fixed.

She swallowed and nodded and knew from the burst of heat on her face that she was blushing.

He drank from his glass. "I realized at that point that I was terrified of losing her. Of course I had to tell her about the surgery. But to ask her to try staying with me afterwards... You must understand, Alexandra, that changing a relationship in such a radical way is traumatic." He seemed to expect a response, so Alexandra nodded again. "And of course part of the post-operative treatment is behavioral therapy. Including aversion-to-women therapy." He took another sip. "Well, one night I finally told her. To my relief, although she was shocked and appalled to learn that executive men did this to themselves, she said that out of love for me, she was willing to try it. So we arranged for her to return to the States and take a few short training courses during the time I was being prepped for surgery, having the surgery, and going through the post-operative psych therapy. The idea was that I'd be stabilized by the time she returned. She said she was terrified of what she'd find when she got back. She seemed to think the psych therapy would destroy my love for her." He grimaced. "That's not what happened. The psych therapy affected me, yes, but it did nothing to lessen my passionate attachment to her."

He sank down into his chair and poured more wine into his glass. The life had gone out his face, and his shoulders slumped. "It was a disaster," he said, sighing. "I didn't trust her motives for sticking with me. I was always suspicious that she was hoping to use me—and that she was seeing other men. The thought of her being with another man—for the first time, for I'd hardly experienced jealousy at all in my life up to that point—the idea of someone else touching her—Christ, it drove me half out of my mind. To put it briefly, for months I was out of control and abusive. Yes, out of control: that was the key to it. Instead of gaining control from my surgery, I seemed to have lost it entirely. I couldn't understand what was happening—I understand it now, of course, but at the time I blamed *her* for my lack of control. I realize now that I made life hell for her. She tried talking to me about separating—we were living together at this point, you understand; I'd insisted on her moving in with me once the GFI project had broken. But every time she even hinted at leaving me, I used violence against her. And then came the day she said she wanted to leave the Company." He glanced over at Alexandra for a few seconds. Staring down into his glass, he said, "I was so rough with her that time that she never brought up the subject again." He swallowed more wine. "Instead, she wrote a letter of resignation, sent it to Washington rather than give it to me, packed up, and left."

He stood. "I want to show you something," he said. "Come upstairs with me."

Alexandra, getting up from her chair, was surprised to find her legs wobbly. Observing that he did not take his glass or the bottle with him, she concluded they would not be gone long, wherever it was they were going.

He shepherded her toward the front hall. "She didn't even leave me a note," he said as they ascended the staircase. "She simply packed and went. This was long before the Blanket, of course, so it was child's play tracking her to a train en route to Calais. I got there with the boys long before the train got in. No, keep going, Alexandra. We're going all the way up to the top floor." He put his hand on her elbow. "When she got off the train and saw me, she knew."

Knew what? Alexandra wondered.

"She didn't even try to run. I took her passport from her and all of us got into the van and drove to a run-down hotel near the station."

"I didn't know there was anything up here besides the staff's rooms," Alexandra said breathlessly into the silence as they climbed the last flight.

They reached the top of the stairs and turned right, along a dim, uncarpeted hallway. The soles of Alexandra's hard-leather winter boots clattered on the bare wood floor. They stopped before a locked door; he took out his keys, selected one, and fit it into the lock. "This room is different from the rest of the house," he said before turning the key. He looked at her. "It's a reminder to me about the importance of control." His gaze lowered to the lock: he turned the key and pushed the door open. The room was dark, shut up, as though heavy blinds covered the window. Unused cold air and an old musty smell drifted out into the hall. "Go in," he said, holding the door open, waiting for her to pass.

Alexandra hesitated. "Isn't there a light?"

He reached around the doorframe. Alexandra heard a click and a ceiling light went on, casting thin, dingy illumination on a very strange-looking, decrepit scene. She ventured inside, aware of her father moving behind her, and the frigid mustiness of the room seeped into her bones. When she heard the door close, she felt plunged into a world utterly separate from everything she knew. It was as though this room were not really here in this house on this island. The battered old furniture—the stained lampshade on the cheap glass lamp, the ugly iron bedstead—worked malignly on her state of mind. Her father moved past her to the long wooden shutters. He opened them, revealing tall French windows. Daylight filtered into the room, exposing the thick layer of dust coating every visible surface—the floors, dresser-top, even the iron bedstead. Alexandra wrenched her gaze from the objects in the room; looking at his face, she found it displaying yet another mood, another set of expressions from those she had so far seen.

"What is this room?" she whispered. She wrapped her arms around her body. Her teeth were chattering. "Why are we here?"

He went to the bed and stretched out on it. The bedsprings creaked with every movement he made. He folded his arms behind his head and stared up at the ceiling. His lying on the bed that way chased chills down her already icy neck. "Everything in this room," he said, "was in that room at Calais, in that hole of a hotel I dragged her to."

Alexandra took one step backwards, then another. Her legs were shaking, her teeth chattering; she could hardly think for the panic engulfing her—panic at the vertiginous insanity wrapping around them, strangling them, sucking them down into inchoate helplessness.

"I lost control of myself," he said. He hardly seemed aware of her: he stared up at the ceiling and rubbed his fingers over his face in strange vertical patterns. "You see I went into a rage when I discovered she'd left without a word to me. An unthinking rage. When I got her here I cuffed her to this bed and sent the others away." His eyes swiveled to look at Alexandra. "It was necessary to cuff her, you know, for she'd have fought me. I already knew that, of course, from the other times. That's how violent we were, Alexandra. She was almost a match for me. She had no problem defending herself in a fair fight..." He sighed. "What I did to her in this room—"

He was talking as though this were the room, as though this furniture made it the same place he was thinking of!

"When I had her cuffed to this bed, I began—"

"No!"

Alexandra saw that he had stopped and was staring at her. She said quietly, "I don't want to hear. Don't tell me. I don't understand why you're telling me any of this, but I don't want to know what you did to her. It's horrible, this place is horrible, and I want to leave here. Now." She turned and went to the door. Her cold, sweaty hand slipped over the surface of the icy brass knob, but it did not budge. She understood, then, that the door had to be opened with a key.

"I want to tell you because I want you to understand," he said, watching her. "Not only about me, but about how important it is to be controlled. You're coming of sexual age, you know, and—"

"Stop it!" Alexandra shouted, glaring across the room at him.

"Control yourself," he said coldly, watching her through narrowed, glittering eyes.

Alexandra swallowed, drew a deep breath, and moved slowly toward the bed. "Give me the key," she said, holding out her hand.

His eyes examined her as though watching for signs of *her* madness, *her* hysteria. "Sit down, Alexandra." He spoke in his usual monotone, very quietly. "It's essential that you learn to control yourself. You may not like this room, you may not want to hear what I have to say, but such situations do happen, and you must learn to find the inner

resources to cope with your emotional responses, especially considering the sort of responsibilities you will be facing in the future."

After a few long, charged seconds of silence, Alexandra said, "I
don't want to be here. And there's no heat in here. Why can't we talk
downstairs?" To her disgust, her voice shook. She hated for him to see
how thoroughly he had succeeded in intimidating her: for surely that
was his reason for making her stay here like this, for wanting to tell
her all the horrible things he had done to that woman he claimed to
have loved.

"Sit down. We will go downstairs shortly. This part of the story
doesn't take long to tell."

Alexandra lowered herself onto the hard straight chair placed
against the wall between the door and the dresser. He left her no
choice but to endure this situation until he chose to end it: that was
what he was telling her by making her stay here. And wasn't that the
point of his story? That that woman could not escape him?

"At first," he resumed, "I acted out of rage. But then it changed. I
started to believe I could terrorize her into submission. If I'd had any
control at all at that point I would have known that wouldn't work
with Kay. But I was completely out of control. So I beat her and raped
her until I managed to wear her down. Or so I thought."

Alexandra sank her chin into the cowl neck of her sweater. Though
the room itself was icy, his words were like half-frozen droplets of water sliding down her neck, seeping inside her body, crystallizing like
liquid nitrogen within her very bone marrow.

"I know that what I did to her in this room lost her to me forever.
I see that now, looking back. But all I could think at the time was
that I was losing her, that I had to bind her to me, that I must use any
method that had any chance of working. After a long time of this,
maybe as long as forty-eight hours, she wore out. Or so I thought. She
asked my forgiveness, she said she loved me and would stay with me.
And I believed her." His mouth twisted. "In my delusion I thought I
had gotten through to her. I uncuffed her—you understand I'd kept
her handcuffed the entire time except when taking her to the bathroom—and she put her arms around me and comforted me. As though
I were in worse shape than she. I let her take control. She told me to go
out and get coffee and food, that she would bathe while I was out. And

to allay any suspicions I might have, she urged me to take her passport with me. So that I'd know she wasn't plotting to leave the first time my back was turned. But of course we both knew that if she had tried such a thing I would have tracked her down again. So of course taking her passport was only cosmetic. Nevertheless it reinforced my conviction that I'd won her back."

Though nothing in Alexandra's experience remotely resembled the situation he described, she somehow could vividly picture it, could *see* that woman in this room (though it was not in fact the real room, as he seemed to think it was), could *feel* her hatred and desperation, for surely that had been what she had been feeling, not the love he spoke of.

He half-laughed. "But of course she was deceiving me—and I wanted to be deceived. That turned out to be the pattern of our relations in the future: her deceiving me to exploit my delusions, my desires—and I letting her do it. When I came back half an hour later, bringing the fragrance of coffee, fresh bread, cheese, and fruit with me, I found her in bed, wearing a nightgown. She had the chemical smell on her that came from washing in such a bathroom. She smiled at me and held her arms open. I oh-so-eagerly fell into them. Within a minute she had one of my wrists cuffed to the bed and was struggling with me to get the other inside the remaining cuff. She'd had the cuffs prepared, each set already attached to the bed frame, hidden by the pillows. Also under the pillows, a jagged piece of glass. She used it to compel me to put my other hand in the remaining cuff. It was the sight of this makeshift weapon that made me realize she wasn't playing. I have to admit that at first I'd half-thought she *was*. I would have fought harder if I'd known how serious she was."

Alexandra watched warily as her father got up from the bed; she prepared to defend herself should he "do something." But he moved past the mirror at the foot of the bed and opened the door she had assumed belonged to a closet, and she glimpsed through the open doorway a bathroom full of antique fittings. He turned around and faced her. "I later found out that she had broken one of my empty wine bottles in the basin. When she had me cuffed to the bed she dressed, repacked her bags, and took her passport from my tunic pocket. Then she knelt over me and held that piece of glass to my neck." He laid his fingers against a spot just below his earlobe. "Right here. The way she looked at me I thought she meant to cut my throat. Perhaps she did. But if so, she couldn't do it. She couldn't kill me, no matter what she said. I don't believe she ever would have killed me. Somewhere she still loved me, though she never admitted it to herself. 'You are killing me, Robert,' she said to me. 'I'm running for my life.' I told her she hadn't given it long enough, that things would improve. It had been less than a year since my surgery, you understand. But she said, 'It's your life or mine, Robert. If you come after me you'll have to kill me to keep me from killing you.' I knew then that she wouldn't kill me. But she lifted the glass from my neck and put it here." He pointed to the outer corner of his left eye. "Then she drew the edge of the glass down the length of my face, stopping short of the artery in my neck. But that was only the beginning. 'You see what we are,' she said, 'there's only violence between us now, there's not much farther we can go before killing one another.' Looking into her face so swollen and bruised from my beating, I could almost believe what she was saying. And then she made another slash. And another and another. She slashed my cheeks into ribbons. Just my cheeks. She left everything else alone. Which I took as a sign that she really could not hurt me. Then she set the key to the handcuffs where I would able to reach it— though with a certain awkwardness that would mean I'd not be able to free myself immediately—and left. She was betting on my not going after her, on my not sending the gendarmes after her. Assaulting an executive is no light thing. She would have spent the rest of her life in prison if I'd pressed charges. But she knew I wouldn't."

Huddled, shivering, her stomach heaving, Alexandra said, "She should have killed you. After what you'd done to her."

He looked at her; his eyebrow quirked. "You're an executive, Alexandra. That is how executive women think. She was professional. Later when I talked to her about this she claimed that the only reason she hadn't killed me was fear of being caught. But I will never believe that. There were several occasions later when she could have killed me—had she truly hated me—and she did not. Though she could never admit it to herself, she did love me."

In the sudden fall of silence, Alexandra longed to tell him how obviously deluded he still was, that no one could love him, he was too horrible to love, that loving him would be a burden no person should ever have to bear. But she did not speak. She wished it all to be over, she wished to be out of that room, out of his "story."

He moved to the door and unlocked it. "We'll go downstairs now," he said. "And have lunch before I finish telling you the rest."

Lunch? She felt sick to her stomach. She couldn't imagine eating anything. All the time she looked at his face, she imagined it in bloody disarray, strips of skin awash in rivers of blood. That woman should have killed him, Alexandra thought—and then realized that if that woman had killed him, she, Alexandra, would never have been born. It gave her a strange, dizzying feeling to realize at that moment just how closely connected—biologically—her fate was with his. Perhaps that was what people meant when they talked about flesh and blood.

[iii]

Alexandra peered at herself in the mirror and lifted her icy cold, livid white hands to her burning red cheeks. Yes, it was true, in some weird way she *did* look like him. Not the way he was now, of course, but she could see a resemblance to his image in the images taken thirty years ago with *her* that he had shown her.

It must be the wine making her cheeks so red: she'd drunk four glasses of it—one before dinner, two with dinner, and one after dinner. He didn't want to be alone, he said, because the entire night before the anniversary was a terrible time for him. He said that though for months he'd been controlled and moderate in his drinking, tonight was different. She must be there to help him tomorrow, to stop him, to refuse him alcohol if necessary. If she took the responsibility for it, Higgins and the others would do whatever she said. As long as she assumed control, assumed responsibility. Would she do that for him?

*There are much worse things than this story, you know, and you'll eventually have to face them. The work you will do in Security requires toughness.* She needed to ask him about this easy allusion to some future he had planned for her, she needed to make him see that she would never work in Security. She was a pianist. And Mama had said she could be a pianist because she would be maternal-line. But she couldn't discuss this with him now. He was too strange, too alien, too unpredictable this night. So many selves he had. The person upstairs in that room, the person who delivered political science and art history lectures, the person who listened to her music, the person behind that alien—drunken—stare... She would almost rather have him as he had been up in that room than drunk, as he was now.

Sighing, she turned away from the mirror. She would have to go back in there, she could not delay much longer. After a while she could insist on going to bed. She could pretend to fall asleep, if necessary. She would not sit up with him all night as he kept hinting he wanted. He couldn't really be expecting that of her, could he?

Alexandra returned to the Small Study and found him pacing, from the wall with the Turner on it, past the sofa, to the fireplace at the other end of the room. Back and forth, back and forth he paced. Alexandra sat down on the rug near the fireplace where she had earlier piled half a dozen cushions for herself. He stopped within a few feet of her and stared down at her. "First betrayed—by Kay; then exploited—by Weatherall," he said. "Leaving me in the dark, leaving me to speculate. Booth was right to damn my reliance on women. Never again will that happen. I'll never trust a woman again. Never."

Alexandra peered up at him and wondered if he meant her in particular. "Then why tell me anything?" she said, half-fearing an explosion from him.

He frowned down at her. "What are you talking about?"

"I'm a woman," she said. "If you can't trust me, then why tell me so many things?"

"Christ, girl, I didn't mean you. You're my *daughter*. If a man can't trust his own daughter, whom can he trust?" He wheeled around and moved back to the sofa. She thought he meant to fetch his glass, but instead he seated himself at the end nearest the fireplace. "Come sit over here," he said, patting the cushion beside him.

"I'm much more comfortable here," Alexandra said.

"Do me the courtesy of doing as I ask, Alexandra. I want to discuss something of the utmost importance with you." Reluctantly Alexandra rose to her feet and went to the sofa. "I do wish you'd cure yourself of this maternal-line mania for lolling on the floor. His voice rasped with irritation. "You'll notice that the productive majority sit on furniture. Precisely because they can't afford the indolence of lounging around on cushions."

Alexandra bit her lip. How many times today had he attacked things he labeled maternal-line?

"I'd planned to save this as a surprise, until I'd gotten the whole package worked out, but I think I'll tell you now: I talked with Keith McHugh when we were in DC. You can be expecting a letter from Yale any day now."

Alexandra frowned. "Yale? But I'm going to Sarah Lawrence! Yale has nothing to offer someone like me. Sarah Lawrence not only has a great arts faculty, but the best executive child development programs to be found! Mama's always said that if she'd had the—"

Her father, looking furious, interrupted. "So your mother's been plotting behind my back again?"

Alexandra took a deep breath. "This isn't the right time to be talking about it," she said as calmly as she could.

"Get that maternal-line nonsense out of your head once and for all, Alexandra," he said harshly. "I won't stand by and see you turned into a cross between a breeding animal and a vegetable. You've got a brain in your head! You surely don't think you should throw away your natural superiority and your extraordinary privileges by following your mother's example?" He leaned toward her, close enough for her to smell his liquored breath. "Or are you more interested in being like your brother, completely lost to reality?"

"Why can't I just be myself? Why do I have to follow someone else's example?" Alexandra's chin lifted in defiance. "I want to be a pianist. That's *all* I want. And maybe I'll like having children. Most women do, you know."

Though he wasn't drunk enough yet to stumble in his speech or forget what he was talking about, his eyes were impenetrable pools of staring, dull with the deadness of alcohol that Alexandra always found disturbingly withdrawn and sinister. "That's a selfish attitude if ever I heard one." He reached over and took hold of her chin. "Things are in such a mess now that there's no room for that kind of selfishness. The executive system might well be on the brink of collapse. And if it collapses, how then will you live your life of artistic indulgence? Don't you feel at all responsible?" He snorted. "It's being said right now that executive women are totally irresponsible, that they don't give a shit for anything but themselves and their own petty concerns."

He released her chin and retrieved his wine glass from the side table. "I suppose this is the inevitable result of letting your mother and her mother raise you."

"I don't mean to be selfish," Alexandra said, staring down at the purple and black embroidery ornamenting the hem of her tunic. "If you think I have an obligation to be career-line, I don't mind. Maybe there will be something I can do, though I don't see what. But not in Security, Papa, I can't—"

"We'll work together," he said, interrupting. His dull, withdrawn eyes remained fixed on her face. "I'll train you myself. You have only one weakness, and that's your control, which I'm sure will improve. After all, your mother's control is fairly good, and so is mine—except for my drinking, but there's a reason for that, and of course with your help it will no longer be a problem. If that kind of control problem can be worked out, then so can your kind. It's a matter of too much indulgence from your mother and grandmother. You have a good head on your shoulders. You're strong—I can sense that already in you, Alexandra, and you have no problem dealing with people. As I've already told you, you did very well at the Blumenthals, your poise was excellent." He grimaced in what she assumed to be an expression meant to convey approval. "I should have realized from the start that it would be you and not Daniel who would be my successor. Historically, sons have always given fathers a lot of grief. But daughters—daughters are to be counted on. For some reason I forgot that. I suspect people mostly do, they don't pay attention to the facts. The wish is always for sons to follow in the footsteps of their fathers... But such an ambition often remains in only the wishing stage. Sons are inevitably hostile to fathers. As I was, for instance, to mine."

Alexandra, her thoughts a wallow of confusion and consternation, tried to think of something to say. But he'd set it up so that she could only confirm or reject his plan. Would objecting do any good? After all, by the time she turned twenty-one, she would already have finished college. If she had to do exactly as he said, take the curriculum he decided on, go to the college he chose, would she have much choice left in how to dispose the rest of her life? She'd have to give up serious study of the piano if she went to Yale—thus missing four extremely critical years, thus interrupting her work with a significant hiatus. Her technique would slip. And without the child development courses—and she so wanted the special ones at Sarah Lawrence—she would not be properly fit to undertake maternity. And twenty-one was usually the age maternal-lines began their first pregnancy. "Papa," she began, hoping to postpone the discussion to a more favorable occasion, "I think—"

Again he interrupted. "You're old enough to drop this 'Papa' stuff, Alexandra. Not only does it put people off when they're around both of us, but it reeks of immaturity."

Alexandra flushed. He must mean for her to address him as Daniel did—saying "sir" all the time, or else "Father." She couldn't quite recall how she and Daniel had come to address him so differently; it had always seemed to be the case. It would be hard to remember at first, but she might actually feel more comfortable addressing him more formally. And perhaps he might in turn treat her more formally, too. "Yes, sir," she said. "I'll try to remember, but—"

He interrupted. "We aren't a Military family, Alexandra. Don't misunderstand me. You'll call me 'Robert.'"

Alexandra stared at him, shocked. She tried to imagine the shape of the word on her tongue, but could not. "It would make me uncomfortable," she said.

He said, "Why?" Not taking his gaze from her face, he drank down half the wine in his glass. Something in his eyes disturbed, even frightened her. He had thrust her back into the land of unpredictability.

"It seems, well, *wrong*," she said, fighting confusion.

He snorted. "Clarify that." His tone was derisive.

"Well, you're my father. I've never thought of you that way, it's foreign to me. And besides, women never call men by their first names. Not that I've ever heard of."

"Our relationship isn't like others' and never will be—if I can help it." His gaze narrowed. "And it's time you stopped going all childish on me whenever the mood takes you. Your mother and grandmother may think it's cute, but I assure you, I don't. Furthermore, I don't want you making Weatherall's mistake. She always avoided dealing with men. It's what got her into trouble. Your addressing me as I want you to will be one small step along the way to fitting you for real and legitimate power."

Alexandra averted her gaze from his face. What was she going to do? What *could* she do? Maybe it was just this night, and the wine. Maybe all this would pass when this "anniversary" had passed and he was sober again. "It's after midnight," she said, carefully avoiding saying "Papa." "May I go to bed now?"

She glanced at him and saw that his face was now wearing its bleak look. "I thought you were staying up with me." Alexandra waited. He shrugged. "All right. Go on. But you will keep your word about taking control when I need you to tomorrow?"

What a strange, bizarre man he was, Alexandra thought. "Yes, of course," she said and stood up. "You can count on me." She went swiftly to the door, stepped out into the hall, and closed the door behind her. (Swiftly, swiftly, before he changed his mind and chose to order her peremptorily or further importuned her to stay.) For a moment she leaned against the door to steady herself. And then she fairly flew through the house and up the stairs.

*Mama, Grandmother, Elizabeth: where are you now that I need you?* But none of them even knew where she was. It was hopeless, absolutely hopeless. And now she knew she would never dare to run away. Was that why he'd told her that story? But Elizabeth had known the story, too, he'd said. And Elizabeth had run away. Whatever he said about Elizabeth, Alexandra knew that Elizabeth had probably had to go. But how had she stood him for so many years?

She locked the door of her room, went into the bathroom, and drew a hot bath, for she was shivering with tension and cold. Was this the way the "outside world" was? Like *him*? *Had* she been "wrapped in cotton wool" all her life, as he kept claiming?

Alexandra slid down in the tub and immersed herself up to her neck. Maybe when she was twenty-one she could live with Grandmother... But would he *let* her? she wondered for the first time. Would it make any difference, her being twenty-one? Look what had happened to that woman he had constantly talked about all day... Alexandra closed her eyes and called up a memory of lying in the sea below Grandmother's house. So quiet, so warm, so gentle. Barbados, Barbados... That was where she belonged.

But Barbados might as well be on the moon.

# Chapter Four

Crossing the atrium, Hazel paused to look at the towering holograph of one of the Free Zone's "founding mothers" ("their only martyr," as Liz sarcastically put it), Kay Zeldin. Liz had known her personally and described her as "powerful, brilliant, and strong"—strong enough, in fact, to set out to destroy both Security Services and Sedgewick and come close to succeeding. Liz always spoke casually about Kay Zeldin, but Hazel sensed intense feeling streaming powerfully below the surface of what she did and did not say about her. Perhaps Liz wished—in retrospect—that she herself had attempted to pull down Security when she'd gone renegade?

The Women's Patrol applied their detectors to her; as usual, they allowed her the jammer. In the elevator she requested the third floor. She would be seeing someone in Housing, someone she'd never met before, though the woman would probably have heard of *her* and would certainly know about Liz. Since moving to the Free Zone, Hazel was always meeting people she had never heard of, persons quite alien to her, whose fit in this strange society and whose opinions and values she had to divine for herself. Most of them, of course, had some advance impression—often stereotypical—of her.

The Free Zone in general and the Co-op in particular had transformed their world into an enormously complicated tangle of relations and possibilities. In the executive world things had been relatively simple: but she knew now that that simplicity and clarity derived largely from the rigid verticality of its hierarchical and bureaucratic structures. Here, however, the structures were not often perceptibly vertical. Liz said this made it harder to "get things done," but when pressed, she had to agree that what she meant, more specifically, was that it made it harder for someone like her to manage situations and individuals. Not that Liz didn't think management wasn't possible: Martha Greenglass, Liz maintained, managed others better than anyone else in the Free Zone—just not through vertical structures. Such talk confused Hazel and made her wonder what Liz meant by management and what the structures themselves had to do with such management.

Hazel stepped out onto the third floor and found herself in Housing's reception area. This, then, was one of the organized floors. Hazel stepped up to the desk and nodded at the wrinkled, visibly aged woman sitting behind the desk. "I'm looking for Beth Sheldon," she said. "Could you point me in the right direction?" Hazel had learned long ago that telling these people one had an appointment got one nowhere. The only person who would care about the fact of the appointment would be Beth Sheldon herself.

Something in the way the woman held her head reminded Hazel of Aunt Dawn, and the resemblance unleashed a wave of poignance that brought an unexpected rush of tears to her eyes. "It's almost exactly half-way 'round," the old woman said. "You can keep following the corridor, or you can cut across by taking a spoke you'll come on a few yards up the corridor. But if you do that, when you come to the corridor you'll have to turn in the opposite direction than the one you started out with here." The woman's shaggy gray eyebrows knit. "That doesn't sound too clear, does it. Let me put it this way. Say we call the direction you start out in counter-clockwise. Well when you cross by the spoke you'll be turning up the corridor in a *clockwise* position. Do you follow?"

Hazel frowned. "I think I know what you mean," she said. She thanked the woman, then set off up the corridor, watching the inner wall—on her left—for signs of a hallway or "spoke."

Besides Jennifer Urien, Aunt Dawn was the only person from Denver she really missed. And now she would never see her again. It was the one thing she regretted about going renegade with Liz. When she'd moved to DC, she'd had the idea of saving up enough to move Aunt Dawn to DC to live with her. To get her *out* of that hell. It was easy to imagine how much worse it must have been for her without her, Hazel, there to take some of the flak and stand up to Dad for her. Her mother never would, she had learned that very early. And now all possibility of getting her out was lost. No doubt ODS officers had been there and were watching them. Liz had warned her again and again not to assume they'd ever let up on that sort of vigilance.

Hazel located the spoke and took it with some curiosity, but all the doors along it were closed, revealing nothing of how they used the center of the wheel. When she came to the corridor, she turned right. Three doors down she found Beth Sheldon's office. Before knocking on the door, Hazel took the jammer out of her pocket, activated it, and returned it to her pocket. Liz said that most of the building was bugged—though not all of it could be routinely monitored unless the Company had expanded the operations of the station, which was doubtful, considering how thoroughly it had been ravaged the previous spring. Still, they had to take every precaution. Some of the biggest breaks in Company operations were the result of diligent exploitation of fortuitous discoveries and connections.

A tall lanky woman with dark brown—almost black—skin opened the door. "Beth Sheldon?" Hazel queried. "I'm Margie Burroughs."

"Hazel, how do you do," Beth said, standing aside to let Hazel past.

"You do understand that anything that goes down on paper or is said to others can't involve my real name?" Hazel said, glad she'd activated the jammer before knocking.

Beth closed the door. "Yes, of course. But between ourselves we can surely drop pretense?"

Hazel half-smiled. "When it's safe."

"And is it safe now?" Beth asked. "You see, I don't know much about cloak-and-dagger stuff. I certainly don't want to put you in danger, but on the other hand, I'm uncomfortable with pretense."

Hazel loathed the "pretense," as this woman called it, herself. But what choice had they? "We have to keep our backs to the window," she said. "Using telescopes or binoculars, they sometimes read lips." Beth looked sardonic: Hazel wondered whether it was out of doubt of what she said or out of contempt for such maneuvers. "I suppose you've heard about the attack on the house Liz and I were living in?"

Beth's head bobbed on her long slender stalk of a neck. "I imagine everyone in Seattle must have heard about it." She moved one of the chairs away from the window. "Have a seat," she said.

In Seattle nothing was deliberately kept out of the newspapers or off the Freenet or vid. Beth repositioned another chair for herself.

"For the time being," Hazel said, "we've been moving around from one temporary situation to another—staying with people for a night or two and then moving on. We're caught in something of a dilemma." She tried to take her cue from Beth's face, but found it utterly still and watchful. Since reactions, attitudes, and values varied considerably from person to person, Hazel never felt she could predict how Co-op people would react to different ways of putting things. "Because of our special security problems, we can't really expect to live in an ordinary housing situation," she went on. "In a large apartment complex we'd be endangering our neighbors as well as ourselves, since we wouldn't be able to take the kinds of security measures that are necessary for our protection. The same goes for moving into a cooperative living situation. But it's very difficult to find any other kind of housing in Seattle."

Beth nodded, and Hazel felt slightly more confident of a sympathetic reception. "Talking with various members of the Women's Patrol, we learned that one way of getting a house might be to approach an upper-echelon professional and make an offer to buy them out—in standard international credits—for a price high enough to enable them to move out of the Zone and establish themselves in their previous lifestyle somewhere else in the States." Beth's thin, plucked eyebrows soared over her suddenly snapping eyes. "I gather," Hazel rushed on, "that only high-echelon professionals are among those who both owned property before the Blanket and stayed on afterwards. That legally, few other houses are for sale, and that any such "sale" would otherwise be really just a bribe to vacate the house and would be understood as such."

Beth folded her arms over her chest. "I see what you're thinking," she said. "But you realize that no one explicitly connected with the Co-op can participate in such property dealings? If there's one thing the Co-op is firm on, it's the abolition of private real estate, of absentee property rentals, of the sale of property for profit."

Hazel gnawed at her lower lip. "Yes," she said. "I understand the problem. But I thought you might be able to assist us in finding such a situation for us to make use of. We're desperate, and I don't know how else we can manage. Except, of course, to leave Seattle."

"That is a possibility you should consider," Beth said, but not, Hazel thought, with hostility.

"Several people have told us that you are the single most knowledgeable person about the housing situation in Seattle," Hazel said.

"I'm not a real-estate agent."

"But perhaps you could put us on to situations you may have heard about?"

"You're talking about people whom I think would want to leave the Zone but haven't because they feel they'd have too much to lose if they left their house behind?"

"Or felt they wouldn't have the plastic to re-establish themselves elsewhere."

Beth shrugged. "I'm fully prepared to believe such people exist, but *I* don't know any. The most dissatisfied people left within a year of the Withdrawal."

There must, Hazel thought, be hundreds—probably even thousands—of people who'd jump at the chance of leaving the Free Zone with the knowledge that they'd have the plastic to set themselves up comfortably somewhere else. Though she could see that maybe service-techs would be unlikely to want to do so, surely there were a lot of professionals, especially high-echelon types, who'd love to get out of the Free Zone?

"You might," Beth said, "have better luck in the rural areas. Or in Northern California, since its ditching of the executive-system is of more recent origin."

An interesting way to put the Free Zone's annexation of territory, Hazel thought wryly. Liz had assumed when she decided to stay in the Free Zone that using the lure of plastic credit and chances of getting out of the Zone would make it easy for her to accomplish certain things. But after a few months she had started wondering whether a covert action team would find it as easy to recruit agents as they did ten years ago. People in Portland and Seattle in particular seemed to have lost interest in fighting the Co-op, in opposing anarchy—even the males, who were still excluded from Steering Committee meetings. But of course, as Liz had pointed out, not that much was decided at Steering Committee meetings. Though issues and principles came in for discussion at those big public (but all-female) gatherings, most

of the day-to-day decisions seemed to be made by committees and
sub-committees drawn largely from the small specialized co-ops that
the Free Zone appeared to have been organized into, and these included anyone—male or female—who cared to join. Some people,
Liz speculated, might belong to as many as ten or twelve co-ops altogether: neighborhood co-ops, food co-ops, work-oriented co-ops,
environment-oriented co-ops, medical co-ops, arts co-ops, and so on
and so forth. "The name of the game"—in Liz's phrase—seemed to
be something called "coalition politics." At which, Liz said, Martha
Greenglass excelled as a consummate master of strategy and suasion.

The structure and techniques of this sort of politics differed radi-
cally from that of the executive system. Its very alienness frustrated
Liz immensely. But it didn't bother Hazel—except to the extent that
it occasionally made personal encounters difficult. On the contrary,
she rather enjoyed the informality of these people. It was, however,
difficult to get things done when the lines of responsibility and authority were so elusive. Before doing anything, one first had to figure out how to do it—that is, one had to trace out possible paths one
might wish to try along the way: the scattershot method, Liz called
it. Hazel found the lack of executive types wonderfully liberating but
wondered if the price to be paid for such freedom would ultimately
be too high. Certainly this safe housing problem she and Liz faced had
something to do with the general lack of control in the Free Zone. As
for what to do with the naval intelligence people who had broken into
their house: that had been one of the worst dilemmas of all. Martha
Greenglass had urged Liz to have them taken to the border and expelled. "What will keep them from coming back?" Liz had demanded.
"Won't more of these types be sent in if they *aren't* sent back to their
masters?" Martha had pointedly retorted.

"I have the distinct impression you're eager to get us out of
Seattle," Hazel said.

Beth sighed. "All I'm saying is that if you can't find a way to live
within our structures you might find it a lot easier somewhere else.
It's not a matter of what *I* think or want. It's a matter of what *you* and
*she* want—and, possibly, need. As far as I'm concerned, your problems
are special because of what *she* is and what *she* wants—the latter of
which isn't at all clear to me." She looked as if she had suspicions that

she didn't like. And probably, Hazel thought, rightly so. Liz made no secret of her disdain for the Co-op's way of doing things. "If it were just you, Hazel, I'm sure we could figure out a safe and livable situation. But what the two of you want together isn't the responsibility of anyone in the Free Zone to provide." She smiled, her full, plush lips twitching but not opening. Hazel wondered if she were suppressing a laugh. "Considering the kind of protection she's marshaled around her—something like a small army, isn't it? —I wonder that you're calling on me at all."

Hazel began to wonder that herself, until she recalled that she had wanted to "pick Beth's brains" for possible suggestions. "I don't think it's a matter of force," Hazel said quietly. "I personally hate violence. What would be best would be avoiding the kind of situation that forced us to leave our house on Queen Anne Hill. We take precautions, we live carefully. What we want is to keep a low profile. But anywhere we live permanently requires further precautions that would not be possible if many other people were involved. My idea in talking with you was to see if you had any suggestions." Hazel stood up. "I'm sorry I wasted your time."

The handset on Beth's desk chirped. She unfolded it on the second ring and held it to her ear. "Beth Sheldon," she said. "Hmmm...Yes, yes, she's here. Yeah, I'll tell her. No, we're almost finished." She folded the handset and looked at Hazel. "That was Martha Greenglass. She would like you to stop in at her office before you leave the building."

"So much for security," Hazel said under her breath, wondering how Martha had discovered her presence in the building to start with and in Beth's office in particular.

Beth walked her to the door. "If I hear something that might be helpful, I'll let you know, Hazel. But don't get your hopes up. Now if on the other hand you should happen to find yourself on your own, I know for a fact I could help you out." Her eyes stared meaningly into Hazel's, as though to communicate something that she did not care to put into words.

That expression in Beth's eyes preoccupied Hazel as she retraced her steps to the elevator. She had encountered similar attitudes in other women in the Co-op. They all seemed to be hinting that she would be better off leaving Liz and that they believed that she *would*

leave Liz…eventually. Perhaps it was this that Liz sensed and resented and possibly even feared. For all that Liz claimed to be appreciative of and non-prejudiced about service-techs, Hazel felt certain that Liz disliked having to work with them cooperatively.

Hazel found Martha's office door open and Martha seated with her back to it. "Hello," she said from the threshold. "Beth Sheldon said you wanted to see me."

Martha glanced over her shoulder at Hazel, then got to her feet; her face, as she smiled at Hazel, glowed with warmth. "Hey, you. Thanks for stopping by. Come in, won't you?"

"Remember about keeping our backs to the window as we talk?" Hazel said as she entered.

Martha closed the door. "Sure. If you like, we can sit on the floor, out of anyone but a helicopter's line of sight." She fetched a couple of half-liter bottles of water from a cupboard and settled on the carpet, leaning back against the door with her legs stretched before her. Her look up at Hazel, who hadn't expected her to drop to the floor, was as mischievous as a little girl's caught playing with her mother's cosmetics and made Hazel laugh.

So Hazel dropped down onto the carpet, too, and sat facing her, upright and cross-legged. "How did you find out I was in the building?" She twisted the cap off the bottle Martha had handed her.

"Someone happened to see you down in the atrium and mentioned it in the course of a conversation. Since I've been wanting to talk to you or Liz, I called down to the Women's Patrol desk by the elevator and found out you had gotten off on the third floor. After which I called Ellie Jordan, who sits in the reception area on the third floor." Martha grinned. "She of course told me you'd asked how to get to Beth's office. Piece of cake. So how've you been?"

"Well *that's* sobering," Hazel said. "It doesn't quite boost my confidence in my security."

Martha's eyebrows rose. "But you realize that neither the Women's Patrol nor Ellie would have given just anyone that information."

"Still," Hazel said. "It's a sample of how circumstances can work. In another situation…" She shrugged.

"You'd be a hell of a lot safer if you weren't living with Elizabeth Weatherall."

Hazel set the bottle down on the floor beside her. "But I am living with her. And I intend to go on living with her."

Martha gave her a serious look. After several seconds, she said, "It's your decision." She drank from the bottle. "But speaking of security. I'd like you to talk to Elizabeth for me. Or else ask her to get in touch with me herself. You see, as she no doubt expected would be the case, we're not at all happy with her having handed those people over to Louise Simon to use as hostages."

The intensity of Martha's gaze was almost palpable. After several long seconds, Hazel looked down at the carpet and picked up her bottle of water. Then she looked back at Martha. "The way Liz saw it was that these men had intruded into her house with evil intentions. They did so uninvited and aware that if they got caught they'd be subject to retaliation. She couldn't stand the thought of simply turning them loose at the border. See, she had the idea they would have come straight back for another shot at us. So, she reasoned, the best thing would be to make use of them to accomplish something positive. Since the Co-op wasn't interested in using them to bargain for the freedom of political prisoners being held by Military authorities, she decided she'd let Simon use them."

Martha stared hard at Hazel. "We're not about to use human hostages for accomplishing *anything*. It's out of the question. This is essentially the same situation Louise got into herself. Those SIC people she captured were intending *her* harm. And had already been doing harm throughout the Free Zone. Yet that didn't justify her taking them hostage." Martha's eyebrows lifted, then relaxed. "What kind of deal did Elizabeth get out of Louise?"

Hazel frowned. "I don't understand your question, Martha."

"What did Louise give or promise to do for Elizabeth in return for getting three new hostages?"

Hazel grew uneasy. Could Liz have worked some deal that she hadn't told her about? "I don't know that there was that kind of deal," Hazel said, her gaze steady on Martha's.

After a few seconds, Martha shook her head. "It's such a mess," she said. "They've only let two of all those hostages go so far. In return for the release of certain militant activists Louise has been in touch with over the years. I assume they're with her now, wherever she is.

But what is really difficult about all this is that Louise, simply by staying in the Free Zone, is able to claim Marq'ssan protection. We both
know, Hazel, that if it weren't for the protection that extends over
each of the Free Zones, Louise's group would probably have been destroyed by now—hostages notwithstanding."

"I don't know that at all," Hazel said. "They have a cabinet officer's son."

Martha leaned forward. "Listen, Hazel. It's important that
Elizabeth understand that she can't take up that type of activity using
the Free Zone as her base of operations."

Hazel said, "Come on, Martha. Even you must see that that's not
in the cards. I mean, Liz and I are having a hard time just keeping
alive. This Marq'ssan protection you're talking about obviously doesn't
extend to *us*." Hazel brought her knees up, leaned forward, and rested
her elbows on her kneecaps. "Hasn't it occurred to you that the reason
Louise Simon hasn't been attacked isn't because of Marq'ssan protection, but because the Executive doesn't want to kill Mark Goodwin?
And maybe even because Louise Simon's whereabouts aren't known?"
Simon had told Liz that she would be moving out of the Free Zone
in the next few months. And since she'd tried to get Liz to give her
security-related details about the LA area, Liz suspected that Simon
intended to join forces with the Mujeres Libres group.

Martha set her empty bottle on the floor and folded her arms across
her chest. "Did you know, Hazel, that I was once Louise's lover?"

Hazel stared down at her knees. "I'd heard that, yes."

"For some time, although I didn't *like* what I saw Louise doing—
training women in combat skills and forming the Women's Patrol, I
mean—I excused her. Because I loved her." Hazel looked up and met
Martha's intense and demanding gaze. "And because I didn't realize
that the violence implicit in her activities was more than theoretical.
When I found out she was a murderer, she said that she'd thought I'd
known. And she acted surprised at my revulsion and condemnation."
Martha paused. For a long moment their gazes held in a powerful
lock. When Hazel finally broke eye-contact, Martha said, "Learn from
my mistake, Hazel. If there's something you sense is wrong, don't shut
your eyes to it because you love her. It's painful, but believe me, it's far
more painful in the long run to look away. I know."

Hazel rolled the empty plastic water bottle between her palms. She sometimes wondered about herself—wondered how she could stay with Liz after having witnessed her deliberately breaking that man's rib. And yet... It wasn't the same. Breaking someone's rib in the middle of an emergency was totally different from the premeditated murder of Louise Simon's death squad. "Liz isn't Louise," Hazel said, looking into Martha's eyes. "And besides, suppose I were to find out something terrible Liz had done: are you saying that the only decent response would be for me to walk away from her? Because I don't agree. I think that if you really loved Louise you would have loved her enough to try to change her."

Now Martha looked away, but not before Hazel saw the pain in her eyes. "I'm not saying walking away is the right thing to do. I've admitted—and publicly, Hazel—that I lacked a certain personal courage. I don't know if it was a lack of love. But maybe you're right. Maybe it was. All I know is that I wasn't strong enough—or didn't feel myself strong enough at the time—to take on the task of changing her. Right now I tend to think that it would have been a hopeless task that no one could have succeeded at. How well do you know Elizabeth? And how long have you been with her? Louise had had many years of experience different from mine, apart from mine. That kind of thing matters, you know."

"You think anyone who's worked for Security must be evil. Isn't that it?"

Martha half-smiled. "That's not what I'm saying. Actually, I'd be a fool to say that since several people I know who have done a lot for the Free Zone worked at one time or another for Security."

Hazel nodded. "You see, there's always hope, especially where a renegade is involved."

Martha sighed. "At any rate, tell her for me—and for the Co-op—that if she pulls another stunt like this handing of hostages over to Louise, the Co-op—and the Marq'ssan as well—may not be willing to work with her in any way again."

Liz had done a great many useful things for the Co-op. This warning or threat (or whatever it was) was going to make her angry, Hazel felt sure. "Beth Sheldon suggested we leave town," Hazel said.

"Why?"

"I don't know. It was her 'solution' to our safe-housing problem."

Martha frowned. "Elizabeth makes people nervous."

"I see," Hazel said, getting to her feet. "I'll convey your message to her."

Martha stood and opened the door, and her face softened. "Listen, Hazel. If there's anything I can help you with, don't hesitate to ask." Her eyes expressed something more, but to Hazel's relief, she refrained from putting it into words.

Hazel headed for the elevator and what promised to be the least pleasant of the day's Co-op encounters. She and Liz always operated on the assumption that the main entrances to the building were regularly watched. If they were seen going in, they must not be seen coming out. For all their liberty, their lives seemed to be bound by rules. One slip could be the end of that liberty. Danger, all around them, had become just about routine: boring and tedious, often embarrassing and awkward, filled with the terrible need to rely on others to do favors—usually small ones—like the one she would now ask of the Women's Patrol. "You must grow a thicker skin," Liz was always telling her. Hazel stepped into the elevator and requested B1.

Thinking about what Martha had said, she wondered. *Had* fear kept her from intervening at an earlier point? (But Liz had driven her foot into him without warning: how could she have prevented *that?*) Hazel leaned against the wall and (again) faced the fact that she needed somehow to understand these things by herself. There was no one to explain to her, no one to judge for her or advise her. She would not be like her mother, but neither would she be like Martha.

## [ii]

"Well. That decides it," Liz said when Hazel had passed on Martha's message and described Beth's lack of helpfulness. "We're going to have to give up our policy of keeping a low profile."

Hazel paused in the act of pouring coffee from the thermoflask into her cup to turn and look at Liz. "What do you mean?" Liz had that calculating look in her eye that usually indicated certain wheels turning, wheels that would carry them into strange terrain Hazel herself would never imagine visiting.

"It's time to face the fact that we're going to have to come out into the open—at least as far as our living situation is concerned. It will mean elaborate and ostentatious security precautions; it will mean building a mini-fortress; it will mean heavy shielding that can't be penetrated by intruders except through something as drastic as heavy-duty aerial bombardment—which I'm willing to gamble they'll never attempt for fear of encountering surface-to-air missiles—if not severe retaliation from the aliens."

Hazel stared at Liz, for a moment too stupefied to speak. "You're not serious," she finally said.

"I'm dead serious. If Greenglass has decided not to cooperate with us—and I expect that's where the problem with Beth Sheldon really lies—then we have no choice. Though they won't like it, I can tell you that right now."

"I have no trouble believing that," Hazel said drily, thinking of Martha's comments on Liz and what she might be up to.

"Of course one reason they won't like it is because it will draw attention to the obvious dangers of anarchy. That is, that someone can be hunted and killed with impunity around here."

Hazel sighed. "If you think you're going to provoke any popular support following that direction, think again. The murder rate is simply not very high in the Free Zone. And people will say that we brought our illicit connections into the Free Zone with us and that it's no one's problem but our own. Or that if it is, we'll have brought it on innocent people." Liz still cherished illusions about managing popular opinion in Seattle—even though she admitted that the covert action team that had been operating in the area since the Executive Withdrawal had never succeeded in achieving any significant influence over public opinion in the city.

"I think, too," Liz said, ignoring Hazel's comment, "that this swings the balance in favor of my openly taking up contract work."

Hazel carried her cup of coffee to the sofa. "Margot Ganshoff, at least, will be happy."

Liz followed Hazel to the sofa. "Perhaps this is what we needed. Playing cat-and-mouse games stunted my thinking. I was willing to settle for survival, which was stupid, Hazel." Liz reached out and brushed a stray hair off Hazel's forehead. "In the long run, to be controlled by fear is not really to survive. One might stay alive, but that's not the same as really surviving. I'm tired of this nonsense, darling. I'm itching to do something."

It wasn't as though Liz had been doing nothing. All the consultations she had been doing with the International Human Rights Committee, with Louise Simon, and with the Co-op surely counted for something. But perhaps because the consultations involved others' projects Liz did not count them as "doing something"? "What is it you're thinking of 'doing'?" Hazel asked.

A dreamy look came into Liz's eyes. "I don't know, darling. But I feel something stirring below the surface of my mind, something interesting, something *large*. I'm going to give it space and see what happens." Her eyes grew intensely excited.

Hazel couldn't stop thinking of her conversation with Martha. "You're not thinking of anything like the things Simon does, are you?"

Liz's eyes widened. "Lord, darling! Do I strike you as a militant revolutionary? Do I?"

Hazel had to laugh. "No, Liz. But maybe something else militant?"

Liz shook her head. "No, darling, whatever it is that's coming, it's nothing to do with deliberately wreaking violence against people and property. I've no desire to be a general at the head of a crusading army."

"Just checking," Hazel said, her anxiety not in the least allayed. Whatever changes Liz intended to make in their lives, she suspected she wasn't going to like them. She'd have to see if she could change Liz's mind about living "openly" and succeed in finding them another housing situation. There had to be a way, somehow, without resorting to Liz's crazy plan.

"I'm starving," Liz said. "Let's eat an early dinner out before going home."

Hazel smiled. "Okay, Rapunzel. Where do you have in mind?"

"Shirl told me today about a little Asian place in Madison Park that opened last week. Want to try it?"

Hazel slid close to Liz, then straddled her with her knees on either side of Liz's thighs. "What if *they* like Asian food as much as *we* do?" she asked, half-serious.

Liz twined her arms around Hazel's neck. "Then *they're* in trouble, darling." Liz, Hazel knew, was half-serious, too.

Hazel leaned forward, closed her eyes, and engaged Liz in an extended tongue-dance of a kiss. In the dark of the long embrace the aching tingle in her groin and breasts spread over the rest of her body. Breathlessly Hazel withdrew. "Okay, Rapunzel. Let's go."

Liz grinned. "You've got a flush on you, darling. Are you sure you wouldn't rather have an antipasto course here first?" Her hand slid up Hazel's thigh.

Hazel grinned back. "We could have dessert at home instead." She knew better than to postpone food once Liz had announced she was hungry. Liz got horridly cranky when kept from her food.

"You're right," Liz said. "I'm too damned ravenous. I might turn carnivorous." She nibbled delicately on Hazel's neck. "Maybe that's how vampires got started. Sheer hunger at a time of sexual temptation and distraction."

Hazel hopped off Liz's lap in mock alarm. "Not with my body you don't!" she cried, reaching for their outdoor clothing.

Liz got up and took her cloak from Hazel. "Such a spoilsport. Wouldn't I be interesting-looking with fangs for incisors?" She bared her teeth at Hazel.

"Only if you find 'interesting' intimidating every soul you meet," Hazel retorted. Liz's smile faded. Hazel picked up the phone to tell Gerry their plans: back to routine, back to reality. Which she'd somehow have to make Liz see it was necessary to hold on to.

# Chapter Five

## [i]

After hours of working on a brief it was likely no judge would ever read, Celia emerged from the dilapidated old building that housed the Hillcrest Center for Medical and Legal Assistance feeling tired and discouraged. When she glanced up and down the street to place her watchdog, she found him leaning against the hood of a four-seater—along with two other ODS types.

Celia's breath stopped in her throat.

Though their approach was leisurely, their eyes never moved from her body, and one of them dangled a pair of cuffs from his fingers. Celia understood what was happening, of course, but she could hardly believe it. It had been a day like any other. There had been no sign of warning, no reason to believe that this day would not be like any other. When they reached her, they didn't bother to say anything. One of them yanked her arms behind her back, and the cold steel scraped her wrists. Celia flinched at the sound of the cuffs snapping shut. Weary anger washed over her. *Not again.*

As they wedged her between two of them in the backseat of the auto, she remembered the jammer she carried in her pocket. When they found the jammer—and it went without saying that they would—they would have an explicit lead into a subject they'd be only too pleased to explore during interrogation. Everyone who worked at the Center took turns carrying the jammer home with them, as a way of thinning the risk of one particular individual being caught in possession of it. They knew they couldn't leave it overnight at the Center, for the Center was raided every few weeks. If discovered in a raid, the jammer would not only be confiscated, but also lead to new arrests.

The car sped up University. When it successively crossed the intersections of both Fourth and Fifth Avenues without turning, Celia wondered where they could possibly be going that was not via the freeway. To meet someone? Or to show her something?

God. She fought off the gag-reflex tickling her throat. The one on her left who looked as though he hadn't washed his hair in weeks had breath that could kill, as if seeping up from a sewer. The car jolted to a halt, and Celia was thrown sideways against him. In dread of reprisal, she quickly righted herself; but the man only snarled at her. *Worse than a sewer. More like rotting shit. Only shit is already rotting, isn't it?* The anglo sitting in the front passenger seat mumbled into a handset, then said to the driver, "We wait here." Celia felt like throwing up. They had left her alone for more than half a year. Had it been because they had hoped to learn more from her this way, once they'd decided she was "incorrigible"? She imagined them having decided *Let her loose for a few months and see what she gets into with Emily Madden. And then we'll reel her back in, bringing some Big Ones along with her.*

Another four-seater pulled up and parked behind them. "Okay, Espin, out," the one with the foul breath said, opening his door. Awkwardly Celia pushed herself along the seat until she could swing her feet onto the ground. Roughly he grabbed her arm and walked her back to the other car.

An executive got out and came around the front. Celia recognized her as Lisa Mott. Mott took Celia's arm and ordered the man back to the other car to wait. "Walk with me onto the overpass, Celia," the executive said.

As they walked the thirty yards back to the overpass, Celia noted that although Mott's grip on her arm did not hurt, it was not lax, either. When they reached the overpass they leaned against the railing, which reached only as high as Celia's thighs, and stared down at the freeway. Celia fought the panic that rose as she faced such a drop with her hands cuffed behind her back. Tipping her over the railing would be trivial. Absolutely trivial. When in detention one always seemed to be noticing ways one could be killed. Things that would ordinarily never occur to Celia would pop into her head the way speculation about the weather might in more normal circumstances.

"Relax," Mott said. "You needn't look so terrified. I'll have them release you as soon as we've finished talking."

Celia stared into the gold-flecked russet eyes. She trusted this woman no more than she trusted the thugs sitting in the car fifty yards up the street.

"I want you to give Emily Madden a message for me," Mott said, sounding oddly breathless.

This was about Emily? Well. The only thing surprising about that was that Mott would explicitly say so.

Mott bit her lip. "You see, I can't afford to risk contacting her openly. Things are...difficult. Since she hasn't been going to Mytilene much these days, I thought the easiest—though not perhaps the safest—thing would be to contact her through you." She made a disparaging face. "You are, after all, easily accessible...when you're in town." Her face was paler than Celia had ever seen it, showing freckles Celia had never before noticed.

Celia looked down at the oleanders flourishing in the long-abandoned lanes below. Easily accessible? Lisa Mott could have her picked up whenever she liked. Could have her detained whenever she liked for however long she liked. Could have her interrogated whenever she liked... Celia looked into Mott's drawn and haggard face. "Just this morning I was talking to somebody who because of his treatment during an ODS detention lost hearing in an ear. It was hard going, trying to talk with him. Are you ever present when such things are done? Have you yourself ever meted out such treatment? Because I'd like to know—"

"That's enough, Celia," Mott said sharply. "I'll warn you right now that if you attempt to embarrass me, you'll deeply regret it. Your position is vulnerable, to say the least. If you say Word One about the subject of this conversation to anyone but Emily Madden, you'll find yourself in a very unpleasant situation. And the only mischief you'd succeed in working against me would be at most dismissal from my job. I'm a Mott, Celia, and that means something." Her blazing eyes looked almost desperate in her chalk-white face.

Celia assumed the appearance of a calmness she did not feel. "Whatever," she said.

"Tell her that I need to talk to her about Elizabeth Weatherall." She stared uneasily past Celia. "Tell her I may need contacts in the Free Zone, that I'm considering going renegade." Celia gasped, and

Mott looked at her. "Oh yes. I know very well the pair of you have been making trips up there."

Celia's stomach flopped. She felt she should deny this, but found no words ready to hand.

"I've done nothing about it." Mott stared hard into Celia's eyes. "There's certainly enough there for pursuing you both. But I've held off." She paused to draw an audibly ragged breath. "Tell her I must talk to her."

"I will," Celia said hoarsely, trying to control the new waves of fear coursing through her body. "I'll tell her everything you've said."

"I'd like to see her tonight, if possible."

Celia swallowed. "It's probably possible," she said.

"Good. Tell her to visit Mytilene tonight at nine. I'll be there ahead of time so her tail won't see me going over there to meet her."

"She has a tail with access to the Muirlands?"

"Yes," Mott said—indifferently. "I arranged for the gate pass myself."

Was this a trap for Emily? Celia supposed she shouldn't be surprised. Given Mott's position in ODS, nothing could be too nasty for her to dirty her hands with, not even blackmail of another executive.

"We'll go back to the other car now," Mott said. "You'll be free to go then. Don't forget, tonight at nine. And if not tonight, tomorrow night. Clear?"

"Understood," Celia responded, and they began walking back. For the moment all she could think of was getting the cuffs off her wrists. Irrational as it seemed to her, the very fact that she was cuffed and in the vicinity of those four animals—never mind her imminent freedom—dampered her mind, kept her from thinking about anything except getting away from them. Once she was safe and free, then she would be able to consider this new development and what might lie behind it.

[ii]

As Celia awaited Emily's return, she worked on the report she was compiling for the next International Human Rights Committee meeting. She kept here in Emily's house—for it was (so far, anyway) one of the safest places in San Diego County for keeping sensitive documents—the flow of reports pouring in from simpatico attorneys and physicians as far north as Santa Barbara and as far east as Amarillo. Amassing information and attending meetings were among the chief responsibilities she had undertaken when she'd agreed to be named the monitor for the US Southwest. She also traveled around the area to talk to Movement people in person. Such work left little time for actual casework at the Center, but since she could not herself go into court, the job of monitor made her feel less powerless, less passive than she had felt when doing only out-of-court prep work for clients at the Center.

This night, though, Celia found it hard to concentrate. Lisa Mott had seemed genuinely upset and tense, but could she really be considering going renegade? Emily had dismissed Celia's suspicion as absurd. "I've been going out into the desert with that woman for years!" Emily had said. "It's unthinkable she would snare me by trickery. If she *were* my enemy she'd play it openly, fairly. I know executive women, Celia. They don't play those kinds of tricks on one another."

"Even if she thought you a traitor to your own kind?" Celia had said.

But Emily had laughed and replied that she didn't think Lisa was crazy enough to judge her a traitor for the sorts of things she had done.

At 10:30 Celia got up from the desk and looked out the window. Surely they would not talk longer than an hour and a half?

If it were a trap and Emily had been arrested, Celia would be taken here by surprise.

At 11:00, Celia returned the files she had been working on to the safe, found the bottle of gin Emily kept for her, and poured a shot.

At 11:30, Celia's handset buzzed. It was Emily, calling to tell her she was about ready to leave, that Celia was not to worry, that she'd be there in half an hour or less.

Celia poured another shot.

Twenty-five minutes later, Celia heard the gates opening; she went to the window and watched Emily's car pull into the drive. The gates closed, and the headlights went dark. When Celia saw Emily getting out of the car, she ran down the stairs and opened the door. "You took so long, Em!"

Emily locked the door and re-set the security system, then went upstairs with Celia to the main floor. "Lisa had a lot to say." Emily gave Celia a troubled, half-worried look. "I don't understand why she felt so certain I know where Elizabeth Weatherall is and how to contact her. Whenever I asked her about that, she'd start talking about my trips to the Free Zone and how Elizabeth must be there or in Canada, since everyone knew she was somewhere on the continent and that those were the only places she could hope to escape being made."

"I hope you never admitted going to the Free Zone?" Celia said anxiously.

Emily's affectionate smile lit her entire face. "Cee! Surely you don't think I'm *that* naïve!"

When it came to Mott, Celia did indeed think that Emily was that naïve. But Celia had to smile. She sank into the deep, comfortable armchair she liked to use for reading. "So you were discreet? I'm relieved to hear it! But tell me, what did she really, really *want*? Do you know?"

Emily sat on the floor and leaned back against the sofa. "According to Lisa, Security Services has been a shambles since Elizabeth went renegade. Not only has the central core of Security been shaken up and disorganized—purged, I guess most people would characterize it—leaving all the branches and local authorities to cope with either contradictory orders or, mostly, none at all—but the man who has taken over Security from Sedgewick—the previous head of the Justice Department—has instituted a witch hunt. He's trying to root out anyone who may in any way be loyal to Elizabeth Weatherall—never mind that she's long gone—and he's trying to break up what Lisa calls 'the women's network', which she says helped accomplish things by providing unofficial channels for cutting through cumbersome and inertial systems. She talked a long time about this 'women's network,' about how it was something Elizabeth herself had fostered. Not that Elizabeth *invented* it, but she used it in such a way throughout most of the branches of the Executive that it got to be a sort of auxiliary system of communication that allowed her—and others—to get things done. And incidentally was very attractive for a lot of women like Lisa Mott." Emily clasped her hands around her knees. "I gather it shifted a certain amount of power to women that they wouldn't ordinarily have had. Giving them more information to go on, for one thing, and also making it easier to *do* things—without having to deal with men. That was the point, of course. It allowed them to access information without depending on men for it—meaning, mostly, their bosses— and it offered a kind of support system." Emily's mouth twisted. "It isn't all that easy for executive women working under executive men, Celia."

"I wouldn't know about that," Celia said shortly, thinking of how much power Lisa Mott had, of how when Mott had ordered her to be picked up it had been done.

"It's quite true. Almost all executive men despise almost all executive women. Even though they depend on the women. The women are expected to pretend there's no dependency."

"You do this for your father?" Celia asked pointblank.

Emily, not breaking eye-contact, nodded. "I've been doing it for as long as I can remember. Which is why, I think, he never inquires very closely into any of my non-business activities." Emily stretched her legs and looked thoughtfully at her toes. She glanced at Celia, then looked back at her toes and wiggled them. Raising her legs and flexing her ankles, she said, "To make a long story short, the fact that Security fell into a state of chaos after Elizabeth's defection—I gather Sedgewick has been put on leave because he was completely ineffectual, perhaps even broken down, according to what Lisa said—has sent a wave of panic through the executive system." She lowered her ankles and looked at Celia. "Panic about the extent to which women have been running the system through this nonofficial set of channels. Which is to say the men feel they've lost control to the women. And they're obsessed with the fear of women as potential renegades. Á la Elizabeth Weatherall."

"Are you saying the executive system is falling apart, all because Elizabeth Weatherall went renegade?" Celia said incredulously.

Emily frowned. "I don't know, Cee. I don't have enough information to go on. God knows the Executive lost control of this country a long time ago. Since the Blanket, I'd say. Basically they've been struggling to regain control since then. But it seems to me that the system itself is getting crazier. How much crazier it can get without 'falling apart,' as you put it, is anyone's guess."

"This women's thing is that widespread?"

Emily sighed. "One of the best kept secrets of modern times is the extent to which executive women stick together. And I mean *stick*, Cee. We have our own slang, our own principles and ethics. We think of ourselves as a *group*. I don't know what we could expect to happen if, say, a significant portion of that group decided its interests aren't being served by the executive system."

Celia noticed that Emily had switched from talking about executive women as "them" to saying "we." It gave her a strange feeling, thinking of how much Emily was a part of that. "So what is it you're to tell Elizabeth Weatherall?" she asked when Emily, staring off into space, did not go on.

Emily looked at Celia and sighed. "Elizabeth is bound to be suspicious. I have no idea whether anything can be arranged. But basically I'm to tell Elizabeth that Lisa and several others are getting rather desperate and would like to meet with her to see about joining her. If, that is, Elizabeth is up to something. Lisa seems to think she is. And she seems to think that if I tell Elizabeth that Allison Bennett has been tossed out of Security and is enduring harassment by her former colleagues and is thus very much interested in 'going over' to Elizabeth, Elizabeth will agree to a secret meeting somewhere safe. Lisa says they're willing to trust Elizabeth to the point of putting up with whatever arrangements she decides are necessary to safeguard her own position." Emily's eyebrows worried at something. "If I read this situation correctly, there may be an executive revolt underway."

Celia leaned her head against the back of the chair. "What kind of implications would such a revolt have for things in general?"

Emily shrugged. "Who knows? But consider this, Cee. The Executive Transformation of 2041 can be characterized as a revolt within executive ranks. Not that there was this precise grouping we now designate as executives before then. But basically it's something that happened in the upper levels of control. A year ago I would have said that that revolt made a difference, that it improved things for all of society. But today I can't say that. I don't think we know what the differences are. It's something we don't have enough information on. Whether a successful revolt by the women will matter is, to me, doubtful. It *could*—but I think the circumstances—the fact, for instance, that those women seem to want to line up behind Elizabeth Weatherall, of all people—argues against that interpretation." Emily looked into Celia's eyes. "For years, Elizabeth Weatherall ran Security. Which is why it was entirely credible when we heard Sedgewick had been booted out of his position after Elizabeth's defection. The grossest of human rights violations have become routine during the years since the Blanket, which happens to be the period of time Elizabeth Weatherall was running things. I'm not saying that she specifically ordered the abuses—because I don't think she did—but I am saying that she hasn't demonstrated the kind of moral and ethical leadership required for bringing about the kind of revolution we could find useful."

"Then if that's the case, you must be careful not to take any risks at all," Celia said. "For they'd be risks taken in vain."

Emily said, "I've given my word I'll help Lisa."

Celia gaped at her.

Emily gestured. "It seems I feel—in spite of everything—a sense of obligation to render this kind of assistance to other executive women."

Celia shot Emily a look of reproach. She found it difficult to understand how Emily could risk her own safety as well as that—possibly— of the Movement for an anglo bitch like Mott who daily gave orders to ODS creeps. Was there a difference between Elizabeth Weatherall as Emily described her and Lisa Mott? And would Emily do the same for Elizabeth Weatherall, simply because she was an executive woman? This manifestation of class loyalty disturbed Celia. But she said nothing, feeling uncertain and badly informed. She got to her feet. "I'm absolutely wiped," she said. "I think I'll go to bed now."

"It's been a long day. As for me, I think I want to do a bit more thinking about my conversation with Lisa."

"Are you going to make a special trip to the Free Zone to contact Weatherall?"

Emily tilted her head back to look at Celia. "That's something I'm going to have to think about. Probably. Because I don't want to mix up Movement business with this executive women's affair. Best to keep them as separate as possible."

Celia wholeheartedly agreed with *that.* For whether Emily admitted it or not, the Movement could be imperiled by these sorts of machinations. She must try to make Emily see that Mott would be an ODS executive first and an executive woman second. And not vice versa.

Celia said good night and went to her room. It had been a long and exhausting day, and the gin had made her sleepy. She cracked the window, turned off the light, and crawled between the sheets. She was safe, and free, and comfortable. It had been a couple of weeks since her last nightmare. She smoothed her fingers over the soft clean cotton pillow slip and drew the fresh ocean air deep into her lungs. Before she finished exhaling that breath, she had dropped into sleep.

# Chapter Six

## [i]

As always before tea on the second and fourth Thursdays in the month, Alexandra went down after her piano lesson to Nicole's little office behind the kitchen. She tapped on the open door, and Nicole looked up from the terminal on her desk. "Well, if it isn't Ms. Sedgewick. I'm deeply honored, I'm sure."

Alexandra sensed from Nicole's drawl and her flinty glance that she was not meant to mistake this sarcasm for the affectionate teasing Nicole favored her with in playful moods. Nicole seemed for once to be in a *bad* mood. Alexandra stood very still and watched Nicole's face. "Have I in some way offended you, Nicole?" she asked—and immediately regretted her own gaucheness. Neither Mama nor Elizabeth would have been so blunt. She could be so stupid sometimes...

"Sit down," Nicole said. "I assume you've come about the menus?"

Warily, Alexandra took the chair on the side of the desk. "It *is* the fourth Thursday of the month, isn't it?"

Nicole's mouth stretched into a tight smile. "Of course. What other possible reason could Ms. Sedgewick have to see her cook?"

Alexandra flushed. Nicole *was* angry at her... For not visiting her lately? Surely it hadn't been that long since...*Oh.* Alexandra realized that she hadn't seen Nicole even once over the last two weeks. Clarice had insisted on doing all the fetching from the kitchen, and somehow Alexandra had never felt driven—as she had often felt before Clarice came—to go to Nicole just to chat, to yack at Nicole "a mile a minute" as Nicole liked to put it. "I didn't realize, Nicole. I'm sorry, I guess I just..."

"No, of course you didn't realize, and why should you? Now that you have your high-priced cut of filet mignon, what could you want with old mutton like me?"

"Nicole!" Alexandra was shocked. "Please! Don't talk like that! It's just that...Well, admit it: I've been a terrible pest. I know I have. And now you don't have to put up with my bugging you."

Nicole snorted. "Did I have to 'put up with it' before, do you think? May I point out there's nothing in my contract about doing anything in this house other than preparing food for the household. Nothing about talking to the lady of the house, nothing about 'putting up with her.' So you think I *had* to put up with you? But that's a contradiction, isn't it, since you people seem to assume that people will only do the things they're paid for." Nicole's fingers flurried across the keyboard, setting up a noisy, angry clatter.

"That's *not* what I think!" Alexandra struggled against tears; she couldn't stand to have Nicole, her only friend in the house until Clarice had come, be mad at her. "It's just that Clarice..." She gestured, unable to explain about the way Clarice always seemed to be arranging things.

The printer whirred, then fell silent; Nicole ripped out the flimsy and handed it to Alexandra. The flimsy listed the menus Nicole was proposing and that Alexandra had to approve. "Oh, *her*." Again Nicole snorted. "That one is the worst of all her type I've yet to see. That one your mother had in the Georgetown house, she was bad enough—another Italian, too. But you can bet this one is much higher priced even than that one. She's too good for all the rest of us. The way she minces around this house, informing us that she's already had *two* longevity treatments and isn't yet thirty-five. It's a cinch you're not paying her that kind of a salary for keeping your clothes in order."

"I don't know how much she makes," Alexandra said, bewildered. "I don't know anything about that end of it. She was a present from Mama."

Nicole's head snapped around. She gave Alexandra a stare so hard it made her wonder what terrible *faux pas* she'd committed now. "She was a *present*? That takes the cake."

Again Alexandra's cheeks heated. "Her services, I mean. You know what I mean, Nicole. Mama is paying her salary. As a Christmas present."

Nicole's stare did not waver. "You people are...*corrupt*. The very idea of your mother giving you, *as a present*, those kinds of services!"

"You don't know what you're talking about!" Alexandra said, her voice rising in anger. "Who're you to judge what my mother does, who're you to say *I'm* corrupt?"

After about ten long, terrible seconds, Nicole said, "Me, I'm Nicole Dugas, that's who I am. Not Ms. Sedgewick, that's true. Just Nicole Dugas, Ms. Sedgewick's cook." After another silence during which Alexandra stared down at her tightly clasped hands and battled her miserable speechlessness, Nicole said, "And now if you'd look at those menus, maybe we could get on with it."

Narrow-minded service-tech, Alexandra told herself as she fixed her gaze on the flimsy. All those ignorant prejudices Mama had warned her about were coming to the surface. It didn't matter that most service-techs thought it wrong. Mama said they didn't matter at all, those people... But Alexandra found it hard to convince herself. Until Clarice had come, Nicole had been her only friend in this awful, desolate place. Without Nicole, life here would have been unbearable. She *did* care what Nicole thought.

[ii]

All through dinner Alexandra brooded over the things Nicole had said, and a strange thing happened: as her anger at the way Nicole had talked about her mother drained away, she began to play with the main thing Nicole had implied—namely the nature of the "services" for which Mama was paying. Ever since Clarice's arrival, Alexandra had been experiencing feelings and sensations that made every physical contact with Clarice almost unbearably exciting. Every night after her bath and before bed, Clarice gave her a body massage because Mama had said that since this house had no Jacuzzi (Alexandra had complained about it to her) a nightly massage would be the next best thing for easing away the tension in her neck and shoulders she suffered from practicing the piano a minimum of four hours a day. These massages had become the high point of her day, something she looked forward to with increasing anticipation. After the massages, she and Clarice would lounge on cushions in front of the fireplace, drinking hot chocolate and talking about all sorts of things. Clarice had traveled a lot; she had been in Europe for part of the war and had hairraising stories to tell about things that had happened to people she had known. Her voice—dark and deep and dramatic, heavily accent-ed—would drop very low, her shining eyes would widen or narrow, her graceful hands flutter or swoop, always punctuating her narrative as she drew Alexandra into a past so vividly revealed that she could almost imagine feeling all the things Clarice described.

"Alexandra!" Her father's voice broke into her speculations about whether her mother had intended Clarice to be her first lover.

Alexandra withdrew her gaze from the candle flame she had been staring at, blinked, and looked at her father. "Yes?"

"You haven't heard a thing I've been saying, have you."

Alexandra bit her lip. "I'm sorry. I guess I was...wool-gathering."

"It's very rude to do that at the dinner table. I can assure you it would be considered extremely offensive in polite company."

"I'm sorry," Alexandra repeated.

"Contrary to what you may think," he said, "boredom does not ex-cuse that kind of rudeness. This is at least the second time this week." His lips tightened. "The next time it happens you'll be barred from the Music Room for the subsequent twenty-four hours. Clear?"

Alexandra stared down at her plate. "Understood," she said very low. She hated it when he talked to her with that nasty rasp in his voice and that rigid look of contempt on his face. As though she were some miserable subordinate who had to be shown her place. It was exactly the way he talked to Mama. How had Mama stood it for all those years that they had lived together? And why had she never an-swered him in kind? He couldn't, after all, punish Mama the way he could punish her. But Mama wouldn't talk about that. "It's none of your business, Alexandra," she had snapped that one time Alexandra had asked her about it.

"Now if I have your attention—?"

Alexandra lifted her eyes from her plate. "Yes?" she said, trying to look attentive.

"I've decided that we'll spend most of March at the winery. With one or two social excursions of the sort we had at the Blumenthals."

At once, under a deluge of emotion, Alexandra's eyes filled. "But there's no piano there!" She knew this because during that long stand-off between them when she had refused to speak to him (she knew exactly how to get at him: if there was one thing he couldn't stand,

it was being ignored) he had threatened to send her—by herself—to
the house at the winery and had let her know, to break her resistance,
that there was no piano there.

"I'm sure you can live without a piano for a month. If you can't,
you've got a problem."

"And besides," Alexandra rushed on without thinking, "those
men don't want a female around. Do you have any idea how it feels to
be so patently unwanted? To be the only female is bad enough, Papa,
but to know that the ones who bother with me would ignore me like
the others if they dared to is even worse! If they don't trust women,
why should they trust me? I'm not *their* daughter!"

He laid down his knife and fork. "Calm yourself," he said coldly.
"You're running on like an hysteric wildly out of control. And you're
being tediously childish." He paused, and she realized she had called
him "Papa"—after weeks of being excruciatingly careful not to call
him anything at all. "In the first place you're not just any woman,
you're *my* daughter. And in the second place, the women who are
found to be disloyal are never in any case *daughters*." He leaned forward, suddenly interested in his own words. "We've taken these career-
line women, as they've come to be called, and plugged them in here
and there, at random, into the system. As though they were to be used
like men. But that's been the mistake, since women are never loyal
to *systems* or anything abstract, but to *persons*, to those with whom
they've developed ties. And since women only consort with women,
their ties are to one another, and not to their men. Whom they do
not, in any case, work for or with. The obvious solution is for fathers
to bring their daughters into the system." His eyes narrowed. "And
considering what a liability the sons have proven to be, it's certainly
worth a try. As an experiment."

So she was to think of herself as an experiment? "But what about
the problem of—" she blushed—"sexuality? I thought that's the main
reason women can't hold positions of responsibility."

He snorted. "You must know by now that I consider that to be
nonsense. Of course one must pay lip service to it, since the surgery is
after all a fundamental executive institution. But quite obviously the
surgery did not improve my control—there was nothing in the least
wrong with my control before I had the surgery—and quite obvious-

ly some very sexual women manage their control quite adequately. Weatherall, for instance, had superb control. And I'd be hard put to think of anyone more libidinous than she."

Alexandra's mind raced at this heresy. Perhaps he was saying it because Daniel had been such a disappointment to him? And because he held his own surgery responsible for his having lost that woman?

"I'm not of course saying that men shouldn't keep things in hand," he said abruptly. "Because there *is* this loyalty problem which is all wrapped up in woman's particularity and their tendency to favor particularities over abstract principles. Even the ones who have brilliant minds that play with the abstract with ease ultimately fall into traps of particularity." He sighed. "Which is why in the end the system will depend upon overall male control. But that doesn't negate the possibility of our bringing our daughters more directly into it. It's a curious thing that traditionally men have brought their sons into the system in order to protect it from rebellious sabotage and usurpation while ignoring their daughters, since their daughters would never in any case usurp power or destroy the system. Thus we fail to realize the resource that daughters are—because, I suppose, of this emphasis on the negative."

"I don't understand," Alexandra said, "why you say sons are so dangerous." What could he be talking about? Daniel cared nothing for "usurping power" or destroying the system: all *that* guy wanted was to plug in, to gamble, to spend all his time with his friends. At least that's what Papa was always saying.

"I'm talking in abstract terms, Alexandra, with reference to long-established archetypes that have been with us since primeval times. You have, I assume," he said, his voice bitingly sarcastic, "heard of the Oedipus Complex?"

"Oh," Alexandra said as certain things fell into place. The Oedipus Complex, her social science tutor had said, was the basis of civilization. Without it people would be savages, do whatever they liked whenever they liked to whomever they liked. There would be no control at all in the world.

"Yes, *oh*," he mimicked her. "Are you going to have this course cleared or what? We could, I suppose, sit here all night if that's what you want, but if so I'll need another bottle of the one we just finished."

Alexandra jammed her thumb against the call button and reached for her water glass. She knew those men wouldn't agree with him, not about accepting her as his daughter, nor about any of the rest of it. But how to get him to see that and allow her to stay here—or visit Barbados—while he went to California?

Penderel came in and cleared the main course and set out the salad, cheese, and fruit. Maybe since they'd sat so long over dinner he'd let her skip the session upstairs in the Music Room. Just thinking about finding Clarice in her room made her wet and tingly all over. Maybe it wouldn't be so bad going to California, since she'd have Clarice with her. What would he say if he knew? What would Mama say? Alexandra suppressed a giggle as she thought of what *Elizabeth* would say.

But it didn't matter what *anyone* said, because she was grown up now and Clarice was *her* service-tech, the way Marie had been Mama's so long ago...

[iii]

Daydreaming, Alexandra forgot to hold the washcloth with her feet against the safety-drain, and the level of the water in the enormous claw-foot tub fell. Idly, without paying much attention to what she was doing, she rocked the water with her knees so that it washed in waves over her body, covering and receding in a repeated sensual rhythm. But the *feel* of the water playing over her body this way caught her by surprise, intensifying all those delicious aching sensations already permeating it. That water could make her feel like *this*! She had always loved taking baths, but couldn't remember feeling these sorts of sensations in her bath before. Had this pleasure always been there, waiting to be discovered, or was it something new that had to do with what she had recently begun feeling? Was it all because Clarice provoked so many exciting feelings?

Alexandra closed her eyes. What would it be like to kiss Clarice? She wanted to know, wanted to find out... But how to do it without making an idiot of herself? Perhaps Clarice would mind? Those massages, when Clarice's fingers touched her that way in those places... Surely that *was* part of why Mama had sent her—wasn't it? Wasn't she *meant* to make love to Clarice? But how to do such a thing? She had no idea of how even to kiss her. She couldn't just grab her. Couldn't just *ask*—or was that the way it was done? How did it happen in books? For some reason, her mind was just *blank*. If only she had someone to talk to about this, someone who knew but wouldn't laugh at her for being so ignorant. To make love to someone like Clarice, someone so sophisticated... If that's why Mama had sent her, it had been a mistake. Better if it had been somebody equally inexperienced, somebody young. Clarice had been loved by many women, women from all over the world. While she, Alexandra, had never even kissed anyone...

She got out of the tub and toweled dry. Mama probably hadn't realized how inadequate she'd feel: Mama always thought about quality first, as when Mama took her here or there because it was "the best" or introduced her to someone because she was among "the best," never paying the slightest attention to her preference to settle for something less superior in the face of her inexperienced awkwardness. Like going to restaurants that were mixed, where they always had creepy male servers, unlike the more comfortable women-only places where only girls—smiling, friendly, flirtatious—served.

As she brushed her hair, Alexandra stared at her body in the mirror. Though it wasn't apparent when she was fully clothed—mostly because of that stretchy chemise Mama had made her start wearing two years ago—when naked, she could see that her breasts were getting fuller. She looked so different without clothing that sometimes she felt as though she were two different people depending on whether or not she wore full clothing or went nude (or wore a dressing gown, which was almost nude). "Don't make a big deal of it, Alexandra," Mama had said when Alexandra first remarked on the swelling of her breasts. "That's for the others. Executive women don't make fetishes of their bodies. Their bodies are no one's business but their own. And once you take away the fetish aspect there's no big deal. You want to fetishize, concentrate on someone like Janice. Or someone like *her*," Mama had said, nodding at a girl serving at another table.

Alexandra slipped on her gown (even though she knew she would be taking it right off again for the massage), opened the door, and went out into the bedroom. Clarice, her body one long fluid rolling line, was lying on the bed on her side with her head propped up on her arm. "Such a lengthy bath, *bellina*," she said with her slow smile. "Forty-five minutes at least!"

"That long!" Alexandra was surprised. She crossed the room to the vase of parsley she kept on the table by the window, pulled out a stem, and nibbled it.

Moving slowly and sinuously—with so much supple grace she could have been a dancer, Alexandra thought—Clarice got up from the bed, tossed her long honey-colored hair over her shoulder, and went into the dressing room. Seconds later she returned with the little pot of oil that had been sitting in a pan of hot water on the dressing table. Alexandra removed her gown, draped it over a chair, and sank down onto the sheet Clarice had spread before the fireplace. "*La donna del prezzemolo* loves—" Clarice's shivery alto drew out the word—"her baths." Alexandra closed her eyes as Clarice's oil-slick hands kneaded the bottom of her right foot. "Baths are deliciously sensuous, and you, *bellina*, appreciate everything sensuous. But the parsley? I haven't been able to figure that one out. What could the attraction of parsley possibly be? Such a mystery, *carina*!"

Alexandra sighed with pleasure as the strong fingers kneaded her ankles. "I like the taste, the crispness, the freshness. The texture may-be most of all." Alexandra thought of how parsley had replaced pen-cil erasers. Who was it who had caught her chewing an entire block of eraser in one sitting? Perhaps she would still prefer erasers, but parsley, at least, was real food. Sort of. More like grass, she supposed. But people *did* eat it.

"*La donna del prezzemolo*," Clarice said softly. "I once knew a lady who ate certain flowers. No, she did not *eat* them, I don't think that's correct. She never swallowed them. But she'd lick them and chew on them and then, at the last minute, spit them out. She was very pecu-liar, *bellina*, but very beautiful. She had long narrow eyes very deeply set, and a lovely long neck. She always wore fresh flowers, but they had to be replenished throughout the day because she would always be absent-mindedly picking them out of her hair or off her clothing to nibble."

Alexandra giggled. "You're making it up, Clarice! I'm not *that* gullible."

"No, no, I swear to you it's true. When I knew her she lived in Sydney. She may still be there, for she wasn't the traveling type."

"Sydney, Australia?" Alexandra asked out of curiosity. "You've lived in Australia?"

"Only in Sydney," Clarice said firmly. "I have very very distant relatives there."

"And did you meet them when you lived in Sydney?"

Clarice sighed. "No. It's best not to mix things up. Their world would have been very very different from the one I live in. It would have been uncomfortable, maybe even unpleasant. So I didn't even think of it." Clarice kneaded in silence for a while, working her way up Alexandra's legs, alternating between left and right as she went. As Clarice's fingers inched higher and higher up her thighs, Alexandra lost track of everything but the exquisite feelings throbbing exciting permeating her body. But Clarice, not going even as far as she had the last few nights when her touches had grown more and more intimate and exciting, suddenly shifted to work on her neck.

Impetuously Alexandra rolled over, away from where Clarice knelt. Clarice's face, usually lively and bright and flashing with warmth, looked almost mask-like in its smoothness, the downcast eyes offering only inscrutable eyelids, mysterious and private. "Why did you stop?" Alexandra whispered—and noticed that her breath was coming in short gasps that made her almost too breathless to speak.

Clarice's eyelids lifted slightly to reveal thin slits of gleaming brown, though not enough to meet Alexandra's gaze directly. "It is for you to say, *carina*. You haven't said anything at all. I didn't know your pleasure." Her eyes widened, and all their radiant heat flooded Alexandra, overwhelming her.

"Kiss me, Clarice," Alexandra whispered without thinking, reaching up to touch Clarice's silky face, to trace the outlines of Clarice's prominent cheekbones.

Clarice's lips curved slowly in a mysterious smile, and her eyelids again descended. She lowered her head, bringing her face nearer and nearer until her lips lightly touched Alexandra's. Alexandra closed her eyes; trembling, she slid her arms around Clarice's neck and at first hesitantly, then boldly, avidly, pressed her lips to Clarice's and slipped her tongue against the girl's smooth, sharp-edged teeth. A warm dark cave they made together through this seeking offering taking of one another, a cave they made with their mouths, yet which surrounded them to hold close their warmth as they melted and poured into one another, while at the same time all her body, throbbing burning aching seemed frighteningly yet deliciously out of control.

When Clarice—expanding the cave letting light into it creating a space a distance an absence Alexandra grew hungry to close up— moved her mouth from Alexandra's, along her neck, tonguing her ear, the sensations—multiplying there on in around that patch of skin and then around and in her ear—grew unbearable in their intensity. Crying out, she clutched at Clarice and, flailing, dimly recognized the waves rocking and convulsing her as distantly similar to that which she did for herself at night alone in bed before sleeping. Yet how different, this explosion infusing *all* of her body, not just that one part, and how could it be so, like that, there in through on that place on her neck...?

Clarice chuckled softly. Alexandra opened her eyes, and saw the girl's flushed cheeks and sparkling eyes looming over her, the beautiful teeth wetly glistening as she laughed. "So soon, *carina*, and we'd only just started." And she ran her fingers lightly down Alexandra's body from neck to navel, leaving a trail of exquisite sensations wherever her fingers touched.

"Oh," Alexandra gasped, "I can't bear this!"

"Shall I stop, *carina*?" Clarice said in a teasing voice.

"No, no, don't stop," Alexandra whispered and closed her eyes to seek again the cave she longed to be woven again around them.

## [iv]

Only when Clarice asked Alexandra if she wanted her to stay and sleep with her did Alexandra recall that long talk her mother had given her during dinner at the Diana before she went away to Crowder's, a talk instructing her in "certain matters of etiquette." At the time, Alexandra had been fascinated because her mother's talking to her about such things implied that she expected that Alexandra would soon begin having lovers. She had not been able to get anything about the things she *really* wanted to know out of her mother, though. "Executive women do not talk about such things with one another,

Alexandra," her mother said when she tried questioning her. "Just as they never *do* such things together, either." But now, remembering the conversation, she recalled that she had given her mother her word that she would not allow her lovers to sleep the night with her. "Someday you'll understand this. Although you will probably want to do it when the time comes, later you will see that it's necessary to keep a certain distance, to retain some privacy, especially if the girl in question is your employee. Give me your word, Alexandra, as an executive woman... We must stick together on certain things, you know. And as the girls will never control themselves in that way, we must take the responsibility."

Lying like this with Clarice's head on her breasts, stroking Clarice's beautiful long hair, bursting with love and closeness, Alexandra battled herself—and resented her mother for having extracted her word on something she had known nothing about. "Better not," Alexandra said, very low, and heard with poignancy Clarice's sigh. But recalling that conversation, she remembered that she must also think of a gift for Clarice. With a lover one gave special gifts after special occasions, though mostly intermittently without calling attention to the reason for the gifts—the love-making itself. Never ever money (even if the girl hinted at it)—monetary payment was handled for certain situations in other ways—mostly through wages for other services, or delicately, when arranging a lover for another person, but never for oneself. And with the occasional lover one never expected to see again one gave a trifle immediately after.

But what could she give Clarice, considering how there could be no shopping for appropriate gifts because they were so cut off from the world here? Perfume, jewelry, clothing... Because it had been her first time, because Clarice was so beautiful and had created—*that*... Perhaps the pearl pendant on the thin gold chain that Papa had given her? Alexandra felt certain Clarice would like it. (Gifts of jewelry could always be sold, Mama had cynically pointed out.) So Alexandra went into the dressing room and took the pendant from her smaller jewel box. When she came back into the bedroom, she found the girl, now dressed, folding the sheet they had lain on. Alexandra leaned against the doorframe and dreamily watched as Clarice put the sheet and the oil away in one of the dressing-room closets.

"You're smiling, *bellina*," Clarice said, pausing near Alexandra on her way out of the dressing room. She slid her arms around Alexandra's waist and laid her head on Alexandra's shoulder.

Alexandra nuzzled her neck and wished again that they could stay together the whole night, lying close, their flesh melting into one another, sharing that feeling that made her burst with warmth and a love close to adoration. "My first time, and it was beautiful," she said. And she fastened the necklace around Clarice's neck.

Clarice bent her head to see it. "Pearls," she breathed. "Oh, they're beautiful, *carina*!" She squeezed Alexandra tightly and kissed her cheek. "*Mille gratias, carissima!*" Alexandra swelled with elation at Clarice's obvious pleasure.

When Alexandra finally got into bed, she found herself struggling against loneliness and a depressing sense of deprivation, though excited thoughts of how she was now a "real woman" and had a lover rewove some of that cocoon of pleasure and warmth and affection around her. Minutes later, before even invoking the mnemonic—for she had intended to lie awake and savor each detail over and over and over again—she fell asleep.

Her last waking thought was a resolution to write her mother requesting her to find things that would make appropriate gifts for Clarice.

# Chapter Seven

## [i]

"Pull over here."

Jolted by the raw tension in Liz's voice, Hazel glanced at her out of the corner of her eye and went cold when she saw how tightly Liz gripped the fully extended M-19 she held muzzle to floor. The wheels of the van crunched over the debris of leaves and branches littering the narrow dirt shoulder. Hazel flipped on the emergency brake and looked at Liz. "We wait here?"

"You wait here," Liz said, opening her door. "I'm going to walk the few yards that will put me within view of the area I designated for their landing. I want to be in position to watch every damned thing that happens."

"But wouldn't it be better to take the van—"

"No," Liz said impatiently. "The van is a sitting duck. Parked here, it won't be easily visible from the air." Hazel had noticed that the branches of the trees on both sides of the road arched to form a kind of leafy ceiling, but hadn't taken in more than its prettiness. "I'll have a head start on them if it turns out to be necessary for us to cut and run." Her eyes narrowed. "And I'm fast. What I want you to do now is turn the van around and watch in your rear view mirror. If you see me running, I'll want you to start the motor, reverse toward me, and be ready to drive hell for leather along the route we planned as Contingency B."

"All right, Liz. But it's a full twenty minutes before they're supposed to land."

"If it's treachery, they certainly won't bother to follow instructions," Liz said, getting out of the car.

"Be careful, Rapunzel," Hazel called after her, all too aware of that long, evil weapon in her lover's hands.

As soon as Liz had gotten clear, Hazel turned the van around and parked, pointing its nose downhill. She realized that Liz had planned even for the terrain to be to their advantage. Going downhill, it would be easy to accelerate to the maximum speed they could take on such a winding road, which they had, after all, practiced driving more than a dozen times.

Every two or three minutes Hazel checked her watch—amazed at how slowly the time crawled—and strained to hear the sound of an approaching helicopter or road vehicle. Hazel did not believe they would meet with disaster, for Margot was handling the air transport. "Don't underestimate Company craft," Liz had said, dismissing Hazel's confidence. When Hazel had asked why if she was so worried about treachery she was taking such a risk, Liz had looked her in the eye and said, "Sometimes it's necessary to take chances." Though Liz did not say so, Hazel believed it was Allison's involvement in the plan that made it "necessary." If the plan were on the level, Allison would be counting on her to help her go renegade. If the plan were a design for betrayal, then Allison herself would likely be in danger. Liz, Hazel guessed, could not face the possibility that Allison might deliberately betray her.

At last Hazel heard the drone of a chopper. She looked at her watch: exactly three on the dot. Butterflies fluttered in her stomach. She kept her eyes glued to the rearview mirror as she listened to the *chop-chop-chop* grow louder and louder. Finally, after a long breathless wait, the sound receded quickly, into a low, distant drone. Now, she thought, now it would become clear whether the rendezvous was a setup. She watched the mirror and waited. Once she glanced at her watch and saw that eight minutes had passed since she'd first heard the sound of the chopper. The wait dragged on. And then at last they appeared, all five of them, with Liz—the M-19 pointed down toward the ground—walking beside Allison Bennett. Hazel recognized Lisa Mott on the other side of Allison but did not know the two service-techs walking behind the executives. She had known, of course, that there would be two service-techs in the party because Elizabeth had made a special point of Margot's having their implants disabled since all implants came furnished with GPS.

When they reached the van, Liz thrust the sliding door open, and the four of them climbed into the back. Liz claimed the front passenger seat and laid the M-19 across her lap. "Let's go, darling," she said, nodding at Hazel. Her face still wore the look of strain, but her voice had relaxed. Of course they still had to face the problem of whether or not these women would betray them sometime in the future. Liz had said that they would never be completely sure, at least not during the first few months, that it wasn't a Company penetration.

As Hazel drove to the house on the Suiattle River she listened to the women in the back admiring the lushness of the cedars and firs towering on either side of the road. She recalled the first morning she had woken and smelled the trees and how, looking out the bedroom window, she had been amazed at the thick deep green that seemed to permeate the very light itself. Liz said little and smiled hardly at all. The intensity of her watchfulness seemed not to touch the others, but Hazel felt it damping the atmosphere. When for a brief moment her eyes encountered Lisa Mott's in the mirror, though, Hazel realized the others were probably not unaware of Liz's watchfulness.

The van's radio signal opened the gates. The women fell silent as Hazel drove up the twisty drive and parked inside the garage. "It's a fairly comfortable house," Liz said as she got out of the van. They trooped through the garage door into the house, everyone but Liz laden with luggage (which Hazel knew that both Margot and Liz would already have examined). Liz still carried the M-19.

When they had deposited the luggage in two of the guest rooms and the six of them were standing awkwardly around the living room, Liz looked at Hazel and said, "Take the girls for a tour of the house. And maybe a walk along the river. I'm sure they'll find it very beautiful. And then maybe the hot tub?"

Hazel glanced at the others—seeing clearly for the first time the three executives as separate from the service-techs—and looked back at Liz. Obviously Liz had the idea that the executives should be separate from the service-techs, even in this new situation. This attitude troubled her, for apart from her meetings with Margot, Liz had not excluded her, Hazel, from any meeting or discussion since they had gone renegade. Much of the time she had forgotten this difference, for here in the Free Zone where most of their acquaintances were service-techs Liz tended to ignore or underplay the difference. But now, her eyes distant, her voice remote, she faced Hazel with it from across the room.

Hazel turned away from the look on Elizabeth's face and said to Anne and Ginger, "This is a really relaxing place. And it's true that if we don't go for our walk now, it'll soon be dark. It gets dark early here." The three of them filed out of the room, and Hazel closed the tall cedar doors after them. The executives could see to their own refreshment, Hazel thought, still perturbed. As she led the others outdoors she realized that she would have no idea of what was said in that room. Had that been the reason Liz had excluded them?

"Is all the Free Zone like this?" Ginger asked in a high, thin, quavery voice.

Hazel unlocked the gate to the path that ran along the bank of the river. "No, but a lot of it is." She held the gate open and gestured for the others to pass.

"It reminds me a little of Colorado," Anne murmured.

"You've been to Colorado?" Hazel exclaimed.

"Yes, during the war."

"I was born and raised in Denver," Hazel said.

"And you miss it?" Anne said.

"Sometimes," Hazel said. "Sometimes." She closed and locked the gate and led the way along the path. How strange, how very strange to be walking here with these women whom she would ordinarily think of as appendages of the executives they had left in the living room. And would they think that of her? she wondered. Was that what people saw when they saw her and Liz together? But she already knew some of that, didn't she, given how Shoshana and some of the other Women's Patrol treated her, teased her.

It wasn't right, she thought as they walked. It wasn't right that Liz had sent them away. She decided she would tell Liz that, even though it would make her angry. Something about it hurt, and she must make Liz see that it did. And did these women feel the same? Hazel wondered, glancing over her shoulder at Anne, whose eyes gazed out at the slow green water. Or hadn't they noticed? She stopped, and they stopped, and she considered asking them. But something held her back, kept her from putting the thoughts into words, as though saying such things out loud to them might in some way scald them all. No, she could not speak to them about it. But she would speak to Liz. That she promised herself.

[ii]

Hazel followed Liz's simple instructions for finishing the food preparation (most of which she and Liz had done that morning) without Liz's expert supervision, while Anne and Ginger, perched on stools on the other side of the central worktable, watched and chatted. Ginger kept offering to help and informed Hazel at frequent intervals that she did most of the cooking in Lisa Mott's household. Hazel tried not to be irritated with her officiousness, for it was obvious that Ginger was deeply upset, even unnerved by the radical change in her life. Anne, on the other hand, seemed cool, almost unconcerned, maybe even curious (though it might simply seem so in contrast with Ginger's fluttery distress). When they'd first followed her into the kitchen—apparently unwilling to be by themselves—Anne had said she'd be willing to help as best she could, but that she had no idea how to do anything besides make sandwiches, tea, and coffee and load the dishwasher. Anne, it turned out, had had a job similar to the job Hazel had had in the Justice Department. Hazel felt certain that Anne had been super-competent: it was written all over her. The fact that after the Blanket she had been evacuated from DC to that underground place in the mountains and then brought back to DC after the end of the war testified to executive appreciation of that competence, too.

"But is it safe to live in Seattle?" Ginger asked.

Hazel opened a drawer and hunted for a long-handled fork. "It's safer than most places," she said as she spotted the fork. "I don't know about you, but there are neighborhoods in almost every city that I'd be afraid to live in. And even in the safest areas I never really felt safe. Somebody or other always seems to hassle you, or worse." She began jabbing holes into the potatoes she'd already brushed with oil.

"For sure," Anne said vehemently. "And I don't think it even has all that much to do with neighborhoods. It can happen in very closed and controlled places. At work, even."

"Well in La Jolla," Ginger said, "we lived in a *very* exclusive neighborhood, and I *always* felt safe. You had to have a special pass to get in at the guard post. Not just anybody could drive in."

Anne snorted. "That wouldn't make *me* feel safe."

"At any rate," Hazel said, sensing possible acrimony, "after a while you won't even remember that Seattle doesn't have jails, police, or law courts." She laughed without humor. "To tell the truth, our biggest problem has been protecting ourselves against Security and Military agents. Which has nothing to do with the general level of public safety around here and everything to do with our having gone renegade."

A heavy silence fell. Hazel put the potatoes in the small upper oven and checked her watch. The meal preparation was going exactly as planned. "Let's see," she said, hoping to break the tension. "The next thing I need to do is set the table."

"I can do that," Ginger said.

Anne laughed sheepishly. "I haven't the faintest idea about arranging things on tables."

Hazel led Ginger into the dining room and showed her where the china, silver, linen, and crystal were kept, then returned to the kitchen.

Anne said, "She's been so hyper I keep wondering if she's going to explode from the stress."

"Either that or implode," Hazel said, taking Ginger's stool. "I wonder if it wouldn't have been better for her to have stayed where she was."

"Do you know how long she's been with Mott?"

Hazel shook her head.

"More than twenty years. Doing the housework and shopping, taking care of Mott's clothes and all that kind of stuff." She wrinkled her nose. "She'd do anything for her, and I mean anything. I don't think she could imagine not following Mott to the ends of the earth— if necessary."

Hazel looked long into Anne's dark, serious eyes. "You and I followed our lovers," she said softly.

"That's different, Hazel. We're lovers, not drudges. Lise would never let me do her laundry or housework, much less ask me to. She's always had an employee do that. Which is maybe my point: we're not their employees, while she is. As well as Mott's lover."

Hazel averted her eyes in embarrassment. "Liz was my employer," she said. "And still is."

"But not in the same way," Anne said. "It's a big difference."

Hazel, studying her hands, noticed that her cuticles had crept, untended, up over the base of each fingernail. She saw Anne's well-tended hands lying on the counter and knew she must spend hours grooming herself. "I hope so," she said. She looked up. "Are you going to look for a new job in Seattle?"

Anne bit her lip. "I'll have to get a new implant first, since Ms. Weatherall required the disabling of our old implants. But to tell the truth, I don't really have any idea what I'm going to do yet. I guess I'll have to wait and see."

"You mean depending upon what Ms. Bennett does?"

Anne looked directly into Hazel's eyes. "I came because I wanted to be with Lise. Going renegade was never my idea. My job was never in danger. And I was only questioned that one time immediately after Ms. Weatherall left. It was Lise they were after."

Hazel heard the kitchen door swing open and assumed it was Ginger. "Did the decision to leave happen very suddenly?" she asked, curious. "Or was there time to get used to the idea?" What she really wanted to know was whether Bennett had talked it over with Anne well in advance, when she first began considering going renegade, or whether she had announced her decision as a *fait accompli.*

"Gossiping, girls?" Liz said softly, her lips inches from Hazel's ear. She put her hands on Hazel's shoulders.

Hazel turned her head to try to catch a glimpse of Liz's face, but the grip of Liz's fingers on her shoulders told her all she needed to know about Liz's level of tension. "We're right on schedule," she said in her calmest, steadiest voice.

"I happened to glance at the dining room on my way back here and saw Ginger setting the table. You must have forgotten to tell her about Ganshoff and Madden, darling."

"Oh," Hazel said. "You're right. I'll go tell her now." She made to get up from the stool, but Liz's hands held her down.

"Not necessary, darling, I've already told her."

Anne slid off her stool. "I'll go see what I can do to help." Before Hazel could stop her, she had gone.

"What a bore for you to be stuck with them," Liz said, wrapping her arms around Hazel's body, bending her head and putting her lips to Hazel's neck. "But it can't be helped."

"They're nice people," Hazel said, irritated at Liz's dismissal of them. "And I can tell Anne is really smart."

Liz snorted. "Smart enough certainly to have taken Allison in. And for how many years now? Too many, that's certain."

Hazel stiffened. "Your attitude is insulting, Liz. Why should it matter to you that Ms. Bennett and Anne love one another? If you can say that about them, then you'd have to say the same thing about us."

"It's not the same at all," Liz said sharply. "You know nothing of that situation. You have no idea about the circumstances under which Allison met that girl, or even what kind of girl she is. She's nothing like you, darling. And I know for a fact that Allison doesn't love her as I do you. Her reasons for going on with that girl are all the wrong ones. Don't make comparisons when you know nothing about that situation."

"Isn't it enough that Anne uprooted herself and her own stable work relationship to follow Ms. Bennett?" Hazel said, trying to pull Liz's hands away.

"Such a dreary thing to talk about, darling," Liz said, pressing herself more tightly against Hazel. "Why must you argue with me when all I came out here for was to snatch a minute with you?"

"Do you still distrust them?" Hazel asked, dropping her voice almost to a whisper.

"They say Security is in a shambles and that the entire damned Executive is in disarray," Liz whispered back. "Allison claims that a lot of women are deeply upset and would be easily recruitable."

"Recruitable?" Something in that word reminded Hazel of some of the innuendos about Liz she'd been hearing from Co-op people, and she wondered: Is it possible she really *is* up to something? "Recruitable for what?"

Liz's sigh whooshed in Hazel's ear. "Never mind, darling—I'll tell you more about it later. It's all pretty fuzzy just now. But there are possibilities I hadn't seen before...if, that is, they aren't setting me up."

"It's terrible that you can't trust someone you've felt so close to," Hazel said, thinking of how just before going renegade Liz had made over all her real estate holdings to Allison, and of how she carried photos of Allison as well as Allison's mother and Maxine around with her. Liz had been worrying about Allison for months. But to at the same time distrust her so profoundly as to imagine her involved in a treacherous plot to destroy her? It was hard to comprehend.

"Simply good sense," Liz said bitterly. "And Lisa Mott is still, when all is said and done, the niece of a Cabinet officer. I can't forget that. Nor her long years in the Company." Liz sighed. "Well, I'd better go back now. I wanted to remind you to watch for Ganshoff and Madden. They should be here any time." Liz planted a noisy kiss on Hazel's cheek, released her, and rustled out of the kitchen.

Hazel slipped off the stool and loaded a tray with things that were to be put on the sideboard and carried it into the dining room. Ginger and Anne stood on opposite sides of the table, desultorily chatting—obviously avoiding going into the kitchen for as long as they thought Liz might be there. She had noticed almost at once how strained they were around Liz. Since this was often the case with service-techs (except for the ones Liz flirted with), this observation came as no great surprise, yet it still managed to add to Hazel's discomfort. She slid the tray onto the sideboard and unloaded the baskets, bowls, and platters of salads, breads, cheese, fruit, and nuts.

"Ms. Weatherall said there would be two more for dinner," Ginger said nervously.

"Both executives," Hazel said, turning to look at the table. She frowned and counted place settings. Though she didn't like questioning Ginger's arithmetic, there seemed too few settings. "Ginger, you're short three settings," Hazel said after she'd finished counting. "There should be eight, but you've only set five places."

Ginger looked confused. "Eight? But Ms. Weatherall only told me to add two more!"

Hazel shook her head. "There were originally six of us," she said. "And we'll be adding two. That makes eight."

"Six?" Ginger said, looking even more confused. "But I counted three." She held up her hand to tick off names. "Lisa, Ms. Weatherall, and Ms. Bennett." The look on her face suggested extreme disorientation, Hazel thought. "Are there others that I somehow have missed noticing?"

Hazel realized Ginger had only been counting the executives. "Us, Ginger, *us*! You, Anne, and me." She knelt to get out more china and napkins from the cupboards built into the sideboard.

"Us?" Ginger said doubtfully. "You mean we'll be eating with them?"

Hazel got out three place settings of china, stacked them, and handed them up to Ginger. "What else? Or maybe you think we should eat in the kitchen?" Her tone, of course, was sarcastic.

"I don't think Ms. Weatherall—" Ginger said, but Hazel interrupted:

"Don't be absurd."

"Ginger's right," Anne said. "We'd be terribly uncomfortable eating with them. And it's clear they have things to talk about among themselves."

Ginger gently set the china Hazel had handed her onto the sideboard. She said, "And Ms. Weatherall asked me to serve, Hazel."

"You don't work for her!"

Ginger flushed. "Maybe not, but I work for Lisa. And I'm the only one of us who *can* serve. Neither of you have the training to do it." Ginger announced this as though serving were a special skill she was fortunate to possess.

"She shouldn't be making that kind of demand of you," Hazel said, angry that Ginger hadn't refused, upset at the thought of Liz continuing this exclusion as though the three of them weren't also renegades now, too, as though the things the executives discussed weren't of concern to the three of them whose lives were so closely intertwined with the executives'.

"What could I say?" Ginger said defensively, wringing her hands, staring at Hazel with pleading, placating eyes. "How could I refuse?"

Hazel tried to smile. "Sorry for jumping on you, Ginger. I do understand." How could someone like Ginger refuse to do what an executive told her to do? Refusing probably wasn't conceivable to her. Certainly she was terribly vulnerable—now, more than ever—to the sorts of put-downs Liz could so effectively deliver. After all, until recently she herself had found it hard being anything but subservient to Margot Ganshoff or any other executive who crossed their paths. Being in the Free Zone didn't magically change all that in one swift stroke. As it was, she knew she would find it hard to handle Liz's executive snubs and put-downs but for the leverage their relationship gave her.

"Please, Hazel, don't make an issue of this," Anne said. "I would be truly uncomfortable sitting at a table with all those executives. I've never eaten with any executive other than Allison, and she and I always eat informally. I wouldn't know how to behave, and I'd be horribly self-conscious. If you want to know the truth, I'd prefer for us to eat separately."

Hazel returned the china back to the cupboard. "Okay. I see your point. You're probably right. And they'd badly outnumber us, too."

The three of them returned to the kitchen, and Hazel finished the preparations. Seeing how these new renegades had brought their world with them made the difference between the Free Zone and the world she had gone renegade from crystal clear. It seemed that one's "world" had little to do with geography. The Free Zone or DC or La Jolla—sometimes it could all be the same.

[iii]

"You're not even listening, are you," Hazel interrupted herself to say.

Liz drew the brush through her hair quickly, with force. "I'm sorry, darling, but I've too many important things on my mind to bother right now with trivialities. Do you mind postponing this discussion to another time?"

"Important things that you consider none of my business," Hazel said angrily. "I see. Anything to do with executives is important, while anything to do with the rest of us—the lowest of the low—is trivial."

Liz turned away from the mirror to face her. "Listen to yourself, darling. You're positively shrill. As you always are when you start raging against my being executive." Their gazes locked. "I'm having such a difficult time, things are so damned tricky, Hazel, and I thought I could count on you for support. Instead, you nag and whine at me about feeling excluded. Which is ridiculous. Can you imagine those girls participating in significant discussions? It's not as though they're like the service-techs who are running the Free Zone." Liz turned back to the mirror and continued brushing. "All this comes from living in the Free Zone, doesn't it. You wouldn't have carried on like this in DC, I know that."

"And I know that our relationship wouldn't have lasted there as long as it has, either," Hazel said.

Liz whirled around. "What the hell is *that* supposed to mean?"

Hazel groped to understand the half-formed ideas swirling elusively through her mind. "I told you at the beginning that I was reluctant to get involved with an executive. As long as I could keep in place certain barriers in my mind it didn't matter about these things. Executives were simply facts of life—bosses, mainly—that one had to deal with, as impersonally and with as much detachment as possible. I'd think to myself it didn't matter what they thought of me or how they treated me because they couldn't touch a certain part of me that was mine. That must be why I didn't ever want to get involved sexually with an executive. Because I knew it would be harder to keep my self-respect. I had terrible misgivings about you all the time, you know, but my feelings were so strong that I couldn't help myself, especially since you went out of your way to disguise so much of this that had a bearing on our relationship." Liz opened her mouth to speak, but Hazel plowed on. "Here we are, you and I, sharing this close intimate life, up till now hiding nothing from one another. I have no way of protecting myself from the stings and pain of those kinds of wounds, Liz, because I'm completely open—and therefore vulnerable—to you. On top of that, you've been this one way with me for months and months. And now suddenly you revert to this other way that's so hateful to me. It's horrible. And at the same time you've begun keeping things from me. Things you call important and significant. While you call everything else trivial—the things you say I should concern myself with." Hazel swallowed, then said, "Do you have any idea how much this hurts me, Liz?" She blinked to stave off the tears threatening her composure.

Liz laid her hairbrush down on the dressing table and came over to the bed. "I don't understand why you're so upset about this. You must know those girls wouldn't have wanted to eat with the executives!" She sat on the bed and reached for Hazel.

Hazel wouldn't let Liz embrace her. "And that's another thing," she said. "The way they are so obviously afraid of you."

"Afraid of me!" Liz laughed. "That's ridiculous! You're imagining things, darling."

"At the very least uncomfortable around you," Hazel said. "The fact that Ginger finds it unthinkable not to do whatever you tell her to—"

"For godsake, Hazel, she's paid to do what she's told!"

"Not by you, she isn't! If you, my employer, tell me to prepare a report or make an appointment for you, then of course I do it, and without thinking twice about it. But I doubt if I'd automatically do that for any executive who happened to ask it of me. Nor would I necessarily do just anything an employer told me to do, either. I certainly wouldn't serve dinner to Bennett and Mott if one of them asked me to."

"You are way off base, darling," Liz said coldly. She got up, went to the dressing table, and turned off the lamp. "And I can tell you another thing, those girls wouldn't appreciate your attitude, either." She went around to the other side of the bed and got in, turned the light off, moved into the center of the bed, and put her arms around Hazel.

Hazel rolled onto her side, away from Liz. "Don't, Liz," she said.

Liz moved in the bed, and then the light went on again. "All right, Hazel, let's have this out right now," Liz said, openly angry. "And turn around! I have no intention of talking to your back, considering how fucking important you're making this out to be."

"Now who's making a big deal?" Hazel said wearily, rolling over to face Liz. "Why can't we just go to sleep?"

"When you're playing your cold-shoulder games again? Every time you don't like something I've done, you blackmail me." Liz's eyes blazed; her cheeks flamed. "So what is it you want this time, Hazel?"

"Why are you talking to me this way?" Angrily Hazel brushed away her tears. "Why do you expect me to pretend that nothing has happened when I'm feeling upset and hurt? Basically what you're saying is that you want to treat me one way when we're in bed and another way when we're not. Turn off the light and everything changes, is that it? Don't my feelings matter at all, Liz?"

"Of course they matter," Liz said impatiently. "Tell me what you want of me."

"I'm being so inconvenient for you, aren't I," Hazel said bitterly. What a mistake to think she could live with Liz. As long as everything centered on Liz's needs, Liz's feelings, Liz's wants, everything went beautifully and Hazel was the perfect angel. The minute she tried to talk about her own needs, feelings, and wants it all became a question of manipulation or emotional blackmail.

"That's very good, Hazel, very good. Sometimes I have to wonder about the level of your emotional maturity."

Hazel got out of bed, snatched up her pillow, and headed for the dressing room.

"Just what do you think you're doing now, Hazel?"

Hazel turned. "I'm sleeping on the lounge in the dressing room."

"There's no need for dramatics, Hazel. I won't lay a finger on you if that's what you're so concerned about."

"I want to be by myself," Hazel said. She turned and went into the dressing room, where she took a blanket from the closet and settled herself on the lounge, which though comfortably firm was a little narrow.

Liz strode into the dressing room and turned on the light. "You're being ridiculous, Hazel. You're blowing this way out of proportion."

"Let's discuss this sometime else," Hazel said. She wanted—needed—to be by herself now, to collect herself and think about what was happening here.

"Fine," Liz said, "but come back to bed. We have a long day tomorrow, and you'll need a good night's sleep."

"The way I'm feeling, I'll sleep better in here. Go to bed, Liz."

Liz folded her arms over her breasts. "If you're going to make a major production of this, then we'll discuss it now. I want to know what the hell is going on, Hazel."

"I need to be by myself," Hazel said—and realized she was no longer angry.

"Why? Will you please tell me why, goddam it?"

"You don't want to know," Hazel said. "Please, Liz, go to bed. We'll talk about it some other time. As you say, it's only a triviality." Hazel now ran up against the bitterness she had for a moment thought subdued and knew she must still be angry to have made such a crack.

"For someone so loving, you sure can be a selfish, mean, manipulative bitch," Liz said. "Your pettiness knows no bounds. When you can't win an argument with me, you know just how to take it out on me, don't you."

"I'm tired," Hazel said. "Since I'm so mean and selfish and petty I don't know why you're standing there shivering in the cold when you could be instantly asleep in bed."

"I insist you come to bed."

Baffled and uneasy at the ragged edge that had crept into Liz's voice, Hazel studied Liz's face. "If it bothers you so much to have me sleeping in here, I'll go sleep on the sofa in the study."

"You're not leaving the bedroom," Liz warned.

"Oh for godsake, Liz, this is crazy."

"You have some nerve talking about craziness. It's crazy for you not to sleep in that large comfortable bed. I've told you I won't touch you, so why make such a point of it?"

Hazel stared at her for a long time and then, sighing, got up, took her pillow, and marched past Liz into the bedroom. She climbed into bed and lay on her side with her back to Liz's side of the bed. "Good night," she said coldly.

Liz got into bed and turned off the light. "Good night, darling," Liz said softly. "Sleep well."

Hazel, weeping hot silent tears, listened to Liz go immediately to sleep as she always did. And the thought seared her: tomorrow, when they got back to Seattle, she would tell Liz that they were through. She couldn't live like this. If her feelings were petty to Liz, then she would take them elsewhere. Liz called her pain trivial. Ergo, it wouldn't matter that much to her whether they broke up. This Hazel said to herself bitterly and ironically, knowing full well Liz would be upset. But the more she lay awake reviewing the words they had flung at one another and what she had seen and heard since the new renegades' arrival, the angrier and more upset she grew, until finally she believed she no longer cared how Liz would react to her leaving. I need my self-respect, she repeated again and again. I can't let her treat me like an inferior or a child whose feelings and reactions are immature and therefore petty. Better to live alone. Better to strike off on my own, to find a more comfortable world than the one Liz seemed to be intent upon recreating. She would never go back to that world, never.

It dawned on her that she had changed, profoundly, since leaving DC: she had become anti-executive; she had come to expect certain things because of the way she had been living in the Free Zone over the last nine months. She looked at things differently, she looked at *herself* differently. She hadn't realized how much she had changed. Only now, in the middle of the night, did she see how far she had come. Partly because Liz had encouraged her, she did see that. It had been mostly convenient to Liz for Hazel to adapt to certain Free Zone ways and mores. And when in serious conflict, Liz had always yielded to Hazel's insistence, as when Liz had tried to wrest information out of the naval intelligence agent—until now. This was somehow different. How it was different, Hazel did not understand. But then there was so much about Liz she could not understand, least of all her near-hysterical insistence on Hazel's sharing her bed.

# Chapter Eight

The wind whined and whistled through minute cracks between the windows and their frames as it battered and buffeted the van and flung rain against the windshield. Hazel's shoulders and arms, shaky and weak from insomnia, trembled with the strain of holding the van steady. Several times she decided to ask Liz to take the wheel, then faltered. She could not bring herself to break the silence so thick between them. She knew Liz. If she confessed to this physical weakness, Liz would seize the chance to lavish tender concern on her weaker and needier companion. And if Liz were to become solicitous over Hazel's manifest weakness, then Hazel would no longer be able to maintain her position that Liz cared nothing about her feelings. Hazel was determined not to give her *that*. Wrapped in the armor of coldness, absorbed by the necessity of wrestling the wind just to keep the van on the road, Hazel persevered.

They passed the first Everett exit, and Liz broke the silence. "This is it."

Hazel punched the turn indicator and, pulling over, stopped within inches of the mileage marker. She had remembered, but Liz could not know that. She watched in the mirror as Margot and Emily zoomed past, trailing two spitting plumes of water flung off the rear tires of their vehicle. Afterwards, there was only the sound of the wind and the drumming of rain on the roof and hood. Hazel stared straight ahead at the dark gray sky and tried to relax her arms and shoulders. The pain wrenching her neck reminded her of the discomfort she suffered whenever she did long inputs without benefit of an ergonomic chair.

After about a minute, a two-seater pulled up behind them. Liz got out and slammed the door. Hazel watched in the mirror as she strode back to the other car. When Liz reached the car she bent down over the window on the driver's side, which the woman in the other car—one of Liz's "amazons"—had lowered. After a minute at most Liz returned to the van, and Hazel pulled back onto the road. "It's in Madison Park, for the entire next week," Liz said, tapping an address into the vehicle's processor. "The house is shared by three professional couples, who will be staying in a downtown hotel for the week."

As Liz relayed the rest of what the contact had said, Hazel surmised that their accommodations for the week had again involved a mixture of bribe and favor. Six professionals sharing a house probably had something nice. Liz said that a friend of a friend of Gillian knew one of the women, who had originally been a Boeing researcher. Apparently the professionals had been willing to give up their house for a week of luxury because they were extremely anti-executive-system, and giving aid and comfort to an enemy of the Executive suited their inclinations.

Hazel located the address without difficulty and parked in the garage behind the house. Shirl was waiting for them at the back door. "Everything checks out," she said. "There's an electronic alarm system, but it's doubtful you'll have any problem. Unless you were followed, of course."

"We weren't," Liz said. "And we went over the van with the scanner before exiting the freeway."

Shirl handed Liz a set of keys. "And of course you'll want the sanction that gets you past the alarm system." She pulled a long thin strip of plastic out of her tunic pocket and handed it to Liz. "You can only insert it back here, so you'll always be coming in through the back door, unless for some reason you decide to turn off the alarm. Since the neighbors would notice your going in the front door, I don't advise that. They're extremely tight in this neighborhood. As it is…" Shirl shrugged. "The people whose house this is did tell the people living on either side that they would be having guests this week. But I wouldn't advertise."

Liz fed the plastic into the slot to one side of the door—a slot Hazel had not even noticed, for it blended into the shingles—and started trying keys in the door's three locks. Hazel wondered why Shirl bothered to tell Liz all these things: surely she must know that Liz was always ahead of her when it came to security precautions? One by one Liz opened the locks. When she'd gotten the door open, she retrieved the plastic strip from the slot and nodded at Shirl. "Thanks, Shirl. We're all set then."

"I'm parked half a block south," Shirl said. And she padded away on her soft soles.

Hazel and Liz carried their luggage through the house, Liz turning on lights as they went. While Liz explored, Hazel dumped Liz's luggage in the bedroom that had the largest bed and carried her own to one of the other bedrooms. Her first order of business was finding a bath tub (which a lot of professionals did not have) or a shower (which, if it was powerful enough and had a massage setting, would do just as well). Bathing or showering might loosen the pain in her neck, which she was sure was causing her headache.

Liz came in as Hazel unpacked her bath and night things. "Thank god they've got a small Jacuzzi in the master bedroom, darling—with untreated water, too! I can tell your shoulders ache by the way you keep rubbing your neck." She moved up behind Hazel, put her hands on Hazel's shoulders, and kneaded them. "You're all knotted up. If I give you a good massage and you sit in the Jacuzzi, I'm sure you'll be able to work the knot out."

Hazel remained still for a moment, then broke away. "For professionals, these people do pretty well for themselves," she said, draping the gown she had laid on the bed over her arm.

"Please, darling, can't we make up now?" Liz asked softly. "While you sit in the Jacuzzi I could make us dinner and then when you got out we could eat, and then we'd have the whole rest of the evening to talk. About whatever you want, darling. Now that we're alone, now that we're in a less precarious situation."

Hazel lifted her eyes to Liz's face. "Please, let's just have a quiet night. I don't think there's any more point in talking."

Liz did a slow blink. "What do you mean? Of course there's a point in talking! I know you're upset, darling. It's written all over you!"

Hazel took soap and powder from her suitcase. "Tomorrow I'm going to start looking for a new place to stay. By myself. And a new job." Hazel stood holding the things she needed for the bath, wishing Liz were not between her and the door.

"But why?" Liz's voice trembled. "Why a new job? Why live alone? But you *can't* live alone," she said in a rush. "You wouldn't be safe on your own, Hazel, you *know* that!"

"I've been told by any number of people that by myself my safety can be assured. And I believe them." Hazel drew a deep breath and moved past Liz to the door. Liz followed her into the hall and on into the master bedroom. Hazel passed through to the bathroom, dropped her things on a chair, and knelt on the floor near the head of the sunken tub, which though made of white Plexiglass, was encased in a rich, lustrous cedar cabinet and graced with gleaming brass taps and faucet.

"It's Martha Greenglass, isn't it," Liz said.

Hazel opened the taps, then busied herself with finding towels and wash cloths and setting her soap in the glass and brass soap dish that shared the same flaring curves that made the taps and faucet so aesthetically pleasing.

"She's poisoned you against me." Liz's voice was accusing. "She's been trying to do that since the first time she laid eyes on you."

Hazel looked over her shoulder, up at Liz. "Thanks very much, Liz, for your show of confidence in my affection and judgment. But then I should have known you don't think much of my mind."

"That's ridiculous! Do you think I'm *blind?* Do you think I can't see that Greenglass's hatred for executives has finally gotten to you?"

"You *are* blind," Hazel said. "If you weren't, you'd realize that I'm leaving you because I can't accept that in our relationship my feelings and concerns count as trivialities, while your feelings and concerns count as important. It's that simple."

"You're *leaving* me? You mean—completely?"

Hazel stripped, then draped her clothing over the chair. She knelt at the edge of the tub and tested the water against her fingers. After adjusting the ratio of hot to cold water filling the tub, she moved down to the other end of the tub and got in.

Liz undressed. "I can't believe you're putting it so simplistically. In the first place, you're taking a remark I made yesterday out of context and generalizing from it as though it were representative of our relations. My saying your concern about the executives eating apart from the girls was trivial by comparison with all the heavy things on my mind can't *possibly* be construed to mean that I consider your feelings and concerns trivial. Second, you know damned well I care about your feelings and concerns. If I didn't, I wouldn't let you browbeat and blackmail me into doing so many things your way." Liz leaned forward and turned off the taps, changed the settings for the whirl-pool, and flipped the switch that started the whirlpool—without ask-ing Hazel for *her* preferences. "Whenever things don't go as you think they should," she said, raising her voice to be heard above the roar of the churning water, "you threaten either to withdraw your love or to outright leave me." She dropped into the tub, and Hazel had to shift to keep from being squashed. "And why do you do that, Hazel? Precisely because I care so much for you that you know I'll give in to your threats."

In the narrow bit of space allotted her, Hazel squirmed to posi-tion herself so that the jet nearest her hit the knot in her shoulders. Leave it to Liz to wreck her bath, which was supposed to relax her neck and shoulders and chase away her tension headache, without so much as a passing remark about (much less apology for) her intrusion. "What a pretty picture you draw of our relationship," she said. "Let me rephrase it: the way our relationship works, I'm almost always very aware and sensitive to your moods, feelings, and needs. Not to men-tion your wants. I pay attention and do what I can to respond. Because I love you. But you, on the other hand, notice very little about my moods, feelings, and needs except when they get in your way. In this sense especially we're not reciprocal. I know very well you feel that all your energy must go into the things you call important. Everything else, you think, will just take care of itself. Which translates into *my* taking care of all those things, mostly without your being aware of them." Hazel shifted both of her legs to one side so that they would not touch Liz's. "This tub is too small for both of us," she said.

Liz stretched her arms and fingers over the surface of the water. "Nonsense, darling."

"Are you even bothering to listen to me?" Hazel said, distracted by Liz's crowding, naked presence.

Liz, her eyes glassy with threatening tears, gave Hazel a reproach-ful look. "Of course, darling. You were just telling me what an insensi-tive bitch I am."

"You're such an expert at loading things. But the fact of the matter is that if you paid the slightest attention to my feelings we wouldn't have these show-downs. Which you insist on seeing as manipulation. Or blackmail. It says a lot, how you begrudge any responsiveness to whatever conflicts with your convenience, which is, I guess, why you feel I extort concessions from you. You push me to it, Liz, when you refuse to pay attention otherwise."

The heat of the water had already made Liz's face flushed and damp, so sensitive was her pearl and rose complexion. "Don't you think you're a little old to be throwing tantrums?" Liz said, her voice infuriatingly silky, even pitched to be heard over the churning rumble of the whirlpool.

Determined to get out of the tub as quickly as possible, Hazel reached for the soap. She lathered without speaking, aware of Liz's intense—and now sexual—stare. "Your calling my insistence on having an independent point of view a tantrum says it all." Quickly Hazel rinsed. "In fact everything you've said makes it clear that we can't go on like this." She hoisted herself out of the tub and grabbed a towel.

"What about love, Hazel? Why doesn't that figure into your equations?"

"Love has been the glue," Hazel said as she rubbed the towel over her skin. "But even glue can give way under certain strains." She dropped the towel, powdered herself, and stepped into the gown. She stared down into Liz's eyes. "Love has reached its limits, Liz. There are things in you I've never loved and will never love. And those things seem to be dominating you lately." Hazel turned to leave.

"Now you're talking about something different," Liz yelled after her.

Hazel went back to her room and crawled into bed. All she wanted was to black out so she wouldn't have to think any more. She felt hollow, empty, worn out. As though her heart and mind had gone blank. She knew she was very angry, but did not feel the anger, except as this blankness, blankness that allowed her not to care about what Liz was feeling or about what she herself might feel once she had cut Liz out of her life. She had become a machine for carrying out her decision to leave Liz.

Some time later Liz appeared in the doorway, carrying a tray. "I've made us toasted Gruyère and tomato sandwiches and hot spicy cider," she said.

"I'm not hungry," Hazel said.

Liz came into the room. "At least sip the cider while I eat." She balanced the tray on the nightstand, then sat on the edge of the bed near Hazel.

Hazel made herself sit up and accept the cup of cider Liz was holding out to her. She knew that Liz would make her feel mean and boorish if she didn't.

"I take back what I said about your throwing tantrums, Hazel." Liz spread a napkin in her lap and took one of the steaming plates from the tray. "I didn't mean it, even when I said it. I've never thought of you as unfairly extorting concessions from me." She looked Hazel in the eye. "You place a check on my worst impulses. You were right about that naval intelligence officer. You were right to stop me, and I know it. I was half out of my head that night, panicking. The truth is, you bring out the best in me, darling, because you expect it of me."

Liz's voice stopped, and Hazel, staring down into her cider, was aware of Liz setting her plate back on the tray. She watched the flecks of cinnamon dotting the steaming surface of the cider swirl slowly in a spiral, as though they could save her from having to get through this scene. She was so tired. She just wished Liz would leave her *alone.*

"Please, darling, please don't walk away from me now," Liz said in a near-whisper. "I want to understand. You know I'm not used to having this kind of relationship. If I don't seem sensitive enough it's because I'm inexperienced, I'm still learning about this kind of love. Please, Hazel, won't you even look at me?"

Hazel lifted her gaze from the cider and saw that Liz was crying.

"I don't understand why you're so angry with me. I *want* to understand, believe me I do."

Hazel's throat tightened; her stomach was so upset she thought she might throw up.

"You won't even speak to me?"

Hazel found it hard to start, but once she began, her words rushed out of her as though they had been pent up under duress and given an avenue of escape would not be stopped. "I'm angry with you because you think my feelings—my hurt, my anger—are trivialities. Now you come in here and claim they do matter—because you don't want me to leave. What is there for me to say, Liz?" Hazel tried to ignore the tears that had begun flowing from her own eyes, as though in response to Liz's tears.

"I never meant that your *hurt* was a triviality, Hazel. What I felt was a triviality was all this nonsense about those girls, who would have freaked out if they'd been forced to eat with the executives *en masse*. You're not like them, darling, no matter what you think."

"It's not just their—and my—exclusion from the meal, Liz. But our exclusion from whatever it was you were discussing. They went renegade, too, you know. They followed their lovers, damn it, which means that anything Bennett and Mott decide to do will affect their lives. Don't they have any right to be in on that?"

"Oh darling you're so mixed up!" Liz wiped her eyes with the back of her hand. "Can you see that girl Ginger sitting in a serious meeting, able to understand much less participate in any serious kind of discussion? It would only worry her, Hazel! We were mainly talking about future security arrangements—and they were telling me about the general situation within Security since I left. And about other women thinking of leaving. What could Ginger or Anne have to do with any of that?"

"You could have *asked* us, instead of simply ordering me to get them out of your hair!" Hazel cried. "You were moving us around, Liz, like chess pieces on a board, and assuming we'd obey. And of course we did. All the time I watched Ginger going in and out of the kitchen back and forth to the dining room, I kept thinking of how each of us ordinarily takes meals with one of the women sitting in that dining room. It was a strange feeling, Liz. An *ugly* feeling. It made me so inferior. Not good enough to eat with the company. Someone kept around for when there's nobody else available to amuse you."

"My god, Hazel, how can you say that!"

"I'm telling you, Liz, how I *felt*. That's all I know, my feelings. I don't have your kind of education, so I can't put it any other way. It felt awful. It feels wrong, your making these assumptions about us, your treating us differently."

"And what did those girls feel?"

"They of course were in a kind of numb state because of the shock of going renegade, of overturning their lives. I suppose they felt it was appropriate. But that doesn't mean that I should have felt the same way, Liz."

"Oh darling, don't you see, it's your *perceptions* that are the problem? If I'd done things your way, those girls would have been *wretchedly* uncomfortable. I would have preferred to have had you there with us, but I knew it wouldn't look right to have you and not them. And they needed someone to make them feel comfortable in such new and alien surroundings."

"Maybe you're right, Liz. I don't really know." There was a lot of phlegm in Hazel's throat that she was having trouble clearing; her sinuses had filled with fluid and gotten all clogged up. "I'm sure they would have been uncomfortable, but I think it would have been better to have included them—and me—anyway. The first few times would be uncomfortable, maybe, but then, after a while, especially if the executives tried to make them feel welcome, things would change. As in my case."

Liz smiled sadly. "I don't believe you'd really be comfortable being in the minority in a room full of executives, darling. Whatever you say now."

Hazel bit her lip. "You're probably right, I probably wouldn't be comfortable. But I'm not sure that's the point."

"You confuse me, darling." Liz sighed. "But if you want me to try to include those girls whenever we're all together again, I will."

"To humor me."

"To keep from hurting you," Liz corrected. She held out her hand. "You're not drinking your cider. Let me put it back on the tray for you." Hazel handed her the full mug, and Liz set it on the tray. "Please tell me you'll stay, darling," she said.

Hazel's gaze met Liz's; she noticed that tears had matted the thick, dark eyelashes into clumps. Liz didn't understand. She just didn't get it. But in spite of that, she was willing to change her behavior—once again. To keep Hazel from leaving. Because really, Liz did love her. But though Liz talked about how wrong Hazel's perceptions were, it was *Liz's* perceptions that needed to change. Would a change in behavior help bring that about? Hazel struggled to smile. "Yes, Rapunzel, I'll stay," she said very low. But she felt bad, felt as though she had failed to make the point, as though Liz had done another one of her end-runs around her.

Liz threw herself into Hazel's arms and laid her head on Hazel's breast. Hazel stroked Liz's hair and drew a deep shuddering breath. She couldn't leave Liz, not when she was like this. Her anger dissolved in a hazy flood of feeling, of aching heart and yearning desire for the closeness and warmth and fullness they often shared. And Liz's need...Liz's need moved her profoundly, in spite of Liz's selfishness. This soft, vulnerable Liz was the Liz she knew and loved. *This* Liz had not a cold mean bone in her body.

Liz lifted her head and sought Hazel's mouth. After a while, she withdrew a little to say, "I love you, Hazel, for you fill my heart and soul."

"Yes," Hazel murmured, closing her eyes as Liz's lips brushed her neck. "Yes, love—" her words issued from her mouth like a sigh— "I know."

## [ii]

Half-asleep, Hazel maneuvered out of Liz's embrace to roll over, for her shoulder and arm were stiff from having been in one position too long. Liz moved onto her back. "Are you awake, my precious?" she said. Hazel grunted. "Lie on me, won't you, it'll be so cozy." Hazel moved closer to Liz and found a comfortable spot for her head in the area below Liz's neck and above her breasts. When she was settled, Liz moved her fingers almost gently back and forth against Hazel's. "It's almost time for me to go make us coffee," Liz said after awhile. "I slept wonderfully. How about you?"

"Dreams," Hazel muttered, finding it hard to form sentences. "Lots of dreams."

"It's going to be an exciting week, darling. Maybe by the end of it we'll be ready to move into the Redmond house."

"So far," Hazel complained. "Long drive there and back."

"Well we won't often be coming into Seattle, darling. The point is, we'll have lots of privacy and space and a good armed fortification."

"You're so damned overconfident. If they find it they'll bomb it," Hazel said, suddenly awake.

"Don't be such a pessimist, darling," Liz said. "The procedures I've set up will be more than adequate."

Hazel, remembering the new renegades, said, "Will Bennett and the rest be staying in the mountains for long?"

"For the week," Liz said slowly. "Partly to give me a chance to think things through. I'm almost sorry I didn't agree to see Lisa before she performed the acts of sabotage I required of her. It would have been useful to have her still in place, if what she says about others wanting to go renegade is true."

"Are you going to give those files to Martha?"

"Emily's already passed them along to the International Human Rights people, darling. That was part of the deal."

"Mott and Bennett could still go somewhere out of the Free Zone, the way we originally planned for ourselves," Hazel said.

"No, darling. They can't. Neither Lisa nor Allison were able to eradicate their identities from Security's processing system. Nor could they get new plastic. No, they're in much more of a box than we were. Lisa was able to convert some of her assets into M-dollars. But she's taking a beating on everything else. Though I do have this idea about stock…especially if others go renegade."

"What idea?"

"Stocks and bonds cannot be simply confiscated, the way real estate can sometimes be. I'm wondering whether if we recruit enough women we can't somehow make ourselves felt in the financial markets."

"That sounds far-fetched."

"Yes, darling, you're right. Just a fantasy. However." She chuckled. "One bit of gossip Allison and Lisa had to pass on tickles me no end. Booth has been so hard hit by the aliens' targeting the corporations in which he has so heavily concentrated himself, they say they've heard he's begun selling off some of his art. I wonder just how much power he'll have left by the time I'm through with him."

"Why are you so set on destroying him, Liz? I would have thought it was Sedgewick you'd want to go after."

"Sedgewick? Oh darling, he's just pathetic. My real enemy all along was Booth, not Sedgewick. I keep kicking myself when I think of how all those years I could have been undermining him if I'd wanted to. With the kind of power I had…"

"You sound wistful for the good old days, Liz," Hazel said acidly.

"I played by the rules, darling. Which was so damned stupid. During the Civil War, I could have…" She sighed. "What's the point of thinking backwards like that? We've got a whole new future ahead of us; it's that I should be daydreaming about."

"I wish I knew what you had in mind," Hazel said.

"Something big, Hazel. I'm going to see if I can reorganize the executive system. It depends on how much support I can drum up. I'm not thinking only of leading a band of renegades, darling. I'm thinking of marshaling support for a major reorganization at all levels, forcing the Executive to change its ways. To get rid of the dead weight, for one thing. All the drunks and do-nothings and burnt-out males who've been in place for the last thirty years. There's been very little movement upwards, Hazel. Largely the same men hold the same positions with the same ideas they had thirty years ago: while the world has changed. As far as I'm concerned, they're all living in a dream world. Which is why they've lost control of this country."

"This is what you were talking about with the other executives?"

Liz said, "No. Not at all. Neither Allison nor Lisa thinks in very large terms, darling. Now Margot, she's had a similar idea for some time. And Emily? Who knows with her. She's a wild card, darling. She's incredibly cynical, I'll tell you that much. It's almost shocking, but I suppose that's what comes of having lived so close to a man like Barclay Madden."

"I like her a lot," Hazel said, thinking of how Emily was the only one of the executives who seemed even to see her. Emily never failed to speak to her or bring her into the discussion. And her interest wasn't like Margot's, which Hazel judged to be purely sexual; she never ogled her or stroked or pinched her. She listened with a serious expression in her eyes whenever Hazel had anything to say to her.

"Lord look at the time!" Liz sat up and leaped out of bed.

Hazel snuggled down into the warm place Liz had left behind and watched her throw on her robe and stride into the bathroom. Such a beautiful, magnificent woman, she thought, amazed as she sometimes was at seeing Liz as others must see her. How very strange that Liz had chosen her, such an ordinary person. Liz was a mystery, yes.

# Chapter Nine

Such joy, such serenity! Sunk within the richest silm in Marqeuei, thick with bubbles of every size—teeming with a myriad organisms—Astrea's field expands and extends until that one's self becomes nearly one with the planet. Sensibilitizing, that one forgets having sent an urgent call to Dghatd l Merr san Fehln, forgets, in bliss, everything but the pleasures of enfolding so many creatures within one's field, of imagining self without borders or wish for borders. Nurturing within itself so many lives and such life-and-death dramas, this *cthollasq* of silm constitutes a small world of its own, mysterious, vital, and hospitable to Marq'ssan.

Only when Dghatd l Merr san Fehln, approaching, slithers into the silm and settles into a nearby furrow does Astrea recollect that life exists outside this *cthollasq*.

"In response, Astrea l Betut san Imu."

Astrea inches closer to Dghatd l Merr. "I call on your expertise, Dghatd l Merr: I'm blocked from enfolding human languages. A barrier holds me at a distance, blocking me from synthesizing the syntactical nexus characteristic of these languages. The xenographers in-struct emphasis on representation and politically marked pseudo-equivalence, the binary structure they say embeds all human institutions and the humans' obsession with origin. This, I think, con-structs the barrier to enfoldment. Can you propose other approaches, Dghatd l Merr?" And: "Never have I constructed closure against any Marq'ssan language—of which I now circulate fifty-nine."

Almost at once, Astrea becomes conscious of offering this addendum to impress Dghatd.

Sunk deep within the thickest layers of silm, Dghatd feathers scales, laterals, and busks with the steaming froth bubbling at the thin surface. "Lying in your furrow may contribute to the con-struction of the barrier you imagine, Astrea l Betut. Among humans, you will live constantly within con-fining structures, you will be constantly compartmentalized and de-fined, physically and conceptually. Harshest of all, you will be forced to hold that one self-con-structing image rigidly to de-finitize a self-presentation for the humans you encounter. You must conceive, Astrea l Betut, that enfoldment of human languages enfolds this de-finitization." Dghatd's laterals stir. "Which is the reason that I wonder whether it's possible to enfold anything truly human while sensibilitizing within silm."

Astrea's laterals lift, breaking the surface, to emerge into the thick rich cloud hanging over the silm. "I'll take your suggestion, Dghatd l Merr, and will separate, divide, and define. It occurs to me to draw connection with the old Bolddan before my birth. Would that be useful, Dghatd l Merr?"

"You will find no equivalence, but perhaps useful connection." Dghatd l Merr in-structs Astrea, one too young to have immediately experienced the old Bolddan tyranny. "Imagine Marq'ssan without Immeni or Omauo. Especially without Omauo. Humans have no language enfolding those processes peculiar to Omauo. The closest they approximate those processes is through nonverbal forms, which they circulate haphazardly, carelessly, or not at all. They hold such forms at a distance, a-part, never integrating them into their other sensibilities or communications. Above all they break processes into de-finitized compartments, pre-cluding both circulation and synthesis. One problem for those who go among humans is this need to de-finitize in order to enfold human processes. This throws up barriers, Astrea l Betut, and con-structs Marq'ssan separate and de-finitized within and without. This is a danger you've heard much of since the Task Force returned. But perceive: this same problem of alteration throws up the barrier holding you away from enfolding human languages."

Astrea contemplates Dghatd's understanding of the problem. Never to flow among Boldeni, Immeni, and Omauo spontaneously? To separate these languages as entire de-finitized systems a-part from the others? (As though languages could ever be a-part from one another?) Astrea rises further, until almost fully extended, surrounded by and within the cloud. "Boldeni fantasizes exact representations which enable certain manipulations and the illusion of exchange."

Astrea wonders: "Shall I imagine such equivalences solely in-forming human language?"

Dghatd l Merr—one who had immediate experience of old Bolddan—inquires: "Have you immersed yourself in the relations of old Bolddan?"

Astrea offers her understanding of those relations: "The structures divided all, the structures in-fined an all-demanding ordering where-in the origin and end were de-fined (whence the privilege of prior-ity), preventing integration of processes, which were re-presented as separate and sub-ordinate to the structures. Whence the death and de-struction which the in-fining of structures implies and impels, whence the attempts of Bolddan to ob-literate Omauo. Without Omauo, oh how dry how arid how abrasive how separate how blocked and locked away Marq'ssan would be!" Astrea—though incredulous—grieves at the image that one has conjured. "Without Omauo, Immeni would bear a special rigid sub-ordinate relation to Boldeni and serve as func-tionary to Boldeni's divisions and in-fining of order."

Dghatd l Merr gurgles, spewing bubbles through the frothy sur-face of silm, though not rising above the surface to be enfolded within the cloud. "A nice summary, Astrea l Betut." Dghatd speaks as elder to younger, though Astrea is—barely—no adolescent. "But can you enfold the entire surface of useful connections? I imagine that if you can, the human languages will be less baffling. The re-presentations all of them posit are con-structed as absolutes, disguised configura-tions and consolidations of power through which they rob themselves. This, the xenologists agree, is the condition of their language, origin-mad as they are. By these con-structions they convince themselves that they have neither responsibility nor power except in relation to these con-structs they worship. Oh the frustrations on board *s'sbeyl*, trying to help them open up ways for mediating among themselves! Consider their de-finitive terms 'Truth' and 'Law' and 'Justice': these power-consolidations they use to construct themselves a-part. Always humans hold these terms above themselves, beyond themselves, out-side themselves, imagined absolute referents independent of their ex-istences and processes. They use these power-consolidations to evade responsibility by referring to them as though they exist above and a-part from those who con-structed them, independent of those who imagine them, as pretexts for averting their senses.

This barrier, I fear, we will never destructure. How to do so, with only one form of language that can only keep them a-part? Oh these com-part-mentalizations! Oh these deferences! Through their re-presentations and divisions they invest the proposed origin of their representations—the abstractions they believe to be prior and supe-rior equivalences to the supposed symbols they manipulate. And then again they replicate this binary pattern in less equivalent ways, thereby dividing and de-finitizing all things they perceive in their world. *All* things, Astrea. Into com-part-mentalized processes! And they assign one priority to this binary, that always and already one term—which replicates in every way imaginable or perceptible—takes precedence over the other, thus fore-closing the other, sub-ordinating it with ref-erence to the imagined absolute origin."

Astrea proposes, speculating: "As with old Bolddan."

Dghatd corrects Astrea's inference: "But in humans the binary cuts primarily along constructed gender and racial rather than ambi-ent lines, as was the case with the old Bolddan."

Astrea trumpets a sudden sense of access. "Yes—yes—yes—which im-parts to me the choice for Marq'ssan to de-finitize on earth within female forms only!"

Dghatd l Merr offers a response slightly dry, evaporating the froth of Astrea's excess: "Again I advise you, go within structures and de-finitize yourself as a human female representation. And then see if you en-circle your barrier. I warn you in advance, and others have said the same: you will never be truly Marq'ssan while immediately within human structures and language. Human con-structs refuse integra-tion and incorporation. To be human as they are now con-structed *is* to be a-part. You will experience barriers and com-partments as you enfold. The contradiction is painful, Astrea. And won't be transcended until humans re-construct and in-corporate."

Astrea goes from the furrow, leaving Dghatd l Merr to sensibil-itize in the silm. Being young, contradictions do not yet pain Astrea as they do the mature. Astrea does not know the experience of being a-part, and though a little frightened considers the prospect intriguing, as with everything different from the life so wetly enfolded within post-Bolddan Marq'ssan. To understand the older ones, to perceive immediately something approaching what they themselves emerged from? A less safe immersion, yes, but different—and surely expansive? A Marq'ssan could not lie sunk in the furrow sensibilitizing without losing structure and materiality. Better this even than going to Bol, better this than going to Androst. No equivalences going to the humans, only connections. And therein frothed the excitement.

# Chapter Ten

Meeting her father at the front door, Alexandra saw at a glance that he retained his amazing good mood. Because of that continuing good mood—which approved of her new hairstyle and allowed her a piano here ("though not another Bechstein, Alexandra, I won't run to that level of extravagance")—Alexandra decided she would ask him to allow Clarice to ride in the car with them. The thought of Clarice riding in the van with five gorillas gave her the shudders. She vowed that if he said yes she would kiss his cheek as she had when he'd promised her the piano; and then his mood would be guaranteed pleasant.

So as they stood on the verge of going out the door, Alexandra nerved herself to speak. "Could Clarice ride with us?" It was a rule that a gorilla had to ride beside the driver, so naturally she never even thought of asking that Clarice be given a seat in the front.

His gaze swept past her to stare at Clarice, who stood beside Alexandra with the luggage. His eyes locked onto something in particular; curious, Alexandra turned to look, to trace the source of his interest. She located it almost at once in the gold chain fastened around the girl's long, graceful neck, its pearl pendant nestled against the black angora in the valley between the full mounds of her breasts, rising and falling with Clarice's every breath.

After a long half-minute he looked back at Alexandra. She flinched at the frigid remoteness now in possession of his eyes. "Perhaps it was a mistake to include her in the party at all," he said, his voice low but distinct. And before Alexandra could think of a reply, he flung open the door and stalked out to the car.

Alexandra threw Clarice a look over her shoulder and hurried after him. Clearly he had recognized the pendant, clearly its presence on Clarice's breast angered him. The drive down to Lucia was now guaranteed to be a fiasco. Depressed, Alexandra got into the car and tried to efface herself: she stared out the window at the endless rows of grapevines and kept silent.

This car, he had told her when they had driven out in it earlier in the week, had a special internal combustion engine and ran on a combination of battery power and combustible fuel—of which he had a great deal stored in tanks near the winery proper. To drive it cost—when one had not gotten the fuel through the Executive as he had—one hundred times more than to drive a car of comparable size that did not have a combustion engine. Also, he said, this car had a more powerful engine. And it could run for long distances without requiring its battery to be changed or recharged.

He did not speak until they had accessed the road that would take them to the coastal highway. Aware of the gorillas' van not far behind, Alexandra knew that Clarice would be hating this part of the trip. Still, she had expressed pleasure at going along. Alexandra knew that given the kind of life she was accustomed to, being cooped up with only her, Alexandra, for company must be difficult. "In the future, Alexandra—" her father's voice suddenly split open the long tense silence—"keep your cunts out of my sight. If you ever again presume to force this one on me I'll ship her back to her owner without another word. Clear?"

A fiery wave washed over her, paralyzing her as the violence and contempt of his words reverberated in her head. Her eyes, fixed on the passing scenery, filmed over. "You make it so ugly," she said, barely able to jerk the words out but needing to protest.

"*I* make it ugly?" he said. "For all the women I had when I was sexually active, Alexandra, never did I stoop to using a whore. My taste simply did not run to purchased flesh." He snorted. "In retrospect I can hardly be amazed that your mother managed to teach you her tastes... I suppose I should have expected it. But then what would you do with a real woman, intelligent and honest? Unable to buy her, you wouldn't have the faintest idea of how to attract and keep her. But why bother when you can deform your taste enough to focus on the easily bought? Slimy tentacled clinging saccharine exploitation." The words flew out of his mouth like missiles of spit. "On both sides. Since anything else would be too dangerous. Nice pat roles, all contingencies overdetermined by the purchase. You think I don't see through it?"

His virulence pounded away at her, savage and suffocating. He was furious as she'd never before seen him. And he had not been drinking. This virulence seemed to spew raw and fetid from some deep well of pollution she had somehow stirred up; not that she hadn't before now sensed deep polluted wells poisoning his entire being, spilling over on her and anyone else who came near him. But this outburst struck her as something new, as some untapped well suddenly provoked into eruption. Certainly it was the most direct assault—apart from that one scene about Elizabeth when he had hit her—she had yet sustained from him. What she hated most, though, was that his ugliness threatened the beautiful and exciting thing she and Clarice shared.

Alexandra knew she should keep quiet, but she couldn't stop herself. "Everything for you is hateful and filthy, there's nothing beautiful in your world. You want to trap everyone inside your prison, you loathe anything pleasurable and beautiful because you're so miserable and grudging and decrepit yourself!"

Rage flared in his eyes; she watched his face tighten and shut down for one brief moment before his hand shot out and his fingers took hold of her hair and jerked her forward and sideways, pulling her sprawling off the seat. "Your control is pathetic," he said.

The car lurched around a curve, again thrusting Alexandra off balance. Clutching the edge of the seat, she waited for him to let go of her hair so that she could get off the floor. "I apologize," she said stiffly, quietly.

Almost at once he released her hair. Alexandra resumed her seat and smoothed her tunic and trousers, patted and fluffed her hair, as though such gestures could wipe the humiliation from her mind. No one had ever treated her as he did. *Bastard!* she silently raged. But though this treatment angered her, it also shamed her. He never would have treated her so contemptuously if she hadn't indulged in that outburst against him. *Your control is pathetic*: a rebuke all the more stinging for its appropriateness. *Bastard, bastard...* She stared out the window and tried to collect herself. Mama would certainly not sympathize with her; Mama thought she should be able to manipulate him. It had been stupid to bring Clarice to his attention, incredibly stupid. What had gotten into her? Simply because his mood had been so good, so pleasant?

"Your sexual conduct," his voice—now in lecturing mode—cut through her self-recriminations, "is your own affair, as long as you keep it discreet, and as long as you know what you're doing. I'm positively astonished that your mother has failed to instruct you properly about either of these things. But since she has, I obviously will have to make up for the omission."

Of course, Alexandra thought, he would have to use my offenses against Mama. Every fault he picked at he held Mama responsible for. While every manifestation of personality or aptitude he regarded as positive he attributed to resemblance to himself.

"And you will do me the courtesy of looking at me when I'm speaking to you."

Alexandra dragged her head around to face him. She swallowed and said, "Mama *has* instructed me about the need to be discreet. I do understand about it. It's my own fault. For some reason I wasn't thinking. I beg your pardon."

"For some reason you weren't thinking," he repeated. "Let's discuss that 'some reason.'"

Alexandra searched his face. He didn't mean her trading on his good mood, did he? "I meant that vaguely," she said. "It was carelessness, not due to some special reason."

He snorted. "Not some special reason? Who're you trying to kid? Let's go back to the scene, shall we?" His mouth twisted into one of his nastier smiles. "There we all are, standing in the hall by the front door. What is on your mind as you're standing there?"

At a loss, Alexandra shook her head. "The trip. I was thinking about how we were going on this trip." And of how it might actually be enjoyable because his good mood was holding.

"What else? Come on, Alexandra. Just before you spoke to me about your cunt, what were you thinking."

Alexandra's face burned. "I was thinking about how unpleasant it would be for Clarice to ride in the other car with the escort."

"Don't give them names when you talk to me. I prefer to know as little about them as possible. Clear?"

Alexandra lowered her eyes. "Understood."

"So you were thinking about the girl. And why were you thinking about the girl when you were standing there in the hall with me?" His hand darted out, grabbed her chin, and jerked it up. "Look at me when I'm talking to you." She looked carefully into his eyes. "Now answer my question," he said when she did not speak.

Alexandra's breath came fast, and her confusion mounted. "Because I was concerned about her."

"And why were you concerned about her?"

"Because I thought she would feel uncomfortable—"

He interrupted. "That wasn't my question. You're telling me the nature of your concern for her. What I asked you was why you were concerned."

Alexandra frowned. It was hard to think with his fingers gripping her chin. "You mean the fact that I would even be concerned about her at all?"

"You wouldn't, for instance, be concerned about whether or not Lamont would be comfortable or uncomfortable at any given time."

Alexandra bit her lip. "I'm concerned about her because I like her."

Finally, finally, he took his hand from her chin. "You like her," he repeated sarcastically. "Tell me. In what way do you *like* her."

"You can't understand, so could we please not talk about it?"

He grinned, showing his teeth. "Oh I understand all right. Do you imagine I didn't experience sexual infatuations myself when I was your age?" When she—embarrassed that he, an executive male, was talking (again!) about previous sexual experiences—said nothing, he continued, "For that's what this is, Alexandra. Because it's—I as-sume—your first, you have no perspective on the subject whatsoever. Christ, I should have thought of this and insisted that Weatherall take you out last spring. With a little wider experience and more guidance than your mother apparently sees fit to offer, you wouldn't be making such an idiot of yourself. As it is, you're wallowing in the most absurd confusion. Which, my dear, must be cleared up. One way or another."

What was he *talking* about? Sometimes the things he said were so impenetrable that she had not the faintest glimmer of understanding of what he was saying.

"Tell me how you view your, ah, relationship with this girl," he said in that same mocking, peremptory tone of voice.

Why did he keep asking her to talk about Clarice when he'd told her she wasn't supposed to bring her up at all? Why was he *harping* on this? Alexandra remembered the look on his face when he was gazing at the pearl pendant, and it occurred to her that he was forcing this conversation on her to punish her for having given his gift to Clarice. "I like being with her," she said woodenly.

"You like being with her. I see. And does she *like* being with you?"

"I think so."

"You think so, but you don't know for sure? And why is that, do you suppose?"

Alexandra flushed. "She's used to being with very sophisticated women. It might be that somebody as young and inexperienced as I am bores her."

He shook his head. "You answered the wrong question again, Alexandra. Try again."

She swallowed. "I don't understand."

"I asked you why you don't know for sure whether or not she 'likes' being with you. You told me why she might not like being with you. But I didn't ask about her, Alexandra, I asked about you, about why you should have to wonder about interpreting her, ah, feelings."

The sneer with which he said these things made Alexandra cringe. "I still don't understand," she said. And now her voice trembled.

"Let me ask you this, then. Do you wonder at your mother's or grandmother's motives when they lavish affection on you?"

Alexandra shook her head. "Of course not. Why would I?"

"Precisely. Why would you? You're not, after all, paying them, are you. You don't have to mistrust their motives—at least not when it comes to certain things you've known all your life. But you will find, Alexandra, as an executive in the first place, but more especially because you are my daughter, that you will not so readily be able to interpret others' motives when it comes to such personal matters as affection. But when it comes to an employee, especially one who is being paid to amuse you personally, then the whole matter becomes absurd. That cunt has greed written all over her, and you know it, whether you want to admit it to yourself or not. She's out for everything she can get from you. My point is that if you want to play with whores you'd better keep clear exactly what it is you're doing."

"You make it sound so ugly," Alexandra said, very low.

"Mixing economic transactions into personal affairs *is* ugly," he said. "And now, we will go on to the second point I want to make. To return to the scene, where we were all standing by the front door and you were thinking of your cunt. Let me put it this way. Neither your mother nor Weatherall would at that particular moment have been thinking about the girl standing beside them, even if they'd moments before been inside her legs. Shall I tell you why?"

"I can't stand your talking this way," Alexandra said, finding it almost impossible now to hold back her tears.

"You introduced the subject yourself. One always has to live with the consequences of one's mistakes. To continue. Perhaps you can explain to me why neither your mother nor Weatherall would have been thinking about the girl if they'd been in your situation."

Alexandra, not trusting her voice, shook her head.

He leaned forward, opened the middle of the three compartments built into the partition between the front and back seat, and extracted two bottles of water and glasses. He handed her one of the glasses and a bottle. "Standing there in the hall with me they both of them would have bent their entire attention on me. *That's* why. If it had been another executive instead of myself, they would have bent their attention on him. Or her. They have priorities, Alexandra. They never allow their sexual interests to get in the way of the things that count. You do understand that one aspect of the theory behind surgical alteration is the very practical problem of men of power allowing themselves to be distracted into irresponsibility. That that need not be the case is, I think, amply demonstrated by Weatherall. Though it often is the case that sexually-oriented persons lack sufficient control over their sexuality to function as they should. If you want to play around, fine—provided you can keep your play from interfering with what counts, provided you can keep yourself free from the manipulation of your cunts. This one has been doing a pretty fair job on you, it's obvious." He twisted the cap off the bottle and poured water into his glass. After recapping the bottle and setting it into the holder in his armrest, he said, "Do you understand what I'm saying, Alexandra?"

"Yes." Her voice was almost inaudible. "I understand."

His gaze bored into hers. "I hope so. For your sake." He drank from the glass, his eyes never leaving hers. "And by the way, perhaps you would be interested to know that I find it extremely obnoxious of you never to address me by name."

Alexandra lowered her eyes to the bottle she held and slowly broke the seal and removed the cap. "It makes me uncomfortable to call you by your first name," she said into the silence.

"That's too bad," he said. "Perhaps if you were made more uncomfortable by avoiding it you might change your mind."

Alexandra poured water into the glass and gulped some before recapping the bottle. "I'm sorry for seeming obnoxious," she said. She drew a deep breath. And added—"Robert." And at once felt her face heat up.

He glanced past her. "Look. We're almost at Carmel." He smiled slightly and his face lost some of its stiffness. "I'm sure you'll enjoy lunch. I haven't been to this place in years, but I hear the same chef is still there. And the view is as good as the food. And then afterwards comes the best part of the drive."

Alexandra sipped the water and stared out the window. She felt numb, confused, disoriented. The important thing was to keep herself from falling apart, to hold together as best she could. She took another swallow of water and set her glass in the holder in her armrest. Once they reached Buchanan's she would be able to get off by herself and think. She needed to think, to clear her head of all the muck he'd flung at her. And then she would be all right again, she wouldn't feel so sick to her stomach, so sick at heart. It was all *him*, all *his* sickness. He made everything ugly.

She wished she could talk to Elizabeth. Elizabeth would understand, Elizabeth would know, Elizabeth would be able to explain.

[ii]

Delicately Alexandra speared a grapefruit section—*whoever heard of eating grapefruit between courses? Sorbet, melon, or strawberries, yes, but grapefruit!*—and slipped it into her mouth. "What concerns me," Whitman, the food producer, said, "is not only the question of whether the country is in danger of becoming ungovernable, but the more immediate problem of Military's getting the upper hand in the

Executive." All of the men sitting at this table, Alexandra knew, had interests closely tied with Security, some of them in strong opposition to interests fostered by Military. Buchanan, on Alexandra's right, smiled at her. "You see, Madam, what a disservice your father has done us by dropping the reins." Buchanan had been paying her steady, scrupulous attention, even going so far as to seat her beside himself, at the end that counted, partly, she thought, because he wanted to please her father, and partly because of that long tedious session in his study that afternoon when—prefaced for Alexandra by lengthy briefings conducted by that obsequious professional from Brace who specially handled her father's portfolio—Papa had told him that he intended for her to begin taking an active role in his financial affairs. TNC had serious problems because most of its satellites were now defunct. Her father had a twenty-nine percent interest in TNC and controlled the voting proxies of thirteen percent more. Naturally the CEO and chairman of the board of TNC would be anxious to ingratiate himself with such shareholding power. The fact that her father had been taking little interest in the actual operation of TNC did not mean that he might never exercise his prerogatives. Papa had suggested to Buchanan that he begin thinking of Alexandra's being made a director.

What to reply to this piece of flattery? Glancing out of the corner of her eye at her father (diagonally across the table from her), she said, "Perhaps it is only temporary." And she forced a smile.

"Let us hope," Steadman, on Alexandra's left, said. "I, frankly, am more concerned about the deterioration of public order and the demoralization of the labor force than I am about Executive politics." Of course, Alexandra thought, a banker would tend to think that way. "Hill strikes me as weak," he added. "Whyever was he appointed Acting Chief, Robert?"

All this was so absurd, Alexandra thought, tensing as she waited for her father's response. These men seemed to believe that her father had gone on leave because of a dispute within the Executive. When she thought of his condition when he'd summoned her away from Crowder's, the entire scenario these men apparently held to seemed an enormous joke that everyone was solemnly pretending to take seriously. Not that he'd ever done more than hint to her the reason he'd "gone on leave." But she found it easy enough to guess for herself. Of course, given the way he sat there—drinking only one glass of wine with each course—handling these men with such ease, only someone who knew him well could suspect that he could be anything other than in total control.

Ingersoll, the man seated on the other side of her father, said, "The entire problem of public order and morale would be solved if we could just manage to keep our fucking com sats operational. We have public control down to a science—when basic technology is functioning, that is. This piecemeal approach to distribution of DVDs, for instance, is simply inadequate. Restore the technology and protect it, and that entire area of concern will melt away." Ingersoll, Alexandra recalled, headed American Vid Productions. "Take, for instance, the cost and inconvenience of sectoring LA. Getting my people to work on time is a major concern. The time they spend going through sector control is costing us our profit. And think of what such elaborate personnel-intensive security systems must cost in and of themselves! And all because LA and Boston would be burnt to the ground without sectoring?" He shrugged. "It's absurd, considering the state of the art of operant social psychology!"

"And they say Houston is next," Pearce, the only dark-skinned executive Alexandra had met outside of Barbados, said glumly.

"What's more, where the aliens are concerned, one cannot really assume with any certainty that any technology restored won't be knocked out again," Whitman said. "Look at Washington! It's just not possible for us to keep *all* our systems underground or surrounded by lead shielding. It's simply not practical. In ten years we've fallen a hundred years behind the times!"

"Is it true," asked Steadman, on Alexandra's left, "that Booth has somehow gotten onto the aliens' hit-list?"

Alexandra observed the grin spreading over her father's face and wondered at the negativity toward Booth that he'd been advertising since his arrival. He hadn't shown such negativity at Blumenthal's. "I imagine so," he replied. "The evidence seems indisputable, and I've got a pretty fair notion of what's behind it, too. I've heard he's dumped all his shares in GE-Westinghouse and plunged into water purification. I surmise that's on the assumption that the aliens won't touch such vital public utilities."

"There's a story there, Robert," Steadman said. "Now that you've waved it under our noses, don't you think you have an obligation to tell it?"

Papa leaned back in his chair and glanced around the table. "I must extract a promise of honor from each of you in respect for the confidentiality of what I'm about to tell you."

Astonished, Alexandra watched as everyone—including Judith MacLaury, sitting at the foot of the table directing the service—gave their solemn word not to divulge the story.

The air fairly crackled with excitement when the service-techs were sent out of the room (carrying the grapefruit plates away with them). An expectant hush fell. Papa began: "The key to the story is, of course, Weatherall—my bitch gone renegade." Someone gasped. Alexandra tensed with suspense at the prospect of his talking about Elizabeth. "You all know her reputation." His mouth quirked in a sardonic half-smile, and his eyes glittered. "Quite frankly, she terrorized most of the Executive. She was really quite superb." He sipped from his water glass. "In fact she was the source of the, ah, dispute between George Booth and myself. He's never fully recovered, you know, from the weakness he betrayed during the Civil War, or from his consciousness that Security alone kept the Executive alive and functioning during that period, or from the fact that Security brought about the settlement of the War, too. Let's face it, George Booth hasn't actually been in control since the Blanket."

Papa's mouth tightened. "Which is probably why he found it so difficult accepting Weatherall. The very idea of my bitch—a woman—being that strong was more than he could handle. He gradually lost even the semblance of control whenever he was around her. She, of course, was enacting my orders with consummate efficiency and effectiveness. Yet George grew positively irrational on the subject." Alexandra caught her breath: could all this be true? "His irrationality peaked when Weatherall—following my instructions—was in the process of working out an agreement with the Free Zone and the aliens that would have settled the satellite issue once and for all." He glanced at Ingersoll and nodded slightly. Ingersoll looked intensely interested.

"In the midst of a discussion about these matters with George—when, that is, it became clear to him that I'd delegated the responsibility for negotiations to Weatherall—he blew up. He declared that the Executive would not countenance negotiations. He had originally been amenable to negotiations, you understand, but once he heard of Weatherall's role, he flipped." He snorted. "Not only must the negotiations be halted, but Weatherall must be terminated: thus he put it to me. And he of course won a great deal of sympathy for this position from several people in the Executive, who'd been fearing her and hating her guts for years and years—precisely because she served me so well. I might also point out that half the Executive are anti-Security in a closet way, and that's not including the Pentagon and its vassals. All, right, George, I said, if Weatherall goes, I'm taking an extended vacation. George dared me to carry through my ultimatum. So I took indefinite leave and Weatherall went renegade. And George proceeded to try to clear out of Security anyone he suspected of alignment with Weatherall. The result is obvious: Security has been decimated. And as far as I can tell, the entire organization is in chaos."

"My god, Robert, this is incredible!" Steadman looked positively gleeful. Alexandra wondered how long he'd be able to keep his oath of secrecy. "All because of Booth's paranoia and sense of inadequacy at your bitch's efficiency? It's scandalous!"

Papa nodded. "Indeed. But there's more." As he drank again from his water glass Alexandra caught excited and pregnant glances flying about the table. She could hardly believe what he had said; but why would he invent such a tale? Surely if he told the story in all seriousness it must be true? Her father cleared his throat. "Weatherall never liked George to start with. And she kept tabs on a lot of people for me. Including George." A smile—showing his teeth—flashed briefly over his face. Alexandra imagined a shiver running around the table, a shiver of uneasiness over whether or not he—and Elizabeth—had been "keeping tabs" on them, too. "But of course, gentlemen, it's Security's business to acquire and use intelligence for the sake of the executive system. Keeping track of the holdings of members of the Executive is routine. Who is it do you think who tipped off the aliens about George's holdings? I imagine she drove a hard bargain with them, though I could also picture her volunteering the information

solely in the service of vengeance." He bent a strangely sinister look
on each of the men sitting around the table, in turn.

"She's gone over to the *aliens*?" Judge Feldman asked, breaking
the thick, tense silence.

Papa shook his head. "I seriously doubt it. I'd as soon expect her
to go over to the Greens. Or the Russians. Or the Southern Front. She
isn't a traitor. I know my bitch. She's simply vengeful. Frankly, I still
see her as potentially useful to the Executive."

Alexandra tried not to goggle at him. He was talking as though
he could still control Elizabeth, as though Elizabeth had not left
him—contradicting everything he had told her about Elizabeth's going renegade!

"A renegade, Robert?" Steadman said, clearly uneasy at the
thought of Elizabeth's coming back into the system.

Papa stared straight across the table at Steadman. "I'll tell you this,
Gerald. If Weatherall had wanted to wreak major and catastrophic
sabotage against the system when she went, she could have."

"Apart from which, Sedgewick," Buchanan said, "who in the
Executive would be both willing and able to take on a bitch like that?
She's ruining George Booth for godsake!"

He's afraid of Elizabeth, Alexandra thought. All these men were
both fascinated and fearful!

Her father laughed in a way that shot icicles down Alexandra's
spine. "Who? Who else would be both willing and able but me?" His
words were a challenge.

Alexandra caught Buchanan nodding down the table at Judith.
Two seconds later the door opened and a wave of service-techs poured
into the room. Alexandra felt a great sense of relief as they began
serving the next course. Much more of this tension and they would all
be jumping out of their skins or hysterical.

They were afraid of her father, every last one of these men. And
he knew it.

[iii]

Alexandra managed to escape the men when they turned to gambling, though her father offered to stake her. She desperately needed
time alone, time to take in the successive shocks her father had been

administering throughout the day and evening. She did not know
what to make of all he had said about Elizabeth. Could he actually
be thinking of her returning to him and Security? Certainly he was
thinking of his own return to Security, for what other reason could
he have to be talking like that to these men? And that story about
his breaking with Booth because of Booth's wanting him to terminate Elizabeth: could that possibly be true? Could it be that he had
declined into drunkenness only after Elizabeth had gone renegade?
And why *had* Elizabeth gone renegade, anyway? Her letter had been
vague, totally non-specific about the precipitating factors. *Could* he
be telling the truth? But if so, why had he spoken so hatefully to her
about Elizabeth, to the point of shouting at and hitting her when she
had dared to express neutrality?

All these questions proposed themselves as she walked from the
dining room to the suite she had been assigned. As for everything he
had said about her relations with Clarice... Alexandra pushed the subject away, unable to face it at that moment. She wanted a long soak in
the tub and then to go straight to sleep. Or maybe she would put on the
headphones and lie in the dark and listen to Chopin piano concerti.

When she entered her room she found Clarice sitting on the bed
brushing her hair. She smiled at Alexandra, and Alexandra's heart
sank. "*Bellissima*, you're early, how charming! I can't get over how
lovely you are in your evening clothes."

Alexandra bit her lip. "I thought you'd be socializing tonight."

Clarice shrugged. "Such a drab household. That girl Petra has got
to be one of the most boring I've ever met. Can you imagine, she's
been with the same lover for twenty years?" She tilted her head to one
side. "You should wear that shade of brown more often, *carina*. It suits
you marvelously."

Alexandra crossed to the bathroom and started her bath running.
When she came out into the bedroom, Clarice said, "Your routine,
even here?" and smiled slyly. "I brought the massage oil."

Alexandra went to the closet and opened it. She stared for a moment at the things hanging in the closet and then turned around.
"Let's skip the massage tonight," she said. "I think I'll want to go
straight to sleep after the bath. I'm almost ready to sleep now." That

was a lie, but she did not know how else to get Clarice out without being rude.

She turned back to the closet and chose a lounging gown. To her acute discomfort, the girl got up from the bed and came and laid her fingers on her arm. "You sound sad or angry, *carina*. Is it anything to do with me?"

Alexandra looked at Clarice's face for the first time since coming into the room. The intent, watchful look in the girl's eyes disturbed her. Concerned, or calculating? She could no longer tell. "No, love," she said, "it's nothing to do with you. But I do want some time alone."

Clarice slid her arms around Alexandra and hugged her. "*Buona notte, bellissima,*" she said in an especially caressing, silky voice.

Alexandra kissed Clarice's forehead and disentangled herself from the embrace. "Good night, love," she said and headed for the bathroom. She turned off the taps and heard the door to the hall open and close. She sighed with huge relief—at the same time she damned herself for the coldness she was feeling toward Clarice. She knew that she had grown (unfairly) suspicious because of what her father had said to her. *That cunt has greed written all over her, and you know it, whether you want to admit it to yourself or not.* Was everything ruined, or was this only a passing phase?

Just as she was about to step into the tub, the suite's phones rang. Startled, Alexandra picked up the handset positioned conveniently close to the tub. Her father? Or Clarice? "Yes?" she said.

"Alexandra, Judith here. I was wondering if you'd care to join me for a cup of tea in my sitting room."

Judith MacLaury: Alexandra had immediately liked the sight of her and knew she wanted to join her. But her father had given her two absolute prohibitions for their visit to this household: not to divulge her pianistic ability and on no account to socialize with their hostess. "Actually," Alexandra said hesitantly, "I would, but…"

"I won't twist your arm," Judith said crisply.

"But I really would like to," Alexandra said. To hell with the prohibition. If it spoiled his attempt to pass her off as a male, *tant pis.* "It's just that I was on the verge of getting into the bath. Perhaps in half an hour?"

"Lovely," Judith said. "I'll send my girl to you then, to show you the way. Do you know, I had the impression during that intriguing conversation at dinner that you knew the renegade they were talking about."

"Oh," Alexandra said, realizing that Judith intended to pump her. "You mean Elizabeth."

"Then you did know her."

"A little."

"Splendid," Judith breathed. "I'm very much looking forward to our chat. Have a pleasant bath, Alexandra."

Alexandra put the handset down. Her father, if he found out, would consider this disobedience a betrayal. But she had no intention of giving up her bond with executive women just to please him. The only way he could make her do that was by keeping her isolated on his island or locked in a dungeon. And she'd be no good to him there. Therefore he would just have to accept it when he found out.

Knowing her father, she felt sure he would find out. *Tant pis*, she thought again, and submerged. *Tant pis*.

# Chapter Eleven

[i]

Maureen and Susan were too damned trusting, Celia thought. They seemed to have no conception of who they were dealing with— as though the word *renegade* could in one stroke wipe out all that a person had previously done and been. "Yes," she said to them. "It's true that Mott's destruction of ODS files has helped a lot of people. And it's also true that the mountains of flimsy she printed out from those files before destroying them is enormously important. But I don't know if we should go so far as to trust her on that account."

"But Celia!" Susan leaned forward and fixed Celia with a pained, earnest gaze. "Think of the people in those detention centers! Surely their plight must compel us to take the risk!"

Celia flinched. "I have an uncle in one of those places," she said to this so-sensitive, delicate-featured woman. "I can't tell you how happy I would be to secure his freedom. But I don't believe anything that bitch says." A quick surge of anger flooded Celia, knocking aside her concern for Susan's fragility. "She's one of *them*."

Maureen poured more tea into her cup. "More tea?" she asked Celia.

Celia shook her head.

Maureen set the pot down and looked at Celia. "Could you be more specific, please? You're not, for instance, saying she's been directly involved in detentions or torture, are you?"

"She had the power to take me out of a detention camp. She had the power to have me picked up by ODS thugs. She also arranged for me to visit my uncle in prison, with a lawyer—as a favor to Emily Madden, executive to executive. And I gather interrogations of my uncle stopped at the same time. That is, I think, enough. Don't you?"

Maureen tilted her head to the side. After a moment of considering, she said, "I think we have to draw a distinction between complicity and actual participation. If you can tell me she's either directly ordered or actually taken part in torture, then that is one thing. But if you can't say more than that she's been passively complicitous, that's another. The woman has gone renegade, Celia. We know that for a fact. And we know she's burned her bridges behind her. She *can't* go back."

"Unless it's all a plot," Celia said. She pushed her tea cup away from her and centered her yellow legal pad exactly before her. "They could have stored the files elsewhere and gone along with destroying all known files."

"But she's given us the names and personnel files of all the people who have been directly involved in ODS detentions and torture!" Maureen exclaimed. "I can't believe they would have gone along with *that*."

Celia felt the stir of doubt in her wary, angry heart. "I don't know," she said doggedly. "You could be right. But I still don't trust her. The very sight of her turns my stomach."

"Besides," Susan said softly. "If the Marq'ssan decide to do this, you can be sure they'll be capable of handling the risks."

"Yes, but if you're depending on Lisa Mott's blueprints of the detention centers——"

"Believe me," Maureen said, "the Marq'ssan are fully capable of taking care of themselves. And they won't allow humans to endanger themselves, either. I don't understand why you aren't thinking of this from the prisoners' point of view."

"Two detention centers," Celia said bitterly. "Of thousands."

"The first ones to be liberated," Susan said. "Leading to the first of many public trials."

"Trials?" Celia said. "Not really. Public revelation and exposure. But not *legal* trials."

"Hold your judgment, Celia," Maureen said shortly. "You still think the judicial system is the only method of achieving fairness. But I don't see that it's gotten anyone justice. Judicial systems legitimate the caging and abuse of human beings. That's *all* they do."

"You're talking about abuse of a system," Celia said wearily. "That doesn't mean the system itself is evil."

"Do you believe the executive system is good?" Maureen asked.

Celia stared at her. "Of course not. But the executive system is not synonymous with the judicial system. The judicial system has roots more than a thousand years old." Careful not to bump her empty cup, Celia reached for one of the short bottles of water clumped in the middle of the table. "The executive system has perverted the judicial system. Inhumane treatment is not inherent in judicial systems." She twisted the cap off the bottle and poured water into her cup.

"I believe that judicial systems are inherently abusable," Susan said. "That whoever is in power will use them to sanction their own ends. And I certainly don't believe that in the history of the judicial system you're talking about there has ever been freedom from inhumane treatment."

Celia sighed. Lay people—and anarchists at that—simply were not well enough informed to be able to talk reasonably about basic concepts of law. It was a waste of time trying to discuss something they would never understand. "The next item on our agenda," she said, "is to try to come to a decision about whether to immediately expose the ODS personnel Mott has given us, or whether we should wait until after the rescue attempt." She saw them exchanging glances—probably at her implied capitulation to the rescue plan. "I think we should decide this before meeting with Cora," she added.

Maureen snorted. "That's for sure. Best never to go indecisive to a meeting with Cora Harris. Not unless you want her to wipe the floor with you."

"I have an idea," Susan said. "But I don't know how risky it would be to carry out. We'd need the Marq'ssan to help us, and maybe you and Emily, too. But I think it could be interesting to begin a series of profiles of these people, one at a time. Sort of a biography with interviews of people who know them, the neighborhoods they live in, in order to force not only public but also individual family and social attention on them. So that they'll *feel* it. We wouldn't even necessarily have to expose them to the people we interview."

"Too bad we couldn't capture the beasts and forcibly interview *them*," Celia said savagely.

"The Marq'ssan would never allow themselves to be used to implement anything intrinsically violent," Maureen said. "Though I suppose I could imagine certain militant-type feminists being more than happy to help. But I doubt if that's what *we* want. That's not what *you* had in mind, Sue, was it?"

Susan's short soft curls swirled and bobbed as she shook her head. "Not at all. That kind of thing could ruin the entire project. We want to shame them, not give them a pretext for more violence."

An image came into Celia's mind, but she pushed it away. She knew he was not ODS and thus would not be included in the files Lisa Mott had given them. "It's a good idea," Celia said.

"I think so too, Sue," Maureen said. "But it would take a lot of doing. So Celia: if we can get Sorben to ferry all of us down there, can you and Emily assist us locally?"

"We're willing to do what we can," Celia said. "Though I'm not sure I know what sort of things you're going to need help with."

"Ground transport, for one thing," Maureen said.

"Sure," Celia said. "That would be no problem."

"So we begin by undermining morale and alerting torturers that they may be facing exposure to, literally, the entire world," Susan said. "And then we rescue prisoners and dismantle the prisons they're being kept in."

Unless, Celia thought sourly, Lisa Mott managed to pull the plug on them first.

### [ii]

"You're paranoid, Cee," Emily said when Celia told her about the meeting with Susan Sweetwater and Maureen Sanders. "I know exactly why Lisa suggested that particular project to Martha Greenglass."

Celia poured boiling water into the teapot. "You mean you have a theory?"

"Knowledge, not theory. Elizabeth insisted she do it. To prove that she wasn't laying an ambush. And to make it absolutely impossible for Lisa ever to go back to Security. Once she participates in destroying two prisons and freeing the prisoners in those prisons, she will be forever tied to Elizabeth."

"You mean it's a kind of test?" My god. To do that to one of her closest colleagues? Elizabeth Weatherall was some piece of work. Just thinking about it gave Celia the shivers.

"Not very pretty, is it. I don't blame Elizabeth for being paranoid, but still, from Lisa's point of view it's damned rough."

Celia shook her head. "While if it works, prisoners will be the beneficiaries—inadvertently."

Emily smiled wryly. "I was there when Elizabeth and Lisa were discussing this. I don't think Elizabeth was all that thrilled about letting prisoners loose—political or otherwise. Still, she has a shrewd sense of public relations. I have the sneaking suspicion—though I don't know for sure—that she intends for Allison Bennett—the executive that defected with Lisa—to mount some sort of public relations campaign for her here in the Free Zone. They're to have their own newspaper. That much I do know."

Celia checked the tea and decided it was strong enough. "Those people give me the creeps." Celia poured out two cups and handed one to Emily. "Don't the Co-op women see through them? They could be dangerous."

They carried their cups to the other end of the room. Emily sat on the floor, and Celia curled up on the sofa. "They're being very careful, I think. Remember, they're anarchists, Cee. They're not likely to be trusting or open with someone like Elizabeth."

"But Elizabeth Weatherall has something of a following, doesn't she?"

Emily ventured a cautious sip. "I'm not sure I'd call it a following exactly. All the service-techs in her retinue are her employees."

"I don't understand about employment in the Free Zone, or money, or anything," Celia said. "Or why these women would be working for her."

"Some of them were followers of Louise Simon." Emily frowned. "For some reason, the ones who didn't want to follow her into terrorism were also reluctant to give up their militant life-style. I guess that's what you'd call it. Working for Elizabeth probably seems preferable to working as hired security guards for a business."

Celia had never met Elizabeth Weatherall, but whenever she heard her name mentioned she always conjured up the image Luis's description of the woman had first evoked. What Emily had told her about Weatherall's having "run" Security Services for years made that image all the more sinister. Celia said, "I can almost think of executives involved with ODS or SIC as similar to extreme militants. I suppose it makes a kind of sense."

Emily shook her head. "These women aren't militants, Cee. If they were, they would have gone off with Louise Simon."

They fell silent, and Celia listened to the rain pattering against the windows. Calm, steady rain was so rare in her experience that listening to it while sipping tea struck her as an exotic treat.

"You're very hard on people," Emily said.

Startled, Celia set down her cup. "What do you mean?"

"You blame the Co-op women for having created an anarchy as an alternative to the executive system. You blame renegades like Elizabeth and Lisa for having for years been complicit with the system in which they were raised. And you blame militant anti-executive groups for their militancy." Emily pushed her hair behind her ears. "But I'm not sure, Cee, that there is a correct way for people to oppose the system. All these people were produced by the system, all have found their own needs and ways of resisting or opposing it. I agree that some of those ways are extremely undesirable. But who has the right answer, if there is one? I can't, for instance, feel about law the way you do. I know that's because I grew up around people who exploited the law to their own ends, and thus I think of the law as a powerful tool for exploiting others and not as a means of ordering human behavior. Because playing it your way, ultimately the ODS and SIC types would always be around, would always be considered necessary for—again—enforcing the law."

"The bestial types could be screened out," Celia said. "The law could be purified, and those upholding the law carefully selected. The beasts *must* be controlled!"

"Those controlling beasts become beasts themselves," Emily said.

Celia leaned forward and poured more tea into her cup. "Your problem is you're cynical, Em." Celia resettled herself. "You think that because the executive system didn't work all systems are inherently corrupt."

Emily pulled a small object, shiny green and compact, out of the pouch at her hip. "I have to admit," she said, "that the Free Zone experiment appeals to me more all the time." She unfolded the object, and Celia saw that it was a hair brush. "There's so much more activity, so much more creativity and energy here, you can feel it all around you in almost every part of the city."

"We'd have that in San Diego if we could return to true law and order," Celia said. "You're just talking about the difference between a place in which repression is the means of governing and a place free of repression. The system I envisage would not be a place of repression."

Emily began brushing her hair. "Perhaps." She sighed. "It's possible you have more in common with Elizabeth and Lisa than you might think. They'd like a nice orderly world, too. And they're not enamored of repression as a means of governing, whatever you might think. I *know* they aren't. But they, too, think in terms of beasts and necessity. Their beasts are just different from yours."

Celia set down her cup. "The thought of being considered similar to them turns my stomach, Emily." She got to her feet and started for her room.

"Cee?" Emily called to Celia as she opened the door to her room. "I didn't mean that the way you think."

Celia closed the door behind her, crawled under the bedspread, and clutched a pillow to her breast. She hadn't been exaggerating: her stomach was heaving with revulsion. All this time Emily had understood nothing, nothing at all about who and what she was. It was her bond with other executive women: Celia could see now that that had always been an obstacle between their ever understanding one another. What did it matter that Emily—theoretically, at least—rejected the executive system? Emotionally she was still tied to other executives, emotionally she *was* executive, to the core. They could work together, yes, on common goals. But the emotional tie Celia had allowed to develop could only bring her pain. She saw that now. Because of who she was, Emily had to perceive her, Celia, as being like an executive woman, not recognizing her for what she was, but making her over into something she could accept. As though only externally was Celia not an executive woman, perhaps through an accident of misfortune.

To be like Lisa Mott... Celia squeezed her eyes shut and pulled the pillow more tightly against her body. Empty, empty, she felt so terribly empty.

[iii]

Trying to suppress the anxiety such places evoked in her, Celia waited in the hotel garage for Maureen, Cora, and Susan to pick her up. Though she did her best to be careful, she thought it impossible that her involvement with people in the Free Zone would escape detection indefinitely. And so, two scenarios frequently played themselves out in her imagination since she had first visited the Free Zone. In one scenario she was outright murdered in a place like this enormous deserted garage; in the other, after returning home from one of her trips, she was picked up because they knew for certain she had just been in the Free Zone. The fact was, people in the Free Zone not only talked interminably about how the place was swarming with SIC agents, but also went to great lengths to make certain they weren't being bugged or followed. And Celia had no doubt that if she were ever identified while being here—through, for example, fingerprints left in their hotel suite—she would lose her freedom for good. Given the tenuousness of her position, she felt torn between the option of handling even the tiniest details to do with monitoring human rights in the Southwest US herself so as to avoid placing another person at risk, and that of sharing all the tasks with someone who could quickly take them over if she were arrested. So far she had chosen to handle everything herself, on the assumption that Emily could help whoever took her place.

When she heard a vehicle approaching, Celia stepped back behind the nearest pillar. She peered cautiously around the pillar and when she recognized Maureen as the driver, stepped forward and flagged her down. Maureen pulled up and called a cheerful greeting through her open window. Celia squeezed into the back with Susan. "Martha's meeting us at Sand Point," Maureen said, swinging the car around the end of the row and heading back toward the exit.

"That's where the—" Celia swallowed nervously—"Marq'ssan will be landing?" It was right in her face, the thing that she had not allowed herself to think about—that she would actually be meeting an alien, who until now might as well have been mythological.

Susan's hand lighted briefly on Celia's arm. "Sorben's very nice, Celia. The Marq'ssan are truly *good*. It's hard to explain, but you'll know when you meet Sorben."

They said little as they drove through the dark to a park on the edge of Lake Washington that until the Marq'ssan had destroyed it had been the regional headquarters for the National Guard. According to Maureen, the site had originally been a federal military base and then a city park before the National Guard had taken possession.

They found Martha Greenglass there, waiting in her parked two-seater. She waved but did not get out of her car.

As they waited for the Marq'ssan, Celia's tension grew. The Marq'ssan were not known to be dangerous to humans per se, only to their property. How many worse things had she faced! Yet the many things people had said to her about their "special powers" crowded her thoughts. That they could see inside one's body, for instance. That they were impossibly wise. That they could destroy objects without using any weapons other than their minds. That they could heal people without medicine or instruments. That they could make themselves—and others—invisible.

Susan's rain gear rustled as she shifted in her seat. Celia tried to think about what Susan had told her about having once worked for ODS. She had gotten involved with the Sweetwaters solely to infiltrate them, but having come to love them, she had submitted false reports, with the result that in ODS's first big wave of repression at the onset of the Blanket they had gone to Sweetwater and had specially detained her because they suspected her of doubling. "So you see, Celia," Susan had said after telling her story, "you mustn't make hard and fast judgments about people simply because they once worked for those you call beasts. Kay Zeldin was another example of a renegade. Lisa Mott must be encouraged and brought along, not made a pariah."

Drifting into thoughts of how estranged she and Emily had become, Celia, folded her arms over her chest. *You're very hard on people.* But there was a world of difference between a Lisa Mott and a Susan Sweetwater. Susan had been in a position similar to that of poor young Angela, who had quivered with fear of the people she worked for and with. One could not compare Angela and Susan with Lisa Mott. The very idea was obscene.

"There it is!" Cora said. Her excitement was palpable. "Do you see how that patch of water has been suddenly blotted out? That's how you can tell." She pointed. "See?" She opened her door.

They all piled out of the car and walked with Martha toward what looked like a shadow barely perceptible in the faint light of the half moon. But as they approached, Celia made out a shadow-like domed shape. When they were within two yards of the dome, a lift—which Celia recognized from the oft-reproduced photographs of the Marq'ssan vehicle that had landed in the California desert ten years past—became visible.

Each of them took the lift in turn, alone. Celia's stomach fluttered when Maureen urged her forward. She stepped onto the little platform and gripped the handrail as it lifted and retracted into the dome. Inside, Martha introduced her to a short-haired, gray-eyed woman who looked perfectly ordinary and human. "Celia, this is Sorben. Sorben, this is Celia Espin, the monitor for the southwestern US."

Sorben smiled slightly and nodded. "If the flight makes you queasy or in any other way uncomfortable, let me know and I'll help you to calm your stomach. It sometimes does upset people's stomachs, especially when we have a lot of ups and downs to make, as we do tonight."

Martha led Celia to a flight couch and showed her how to strap in. Celia glanced curiously around the interior, but the dim lighting revealed little beyond two dozen or more flight couches. She saw no signs of anything that looked alien or particularly high-tech. In fact, she was surprised not to see anything resembling instrument panels or switches. A single terminal attached to the rear-most flight couch seemed to be the only possible pilot's seat. Unless there was another space blocked off from this main area?

When they had all boarded and strapped in, Sorben took the flight couch with the terminal. An amber light flashed; Celia felt a lurch in the pit of her stomach and a tremendous weight pressing her down into the couch. "In case you're wondering, the meeting is at a place near Quito," Martha said.

"Quito, Ecuador?" Cora said sharply.

"Yep," Martha said. "High, high in the mountains. Hope we don't get altitude sickness!"

So they were flying to another continent! Martha had said nothing about going outside the United States. She had insisted that Celia travel with them—and not on her own—for "security reasons" and had refused to divulge the location, which had reassured Celia. What an adventure, what an incredible adventure, flying through the night in a strange craft, eventually to land in the Andes. And what a pity Emily hadn't been able to go. But at the thought of Emily, Celia remembered, and depression washed back over her. She closed her eyes and decided to try to sleep. Tomorrow would be a long and exhausting day, a day full of talking and thinking and listening. Best to sleep now, while she had the chance.

[iv]

Celia woke with the fragrance of coffee in her nostrils. She opened her eyes and peered around the bunk-crowded "cell" (which was what they called the sleeping rooms in this former monastery).

"Morning," someone said. Celia looked around. It was one of the women she'd been introduced to on the pod the night before. Tall, professional, black. "Want some coffee? I brought enough in case you wanted some, too. I can't, myself, face hordes of people before I've drunk my first cup of the day. And coffee is so plentiful around here that they keep a couple of thermoflasks of it in that little lounge down the hall." As she spoke, the woman poured coffee from a thermoflask into a disposable cup. She handed the cup to Celia. "Here. It's wonderful, totally authentic stuff. Guess it should be, since we're in the heart of Coffee Country."

Celia smiled with pleasure as she took the cup: it smelled wonderful. "Thanks," she said. "I'm feeling pretty dead."

The other woman nodded. "Amazing, isn't it, the way the others"—the woman nodded at the empty bunks all around them—"are already at it. I'll bet Greenglass was first up. She never misses a chance at these affairs."

Celia sipped the coffee and struggled to remember this woman's name. From Boston, wasn't she? "You've been to similar meetings?"

The woman snorted. "Are you kidding? Been doing it since the Marq'ssan's first shindig on their starship. And you can take it from me, they're all practically the same. The only things that vary are the topics of the meeting and a few of the faces. Usually the arguments all come out the same. Me and a few like me against Greenglass. And Greenglass always wins." She made a face. "Mostly always," she amended.

"You're not a fan of hers, then," Celia said dryly.

The woman flicked an eyebrow at her. "And you're not rising hotly to her defense."

Celia swallowed another sip. The coffee tasted as good as it smelled, which in her life wasn't often the case. "Should I be?"

The woman's intense dark eyes narrowed. "Perhaps. After all, your project is getting the kind of attention from the Marq'ssan I've never managed to attract after all these years. The Marq'ssan ration their favors damned carefully."

Celia realized this woman had picked up a lot about her already. Had she learned all this on the pod? "I know little about the Marq'ssan or about these kinds of meetings," Celia said. "Until recently, it never occurred to me to have anything to do with either the Free Zone or the Marq'ssan."

"Just the usual long, plodding effort of local action," the woman said.

"Yeah. That's as good a description as any. Mainly trying to find people who've disappeared and trying to get people out of detention. A largely losing battle."

The woman eyed her sharply. "You've been there too, haven't you," she said.

Celia's throat tightened. "What do you mean?"

"Detention... and all the rest."

"It shows?" Had she cried out in her sleep? Both her mother and Emily said she often did.

"To me, yes."

"It wasn't much," Celia said. "As you can see, I'm still alive and in one piece. No permanent injury. You might say I'm one of the lucky ones."

The woman's mouth twisted; she drank more coffee. "What organization are you with?"

Celia shook her head. "No organization in particular, if you mean political organization. I work for a center that gives medical and legal advice, but it's not exactly political in the sense that it has no agenda besides stopping violence against the people."

"Doctor, lawyer, or other?"

"Lawyer."

The woman's mouth split into a grin. "Howdy, colleague. At last. A comrade to back me up against these damned anarchists. I knew there was something right about you the minute I laid eyes on you."

"You're a lawyer, too, then?"

"I'm with the Boston Collective. Which quite definitely is political. Militantly political, not that all of us support the use of violence, but since we're not all tuned in to the same political principles when we can't reach what the ladies around here like to call consensus, why then we go with the old-fashioned Majority Rules method. Hence we're militant. We blew up a bank just last week, as a matter of fact. It warmed the hearts of certain elements in the Collective, but it also resulted in a further tightening of the pass-checks we have in Boston. I—and nearly everyone else in the Collective—have been underground since the Blanket. Ergo, I can't do much practicing of law."

"I was named last year," Celia said, "so I can't represent clients in court myself."

"But you're not underground," the woman said.

Celia shook her head. "That might be almost impossible in San Diego, it's got such a sparse population. I'd have to go to LA or the Bay area if I were."

"And I take it you have interests preventing you from running."

Celia nodded.

"You're either very foolish or very brave," the woman said.

Celia smiled weakly. "Very foolish, I think." She drank the last of the coffee in her cup and decided to admit her social lapse. "By the way, I was half-asleep last night when they introduced me to you. What is your name?"

The woman offered Celia a glittering but warm smile. "Jo Josepha. And I'm extremely pleased to meet you, Celia Espin."

Celia got out of bed to pour more coffee into her cup. This frank and open woman was the first person among those she'd met through Greenglass that she could actually feel comfortable with. This meeting might prove very interesting indeed.

# Chapter Twelve

## [i]

When the executives gathered around the conference table in Liz's office to discuss "strategy" (as Liz called it), Hazel sat with them to take notes. Her NoteMaster recorded everything so that a verbatim transcript could be prepared afterwards. But Hazel also kept notes herself for possible clarification of previously-made points while the meeting was in progress.

After Liz put Bennett and Mott through some rigorous Q&A, she said, "So the main question facing us seems to be whether to encourage defections *en masse*, or to draw out the defections for as long as possible. Besides giving us certain psychological advantages, the latter option would also allow us to keep useful lines of communication open." Liz looked from Bennett to Mott. "I would expect that as word gets out about what we're up to—and about how well we're surviving in the wilds of the Free Zone—we'll attract more than this tentative list of a couple dozen or so that you two feel confident of." Liz drank from her water glass. "The fact is, all these women on our list are in Security or Com & Tran. We should be able to attract women from other departments, as well. Assuming the repression is an Executive-wide phenomenon."

"I think it must be," Bennett said. "It's just that Lisa and I haven't been in contact with anyone but people in Security and Com & Tran."

"When my final project goes through we may lose some people," Mott said. "Have you considered that, Elizabeth?"

Liz made a face. "Yes, Lisa, I *have*. But it *will* make a splash—and a point. And my god, it will put those bastards on the run like nothing you've ever seen. Security will be shaken to its goddam foundations. A greater embarrassment can hardly be imagined. I'd be surprised if the Executive didn't panic and order a replacement for Hill." She snorted.

"They might even bring back Sedgewick." A grin spread over Liz's face. "And as we all know, that would just about do the Executive in."

"I wouldn't count on that," Mott said. "I have the distinct impression that *most* executives would feel safer with Sedgewick back in. There's a general perception that he's super-tough, you know."

"Which you mistakenly share. Sedgewick is absolutely helpless on his own. He's drunk three-fourths of the time and crazy the rest. Ever since the Blanket he's been off his rocker. I should know."

"But does it matter whether he's competent or not?"

Liz shrugged. "Perhaps, perhaps not. But if he is brought back—by popular demand—" Abruptly she hooted with laughter in a hilarity no one else shared. The others waited patiently for her mirth to subside; and seeing this, Liz quickly controlled herself. "Sorry, the thought of Sedgewick's having a quote popular unquote following completely cracks me up. But then we *are* talking exclusively about executives, aren't we." The grin popped out again, but was immediately repressed. "What I was saying," she said, "was that if Sedgewick is brought back, things will fall apart even faster. You see, there will be almost no orders downward. Each station and branch will be left to its own devices. Because Sedgewick would do nothing. Nothing at all. Unless someone managed to get hold of him and take control…which is doubtful, for I can't see him at this point allowing anyone but a woman to do that to him, which possibility is in itself highly dubious since there's not a woman within miles of him."

Mott looked puzzled. "Why a woman?"

Liz smiled scornfully. "Because of the nature of his, ah, psychosis. I suppose that's the correct word for describing his problem?" She glanced at Bennett. "Wouldn't you say, Allison, that Sedgewick is psychotic?"

Bennett's nose scrunched up. "I don't know anything about psychiatry, Elizabeth. I would agree with you that he has a problem, yes. But I've never gotten close enough to see much."

Liz threw Mott a strangely wry look. "This woman kept her distance as best she could. And he *liked* her—somewhat."

"Compared with the way he felt about me?" Mott said. Her lips were so tight and stiff that the words she spoke sounded as though she'd been chewing them before spitting them out. "The man hates women more than most of the males do. Which is why I can't buy your theory about his letting only a woman control him."

Liz produced one of her exaggerated, world-weary sighs. "Take my word for it, I know that man inside out." And now, like clockwork, came the bitter, knowing smile. "His attitude toward women isn't comparable with the usual male attitude because he's so thoroughly fucked-up. There's no common basis upon which to make a measurement. He wasn't raised an executive, you know."

Mott rolled her eyes. "Yes, we all know that. Leland will always like him for it."

"So where were we?" Liz said. "When we got off on this sidetrack?" She looked at Hazel. "Can you pull us back onto the straight and narrow, darling?"

Hazel glanced down at the notes she'd been inputting by keyboard. "You were discussing the possible effects of the detention centers project on women thinking about going renegade."

"Right. So, what I suggest is that we see what we can do with some of the names on our list, even before Lisa's final project goes through. We'll have to work mainly through a mail service, which is a drawback, since we can't risk much personal or phone contact, and especially not email. Which means the women going renegade will have to handle all the details at their end themselves. This is regrettable, but I don't see how we can do it any other way. At the same time, I want to start using some of the dirt I input into my personal terminal before blowing up Sedgewick's office. He, of course, has copies of some of that stuff stashed away in other locations, but I doubt if he's together enough to think about checking on whether or not I'm using it." Liz's mouth pressed into a small, tight smile. "And I've collected dirt on my own for years, too. But somehow I just can't see Sedgewick thinking to cover the dirt angle as a possibility." She snickered. "Let's face it, at this moment, the man is probably semi-conscious at best."

"You're talking about blackmail?" Mott asked.

"Certainly. And don't give me that look, Lisa. Not considering your own experiences working for Security."

"Why must *we* use such methods? Why can't we free ourselves from all that now?"

"Because, my dear," Liz said with that attitude of visible patience that Hazel knew well, "we must do whatever is necessary to survive."

"Not to survive, Liz," Hazel said quietly. "I don't think our survival is in question, do you?" She sensed Mott and Bennett staring at her in surprise. Never before in their meetings had she volunteered an opinion.

Liz, of course, did not look surprised: she looked, on the contrary, wary. "I'm talking now not about personal survival, Hazel, but about survival of the system." Liz paused, as though waiting for Hazel to nod agreement, but Hazel waited for Liz to go on. Finally, Liz asked, "You don't think that's a strong enough reason to pressure people we'd all agree are basic shits?"

Hazel held Liz's gaze. How strange it was that they were having one of their "show-downs" in the middle of an executive strategy meeting. It made Hazel light-headed. "Blackmail is a terrible thing," she said.

Bennett reentered the discussion. "Why not think of it as a last resort, Elizabeth?"

"Because I would like some information," Liz said, still locked eye-to-eye with Hazel. "We're operating in the dark, and we needn't be. There's no department of the Executive I can't get information from—using the information I already have to pressure well-placed sources."

Mott looked disgusted. "Well don't ask me to help you do it," she said. "I don't want to know anything about it. Of Company methods, I've always found blackmail to be among the most despicable."

"And utilitarian," Liz said.

"It's almost one," Hazel said, sensing that the argument had been lost—this round.

Liz checked her watch. "We're about ready to adjourn, aren't we?" she said, glancing at the other two executives. "So we're agreed about the round robin Allison will make up. I'll draft something this afternoon to give to you, Allison, and will start making a list of all the women I can think of to send it to. And both of you will do likewise. And then we'll meet again to combine our lists and talk over the drafts. Agreed?"

Bennett and Mott shoved their chairs back from the table. Hazel pressed the off-button on her NoteMaster's recorder and went out to the outer office and locked the NoteMaster in her desk. Mott and Bennett passed through and left by the outer door.

"Hazel."

Hazel turned.

Liz was standing in the doorway, one hand gripping the door-frame, her feet planted at least half a meter apart. "You don't know these men the way I do," she said. "We can't afford to be soft on them. If you knew anything about them, I don't think you'd be so eager to protect them."

Hazel shook her head. "It's not them I'm thinking of. And I don't think Mott is, either."

"Lisa would simply rather not know anything. She's a shirker of responsibility, Hazel. I've noticed that about her. It's a completely non-executive attitude, wanting to close her eyes and ears to the things going on around her."

"Is that what you think about me?" Hazel asked curiously.

"No, darling, not at all. On the contrary. You could have been an executive. But what I think is that you don't fully understand the implications of things. If you did, you would not be so quick to take stands. If you understood the kind of difference using or not using these potential sources would make…" She shrugged. "But then you're simply not well enough informed, darling. Yet, anyway."

"You don't think I understood what was at stake in the case of the naval intelligence officer?" Hazel asked.

Liz bit her lip. "That was different from this. That was…extreme. And simple. And immediate. Here we're talking about long-range consequences, which I don't think you can conceptualize. I don't think you have any idea about the importance of acquired and secret intelligence."

"You believe then that the ends always justify the means?"

"You're saying that you were thinking of how *we* would feel when you objected to my pressuring these potential intelligence sources. But I'll tell you right now, *I'd* feel no compunction, Hazel, none whatsoever. I'm not squeamish. I'll do what I have to do and live with the consequences."

Hazel jammed her hands into her pockets. "You mean you're go-ing to go ahead with this and simply not tell either Mott or me. Since we're such delicate *soft* creatures."

"You have a nasty way of putting things, darling."

"Well let me ask you this. Let's suppose that you could instantly transform the executive system into whatever it is you want by simply killing one person."

"Don't be ridiculous—" Liz started, but Hazel interrupted:

"No, we're playing pretend, Liz. Just suppose that by magic you would be given everything you wanted simply by killing one person. Would you do it?"

Liz's eyes flickered. "That's a damned loaded question if I ever heard one, Hazel. I'm not about to play your game. In case you're wondering, I've never killed anyone. Ever."

"Directly," Hazel said without thinking.

Liz paled. "What are you accusing me of?" she cried, taking sev-eral steps towards Hazel. "I insist you tell me, Hazel. What is it you think I'm guilty of?"

Between the things Martha Greenglass had said and what Anne had told her about Liz's supreme authority within Security, Hazel had from time to time been afflicted—especially in the late night hours when Liz lay snoring beside her—with the obvious implications of that supreme authority. "You were mostly in control in Security, weren't you?" Hazel said. "According to Anne, no one there—"

Liz closed the space between them and grabbed Hazel by the shoulders. "Anne! What has that treacherous little cunt been saying about me?" Hazel recoiled from the expression in those now blazing blue eyes and fought a sudden blast of fear. "Tell me, damn you!" Liz, shaking her by the shoulders, cried.

"Stop it, Liz!" Hazel glared at her. "Stop it *now!*"

Liz released her and sagged back against the desk. She put her hands to her cheeks. "Your lack of trust in me is going to destroy us," she said, her voice low and husky. "I can't take all this moralizing. You always seem to suspect the worst of me. It's getting so that I never know what you're thinking when you look at me the way you looked at me across that table a little while ago."

Hazel swallowed. "You talk so much about responsibility. Do you ever wonder how many people's deaths you are indirectly responsible for, Liz?"

Liz took her hands from her face and stared at Hazel. "Why are you doing this to me?"

"I think your idea of responsibility is lopsided," Hazel said. "Always you talk about responsibility. But you never talk about *that* kind of responsibility. And I bet you don't think about it, either. Being squeamish, you call it. I wonder what that means, Liz."

Liz slowly straightened up. "They'll be waiting lunch for us. All of them. We'll have to continue this discussion another time."

*All of them*: of course—Liz wanted to remind her of how she was including the service-techs in meals with the executives. Hazel followed Liz out of the office, then locked the door before following her to the dining room.

Whatever Liz might say, she had a guilty conscience about something, that was clear. Which meant she wasn't quite as calloused as she claimed.

## [ii]

Hazel got back from her trip into the city at about a quarter after six, her thoughts full of the Co-op's plans for the eleventh anniversary celebration of the Executive Withdrawal. She had an idea Liz was going to be annoyed at the amount of fuss the Co-op intended to make over the anniversary, considering how vexed she had been at the Free Zone's celebration of Kay Zeldin Day last October, an annual holiday commemorating Zeldin's martyrdom. To commemorate the Executive Withdrawal, the Rainbow Press was bringing out a new edition of Zeldin's book, adding new appendices that included a biography of Zeldin, essays on the first ten years of the Free Zone, as well as tributes to Zeldin's "contributions and legacies." Several films were to be premiered during the anniversary celebration, both documentaries and "re-creations of history." "More Than A Decade of Freedom" was to be the theme associated with the anniversary celebration. Yes, Hazel thought as she parked the single-seater in the garage, Liz was going to absolutely hate it.

The eternal routine of having to rendezvous with Betsy, drop off the van, and switch to the single-seater, all the while checking for a possible tail, was enough to drive a person crazy. And the radio-contact routine, too, had gotten old fast. But it was essential that they not give away their (hopefully) permanent "headquarters" as Liz called the new house. As for the nonsense of bringing people here in the back of a closed van, she had to wonder how the new renegades—all ex-ecutives—stood it. But Liz was adamant about the policy, determined that only a handful of its denizens would ever know the exact loca-tion of the house. One of the items at the top of her list of "contra-band" was anything that had global positioning capability. Since most NoteMasters came equipped with that capability, Liz had assigned Bennett responsibility for detecting and disabling it when newcom-ers, who always brought NoteMasters with them, arrived.

Hazel walked the short distance from the garage to the back porch, feasting her eyes on the velvety, deep rose perfection of the camellias and the thick, profuse purple, white, and crimson rhododendrons that dominated the landscaping. Liz swore she'd have at least half the rho-dodendrons pulled out before the next spring came around. She said she hated them and wanted more lilacs and lilies and other spring flowers. "Overbearing, insufferable show-offs," she called them.

When Hazel opened the plate-glass door into the glassed-in porch, she found Lacie scrunched up on a pile of cushions, sobbing. At the sound of the door closing, Lacie looked up in resentful panic. Hazel dropped her packages onto a table and knelt beside her. "What is it, Lacie? What's wrong?"

The flaming rays of the setting sun tinted Lacie's pale hair a bril-liant orange, a not very attractive framing of her tear-swollen face.

"Everything," she sobbed.

Hazel's heart sank. Ever since Lacie's arrival here she had been waiting for this to happen—for Lacie to find the security require-ments combined with being away from home for the first time in her life too hard to bear, or to find the strangeness of being a heterosexual female living among almost exclusively lesbian women either fright-ening or oppressive. Hazel had stopped worrying about the latter a few weeks ago. But it had struck her as all too likely that Lacie's feel-ings of alienation had simply gone underground. "Can you tell me about it, dear?" Hazel said, wondering whether she should put her arm around her.

"It's that horrible Ginger!" Lacie burst out. "She never stops bossing me around, it's like she follows me all over the house, I never do anything good enough for her! She's always screaming at me about there being one way of doing things, the right way, and that no other way is good enough for executives. I don't make the beds right. I don't chop the vegetables nicely enough. I don't arrange the towels perfectly. I can't stand it another minute, Hazel, I just can't!"

"Oh, Lacie," Hazel said, taking her hand, "I'm so sorry about Ginger. I know it's hard for you to understand, she's so different from anybody you've ever known. I sometimes find her a little hard to take too."

Lacie awkwardly wiped her nose with the soggy tissue she clutched in her free hand. "She's a perfectionist and a snob! I think she hates me."

Hazel sighed. "She's very frightened, I think. She's in a new environment unlike any she's ever known. And because you're so young, she thinks she can take it out on you."

"It's not fair. Liz *never* complains about the way I do things!" Lacie sniffed. "I know Liz likes me," she said passionately. "I can tell. But that Ginger acts as if she and not Liz owns the place!"

Liz had done quite a job on Lacie, Hazel reflected. When she wanted to, she could really turn it on. Lacie idolized her to the point that she'd do almost anything for her; she cherished and savored every smallest word of praise (or flattery) or slightest sign of attention that Liz bestowed on her. It was always Liz this and Liz that from Lacie, which had to rub Ginger raw. "Well think of this," Hazel said. "Ginger is probably jealous *because* Liz likes you. Liz doesn't like Ginger much, as you must have noticed. Liz hasn't liked Ginger for years, and Ginger knows it. I'm sure that rankles. Don't you think?"

Lacie brightened as she considered this. "Oh," she said. "I guess that explains a lot."

"Yes, I guess it does. That and Ginger's feeling so lost now that she's left home for good."

"What about me?" Lacie said, her tone somewhere between petulance and irritation. "I know from what you've told me that Carnation

isn't far from here, but since I only get to leave on pre-arranged weekends, I get homesick, too. But Ginger doesn't think that counts."

"She's not your boss, you know," Hazel said. "You don't have to
put up with her bossing you around. I've tried talking to her about it,
but it goes in one ear and out the other. The only way Ginger will stop
bossing you around is for you not to let her do it."

Lacie grimaced. "She gets me so upset."

"Yes, but think about the rest of us in this house. We all of us
like you, Lacie. And we're not dissatisfied with your work. I know for
a fact that Anne likes you. Liz likes you. I like you, a lot. And I think
Ms. Mott and Ms. Bennett like you, too. Just remember, Ginger has
her own problems. If you can get past being on the defensive with her,
can keep her from riling you, then you'll feel much better, and maybe
you'll be able to understand Ginger better. She doesn't have the best
life, Lacie."

"The way she goes on all the time about living in La Jolla California
and about executives and the Good Life, you'd think she'd had the best
life there was."

Hazel smiled. "Don't you believe it for a minute. It's nothing compared to yours growing up in the Free Zone. You'll see when you get
older that people are scared of big changes. Ginger is in the middle
of a terribly big change, and her response is to cling to everything
she knows."

Lacie's hand squeezed Hazel's. "You make everything look, different, Hazel. You're so *good*. I can see why Liz can't help but love you."
She blushed and looked down at their clasped hands.

"That's a lovely compliment, Lacie, but I don't think I deserve it,"
Hazel said, embarrassed.

"You're so understanding," Lacie mumbled.

"You feel better now?"

Lacie nodded.

"Good." Hazel gave Lacie's hand one last squeeze and dropped it.
"Let's go inside now. You'll want to wash your face, I know I always
do after having a long hard cry. And some of the stuff I brought back
is food that needs to be refrigerated."

They got up from the cushions and Lacie helped Hazel carry the
packages inside. As she put away the groceries Hazel thought about

the talk she would have to have with Ginger. And with Liz. There was no question that Liz was going to have to change her attitude toward Ginger. If she didn't, they'd all be going crazy in no time.

[iii]

Hazel heaped her plate with food and carried it to the table. Ginger, obsessed with times past, had been the only one to fuss about all of them regularly eating together, serving themselves from the buffet. Although the first few meals had been awkward, everyone else had soon gotten used to it and had at times even begun to enjoy the communal meals, despite odd or tense moments that crept in. Liz had decreed from the beginning that they were to eat breakfast and dinner in whatever attire each individual chose to wear and had herself promptly begun wearing lounging gowns during dinner. Most of the others—excepting whichever amazons happened to be dining with them—had taken to doing the same. And now, finally, Lacie had been able to adopt the custom, for one of the things Hazel had brought from town was a lounging gown for Lacie—as a gift from Liz. Just before dinner she had sailed into the kitchen showing off the new gown. Ginger had taken Hazel aside. "You'd better watch it, Hazel," she had whispered. "You know what Ms. Weatherall's like. The way she's going, that girl will have her in bed in no time." Hazel had given her a cold stare and said, "That's hardly flattering to Liz. I've heard a lot of gossip about her, but never that she seduced seventeen-year-old heteros." "So you *are* jealous," Ginger had retorted. This backbiting was tiresome nonsense, but nonsense that could make life miserable. She hoped Liz would—as she had just promised Hazel—take pains to be nicer to Ginger. It could make all the difference to the household.

Hazel bit into the tartlet she had taken and discovered under the flaky crust a rich luscious mushroom filling. "Mmm, this is *wonderful*," she said, hoping Ginger and not Bennett or Lacie had prepared it.

Ginger's head jerked up. "Thanks, Hazel," she said, obviously pleased.

"Don't you think, Liz?" Hazel said, wishing Liz were sitting beside her so that she could elbow her into a compliment.

Liz looked across the table at Hazel. "Sorry darling?"

"Don't you think Ginger's tartlets are scrumptious?"

Liz flashed a smile at Ginger. "Luscious delicious, Ginger."

Ginger beamed. And then Hazel grew aware of Lacie's eyes moving from Hazel to Liz to Ginger and back to Hazel. She's quick, Hazel thought. Amazingly quick. If she didn't dislike Ginger so much, she'd easily find a way to deal with her.

"So you went into Seattle this afternoon?" Bennett asked.

"Yes, my excitement for the day," Hazel said. "Mainly to shop, though I did stop in at the Co-op to see Maureen Sanders."

Bennett glanced down the table at Mott but said nothing. She would of course know that Hazel would have been seeing Maureen to continue working out the details of the upcoming operation against the detention centers in southern California. "I keep wondering," Bennett said after a while, "what Seattle is like now. When I was here nine years ago, I found it incredibly different from what I remembered from my graduate student days. I imagine it must be even more different now."

She sounds wistful, Hazel thought.

"Why don't you go into town one of these times?" Liz said. "It *can* be worked out, you know. You could visit Margot and surf the galleries and import shops in Pioneer Square."

Bennett sighed. "I suppose so. And I know Anne would like to hit the bookstores. It's just that I feel so security-anxious. For all I know, they have Wanted posters out, circulating among all the local agents the station controls."

"Christ," Liz said. "I'd like to get a handle on *that* situation. On whether they've set up a new station and who the hell is running it if they have. But you do realize, Allison, that they've probably lost all contact with their stable of local agents, with all the station's officers gone now. And besides, I doubt if Central would advise any future CAT to cultivate the same agents for the simple reason that they'd expect all of them to have been exposed to Simon. And as a matter of fact, Simon did provide a list to the Women's Patrol. No, I imagine you'd be pretty safe, Allison." She rose and went to the buffet. Taking a fresh plate, she assembled her second course.

"I was surprised by Seattle," Mott said. "In so many ways. One rather expects a sort of bad-section-of-town atmosphere to prevail everywhere, but no such thing. And of course I expected it to be drab and without any shopping or cultural interest. The only thing I've found lacking is the usual executive facilities. Clubs and first class restaurants and so on."

"There's a club," Liz said, "but we don't use it for obvious reasons." She returned to the table; her plate was heaped with what looked like three-quarters of a chicken, a mound of broccoli, and an enormous baked potato topped with sour cream. Among the amazons Liz's appetite was legendary. The amusing thought occurred to Hazel that Liz's appetite might—but also might not—have something to do with why the amazons called her "Big Liz" behind her back. "You know, Allison," Liz said after swallowing a bite of chicken, "you might want to attend a symphony concert. Margot says the symphony here is quite decent."

Bennett looked wistful. "Anne might like that, too," she said, catching Anne's eye. "Wouldn't you, love? You go in for such things more than any of us, I think."

Anne smiled. "I'd love to have an excursion away from this house. It's a nice place, but I guess I'm getting a bit stir-crazy."

"Then I'll have someone get in touch with Margot and get you tickets for the next concert," Liz said.

"Well..." Bennett hesitated.

"I'm sure you'll be perfectly safe," Mott said. "I've been into town several times now in broad daylight without getting the slightest hint of interest from anyone remotely likely to be in the pay of an intelligence service."

That seemed to do it. "Then yes," Bennett said. "And we'll go early enough so that Anne can do some bookstore-hopping." She smiled at Anne. "To stock you up for our long, long siege."

Siege? Hazel wondered. Is that how these renegades thought of it? If so, they were likely to be miserable. No wonder Ginger clung so tenaciously to the old ways. None of them believed their renegade days would last.

## [iv]

Hazel woke to find Liz in the throes of one of her dreams. She leaned over her and gripped her shoulders. "Liz. Wake up, Liz, wake up now, it's all right, wake up, Liz."

"What—" Liz gasped, and Hazel knew she was at least partially awake.

"It's all right, Rapunzel, it's just a dream, all you have to do is wake up, sweetheart." Liz clutched her and after about a minute of Hazel's soothing words, quieted. "The same dream, Rapunzel?" Hazel asked, stroking Liz's hair and neck.

"Yes. A variation. Awful."

"Want to talk about it?" Hazel asked as she always did.

Liz shuddered. "No. No. Want to forget it. Let's not talk about it. May we have the light on, darling?"

Hazel rolled over to her edge of the bed and switched on the reading light. As she always did, she took a half-liter bottle of water out of the nightstand, poured out a glass, and handed the glass to Liz.

Liz gulped the water like a child. "I'm sorry," she said when she finished. Hazel set the glass on the nightstand. "I seem to be doing this to you a lot lately."

"Two nights in a row. Which you've never done before."

Liz's eyes, strangely dark and frightened, flickered. "It does seem to be getting worse," she said.

"Maybe you should think about the dream, Rapunzel. Maybe your unconscious is trying to tell you something. Don't you think?"

Liz swallowed. "I can't bear to think about it."

"Even in the daytime?"

Liz half-laughed. "In the daytime, it doesn't seem important, darling. It seems absurd to me then that I could get so frightened by such a silly dream."

Hazel sighed. "I don't think denial is going to make it go away. Unless you can hypnotize yourself into repressing the dream?"

Liz shook her head. "I tried that. Months ago. Which is when the dream changed. All that would happen if I tried doing it again would be getting a new—and possibly worse—dream. No, I'm stuck with it." Liz's mouth trembled. "Please, darling, hold me."

Hazel lay back down and opened her arms. Liz snuggled close and Hazel rhythmically stroked her back.

After about fifteen minutes, Liz went back to sleep. Hazel shifted Liz off her, reached over, and turned off the light. It took her a long time to go back to sleep, and she lay wondering about the dream and why Liz was having it so often lately. What are you running from, Rapunzel? she silently asked her sleeping lover. One day Liz would have to tell her. It wasn't possible to keep running and evading indefinitely—not from a dream this powerful, however easily she could dismiss it in the daytime.

# Chapter Thirteen

## [i]

From her favorite vantage point on the bluff, Alexandra stared down at the sea and watched the waves roll in. This was spring, she told herself, remembering Elizabeth's enthusiasm for the season last year in DC. It didn't at all resemble spring in DC, though. Still, the air was different from what it had been. And under the cloudless blue sky the ocean seemed relatively mild, relatively calm, and deep, deep blue.

Alexandra found herself at odds with this serenity. In her pocket she carried four of her mother's letters. *Why don't you answer me, Alexandra? Don't you realize I have no way of knowing whether you're ill or well or any other thing about you? I can't reach you by phone, email, or in person. I don't even know where you are! Please answer me, Alexandra, I'm worried sick about you.* But answer what? What was there that she could write?

Alexandra turned her back on the ocean and wandered into the woods. She didn't know the names of any of the flowers in bloom. She thought again of Elizabeth, chatting about spring, and realized that she had been here for nearly a year.

Now *that* was a depressing thought.

*You are going to have to be stronger than that, Alexandra. I've told you and told you that your father, like all males, considers any sexuality obscene. When he talks to you that way you must always consider the source. As for your waning interest in Clarice, it must be that you've already tired of her. If you enjoyed her at first it isn't likely you won't enjoy other girls. I simply don't believe you will feel this way toward all of them. But how tiresome of you, Alexandra, to have such a short attention span. Still, I can understand. I've known other women to be the same way. But what shall we do about it? It will take some time to arrange something new for the girl—she's expensive, you know—and there are problems in replacing her, not least of which will be probable interference from your father. Think about this before making a decision. It's your decision, dear, but don't be too hasty.*

How *could* she answer such a response to what she had written about how sick she felt? Mama seemed not to understand what she had tried so hard to tell her. Or was it one of those things one never talked about?

Alexandra leaned against a tree and listened to the birds twitter. Everything was always so complicated. And judging by her own experience, everything just kept getting more complicated the older you got. *That's how the males think of the girls, Alexandra. Their conditioning makes them find women's genitals loathsome and disgusting. You must learn to ignore that contempt. We all have to put up with it. After a while one doesn't even hear the words they're saying or the tone of voice. It is they who are deprived, dear. Remember that.* None of this advice could help her. As for ignoring her father, how could she? As soon ignore the need to drink water or ignore the weather when deciding what to wear.

Mama must not remember what he's like, Alexandra thought. Or else he never talked to her quite that way. She would understand if she could remember. Had Grandfather Raines ever talked to her mother that way? It was hard to imagine, when he was so kind to her, Alexandra. He was so nice, so gentle that she even liked it when he hugged her. But of course that had been before she had become a woman. Maybe everything would be changed now. Maybe he would be horrid to her if he knew about Clarice. How could she tell? Maybe everything changed when you became a woman. After all, Grandfather Raines wasn't especially nice to Mama. Not mean, but not kind, the way he was to her.

Alexandra stepped a few inches away from the tree and brushed the toe of her boot over the clump of fungus, a rich dark shade of red that reminded her of merlot, growing at the base of the tree. Things used to be so clear, so sharp, so easily understood. Now everything was a mush of confusion and uncertainty. Even Papa, who liked to think of himself as "teaching" her about everything he considered to be important, seemed to muddle her, maybe even deliberately. The only person who—at least since Alexandra had come North—had ever made things clear and comprehensible was Elizabeth. Of all the people in the world, it was Elizabeth Alexandra most longed to see. Cuddling with Mama or Grandmother would be nice, but would not make the messy confusion go away. Elizabeth, Alexandra felt confident, would.

Alexandra kicked at the fungus until she'd smashed all of it against the rough bark of the tree. There was no way out, no way out at all. And after last night she felt as though she hated Clarice. The very thought of seeing her again made her flesh shrink with disgust. *Dear Mama,* she imagined writing, *the very sight of Clarice makes me sick, makes my stomach churn. I don't ever want to see her again, please take her back.*

But she couldn't write that, the whole thing was unfair to Clarice. It wasn't her fault. Clarice had a *contract.* As both Papa and Mama said. What else could she do?

Not slyly seduce me, Alexandra thought in angry rebuttal. She had no right, no right at all to do that. She knew I didn't want her. She was hoping for another present.

Alexandra moved through the trees. She knew she was thinking these things about Clarice because of what *he* had said. He had poisoned her feelings for the girl. She knew that. It wasn't fair, because he couldn't—wouldn't!—see Clarice as a person. Stuck here on this island, Clarice was probably as lonely as she was. Maybe even more so. And she, Alexandra, had been diffident, reserved, sometimes cold to her, had hardly talked to her at all for weeks now. *I had begun to think you'd already gotten tired of me, carina.* And so after refusing the girl's advances, she'd given her the perfume Mama had sent to be used as a present. That had probably been a mistake, because the girl had probably read the gesture as a promise rather than a guilt-offering. But what would she say to her tonight? That the very sight of her turned her stomach?

The woods blurred into a mass of green as Alexandra stumbled along the path. When she emerged onto the western headland she sank down onto the wet ground, oblivious of mud and damp, facing the ocean but not really seeing it. She imagined a never-ending string of horrible meetings and dinner parties lined up down the years, imagined sitting around talking about financial affairs, listening to people gossip about the Executive...

The only person in that house who had shown a breath of life had been Judith MacLaury, and she had been off-limits. "To see those bastards shaking in their boots...! What a pleasure!" Judith had crowed. "A woman like that... But if there were many like her, we wouldn't last, you know." This had seemed to be a reminder and, possibly, an excuse, Alexandra thought. An excuse for why more women weren't like Elizabeth. "They're so easily threatened," Judith had whispered. "And they say *we're* hysterical!" Judith did not have a maternity contract with Buchanan; she was career-line: a kind of PA, hostess, and confidante all wrapped into one package, her duties and functions specified in a long detailed contract. She did not live away from Buchanan, except during vacations. She said that one day she would do well for herself and would find that the grind had been worth it. Delayed gratification, she called it. But she wanted to know everything about Elizabeth Alexandra had ever heard. Elizabeth fired her imagination, provoked fantasies of vengeance against males like Buchanan, like Booth, perhaps even like Papa.

Alexandra's watch chimed. Reluctantly she stood up and brushed off the back of her tunic and trousers. Right up against the limit of tardiness her father would tolerate, she dared not put off going in for tea.

## [ii]

She checked her appearance in the hall mirror. Presentable, she decided as she fluffed her hair. Before turning away she caught a fleeting expression on her mirrored face that reminded her of her father. It was the haircut, she thought. No wonder he liked it. Even if her hair was chestnut and textured like Mama's...

Alexandra opened the door to the Small Study and stopped short on the threshold. Though it was only 4:30 in the afternoon, he was lying on the sofa—in nightshirt and robe, unshaven—drinking what she knew must be scotch and listening to that same infernal symphony. As she hesitated, he turned his head and saw her. He fumbled with the remote control lying on his chest and the music ceased. Alexandra thought back to the previous evening—before Clarice had seduced her—and tried to remember how he had been then. No mail on Thursdays, after all, and there had been no off-island visitors that she knew of. So it must have been something last night that had set him off...

Oh, she thought, remembering. The aliens' vid broadcast. They had watched part of it, and then he'd offed it and begun ranting about how the program was more of Elizabeth's treachery. He had been drinking pretty steadily when she'd gone upstairs for the night, but not scotch. That must have come later. Yet he was in nightshirt and robe... Surely he hadn't been drinking nonstop since then? But what she most wanted to know was where Higgins was and why he hadn't told her about this. Alexandra closed the door behind her and walked over to the sofa. "Give me your glass," she said calmly, staring down at him.

His bleary, bloodshot eyes peered up at her. "So there you are."

"That's scotch, isn't it." She held out her hand. "Give me your glass. You know you're not supposed to drink scotch. You told me you wouldn't. Remember?"

"My prerogative to change my mind," he said, his eyes straying away from hers to fix on his glass.

"You know you can't handle scotch," Alexandra said. "Give me your glass."

"You sound like her," he complained.

"Let me put it this way." Alexandra glared at him. "If you don't give me your glass I'll just take the bottle and leave you by yourself." She glanced around for it and wondered if he had secreted it in the crack between the cushions and the back of the sofa.

"Bossy." He put the glass to his lips and took enough scotch in his mouth to require several swallows. "Sign this, she'd say. Read that. Go to this meeting. Talk to that asshole on the phone. Bossy bossy bossy bitch."

"If I have to I'll get Forbes and Higgins in here and have *them* find the bottle," Alexandra said. "You want to spend the whole evening alone?"

His eyes filled with tears. "Just this glass. I'll give you the bottle, if I can keep the glass?" He dug the bottle from where she'd guessed he'd hidden it and awkwardly handed it to her.

"Thank you," she said. "And now the glass." She shifted the bottle to her left hand and again held out her right.

"You'll stay?"

"Yes," Alexandra said wearily, resigning herself to hours of excruciating boredom. "I'll stay."

"Give me your word."

This mania for promises he had when he was drunk drove her wild. He himself was incapable of keeping promises. He had told her several times over the last year that he had sworn to himself not to drink scotch again, for he knew that scotch was his downfall, that scotch sent him totally out of control. "I give you my word I'll spend the evening with you," she said.

"One last sip?"

"No," Alexandra said sternly. "If you drink from that glass again I'm leaving. That's the bargain. Clear?" Solemnly he held the glass out to her. She carried it and the bottle to the desk. Then she picked up the house handset and buzzed Higgins' room. Higgins answered on the third ring, sounding so groggy that for a moment Alexandra wondered whether he had been drinking with her father when he should have been stopping him. "I need you *now* in the Small Study," Alexandra said. He mumbled a yesmadam, and she disconnected and buzzed the kitchen and asked Nicole to include on the tea tray a pot of detox coffee.

When Alexandra finished her calls she crossed the room to the fireplace. She would make a fire and settle herself on cushions in front of it. She would be physically comfortable, if nothing else. He would not dare to complain about her "maternal-line habits" lest she take umbrage and leave. He seemed peculiarly powerless when he got this intoxicated. It was a thing she did not understand the reasons for, though she knew intuitively how to use it. As she arranged the kindling she heard him mumbling something at her. "Just a minute," she said to him over her shoulder, "let me get the fire started and then I'll come sit by you for a while." It would be preferable to get him to sleep, but from everything Higgins had told her last January about the patterns of his drunks, she knew that wasn't likely.

By the time she had gotten the fire going and had a big chunk of log burning, Higgins arrived. He looked even pastier than usual. "Get rid of that glass and bottle on the desk," she told him. "Then bring my father an oxy pill and a B-complex injection. And let the staff know that my father is not to be given anything alcoholic until further notice from me. Clear?"

"Understood." Higgins shuffled to the desk.

Alexandra got up and followed him. "Why didn't you call me, Higgins?"

"He slipped something into my wine last night," Higgins said, not meeting her eyes.

"What!"

"He insisted I join him in a glass of wine."

Alexandra, astonished, glared at him.

"I didn't see the harm drinking just one glass," he said quickly. "I mean, we made a deal that I'd drink that glass of wine with him, and then he'd go to bed. Everything went fine. We drank the wine and then went up to his room. He changed into his nightshirt and robe and dismissed me. I could hardly make it to bed I was so tired. I only realized when I woke up a little while ago what he'd done. He can be quite crafty sometimes, Madam."

"Which you should have been smart enough to catch."

"I'm afraid I slept most of the day. It must have been something strong to keep me knocked out for just about fifteen hours."

Alexandra barely kept herself from treating him to a lecture about the stupidity of making deals involving alcohol with her father. "Just get this stuff out of here and get the oxy and B-complex into him. I've already ordered that detox stuff. I'll be spending the evening with him. As soon as he's started sobering up, you can go back to bed if you want. I'll call you if I need you."

He thanked her, then shuffled out of the room with the glass and bottle. Alexandra noticed he didn't even look at her father. She supposed he must feel chagrined; she could hardly blame him. Papa could be very insistent, and anyway who would guess—except, perhaps, Higgins—that he would be that sneaky, that greedy for scotch? He must have taken Higgins' keys, too, to have been able to get inside the locked liquor cabinet.

Alexandra settled on the floor beside the sofa with her knees tucked under her chin. "Higgins told me what you did," she said.

He grinned. "Higgins is an idiot." So he remembered? She wished she knew more about the symptoms of drunkenness. Did the fact that he remembered something that had happened so many hours ago mean he wasn't *that* drunk? Then why act this way if he wasn't?

"Oh?" Alexandra raised her eyebrows. "Is that why he's stayed with you for so many years?"

His face sagged. "Aren't you going to be nice to me now?"

Why why why did he talk this way when she took away the scotch? Had he always done the same with Elizabeth? It was as though he *liked* the whole thing, he *liked* being babyish. "Only if you drink your coffee when it comes," she said.

He sighed. "If you hold my hand," he bargained.

"All right," Alexandra said and made herself take his hand. His cold clammy fingers squeezed hers tightly, then loosened to a strangely repellent limpness.

"You're never affectionate with me." She *hated* it when he whined; somehow that was even worse than when he got teary-eyed and maudlin. "It's not natural in a daughter to be so cold to her father."

God. How could he talk this way to her? He was like two people inhabiting the same body. "I barely know you," she said, a thing she would probably not say if he were sober.

"You barely know that cunt of yours," he said, "yet you *lavish* affection on her."

She jerked her hand away from him. "If you're going to talk that way I'll go sit by the fire."

Higgins returned and gave her father the shot and had him swallow the pill. And then Penderel wheeled in the tea tray. Alexandra showed him where to place it and sent him away. Feeling more and more irritable, she poured some of the detox coffee into a mug and took it to her father. "Sit up now," she said, "and drink the coffee as you promised." He struggled into a sitting position and accepted the half-full mug, his hands unsteady enough to make the coffee rock up the sides. He's like a baby, she thought as she coaxed and chided him into drinking each successive swallow, and the thought somehow made her feel more indulgent towards him. When he'd finished what she'd given him, she took the empty mug and set it back on the cart. She would give him more later, but the next step was to get as much water down him as possible. "Do you want some poppyseed cake?" she asked, certain he would refuse. But he said he'd eat some; she cut him a piece and put it on a plate. "Fingers or fork?" she asked, thinking of how he might make a mess of trying to eat with a fork while holding the plate in his other hand.

"Fingers," he said, and she handed him the plate.

Slowly, painfully they worked their way through tea. He did everything she ordered and nothing she did not explicitly tell him to do. "It has to be her behind it," he said when he'd almost finished the glass of water she'd given him to drink.

"Behind what?" she asked, knowing he had to be referring to Elizabeth, for with him "her" could refer to only one of two women.

"That trash on vid last night. She's giving the enemy our files. Which means she's broken the new code they installed last winter. The opposition aren't clever enough to be able to do that kind of thing by themselves. But why? Why's she doing it?"

Alexandra poured more tea into her cup. "I don't believe it's Weatherall," she said.

The house phone buzzed. "No one else would or could do it," he said. The phone buzzed again. "Don't you hear the phone?"

Alexandra set her cup down and got up and went to answer it. Undoubtedly they'd want to know something stupid about where to serve dinner or whether or not to serve a cheese course before dessert. "Yes," she said into the handset.

"Mr. Sedgewick, please," a male voice not immediately recognizable said.

"He's not available. This is Ms. Sedgewick. What is it you want?"

There was a pause. Then, "This is Marlin, Madam." Marlin, Alexandra recalled, was the gorilla in charge of the entire security detail. "We've had a call saying that Mr. Wedgewood will be landing here in twenty-five minutes."

"Just a minute, Marlin." Alexandra put the line on hold and walked over to the foot of the sofa. "Marlin says Wedgewood is landing here in twenty-five minutes. Were you expecting him?"

Her father frowned and slowly shook his head. "No, don't think so. Don't remember a meeting. He was here just last week."

"Well should I tell Marlin that Wedgewood's plane has clearance to land?"

"Of course," he said.

Alexandra returned to the phone and relayed the message to Marlin. "You're going to have to drink more coffee then," she told her father when she had finished talking to Marlin. "Otherwise how will you make sense of anything he's come to see you about?"

"I'm perfectly competent now," he said, and gave her a surprisingly steady look.

Quick-change artist, she thought. What in *hell* was going on inside him? "Still, you could probably use some more coffee," she said and poured more of the detox stuff into his mug.

He accepted the mug, chugged every last drop in it, and held it out to her for a refill. "You'll have to give orders that he's to dine with us," he said. "And this time I'll want you to stay down here while I talk with him." Every trace of his infantile posture had vanished.

Cold claws of fear scraped the walls of her stomach. "No," she said. "I don't want to know anything about the business he has with you." As she spoke she refilled his mug and handed it back to him.

He downed the refill and set the mug back on the cart. "I insist. I also want you to give him something to drink and make smalltalk with him while I'm showering and dressing." He stood up. "Call my valet for me and get him upstairs to my room. I'll want him to shave me after I've showered." And to Alexandra's amazement, he walked out of the room, steady though stiff and careful. Had the detox worked that quickly and effectively? It had taken so much longer the last time. It was almost as though the mere mention of Wedgewood had instantly sobered him up—enough so that she knew she would have trouble evading his demand that she sit in on their meeting.

### [iii]

Alexandra watched in near disbelief as her father poured only one cognac, handed it to Philip Wedgewood, and asked Alexandra to pour him a cup of coffee. He had drunk no wine with dinner, either, though wine had been served to Wedgewood and herself. She poured out a cup from the thermoflask on the tray Penderel had placed on the table near her chair, got up, and carried it over to him. She herself drank water.

"So, Wedgewood, why the visit?" Papa asked pointblank.

They had discussed nothing but DC gossip and cultural events through pre-dinner drinks and dinner. Alexandra was not surprised at Wedgewood's expressive glance at her. "Shall I leave?" she asked, though without much hope.

"Certainly not," her father said, frowning at her. He looked at Wedgewood. "You can talk freely, Wedgewood. My daughter is in my confidence."

Wedgewood's prissy lips tightened and his blond eyebrows drew down into a vee. "This is an extremely sensitive matter, Sedgewick."

"Naturally," Papa said drily. "I suppose it's about that vid-display the aliens forced on the world last night?"

"On the continent," Wedgewood said. "They've stopped globe-wide vid broadcasts. God knows why, but I suppose we should be thankful for that."

"Since when have they restricted their vid output?"

Wedgewood shrugged. "For a long time now."

Papa bit his lip. "But that vid-display is relevant to your reasons for flying up here."

"Yes. From what they said at the beginning and then again at the end of the broadcast, there will be more of this kind of propaganda, considerably more."

"The first question being, how they got hold of so much information. As far as I can tell the entire broadcast was aimed at ODS."

"Didn't touch anybody else," Wedgewood agreed.

"So you're shaking the Southern California station upside down."

"It's in chaos," Wedgewood said. He held the balloon snifter to his face and took a swallow of cognac. "Leland sent in his resignation three weeks ago. Effective next Friday."

"Leland's quit? But why? I thought he'd continue there forever!"

Wedgewood rolled the glass between his palms. "Don't know for sure, since he gave no specific reason, but rumor has it that he quit because his PA went renegade."

Papa's eyes narrowed. "That Mott bitch? *She* went renegade?" He looked incredulous. "When?"

"A month and a half ago. And then when Mott left, she sabotaged most of the local data system, including every goddam last ODS file, and things more or less fell apart. They even lost the inmates' records at the two federal detention centers in that territory."

Papa shook his head. "I'd never have figured *her* for that kind of action." He stared down into his coffee cup, then suddenly looked up at Wedgewood. "It's Weatherall, isn't it. She's behind Mott's defection. I'm beginning to see a pattern, damn it!"

Wedgewood, frowning, shook his head. "What has Weatherall to do with Mott going renegade?"

Papa snorted. "Everything. That bitch is up to something, something that's going to cost the Executive dearly. Take my word for it. She's at the heart of this. I wouldn't be surprised if this pattern were to repeat itself in other places too."

"Maybe it's a copycat thing. I don't see how Weatherall could have controlled Mott from that great a distance. We'd *know* if Weatherall was anywhere near the vicinity of that station."

Papa made a sound of disgust with his tongue against his teeth. "Don't be an idiot, Wedgewood. It would have been child's play for Mott to suppress information revealing Weatherall's presence in San Diego if she so chose. Who's to have checked on her other than Leland? And Leland had complete confidence in her. I know, I've seen them in action. There's nothing that went on at that station that that bitch didn't know about. And she's Michael Mott's niece for fuck's sake. She's been with the Company since she got out of college god knows how many years ago. No one would ever dream she'd think of going renegade, much less commit sabotage."

Wedgewood steepled his fingers—knuckle-deep in chunky gold rings—against his nose and moved them up and down, up and down, rubbing hard enough to stretch the skin and pull the lower lids of his eyes away from his eyeballs, revealing the pink inner flesh of his lower lids and the red-veined protuberant whites extending far beneath the blue irises of his eyes. Alexandra watched with unwilling fascination. "I hope to hell you're wrong, Sedgewick," he finally said. "Because if you're right about this..." He swallowed and sucked in a deep breath. "If you're right about this, we'll soon be up shit creek.

Without a paddle. And with holes springing unpredictably anywhere along the hull of our goddam boat."

Papa's lips curved a little, into more of a grim smile than a sneer. After a couple of beats, he said, "Precisely. If Weatherall has started something, if she has found a means of recruiting bitches in strategically crucial positions, we're fucked. Which is to say, you'd better find her, fast. Or else try to deal with her."

Wedgewood's mouth dropped open. "*Deal* with Weatherall!" His voice cracked, which Alexandra had not realized adult male voices could do. "Deal with one of the worst cases of treachery in the history of the Company? Are you *nuts?*"

This time Papa's mouth unambiguously formed a smile—one of his nastier, sneerier efforts. "Your only other alternative," he said slowly, enunciating every syllable of every word distinctly, "is to terminate every damned bitch in the Company. Without exception." He paused dramatically, then said "Do you think anyone will be interested in doing that, Wedgewood?"

Wedgewood seized his glass and gulped down several swallows in quick succession. "But that's presuming you're correct," he said. "We have no compelling reason for believing Weatherall is behind everything. Besides, Sedgewick, Booth would never stand for dealing with her. You know he wouldn't. And as for firing all our bitches..." He shook his head. "The very idea is *insane*. How would we deal with all the crap, all the millions of details? And with managing the service-techs? For the birthing fuck, man, we'd be mired in shit up to our eyeballs, 24/7. We'd never get anything done!"

"Well that's my advice, for what it's worth. Unless, of course, you can find her. Naturally that would be the optimal solution. But if you haven't found her yet..." Papa shrugged. "I doubt you'll find her now. It would be like trying to find either one of us if *we* decided to take a powder."

"She did field work all those years ago, it's true," Wedgewood said glumly. "Most people forget tradecraft when they've sat behind a desk for as many years as she has."

Papa's voice rasped with irritation. "Don't be absurd, Wedgewood. Those kind of things you don't forget, not if you've been living the way she has. She dodged Military's excision specialists through the entire Civil War. She developed habits. And she kept up with her martial arts skills, too. She could take every damned one of my escort in one-on-one combat, you know. I myself have seen her take Lamont."

"Yeah, I know. I've seen her work out myself." Wedgewood picked up the snifter. "She took me several times, too, until I admitted we weren't anywhere in the neighborhood of being matched."

Her father indulged one of his weird bouts of laughter, and the sound of it sent a shiver up Alexandra's spine. Wedgewood looked into his empty snifter and fingered its stem.

When Papa finished laughing, he picked up his cup and sipped his coffee. Putting the cup down, he grinned. "So how's Booth taking it? Is he panicking yet?"

Wedgewood set the snifter down and sighed. Looking at Papa, he bit his lip and stroked his moustache. Though he wore his usual stone face, Alexandra could almost swear he was about to break into a nervous sweat. "Rumor says he's about ready to can Hill," he finally said. "But one of my sources close to Booth tells me he's thinking of sending Hill back to Justice."

Papa's eyebrows raised. "Oh? And who's he going to replace Hill with?"

Wedgewood brushed at his sleeve several times, presumably to remove a speck of lint from it. "Haven't heard Word One on that." He glanced at Papa, then looked down at his sleeve and picked at it with his fingernails. "Naturally there are plenty of rumors. About bringing in somebody from Military, about bringing in some corporation type. The wilder the possibility the more people play with it."

"More cognac?"

"Please."

Papa looked at her; Alexandra rose, fetched the bottle from the liquor tray, and poured a couple more shots into Wedgewood's snifter. She reseated herself. "Tell us, Alexandra," Papa said, "how *you* think Weatherall might be recruiting and keeping in contact with Mott and anyone else who might entertain ideas of going renegade."

Taken by surprise and acutely aware of both pairs of eyes focused on her, Alexandra struggled against the blush she felt spreading inch by inch over her face; she hoped she did not look as guilty as she felt. If they had any idea she had heard from Elizabeth *twice* since Elizabeth had gone renegade, they would... Well. They would consider her a traitor, and they would know where to start looking, and would also start watching her mail. She swallowed. "I have no idea," she said. "I'm very inexperienced at this sort of thing."

"Yes," Papa said impatiently, "but you know how executive women think, and you know the ways of executive women. Surely you must have *some* ideas of how she might be working it?"

Alexandra shook her head. "I'm sorry, but I don't. I've only lived here and in Barbados. How would I know such things?"

Papa gave her a thoughtful look. "You probably don't realize just how much you do know," he said. "Think about it, Alexandra, and if you come up with any ideas, let me know. You may surprise yourself."

Alexandra poured herself another glass of water. Wedgewood turned the conversation to a discussion of what could be done to resurrect morale in the Southern California station, and Alexandra felt as though a dangerous moment had passed. All she had to do was efface herself, and they would not notice her or make demands on her again.

What a terrible thing it would be if her father were right and she *did* know about the things he had asked her about and, knowing, betrayed Elizabeth and any other executive women involved. She would never forgive herself if she ever in any way let down other executive women. As Mama and Grandmother always said, because everybody else in the world hated them, executive women *had* to stick together.

### [iv]

Alexandra got away from the males' discussion around midnight. En route to her room she had two things on her mind: the need to go to sleep immediately because she would have to get up early to write the social psychology essay that was due at 10 a.m., and a good chew of parsley. And so when she opened the door to her bedroom suite she went straight to the vase of parsley and pulled out four or five stems. She stuck one into her mouth and began unfastening her tunic. As she struggled one-handed to get out of the tunic, she heard a sound, whirled, and found Clarice coming towards her. "What are you doing here?" she said sharply. She'd told Clarice before dinner that she would not be wanting her tonight.

Clarice helped her out of the tunic. "I thought you might change your mind," she said, smiling as she draped the tunic over her arm.

Alexandra scowled. "If I'd changed my mind I would have called you," she said as she stepped out of her trousers.

Clarice carried the tunic and trousers into the dressing room. Alexandra laid the remaining parsley stems on the night table, stripped off her underwear, and got into bed. Clarice slithered back into the room, came over to the bed, and sat on the edge. "Don't be cross with me, *carina.* I've missed you." Her smile grew coy. "I thought you gave me the perfume because you wanted me to wear it for you?"

"I have to get up early and write an essay," Alexandra said. "Good night, Clarice."

Clarice made one of her pouting faces. "You'll have a nicer sleep if—"

A wave of fury rushed over Alexandra, and she cut Clarice off: "Will you please shut up!"

Clarice's eyes widened and burned with resentment. Alexandra realized she had shouted at the girl, something she had never before done. She swallowed. "I'm sorry, dear, for shouting at you. But I can't stand your manipulating me. I'm tired, I don't want you here right now."

"You're angry at me?" Clarice looked as though she might cry.

Alexandra shook her head. "Just exasperated. I want you to go away now, so I can sleep. Will you please do that, dear?"

Clarice mustered a smile. "Good night, *carina.* Sleep well." She moved to the door, threw Alexandra a sad look over her shoulder, and went out. Alexandra released the breath she'd been holding while waiting to see if Clarice would agree to end the scene, then grabbed her parsley and turned out the light. Clarice would have to go. There was no way she was going to be able to stand the girl for the full two years of her contract. She would write to Mama tomorrow afternoon and tell her to start making arrangements.

After swallowing her mouthful of parsley, Alexandra subvocalized the prompt. Within moments, she had escaped into sleep.

# Chapter Fourteen

## [i]

Aridity and relatively low gravity, threatening dissolution/ merging/ scattering/ collision, overwhelm Astrea until self comprehends the need to pull one's field within and make tight, definite physical aspects of self. Obedience to Starfleet cadre's exhortation that those without star-travel experience occupy the small box-compartments separating self from other Marq'ssan grows increasingly attractive despite self's lack of physical ill-effects.

Not to circulate, not to attempt to sensibilitize with this bizarre material world so thinly shielded by the physical lineaments of the ship seems no longer a disturbing suggestion for adopting a mode abhorrently passive for any Marq'ssan. The prospect of sleeping and occasionally dreaming offers stability.

Astrea knows that by sleeping, the star-traveling Marq'ssan avoids the necessity to utilize the digestive track for nourishment not otherwise available in transit.

Now without reservation, Astrea inserts self into the compartment and its surrounding field-resistant walls in easy confidence that self cannot disturb others during sleep, that self will find meditation possible, that self while sleeping will not mind such solitude and apartness...

Yet dreaming and eating—which Astrea deems among the most primitive of activities that sentients have been known to depend on—are advised by the xenologists as useful preparation for meeting humans. Humans sustain themselves by crude digestion and dream. Humans do not sensibilitize. Their metabolism is inefficient, wasteful, and dependant on a haphazard digestion only dimly understood by humans themselves.

Thinking of this before spilling into dream-sleep, Astrea recalls the xenologists' warning that to date, each Marq'ssan's first reaction to these disgusting primitive dependencies has been repulsion. The xenologists claim that the continual digestion of animal and vegetable lifeforms and its resultant crude metabolism bear no resemblance to *s'sbeylassan.*

Astrea settles into an ultra-low metabolic state. Sleeping, self dreams about sensibilitizing in silm.

[ii]

After an interval, Astrea wakes.

Dream fragments drift in and out of self's five levels of consciousness. Metabolism so slow, so sluggish, Astrea chooses to step outside the compartment to seek position.

Eflhanyyt l Mohr san Androst assures Astrea that *s'chorl* is only a third of the way to its destination, and Astrea re-turns self within the compartment, intending to meditate. But sluggishness conduces to such aimless diffusion that self slips again into sleep, storing for recall upon waking the in-sight that ingestion of food must be undertaken and half-hoping self will waken only when they have reached Ambient Sol, which would preclude the need.

[iii]

The second, protracted waking comes as self floats in and out of the less verbal levels of consciousness. Images flash briefly, sometimes for long enough to be consciously grasped, often for such fleeting duration that they blink in and out of consciousness never to be recalled again. In confusion, Astrea imagines enfoldment within silm, for the en-rapture of silm weaves in and out of the long sleep's dreams.

But recollection of the need for ingestion of food and production of energy prods self toward full-waking, overriding the lethargy, diffusion, and the disgust for digestion, a process self knows to be essential now for survival.

Astrea flows along *s'chorl*'s conduits to the compartments designated for alimentation. Several compartments are unoccupied; Astrea chooses one of these and folds self within, certain of privacy into which no Marq'ssan would conceive of intruding. Amenities in the alimentation compartment include packets of organic matter of several sorts, packets of fluid necessary for aiding disposal of waste that such primitive ingestion and metabolism incur, and facilities for private and sanitary elimination of waste products.

Astrea takes a packet containing a solution of minerals, sugar, and amino acids and injects the solution into a blood vessel, forcing circulation of relatively quick-access sources for metabolism. After a brief interval, Astrea consumes through laterals a packet of fluid. These first steps of primitive alimentation are the easiest.

The next step is the worst, worse even than the various aspects of waste elimination. Astrea procrastinates and feebly argues against sense that the previous ingestion will suffice.

After a struggle self becomes unified in the determination to do what must be done: and opens one of the packets, the contents of which must be intaken by mouth, and imposes on self the disgusting process of chewing, swallowing, taking more, all the while shrinking from the intrinsic horror such barbarism inflicts.

When finished intaking the packet, self sinks into lethargy, prepared to sleep until driven to eliminate the waste products of a completed digestion and metabolism. Starship cadre say that the dreams following such alimentation are twisted, perverse, bizarre—and no reflection on anything but the loathsome primitive process.

## [iv]

"This, the largest planet in the Sol Ambient," Sbina l Sellyyn san Bol informs the first-timers, "is most like Marqeuei in size, gravity, and atmosphere, as well as being the most beautiful of all Sol's satellites." Astrea scans far outward with great elation, pleased to be once again in a space self can fully perceive, scan, and enfold.

Soon they will be reaching Earth, soon they will be meeting with the six Marq'ssan who stayed. Astrea's metabolism stirs with excitement as the unknown approaches.

Yet self admits to doubts:

Will the shape and size (enormous!) of the human form chafe self?

Will the relative lack of Earth's gravity make movement ridiculously awkward or even induce diffusion or other obstacles to centering?

Will the arid and impoverished atmosphere render metabolism stressful?

While most Marq'ssan who have visited Earth have not experienced substantial difficulties, a few—unable to bear the misery their physical responses to Earth inflicted upon selves—have found physical adaptation intolerable.

These worries, though, resemble certain of the tiniest creatures that live entirely within silm that gnaw or burrow beneath one's flesh; one lives with them for the sake of the greater experience, for they may even form a part of the ambient itself.

Dghatd l Merr san Fehln has warned again and again about the need for regular sleep and dream periods for as long as they physically adapt selves to human form, to Earth ambient, but has also said:

"It will get easier the longer you stay."

Astrea looks now at Dghatd already in human form and wonders what memories that Marq'ssan has from the previous trip, which Astrea knows lasted far into Dghatd's second-phase...

Astrea thinks, staring out at one of the beautiful moons of Sol's largest planet: Soon they will see Earth (which will not be so pretty). What a pity they can not stop and sample this planet. Perhaps it even has silm.

Everyone knows that Earth does not.

# Chapter Fifteen

[i]

The pod landed on Emily's beach just after dark. As they hurried to it Celia wondered whether it had created radio disturbance in the neighborhood. She knew they could no longer be certain who might be watching. Since Mott's defection, Emily's tails had been dropped, and in the last week Celia had found herself with only one of the two tails that had been persistently following her over the last year. She and Emily had concluded that ODS must indeed have fallen into disarray. Although most newspaper editorials argued that ODS's abuses were justified, Celia knew that the vid programs exposing individuals working for ODS must be exercising an enormous influence on everyone employed by the agency. If only, if only they could do this to *all* repressive forces around the country. Still…the prospect of freeing all the political prisoners in those two detention facilities made her wild with anticipation.

Before they strapped in, Maureen Sanders introduced Celia and Emily to all the Marq'ssan and humans the two of them had not yet met. "You already know Sorben," Maureen said to Celia, "but Emily, I don't think you do. So please, Emily, meet Sorben. And Celia and Emily, these are Tyln and Magyyt and Flahn." Unable to suppress a shudder at having *four* of them present all at once, Celia nodded at the new faces and tried to look calm. Considering what they were up against, the more of these powerful beings the better. "And this is Paulette Liya, an observer for the government of Cameroon." Celia and Emily each shook hands with the woman, then Maureen moved to the next flight couch and continued, "and this is Ariana Vargas, an observer for the government of Greece." And again shook hands. "And Juliann Djikstra, an observer for the government of the Netherlands." Celia saw that the next passenger was a male executive and felt uneasy surprise. "This is Heinrich Epstein, an observer for the government of Austria." Emily nodded at him but did not offer her hand for shaking, and Celia imitated her; he nodded coolly at them. "And finally, Dr. Simona Santos, a medical observer for the United Nations." After they had shaken hands with this last observer, Maureen said, "I think you know the rest of us?"

Everyone, Celia could see, was waiting, waiting, waiting: for once they lifted off this beach, they would be less than five minutes from El Cajon... She seated herself and fumbled with the straps. She could feel the others concentrating on her slowness, could feel the level of tension rising.

Sorben addressed the group at large. "Before landing we will hover—in full camouflage—above the prison to scan the entire set of structures. We will input data from the scan into the processor to assist Lisa's team in determining how best to proceed with its assigned tasks. Next we will create a localized EMP, which will have the effect of disabling most of their weapons, as well as plunging the prison into darkness and releasing the electronic locking mechanisms. At the same time, we will begin destructuring all remaining mechanical weapons. Then we will land, and Tyln and Magyyt will go ahead; they will be followed by me with Lisa's team, to be followed by Flahn and the medical team and the observers. Only after we have begun an orderly evacuation will the media team move in. The highest priority will be given to loading those who require medical attention." Sorben looked at Lisa. "Your team has reviewed a number of contingency plans for how to deal with the prison personnel. I hope there is no question about the principles we agreed upon in advance?"

"Everything is very clear," Lisa said. "And as I'm sure you must already know, none of us are carrying weapons of any sort."

No weapons! What could they be thinking of? If she were setting a trap, surely Lisa would *prefer* them not to be carrying weapons? Celia glanced sidelong at Emily. Emily shrugged and fingered her mask. Emily must have known, Celia thought, for she was going in as part of Lisa's team of women trained in unarmed hand-to-hand combat. Yet she had said nothing. The thought chilled Celia, for it was another sign of the rift growing between them.

Sorben strapped in, the amber light flashed, and Celia felt the pod lifting. Images flowed over the data screens distributed among the flight couches. Leaning forward toward her own screen, Emily called up each and every component of the prison structures and studied them; Celia was content to follow along.

After a few minutes, the pod dropped and the disembark light came on. To Celia's astonishment, three of the cabin's walls rolled back to reveal hundreds of vacant flight couches in adjoining cabins. Everyone in the pod unstrapped as Sorben issued more detailed instructions. "Once we've destructured their projectile weapons, Magyyt and Tyln will work their way to the administrative section. Lisa, now that you have data from the scan, have you decided which plan your group will be using?"

Emily got up from her couch and moved away. Celia fiddled with her mask and glanced around the cabin. Her blood fairly froze in her veins when she saw the three other Marq'ssan sitting apart, their eyes closed, their faces vacant. They were *doing* things. They must be doing what they called 'destructuring'! She glanced at a data screen and saw that the images were constantly changing.

Celia averted her eyes from the screen and noted that a few dozen people were spreading out in a section of the cabin that was now without flight couches and launching into vigorous warm-up exercises; Emily, she saw, was among them. Impressed by the sight, Celia made a quick count of the number exercising and came up with forty-nine. Forty women, most of them Free Zone Women's Patrol, and nine men. Forty-nine seemed a lot—but since none of them were armed... Would Luis be there? Or had they moved him? What would they find? Celia shivered. Did any of these women understand what they might be getting into? Maureen, at least, must have some idea... Celia pushed away the terrible memories of detention. She needed to be clear-eyed, hard, efficient. This was no time for weakness.

A stir rustled through the humans: two of the Marq'ssan were disembarking. The data screens all cleared simultaneously and reformed. Celia stared at the new image for several seconds before realizing it was tracking the movements of the two Marq'ssan who had gone first. A thick silence held as the two stick-figures on the screen moved from the round circle toward the lines representing the perimeter of the prison compound. The stick-figures halted at the outer wall. Suddenly the line of the wall disappeared. One of the Free Zone women cheered, but everyone else waited tensely. Celia realized she had been holding her breath when Sorben said, "The guard post and the road are at the other end of the prison. They've gone through an unguarded section of wall. As you can see, they're now approaching one of the outer buildings."

"That's the main physical plant," Lisa said.

Celia glanced at the remaining one of the three Marq'ssan who had been doing their thing before the first two had gone in and saw that the alien called Flahn still had her eyes closed. She must be "scanning" all the time, Celia thought. The screen now showed diagrams of three separate floors of a building. Numerous red stick-figures were converging on one large room on the ground floor. Probably a control room, Celia guessed. She looked for the Marq'ssan and saw the two black stick-figures were still positioned outside the physical plant. She wondered why, for since the EMP had immobilized the physical plant, there could be no point in giving further attention to this peripheral building. But then she saw something strange happen: all the red stick-figures began moving in an orderly line through the building. "They've probably warned the people inside that the building is going to be destroyed," Sorben said. "Once everyone has left the building, they'll destructure it."

"And what will happen to the people they've persuaded to evacuate the building?" someone on the medical team asked.

"They'll temporarily place a barrier around them," Sorben said. "Which is what we intend to do with all the prison personnel as we disarm them. And then when everyone is safely on board, we'll destructure the barriers."

Sure enough, once all the red stick-figures had left the building, a new line, bright red, encircled them. And then the building was gone and the black stick-figures were moving on. What she saw on the screen seemed so fantastic that Celia found it hard to believe it bore any relation to reality.

Now the black stick-figures were crossing a large empty space. "There," Lisa said. "They're approaching Cell Block C now."

"They'll be going on to the central core," Sorben said. "It's time for Lisa's group to move."

The forty women and nine men moved in an orderly file to the lift. Celia looked around her until she found Emily standing nearby, fastening her mask. "Be careful, Em," Celia said hoarsely.

Emily nodded. "Thanks, Cee. I will." She must be nervous, even frightened, Celia thought. But she knew Emily was really into it, too. From the time she had learned of the plan she had been excited at having the opportunity to take this kind of action. The only thing she had worried about was the risk of being identified later. But they knew that as long as she and Celia kept their masks on they should be able to remain anonymous. There would be no fingerprints or other forensic evidence left to be used against them.

One after another, the members of Lisa's group took the lift. "From now on, if there are any questions, ask Flahn," Sorben said to those who remained, then stepped into the lift herself. The data screen split in half, and a new diagram, depicting Sorben and Lisa's group, appeared. All but one of the stick-figures were blue; so Celia guessed that the single black stick-figure must be Sorben.

The pair of Marq'ssan who had gone ahead destructured one of Cell Block C's walls and moved quickly along a corridor. Celia shivered as she saw all the stick-figures in the vicinity of their passage appear on the screen. The single red stick-figures dotted in one partitioned space after another must be prisoners in cells; the other red stick-figures she assumed to be warders. As the Marq'ssan passed them, the figures Celia took for warders did not move in pursuit. Celia wondered about this, then remembered that it must be dark inside the prison—and that the aliens could make themselves invisible.

She watched the movement on the right half of the screen depicting the long line of figures in Sorben's and Mott's group moving steadily toward Cell Block C. They would liberate it first, then D, then B, and last A, for the prisoners in A were, according to Mott, not politicals. Once the guards in Cell Block C had been neutralized, the medical team was to go in and Mott's group was to move on to Cell Block D. Celia and the observers were to accompany the medical team. The media crew was to go in only after all the prisoners had been evacuated; and no prisoners were to be filmed or interviewed on site: Celia and Maureen had insisted on that. The prisoners would at the very least be disoriented by their sudden liberation. And likely some of them would be in a traumatized condition.

Sorben's group poured through the breach in the wall of Cell Block C and went straight to a room containing three red stick-figures. Sorben's stick-figure paused outside the door to the room, and a line circled the three inside. Ten of the blue stick-figures moved down the corridor almost as far as the central core, then retraced their steps, stopping several times along the way to bring red stick-figures along with them. Where had the others gone? Celia wondered. To another level? She had lost track of Sorben. She watched the blue and red stick-figures as they moved toward the breach in the wall of the cell block. They exited the building, and Celia could see no more red stick-figures inside.

The screen refreshed. After a few seconds, Celia realized that it now displayed a different level of the building.

The process of liberating Cell Block C seemed interminable. Celia's eyes never left the screen; her body trembled with tension as she waited for something terrible to happen, and the hard clench of her neck and shoulders spread through her skull, making her head ache. According to the visuals, everything was going smoothly. But it felt as though it were taking too long.

At last Flahn stood up and made the announcement: "Cell Block C is open. The medical team and observers can go in now."

Mechanically Celia donned her mask, glad to finally be *doing* something—then saw the med team tucking collapsed stretchers and med-kits under their arms. A realization of what they might be walking into slammed her like a kick in the gut. Maureen moved close and touched her arm. "Don't worry, Celia. All this equipment is precautionary," she whispered. "It's only because we have no idea what we'll find in there." Celia shared the lift with a woman carrying an enormous med-kit. Outside, on firm ground, she found it hard to stand because her knees were shaking so badly. The Milky Way stretched overhead; perhaps because she had become so acutely aware of the Marq'ssan's presence among them, she felt as if the stars out there were watching, waiting, judging, not a blind and indifferent backdrop to life or pretty objects to enjoy in life's occasional pauses.

After the medical team and observers finished disembarking, they all set off for Cell Block C. It looked very different outside than it had on screen. The ground was rough, strewn with rocks and desert scrub. Since the moon had not yet come up, they had to use flashlights to light a way for their feet. "Once the entire prison has been liberated, we'll illuminate this area so that it will be easier to walk," Flahn called over her shoulder. After passing through the ashy rubble left from the destructuring of the outer wall, they walked perhaps one hundred yards before reaching the physical plant. One of the observers played her flashlight around the area to locate the structure the Marq'ssan had put around the personnel they had taken from it. What could those people possibly be thinking? Celia shivered. "We're almost there," Flahn said. "Just a few more yards." Celia wondered why they hadn't landed the pod closer to the main buildings, inside the walls. If any of the prisoners were unable to walk or had difficulty walking, the distance would be a problem.

Two women from Mott's team met them at the place where Cell Block C's outer wall had been breached. One tapped her com unit and said, "So far everything's going according to plan. We've another pair posted at the main entrance to this section of the prison, and they report that everything continues quiet."

The people carrying portable lights set one just inside the building and continued setting up lighting in the corridors in advance of the med-team. Flahn stood very still with her eyes closed for a moment, then said, "I don't understand it. None of the prisoners have stirred from their cells though all the locks have been opened and the guards removed."

"Maybe they're too frightened," Maureen said. "Maybe they don't know the guards are gone."

They stood silent, listening. Celia realized that except for the noise the people with the lights were making, the night was utterly still. And with the silence, entered dread. Celia's pulse beat violently in her temples and ears.

After perhaps half a minute, Flahn spoke, suggesting that Maureen and the observers walk with her and that the medical people follow, then led the way into the corridor. She stopped at the first closed door they came to. "Celia?" she said, gesturing.

Celia wrestled with the door, one that usually operated electronically that now had to be forced along its track. When she got it open, she stood in the doorway and peered into the cell, lit by the scanty light spilling into its darkness. After a few seconds, she made out a bundle humped in one corner. Celia inched forward. She wished she knew the gender of the person lying there so that she could address him or her as "sir" or "ma'am." "Hello," she said unsteadily. "I'm Celia Espin with the International Human Rights Committee. We're here to offer you and your family asylum or transportation to a location of your choice." Celia waited for a response. Her heart pounded harder and harder as she forced herself closer. Was the prisoner too ill to respond, or perhaps deaf? "Are you all right?" she said, kneeling on the concrete floor beside the prisoner (whose gender she still could not make out). She touched a shoulder, but received no reaction whatsoever. A sudden terror that the prisoner was dead streaked through her, and she looked over her shoulder to the others standing in the doorway. "This person isn't responding at all," she said in a trembly voice. "Maureen?"

After a few seconds, Flahn said, "I've just scanned him, and he's heavily drugged. It will be difficult waking him."

Maureen and one of the doctors came into the cell, took the man by the shoulders, and rolled him onto his back. Still he did not waken. The doctor knelt beside him and measured the man's blood pressure. "He's going to need help getting back to the pod," she said.

"I've just been scanning the other prisoners on this floor," Flahn said, "and all but one are as drugged as he is."

Celia had known from the files Mott had given her that prisoners were being drugged, but she had not expected such a heavy dosage. "There's nothing you can give them to counteract the drug?" Celia asked the doctor.

"Too risky. I think we must simply allow it to wear off." She rose to her feet and moved to the doorway. "Let's get going then with the stretchers," she said. "We've got strenuous work ahead of us."

How bizarre, Celia thought. How absolutely bizarre prisons are.

When the prisoners woke they would find themselves somewhere else with no memory of how they had gotten there. That alone would be disorienting. But if they'd been living in a drugged fog for who knew how long? Would they ever be able to make sense of their lives?

Celia went out of the cell and, for form's sake, went on to the next one with Maureen, the doctor, Flahn, and the observers. With the prisoners in such a condition, evacuating them could take all night, which meant they'd have to do the other prison the next night. They'd be exhausted by the time they'd moved everyone onto the pod.

## [ii]

The night seemed to go on forever. Luis was one of the roughly one-fifth who could be waked into sufficient awareness to walk with assistance. Celia found him in Cell Block D and for a few minutes felt ecstatically happy, although she had to watch him be helped away by med-team people since she was obliged to complete the process they'd determined on. But her burst of joy faded, and she found it cumulatively harder and harder going; her queasy stomach roiled several times into violent spasms of vomiting; the smells in some of the cells were wrenchingly vile, and some of the sights they had seen were revolting. The only people who hadn't been drugged were those recently tortured or in the process of being tortured. They had found eight people in Cell Blocks B, C, and D whose torture had obviously been interrupted by the EMP. The four observers had begun dictating notes on these eight prisoners' conditions into their tape-recorders even as on-site medical care was being administered. Celia had had to wait for the observers before going on and had hated them for making her stay there, had hated them for making a catalogue of the injuries they could immediately see. "There will be medical examinations and doctors' reports that will be made available to you," Celia said the first time this had happened. But the observers insisted on making detailed notes of what they themselves could see with their own eyes, though they did not make notes about the other prisoners. Celia wondered whether they would ask to talk with the others when the drugs had worn off, or whether only those in the most extreme condition were of interest to them.

When they had finally boarded all the prisoners from Cell Blocks B, C, and D, and when the media crew had finished shooting in Cell Block C, only Cell Block A, which contained non-political prisoners, remained. And here the observers balked. Celia had already agreed—reluctantly, without a sense of real choice—to do the same for these prisoners as for the politicals. The other observers jointly made a statement protesting this violation of law and returned with Flahn and the remainder of the medical team to the ship. Celia swallowed her distaste and went through her routine, this time to six persons per cell, each of them drugged—though more lightly than any of the politicals—and as she moved from cell to cell began to think that the observers should have stayed with them, since the conditions in which these prisoners were being kept could not by any stretch of the imagination be called humane. The filth, the stench, the crowding, the dazed state of the prisoners—who were easily led without fuss to the pod, as though zombies without a will of their own—sickened her almost as much as conditions in the other Cell Blocks had. Exhausted emotionally and physically, Celia hovered on the edge of hysteria and in each cell rushed through the formula as quickly as she could, never looking at the faces of the people staring bemusedly at her and the others.

It was almost dawn when everyone had been boarded onto the pod—or, rather, what Sorben now called the "quadri-pod." Everyone moved wearily, quietly, heavily. Even the Marq'ssan moved slowly.

Lying flat on her flight couch, Celia sleepily watched the screen and saw done what the Marq'ssan had said they would do: one by one the lines designating the prison buildings disappeared until all that remained were the enclosures surrounding dozens of red stick-figures. "Do you see, Luis?" Celia whispered to her uncle. She turned her head to look at him and saw he was sleeping. Celia looked back at the screen; two of the enclosures' walls had been breached and red stick-figures had begun moving out. Wild joy surged through her as she imagined how in the bare dawn light the ODS people remaining would see nothing but miles and miles of uninhabited desert—and one another.

When all the red stick-figures had been freed, the amber light went on and the pod lifted. Celia glanced once more around the cabin. Almost all the other humans had arranged their couches in the flat position and were lying silent, their eyes closed. Celia found the silence strange—though vastly different from that they had encountered in the cell blocks. Luis was safe, Emily was safe, and all these prisoners were safe. The world felt different, as though something momentous had happened, as though some great change had been set into motion. For the first time in more than a year, Celia felt hopeful.

[iii]

The quadri-pod landed first at the Whidbey clinic-retreat to drop off the eight prisoners in the worst shape, then went on to Seattle, where they landed on the roof of the big stadium parking garage less than a mile from the hotel they had rented. For the first two or three days the remainder of the freed prisoners were to be housed in a large downtown hotel the Co-op had rented for the purpose.

Celia sat beside Luis for the short shuttle ride to the hotel. She noticed he was looking slightly more alert and was pleased when he whispered, "Where are we, Celia?"

She took his hand between both of hers. "In Seattle, Luis. There's nothing to worry about, you're safe now."

"Seattle," he repeated, as though unable to make sense of the word.

"We're going to a hotel," Celia said, repeating what Maureen had already said to the group at large. "Once you've rested you'll be able to decide what you want to do next. But there's no hurry, Luis." Celia hadn't thought at all about what Luis might want to do—she hadn't dared to believe this would actually be happening. Now, half-asleep herself, she wondered. As a doctor he would be more than welcome almost anywhere. But a worm of fear worked its way into her gut as she faced the likelihood that Luis would insist on going back to San Diego to work underground. She would try to keep him from doing that, for surely *they*—desiring vengeance—would be hunting all those who had been released.

The bus parked in front of the hotel, and the passengers—a mixture of rescuers and rescued—filed out. Celia greeted the fresh team awaiting them, with great relief. "Why don't you go on up to the fifth floor, Celia, where we're putting all the rescue workers?" Ida said to Celia. "You look utterly done in."

"I want to see my uncle settled first," Celia said. She turned to Luis. "Luis, this is Ida Grayson. Ida, this is Luis Salgado, my uncle. He was in the El Cajon prison."

Ida, who had been smiling rather automatically at Luis, gasped; her gaze darted back to Celia's face. "Your uncle! Oh, Celia! Did you have any idea?"

Celia mustered a smile. "I hoped, Ida, I hoped." She noticed that Luis had barely taken in the introduction and that as they lingered here in the lobby he was tugging the blanket he'd been given more tightly around himself.

"We're putting men on the first three floors and women on the fourth," Ida said. "We're not bothering with making room assignments or anything like that—the idea being to hold up on the red tape until people are better able to cope with it."

"Which is where I'll come in," Celia said dryly. She and Luis joined the group of people clustered near the elevators. As they waited, she put her arm around him and said, "Soon, Luis. You can go to bed soon." A real bed, she thought, for the first time in more than a year. Perhaps he wouldn't even want to lie on a bed. Tears came into her eyes as she tried to imagine how Luis must be feeling now and how he would feel later, when he woke up free of the drug. Beneath her hand his trembling shoulder felt so frail, she worried that she might hurt him by holding him too hard.

When an elevator arrived, the crowd surged forward. Celia hesitated, then heard another elevator bell ring. "Over there, Luis," she said. "It'll be less crowded."

"I'm tired, Celia," he said as she guided him into the second car. She couldn't remember ever having heard her uncle complain about his own physical state before.

"I know, Luis. I know," Celia soothed. "We're almost there." The doors opened onto the third floor, and everyone poured out. It occurred to Celia that it might be best for Luis not to be by himself, since when he woke later he might not remember or understand anything that had happened, and so she arranged for him to share a double room with another man. Maureen had said there would be med people stationed on each floor making rounds every hour. Given the drugged state of those they'd rescued, that now seemed inadequate.

Luis crawled under the covers without bothering to remove his plastic prison coverall. After Celia smoothed the covers over him, she kissed Luis's forehead—and saw that he had already fallen asleep.

Staring down at him, she felt happy imagining her mother's joy. Her pleasure faded as another picture came into her head, a picture of herself telling her mother of Luis' decision to return to San Diego.

She found the fire stairs and climbed to the fifth floor. Women were standing about in the corridor in small groups, talking; Celia supposed they were too stimulated to settle down to sleep. She herself longed to bed down, for she was beyond excitement. But she knew that before sleeping she needed to find Emily first.

"Have you seen Emily Madden?" Celia asked each group of women she came to. A woman Celia recognized as one of Mott's group said she'd just seen her in a room at the end of the corridor. Her vision blurring, her limbs trembling, Celia stumbled on. She peered into each open doorway that she passed and wondered if Emily were already in bed behind one of the closed doors hung with **DO NOT DISTURB** signs. But two doors from the end she found her—locked in a hug with someone who looked from the back like Lisa Mott. Celia sagged against the doorframe, unsure whether to go or stay.

Emily saw her. "Celia," she said. Mott turned, and Celia saw she had been crying.

Celia inched backwards, out into the corridor. "I'll come back later," she said.

"No, Cee, wait." Emily took a step toward her, then stopped.

Lisa Mott put her hands to her face, went into the bathroom, and closed the door.

"How is your uncle?"

"I've just got him to bed now," Celia said.

"You look wiped. Why don't you lie down, at least for a while, and try to sleep? I know you have a lot to do, but surely it can wait?"

Celia hugged herself and fought back the giggle that suddenly shook her chest. "In here? But what about her?" Celia jerked her head toward the bathroom door.

Emily's eyes stared into Celia's, and Celia wondered what it was that Emily was not saying. "Lisa will be leaving. Someone will be downstairs to pick her up fairly soon." Emily started again toward her. "Please don't go on her account, Cee."

Emily crossed the room. "All right. Not if she's going to be leaving." The words fairly caught in her throat. What did it matter? Lisa

Mott had not led them into a trap. Whatever her motives had been she had worked as hard as any of them to free the prisoners.

"Come in then." Emily laid a gentle hand on Celia's shoulder.

Without realizing she was going to do it, Celia threw her arms around Emily. And then great choking sobs were tearing out of her, and her body convulsed with unspeakable sadness. After a while she grew aware of Emily's hand rhythmically stroking her back and of Emily's voice murmuring, "So awful for you especially, Cee. And now you're just terribly terribly tired."

Celia pulled away and used her sleeve to wipe her eyes and nose. "I haven't been sleeping well because I was so worried. Couldn't sleep the last two nights at all... Yeah, I'm just tired, that's all. That must be why I feel so..."

"Can you sleep now, Cee?"

"A shower first." From the moment she had first set foot in that prison she had felt almost constantly in need of a shower; the feel of the place, the smells, the filth had crawled over her as they always did in such spaces.

"It's only a chemical shower," Emily said.

"I don't care." Celia moved to one of the beds and lay down on top of the bedcover. "At least I'll be clean." Unlike Emily, Celia did not enjoy the luxury of daily water showers—except when staying with Emily, of course. A chemical shower was no big deal. She closed her eyes, but her mind filled with a vision of layers of scum covering the surface of her body, excepting her face, where hot salty tears had dried and stretched the skin over her nose and cheeks.

Mott stayed in the bathroom a long time. As Celia waited for the shower, she recalled the promise Emily had extracted from her, that she never tell a soul about Emily's sexual involvement with Dash, Martha Greenglass's new Trade Facilitation apprentice. When Celia had asked her why it mattered, if it was because she was ashamed of having been to bed with a service-tech, Emily had said "It's hard to explain, Celia. But the fact is, I would be ostracized by all executives—because Dash is male." Celia had at first been incredulous, but when she saw that Emily was serious, she decided that it must be true. Talk about screwed up! No wonder she and Emily had such a hard time communicating. The worlds they each inhabited were so incommensurable it was a miracle they had as much of a relationship as they did. She still hadn't really been able to process that new piece of information. And of course she couldn't talk about it with her mother...

Urgent with the need to cleanse her body, Celia was still awake when Mott emerged from the bathroom and stood in the doorway, hesitating. Emily went to her, and they stood there for a while, whispering. And then Lisa moved the few steps to the foot of Celia's bed and stood there, her eyes shifting between Emily and Celia. "Hello, Celia. Emily tells me you did find your uncle last night."

Slowly Celia sat up. "How letting all those people go must gall you," she said to the executive.

Mott shook her head. "You're wrong. I've always thought that was a horrible place. Whatever you might think, I don't like such places. But sometimes it seems that they're necessary."

"Necessary to lock up doctors who are good and decent human beings?"

Mott shrugged. "I don't know," she said dully. "I don't know anything any more."

"You're saying that none of it is your fault?" Celia said.

Mott stared at her. "Just what the fuck do you want of me?"

Celia heaved herself to her feet and went into the bathroom. She discovered that though the shower and toilet were chemical, there was unscented wash water available from the sink's faucet. While the sink filled with hot water, Celia stripped off her clothes and took a washcloth and towel from the wall rack. For fifteen minutes she scrubbed herself. When she went out into the darkened bedroom, Mott was gone and Emily was tucked up in the other bed, already asleep.

Celia slipped under the sheets and closed her eyes. The sleep she craved and had thought inevitable eluded her for more than an hour. Finally, though, exhaustion triumphed, and the night's images removed their grip from her consciousness.

Letting go, Celia dropped into heavy, dream-laden sleep.

## [iv]

Celia nibbled on a buttered slice of crunchy, tasty pumpernickel toast as she filled Luis in on the liberation. "So that's the story as I know it," she said in conclusion. "The word is we'll be going back tomorrow night to liberate the San Bernardino prison. Though I wonder if it won't be guarded to the teeth now, if they won't be expecting us."

Luis snorted. "El Cajon was guarded to the teeth." His eyes gleamed.

Celia couldn't remember the last time food tasted as good as it did this morning. "I can't believe you're here, that you're safe," she whispered. She stretched her hand across the table, palm up. "I was so scared, I didn't know what we'd find."

Luis fingered his newly shaven jaw. "They never actually laid a violent finger on me. And for a long time they didn't drug me, either. Although when I was first brought in, they deprived me of sleep and kept me dangerously short of water."

Celia bit her lip. "It must be because Emily persuaded Mott to give special orders about you." She frowned. "I always wondered what Mott was up to with you. Ever since that Weatherall woman interrogated you I've known that *something* must be going on."

"You think they're serious about transporting people's families to the place of their choice?"

"More coffee?" Celia asked, lifting the thermoflask.

Luis covered his cup with his hand. "Thanks, honey, no. I'm not used to caffeine."

Celia refilled her own cup. "Yes, I believe they are serious, Luis. Speaking of which, as soon as we finish eating, I'll be helping interview the other people we busted out last night. We need to know about human rights violations, about where the freed prisoners will want to live, and so on."

"And if they won't say?"

"You don't think they'll trust us?"

Luis shrugged. "I don't know. If I didn't know you so well myself, I don't know *what* I'd be thinking right now. After who knows how long in a drugged fog, after months of solitary, of having to be careful and paranoid just to survive? Most of us were asleep last night and won't have the faintest glimmer—as I do—of what happened. Can you imagine it, Celia?"

"Yes, Luis. I *can* imagine it." Celia took another swallow of coffee, then put her hand over his. "Will you make the rounds with me?"

She watched his careful, old-seeming eyes. "I need a doctor with me. And I think it would be better if it were you. You would understand so much more than a doctor without your experience." At the visible tightening of certain muscles in his face, Celia hurried on. "But if it would be too much for you, don't even consider it. It's bound to be stressful."

Luis turned his hand over to clasp hers. Calmly, he said, "I'm glad you asked me. I've done nothing for months. I've felt useless, my mind dulled and hazy from their drugs, managing on the best days to at most read over and over the books you brought me, eternally pacing up and down that cramped filthy hole trying to figure out the meaning of their questions, the meaning of their allowing me visits from an attorney and from you and Elena, trying to make sense of so little information." He paused to drink water. "The man who slept in the bed beside me last night has several fractures, you know. He needs attention."

Celia looked down at the remaining food on her plate. "The medical people will take care of all those things. It's more important for you to help me with what I have to do."

Luis took his hand from hers and sipped some water. "You will know best," he said.

Celia looked at him in surprise: never had she gotten such a vote of confidence from him before, except where legal matters were concerned. "And do you have any idea what you yourself will want to do?" Celia asked to cover her confusion.

"I'll have to think about that. I don't know yet what will be most useful."

"Then you aren't set on going back and living underground." Some of the tension in Celia's neck and shoulders eased.

"I will have to think about it," Luis said, apparently refusing to rule out the possibility.

*No!* A streak of fear lanced her stomach with a brief flash of pain, but Celia managed to keep calm.

He said, as though aware of her reaction, "I have a lot of new information to assimilate. And since I know very well that the drugs are still working their way out of my system, it's best that I wait to make such an important decision."

Celia offered him a small, wobbly smile. "I can hardly wait to tell Mama you're safe."

The corners of Luis' mouth lifted slightly. "They've left Elena alone?"

Celia shrugged. "She had some trouble over not writing a report for an emergency room case that someone leaked to ODS. But they only held her a week that time." Celia let her eyes travel across the room from table to table until they reached the windows at the far end. "I don't know if Emily worked something out with Mott that time or not. Emily never said. And I didn't ask her."

"It's a crazy world, Celia." Luis' voice seemed to come from a great distance. Celia returned her gaze to his face and saw that he had grown almost as remote as he had been when they had begun break-fast. She fiddled with her fork and tried to think of something to say. After about a minute he looked directly at her. "I don't understand what they're doing, destroying prisons." He blinked. "I'm wondering, too, about this organization you say you are working for now. Not lo-cal, you say. Tell me more about it, Celia. Who is directing it. Who is paying for all this." He waved his hand—to indicate, Celia thought, the hotel. "Executives like your friend Emily Madden? They're pay-ing for it?"

Celia swallowed. "No, Luis. Not executives, although there are some involved. But the people who run the Free Zone. And the aliens."

"Ah," Luis said. "The people who run the Free Zone. It is a way, then, for them to get at the government."

"They seem to care very much about human rights, Luis." How strange, defending the very people she distrusted herself. Yet thinking of Maureen and Susan and many of the others involved, she realized she believed in their sincerity.

"Perhaps. But we must be careful not to let ourselves be exploited by political groups."

"Of course," Celia said mechanically. "Still, they may manage to stir the public conscience. That is my hope. Since only in that way will the government's vicious methods of repression be stopped."

"But to be connected with anarchists and aliens?"

Celia fingered the handle of her coffee cup. "We thought they were going to stop after the war, remember? And they didn't. Well we

can't go on just waiting for something to happen. This is the first unified push we've been able to make. After what we did last night..."
She smiled earnestly at Luis. "Don't you see? For the first time we have something to hope for."

Luis did not smile. "Have you any idea how enraged—and possibly frightened—they will be?"

"Things can't get any worse than they already are."

Luis raised an eyebrow. "Oh no? They can start killing people rather than harassing or torturing or drugging them, Celia. If, that is, they think that live survivors are more trouble than dead bodies."

Celia pushed her plate to the side. "Are you finished eating? Because I think we should be getting started with our interviews now."

"You think I'm raining on your parade," Luis said as he pushed back his chair and rose to his feet.

Celia stood too. "Not at all," she said. "I know you find it hard to believe. So do I. But you must admit that what happened last night was...different. Was on another scale from anything we could ever have imagined."

"What do you think you're going to do, Celia? Destroy the many thousands of prisons that exist all over the world? What will you do then with the people who make those prisons work?"

"I don't know." Celia took his arm and walked with him to the door. "I just don't know. There must be something."

Luis snorted, but said nothing. What after all was there to say? There was only the work to do, to go on doing, the work that left no time for questions that were, at base, unanswerable.

# Chapter Sixteen

## [i]

At breakfast that morning, Anne asked Hazel if she'd be interested in going for a walk with her that afternoon. Since Anne almost never said anything beyond a mumbled *Good morning* before 10:30 or 11, Hazel figured Anne must have some pretty particular conversation in mind. And so after lunch the two of them crossed the back lawn and entered the woods that extended for several acres behind the house by way of the path that ran along the creek bordering the property. For several minutes they walked without speaking through alternating patches of sunlight and shade as the path, rising, meandered away from the creek. The air smelled earthy and fresh and felt pleasantly humid in the mildness of the day. When Hazel spotted a patch of violets, she exclaimed with delight and crouched to get a closer look. "I've never seen violets in a wood before," she said. She glanced over her shoulder at Anne. "Have you?"

Anne shook her head. "Only in a movie. And of course read about them in books." She knelt beside Hazel and sniffed several times. "Can you smell them? Aren't they supposed to have a scent?"

Hazel brushed her fingertips over a few of the flowers, then grasped one of them by its thin green stem and pulled. She held the small bloom first to her own nose, and then to Anne's. Anne sniffed. "Subtle. Not exactly what I expected."

Hazel made a "hmm" sound in her throat and smiled at Anne. Anne smiled back, and they stood up and continued walking. After a minute or so, Hazel glanced sidelong at Anne and found her scowling fiercely at the ground. Hazel's sense that Anne wanted to talk about something was confirmed. "Anything special on your mind?" she said.

Anne shot Hazel a quick look, then stared again at the ground. "I know something is going on, Hazel. And since you're usually in on what *they're* up to..." Anne looked again at Hazel. "Or is it too secret for me to know about?"

"Allison hasn't told you anything?" Hazel asked, a little surprised.

Anne shook her head. "I don't like to ask Lise questions. And she's been, well... strange, the last couple of days."

Oh yes, Hazel thought, and Mott's been stranger still. Why *hadn't* Allison told Anne about Mott's mission? It wasn't as though the rest of the world wasn't going to know anyway. "It's a long story," Hazel said, "but basically it's this: last night Lisa Mott went on a mission with four of the aliens and a lot of people from the Free Zone to remove prisoners from a detention facility in California, which the aliens then destroyed. Actually, they were supposed to do this to two prisons, but they didn't have enough time because almost all the prisoners were too drugged to walk."

Anne's plucked black eyebrows knit together. "But that sounds crazy! Why would Mott help do a thing like that?"

Hazel sighed. "It's a long story, as I said. But Liz asked her to do it. As a proof of her loyalty."

"But couldn't she have thought of something besides letting criminals loose?"

"Remember those things we've been seeing on vid, produced by the Free Zone?"

Anne swallowed. "You mean all that stuff about abusive cops and prison guards?"

"Yes," Hazel said. "All that. Well the Free Zoners have been wanting to do something about human rights violations. So they used information provided by Mott to produce those vid shows. The men they exposed were responsible for prisoners in the place that was destroyed last night."

Anne stopped and put her hand on Hazel's arm. "You're saying *Lisa Mott* had something to do with those vid shows?"

"She gave them the documents that made the exposés possible."

Anne drew a ragged breath. "So she is in some way connected with all this."

"Sort of," Hazel said cautiously. "Indirectly, I think. I don't know that much about it, Anne."

Though Anne looked off into the middle distance, she continued to hold Hazel's arm, and the two of them stood quietly, without speaking, for what felt to Hazel like a long time. Hazel looked at the ferns glittering in a patch of sunlight a few yards away and listened to the woods. She had been hearing a robin for some time, but now she heard two other birds, one with a mournful two-tone song that repeated over and over and over.

Anne sighed and looked Hazel in the eyes. Her dark, velvety gaze stabbed at Hazel. "Tell me. What has she asked *Lise* to do?"

Hazel was careful to hold Anne's gaze, wanting with all her heart to convey truthfulness. "Nothing that I know of, Anne. Surely Liz trusts Allison. She's known her all her life."

Anne withdrew her hand, and they resumed walking. "I bet there's something," Anne said bitterly. "Maybe it's so awful they're not even telling you. Unless you're lying to me?"

"No," Hazel said vehemently. "I'm not lying to you. I wouldn't do that. Anyway, Liz trusts Allison. I'm sure of it." Or at least she does now, Hazel thought, pushing away the memory of Liz's paranoia when preparing to meet Lisa and Allison at their rendezvous in the mountains.

"I never know what to think about that woman."

After a few seconds, Hazel said, "There's some kind of history between you and Liz, isn't there." She had wondered, and had once asked Liz, but had gotten no reply.

"She doesn't like me, and she doesn't trust me." Anne's voice was hard. "She once did her best to separate me and Lise, but it didn't work, Lise was furious with her for a long time after. She's never forgiven me for that—for Lise's anger, I mean. Of course she didn't like me much from the start. God knows why it mattered so much that Lise had a lover living with her, but it seems it did."

Hazel sighed. "Liz says very little about Allison, but I can tell you this: she always keeps her picture around. She worried a lot about Allison when we went renegade, she worried terribly that Allison might catch a lot of flak."

"Yeah," Anne said, "well she did catch a lot of flak. It's a scary thing, getting interrogated like that. Once a week they had her in for questioning. And they followed her and opened her mail and monitored all her communications. They never *did* anything to her, but they hounded her, Hazel. She was a wreck after only a week of it. Mr. Booth had her in before the Executive once, too. Can you imagine it?"

Hazel shivered. "She must have been glad to go renegade, then."

Anne's mouth tightened. "Oh yes, fairly soon she began to think about doing it. But it wasn't easy for her, you know."

"Nor for you."

Anne kicked an acorn off the path. "I just lost a job, Hazel, and a few friends. I didn't own anything to lose."

"It's better for us here," Hazel said. "If you got outside more, got to the city regularly, you'd see that. There are possibilities for service-techs here that you'll never find anywhere else. I love it here. If I'd known what it was going to be like, I would have come whether Liz came or not."

"All I know is that I'm tired of being cooped up in this one place," Anne said. "I'm not the country type, you know. All my life I've been a city person. I grew up in DC. To be shut up like this..." She wrapped her arms around her body, as though chilled. "It reminds me a little of that weird life we lived in Colorado during the war years."

"You've only been to the city for that one concert," Hazel said sympathetically. "Look, Anne. Why don't you come into Seattle with me some of the times I go in? I'm sure Liz wouldn't mind. As long as you promised to stick with me."

"I'd like that," Anne said wistfully. "It's just that I don't want a hassle with her about it. You know?"

"I'll talk to her myself. You won't even have to mention it to her. How's that?"

"That'd be good," Anne said. "But I'm not counting on it. I know how she is about security. And she doesn't trust me at all."

"Bullshit," Hazel said. "Not liking you isn't the same as not trusting you."

"Huh."

Hazel could see she was interested.

Anne said, "Tell me more—if you can, I mean—about this mission. The more I think about it, the stranger it seems. I mean, Lisa Mott working with the aliens? And what do they think Security will do about it?"

"Good question," Hazel said. "But Liz hasn't discussed it, at least not with me or in my presence. I suppose she's expecting a reaction, but what it is I have no idea."

"Hmmm. Things sure have gotten weird with them."

"I know," Hazel said. "I know."

## [ii]

Returning to the office after her walk with Anne, Hazel realized that getting away from the house for just an hour had cleared her head remarkably. But then she opened the door to Liz's office and found Allison there, and Allison broke off mid-sentence, and she and Liz stared at her without speaking. Hazel said, "Sorry to interrupt" and backed out of the room, closed the door, and sat down at her desk. Allison, she thought, looked troubled. Could Anne have been correct in her suspicions?

Surely not.

Hazel stared at the closed door. Was Liz right to be asking such things of these women? And why was it that she seemed to be in a position to make demands on them at all? It was this last question more than any other that puzzled Hazel. Surely both Allison and Lisa Mott could have gone renegade without Liz's "help." For what did they need her? What was it that she was offering them, what need of theirs was she meeting that she could make such demands on them and constitute herself as their leader?

Liz's recent trip to Toronto and Denver had resulted in arrangements for two more defections. That alone suggested there must be something in particular that Liz had to offer... Liz had said that neither Allison nor Lisa Mott would have gone renegade unless they'd known they'd have her, Liz, to come to. That they would have stuck it out, or somehow exiled themselves, Lisa particularly, since Lisa could have resigned and sunk into obscurity without much trouble and though not fabulously wealthy could have lived without her salary. Yet something had driven her to go renegade, and that something had to do with Liz...

Hazel resumed inputting the report she had been working on before lunch, an analysis of Military Police and Intelligence agencies in the Southern California area that Liz intended to hand over to Maureen Sanders. But after only a few minutes' work, the house phone chirped. Liz, it seemed, wanted her to find Anne. Intrigued, Hazel tracked Anne down by phone and waited impatiently for her arrival. "You've talked to her already?" Anne asked when she came into the outer office.

"No. I haven't talked to her at all. I've no idea what this is about, just that she and Allison were in there when I came back and now want us to join them."

Anne looked worried.

Was this personal or work-related? Or a mixture of the two? Hazel led the way into Liz's office. Liz offered them a friendly face, Allison a neutral one.

"Sit down, girls," Liz said. "Allison and I have been discussing plans for her media organization and would like to run a few ideas past you." She lavished one of her most engaging smiles on Anne. "We're hoping you'll agree to go to work for Allison, Anne. I am of course familiar with your work experience and know how valuable and useful it would be. But Allison has been telling me that she's confident you could handle much more responsibility than you were given working for Alice Warner."

Anne looked from Liz to Allison and gave the latter a questioning look. Allison smiled with visible constraint. "You know you had gotten bored with your job," she said.

Anne looked at Liz. "What is it you have in mind?" she said quietly.

"It's rather complicated," Liz said. She leaned back in her chair and gestured expansively. "Let me start with a bare outline and fill in the details afterwards. Basically what Allison wants to do is to set up some media outlets. Vid, radio, and print publications. To do this she needs people with technical expertise, people with journalistic skills, people with presentational skills, actors, and so on. In addition to administrative staff, of course. Naturally we'd want most of those to be local. And we'd want the focus of the outlets to be chiefly local and the outlets to be self-directed. Overseen from the top, yes, but not micromanaged. One of the first tasks for setting up such an organization, then, becomes one of recruiting competent, creative, responsible staff. We think you could help us with this." Liz leaned forward in her chair. "Allison has persuasively argued that you deserve a change, that you've been wasted as a secretary. You don't have to decide right away, but we think you might like to attend classes at the University. Perhaps one or two to start with—they're very flexible here since they've thrown the University open to anyone qualified to attend—if you didn't want to immerse yourself full-time all at once."

Anne looked bewildered. "College?" she said blankly. "I don't understand. How does that fit in with this job you're talking about?"

Liz flashed a look of surprise at Allison. "You're right, this girl is really on the ball, Allison." She looked back at Anne. "Partly to help train you in the kind of skills you would find useful working in Allison's organization, and partly as means of making contact with local people. Especially if you're taking classes in communications or whatever. Do you see it, Anne?"

"I've never thought of college," Anne said slowly. "I'm a little old to be trying it, don't you think?"

"Nonsense," Liz said. "Hazel's been thinking about it for herself, haven't you, darling?"

Anne looked at Hazel. "Yes," Hazel said, uncomfortable to have a privately-expressed matter being used as a lever of persuasion. "I've been attracted to the idea of taking some courses. Nothing useful, though." She smiled ruefully. "I'm interested in things like literature and history. Because of all my reading, I guess. And maybe psychology. None of which would be useful."

Allison snorted. "Not useful? I took my Masters in History, you know. Precisely for its utility."

"Wouldn't it be easier putting ads in newspapers and using employment agencies?" Anne asked.

"We will be doing that, too," Allison said. "But if you're going to be a part of the organization, well, it would be good for you to be recruiting people personally. Probably better than the other way." She shrugged. "It's hard to explain, Anne. Mainly it's because of the risk involved in hiring people in that other, very impersonal way."

Hazel looked from face to face. What the fuck were they *talking* about?

Liz shifted her attention to Hazel. "What do you think, darling? Would Anne be good at recruiting and helping with the administrative work?"

"Anne's very competent," Hazel said with some discomfort. "But only she can say whether that kind of thing would appeal to her."

"Of course, darling," Liz said warmly. She looked back at Anne. "We wouldn't want to pressure you into something you'd hate doing, Anne. It's just that I had the impression you were restless not working and that you were ready for a challenge, for something new."

"I'm extremely interested in working again," Anne said. "But this is all so different, so sudden..." She bit her lip. "Could I have some time to think about it, Ms. Weatherall?"

"Please, Anne, don't be so formal. Call me Liz. And of course you can have time to think about it." Liz glanced at Hazel. "Hazel's bookmarked the online course catalog for the summer term. Maybe you'd like to scroll through it, see if anything especially interests you. There's plenty of time before you'd have to decide about attending classes, so there's no rush."

"Thank you for thinking of me for this job," Anne said awkwardly. "I appreciate your confidence in me."

Liz bestowed another of her top-flight smiles. "But I want this move to be good for *all* of us, Anne. Change, however challenging, should always be for the positive." Anne smiled fixedly but said nothing. She sat poised on the edge of her seat; her body language plainly broadcast a desire to flee. "I won't keep you any longer, since I know you'll want some time to think about this. You must talk with Allison about it, and Hazel, too. But in any case, whatever you decide will be fine with me, dear."

Anne stood up to go, and to Hazel's surprise, Allison joined her. "I'll talk to you later, Elizabeth," she said and followed Anne out.

Liz gave Hazel a Look. "You could have been a little more enthusiastic, darling. A girl like that needs encouragement."

"But as you said, it's her decision." Hazel warily watched Liz's face.

"We need people we can trust in positions of responsibility."

Hazel crossed her arms over her chest. "Anne just told me a while ago that you don't trust her."

"Nonsense. If I didn't trust her, she wouldn't be here."

"Then why haven't you let her get out more? She's going crazy being cooped up here all the time."

"But I've just suggested that she do something that would have her out of the house every day, darling. How can you complain about that?" Liz got up and went to the little refrigerator. "Would you like some juice?" She got out the two-quart pitcher of grapefruit juice Ginger had squeezed for her that morning and Hazel had placed in the refrigerator right after breakfast as she always did.

"No thanks," Hazel said. Grapefruit juice made her stomach burn and her teeth feel weird. "I'll have some water, though."

Liz poured out a glass of juice and returned the pitcher to the refrigerator, then handed Hazel a half-liter bottle of water and a glass. "Allison thinks the change will be good for Anne," Liz said. "Of course I have reservations about Anne's abilities—she's basically untried in administrative work. But we could entrust her with a little at a time and see how she handles it. Allison's very keen on the idea of Anne working for her, you know. And she's concerned that Anne find a place for herself in this new situation. After all, you've become an integral part of our work here, darling. And Ginger is in her heaven, running this household and taking care of so many people at once. But Anne..." Liz sipped the juice. "I don't know. We must find something for her. We can't have her getting restless and disaffected on us."

"You could put her to work doing what she already knows she can do," Hazel said. "Working for Allison. Surely Allison will need a secretary?"

"She needs an administrative assistant a far sight more than she needs a secretary," Liz said. Her eyes and mouth were thoughtful. "But I suppose you're right. There will be more executives arriving, after all." Liz frowned. "But as for the recruiting... To be frank, darling, we'd rather not have executives handling that aspect. In the Free Zone there's a certain—" Liz smiled at Hazel and gestured. "You do see what I mean?"

"I'm not sure I do," Hazel said—sure, actually, that she didn't. "I only see that you want Anne to do this recruiting for you."

Liz sighed. "Never mind, darling. Just do me a favor and encourage Anne to take the chance. It's to her benefit to do so."

"You said there will be more executives arriving." Hazel sipped some water. "That's firm?"

"Fairly firm." Liz radiated the satisfaction of a cat cleaning the cream off her whiskers. "Unless last night's strike scares them off... Which I seriously doubt. I think, rather, it will impress them. The Executive losing control and all that. While I..." She shrugged with an obviously feigned casualness. "But let's not gloat." And she smiled.

"Lisa looked upset when she came in this morning."

"It was the *coup de grâce* for her, darling. There's no way in hell she can go back now, and she knows it."

Hazel shivered. "Sometimes you're damned cold-blooded, Liz."

Liz's eyes chilled. "We have to survive, Hazel. You and I have a lot at stake. We can't afford to take chances."

Hazel swallowed. "Considering the content of some of the files we gave to the Co-op people, I suppose we can say that last night at least served some positive purpose. What do you think about that, Liz?"

Liz's face closed down. "I don't think about it at all, Hazel. And I don't want to think about it. Thinking about such things can only make you crazy." An edge came into Liz's voice. "As far as the men being pilloried on vid go, they're slightly crazy animals fighting a war. A war against yet another kind of craziness. I've been saying for some time now that our policies have not helped the situation. I've never agreed with Sedgewick's methods. But for the most part, those have been the only methods available to us. I'd like to make changes, Hazel. Obviously an indiscriminate emptying of prisons isn't the way to go about producing public order. We need to work out some kind of understanding with the aliens so that we can resume our com-sat capabilities. We need to come to terms with the situation in the worst of the cities. I think there are ways other than Sedgewick's. But as the Executive is now, it's not possible even to think of these reasonable objectives. Therefore..."

"Therefore you want to destroy the Executive?" Hazel asked incredulously.

"Yes," Liz said. "That's exactly what I want to do."

Hazel gulped another mouthful of water. "And then? After you've destroyed them?" But how could any single individual or group think they could destroy the Executive?

"After we've destroyed them we'll set up a new Executive. One that will include women. An Executive that is not blind; an Executive interested in more than merely preserving its own power."

Liz's cold blue eyes held Hazel's gaze through a long moment of silence. "You really think you can do this?" Hazel finally asked. So this is what Allison and Lisa Mott saw in Liz? This is what they believed in? This is what they looked to her for? Hazel said, "All this time you've been talking about wanting to pull Booth and Security down, it never occurred to me you were thinking about actually trying to destroy the Executive. I thought you were only interested in personal revenge. As for why you were getting others to defect..." Hazel bit her lip. "I guess I never thought very clearly about that. But this! How did you ever come to think you could *do* such a thing, Liz? Or that you even *wanted* to do it?"

"I know how it all works," Liz said. "I know I can do it."

"With the aliens' help," Hazel said. "You needed them to do what they did last night, isn't that right?"

"If we have overlapping interests, there's no reason not to exploit them, Hazel. That's how power works." Liz set her empty glass down and laced her long, strong fingers together and clasped them over her knee.

"Your ambition," Hazel said, trying to take in the enormity of it, trying to connect this plan with Liz herself. "I never dreamed it was so big."

Liz's golden head inclined.

"Allison and Lisa—they knew from the start what you had in mind?"

"Since their arrival in the Free Zone."

Hazel drew a deep breath. "Then you were hiding things from me," she said in a rush. "That first afternoon and evening when all of you were talking together. Emily Madden—is she in on this, too? And Margot Ganshoff?"

"They know, if that's what you mean," Liz said, frowning. "Don't tell me this upsets you, Hazel? I would have thought you'd approve of my reforming the executive system."

"I don't know," Hazel said, her voice a low mumble. "I'm still in a state of shock."

"*Shock?*" Frowning, Liz shook her head. "But surely you had *some* idea of what I've been thinking, darling!"

"Why bother with the media organization and all that if you're just going to be leaving the Free Zone?"

"The Free Zone is our base," Liz said in a tone of patience. "We can't expect to be walking back into the system in a few weeks, you know. This project will take time."

*Project?* Liz called the overturning of the Executive a *project?* The whole thing sounded crazy. "It's very dangerous," Hazel said.

Liz looked unconcerned. "I assure you, darling, that we couldn't possibly get ourselves into more danger than we are already in. There's no question there was a price on my head before last night."

"You think they'll know you were behind the destruction of that prison?" Hazel asked, incredulous.

A big, shit-eating grin spread across Liz's face. "Perhaps, perhaps not. Depends on who's left at Security."

Liz seemed so sure of herself, so confident. Given the things Anne had said about her, Hazel supposed it made a kind of sense for her to think on such a grand scale. But it was scary, associating that kind of thinking with the woman she so often felt close to. And scary, wondering what else Liz wasn't telling her. Hazel sighed and stood up to go back to her desk. She needed time to think, time away by herself, more than she could get taking a stroll in the woods. Maybe she would take tomorrow morning off and go into the city.

# Chapter Seventeen

These Marq'ssan, all six of them, resemble none that Astrea has ever met. They are stiff, they hold their fields always in tight human form, and except for Leleynl l Absq san Phrglu, they stand clumped together even before anyone has spoken anything other than greetings.

Leleynl l Absq—a very old one—speaks first: "Is everything well on Marqeuei?"

It is Senhlis l Fenst san Bol, of course, who replies. "Everything is much the same. All that is new is that the First Council is anxious for news of how things go here. And the Greater Assembly is debating a quarantine of the humans to prevent their wreaking destruction on the rest of the universe."

Sorben l Sorben san Priusq exchanges humanish eye-messages with the other five. And then that one speaks: "What sort of quarantine?"

Again, it is Senhlis l Fenst who replies: "Many think that a permanent barrier should be constructed around Earth, a barrier which would draw its energy from Earth's star. We all know that it is doubtful whether the humans would ever be able to develop the technology much less accumulate the energy necessary for dissipating such a barrier. It would cost us heavily, of course—for it would require a great deal of our own energy to put in place. We'd have to bring several starships full of Marq'ssan here to do it. But if we did, we would never have to worry about the humans' destructiveness again."

Magyyt l Fenst san Bol, her field almost sizzling with anger, glares at her crèche-mate. "And you would trap us here forever, without recourse of leaving?"

And Senhlis l Fenst retorts: "That would be your decision, Magyyt, if you chose to stay in the face of such a Marq'ssan decision."

"Are you saying this has all been decided?" Pendrine l Alyyt san Anz speaks to Magyyt in Immeni. "Didn't you listen to what Senhlis just said? There has been discussion only. Nothing has been decided.

Many of us wanted first to see how things have been going with the humans."

Magyyt's field expands slightly. "The six Free Zones have been learning and are doing relatively well, I think. As for the rest of the world... For several years there was global war. It's our opinion that the war has weakened the major structures of government."

Magyyt l Fenst glances around at the other five selves so sharply different from all other Marq'ssan present. "We all of us feel that change is beginning to come: slowly, yes, almost imperceptibly, yet we feel it is in train. It is necessary to be patient. We Marq'ssan did not change overnight. Certainly not in as short a period as the Greater Assembly seems to have given the few of us to work."

Senhlis l Fenst speaks in Boldeni; that one's tone is clipped and arid. "The Greater Assembly has decided nothing for certain. We would all agree that change comes slowly, yes. But recall, please, that we have from the beginning been concerned that an attempt to move another species from destructiveness is fraught with danger to us. We risk our own sanity. We risk losing our own long-time-in-coming en-foldment. If you could perceive your selves—your human-structured selves—as we fresh from Marqeuei perceive you at this moment, you would wonder, too. You position your selves as adversaries to the rest of us. You speak stiffly, as though you seldom talk in non-human lan-guages. You think of your object among humans before you think of anything else: clearly, Magyyt l Fenst, you've lost sight of circulation. And who can wonder, you who have been deprived of sensibilitizing for so long?"

Dghatd l Merr san Fehln replies in Immeni, using a scolding tone, which Astrea perceives as one-upping Senhlis's overbearing tone:

"Senhlis l Fenst: I urge you to listen to your own words! You sound as if you yourself have been living light years from a silm furrow! The pomposity of those who sit on the First Council threatens to emo-tionally deceive us—and perhaps it even deceives The First Council themselves. Since when did preaching accomplish anything other than humiliation or resentment? Before we initialize the judgments the First Council is so eager for the Greater Assembly to take upon itself, it would seem those of us who have come as observers must, indeed, observe."

Dghatd l Merr moves toward the six. "My mind is open, Magyyt l Fenst. Not all of us have decided in advance as Senhlis l Fenst has."

Pendrine l Alyyt moves with Dghatd and says, "I too wish to see for myself."

One after another most of those fresh from Marqeuei join Dghatd and Pendrine. Astrea, too, makes declaration of self's eagerness to see earth, to encounter humans. Finally, alone a-part from the others, Senhlis l Fenst too agrees that it is necessary to see with open eyes and mind. Astrea moves very close to Magyyt l Fenst, so close that their fields nearly touch. And Astrea, feeling strongly that Magyyt l Fenst has the most of all of the six to teach, to show, to share with self, asks, "May I accompany you as you go among humans?"

Magyyt's field expands, overlapping Astrea's, and Astrea tingles and shimmers with the power of the other's field. And as Magyyt's mouth smiles without the stiffness Astrea has experienced when practicing the movement one's self, that one says: "After I've rested, yes. But just now I'm exhausted." The human eyebrows quirk. "I warn you that it will be strenuous, and perhaps risky. We are engaged in large undertakings at this time—as we haven't been for most of the eleven years since the starships left. But we feel the time is right."

Dghatd l Merr asks the question on Astrea's lips. "Undertakings?"

Sorben 1 Sorben speaks bluntly in Boldeni. "We'll explain after we've rested."

Sbina l Sellyyn san Bol says, "You can find the sleeping compartments yourselves. The rest of us will continue our scan while you rest."

The six leave the mediation chamber. Astrea turns to Dghatd l Merr. "Must they always sleep and dream?"

"Regularly. And the more energy they circulate, the more sleep and dreaming they require. You feel it, don't you, the massive strength of their fields."

Astrea wonders about this but decides to ask Magyyt 1 Fenst later rather than pursue this with the others.

The tensions in this group are uncomfortable—and interesting. But then the making of judgments upon others necessarily produces tensions.

Which is as it should be.

# Chapter Eighteen

Entering the room, Hazel went straight to the buffet and helped herself to bread, butter, and Brie and a bowl of sliced peaches, then carried her plate to a place near the head of the table. Because it was breakfast, a meal at which sociability was considered optional in the household, she merely glanced at Mott and Anne, and nodded. Mott nodded back. Anne, of course, staring down into her bowl of cereal, eating mechanically, looking as though she were still half-asleep, did not notice. Though usually first to the table, she seldom woke up enough to hold a conversation until after she'd finished her cereal and drunk at least a cup and a half of coffee. Hazel had once suggested to her that she ask Ginger or Allison to bring her a cup of coffee while she was dressing, but Anne had said no, no, she *preferred* waking up after she'd finished dressing, that starting the day was always so painful that she liked to do it gradually. As for herself, Hazel never for a minute considered refusing the cup of coffee Liz usually brought her, though she occasionally longed to tell Liz to keep her early morning cheer to herself. Lisa usually took coffee in her room and ate breakfast later in the morning with Liz; Hazel couldn't remember ever seeing her at the table before eight. Yet here she was, drinking coffee and juice—though not eating. Maybe she had asked Ginger for an omelet or other custom-prepared dish?

Hazel had worked about halfway through her bread and cheese when Anne looked up from her cereal. "Good morning, Hazel," she said. "Did you sleep well?"

"Tolerably. And you?"

Anne shook her head. "Had insomnia half the night. Feel like I've been run over by a bus."

"Maybe you should have a Jacuzzi before you start the day," Hazel said. "Or better yet, go back to bed. You don't have anything special on, do you?"

Anne grimaced. "That's the problem, isn't it. Kept thinking all night about the job Allison's offering me. After all, I can't go on like this, can I. It's nice reading novels all day every day for a few weeks, but after a while it begins to feel, well, vegetative. And doing chores for Ginger doesn't make me feel like I'm working, either." Anne reached for the thermoflask to refill her cup.

"I'm going into Seattle today," Hazel said. "Why don't you come along?" Something in the way Lisa's gaze darted to Hazel's face and then instantly away made Hazel wish she had waited to ask Anne when they were alone.

"Today? Sounds wonderful." Anne looked wistful. "But will it be all right with Ms. Weatherall if I go?"

"I'll ask her just to be sure, but I can't imagine her objecting. I'll be going after lunch."

Allison came into the room, said a general "Good morning," and went to the buffet for her invariable yogurt and fruit, croissant and butter and jam. They were all, Hazel thought, creatures of habit. "So," Allison said as she seated herself. She looked across the table at Lisa. "I suppose the timetable is the same as before?"

"Exactly the same," Lisa said. "Only this time we know going in that it will take us all night to do it. And we can expect things to be rougher. One must assume that all federal detention centers will be on Full Alert status. Unless, of course, Security is throwing a vast hysterical fit, as Elizabeth would have it." The sardonic look on Lisa's face made it clear that she did not expect any such thing of Security.

"So you actually got to see four aliens," Allison said, pouring coffee into her mug. "What did you think of them? Were they creepy to be around?"

Lisa leaned back in her chair and wrapped her hands around her own mug. "They were incredibly powerful. Imagine, Allison. Before they even landed they had located every last projectile weapon in the place and input the information into their processor—for our use, not theirs: since they apparently don't need to use processors except to communicate information to humans. They also located all the living human bodies and input that information, too. And *then* they imposed a localized EMP and destroyed all the major stores of weapons and ammunition. Only after doing all that did they land. Well of course the place was pitch black, the physical plant shut down, the roof emplacements utterly demolished, all spotlights non-operational..." Lisa drew a ragged breath. "Two of them then took a stroll through the prison—demolishing first an outer wall and then the physical plant after persuading all the personnel inside to come out, after which they constructed—out of thin air, Allison—a physically impenetrable electromagnetic wall around the personnel they'd evicted. And that was only the beginning. We never had to deal with live weapons. It was simply hard physical labor dragging warders from one place to another, nothing difficult to handle. And then later we had to help carry prisoners too drugged to walk to the transport-thing. The freakiest thing for me is that they seemed to be linked with their processor as well as with each other but without any device apparent to the casual observer. That and their ability to do what they call 'scan.'"

"Did they make themselves invisible?" Allison asked. "Of all the things I've heard about them, that's the one that freaks me most."

"I've no idea. The prison was, as I said, in pitch blackness."

"I almost wish I were going tonight myself," Allison said. "It's such a, well, *unique* situation."

"Lise!"

The executives looked at Anne, startled. As though, Hazel thought wryly, they had forgotten they were not alone.

Allison offered Anne a wry smile. "Come on, love. I could *use* some action." She laughed a little, as though at herself. "I'm as sick of hanging around here as you are. And I'm curious as hell about the aliens. I must be one of the only people in this house who hasn't met even one of them."

"I haven't met one yet," Hazel said, wishing that she could.

Lisa looked Allison in the eye. "I'm sure no one would mind if you came along with us tonight."

A flush crept into Allison's cheeks. After a few seconds, she said— defiantly—"Brief me, Lisa. I want to go if I can."

Anne pushed back from the table and carried her dishes through the swing-door into the kitchen. Allison stared at the door left swinging in Anne's wake and sighed. "Damn." Without a word to anyone, she picked up her mug of coffee and followed Anne into the kitchen, leaving her half-eaten breakfast on the table.

Lisa regarded Hazel with raised eyebrows. "Can you blame her?" she said.

"Who?" Hazel asked. "Allison or Anne?"

Lisa snorted. "That's the problem with talking freely," she said. She scowled. "It's all your fault, you know. Ordinarily Anne wouldn't know shit about Allison's work. Same for Ginger about mine. What's the point of all this carrying on?" When Hazel did not reply, Lisa said, "Would you be kicking up this kind of fuss if Elizabeth chose to get into some action?"

"There would be no point, would there," Hazel said. "I know what Liz is. As it is, she goes on her damned trips into Canada and the States, which given the price on her head is dangerous."

"But you accept her need to do such things."

"I can't lead her life for her, if that's what you mean," Hazel said. "Anymore than she can lead my life for me."

"There you are," Lisa said. "You're different. But Anne and Ginger should never have been told. It upsets them."

Hazel drank the last of the coffee in her mug. "Maybe it upsets them," she said, "but I don't know that that's any reason for whispering behind their backs about things that matter to them. I'd hate not knowing when Liz was risking her neck. I'm pretty sure I'd be angry with her if she withheld such information purely on the grounds that it might upset me." Hazel stacked the dishes she had used.

"But you're different," Lisa said.

Hazel met her gaze. "The longer lovers live together, the greater hand they have in shaping one another. That's my theory of mutual influence. Only in some cases, the influence is less mutual than in others." Hazel, rising to her feet, saw that Lisa looked puzzled. Before Lisa could ask her to explain, she picked up her dishes and went out into the kitchen herself. Anne and Allison, she was relieved to see, had already gone. The household, she thought, was getting to be incredibly involved emotionally. Could they afford to absorb more renegades? It was a question Hazel thought worth pondering. Not that Liz would take such a question seriously, of course. Liz refused to believe such things should be taken into account when making important decisions. Such factors were too irrational to count—according to the executive view of life.

# Chapter Nineteen

Gina leaned forward to look at Celia, who was at the other end of the table. "Won't Luis Salgado be joining us?"

"He's terribly tired," Celia said. "He asked to be excused this time. He said that since he'd already talked with you about specifically medical issues, I could cover on his behalf just about anything else that might come up."

Maureen gnawed at her lip and looked worried. "Maybe we should postpone," she said. "Given the special difficulties we seem to be up against, his particular input seems very important."

"I agree," Susan said.

Gina opened a bottle of water. "Look. We need to discuss these things before we go through the whole process again tonight. Because let's face it, friends. We have a significant problem on our hands and one that we need to find some practical mitigation for. Repeating the same procedures we used on the first group is simply not acceptable."

"The drugging is a definite problem," Maureen said. "But I don't see what we could possibly do to mitigate much less solve it." She glanced around the table. "Any practical suggestions?"

Glum silence.

Everyone had gotten pretty uncomfortable by the time Susan finally spoke. "Why don't we take Luis himself as an example? Consider: he's not as disoriented or as paranoid as the others. Maybe we should look at the reasons for that and see if we can't produce some of the same factors for the other prisoners we free." Susan paused for response.

"Go on, Sue," Maureen said. "Tell us the reasons you see for Luis' being less disoriented and paranoid than the others."

Susan cleared her throat; and it seemed to Celia that she was oddly nervous about speaking. "First," she said, holding up her hand and folding down the index finger with her other hand, "he's got Celia, someone he loves and trusts, someone whose word he can believe.

Second—" Susan pulled down the middle finger of her hand—"he's able to participate in a very constructive way in the project. He's not left in a passive role. Third—" she continued ticking off each point on her fingers—"the drug didn't affect him as strongly as it did most of the others. Which means he was among those who were hazily aware of what was going on during the evacuation. He was able, for instance, to walk out of the prison on his own two feet. Fourth, as a doctor, he understands some of the psychological effects such drugs have, especially when taken over the long term, and thus is able to get a better grip on himself and the understandable tendency to paranoia. Fifth—she closed her thumb around her folded fingers, making a fist—"because he's talked with Celia, he has a broad background on which to draw for putting his experience into a larger context."

Gina had been nodding as Susan made her points. "Yes, yes, I see," she said, speaking rapidly as she always did when she was excited. "Some of the basic problems the evacuees must grapple with are disorientation, the difficulties of establishing a plausible sense of reality, paranoia, affective dysfunction, a sense of powerlessness, and alienation. The drugging exacerbates all these conditions. And Susan has put her finger on the sorts of factors that can alleviate the nexus of symptoms."

"But what can we *do?*" Maureen said dispiritedly. "Luis Salgado is a special case. We can't prevent the drugging. Nor can we bring the evacuees' friends and relatives here since we don't even know who they are or where they live." She tapped her pen on the table in an impatient tattoo. "I suppose we could try to explain the drugs to them, as well as give them as much background as they can absorb. But I bet they'd be suspicious of make-work right off the bat."

"Don't be so negative, Maureen," Susan said. "Just as you were going through your whole list of things we couldn't do, I was one step behind you, thinking of things we *could!* Let's take your points one at a time. First, the drugs. I think we should talk with the Marq'ssan about this. It might be possible for them to find some way to bollox up the drug distribution in advance of our going in."

Maureen shook her head. "We're going in in a matter of hours, Susan!"

"If the Marq'ssan think they can sabotage the drug distribution in advance, we can always postpone for twenty-four hours," Susan said. "It's the obvious thing to do, given the kind of difference we're talking about."

"My god!" Gina said. "Susan's right! A whole set of problems wouldn't exist for us if we could lead people out under their own steam. The entire atmosphere of the liberation would change!"

"But can it be done?" Celia said.

"Only the Marq'ssan can answer that question," Maureen said. "Celia, did Luis say anything about how the drugs were administered?"

"He suspects they lace the food or water."

"If it's the water, the plan is in immediate trouble," Gina said. "The prisoners could afford to miss a meal or two. But if we destroy their water supply, we risk putting them in danger of filter-failure since we don't know how close to the margin they run water distribution. We can assume it's fairly close because they'd consider it uneconomical to let prisoners have more drinking water than they absolutely required for being kept alive."

"Shit," Maureen hissed.

"I think we should ask Lisa Mott about this," Celia said.

"Was there anything in the files she gave you that would clarify this?" Gina asked Maureen.

"I'm trying to think," Maureen said. "Can you remember anything, Celia?"

"Problem is, it's hard to get hold of Lisa," Maureen said. "She lives in hiding, you know. Well, maybe Martha or Shoshana can get hold of her for us." Maureen got up from the table and left the room.

"As for the other things," Susan said. "Off the top of my head it occurs to me that we might consider asking the people who seem to be in the best shape to help with the others. I realize that in many cases this would be a terrible burden, but surely in some cases it would give the person a renewed sense of competence, of participation, and perhaps best of all of knowing what's going on. What I'm saying is, we probably should have included some others besides Luis in this meeting in particular."

Gina said, "Right. I see what you're saying. We need to offer them a kind of immediate hands-on reality situation. Of course Cora's group will in a way be working toward that same end."

"But that's not the same thing, at least not at first," Susan said. "As we all found out yesterday, not that many people are interested in talking—yet. Once they get more involved, their confidence will grow, and they'll be able to begin telling their stories. It may be easiest if they can talk first among themselves. I don't know. We've never had this kind of situation before, have we. The thing is to see how much they can handle and to let them decide, while those of us who are whole and strong stand by ready to offer whatever support they might need of us. I'd like to see us avoid taking these people as cases. As patients. As persons being rescued and helped and so on. This is something Luis has going for him. You see what I'm saying?"

"I agree entirely," Celia said, amazed that Susan should have seen all this by herself. In her own experience it had been only after she'd left Emily's and begun working at the Center in Hillcrest that she'd been able to shake her despair and self-contempt—and the worst edge of her fear, too.

Maureen came back into the room. "We're in luck," she said. "Lisa Mott is due in at any time now. Shoshana says that Lisa agreed to be on hand to review the procedures her team used the other night in preparation for tonight's work."

"You know," Gina said, frowning, "I think we should consider postponing for maybe forty-eight hours, so that we can work out some of the suggestions Susan is proposing."

"And I propose," Susan said, "that before we go any farther we go through all the notes we've taken during our interviews so that we can select people we think might be able to handle sitting in on our meetings."

Her mind buzzing with ideas and plans, Celia realized that her exhaustion had vanished. It was Susan who made the difference, she thought. Somehow she made the impossible seem simple. Celia glanced up from her notes to look at her and by chance caught her eye. Susan smiled slightly, then looked back down at her notes.

Full to bursting, Celia lowered her own—brimming—eyes.

# Chapter Twenty

As they land, Astrea scans like crazy, agog at the prospect of experiencing Earth first-hand.

Magyyt speaks in Boldeni. "You will be seeing some of the best as well as the worst of humans. In this Free Zone we've just landed in, you'll be meeting humans we've been working closely with. We're currently undertaking a special project with them, one which takes us into prisons."

Trying to understand this human word inserted into a Boldeni sentence, Astrea asks, "What are prisons?"

Magyyt now in-structs. "Prisons are places of confinement and torment. Imagine being forcibly kept in the separate compartments we occupy during trans-galactic travel. Imagine not having a choice about being closely confined in such a chamber and being deliberately tormented as well. And, we've just discovered, chemically poisoned, too."

Astrea feels dry patches spot self's pelt until remembering self does not have one just now. "This is something humans do?"

Magyyt's voice is as dry as Astrea's imagined pelt. "Yes, humans do this to one another. It's common. We will be going to one of these places tonight to free the prisoners and destroy the physical structures of the prison."

Astrea glances at Dghatd and perceives that that self's field is troubled. And Dghatd says, "That will be a rather drastic introduction to human culture for Astrea."

Magyyt, so human-seeming, shrugs. "Neither of you need accompany us on our mission. But for now, we're meeting people who oppose such things as prisons."

Astrea does not understand and says so. "How could any human not oppose them?"

Now Sorben l Sorben shrugs, "Perhaps you'll find the answer to that for yourself. But it's more than I've ever been able to learn."

Astrea knows that self must learn to use this human body as naturally as Magyyt and Sorben do. But their gestures, their tone, their attitude disturbs and makes self wonder if taking on such gestures might not profoundly change Marq'ssan.

The six of them leave the pod. In camouflage, they sprint on their human legs.

As they speed through the light gravity like winged creatures, Astrea reflects that if they had these bodies on Marqeuei, they would be too heavy even to move their heads, for the mass they adopt for earth is loosely proportional to earth's gravity.

Their bodies soar over the ground in swift, graceful leaps and bounds, and Astrea sheds the awkwardness that self has come to associate with taking human form. The brilliance of the light, the shimmering clarity of the air startles, though the human-form eyes are suited to it.

Astrea calls to Magyyt, "Those pools of fluid in the ground. They contain the fluid called water, the fluid that covers most of this planet?" It isn't a genuine question, since Astrea knows that they do; nonetheless Magyyt affirms the observation without comment.

Astrea, still scanning, finds that the pools of water contain traces of energy sources, as well, and tries drawing on them without ceasing self's movement. Soon Astrea's field is swelling from the draw, and Magyyt, Sorben, Tyln, and Flahn all laugh as they perceive it.

Magyyt in-forms Astrea, "You will find energy sources everywhere on this planet. The humans produce it as waste products that are poisonous to themselves."

The structures around them grow denser, larger, taller. They fly past humans almost constantly now, but at such a speed that Astrea cannot scan any one individual they pass.

Vehicles crowd the way, and Magyyt warns them to dodge them without dropping camouflage. Astrea wishes to slow down in order to scan more closely, but follows the others' example.

Abruptly they halt outside a rounded structure, and the world becomes stable and even richer with new materials to scan. Magyyt leads the way into the structure and through a cavernous chamber filled with an image of light fashioned to look like a human. They pause at a place where humans sit and Sorben greets one of them:

"Hello, Dana. None of us have weapons, of course."

The human grins at Sorben and looks over the rest of the Marq'ssan. "Six of you today!"

"Yes, two are visiting from Marqeuei, just arrived."

The human's eyes widen and gaze upon the Marq'ssan as though trying to spot the two who are new.

A panel in the wall slides open, revealing a small chamber. They get in, and the panel slides back. Briefly Astrea feels gravitational pressure, and then the panel slides open again.

They follow Sorben out into a rounded narrow conduit they traverse until that one pauses before a door. The door opens and a human appears. The human says, gesturing them to enter, "Sorben, Magyyt, Tyln, Flahn, come in." They pass through the doorway and join several humans in a large chamber filled with what Astrea recognizes from courses on human culture as a table and chairs. Humans prefer to sit and lie on structures specially designed for such functions, though not, according to the xenologists, comfortable or healthful. The xenologists claim that humans often prefer structures to be uncomfortable, for they consider the routine endurance of discomfort to be a sign of efficiency.

"Maureen, these two Marq'ssan are Dghatd 1 Merr san Fehln and Astrea 1 Betut san Imu. They've just arrived from Marqeuei."

Maureen is a female with light brown skin, short-cropped hair, and loose, bright clothing; she smiles at Astrea and Dghatd, though her field, like Dana's, remains exactly as it had been when they entered the room. Dghatd had warned Astrea that humans' fields seldom reflected their attitudes and feelings, but it is disturbing all the same.

"Just arrived from Marqeuei!" Maureen's face is animated, her eyes shining. "Is this the first time you've actually been on Earth?"

For the first time, Astrea speaks to a human in English. *For me, yes. And you're the first human I've spoken to.*

Maureen looks pleased. "It must be very strange for you." A peculiar, nervous laugh ripples through her words.

Dghatd says "But *I've* been to earth before. I lived for a time in Asia. Before we Marq'ssan called attention to our presence on this planet."

"Where specifically in Asia?"

"I concentrated mainly on India, China, and the smaller countries to the south of China and to the east of India."

More humans come into the room.

Maureen says "Shall we get started now?"

Everyone sits on the chairs around the table, and Maureen makes introductions to Astrea and Dghatd. Astrea shifts on the chair, trying to find a comfortable position, glancing at the others for confirmation of what the correct posture is. Maureen speaks again. "We've spent the day reviewing our procedures in light of what we've learned from the El Cajon action. We think it would be best to postpone the next action for either twenty-four or forty-eight hours, in order to improve our preparations."

Maureen's eyes move constantly between Sorben's and Magyyt's faces. "In addition, we need to ask whether the Marq'ssan can take on the advance action of halting the distribution of drugs to the prisoners. The drugs have a pernicious effect—most of the evacuees we brought here the other night have no memory of how they got from the prison to the Free Zone and consequently are disoriented—and not surprisingly, distrustful of us. Also, the fact that we transported them while they were sleeping has increased their sense of helplessness. It would make an immense difference to the prisoners' recovery if we could stop the distribution of drugs well in advance of our going in and liberating the prison."

Maureen raises her eyebrows. "Would you be willing to help us do that?" She looks from Sorben to Magyyt and back to Sorben again.

"Of course," Sorben replies. "Do you want us to do this tonight or tomorrow? How far in advance are you thinking of?"

Maureen looks at another of the humans, one with a pale skin, brown hair, and clothing somehow different from that worn by all the other humans in the room, though Astrea isn't sure in what way exactly it is different. "What do you think, Lisa? What will they do if they discover the gas has been tampered with and the prisoners not getting the drug?"

This human shrugs. "I doubt they'll do anything at first, beyond trying to find out what has happened. If their entire supply is destroyed, they won't be able to get hold of a fresh supply for a couple of days at least. I'd say we could afford to do it twelve to twenty-four hours in advance. But of course if the Chief Warder discovers what's been done, they'll be even more on guard against us than they will already have been."

Maureen moves her gaze from face to face around the table as she says "Anyone else have anything to say?"

The human with the darkest skin and most elongated limbs speaks: "I say we go in tomorrow night. And that the Marq'ssan sabotage the drug supply tonight. That way the prisoners will have a good twelve hours to shake off the effects of the drug. If Lisa is right about their routinely pumping the gas through the ventilation system at six a.m., noon, six p.m., and midnight, they would then miss three doses of the drug before we got to them. "

This human opens a transparent cylindrical container and tilts its opening to her mouth. Astrea, shuddering, looks away.

Lisa says "It's doubtful that they'll realize what has happened. Contact with prisoners isn't usually very frequent. Perhaps an individual case will be discovered, but the assumption will be that something was wrong with that cell's venting, or some other local problem of equipment rather than the drug supply. In any case, I'm certain there's no danger whatsoever of their being able to replenish their drug supply before we arrive on the scene."

Sorben speaks. "And the other things you were hoping to accomplish by delaying twenty-four hours? Do you think twenty-four hours will give you the time you need?"

Astrea wishes they would explain what they are talking about. Magyyt will explain, later, of course. For now it's enough to be able to stare at these strange creatures and listen to their voices—though it would be preferable that they not take fluid into their mouths so openly.

# Chapter Twenty-one

After attending a meeting at the Co-op Building to finalize the plan for the next prison liberation, Celia and Luis took a bus to one of the city's waterfront parks. Luis had been complaining about having gotten out of physical shape after so many months spent "sleeping," as he put it, so Celia had asked Maureen for suggestions of where to walk and then proposed one of them to Luis. This one bordered Lake Washington, in a residential section of the city previously unknown to Celia. Because it had rained the night before, the air sparkled and the water shimmered with a deep, bright blue only slightly darker than the blue of the sky. A gaggle of fat Canada geese waddled about in the grass, fertilizing it with their dung as they grazed, and diverse species of ducks fished and bathed and preened in the water. Bicycles constantly whizzed by on the bike trail a few yards from the path, their riders wearing brightly colored helmets and skin-tight shorts and shirts. The day, Celia thought as they headed south at a good pace, could hardly be more perfect.

They walked in silence for a few minutes, and for the first time in a long time Celia felt happy and calm and right with the world. For these moments, at least, she could believe in her heart that life could be good—which her mother had been telling her for a long time now that she needed to feel and believe.

"There's something I've been wishing, for months, for the chance to say to you, Celia," Luis said.

Celia slid a sidelong glance at him and tensed. Almost she asked him not to go on, to wait to say it another time.

He stopped and took her hand between both of his. "As you know all too well, honey, I have a very bad habit. I take strength and effort and goodness for granted." He squeezed her hand. "So I'll say now what I kept wishing I'd said when I had the chance. Celia, I'm proud of you, more proud of you than I can say. I've always laid extremely high expectations on you. And you've never failed me, not once! You're an extraordinary woman. And you probably don't even realize that." His face might be gaunt from months of imprisonment, but his gaze was steady and loving, and Celia saw herself in it, and her heart overflowed with joy. And for an instant, she was filled with the memory of the night she had stayed up talking and talking and talking with him until four in the morning about her potential, and life, and personal destiny, drinking a delicious white wine that had been a gift from one of his patients, a night that had culminated in her decision to go to law school. She had felt so close to him then, far closer than she had been to her mother in those years.

After a few seconds, he continued. "What you are doing with this human rights project with these Free Zone people: I'm deeply impressed, however skeptical I was at the beginning. From what I can see, this project has changed everything. Potentially for the good, though at the moment it's made the situation for people like us very, very dangerous. Those people must be feeling extremely threatened, Celia. They're on the defensive, which means they're likely to switch from a policy of harassment to more serious measures to silence those who, like us, can and will speak truth to power."

Celia's throat was tight. She said, "As you must have noticed in the last couple of days, working with Gina, there's plenty of work for you to do here that would be an important contribution to the project. You know that if you returned, at the very least they'd recapture you. And what good would you be able to do, stuck in jail and drugged?" Not that Celia believed that's what would happen were he captured now. She could just imagine all the new subjects for interrogation that would be opened up: the human rights project, the aliens, the clinic at Whidbey, plans for future prison liberations… Looking at him, she saw how physically frail he had become, so thin, so drawn, his hair gone completely gray.

"You are right to think they'd return me immediately to jail, Celia." He withdrew his hands from hers and slipped an arm around her shoulder and started them walking again. "And without doubt, if I didn't turn myself in on returning to San Diego, they'd charge me with escaping detention. Which is, as you know, a felony."

Afraid she might say the wrong thing, Celia kept quiet and waited for him to continue. She fixed her gaze on Mount Rainier and realized she had actually gotten used to Seattle, had stopped being fearful of wild, lawless behavior in a city without law or law enforcement.

After they'd walked perhaps fifty yards, Luis said, "So although I don't like leaving Elena and you, especially now that you're in heightened jeopardy, I've decided to stay here for the time being and work with the Whidbey Clinic people and provide medical assistance for prison liberations."

Celia's relief was so great that she started crying. Luis said with mock sternness, "Hey! What is this? Tears? From the tough, indomitable lawyer who won't be silenced?"

Celia laughed and rubbed her eyes with her sleeve. "I'm just so happy," she said. "So happy you're not in prison, so happy you're going to join the project. I can hardly wait to tell Mama!"

A couple of young men holding hands, walking in the other direction, passed them. Luis smiled at Celia. He hadn't been this easy, this relaxed in years.

# Chapter Twenty-two

Following security protocol, Hazel was waiting at the side door when Bobbie, one of the amazons, arrived with Margot Ganshoff to hand off the visitor directly into her charge. Hazel greeted her with a cool smile and led the way to the sitting room Liz had claimed for her own across the hall from her bedroom. But Margot moved up beside Hazel and slipped her arm around Hazel's waist. "It's been too long, sweetie, since we've seen one another."

Why did they have to go through this every time? Hazel wondered as she restrained herself from pulling away from the intrusive touch. "Is that right?" Hazel said in the most saccharine tone she could manage. "Time rushes by so quickly around here that I can't seem to keep track of people's comings and goings."

"Indeed," Margot said drily. "But then that's hardly surprising. I imagine Elizabeth is quite a slave-driver."

"A slave-driver without slaves?" Hazel said archly as they rounded the corner and came to the open sitting-room door.

Margot looked at Liz, who was seated on one of the pair of sofas arranged vis-à-vis. "Why does this girl always defend you?"

Liz raised an eyebrow. "If you'd simply accept that we are absolutely and utterly devoted to one another, she wouldn't need to be defending me, Margot. *Ne c'est pas*, darling?"

"Leave me out of this drama," Hazel said. "Is there anything you want me to do before I run along?"

Margot dropped her hand from Hazel's waist, swished into the room, and seated herself on the sofa facing Liz.

Liz gave Hazel a long, enigmatic look. "Why don't you sit down with us, darling," she said. "Maybe you could keep notes for me?"

"Notes!" Margot exclaimed.

"Just for the purpose of memorandum," Liz said. "Nothing official, I promise you. If you like, we can provide you with a copy."

Margot snorted. "Memoranda, my dear Elizabeth, have been known to get even the most astute players into difficult situations."

"Do sit down, darling."

"I need something with which to take notes," Hazel said.

Liz sighed. "Look in the desk, darling. I'm sure there's a NoteMaster in the drawer." Hazel found the screen and stylus without trouble and took the armchair at a right angle to both Liz and Margot's sofas and flicked it on and started it recording. Liz's long fingers plucked at the fringe on the cushion she held in her lap. She said, "So give me the news, Margot. What—if anything—has gotten out, and what are the general and specific reactions?"

"The big splash will come only after they put out the vid program they're in the process of making," Margot said. "When was it that they expected to broadcast?"

Liz looked at Hazel. "I think they're shooting for tomorrow night," Hazel said.

"Yes," Margot said. "Well, you see what is of greatest concern for my government as well as for the other governments who sent observers is the Executive's reaction against *us*."

Liz snorted. "What possible reaction *can* they have?"

"Come, Elizabeth, you know the kind of pressure they've been putting on us because of our ties with the Free Zone. And I've told you about the pressure the SIC has been putting on our intelligence services. We're justifiably concerned about retaliation."

Liz shook her head. "I don't believe they'll retaliate. They don't want to risk breaking up NATO, now do they. They can't punish one ally without losing several."

"And you, my dear Elizabeth, know that they don't think that way at all: they'd be more afraid *not* to punish an ally they perceive to be out of line. You're not working for them anymore, there's no point in your bullshitting me. So don't." Margot sounded annoyed.

"Well we'll cross that bridge when we come to it," Liz said, unperturbed. "But have you heard anything at all?"

"Well, yes we have." Margot stared hard at Liz. "Some of the warders recognized Lisa Mott. Which I suppose you intended?"

"Yes. That was part of the requirement."

"Unnecessarily severe, my dear. And possibly a mistake. Are you certain you want them to know at this stage who is involved? Wouldn't it have been more interesting to let them think it purely a Free-Zone production?"

"No," Liz said emphatically. "Not at all. I want them to have to confront—immediately—the fact that they're up against me, and that being up against me means something. The sooner they learn this, the sooner they'll be wanting to come to terms with me."

"Who, dear?" Margot queried. "Who will want to be coming to terms with you? Security Services? Sedgewick? Booth? The entire Executive? Or various dissatisfied components of the executive-system?"

Liz smiled scornfully. "All of the above, Margot."

Margot tilted her head to one side. "I see. And which of these do you think you want to accept terms from?"

Liz's smile broadened. "Ah. That's another question entirely, isn't it. I think I might be willing to work with the Executive, though I'd want the most important components kept in my own hands."

Margot nodded. "Yes, all right, Elizabeth. That's fine. Very sensible. No dealing with Sedgewick or Booth. Or Security Services. Unless you simply want your same old curtailed power back. Because what would be the use of it? You might as well not have gone renegade at all if you accept only what you had before—or less."

"I can assure you, I'd never settle for so little."

"Do the Free-Zone people have any glimmering at all of what you intend? What is it they think your interest in this demonstration is?"

Liz's eyes slewed sideways towards Hazel. "Hazel can tell you that better than I can. I hardly see them these days."

Both Margot and Liz stared at her. "They assume it's for two reasons," Hazel said. "Some of them accept both reasons, though most are too distrustful to think anything is involved other than that Liz is testing Lisa."

"And the other reason?"

"I've told them that Liz disapproves of the Executive's human rights abuses." Hazel glanced at Liz. "Whether that's true or not, only Liz herself knows."

"Don't be cynical, darling," Liz snapped. "I don't know why I can't be allowed decent motives."

"Your motives are usually mixed," Hazel said.

"Precisely, darling. Just don't rank me with Hitler, Pol Pot, and all those dreadful Latin Americans."

"Oh Liz, will you please cut it out."

"Just because I'm practical, Hazel worries about my morals, Margot."

Margot gave Liz a questioning look, as though wondering why she was working this nonsense so hard. "We were, after all, talking about our ultimate goal of reforming the executive system," Margot remarked. "What I'm wondering is how much Greenglass has figured out of what you might be up to. Me she doesn't suspect, you know. Given that Austria's interests have become so securely tied with the Free Zone's. If she had any idea of your plan to ultimately win the Free Zone back once you've reformed the executive system, though, she'd stop cold every bit of cooperation between you and the aliens and the Free Zone. As it is, you'd best be warned she isn't stupid. I've told you this before, but I don't think you've quite understood. If she decides you're finished with the aliens, then you are. No more handy help from them, no more cooperative ventures." Margot paused. "So tell me. Do you think you can pull off your operations without the aliens?"

Liz recrossed her legs. "What a foolish question. Of course I can. I don't need the aliens to bring the Executive down. But since we are getting some cooperation from them—cooperation I'd be a fool to pass up—it's all just happening more quickly than it would have. Believe me, I'm not dependent on them, not at all."

"Another matter," Margot said. "What of Emily Madden? Do you think you've got her in your corner?" At Liz's raised eyebrow, Margot went on, "What I mean is, if your action should threaten to bring down her father, where do you think she'll stand?"

Elizabeth lifted her hands and shoulders and then let them drop. "I've no idea, Margot. No idea at all. Any more than I've any idea how you would react in certain tricky circumstances."

Margot looked at Hazel. "Could you get us some tea, Hazel? As well as some water? I'm parched."

"Please, darling," Liz said. "And some grapefruit juice for me."

Hazel put down the NoteMaster and left the executives alone together. So Margot had something to say to Liz that she did not want her to hear. A declaration of intent? Or something more, something to do with the position the Austrian government had determined to take? It must be highly confidential, considering the things they'd been openly discussing in her presence.

Hazel went into the office and refilled the electric tea kettle and switched it on. Thinking a bit more about Margot's sending her out of the room, she decided that whatever Margot had to say out of her presence, she probably didn't want to hear.

# Chapter Twenty-three

Alexandra sank her fingers into the satisfyingly full E-flat major chord; smoothly, lyrically, the long arpeggio rippled up from its root. Then, as the line cascaded down the keyboard in a swift, scintillating sparkle of notes, her watch chimed, its tone and pitch (a slightly sharp A) clashing with the piano's E-flat major overtones still thrumming in the air. Disgusted, she lifted her hands from the keys and switched off the alarm.

Tea time, again.

She crossed the hall to the bathroom to pee. Drying her hands, she stared at her face in the mirror and found that she still could not look herself in the eye. It might as well be his face, she thought, and wondered how much of one's personality was hereditary. But why had she inherited so much from him, rather than from Grandmother, or Mama, or even Grandfather? She turned away from the mirror. If she truly was like him, she would be better off dead. Yet from where else had she gotten her cruel streak? Mama wasn't that way. Mama never even raised her voice. No, of everyone she knew, only he behaved that way.

*It's all a matter of politics. Whether us or them, using the techniques or exposing them, it's all the same. I'm sick to death of this hypocritical tone yammering away at the world as though upon this one thing hinges the fate of civilization. The truth is, the fate of civilization depends upon our protection of it from the great destroyers these rebels and anarchists inevitably are.*

*—But does Security actually do the things they are claiming?*

*You're not a child now, Alexandra, don't think your sniveling is anything but weakness—weakness we can't afford. Unless you want everything to end, unless you want to give the world into the hands of the destroyers of everything that means anything? It's all politics, and you're a fool if you let yourself be duped into thinking otherwise.*

She would have to get his permission before making arrangements with the pilot. And it would have to be today, so that Clarice could leave on the weekend. And then things would get better. Only it would be so horrible bringing up the subject. But the pilot's orders always had to be cleared through him. It was one of the few things he still controlled directly. Maybe once she had asked him her anxiety would ease. And then she could inform Clarice of the arrangements and ask her to stay away.

After she had been told, Clarice would probably be glad to stay away.

Down in the Small Study, Alexandra found her father seated at his desk, awash in paper, much of it purple. Wedgewood, she thought, must have sent him these papers. He glanced up and asked her to pour him another cup of coffee. Hiding her surprise, she took his cup and saucer to the side table, poured coffee from the thermoflask into his cup, added a teaspoon of sugar, and stirred it. When she returned to the desk with it she said, "Shall I go away?"

He removed his glasses. "Not at all. Have a seat." He gestured at the armchair positioned in front of the desk. "It's fascinating having a spectator's position in this battle of wits. It allows me to pose our problems as puzzles, perhaps even as mysteries to be solved with great ingenuity." His lips quirked very slightly. "Only of course I'm not quite the spectator that I appear to be. Like all the other players in this game, I have a great deal to lose. The fact that I'm as yet only a passive player—an odd position for someone like me, wouldn't you say?—lends the sense of spectating rather than playing. But of course that's nonsense." He lifted his cup to his lips and drank.

Alexandra waited patiently for him to explain what he was talking about. He could go on for a long time this way, in monologue, without requiring an explicit response from her. And he often did.

"And what are our puzzles?" he rhetorically asked. "Several, some of which hinge upon the hypothetical outcomes of one another. One of the key questions, of course, is what her intent is, and another, her strategy." His eyes narrowed. "Why connive with the aliens to destroy these prisons?"

"You mean," Alexandra said, taking his cue, "Weatherall had something to do with what the aliens did to the prisons?"

"Yes, yes," he said impatiently, "it's obvious she's behind it. Even if those fools attempting to run Security can't see it. Highlighting Lisa Mott's obvious participation is her calling card. She's telling us that not only can she inflict heavy damage, but that Mott has defected to her." He paused to drink more coffee. "One then must expect more demonstrations of other defections, perhaps—for surely we can consider this more in the way of a demonstration than of deliberate sabotage, whatever those fools think." He frowned. "Perhaps it's a matter of demonstrating a certain grip she still retains? Can it be that simple? Is it possible she's simply demonstrating her potential for sabotage in order to induce a willingness on the part of the Executive to come to terms with her?" He drummed his fingers on the desk and stared at Alexandra. "What other reason could she possibly have for making such demonstrations?"

When Alexandra realized he expected her to answer, she ventured, aware that her suggestion would probably make him scornful if not angry, "Maybe she did it for humanitarian reasons."

She thought she saw a flash of annoyance cross his face, but if it did, all trace of it vanished as quickly as it had appeared. He leaned back in his chair and subjected her face to intense scrutiny. "Humanitarian reasons," he said with a surprising lack of inflection. "Let's see what kind of case you can make for supporting such an argument."

So this was to turn into another political science lesson. As usual she would make an inept case that he would pull apart with a sentence or two, after which he would make her try again. And again. And again, until she came up with the answer he had been looking for. "I'm thinking of something she once said to me." Alexandra hesitated when she saw his eyes narrow. "It was when they first began airing claims of human rights violations last spring. I asked her about it. And she said several things. Very complicated things, I don't know if I can get it exactly right, but—"

"Go on," he said. "Make a stab at it."

"First she said something about how a lot of people in the Company disapproved of such methods and distrusted the crazies who were into that kind of stuff, as she put it. She said that common sense alone made it clear that such methods were inefficient and counterproductive. That they'd only stir up more opposition because they

made people react emotionally. That people aren't capable of thinking things out to the point of seeing what was best, that avoiding such
emotional images was crucial for maintaining control. She said she
herself sometimes felt sick at things she saw and heard about, and that
if she did then people unable to understand where their best interests
lie would also react that way and might even be prodded out of their
inertia because of it. That repression hurt the economy and confused
people with emotional issues." Alexandra twisted her hands in her
lap. "I think that's the gist of what she said. Anyway, she may have felt
strongly enough about it to help the aliens try to stop it."

Her father snorted. "That's all very interesting, but obviously she
left out one important point when talking to you about this. She should
have added that until the aliens fucked up our economy and our transportation and communication systems, repression never came much
into the picture. The idiot dissenters moved in and out of jail quite
mechanically and no one gave it much thought. Where else in the
world could you be arrested dozens of times for seditious activities
without ever being in danger of permanent imprisonment or brutal-
ization? But all that changed when the aliens zapped us. It's the aliens'
fault we now have homegrown terrorist groups that need a tight rein.
And it's the aliens' fault we've been on the brink of collapse for the
last eleven years. Only a tight rein can control this volatile a situation. If people can't behave in a civilized manner, if they can't control
themselves, then repressive tactics are necessary to preserve the freedom of the majority. What is needed now is radical surgery—to clear
out the cancer and allow us to heal. No amount of muddled wishful
thinking will get around this basic problem, Alexandra."

"Weatherall also said," Alexandra said when his silent stare began
to make her uncomfortable, "that people will basically go along with
the status quo as long as the opposition doesn't find sources for emotional manipulation."

"That's in ordinary times," he said impatiently. "But these are
not ordinary times. The aliens have shaken everything up; and as far
as the majority of the people in this country go, the Good Life for all
practical purposes is a thing of the past."

Alexandra stared down at her hands. "Does that mean you think
that only negative methods are useful?"

"I didn't say that." His words were a rebuke. "But we're talking about Security's role now, not the entire Executive. Security's role naturally tends to be fairly negative even at the best of times."

Which was why, Alexandra thought, she intended never to have anything to do with that institution.

# Chapter Twenty-four

Anne and Hazel hopped out of the back of the van and walked briskly down the street without pausing to watch Denise drive away. Everywhere they saw colorful streamers and pots of flowers and posters and banners proclaiming *A Decade and a Year of Freedom!* "Tomorrow's the big day," Hazel said. "There'll be a march from the Co-op Building to the Seattle Center, followed by a big celebration— free food and entertainment, and lots of speeches. Liz wants all of us to boycott it, of course."

Anne gave her a curious look. "But you don't agree?"

Hazel shrugged. "Doesn't matter to me one way or another. I understand how she feels, so I'll avoid coming in to town."

"Do you suppose the aliens will attend?"

Hazel opened one of the building's big, heavy doors. "Probably," she said. "They started it all, didn't they. It would be a little odd if they didn't." The atrium had been decorated with tapestries, mobiles, and a few statues. The result had not been to leech attention from the holograph of Kay Zeldin, but rather to intensify its effect.

Walking to the elevator, they passed a three-dimensional vid about Zeldin and the founding of the Free Zone, which was new. "I remember when they captured Zeldin," Anne whispered when they were alone in the elevator. "Everyone at the Rock talked about it, it seemed like a good sign that such a flagrant traitor had been caught."

"Then it must be strange for you now, seeing how everyone here considers her a hero."

Anne swept her gaze over the walls and the ceiling, as though looking for a microphone. "Sort of makes you realize how we really are living in enemy territory."

"That's a little strong, don't you think?" Hazel said as the doors slid open. She could tell that Anne was wishing that she were whispering, too, but she continued to speak in a normal tone of voice. "I find it hard to consider any of the people in this building my enemy. I know Liz feels that way, of course. But they're such decent people."

As they moved along the curve of the corridor Anne's eyes darted nervously about. How absurd, Hazel thought of the cautions and instructions Liz had given her about Anne. The fact was, Anne was less likely to be "corrupted"—in spite of what Liz claimed about her naiveté—than she, Hazel, was. Anne, Hazel thought, shared some of Allison's paranoia. But as they arrived at Martha's door, she recalled her own paranoia the first few times she had come into this building by herself. She too had thought of these people as her enemies.

"Knock knock," Hazel called out.

Martha glanced over her shoulder, saw Hazel, and smiled. "Hello there, stranger. Haven't seen you in *ages!*"

Hazel grinned back. "Meet Anne Hawthorne, one of our household. Anne, this is Martha Greenglass."

Martha got up from her chair, came forward, and shook Anne's hand. "Nice to meet you, Anne," she said. "Are you another renegade?"

Anne looked uneasy. "Yes," she said hesitantly, as though not certain the designation fit her.

Martha looked back at Hazel. "Coming to the commemoration celebration tomorrow?"

"You weren't expecting any of us, were you?"

Martha's lips twitched, then broke—perhaps unwillingly—into a wry smile. "Not really. Though one can always hope. Want to come in and sit? Or is this a flying visit?"

"There are a few things I wanted to talk about, actually," Hazel said.

Martha gestured them into the room, and when they came in, closed the door after them. Hazel turned her back to the window and sank down onto the floor; Martha got three bottles of water from a cabinet and passed one to each of them. Parched, Hazel sipped before speaking. "We were sorry to hear the news about Cameroon," she said. "Margot Ganshoff told us that her government intends to raise a ruckus in the UN about it, but that she doubts it will mean anything since the US doesn't recognize the UN and the sympathy of most governments will be with the US, not with Cameroon or the people who died in the bombings."

Martha's face clenched with anger. "Those bastards are incredible. You know why they picked on Cameroon, don't you? Cameroon doesn't have much of an air force to speak of and very little financial clout compared with the other three countries involved. Sovereignty," Martha scoffed. "It's incredible that they can talk about prisons in terms of sovereignty!"

"Will the Marq'ssan retaliate?" Hazel asked.

Martha nodded vigorously. "Damned straight they will."

"Do they already have a target in mind?"

Martha tilted her head to one side and regarded Hazel with obvious speculation. "Don't tell me," she said softly. "Elizabeth Weatherall has one in mind."

"The Executive's major propaganda organization," Hazel said apologetically. "The Department of Com & Tran's post-war public education campaign."

Martha's eyes widened. "She can help us wipe out *that?*"

"Are you interested?"

"Very," Martha said. "Though it sounds as if it could be an exceedingly complex and intricate mission."

"Yes," Hazel said, "it would be, since it involves more than one location. Assuming you want to get inside of the whole of Com & Tran's data banks, which are spread out in about thirty different locations across the country."

"I suppose that means you have someone who knows quite a lot about it," Martha said.

"Two people. Liz says that with their combined knowledge, almost the entire picture can be pieced together without much difficulty."

"It's tempting," Martha said. "Very tempting. I'll have to get back to you on it."

"Good. We just didn't know whether it was too late."

"No, I don't think so. The Marq'ssan are extremely busy these days. Especially since a starship load of them just arrived from Marqeuei."

Hazel's stomach dropped. "From their *planet?*" she asked, wondering how many of these powerful creatures might be walking the face of the earth at that very moment.

Martha drank the last swallow of water from her bottle. "I get the itch sometimes to go there and see it for myself." Her smile looked a little sheepish, Hazel thought. "But of course that's out of the question. The Marq'ssan won't even show us what they look like naturally. They say we have a low threshold for tolerating difference."

The image that conjured in Hazel's mind made her shiver, and she hurried to change the subject. "But except for the bombing of the two Cameroon prisons, you must be pleased at the success of the mission."

Martha sobered. "I suppose so," she said. "But people don't seem to be getting our basic point about prisons. The observers, for instance, in every single public statement they've made, register protest for our having freed the non-political prisoners. They've told me they think that in a certain sense we *did* violate the sovereignty of the US by interfering with its lawful system of justice. And that to a certain extent the Executive is justified in calling our liberation of prisons acts of terrorism." Martha snorted. "The gall of those people amazes me. Considering the terrorism they routinely visit on the people kept in those prisons. The drugging alone is heinous! Not to mention all the other abuses prisoners have to endure!"

Hazel glanced sidelong at Anne and saw that she was frowning.

"And who knows how long it will take them to recover," Martha said. "Helping torture victims is an extremely delicate and drawn-out process. It often takes years."

"What about the people *they* hurt?" Anne burst out. "How long do you think it will take *them* to recover? No one cares about them, do they. I don't understand why you're so anxious to free criminals who have made others' lives hell. But then that's been the aim of you people in the so-called Free Zone all along, hasn't it. The first thing you did was to empty the prisons here."

Martha stared in surprise at Anne, then glanced at Hazel—who raised her eyebrows—then back at Anne, who refused to meet Martha's eyes. "None of the people we freed last week had hurt anyone, Anne. They were for the most part political prisoners."

"That's easy for you to say: 'political prisoners.' But included among them were people who set bombs and have otherwise killed or injured people. And besides, even when they don't do that, they want to take away everyone else's freedom."

Martha's eyebrows came down into a frown. "That's simply not true. What harm does someone who is caught passing out censored material do to you?"

"I *know* what political prisoners are," Anne said. "I'm not *stupid*. These people want to deny us our freedoms. They want to take over the government, to force their ideology on the rest of us!"

Hazel watched Martha intently as the Free Zoner leaned forward, her attention entirely on Anne. "Now look, Anne: supposing what you are saying were true—and I'm not saying it is. Just supposing. Does that mean you think such people deserve to be tortured, deserve to be treated inhumanely?"

"I'm not saying I think that kind of thing is right," Anne said angrily. "But that doesn't mean you should go around setting such people free! They're enemies of society and should be prevented from doing harm. I don't condone torturing them, but I don't condone letting them loose, either."

"Oh Anne," Martha said, her eyes big brown pools of sadness. "If only you could meet some of these people you call your enemy. I don't believe you would still feel the same."

A knock on the door ruptured the tension. Martha got up from the floor and went to the door. Before she opened it, she looked over her shoulder at Anne and said, "Think about this, Anne: if you are a renegade, as I assume you are, suppose they captured you: then think how they would treat *you*, and see if you feel the same about it then." Martha pulled open the door.

Hazel looked at Anne and saw that her eyes had gone wide, that her upper lip trembled. Hadn't she thought at all about that possibility? But she *must* have... "Come in, come in," Martha was saying as she ushered more people into her office. Of the four, Hazel recognized only Maureen Sanders and Susan Sweetwater.

"We're just back from touring both the Whidbey Clinic and the Whidbey Health Sciences Center," the professional woman Hazel didn't know said.

"Most impressive," the professional man—middle-aged and on the short side, but with a strong vibe of quiet competence—murmured.

Martha said, "Hazel, I think you already know Maureen and Susan?" Hazel nodded. "But I don't think you know Gina McCartney, the doctor who founded the Whidbey Health Sciences Center, and Dr. Luis Salgado, who's one of the people we brought here from the El Cajon detention facility." Martha looked at the two doctors and said, "Please meet Hazel Bell." Hazel and Anne rose to their feet. Hazel shook hands with the two doctors, then took a second look at the man whose worn and frail appearance now took on a certain significance. "And this is Anne Hawthorne." Laboriously, politely, Martha introduced Anne to all four of them.

"Luis's been offering us many useful suggestions for the Clinic," Gina said after all the introductions had been made. "But then he's had a lot more experience treating torture victims than we have."

"I'm very impressed," Salgado said. "We have no such facilities anywhere in San Diego. But then the fear of recurrence is always one of the greatest preoccupations of the people I've treated there."

"I suppose it must count for something that doctors are willing to treat torture victims at all in San Diego," Susan said. "Dr. Salgado himself was persecuted on that account," she explained to Hazel and Anne.

A shiver ran down Hazel's spine. The things this man must know, she thought. The things he must have seen... "But the reason for our visit, Martha, has to do with other things Luis has told us," Maureen said. "Our timing seems to be lucky, since some of this may involve a liaison with Lisa Mott again." Maureen looked at Hazel. "You will act as mediator again, Hazel?"

Mediator? Is that how they thought of her? All because she went back and forth making arrangements between the executives and the Co-op? "I'll certainly carry a message back to Lisa if you like," Hazel said, smiling into Maureen's eyes. "But perhaps you'd prefer to talk with Lisa herself?"

Maureen glanced at Anne. "It's all right for us to talk?" she asked. Hazel nodded. "Good," Maureen said, shutting the door. Cut off from the corridor, the room shrank and grew crowded with its seven occupants. Maureen looked at Salgado. "Go ahead, Luis. You tell her about the possible extension of the project."

Salgado stood with his arms crossed over his chest. As he talked he occasionally unhooked his right palm from his left elbow to gesture, but having finished the gesture reclasped his elbow. He glanced at

Hazel once as he started talking, then dropped his gaze to stare down at the floor. "I was explaining to the others that only a small fraction of the human rights abuse goes on in the federal detention facilities. That many of those arrested and tortured are never officially acknowledged to be in custody, that there are a large number of small places where the worst things are done." Salgado's distant brown gaze lifted briefly to Hazel's face and fell again. "For instance they seldom murder people who are officially detained. Generally when one is taken to the official facilities one can feel confident that one won't be killed deliberately. Accidentally during torture, perhaps, through a miscalculation, but not by specific intent. In fact we have no idea how many people have been killed. All we know is that there are people missing." He shrugged. "The same old story of practices used in other countries. They've adopted them all here." He made a peculiar gesture, then reclamped his elbow. "And then there are the larger places some of us have been taken to, that seem to be official, but apparently are not. It has been suggested to me that these may be places controlled by the Military—as opposed to ODS. I don't know. They are vile places."

Salgado glanced at Hazel. He continued, "After I told the others about these places and what I knew of them, it was proposed that perhaps we should attempt to do something about them, too. Though one can see without much effort that certain obstacles would stand in our way. Finding the locations of such places, for instance. None of those tortured in such places have ever had any idea where they were taken." Again he shrugged. "Of course, that would not stop the torture. Their instruments and buildings can be destroyed, but torture can be conducted without instruments. As we well know. It is my opinion that those who torture should not be allowed to go free." He raised his eyebrows and grimaced, then shrugged again. "But of course that is not for me to decide."

Hazel looked from Salgado to Maureen. "You'd like me to ask Lisa if she knows any of the locations?" The implications of the words hung in the room, generating a new surge of tension.

Maureen's eyes flickered. "Or if she knows how to discover such locations. If, say, she were to have access to Security's files, or any other files she might think she needed, whether she'd be able to find out."

"I'll ask her," Hazel said, so uncomfortable that she wanted to get out of the room as quickly as possible. Ostentatiously she glanced at her watch. "We have to be going now," she said. "I'll get back to you on this in a day or two."

Martha let them out and, touching Hazel's arm, said, "Sorry we didn't get around to the things you wanted to discuss. Next time?"

"Next time it is."

"Nice meeting you, Anne," Martha said, smiling. "Come back for more talk some time."

Anne mumbled goodbye, and Hazel took her arm and headed for the elevator. She knew it was the flight of a coward, but she felt sure she'd have gotten sick if she'd stayed in that room much longer. The scar on his left hand that she'd only noticed as they were leaving... No, she told herself, don't even think about it, you have no way of knowing how he got that scar, he could have had it since childhood.

In the elevator, Hazel requested the garage level. Anne said, "Do you think he was telling the truth?"

Hazel looked at her. "About what?" she asked, blankly.

"About being tortured for treating people who had been tortured."

"Yes," Hazel said, "I do."

"But that's irrational!" Anne exclaimed. "He must have been involved in terrorism, too?"

"These things are never *rational*, Anne. Ask Allison or Lisa or Liz. I doubt they'd find it hard to believe that doctor's story."

The elevator door opened, and they stepped into the garage, where they found Denise already waiting with the van. Hazel had a strong desire to get home. She wished they didn't have to visit the University and hit the bookstores before going home. But it wouldn't be fair to Anne not to, considering this was her first real excursion (not counting the concerts with Allison).

# Chapter Twenty-five

Her father was relatively abstemious at dinner again. This had been the case every evening since Wedgewood had come to discuss the Free Zone's exposé. In this temperate state Alexandra found him less unpredictable and arbitrary but occasionally more difficult. Rather than boring her with repetitious reminiscences or complaints, he tasked her with lessons on politics and economics. Earlier in the week when he'd discovered how little she knew about the Executive Transformation of 2041, he summoned her social science tutor and rebuked him for her inadequate preparation in history. The tutor had in turn dumped several books on her and assigned a term paper dealing with the causes and effects of the Executive Transformation of 2041.

Now ascending the stairs as they moved from the Informal Dining Room to the Music Room, he continued the lecture he had begun during the soup. "While the tendency to polarization has been inherent in the Executive since the mid-Sixties, the strain of the Blanket and the unrest accompanying it took its toll on the Executive and the executive-system at large. In retrospect I can see that Military's conspiracy with Gates, Larson, and Devito was only the final precipitating factor: that they could conceive such a conspiracy indicates that potential was already strongly present and visible. The amazing thing was that I didn't see it. But then I had my hands full trying to restore the country to a decent civil order." They reached the second floor landing; he took her arm as they turned to walk along the hall. "There's a lesson there, of course," he said. "One must not dismiss tensions where there's any sort of potential for cataclysm. The fact that those individuals collectively commanded so much power should alone have induced me to assign an entire team to keeping a close watch on them. But then," he said, pausing with her as they rounded the corner into the final stretch of hall, "I will never understand how my intelligence within those Departments failed."

His sideways glance moved past her, and his head turned. She realized he was looking at the cloudy, gilt-framed mirror hanging over the low boy. Without warning, he put his hands on her shoulders and pivoted with her to face the mirror. In the gaslight their faces loomed eerily before them, looking, Alexandra saw with a shudder, almost identical. The one difference—their hair coloring—did not show much in the gaslight, and Alexandra could see that since she had gotten her hair cut the bone structure in her face had become more prominent, more obvious in its resemblance to his. "Do you see?" he said, very low. "We are almost identical. If you wore your hair exactly like mine..."

His eyes in the mirror caught Alexandra's. "Do you think it matters?" she whispered. "Heredity, I mean."

His fingers tightened on her shoulders. "Of course it matters."

Could he hear how hard, how loudly her heart was pounding?

"What a mistake I made thinking it would be Daniel who would be like me," he said. "Look here." His right hand lifted from her shoulder to her face. With his index finger he traced the line of her jaw. "That is blood," he said. For several long seconds Alexandra groped for a reply while her mind grew frozen and numb at the thought that he might be right. He turned his head and kissed her cheek. Then, after lightly brushing his fingers over her neck, he drew her along the hall to the Music Room.

"Could we skip my playing for you tonight?" Alexandra said, fighting to keep her voice steady.

He raised an eyebrow. "If you'd told me that earlier we would have stayed downstairs and gone instead into the Small Study."

"Sorry. Do you want to go down now?"

"No, of course not. They've already set out the coffee tray in here." He took the sofa, and she sat in one of the chairs facing it.

"Shall I pour you some coffee now?" she asked.

"Yes."

She poured coffee into one of the cups, added sugar, stirred it, and handed it to him. Then she poured a glass of water for herself. "You'd gotten to the point where you had uncovered the plot following the attempt to assassinate you," Alexandra reminded him.

He drank from his cup, then set it down on the table beside him. "The story goes on and on," he said. "The end result was the Civil War. Which would have been prevented if Kay hadn't abducted me just as I was dealing with the remaining conspirators, Turpin and Devito."

That part of the story Alexandra already knew. She had heard it often enough to have memorized many of the details.

"I suppose the main point to be made is that in spite of the apparent reunification of the Executive, a certain level of polarization still exists. The difference now is that the Executive is largely weighted toward our side of the split rather than Military's." His lips thinned. "But of course at this very moment Security might actually be vulnerable, were Military to decide to take advantage of the current mess things are in."

First this Kay woman, and then Elizabeth, precipitating trouble. No wonder he didn't trust women.

"You're quiet tonight."

Alexandra waited for more, but he seemed not to be irritated.

"They tell me you didn't go to get the mail today."

Alexandra shrugged. "I just didn't feel like going out."

"Is there something bothering you?"

Alexandra remembered about Clarice. Was this the time to get the required permission? "There's nothing bothering me," she said, taking a sip of water. She looked at him. "But I wanted to clear with you my girl's going on the weekend flight with the others."

His face stiffened. "Of course. Just be sure to give her explicit instructions about being on time when the pilot is ready to return."

"She won't be returning." Alexandra flushed, and he gave her a look that made her avert her eyes. "It's all arranged with Mama," she added awkwardly. "There won't be any inconvenience for you."

He recrossed his legs. "So you're tired of her already."

Tears sprang to Alexandra's eyes. "I wish everybody would stop saying that!"

"Everybody?"

Alexandra shook her head. "Can't we please not talk about it?"

"So you *are* upset."

"I don't want to talk about it."

"It's important to talk about such things, Alexandra, when you're *that* upset," he said. "So tell me, why *are* you sending her away?"

"I don't want her around me!" The words burst out of her without intention. "I can't bear the sight of her, she makes me sick!" Alexandra covered her face with her hands and got to her feet. She had to get out of there; she was completely out of control.

But before she had taken more than a couple of steps away from the chair, her father materialized beside her, put his arm around her shoulders, and pulled her over to the sofa. "You'll feel better if you can talk about it," he said, his voice very close to her ear.

Drowning in tears, feeling at that moment that he was a little like Grandfather, she let him press her head against his chest and even clung to him. "I think I must hate her." Alexandra sobbed. "Last night—!" She halted, unable to go on, hearing again Mama's voice saying, accusing, *You must never use violence against a dependent; it's unfair, irresponsible, and above all counter-productive.*

"What about last night?" Papa said softly.

He sounds as though he cares, Alexandra thought. As though he *understands*. She wiped her eyes with her sleeve and struggled to sit up. "I was horrible to her last night." She sniffed to keep her nose from dripping. "I didn't know I could be so mean. But I couldn't help it, she made me so *furious*!" Alexandra sniffed again. "I can't stand her lying to me that way. As though she thinks I'm that gullible, that stupid. That I can be manipulated."

"Why don't you tell me the whole story?"

Alexandra intertwined her fingers, pressing one of her rings tightly into her flesh. "I called her to my room last night," she said, staring down at the livid area of flesh the ring's pressure was creating. "I guess she thought I'd changed my mind and wanted her." She swallowed. "I haven't let her come to my room at night for over a week, only in the day when I'm not there. To take care of my clothes and things. Anyway, I called her last night to tell her about how Mama was making new arrangements for her, that she would be leaving here soon. When I told her, she started crying and saying all kinds of things. It made me so mad. So I said to her that she should be glad that Mama would arrange something that would be at least as lucrative and probably more so than a kid like me. And that's when she really started carrying on, mostly in Italian, and then…and then she claimed…that she *loves* me." Alexandra's cheeks burned; she snatched a shy glance at her father. "I couldn't stand it, it upset me so much, her lying about that kind of thing, that I hit her." Ashamed, she lowered her gaze and wished she hadn't said anything about Clarice at all. Of all people to share her secret with… You weren't ever supposed to talk to males about such things. Though she couldn't imagine ever being able to tell Mama, or Grandmother… They would say she obviously wasn't mature enough to have a lover. And there might be some truth in that. Either that, or she was a monster. Which she probably was, being *his* daughter. "And then afterwards," Alexandra mumbled in miserable conclusion, "she still kept saying it, and I had to physically push her out of my room. It was horrible, horrible!"

"That's all?" he asked, sounding surprised.

Alexandra looked at him. "I feel like such a monster," she said.

"But my dear Alexandra, it's perfectly clear the girl provoked you by trying to manipulate you. God knows when one discovers one's been manipulated the provocation to violence is almost irresistible. The only problem as I see it is your taking such a girl so seriously. It shouldn't matter to you whether or not she thinks she can manipulate you. Such girls are nothing at all. As I said before, if you want to play with them, fine. But don't take such play seriously. If you can't detach your emotions from such play…" He shrugged. "Then perhaps you should give it up."

"I'll never have another lover," Alexandra fiercely vowed. Not because she couldn't detach her emotions, but because it was so ugly, so horrible, manipulation on one side, uncontrollable anger on the other. How could one not hate girls like Clarice? It would be best to stay away from them. Better never to have pleasure than to feel the way Clarice made her feel now.

"So you *are* taking these girls seriously," he said. "Very, *very* seriously."

Alexandra looked at his strangely sympathetic face and wondered how he could be so different now from the way he always was. "It's too ugly," she said. "I would rather be by myself and lonely than have to go through so much ugliness again." To be clean and free of one's own monstrousness, rather than temporarily excited, warm, and obsessed—all the while knowing what would come afterwards.

He got up, poured some cognac into a snifter, and brought it back to the sofa. "Here," he said. "Drink this. It will help."

She had never drunk cognac before. She took the glass from him, held its lovely curves in both hands, and raised it to her mouth—and recoiled from the fumes. Still, she ventured a timid swallow. She almost choked, for the fiery liquid burned as it slid down her throat. Coughing, she said, "It's strong."

"It really is a shame the way the executive system has made such a mess of the sexual function," he said. "In the end, no one is satisfied, and no one seems better controlled than in the past. And as we now see, most of the women are more or less alienated from their men because their affections are no longer engaged." He sighed. "But it's not possible to go back. It's all too well entrenched now as a part of the executive ethos and lifestyle. All we have to do is look at the youngest generation—you, Alexandra, and Daniel." He sighed again. "Drink your cognac, dear. And then choose something for us to listen to. Unless you want to talk more?"

Alexandra shook her head. No, they'd said too much already. But as the cognac warmed her she realized she did feel better, knowing that someone understood her at least a little. She would pick a late Beethoven sonata, she decided—something it would require a great deal of concentration to listen to.

# Chapter Twenty-six

After Liz finished her late dinner—having arrived back from the house on the Suiattle River at 9:30—Hazel briefed her on her meeting with the Co-op people. She ended her report—which included an account of the argument between Martha Greenglass and Anne, since given her paranoia about Martha, Liz always wanted to know exactly what she and Martha talked about—by remarking that while she and Anne were being driven home she had herself put the question Martha had asked Anne.

"So?" Liz said. "What did the girl say?"

"She said that she knew very well she was a renegade and traitor; and for that reason she would deserve any punishment she got for betraying her country."

"She said *that?*"

"Oh yes. And she meant it, too."

Liz looked thoughtful. "Alice Warner sure knows how to pick them. It's amazing that she followed Allison here." She frowned. "Unless…? No, I don't believe she's a plant. What an absurd idea. A girl like that wouldn't have the gumption." Liz's teeth gnawed at her lower lip. "Maybe I should put *her* to the test, too," she said. "Perhaps work something out for the project I have in mind for Cleghorn?"

Cleghorn was the new renegade from Com & Tran. "Liz, you really don't need to test Anne," Hazel said. "She *loves* Allison. So if Allison is with you, you have nothing to fear from Anne."

Liz's eyes gleamed. "Allison will always be my woman," she said softly. "After all we've been through together, I know that as sure as I know my own name."

Hazel swallowed the last of the tea in her cup. She might as well get it over with, she thought, for there would never be the "right moment" for this particular subject. She set down her cup and looked at

Liz. "When the first accusations about human rights violations were made last year, you ordered an investigation, didn't you?"

"Yes, darling, surely you remember typing the final report I wrote?" Liz stretched out full length and tucked a cushion under her head.

"But your investigation found nothing like what was found in those detention facilities last week, or anything that that doctor was talking about this afternoon?"

Liz's eyes searched Hazel's face. "A few incidents, but nothing systematic. As for what the doctor alleges, you must remember that San Diego is run for the most part by Military. God knows what *they* do."

"How thorough was your investigation?"

Liz sighed. "What is it you're getting at, Hazel?"

"I'm trying to understand some things," Hazel said. "The picture I'm getting is horrible. Really horrible. And since you were more or less running Security for all those years, I'm wondering how you could have let that kind of thing happen."

Liz sat up. "Are you holding me responsible for individuals' excesses?"

Hazel swallowed. "Let me ask you this, Liz. You've said several times in the past that there have always been what you call scum in Security. But you've been pretty vague about what you mean by that. Is it Company policy to torture people in certain instances?"

Liz ran her fingers through her hair. "All right, darling. You've asked for it. You're sure you want to know about such things?" Hazel nodded. "Okay. Then yes. There are three categories of instances in which torture is considered. Never is it to be undertaken lightly, though. Not the way these people are talking about." Liz held up her left hand and with the fingers of her right hand bent her index finger back. "First category: certain vital interrogations, mainly abroad. Almost never in this country, except when national security is perceived to be gravely threatened." Liz bent her middle finger, joining it to her index finger. "Second category: occasional assistance in interrogations involving enemy intelligence agents or officers, where such interrogations won't make embarrassing waves in the diplomatic sphere." Liz bent back her ring finger, then dropped her hands onto her thighs. "Third category: punishment of Company or ODS people found to be doubling. In any situation involving American citizens, Wedgewood is required to give formal approval. And usually Wedgewood checks with Sedgewick first." Liz drew a deep breath. "You see, it's not as loose a situation as you seem to think, Hazel."

"Have you ever given *your* approval for someone's being tortured, Liz?"

Liz flushed. "For godsake, Hazel, *no*! I've already told you my feelings on this subject. Why can't you accept what I tell you as truth?"

Why was Liz being so defensive?

Hazel pressed on. "But what about those two prisons? Lisa said she saw with her own eyes that there were victims of torture there! She wouldn't make such a thing up!"

"Yes, darling, I know," Liz said. "I'm not denying what they found. You might wonder why *Lisa* doesn't know more about what was going on under her own nose!" Liz sat up. "I admit I should have conducted a more thorough investigation. I should have sent a team of physicians around. I went about it the wrong way." Liz glared at her. "Is that what you want to hear me say? That I was negligent?"

"Don't shout, Liz. I just...I just need to know about this. I'm trying to understand. How it could happen." A sudden rush of tears took Hazel by surprise. "It's so horrible, it seems important to know how it could happen at all."

"Oh shit," Liz muttered, lying back down. "Listen darling, please. I couldn't root out the scum back when I was running the country. God knows, I tried. If I couldn't do it then, how could I do it later, when I had not only Sedgewick, Wedgewood, Ambrose, and Stevens to deal with, but Booth as well?" Liz stared earnestly into Hazel's eyes. "If anyone consciously promoted the abuses, it was Stevens and Ambrose. In fact, I did find out about the drugs and that Ambrose was making a whopping profit on them, that his father had a big interest in the company producing them. So I sent down an order to stop the drugging. But apparently after I left, Stevens or Ambrose reinstituted the old order. Or else the local people just did as they damned well pleased. You have to understand, Hazel, that I didn't have much contact with ODS. All through the war Ambrose handled domestic order. All I knew was that he was following the lines laid down by Sedgewick at the outset of the Blanket—which was when ODS really started cracking down. That was Sedgewick's way of dealing with the disorder. And my god,

Hazel, I can hardly blame him when I think of those first few weeks after the Blanket. The country practically went up in flames!"

Liz sighed. Staring at her hands, she twined her fingers together. "Anyway, I didn't really want to give my time to matters involving ODS. I didn't feel I could junk Sedgewick's policies—christ I was constantly looking over my shoulder waiting for the Executive to decide they didn't need me and to charge me with god knows what crimes—overstepping my authority, for one thing. If you had any idea, darling, what those days were like! Trying to put up a good show with Sedgewick, when I could hardly get him off his damned island, could hardly get him sober enough to sit up straight in a chair. That little Anne may be telling you stories about my power, but there are certain things it's hard to do when one's power is not quite legitimate. I couldn't be a new broom, Hazel. If I tried axing some of the very people who made my power possible, what do you suppose would have happened?" Liz stretched out her hand and touched Hazel's ankle. "Please don't doubt my morality, darling. I don't think I could bear it if you did."

Hazel extended her own hand and touched Liz's fingers. "Do you think Lisa will be able to work with them on their new project of going after these small places of torture and detention?"

"God darling, I don't know. It sounds pretty doubtful. It's not as though Lisa hung out with ODS types much herself. Of course, she may have some idea of locations of safe-houses and such that might be used for these other purposes..." Liz yawned. "Lord I'm tired. Can we go to bed early, darling? It's been a grueling day—getting up at the crack of dawn to be there for Cleghorn's arrival, then debriefing Cleghorn, and then the drive back."

Hazel sat up. "I'm not tired yet, Liz."

Liz sat up, too, and grinned slyly. "I can fix that," she promised.

They crossed the hall to their bedroom and made love. Afterwards, Liz fell asleep at once. But Hazel did not. She had too many things on her mind to sleep easily, lovemaking notwithstanding.

# Chapter Twenty-seven

"Put it out of your mind, *chere*." Nicole's voice was gruff, but in a good way. "The gardener's out there right now collecting a great big bouquet of it for you to take. Didn't I tell you I'd see to it?"

"I know, Nicole," Alexandra said. "But I just had to make sure. Sorry for bothering you." She disconnected and picked up her pen and ran a line through the item "parsley." Next, packing. That was easy, since it was only for two days and one night. She went into the dressing room, got out a garment bag and picked out one set of evening clothes, a couple of lounging gowns, and two tunic-trousers sets. Not that she'd need two, but in case she had a rip or spilled something on the clothing she was already wearing. She clipped the hangers to the garment bag's rack, tucked the clothing inside the bag, and zipped it. Next she fetched a small case from the closet for her underwear and toiletries; she was tossing into it the odds and ends that struck her as things she might like to have with her, when someone tapped on the door. Impatiently, she crossed the room and opened it.

Clarice confronted her with bloodshot eyes and a blotchy face covered with an unusually thick application of make-up. Alexandra stared at her for a few seconds without speaking. Her heart was pounding so hard she thought the girl could probably hear it. "What do you want?" she said, barely keeping her voice steady.

"I just heard that you're going to Washington for the weekend. I thought you might need help packing."

"It's only an overnight trip." Alexandra's voice, though suddenly hoarse, came out brusque, almost harsh, though she meant it to be neutral. "Why would I need help packing?"

"Please, *carina*," Clarice said, her voice rising. "Please at least say goodbye to me."

Alexandra heard a sound down the hall. Afraid that someone might be eavesdropping, she stepped back and gestured Clarice in. "I don't want a scene," she said coldly, hoping she was giving the impression of being in control. The girl, she saw, was wearing the pearl pendant. She said, more sharply than she intended, "And if you're going to wear that on the plane, put it inside your shirt and wait until I'm out of sight before you display it."

Clarice gave her the look of a hurt puppy. Tears brimmed her eyes as she reached behind her neck and unclasped the chain. "Here," she said, the tears now overflowing. "If that is how you feel, then you must take it back." She poured the chain and pendant into her palm and held it out to Alexandra. "If it angers you to see me wearing it I don't want it."

Alexandra ground her teeth. "Don't be ridiculous," she said, aware that her cheeks were burning with shame. "It's yours now."

Clarice blinked ineffectually against the flood of tears. "I don't want it, not like this."

"Then sell it." Alexandra turned away from the sight of the girl's flowing, reproachful eyes. "I certainly don't want to ever see it again, much less *wear* it." Immediately she regretted the churlishness of her words. Her mother, in this situation, would be gracious rather than grudging.

"I thought it was special," Clarice cried. "I thought you were different!"

Alexandra whirled. "It's not going to work," she shouted. "I know what you're trying to do, but I'm not that easy anymore. For godsake go fix your eyes, your mascara, or whatever that black stuff is that's running all over your face."

Clarice put her hands to her eyes. "I know I'm so ugly today," she wailed.

"The plane is leaving in less than half an hour," Alexandra said more quietly. "Go wash your face while there's still time." Why wouldn't she just go away?

Clarice dropped her hands and caught Alexandra's eye. Flinching, Alexandra looked away. "How can you be so cruel so young?" the girl whispered. "Why did you have to be so kind at first? What is it that I've done? I've gone over and over every word between us, and I can find nothing, nothing at all. Tell me, *carina*, please!"

"You have to go now," Alexandra said wearily.

"Good-bye, *carina*," Clarice said softly after a moment, then turned and went out the door.

Her vision blurred by an uncontrollable rush of tears, wishing she could wipe the very memory of Clarice from her mind, hoping that once the girl was gone she would never think of her again, Alexandra finished packing.

Another tap sounded on the door. Afraid Clarice had returned, Alexandra called, "Who is it?"

"Penderel, madam."

Alexandra opened the door and admitted the butler. "Just the small case and the garment bag," she said. He took them and left. She looked at her watch. Ten more minutes before she had to go downstairs. Fifteen minutes before the plane was scheduled to take off. She moved to the window and stared out at the trees. *You're taking the girl too seriously.* What was happening to her, that she could be so hateful, feel so hateful? Mama would probably say it was a game, that a girl's manipulations were to be expected, that the best thing to do was to let them think they were manipulating you: she could almost hear Mama offering that advice, because Mama had said the same thing in the context of other situations. Well it was a good thing she hadn't let the girl sleep with her: at least she didn't have *that* to be ashamed of. But to find so much meanness in herself... And that they were manipulative like that, willing to say anything if they thought it might serve their purpose. Clarice, standing there crying like that, Clarice whom she'd slapped, came off as a persecuted underdog, a weakling unfairly taken advantage of. Making her, Alexandra, a monster. How could she have so misjudged the girl? How could someone so sophisticated and experienced as Clarice be willing to throw such scenes? And to think she'd imagined that Clarice must regret being stuck with someone so young and gauche. But then Clarice must have misjudged her, too, at the end admitting she found it hard to believe that Alexandra hadn't been what she'd thought.

Alexandra pulled away from the window, picked up the novel she was currently reading, and went down to the Small Study. She found her father putting things into a leather attaché case. A frisson trickled up her spine at the sight of him wedging a handgun among the papers. Why did he do that, when all his gorillas—and the plane itself—were armed to the teeth? But as far as she knew he always carried firearms in his attaché case. Alexandra let her gaze rove and spotted Thursday's *Executive Times* still laid open to the editorial page. Irreverently she wondered if he intended bringing it with him so that he could continue rereading the editor's exhortation to get Robert Sedgewick back onto the job before Security entirely self-destructed... Although he did not say so, she knew the editorial was responsible for his sudden decision to go to DC—and not his desire to see the Saturday night performance of *The Magic Flute* as he alleged. She had never seen him in such an elated mood before. DC was in an uproar over what had been done to those prisons—which was why, according to her father at any rate, Military had been allowed to get away with such a gratuitously stupid act as making air strikes on another country's property. And as her father had also pointed out, the disastrous flooding of the Mississippi and certain of its tributaries hadn't even made the front page: such extensive damage to property and life was considered insignificant by the *Times* in comparison with the crisis in Security.

"All right, I'm ready to go," he said, flipping the tiny switch that electronically locked his attaché case. (What about an EMP? she'd once asked him. Nothing I carry around with me is indispensable, he'd replied. It's more important that access to the things inside be denied to possible thieves than that I be assured of access myself.) Together they left through the east door and strode across the lawn to the landing strip where the sleek silver jet glittered in the sunlight, its engines already whining. Three gorillas—including Blake, one of the pair specially assigned to Alexandra—stood at the foot of the stairs.

Oh these rituals and protocols, Alexandra thought, how useless, how stupid, but how much he loves them: she could see it in the way he held his head and shoulders, in his pretense of unconsciousness of being the center of everyone's attention. Her father dropped her arm to let her ascend the stairs first; he followed close behind, speaking over his shoulder to the gorillas. In the dimness of the shuttered forward cabin she grew conscious of the eyes of the accompanying service-techs, the tutors, the rest of the gorillas, and most especially of Clarice whom she saw out of the corner of her eye sitting at the rear of the cabin. She kept own gaze on the door of the rear cabin and felt her father's hand on her back, urging her on. Relief swept over

her as she passed into the brilliantly sunlit rear cabin. The tutors and
Nicole, the valet, Higgins, and Clarice were not allowed a view out of
the plane for security reasons; only she, her father, the pilot, and the
gorillas knew the island's location, which meant that the shutters on
the windows in the forward cabin could be lifted only when they approached DC.

Her father closed the door between the two cabins and took the
seat beside her. As they buckled in he said, "So she made you a scene
this morning."

Alexandra looked at him in surprise. "How did you know that?"

"Her face is blotchy."

"Oh." If he had figured it out, probably everyone else on the plane
had, too. That was another lesson she had learned from this affair:
privacy where she was concerned could only be illusory. She might as
well be living in an aquarium.

# Chapter Twenty-eight

Celia and Emily waited a long time outside the hospital in the back of Emily's car, though Elena had been due to come off her shift twenty minutes before they had arrived to pick her up. "More coverage of those disgusting protests from the eugenicists," Emily said, her eyes scanning the editorial page of *The San Diego Union*. "It burns me up the way those people are not only allowed to protest for their nauseating fascist ends but are given extensive media attention, while any other kind of protest on any other issue is forbidden. Listen to this: 'If the Department of Health exercised greater selectivity in its criteria for parenthood, unrest would cease to exist. Only those fit to give birth to and raise law-abiding citizens should be allowed the privilege of maternity or paternity. If the Department of Health in its implementation of Birth Limitation cannot serve this country more responsibly, we strongly urge that the Birth Limitation Program be placed under the supervision and authority of Security Services, the one branch of the Executive fully aware of the disruptive elements in our society.'" Emily threw the paper onto the floor. "What a crazy world we live in, Celia."

"Most of those eugenicists are racists, too," Celia said. "They'd like to see only anglos allowed to give birth."

"Really? But who would do all the boring or messy work that needs to be done if there were only whites left?"

"I've heard their arguments," Celia said. "They say there will always be an infinite pool of cheap labor because there will always be people wanting to immigrate. Because the US is such a paradise."

Emily sighed. "Shall one of us go see if your mother's gotten hung up?"

Celia checked her watch and saw that they'd been waiting fifteen minutes already. "I'll go," she said, restless with the usual anxiety that crawled over her whenever things did not go exactly according to plan.

A lot could happen in thirty-five minutes: one never knew if things were going to be "normal" or not. Celia opened the door and swung her legs out—then stopped when she spotted her mother coming out of the hospital. Celia noticed that her shoulders were slumped and that she moved with the heaviness of deep exhaustion or depression. Celia slid closer to Emily to make room.

"Sorry I'm late," Elena said as she got in and closed the door. "There were two things keeping me, which I'll want to discuss with both of you." She glanced across Celia at Emily and said hello. The driver started the car, and Elena leaned back against the seat.

They were quiet for most of the drive to Emily's beach house. Only when the car stopped to wait for the gates to open did Elena speak. "Someone posted one of those cartoons in the staff women's room this morning. It stayed up for a good three hours." Elena half-smiled. "It would be interesting to know who took it down." The car pulled past the gates and parked.

"Probably someone afraid," Celia said. "Fear does most of the work of repression."

"Which cartoon was it?" Emily asked. "I recently saw one on the subject of the prison bombings in Cameroon."

"This one showed the acting head of Security standing before the rest of the Executive wringing his hands, saying something like, 'But I don't know how I lost them. I thought they were all too drugged to move! They must be around here somewhere...' The humor was in the expression on their faces—oh, and off in the corner, peering in through a little window, was the usual alien caricature, with a 'hee-hee' balloon."

They got out of the car and walked into the house. Emily detoured to the kitchen, but Celia and Elena went directly out to the terrace. "What a gorgeous day," Elena said, waving her hands at the hard glittering blue of the sky and sea.

"You should take some time off, Mama," Celia said. "You look so tired."

Elena smiled at Celia in gentle mockery. "You've just noticed? I've been looking tired for years now, Cee."

Celia bit her lip. It was true, she *had* just seen her mother as she came out of the hospital this afternoon as though for the first time in months. She watched her mother hold her face to the breeze ruffling the bougainvillea. "Part of the reason I thought we should come out here was so that we could discuss Luis's situation openly," Celia said. They hadn't been able to talk about Luis at home, confined to scribbling notes to one another that they burned on reading.

Emily arrived with a tray loaded with glasses of juice and water. "It kills me that I haven't had time lately to swim," she said, glancing out at the majestic progression of waves rolling one after another up onto her beach.

"We're all wearing ourselves to the bone," Celia grumbled. "But I guess we don't have any other choice."

Elena reached for a glass of juice. "No, Celia, that's wrong. What we do *is* a choice. A choice that we need to convince others to make."

Emily said, "Is that one of the things you specially wanted to discuss?"

Elena seated herself on a lounge. "Yes. Ever since Celia told me about the project of trying to get up a professional petition—positioning signing as an action one step removed from actually joining a dissenting organization—I've been discreetly sounding out my colleagues at the hospital." Elena took a long sip of juice. "And then today I heard something new."

She shifted her chair to get the sun out of her eyes. "Apparently ODS people are making the rounds of public facilities looking for replacements for the physicians, psychiatrists, and physical therapists who were exposed on the Free Zone's vid programs. The story is they're being transferred somewhere else. Because of their professional and social embarrassment." Elena's mouth tightened. "The very thought of people using their medical expertise to assist or design torture turns my stomach. They should be drummed out of the profession. But I doubt if we can get the AMA even to reprimand them."

"Wait a minute," Celia said. "How can they be needing new medical people when we've eliminated those prisons? It doesn't make sense!"

Elena and Emily stared at her. Finally Emily said, "It must be that those medical people worked not only in the two detention facilities, but in other places as well. In those smaller, unmarked places Luis was talking about."

Celia looked at her mother. "Are the recruiters having any success?"

Elena shrugged. "No one's going to say, are they? Apparently the salaries being offered are double and sometimes triple the usual pay at our hospital. Needless to say, those of us who work in the public sector make such paltry sums by comparison with some of the private practitioners that we may seem to be easier pickings."

Celia's hands clenched into tight, white-knuckled fists. "Reading all that stuff the Committee dug out from the twentieth century made me realize how the entire machinery of violent repression would be impossible without the collaboration and complicity of the profession- al sector. In almost every instance, once the lawyers and doctors dedi- cated themselves to ethical stances and began ostracizing colleagues actively collaborating, it grew harder and harder for the governments to sustain such methods. Why why *why* can't we accomplish that now?" She shook her head; her jaw was as tightly clenched as her fists. "It's as though we're living in the most ethically backwards of times. I tried to explain this to John Daniels yesterday, but I could see that all he could think about was getting me out of his office, out of the build- ing, lest the firm be contaminated by my presence. He made the usual argument about how if the judges wouldn't play, it was pointless for attorneys to sign petitions or go after those who work for the state."

"You don't think that's true, do you," Emily said.

"No," Celia said vehemently. "I don't. There's a legal tradition in this country, one that can touch judges as well as attorneys. But we're up against fear and greed. Fear in the general attitude of complicity maintained by the majority of professionals. And greed on the part of those actively collaborating."

"The fall in the standard of living is difficult for some people to cope with, Cee," Elena said. "I don't know that it's always greed. It may be another form of fear. A fear of squalid poverty. A fear of in- creasingly lower status. I don't think I'd call that *greed*, exactly."

Celia waved her hand in a gesture of dismissal. "Well I've no pa- tience with people who put their own comfort above morality and ethics in the very grossest sense."

"Most people don't know what's going on," Elena said.

Her mother was too easy on people. She wanted so much to think the best of them. Celia said, "That may have been true during the war, but not now. Not after the vid exposés. There's no excuse for anyone, Mama. It drives me crazy, thinking of how at this very second there are people in the most desperate situations right here in San Diego while the world just goes on about its business!"

"It doesn't do any good, Celia, to be judging others so harshly." Elena spoke in one of her most gentle tones of voice.

A silence dropped over them, and Celia felt her anger reverberating in it almost palpably.

"Come," Elena finally said. "Being so righteous and judgmental won't help us establish a resistance. And I do think it's general resistance we need to be thinking about more than anything else now."

Celia stared down at her fists in her lap. "Don't worry," she said, still angry. "I won't let my personal feelings get in the way of the work."

Another silence set in, and Celia stared out at the waves and listened to their rhythms. She thought of a conversation she'd had with her mother recently, while her mother was tending her table of bromeliads, which required constant, daily care. "I don't know why you bother, Mama," Celia had said, thinking of how hard her mother worked and how little time she had for herself. "I bother, Celia, because they're beautiful and demanding and don't have a damned thing to do with work or politics. I bother because they give my heart a lift, every time I see their beauty, see that they're flourishing in this desert climate. And I bother, finally, because I can." Her mother, of course, had been trying to tell her something about the destructiveness of constant, bleak anger. Celia hated being the sour note sounding monotonously and constantly out of turn. But she could not help her anger, for it was directed outward, almost at scattershot random in its generality, at an indifferent world that allowed and enabled the beasts to do their worst. At this very moment, as the three of them sat here and enjoyed the soft ocean breeze and the lovely sound of the surf, people were suffering the most unspeakable torments. Lisa Mott's—indeed all executives'—indifference made them moral monsters, complicit with the beasts.

After about a score of new waves had rolled in, Emily said, "I think I may be able to get some executive women to sign the petition."

Celia didn't take her eyes off the water, which looked utterly implacable today. "Right," she said, pissed that Emily would even think such an endeavor could be viable. "And scientists will next be telling us that the Marq'ssan have turned the moon into green cheese."

"Oh I'm fairly certain I can," Emily said. "But whether their signatures will mean anything is something else."

Celia looked at Emily and raised her eyebrows in a silent query.

Emily produced an uncharacteristically grim smile. "Believe it or not, among women executives, too, there's a certain level of fear. Not of physical retaliation, merely of being socially and even financially penalized."

"And the men?" Elena asked.

"Even more so," Emily said. "But then my contact with male executives is mainly with men concerned to keep in good standing with my father." Her smile became wry and self-mocking. "As you can imagine, conversations with such people about human rights can be pretty weird."

They sipped their drinks in silence and watched the surf. After a minute or so, Elena said, "The other thing I wanted to discuss is the need for evacuating a patient who was brought in and dumped on us by persons unknown." Elena's eyes flashed with irony. "Unknown in the official sense, that is. Needless to say, they were security types. At any rate, this woman is in very bad shape. She was unconscious when they dumped her. She had been abducted with her husband and he had been made to watch her being tortured. When she came to, she was anxious about her cousin and aunt, who live with her, as well as about her husband. She's very worried they'll pick up the aunt and cousin living with them—if they haven't already." Elena sighed. "I myself think they might come back for *her*. They sometimes do. It happened just last week. I have the feeling that the only reason they dumped her on us was because they wanted her patched up enough to be able to take another whack at her." Elena stared out at the waves. "Later, after I'd heard that ODS is actively recruiting medical staff, it occurred to me we may be getting more of this sort of thing."

"So somehow we have to get this woman and her family out of town," Emily said.

"The Marq'ssan's regular pick-up day is Friday," Celia said.

"Almost a whole week away," Emily said. "Look. If there's some way we can dodge watchdogs, I could fly them up to the Free Zone myself."

Celia stared at her in surprise. "But Em, if they catch you—"

"Exactly," Emily interrupted. "That's why I say I'd do it *if* there's some way to elude whatever watchdogs they might have put on the woman and her family. As far as I can see, that's the main problem." She frowned. "We'd have to set up a complicated kind of shuffle designed to confuse them." She looked at Elena. "Unless you think it's possible this woman isn't under surveillance?"

"Not a chance," Elena said. "Otherwise they would have dumped her somewhere else. On an empty lot in one of the abandoned parts of town. Or even in her neighborhood, as an object lesson. But not with us."

"Is she ambulatory?" Celia inquired. That would make a big difference.

Elena shook her head. "No. We had to send her to surgery because she was hemorrhaging internally. She's very weak. And both ankles are fractured."

The graphic details set Celia's stomach churning. "There must be *something* we can do."

"We have to make up some kind of scam with two vans." Emily's tone was blessedly decisive. "We take her out in one van, then switch, maybe in a parking complex. We'll have to ditch the first van since once they find out it's empty the person driving it will be in danger of being stopped and arrested." She looked at Celia. "Can you find volunteers to do the driving?"

"The Center can," she said.

"And we'll need a physician to accompany her," Emily said, looking at Elena.

Elena, her eyes steady, nodded. "I will do it myself," she said.

"No!" The very thought of it made Celia frantic. "They'll *recognize* you. You know they will!"

Elena shook her head. "She's my patient."

"My god," Celia moaned, "You know what will happen the minute you returned to the hospital without her. It has to be somebody else, Mama. Somebody they don't already know."

"We will find a way to work this out," Elena said. "I rather think I might be in less danger than the people on duty in the hospital at the time, who would be held responsible for losing her." Her mouth quirked. "Though I *suppose* they could simply say some armed men came along and took her and the staff thought they were security people. As for being seen—it's not necessary. I can wait inside the van and let others bring her out of the hospital. The only danger will be at the point of switching."

Emily said, "I think she's right, Cee." She looked at Elena. "You'll have to arrange for some time off, though. And make it look as though you're spending it here."

Celia supposed they were right. This was probably the best and safest way. But it would still be dangerous.

# Chapter Twenty-nine

Rather than join Ginger, Lacie, and Anne in devouring the most recent installments of their favorite soap, Hazel lay in the bathtub reading a murder mystery by Michael Innes, her current literary passion, which she had picked up that afternoon in her favorite used book stall in the Pike Place Market. But she made her bath too hot, and after only twenty minutes had to get out. As she was toweling herself, she heard voices, one of them sobbing, coming from the bedroom. She stood very still and strained to hear. But the voices were too muffled to distinguish. Unsure of whether or not to make her presence known, she went to the door of the dressing room and pressed her ear against it.

"Everything's getting crazier and crazier!" Hazel identified the voice as Allison's. "There has to be a better way, Elizabeth! We're sabotaging our own side, for godsake! And you can see what's happening—Military's going to take over and plunge the country into another goddam war." Allison's voice rose to a shriek. "I don't think I can stand it!"

"Ssh, ssh, darling, it's not as bad as you think," Liz's voice soothed.

"It's worse than *you* apparently think! My god we're losing what's left of *Africa* because of those idiots bombing Cameroon! Already five different governments have announced they're evicting our military bases. Can't you *see* what's happening! You have to *do* something! You saw that editorial in the *Times*! Don't you see, if you could get back together with Sedgewick, then—"

"Allison, get hold of yourself," Liz interrupted in that firm, patient tone of voice Hazel couldn't remember ever hearing Liz use to another executive. "We're not going to give ourselves up like that. Do you have any idea of what they'd do to us if we did? They won't be pinning any medals on us, that's certain."

"But if Sedgewick is reinstated—"

"You think *Sedgewick* would welcome us back with open arms?" Liz's tone became harsh. "*Never* are renegades welcomed back, *never!* *Never!* Get that through your head. It's not a possibility. We're over the line, there's no turning back!" Allison's response was too muffled for Hazel to hear. "No, no. No despair, darling." Liz's voice softened to a murmur. "I promise you, I give you my word that it will work out, that we will eventually go back, that I won't allow disaster to strike, I promise, love. You know I keep my word..."

And then Allison's sobbing ceased and Hazel heard nothing. She stood frozen, wishing she could disappear, afraid to move lest she reveal her presence, trapped in an embarrassing situation.

"Is this what you want, darling?" Liz's voice dropped into its huskiest register. "Are you sure?"

"Oh damn it Elizabeth I've never stopped wanting you," Allison gasped. "All these years—"

"Sssh, let's not talk, love," Elizabeth cooed. Oh god, Hazel thought, they're going to make love now. And here I am, eavesdropping. She stepped quietly back into the bathroom and eased the door shut. Then she sat down on the tile floor, leaned her head back against the wall, and picked up her murder mystery.

Some time later—unable to concentrate on the book, Hazel had read the same page over about ten times—the door opened and Liz came in, naked, and went to the toilet. When about a second after she started peeing she saw Hazel, she gasped. "My god! What are you—" she broke off. "Oh, I see," she said jerkily, her breath coming in gasps. "You were bathing. When Allison and I came in. And then when you heard or saw us..." Her eyebrow quirked sardonically. "Is that it?"

"Sorry," Hazel said, wondering at Liz's being so flustered. "If you like, in the future I can bathe in one of the baths the others share. There *are* problems, you see, in our sharing a room. It is very awkward, my getting in the way of your privacy. Maybe I should have my own room, Liz?"

"Don't be ridiculous," Liz said in her haughtiest voice.

Hazel got to her feet. "I'm thinking of you. Obviously you didn't mean for me to be privy to the full nature of your relationship with Allison. Therefore—"

"It's your damned jealousy again," Liz said. "Wanting to punish me for being with another woman. Must we go through this again?"

"That's not what I meant," Hazel said slowly. "I was just thinking of your convenience. Naturally I'm willing to keep this arrangement, but surely you see it's awkward?"

"I suppose you're going to spread this around the household, too."

"Why would I do that? It's your and Allison's business. Why are you so upset, Liz?"

Liz gave her a strange look. "Don't you understand? If word of this ever got out, Allison and I would be socially ruined. We'd be ostracized by all other executive women!"

"But that's crazy! Why would it matter?"

Liz's eyes glittered dangerously. "Because executives don't have sex with executives!"

Hazel strove to reassure Liz with her eyes. "You can trust me, Liz. I'll never tell a soul." Thinking about how many years this must have been between Allison and Liz, she added, "But I see now why you're so hostile to Anne. It's really not fair, you know." To think that Liz was jealous of a service-tech! Up until a few minutes ago, if someone had suggested such a thing to her she would have said it was impossible.

"I'm not hostile to Allison's little service-tech." Liz yanked a handful of toilet paper off the roll. "As you very well know I've just offered her a job, and you've never seen me being rude to her, because I never have been rude to her."

"Always calling her 'little,'" Hazel mused. "There's hostility in that, I think."

Liz got up from the toilet. "You don't know what you're talking about." She moved to the door, then paused to say, "And you don't have to go on sitting in here. Allison's already dressed and gone."

Hazel levered herself to her feet and followed Liz into the dressing room. Why was she so testy? "Allison seemed upset," Hazel said, to change the subject.

Liz got down on the rug and began doing push-ups. "She drinks too much," Liz said as she raised her body from the floor.

"You don't think she's deeply upset?"

Liz did another push-up. "Of course she's upset. That goes without saying. But it's a matter of her handling it. When she drinks as much as she has tonight, she can't handle it." She did another push-up. "And that little Anne doesn't help. She feeds Allison's doubts instead of giving her the support she needs." Liz did another push-up. "You're going to have to work on her, darling. Get her to take a more positive attitude about what we're doing. And even about the Free Zone. She's *too* brainwashed."

What the hell did that mean? *Too* brainwashed? "Brainwashed?" she said. "In what way is Anne brainwashed?"

Liz rolled over onto her back and began doing leg-lifts. "She believes everything the media has fed her over her entire adult life. Which is to say she can't seem to make the kind of attitudinal adjustments that are necessary now."

Attitudinal adjustments?

"You've got to foster some tolerance in her for the possibility that the Executive may be temporarily off the rails. Yes, that's a good way to put it," Liz said thoughtfully. "And for godsake help her accept our dealing with Co-op people. If she can't, we'll have to keep her away from them."

Hazel shook her head. "I don't understand you, Liz. On the one hand you worry about Martha Greenglass corrupting me, while on the other you seem to be worrying about Anne alienating the Co-op people by not being flexible enough."

"I don't worry about Greenglass corrupting you, darling," Liz snapped. "I just don't want her seducing you away from me. Which is a different matter entirely." She sat up and glared at Hazel. "And don't look at me that way. You know damned well what I'm talking about."

Hazel sighed. "You know I'm not sexually attracted to Martha. At least not very much," she added mischievously. "No, no, I'm just teasing, Liz, don't look at me that way. You know I'm monogamous."

"Yes," Liz retorted, "that's precisely what worries me."

"It's so silly, Rapunzel," Hazel said softly, smiling. "You know you're beautiful and that I love you. What has Martha Greenglass got that I could suddenly stop desiring and loving you and switch my affections to her?"

Liz stood up in one astonishingly fluid movement. "I suppose it's because of all people it would most hurt me for you to go to her," she said. "Yes, I think that must be it."

"Silly Rapunzel," Hazel said, still smiling. She went to Liz and wrapped her arms tightly around her.

"Will you take another bath with me?" Liz murmured into Hazel's ear.

Hazel, laughing, let herself be drawn back into the bathroom. But she wondered why Liz was so upset, even now that they had talked. In spite of Liz's continual show of confidence and strength, Hazel sensed that she was profoundly disturbed. Her recurring dream, her lack of faith in Hazel's loyalty, her testiness all pointed to trouble beneath the surface. Even if she wouldn't admit it.

# Chapter Thirty

## [i]

Alexandra looped the long string of pearls twice around her neck. She stared in the mirror for a minute or so and debated making another loop, but decided she liked the way they hung past the wide band of sash at her waist. Then, checking herself out from several angles, she scrutinized her appearance *in toto*: better that she find any flaws than her father. She took an especially long look at her new hairstyle, about which she had serious misgivings. She had had it done exactly as he'd asked, almost without thinking about it. But now she had to live with it—for a few weeks at least. What would he say when he saw it?

She seated herself at the dressing table. The problem was, she didn't feel quite like herself. Her ears felt exposed, and in the mirror she looked like a stranger even her mother might not recognize at first sight. Staring at her naked ears, she worried about whether or not to wear earrings. Would earrings call further attention to her ears, or would the hairstyle automatically do that and the lack of earrings only emphasize their nakedness? Alexandra went to her earring box and sifted through its contents. What could one wear with pearls? And with rose silk already honeycombed with little inset pleats crusted with various bric-a-brac? Wouldn't earrings be too much? She looked at the tiniest pair she could find, thin gold rings. No matter what she did her ears would be conspicuous. Impulsively, with mischief aforethought, Alexandra fastened one of the earrings to her right ear and left the other one naked. In a late twentieth-century novel she had recently read the characters wore only one earring, or else wore unmatched earrings, or sometimes more than one earring on an ear. Should anyone ask, she would say she was interested in old-fashioned styles. After all, if the service-techs could wear dresses, surely executives could wear a single earring if they chose.

When she had satisfied herself that she looked presentable, Alexandra went down to her father's study. "Oh!" she cried when she saw him standing with one elbow on the mantelshelf above the fireplace, reading a sheaf of flimsy. He looked over at her, smiled, and removed his glasses. "It's beautiful," she gushed, wanting to touch the gorgeous silk, to feel its sculptured pattern on her fingers.

"I ordered it a year ago last spring," he said, "but have never worn it. The silk was designed for this suit especially."

It had to be jouissance silk, Alexandra thought. And she'd never seen him in the post-war style before, either. The part of the sash falling diagonally from his left shoulder was studded with a border of tiny red stones—rubies, probably. They wouldn't sew glass onto jouissance silk, it would be unspeakably tacky even to consider it. "You look very distinguished," she said shyly. And not only that: tonight he looked fit, healthy, energetic. And perhaps because of the midnight blue woven into the fabric, the color did not seem as somber—or sinister, as he sometimes looked in black—as it might have.

"Then we make a perfect pair," he said, still(!) smiling. He glanced at his watch. "We don't have time for a drink. I hope you ate enough to tide you over?" Alexandra nodded. "Then *avanti*," he said, taking her arm.

In the foyer he stopped before the long, ornately framed mirror. Astonished, Alexandra stared at the closeness of their resemblance. With their hair styled exactly the same and their clothing—beyond the colors, and his diagonal sash opposed to her pearls—almost identical in style and cut, the resemblance made Alexandra feel strange, as though she were no longer herself. But she could see how pleased and even excited he was, so she kept her sense of strangeness to herself. "We could be brother and sister," he said. "Twins, even."

"I'm shorter than you are."

He snorted. "By at most half an inch."

In the car—not only one of the internal combustion types so rare even here in DC, but an exquisitely preserved antique—she let herself think about the prospect of a live performance of opera. She could count on the fingers of both hands the number of live performances—dance, symphony, chamber, and opera—she had attended in her life. Live performances, though imperfect and raw—so unlike the perfection of digitized recordings—imparted a magical excitement to the music, adding a frisson to the passion and a sort of wild elation that seemed to do with being there at the moment the music was produced, at seeing and feeling firsthand that musicians make music in a shared moment of creation. The first time she had attended a live concert she had conceived a longing to play with others, to be part of a group making music together, something she was deprived of playing the piano alone. Chamber music and concerti had thus taken on the seductive allure of something she might some day participate in. In college, perhaps.

As for this particular opera, she had seen video recordings of it, with subtitles, and of course had many times listened to the version of it she had on her data disk. She loved the music, but the story, as was characteristic of most opera libretti, was horrible. In fact, the story might be considered worse than the usual, for it revolved around the struggle between the evil fairy mother and the benevolent sorcerer father for their daughter. Alexandra had never been able to believe in the fairy mother's evil; in the opera, the daughter is only told her mother is evil by her father, and no proof seemed to be necessary for the daughter's turning away from her mother to her father (and—ugh—a male lover). Thinking about the opera's story, Alexandra glanced sidelong at her father. Would she be uncomfortable seeing this opera with him? It occurred to her to wonder if he had chosen to take her *because* of the story. But no. She knew that couldn't be the case, for the opera was an excuse to come to DC; his real reason had to do with the editorial about him. That *The Magic Flute* had been playing this weekend had been purely fortuitous.

"Where *is* the opera house?" Alexandra asked when it became clear they were heading away from the city. She had attended once a long time ago, but she'd been too little to know its actual location.

"Believe it or not, it's in McLean," her father said.

"McLean! Why would anyone build an opera house in McLean?" Where *was* McLean, anyway?

"Good question. Though it's true that not everyone lives in Georgetown. At any rate, it isn't far. And the acoustics are superb."

Alexandra fidgeted with her sash until the car pulled up before an enormous building that offered the illusion of having been constructed out of a series of dazzling white and chrome interlocking arches that looked as though they were about to fly apart. "A remnant of the short-lived Cosmic Phase," her father said. "The irony of anything called *cosmic* being found in McLean is almost cosmic itself." As one of the gorillas came around to open the door on her father's side, he added, "And by the way, make sure Blake is always within sight. I hope I don't have to explain to you how important security considerations are?"

"I'll be careful," Alexandra said, sliding along the seat to get out after him.

The pair of them walked up the shallow stairs (trailed by at least three gorillas) and into the cathedral-ceilinged lobby. Everywhere she looked she saw that same glittering white surface—what *was* it, she wondered? It was as smooth and shiny as chrome but veined like marble—and chrome, and holographic projections that people were avoiding walking into. They passed through the lobby unchallenged and ascended the winding chrome open-step staircase. She sensed eyes watching them. But perhaps everyone recognized her father, who must always attract stares among executives?

At the top of the staircase an usher greeted them by name and led them along the hall (lined with that same white material) past several open doorways through which Alexandra snatched glimpses of the theater. As they rounded the curve of the hall Alexandra spotted Marlin a few doors down, standing beside a closed door. Of course, he must have been sent to check everything out in advance. That was the way her father's security team operated. The usher stopped before the door that Marlin guarded, opened it, handed them programs, and wished them "a pleasant evening." Blake followed them inside; the other gorillas did not.

This box, Alexandra saw, did not adjoin the open boxes of the loggia but was one of four physically isolated from it. It held only nine seats—armchairs, really, none of them fastened to the floor. The walls here had been covered with black linen, and there wasn't a bit of chrome in sight. A low cabinet occupied a niche on the back wall; its open doors revealed champagne flutes and wine glasses of various shapes and half-liter bottles of water. Alexandra chose the middle seat in the first of the three rows; her father sat to her left. As they waited, she found it hard to be still and kept leaning forward to stare out at the theater and the people in evening dress who filled it.

"I don't think I've ever seen you so excited," her father said.

Avidly Alexandra scanned the audience in the seats below and in the loggia to her left. "I *love* Mozart! I *love* live performances!"

"Is that so?"

Alexandra pulled her gaze from the glittering crowd and noticed he was smiling *again*. And not his usual ghastly grimace, either, but a smile full of warmth. "I've never seen so many executives in one place together," she said. Of the hundreds of people seated within her range of vision (i.e., those in the orchestra and loggia), only a couple dozen appeared to be professionals. And the only service-techs besides the ushers were stunningly gorgeous girls dressed in floor-length dresses of deep décolletage, sitting beside executive women.

"Yes, there's a lot of money present," her father said drily.

Alexandra thought she saw a familiar face in the loggia: could that woman in the blousy cocoa tunic with sheer sleeves be Madeleine Bardeen, a friend of her mother's who sometimes visited them in Barbados? Uncertain, Alexandra took care not to catch the woman's eye or to seem to be staring at her—even though at least a quarter of the people in the loggia seemed to be staring at *her*.

The door behind them opened and Marlin stepped in. "Excuse me, sir. An usher just brought this for you."

Her father accepted the folded slip of paper and opened it. After a few seconds he took his Mont Blanc pen from his pocket, uncapped it, and scrawled a dozen or so words on the paper, refolded it, and handed it back to Marlin. "Here's the reply. See to it that Mr. Goodwin gets it." Marlin left with the note, and her father turned his gaze onto the loggia. "I've invited Edwin Goodwin to have a drink with us during intermission, Alexandra. Ah, there he is, at the far end. Not surprising to see him here, I suppose, since he's such an opera buff, though the nineteenth- and twentieth-century repertoire are more to his taste." He turned his head to look at Alexandra.

"Oh," Alexandra said. She had never met anyone—besides her father of course—in the Cabinet. She drew a deep breath. "*Are* people staring at us? Or am I imagining it?"

Her father chuckled. "Certainly there are people staring at us. By tomorrow noon everyone in DC will know we attended this opera. And I wouldn't be surprised if it rated a mention in tomorrow's *Executive Times*."

He sounds satisfied, Alexandra thought. She considered asking him more directly the reason he thought they were attracting attention, but the house lights dimmed and the concertmistress walked out and commenced the ceremonial tuning of the rather small orchestra. When the cacophony of A's sounded by all the variable-pitched instruments in the orchestra ceased, the conductor strode out and a light chatter of applause rippled through the audience.

The first chords of the overture sounded. Excited almost past bearing, Alexandra at once slipped into an elated state of intense concentration and forgot everything but the music, the performers, and their creation.

[ii]

At intermission Alexandra excused herself to go to the women's room. Her father said, "Meet me at the bar, then. And take Blake with you."

"Into the women's room?" Alexandra gaily retorted. "He'd be massacred in no time at all!" An image of her gorilla's being torn limb from limb by an angry crowd of executive women tickled her fancy.

"Don't be saucy," her father said, but with a smile.

Alexandra glanced at Blake as she moved to the door. He sprang to his feet and opened the door and held it for her. She didn't care whether he'd heard her joke or not. In spite of what her father had once advised about developing a "rapport" with the gorillas he'd assigned to her, she could not think of them as very human. Though it was true that of all her father's gorillas she found Blake the least objectionable, still, she couldn't remember ever managing to hold a conversation with him about anything besides working out or the weather. Gliding through the crowded corridor on the surge flowing toward the bar and lounges and restrooms, Alexandra pretended he wasn't there.

"It *is* Alexandra Sedgewick, isn't it," a woman's voice said.

Alexandra looked in the direction of the voice and saw the woman she had thought she recognized. "Madeleine Bardeen?" Alexandra said.

The woman smiled; she pressed through the crowd until she reached Alexandra. "Hello, dear, how nice to see you." She took Alexandra's arm. "Your mother didn't tell me you were in DC."

They reached the mezzanine level's main lounge. "I'm on my way to the women's room," Alexandra said.

Madeleine squeezed her arm. "We can wait in line together." Gazing into one of the enormous mirrors lining the walls, Alexandra did a double take when she realized it was her own image she had been staring at. "So what do you make of this vile opera?" Madeleine asked, steering them toward the women's room.

"Of course the *story's* dreadful," Alexandra said. "But the *music* is *divine*! And *Papagena*!" Alexandra rolled her eyes sideways and grinned. "Isn't she luscious!" Alexandra felt so grown-up and sophisticated that she had a momentary fantasy of running into Elizabeth, who would then sweep her off to the Diana for an evening of excitement and glamour of the sort she'd never be able to experience in company with her father.

Madeleine pushed open the door to the women's room. "Mmm, yes, you're right, she *is* a treat to watch. Especially compared to the pallid Pamina."

"I bet you're just prejudiced against her," Alexandra said. "Because she betrays her mother in the second act."

They joined the queue, and Alexandra stared in the mirror at the glitter of executives chattering and gossiping all around her. "Is there some significance to your hairstyle?" Madeleine said.

Alexandra's eyes darted to the other woman's face to look for the edge absent from her voice, and her sense of being a grown-up among grown-ups vanished. "What do you mean?" she said guardedly.

Ah yes. *Now* Madeleine's smile acquired the edge Alexandra had been looking for. "Come, dear, you surely don't expect people to pretend not to see? I wonder that you haven't dyed your hair, too."

Alexandra swallowed. "I'm just trying it out," she said as frigidly as she could, hoping Madeleine would hear the 'mind your own business' she meant to convey through her tone of voice, rather than the quivering, childish defensiveness she was feeling.

"*Both* the men and the women will be gossiping about *this*," Madeleine said. "Has your mother seen it?"

Alexandra flushed. She was not about to explain to this woman that her father did not allow her to see her mother. A suspicion came to her that Madeleine might be fishing for inside information. "People will gossip about anything," Alexandra said. "Especially when it involves men as important as my father."

"Such father-daughter solidarity is rare," Madeleine said. "You must see that it's bound to provoke interest."

Alexandra's turn came and she was relieved to shut herself into a stall, away from Madeleine. As she peed, she realized that not only would Madeleine gossip about having talked with her, but she would also probably get in touch with Mama to tell her about the hairstyle and her appearing in public side by side with Papa. She finished, hastily washed her hands, and rushed to exit the women's room before Madeleine could reclaim her. Blake fell in step behind her, and she hurried to the bar.

Alexandra stood on the threshold and scanned the room for her father. Since there were no women in it at all, she thought it no wonder that people were staring at her. Having no success at spotting him, she said to Blake, "Do you see my father anywhere?"

"No, madam. He's definitely not in this room."

An usher approached. "Ms. Sedgewick? Mr. Sedgewick asked me to request you to return to his box."

Alexandra strode at a brisk pace across the mezzanine, Blake at her heels, wishing operas did not have intermissions. Bad enough the scene with Madeleine and her faintly conveyed disapproval of Alexandra's apparent disloyalty to the women's code, but then to enter a wholly male preserve like that bar, by herself, and stand there like a fool... And now to have to deal with males back at the box...

But only one male sat with her father. "Alexandra, come meet Edwin Goodwin," he said, pausing in the act of lifting a glass of wine to his lips. "This is my daughter Alexandra, Ed."

Alexandra nodded at the haggard-looking man and held out her hand. *On those occasions when I go to the trouble of introducing you to someone you will shake hands with him. Clear?*

Clearly surprised, Goodwin accepted her hand and limply shook it. "I don't believe I've met you," he said, his eyes moving back and forth between Alexandra's face and her father's. "The resemblance is uncanny, Robert."

"There's a glass already poured for you, Alexandra," her father said, gesturing at the tray sitting on top of the cabinet.

Conscious of her father's eyes on her, Alexandra went through all the steps he required of her at home before drinking the first glass of each bottle—looking at its color (though the light was so bad that it seemed ludicrous even to make a show of it) and its legs, inhaling its scent, and then finally taking the first careful mouthful. Suddenly aware that both men were watching her, she flushed and set her glass down on the narrow arm of her chair.

"That too?" Goodwin said. "I don't believe I've *ever* seen a woman do that before."

"She's not very experienced yet. So, what's the verdict, Alexandra?"

Goodwin's amusement embarrassed her. "Must I?"

"Of course. Go ahead. We'll take into account that you've been drinking wine for less than a year."

Alexandra swallowed. "The color is almost black, the legs pronounced, the bouquet very rich, and the body—big! It tastes highly tannic and very dry, in fact so dry I can feel it pulling away from my teeth. The aftertaste reminds me a little of olives. Could it be a mature petit syrah, perhaps blended with a little cabernet?" Her father showed her the bottle, and she saw she'd gotten it right. And was the demonstration now over? she wondered, glancing at Goodwin, who was looking impatient.

"I fully sympathize with your plight, Ed" her father said, presumably resuming the conversation her entrance had interrupted.

"It's so damned frustrating trying to deal with Jack Hill. I never realized what a cautious do-nothing he was. And to think he's been in the Cabinet for the last fifteen years!"

"To be honest, I don't think my talking to him will help the situation."

The lines in Goodwin's face deepened. "If you had any idea, Robert, any idea at all. And then when they managed an exchange of prisoners for Lauder and the naval intelligence man—" Goodwin, frowning, interrupted himself. "You did hear what your bitch did, didn't you?"

"You mean capturing the three navy men who located and tried to take her and then handing them over to that Simon woman?"

"Yes. Anyway, Military was willing to make the exchange for one of their men, and Hill did the same—for Lauder. Just Lauder, damn it. Putting that washed-up old bastard first."

"I understand your frustration, but Lauder outranks Mark where most Company people are concerned."

Goodwin's face darkened. "I don't believe for a second you would have sold my interests down the river like that, Robert."

"Perhaps Simon didn't give him a choice."

"Are you siding with Hill?"

"Not at all, Ed. But you know I haven't got anything to say about what goes on in Security Services now." Papa sipped from his wine glass.

"God knows you're thriving in your leisure," Goodwin grumbled. "I haven't seen you look this fit in years."

Papa smiled. "I even beat Alexandra at racquet ball last week. She usually knocks the shit out of me. But you know, Ed, going on leave wasn't my choice."

"Damn it, Robert. The situation is serious. Booth is outright losing it! Executive meetings are like—" A trumpet flourish cut him off. When the sound ceased, Goodwin said, "I suppose I'd better return to my seat. Is there any chance of our meeting tomorrow to discuss these things?"

"Certainly. Come around noon. We can talk, and lunch afterwards."

"I'm serious, Robert," Goodwin said, and stood up. "It's time for a change. Things can't continue this way."

"We'll talk about it tomorrow." Her father's voice was smooth as cream.

After Goodwin left he said, "The Free Zone terrorists have Goodwin's son. They've had him for a year now. Goodwin looks as though he's been in hell, it's incredible how this thing is marking him.

He was telling me when you came in that he hasn't been able to talk to either of the two hostages the terrorists released some weeks ago. When he'd first heard of their release he'd thought he could at least get news of his son. But both Hill and Whitney are stonewalling and not allowing even Cabinet officers access to the released hostages."

Talk about excitement! Alexandra had never seen such intense interest, passion, and self-confidence on his face before.

The houselights dimmed. Alexandra, sipping her wine, let the overture sweep her back into the opera, which she had somehow forgotten during intermission. How strange it was, moving from one world to another, back and forth, as though dipping in and out of different novels, different universes...

[iii]

After the opera, the car took them back to Georgetown, to Stefano's, a restaurant specializing in Mediterranean cuisine. Lamont had done the advance work there and was standing beside the Maitre d'hotel when the latter greeted them at the door. "Please follow me, madam," the Maitre d' said, bowing. A little elated at taking the role that usually went to her mother when the two of them were out together, Alexandra strode after the man in the antique-styled suit, following him through the main dining room and up a short flight of maroon-carpeted stairs. She could not help being conscious of attracting the attention of many of the executives they swept past.

The Maitre d' showed them into a private room with windows looking out over the main dining room. The other side of the windows, Alexandra realized, were mirrors. After the separate box at the opera, their being seated in a private dining room did not surprise her much, though she wondered why her father bothered. Did it matter to him so much to be separate from the others? Was it a status thing? Or a neurotic need to shield himself from the scrutiny of the executive world at large? A bottle of Saint-Emilion stood open on the table; the Maitre d' seated first Alexandra and then her father, poured glasses of wine for each of them, promised that their first course would be served "at once," and left.

Only two place-settings had been laid, Alexandra observed. Her father had refused several invitations tendered to him after the opera as the two of them had moved down the staircase and through the lobby. She considered asking him about it now, but decided not to rock the boat. Over the months she had noticed that the better things were going between them the more irate he tended to be when his good mood broke.

Once they got through the ritual with the wine, he said, "You enjoyed that, I think. I could see how intensely you felt the music."

"It's so different when it's live," Alexandra said. "And then Mozart—well! How could one not be intense?"

The door opened, and a waiter carried in a platter, set it down on the table, and left. "We should be drinking something white and dry," Papa said, serving himself from the platter, "since there's so much seafood here, but I didn't have the patience for white wine tonight. Anyway, there's *pâté de fois gras*, so I suppose one could justify the Bordeaux..." Alexandra ignored the pâté and helped herself to the shrimp, scallops, and crab. "You realize that's another thing you inherited from me," he said, spreading pâté on a thin round of toast.

Alexandra raised her eyebrows at him, wondering what he could possibly be talking about.

"Your musical ability and taste, Alexandra," he said in a tone that suggested she should have known what he meant. "My mother could have been a professional cellist, but she chose the law instead and played solely for pleasure."

Alexandra's longtime curiosity about her paternal grandparents flared. "I know nothing about your parents," she said, "not even their names." Mama couldn't tell her even that much, much less anything about them personally, or even whether they were alive or dead.

He ate a bite of the pâté-laden toast. "My mother's name was Rosemary Sedgewick. It was her name I took, not my father's."

How bizarre. Alexandra couldn't remember ever having heard of such a thing. "Would you tell me a little about her, please?" she said softly, afraid he would refuse, afraid her request might provoke irritation.

But he seemed pleased at the question. "She looked like us, the shape of her face, the line of her jaw, the nose... She was extremely intelligent, strong, powerful. An incredible woman. Who could say what she might have been if she and my father hadn't been assassinated?"

"Assassinated!" Alexandra cried. "Why would anyone assassinate them?" They weren't even executives—that much Alexandra knew, as everyone did—which meant they couldn't have been very important.

Her father gave her a distinctly dry (though brooding) look. "For one of two reasons." He touched the stem of his glass with just the tips of his fingers. "The Federal Bureau of Investigation never could decide which of the two reasons was the true one." He picked up the glass and drank. "They ran the investigation, you see. I suppose nowadays ODS would handle such a case, I don't know, it's a rather borderline thing. But at the time ODS was only an idea in Frank Snelling's mind." His eyes moved from his glass to Alexandra's face. "They were killed in 2043, two years after the Executive Transformation. Sprayed with Uzi fire in the lobby of their apartment building. In New York, where they lived. It was undoubtedly the work of an excision specialist hired by someone resentful of the things one of them had done to help bring about the Transformation."

"How awful for you," she said. "You were so young then." And she tried to imagine what he could have been like, so young. Surely not at all like *Daniel?*

He shrugged. "Twenty-four, not so young. I was very bitter about losing my mother. But my father?" His mouth twisted. "I thought of his death as good riddance." He took another sip of wine. "My father was an arrogant, opportunistic prick. I doubt if anyone missed him after his death. Unlike my mother..."

Embarrassed, Alexandra asked, "What did your parents do that made them such targets?" She could not remember ever hearing anyone use—except in books and movies—the epithet *prick.*

"My mother worked in the corporate section of the Justice Department—the original Justice Department, that is. She not only helped draft the new constitution—they of course needed corporate specialists to collaborate with the constitutional specialists, since without certain protections the corporations would never have agreed to the compact—but she also helped implement it, which entailed breaking several highly placed hold-out families and corporations." Papa sighed. "You realize the Transformation wasn't a nice neat agreement among gentlemen... There was a certain amount of bloodshed, though far less than usual in revolutions of comparable scope. Those corporations that would not play the new game were ruthlessly destroyed. My mother had a hand in three of the more spectacular destructions." He smiled rather grimly. "In fact, as the Bureau told it to me, she was largely responsible for bringing down the wealthiest family in this country at the time of the Transformation." He paused to finish the wine in his glass.

"And your father?" Alexandra prompted when he did not immediately continue.

"Ah, my father. Yes. His demise may have been desirable for less rational reasons. And by any number of men." He refilled his glass and half-smiled at Alexandra with one of his nastier efforts. "My father belonged to the group of shrinks who devised the theory and practice for de-sexualizing executive males." Alexandra gaped at him, shocked. "Oh yes, he was among the group that dreamed up that little nightmare. If my mother in her field encountered resistance, imagine what my father was up against." He laughed shortly. "He practiced first on prison inmates. Mostly lifers. His special contribution was the theorization of the projective sublimation aspect—claiming that the 'drive energy' as they call it would be channeled into high achievement. He was rather bored with the rest of it. I had the impression that sexuality per se bored him. A rather strange attitude for a shrink. But then he was a Behavioralist."

Alexandra, biting into a shrimp, hit a concentrated spot of red pepper. Her eyes filled with tears, and she reached for her water glass. This was one of the first spicy dishes she'd had since leaving Barbados. Nicole seemed not to realize that red pepper and ginger existed. She choked for several long seconds, then forced down small sips of water.

"Are you all right?" her father said, watching her closely.

"I'm fine," she said—and started coughing again. "Pepper hit a sensitive spot in my throat," she managed to get out between coughs. She coughed some more and took a few more sips of water. Dabbing her face with her napkin to mop up the tears, she said finally, when she could manage to speak without coughing, "It's strange, thinking of your father as a psychiatrist." Quickly she gulped several swallows of water, to keep the coughing at bay.

Her father snorted. "He was a cold, sadistic shit. It's a tribute to my mother's control that she was able to live with him for so long. She did it for me, of course. Her salary alone would never have paid for my education, but she saw to it that I went to Harvard Law School, as she herself had." He swallowed some wine, then continued, his voice harsh and sneering, "Here's an example of life with my father: until I was eighteen he carried a squirt gun around the house with him. At dinner it sat beside his plate. Whenever he judged my speech or behavior undesirable, he squirted me. This of course meant different things to me at different ages...but at all ages there was something horrible about it. Of course his reason for living with my mother all those years was his own comfort: professionals of even their status back then could not live a decently comfortable life alone, they had to pool their resources, whether through marriage-bonding or other sorts of group arrangements, almost always contractual." He stabbed his fork into a shrimp. "What a mania those people had for contracts! But then everything was so damned expensive. Fortunately, though, the Executive Transformation eventually eased things for upper-level professionals."

After eating the shrimp, he stared at his wine glass and rolled its stem between his fingers for a few seconds before going on. "Considering their contributions to the creation of the executive system, they should both have been executives. Yet my father and the other shrinks who developed the de-sexualization theory and technique would of course be about the last persons to be rewarded with executivehood. As for my mother..." He shrugged. "They probably would have given her a judgeship, once she'd completed her work of ramming the compact through. Though who knows?" He sipped his wine. "They might have come to see her as an inconvenient reminder of something they'd prefer to forget and thus buried her in obscurity."

He leaned back in his chair. "However that might be, after their death I haunted the Bureau officers who were handling the case. Either one of them, or a connection of my mother's—I'll never know, it wasn't in my Company file at the time I was made Chief—judged me a good recruit for Frank Snelling's hand-picked young group that was to form the cream of the Company. He was asked to help form Security, both he and the old director of the CIA, who was made the first Chief of Security Services. Frank was given the task of training and organizing an elite corps of men who were to be cadre for a new intelligence service—the SIC, of course. Old-timers were incorporated into the new Company, but fresh new cadre like me were given a marked preference. After my training they sent me to Asia. And then on my next tour of duty they handed me the Western Europe desk." He grinned. "Hard to believe, isn't it? That they would give a kid like me that kind of power and responsibility? But Snelling was bold, daring, gutsy. He commanded total loyalty from his recruits and inspired a certain ruthlessness in dealing with CIA and NSA hangovers that he never would have gotten from the old-timers. Which meant he revolutionized the intelligence services. At the time of the Transformation there were at least seventy-five different branches of intelligence, and that's not counting those that belonged to Military. Snelling consolidated them and put an end to internecine strife between branches."

The door opened and the waiter wheeled in a cart. They kept silent as the courses were changed, except for her father's direction to the waiter to have a second bottle opened. When the waiter had gone, Alexandra said, "What a strange life you've led."

"Only from your perspective, based as it is on such very limited experience," he retorted.

Alexandra ate a bite of the lamb and found it tender, juicy—and spicy. "It's a romantic story," she said, forgetting to be careful.

He smiled warmly, indulgently. "Oh but that's the least romantic part of my story." He ate a bite and warned, "You do realize all this is highly confidential. At the time I was made Chief, I deleted from my personnel file all mention of my own history from before my name change at the time I was recruited by Snelling. None of that is anyone's business but my own. And, perhaps, yours. You should know about your grandmother, you should know what you are a part of, what you share with me."

He drank again and refilled his glass. "On the day I was invested by the Cabinet, I had two desires—that my mother could be there, could see how I'd succeeded, and that Kay know and share my triumph." He laughed shortly. "The first was manifestly impossible. As for the second—well, as I should have suspected and later found out, Kay didn't exactly appreciate my accomplishment." He speared a piece of meat. "I suppose part of it was that she was so much smarter than I that my achievements couldn't possibly impress her. And, too, when she left the Company she became such a determined provincial that she didn't pay the slightest attention to anything happening outside her academic milieu."

"You must have resented her for that attitude," Alexandra said, continuing to respond with a rash lack of inhibition.

"Actually, I didn't. When I re-recruited her, none of her past attitudes meant anything, for provincialism doesn't survive very well within the milieu of the Executive." He paused to drink. "I wish you could have known my mother. She was nothing like any of the women you've ever known. The closest person you know to being anything like her was Weatherall, and Weatherall is nothing like her." His eyes grew misty. "My mother fought so damned hard for the Executive Transformation. Nothing would have brought her to betray either her country or the system she helped create. She was too strong, too resourceful, too full of integrity to take such a way out."

"And she played the cello?" Alexandra said wistfully.

A tender smile warmed his face; he reached across the table and took her hand. "And she played the cello, beautifully. You should have heard her play the Bach unaccompanied cello suites. Such purity of tone, such precision, such controlled passion... You see, there is a place for your music, sweetheart. But it must have its place, you must not think of it as an end in itself. That would be too selfish, too effete."

A rush of warmth flooded Alexandra; with joy and pleasure she smiled back at him. He loved her, he understood her. Everything would be all right, she could see that now. He made everything so beautifully clear in all its rich complexity.

Best of all, he held out to her the hope that heredity was not a curse so much as a promise.

# Chapter Thirty-one

## [i]

After Hazel forced the plastic gloves over her hands, she removed the sheets of labels from the hopper and carried them into the conference room where she laid them on the table beside the stacks of envelopes and the printed material that was to be mailed out. Then she stripped off the gloves and knocked on the door to Allison and Lisa's office. "Come in," Allison called.

Hazel opened the door and stood on the threshold. Lisa and Allison were sitting at their desks, staring at their monitors. "I've got the mailing materials all set up," Hazel said.

Allison flicked an uneasy glance at Lisa, then looked at Hazel and made eye-contact. "Fetch Valerie and Carol, and I'll meet you all in the conference room," she said.

Hazel had no trouble guessing that Allison and Lisa found the prospect of watching Cleghorn and Burns implicating themselves disagreeable. But Liz, of course, had ordered them to "oversee" it.

Hazel tracked Burns and Cleghorn to the veranda, where they were drinking fruit juice and chatting as though they hadn't a care in the world. "Allison's ready for you now," she said shortly.

In silence they got to their feet and followed her back to the office wing. Neither of them could be looking forward to doing the physical work of the mailing, leaving fingerprints all over the letters and envelopes and mailing labels that would be going out to twelve thousand selected executives. So far, of all the executives who had followed Liz into the Free Zone, only Allison had not yet exposed herself as a renegade. Did Liz have something special in mind for her? Or did she exempt Allison out of affection, despite her frequent declaration that she never mixed public affairs with private?

When the three of them trooped into the conference room, Allison dismissed Hazel, and Hazel returned to her desk, inserted the earphone, and began transcribing Liz's dictation. According to Liz, if the secretaries Margot had brought over from Austria passed the series of loquazene examinations Lisa and Burns would be administering next week, much of Liz's swelling correspondence could be handled by one of them, since the bulk of the correspondence was the least "sensitive" of secretarial and clerical tasks that had begun proliferating in the office.

When she finished keying in a letter to the members of the board of a prominent chemical corporation—two of whom Liz obviously knew personally, since she dictated significantly personalized versions for two of the letters—Hazel wondered again at the willingness of the Austrians to associate themselves so closely with Liz. She really didn't get it. All return correspondence was to be forwarded to Liz through Austria's Foreign Ministry. And since many of the people Liz had begun writing to either worked for Departments of the Executive or for private corporations with strong ties to the Executive, Security and the Pentagon would of course be aware of the Austrian government's assistance to Liz. Hazel moved her foot to switch the data feed back on. Margot Ganshoff and the Austrian government, she thought, would not be risking their relations with the US if they did not see some decisive advantage to the association. Was it possible they believed Liz could pull off whatever it was she contemplated? But what reasons would they have for believing she could? Liz had no armed forces at her command and not that much capital behind her (or so Hazel surmised). From whence did their confidence spring?

Hazel worked steadily through the morning without interruption. No regular phone connection with the outside world (a security measure against being traced and bugged) was in some sense a blessing. When she finished preparing all versions of the letter going out to the board members, she turned to her least favorite task, that of comparing the tapes of Cleghorn and Burns's debriefings with the processor's automatic transcription of them. About two or three times a minute she had to stop the recording and correct the processor's spelling or interpretation. Cleghorn, especially, frequently garbled her words; she seemed unable to remember to speak slowly and clearly enough for the processor to copy. Also, she had a slight Bostonian accent that regularly distorted her vowels.

Before going renegade, Valerie Cleghorn had been a senior financial specialist in Com & Tran. Like many of the reports she had typed for Liz when they both still worked for Security, this transcribed material troubled Hazel. Perhaps, she thought, that was why she had taken a dislike to Cleghorn. But then Allison had been in on most of what Cleghorn reported on (and indeed had been Cleghorn's superior some of the time), and she didn't dislike Allison...

Hazel paused the recording and stared for a minute at the screen without really seeing it. Enough, she finally told herself. She needed to focus strictly on the work. She could think about it later, when she had more time—or better yet, not think about it again at all.

Liz came in some time later and put her hands on Hazel's sore, tired shoulders. "How's it going, darling?"

Hazel paused the recording. "I need some help," she said, leaning her head back against Liz's belly. "It's too much for one person, even if I skip all the other work. Couldn't Anne do some of the corrective readings of the processor transcripts?"

Liz sighed. "If you think it's absolutely essential. I suppose we can trust her."

"Come *on*, Liz, don't be silly," Hazel said. "You know as well as I do that Anne is as straight an arrow as you'll ever find."

Liz kneaded Hazel's shoulders. "And of course the whole process will take at least a couple of weeks from start to finish," Liz said. "This kind of debriefing is so damned time-consuming, and with only Lisa and Allison to help... And Lisa has these meetings with the Co-op people for the next piece of action."

"Can't you just ask these women to debrief themselves? To write super-comprehensive reports?"

"No, darling, not possible. In the first place, people miss things because they take them for granted. In the second place, I'm not going to trust them that far. At least not until each of them have had *their* baptisms by fire."

"And you say there's another pair arriving at the end of the week?"

"They won't be coming here yet, darling. We'll have some breathing space."

"I don't know how you expect this house to absorb an infinite number of executives," Hazel said. "I can't imagine their agreeing to share bedrooms. And as for the demands they put on Lacie and Ginger: these two in particular seem to be constantly insisting on special services."

"You're a worrier, darling." Liz's fingers worked at the central knot in Hazel's neck. "In the first place, they damned well better be prepared for some personal inconvenience. We'll have to set up some ground rules fairly soon, I imagine. For allocating space and for making things as bearable as possible. Second, we'll bring in another service-tech to help Ginger and Lacie. You can start looking tomorrow."

Hazel sighed. She could see the writing on the wall: obviously Liz would be leaving it all to her to manage, to organize, to placate the inevitably disgruntled executives. "Working for you is certainly not a nine-to-five job," she said. "You're turning into a tyrant, Liz."

"Nonsense, darling." Liz kissed Hazel's neck. "But speaking of work, Cleghorn and Burns have almost finished stuffing those envelopes. We're just about ready to resume the debriefings." Liz usually floated between the two debriefings, supervising. "What I came out here for was to ask you to get Anne in here this afternoon at four. I want both you and her to sit in on the meeting I'm having with Lisa and Allison."

"Cleghorn and Burns won't be attending?"

"They'll be included in executive meetings only after we've finished debriefing—and after they've proven their loyalty." Liz's hands lifted from Hazel's shoulders. "We need Anne, you know," Liz said, moving towards the door to her office. She stopped and looked back at Hazel.

Hazel met her gaze. "Yes?" she said.

"We're stretching ourselves too thin," Liz said. "And I'm not talking about clerical work, either." Liz half-smiled, then turned and went into her office. Hazel switched the tape back on and resumed the transcript work. She would think about what Liz might have in mind for Anne later. As for Liz's multitude of projects...that, too, was something to consider—when she had time.

[ii]

Hazel sat with her NoteMaster on her knee and watched to see what Anne's response would be. Liz, it seemed, could still surprise her.

Anne's gaze moved back and forth between Liz and Allison's faces. "What you're talking about—" her voice was hesitant—"is that you want me to...spy? Is that it?"

"'Spy' is perhaps too, ah, *specific* a word to use." Liz smiled. "But it's true I'm concerned about establishing sources of intelligence within the inner circles of the Co-op."

Anne's shoulders hunched, and the fingers of her right hand fidgeted with the lovely opal ring—a commitment ring from Allison—she wore on the third finger of her left hand. "But wouldn't Hazel be better able to do that? I mean, she already has a kind of rapport established with Martha Greenglass, and—"

"No, no," Liz interrupted, "that wouldn't do at all! In the first place, I need Hazel here. And in the second place, they would be suspicious of her. After all, they know she's my lover."

Hazel didn't buy it. The real reason was that Liz didn't trust her around Martha Greenglass. And probably, there was a second reason, too—that Liz would hate having her live away from her. She made such a fuss about her sharing her bed...

Anne's even, white teeth gnawed at her plush lower lip. "I don't see them trusting me," she said. "I've only met Martha Greenglass once, and that one time I got into an argument with her."

"Doesn't matter, dear." Liz smiled at Anne, turning on the warmth full throttle. Hazel glanced at Allison and realized that she had known Liz was going to propose this. She must approve of it! But *why?* "Now listen," Liz said. "Here's the cover story. You and I have had a serious falling out, making it impossible for you to go on living here. You need a place to live, and a job. Now one obvious aspect of your going to the Co-op people is that you're black. You can hint or say baldly something to the effect that you're impressed that the Co-op has so many black women in leadership positions...that you'd like to get involved, too." Anne's face darkened to a deep aubergine: in acute embarrassment, Hazel guessed. "You can even say you're not sure of your feelings about the Free Zone, but that you know you can't go on living here and working for me. And that you can't go back, either. That your situation is difficult." Liz's smile flashed out. "Believe me, they'll grab you up, Anne, eager to make a convert out of one of my people. For their own reasons." Liz darted a sardonic look at Hazel, making Hazel wonder what *that* crack was supposed to mean.

"I'm terribly uncomfortable with the scenario you propose," Anne said after a pause. "Especially with the aspect of using my being black." She pressed her plush, sensuous lips together. After a few seconds of silence, she said, "I mean, what am I supposed to say? That I think being black has counted against me in the executive system? Or counted against me working for you?" Anne looked at Allison and then back at Liz. "And then there's the point of my having to be isolated from the only secure and comfortable situation available to me. Would this mean I have to give up seeing everyone here? That I'd be completely off on my own? Because I don't know if I have the kind of inner resources such isolation would require. It hasn't been easy for me, going renegade..." Anne looked at Hazel, as though asking for help.

"We could still see one another," Allison said. "The story would be that you had a falling out with Liz, not me. And you could see Hazel, as well. I don't know what would happen, of course, if you played the role of political convert. That might create difficulties. But we wouldn't be abandoning you, Anne. I'd come in to Seattle often and spend a lot of time with you."

"It sounds so...scary."

Hazel's throat tightened. She could see Anne didn't want to do this, she could see Anne groping for ways out of Liz's net. Hazel turned to Liz. "It's not fair of you to ask this of Anne," she said. "Anyone can see she doesn't want to do it."

Liz's face smoothed into blankness: sure sign that Hazel's interference was irritating her. "This is extremely important, darling, or I wouldn't ask it of her. I know Anne is very loyal and is as concerned about the situation as the rest of us. We're all making sacrifices, we're all risking ourselves. Don't you think it's a bit patronizing of you to assume Anne needs to be shielded from taking on the same level of commitment and sacrifice as the rest of us?"

Hazel looked away from Liz, at Anne: yes, of course, Liz's words were acting on her, and strongly. Liz was a master manager. Hazel looked back at Liz and sent her a pregnant look—which Liz ignored. Liz had outmaneuvered her. She could not think of a thing to say that would be effective now.

"It's true," Anne said, "that I've done very little since I've been here. You've asked little of me. And I've felt out of it for that reason. I suppose…but it is so hard for me. I've never done anything like this before." She looked at Allison. "What about that other project, of recruiting people for your media organization?"

"This is more important, Anne," Allison said. "There's hardly anyone we could ask to do this, or could *trust* to do it."

Anne nodded. "All right then. I'll do it." She sounded resigned.

Liz beamed approval on Anne. "I knew you would help us out, as soon as you understood how much we need you," she said. "Welcome to the team, Anne."

Hazel stared down at the screen of her NoteMaster and imagined herself getting up and walking out. But she'd never get Liz to see this thing in a reasonable perspective if she reacted so adamantly.

Patience, she told herself, fighting the wave of anxiety washing over her. Patience.

### [iii]

Hazel paced back and forth from bath to dressing room to bedroom, one slow, even step after another, staring down at the pale pink silk slippers Liz had given her, preparing, as she paced, to confront Liz. Liz would try to brush her off, of course, would try coaxing her to discuss it on another occasion, on the grounds that it was late and they both needed their sleep. And then finally she'd display annoyance and be disagreeable and threaten Hazel with coldness—probably telling her to mind her own business, to leave work-related matters to her, pointing out that she, Hazel, was a secretary, not an executive… No, she wouldn't use those words: Liz would never be so crude. But that would be the implication of whatever she said. She would be willing to use the threat of anger and irritation and tension to get Hazel to drop the subject. *Let's have peace, darling, why must we quarrel, it's so unnecessary, why can't you just leave these things be? Why fuss fuss fuss so?*

Hazel caught sight of herself in the mirror and smiled wryly: even knowing what she was starting she would still make herself go through with it. Sometimes Liz could be reasoned with. At the very least she had to make Liz see what she thought of her machinations. She would not be silent, even if that was the easiest and least tension-producing way.

It was after midnight when Liz finally showed up: having spent hours socializing—or had they been strategizing?—with the four other executive women of the household. Of course she might not have spent *all* those hours with all of the executive women. She could have been across the hall in her sitting room, for instance, with Allison...

"What, still up, darling?" Liz stepped out of her gown. "I thought you'd be long asleep."

Hazel leaned against the door frame. "I wanted to talk with you," she said quietly.

Liz shot her a quick, suspicious look, then smiling, came over to where Hazel stood. "It's too late to be serious tonight," she said. "And you do look terribly serious. Are you going to scold me?" She took Hazel's hand and pressed it against her breast.

This gesture so infuriated Hazel that she dropped her planned strategy and said, "You must be pleased with yourself, at finally managing to physically separate Allison from Anne."

Liz released Hazel's hand and moved away. "That remark hardly seems worthy of you, darling. I never realized you had such a streak of cattiness in you. In general you're not at all like other girls."

"Well Anne is a special inconvenience, isn't she," Hazel retorted. "I imagine her not being in Allison's bed at night will make things much easier for you."

Liz climbed in between the sheets. "Your jealousy is carrying you away," she said softly. "I never make work-related decisions on the basis of personal motives. I would be a fool if I did."

Hazel's cheeks warmed. "And god knows you're not a fool," she said. "Considering the unscrupulous way you managed Anne, that's one thing no one would ever call *you*. You didn't care for a second about what she'll be giving up or about how she feels. Anything to get your way, right Liz?"

Liz turned off the light on her side of the bed. "I'm tired, darling, and you're obviously too emotionally wrought up to make real discussion possible. I'm going to sleep. We have a long day ahead of us tomorrow."

By the time Hazel had turned off all the lights and slipped into bed, Liz had fallen asleep. Of course with her damned self-hypnosis training, Liz slept at will.

Stupid, she had been terribly stupid. Why had she dragged Liz's sexual relationship with Allison into the discussion? She had sabotaged her own effort, right off. What was the matter with her? Was it true that she was jealous, as Liz kept insisting?

Hazel rolled onto her stomach and turned her pillow over. She hadn't helped Anne in the least. All she had done was to confirm Liz in her view of things. It would have been better if she'd kept quiet, better if she had waited.

# Chapter Thirty-two

## [i]

Celia woke abruptly. Heart in mouth, she sat up and listened to what sounded like the splintering of the front door.

Without thinking, she leaped out of bed, heaved herself over the window sill, and dropped down onto the rocky sand below. As she scrambled barefoot through the dark, lights went on all over the house and male voices shouted. The ravine was her single thought: she must crawl down into the ravine. Down there they would be unable to find her until daylight—unless, of course, they had searchlights or infrared goggles. Stepping into something prickly, she suppressed the yelp of pain that rose into her fear-dried throat, backed away, and groped stealthily around it.

"She was here, she's bolted," a male voice yelled. "Out into the back, all of you." Celia trembled violently, and her breath came in gasps. They would find her, she would never make it into the ravine before they caught her, not while trying to negotiate the descent in the dark, barefoot. Still she pressed on down the slope, her toes digging into the dirt as the terrain grew precipitously steep. Snatching a glance over her shoulder she saw wide beams of light spraying the area. Speared by a fresh spurt of fear, she slipped and fell and rolled until she managed to catch hold of a piece of scrub. Terrified that the noise she had made would bring them straight to her, she ignored the abrasions of the scrub and loose gravelly sand against her naked arms and legs. Unable any longer to negotiate such steep terrain on foot, Celia crawled, clawing at whatever vegetation came to hand. "You can see she came this way," one of them said, his voice sounding so close she could hardly move for the violence of her trembling. "Over here, boys, light up the area down there real good."

Celia knew it was all over when the ground around her lit up as clear as day. Still adrenalized, she perceived the world with amazingly sensual clarity: smelling the sharp scent of the juice of the leaves she had inadvertently crushed on her hands, feeling the coolness of the night air on her sweaty, heated flesh, seeing the green and gray and silver foliage of the scrub that she desperately clutched brilliantly and vividly revealed, cringing at the shrillness of her pursuers' crows of triumph at having exposed her in the beams of their floodlights. "That's it, Celia," the voice promised with hateful glee. "You've had it, babe. Give it up. You've got ten seconds to get your ass up here or we'll jolt you but good."

Sobbing, Celia released her grip on the prickly leaves tearing into her palms and went rolling downwards—out of the range of the light, she hoped. But before she reached bottom, her consciousness ebbed into the blankness of vacancy, and she lost herself, aware only of a mass of pained confused sensations...

When she returned to full awareness, she did not at first know where she was or what had happened. Her ankles were on fire, the skin on them being scraped raw, and she realized she was being dragged over concrete. She struggled against the grip tearing at her arms, which she feared would pull her joints out of their sockets. "She's coming to," somebody said. "Stand up, bitch, and walk, damn you." The men who had been dragging her stopped to let Celia stand, and then hurried her toward the street. When she saw that she was being led to one of two long gray vans, a prolonged moan escaped from her, unwilled, as though it were a sound being made by someone else. About a yard from the van the man who had told her to stand up said with a laugh in his voice, "I can handle her."

"I just bet you can," the other one drawled. "Enjoy yourself, Romeo." As the man moved away he passed under a streetlamp, and Celia saw that a hood covered his head. The sight of it sent a fresh wave of terror washing over her. Never never did they cover their faces. Why were these men wearing hoods? For she saw now that the man she had been left with was also wearing one. And a uniform. *He was wearing a Navy uniform.*

"I earned this," her captor announced as he pulled opened the doors. "I was the one that hit you. There's a bonus because you tried to run, bitch." He shoved her against the back of the van, pushing her up against it. "Get in, cunt," he snarled. With her hands cuffed behind her she had to use her shoulders and stomach and knees to work her way inside, but impatient, he grabbed her buttocks and shoved her from behind, scraping more of her already scratched and abrasion-tormented skin. It was then that she realized she wore only a tee-shirt and underpants. The Santa Ana had made wearing pajamas too uncomfortable. And of course when she went out the window she had been thinking about nothing except getting away. No clothes, no shoes: the lack was an added vulnerability she didn't need.

He crawled in beside her and slammed the doors shut, plunging the back of the van into inky darkness. This was a nightmare, this couldn't be happening to her, she couldn't be lying here on the cold metal floor of this van, shut in with the hooded man who had shot her with a stun-gun. Roughly he rolled her onto her back, forcing her to lie on her arms and her steel-cuffed wrists. A painful yank on her hair forced her head back, and Celia wriggled her body backwards to ac-commodate. A fiery wave of pain engulfed her back, inflaming abra-sions she hadn't known she had. They must have dragged her along the ground on her back while she was lost in the neuro-seizure after the stun. "What, moaning already?" He chuckled. "Such anticipa-tion!" He stopped pulling on her hair. "You're something special, you know that? We've got instructions to be thorough." His hands groped her body and shoved her tee-shirt up and bunched it around her neck. "You know what *thorough* means? It means tearing up every little thing inside your house looking for evidence." His fingers found her nipple and squeezed and twisted and pulled it. "Yessir, it'll take the boys some time to get through that entire house. Four rooms, right? Maybe an hour per room. Who knows? Only thing is, we've got to be done by dawn. Long as we operate when nobody's looking it's just fine. 'Course, all your neighbors will know. Which is all to the good. People like to know terrorists are being taken care of. You know?"

Celia lay rigid and shivering, her teeth clenched, trying not to cry out, not paying attention to his voice, which went on and on and on, thinking about how she had failed to dispose of her attaché case. She had gone out the window without thinking. She had always planned under such circumstances to take it with her, but she had forgotten,

she'd panicked and bolted. It would have been better if she'd run outside with it and set the papers inside it on fire. Thank god she had
convinced them at the Center that she should not be carrying the jammer while her mother was away on this risky evacuation mission. But
there were other things—the human rights petition, for one thing,
which had the signatures of seven attorneys on it. And her dossier of
disappearances, everything fresh and current, since all the older stuff
was kept at Emily's.

A sudden jab in her solar plexus made her gasp. "You *answer* me
when I ask you a question," he hissed in her ear.

"Didn't hear," Celia panted.

He grabbed her nipple again and drove his fingernails into it.
Unable to stop herself, Celia cried out. "Shut up," he hissed. "You
don't want a crowd out here watching, do you? Are you listening to me
now, bitch?"

"Yes," Celia whimpered.

"What I said before was, we got orders not to mark you. And I was
asking you if you didn't think you were pretty damn lucky for that."

"I don't know." Celia could hardly get the words out. "I don't know."

"Well me *I'm* pretty lucky I get to fuck a terrorist for my country,
it's the least I can get out of hauling your twitching deadweight body
up the fucking gully, don't you think, bitch?" His hand released her
nipple. And then without warning he threw himself on top of her,
pushing the breath out of her body, pressing her elbows so hard into
the floor she thought they might break, jamming the steel edge of the
cuffs into her tailbone. And then his weight shifted almost entirely
onto her thorax, shoulders, and breasts, filling her with the panic of
suffocation. His hand jerked at her underpants, and she heard them
tear, and his fingers dug into her genitals. He panted out something
she thought must be "terrorist pussy." And then his weight shifted,
and she could take a breath, but with breath she began to whimper,
certain her arms were breaking and so inescapably sharply aware of
the painful things he was doing to her genitals. She shut out the words,
trying not to hear him, trying to blank her mind, swallowed up by the
consciousness of a world empty of all but this beast and the pain he
inflicted. The sudden rending intrusion of his penis into her vagina,
however, took her by surprise, and she yelped. His hand groped over

her face, found her mouth, and clamped down hard against both mouth and nose, and again she was consumed with the fear of suffocation.

It went on and on and on, his penis pounding into her, his words defiling her, his hands tearing at her. And it just kept going on and on. Only when the doors were opened from the outside did he stop. "Everything all right in there?" a voice said into the dark.

"Affirmative, sir," the beast said jauntily as he withdrew his penis from Celia's vagina to ejaculate over her thighs and belly.

"We've finished inside. We're on our way now."

The doors slammed shut, and again he took her by the hair. "Yep," he said, "we're just fine in here, me and this terrorist trash. You just wait, Celia, there's plenty more to come. You can take my word for it."

The van's motor started. Weeping, Celia thought of the semen and other substances covering her body, of the shambles her tee-shirt and underpants had been reduced to, and of how they usually made her wait for hours in some corridor or tied to a chair in some public spot before putting her in a cell. She had so much to hide. This time she was no longer merely a simpatico whose assistance to prisoners must be discouraged, this time she was guilty of breaking their damned unfair laws. And this time, if she weren't careful, she could hurt her mother and Emily and many others.

This time was something else entirely.

[ii]

*Time*: Celia lost track of it almost at once.

Before they took her out of the van they blindfolded her. Then they pushed and shoved and grabbed her, and made obscene jokes about "Romeo," as they called him, having "made" her. They forced her down a scary flight of stairs and locked her in a cell without removing either the blindfold or the cuffs. She stumbled about the cubicle trying to perceive it by touch and discovered it was very small, perhaps four by five or six. It had no toilet, no platform, nothing but the walls and the floor. Slowly, painfully Celia dropped to her knees. She knew from what her bare feet told her that the floor must be filthy, but her body was shaking violently, her muscles cramped, and she did not think she could stand for long.

And if they came in and ordered her to stand?

No, she would not anticipate, she would concentrate on getting through each moment as it came. How to ignore the aches and pains and burning in so much of her body? Though they had not beaten her yet, it felt as if they had. *We got orders not to mark you.* It wouldn't be a beating, then, anyway. They would use other techniques... *No Celia don't think of that, think of who it is. They wore Navy uniforms, so they must be Military not ODS. What do they want? Not the woman evacuated, that must have been ODS because why else dump her, and Military has plenty of medical staff to patch her up. No it must be something else... Maybe they found out about the Human Rights Committee, maybe somebody in Ecuador was working for one of them and fingered me, maybe it's the petition—what* is *it they want with me?*

An eternity passed before the cell door was unlocked. "In here, doc," a smooth male voice said. Celia braced herself for a command to rise to her feet. She heard a shuffling of shoes on the floor and sensed that if she leaned forward even an inch she would find herself brushing against their clothing. "Everything needs to be made perfectly clear, Celia," the same voice said, very low. "So we'll start with an injection before we begin interrogation. That way you'll understand what you can expect if your participation during interrogations doesn't meet our expectations. You know what sulfizine is, Celia?"

"I've heard of it," Celia said hoarsely.

"This is a variant of sulfizine. Its effects are extremely unpleasant," the voice instructed. "After you've experienced it you'll probably do anything to avoid a second injection, although we're prepared to use it for as long as you make it necessary. All right, doc, proceed with the injection."

"She'll have to lie down, it must be given in the hip," a second male voice said.

She heard movement and felt one of them brushing against her and realized her cuffs were being removed. "Lie down, Celia," the first voice ordered when the cuffs were off.

Stiffly Celia shifted and lay down on her side. A cold swab brushed the skin on her hip and she felt the needle going in. As soon as the needle was withdrawn the two men left.

Celia removed the blindfold and blinked against the painfully bright light. The room was not large enough for her to stretch out in except diagonally, and that with her knees bent. The door was of thick metal with a mirrored pane of glass inset behind scratched, filthy wire-threaded Plexiglass. Fluorescent lights hung high above. Beyond that, there was nothing. Celia lay quietly in fetal position with her arm over her eyes, waiting for the drug to make her sick. Convulsions, she thought, fever and convulsions and excruciating pain. Unbearable, one of the people taken from San Bernardino had said. Utterly unbearable. *It makes you want to die.*

Celia tried to empty her mind, tried to keep from being swallowed up by fear. Fear as much as pain had become her enemy now.

# Chapter Thirty-three

## [i]

Celia squatted over the bucket, so weak that she could hardly hold herself in position long enough for the urine and diarrhea to finish streaming and spasming out of her. "If you don't want to go into filter failure you'd better drink as much water as you can," the doctor had said to her on his last visit. "You've lost a dangerous amount of fluid through sweating and diarrhea. And your system is loaded with toxins that are straining your filter. So drink every damned bottle you're given." A guard had brought her four liters and the bucket, making a crack about how they wouldn't even consider taking her to the bathroom because of her stench.

The fever was receding, the grinding, rending pain had ebbed to dullness—except for the blinding headache—and her muscles twitched only slightly now, whether from weakness or a residue of the drug in her system she did not know. The hallucinations, too, had gone, though she felt strange, as though her eyes could not properly gauge depth or distance, as though her hearing might still be hallucinatory.

Falling back onto the floor, it seemed to her that the sound of her joints creaking came from an echoey distance somewhere far outside her body. She closed her eyes against the harshness of the light and laid the blindfold loosely over them. The nausea had become the worst of her torments; it had probably always been there but she hadn't noticed it under the assault of inexorable pain.

Drink, she told herself. Drink, they would let you die, they wouldn't care, drink, Celia. Yet the effort it took and the discomfort of the water in her heaving stomach—already awash with liquid she could hear rolling around inside her body—held her back. Only when the dryness and the horrid taste in her mouth grew too uncomfortable did she pick up the plastic bottle to drink. After perhaps a minute of trembling struggle the cap flew off and rolled away from her. Celia put the mouth of the bottle to her lips and sipped from it without lifting her head; she held it there until she had finished the bottle. Then she dropped it and waited for the need to pee to grow too strong or the gush of diarrhea too pressing to resist.

[ii]

Later, when the spasms of diarrhea had grown less frequent and violent and she had drunk almost all of the four liters, the guard, speaking through the intercom, ordered her to put on the blindfold. She obeyed and worried that the doctor was coming to see her again. But this time two guards prodded her onto her feet and out of the cell, cursing her when they had to half-drag her because of the weakness that made it difficult for her to stand, much less walk. They brought her to a place that seemed a long distance from the cell and told her she was to be "cleaned up." There they took her one remaining piece of clothing—her tee-shirt—from her, put a tube of soap gel into her hand, shoved her under a chilly chemical-treated shower, and told her to wash herself. The cold scalded her burning flesh and seeped into her bones. Teeth chattering, leaning against the cold metal wall for support, she struggled to wash herself. At least, she told herself as the soap irritated her cuts, at least the excretions crusted over her body were coming off her, at least she would be clean.

They gave her a small, thin towel for drying herself, then pulled a tunic over her head, cuffed her, and again half-dragged her to somewhere other than her cell. There they removed her cuffs and pushed her into a chair. An authoritative female voice told the guards to wait outside. Celia heard the door shut; hands coming from behind removed the sopping wet blindfold. Celia blinked and rubbed her goose-fleshed arms. When she saw that she was seated at a table on which food had been set, she made to turn her head to look around her. But the hands pressed against the sides of her head and held it still, and the voice said, "No, don't turn your head, Celia. Or we'll have to have your blindfold back on. Just look straight ahead. Clear?"

"Understood," Celia said, finding her voice very hoarse.

"The food is for you," the woman said. "You must be famished. Certainly you're very weak, aren't you."

Celia stared at the food in astonishment. It had not come from a tube but was real—a big steaming bowl of stew, rolls and butter, a glass of milk, and a banana. "My stomach is upset," she said.

"Even so, you need to eat. Do the best you can, Celia, for you need your strength. You know you do, don't you?" The voice sounded warm and sympathetic, as though the woman was genuinely concerned about Celia's welfare.

Celia picked up the spoon and dipped it into the stew. Slowly, with shaking fingers, she conveyed pieces of carrot and potato to her mouth. Mechanically she chewed and swallowed, then took a bite of the roll. Her stomach roiled. "I'm afraid I'll be sick," she said.

"I'm sure you can manage the banana and roll," the woman said encouragingly. "They tell me you have an interrogation to face, so I'd eat as much as I could if I were you."

*If I were you*: such mockery, Celia thought, chewing a bite of roll. Such a mockery of sympathy.

"I'm going to take your pulse and blood pressure, Celia. Just go on eating," the voice said after Celia had peeled the banana and broken off a piece. She took Celia's left arm and wrapped a cuff around it. Celia stared down at the white hand and the navy blue sleeve with its gold stripes on the cuff: obviously another Navy person, she was probably a nurse. The cuff self-inflated, then slowly released the air. Celia heard a tapping of fingers on a keyboard and guessed the officer was recording the data. "When you've had enough to eat I'll weigh you," the woman added. "I'm going to try to take very good care of you while you're here, Celia, but you'll have to work at it, too."

Anger choked her; the banana she had swallowed came back up in a wash of acid into her throat. Gagging, Celia clapped her hand over her mouth. After the heaving stopped, she made herself swallow the vomit. Quickly she downed a mouthful of milk to try to wash the taste away, to soothe the burning in her throat.

When Celia announced she could eat no more, the woman re-blindfolded Celia, helped her out of the chair, and led her several steps away from the table. "The scale's right in front of you. Step up onto it, Celia." Celia obeyed and again listened to the tapping of fingers on a keyboard. "Okay, very good," she said, patting Celia's shoulder. "Remember now, drink as much water as you can and eat whatever they bring you. And try to sleep. Your body must be exhausted from its struggle. One step down and backwards, Celia." Celia moved as she was directed; she felt and heard the woman moving away. There was the sound of knocking and then of the door opening. "She's all yours," the woman said, and the words let loose a powerful flood of emotion that nearly knocked Celia, already trembling from the effort of standing upright, off her feet.

She knows, Celia thought as they cuffed her hands and forced her through the halls. She knows and she isn't crazy the way these others are, she knows and she can talk to me like that, and then to them, as though this were nothing, as though it weren't a perversion of reality, an obscenity tainting her, too.

They left her in the cell with a small sponge and a basin of blue-tinted water with which she was supposed to clean up her "own filth." The bucket of excrement was still there as well as her diarrhea-sodden underwear. She saw that they had also brought her another liter of drinking water: obviously under the doctor's orders. She imagined for a moment having to go through it again. Her head swam with dizziness, and she thought about not drinking the water, about not trying to survive.

No, Celia, you're not that weak, she told herself, dipping the sponge into the water. You must not let them kill you, you must not. You're stronger than that, Celia Speranza Espin. You *will* survive.

# Chapter Thirty-four

As she ate lunch Hazel listened to Lacie telling her about her parents' annual vegetable garden and tried to imagine the world Lacie had grown up in, a world so different from that of her own childhood. "Even though it was the hardest part, I think maybe preparing the beds and planting them was the most exciting part, because of all the expectation," Lacie said. "When we planted the peas in February, I'd go out there every morning and stare at the ground, watching for the first sprouts. And then I'd watch each stalk shoot out leaves, and so on and so on. For a while I'd know exactly how many leaves each stalk had. Until finally they flowered..." Lacie took a bite of her sandwich. Still chewing, she continued, "Of course the first harvest was always exciting. But eventually that part of it would get to be kind of old, just a chore, having to go out there picking all those vegetables night after night after night. I remember one time when—"

"Excuse me, Hazel dear." The tone of Valerie Cleghorn's voice claimed Hazel's attention. Hazel patted Lacie's arm and raised her eyebrows at Cleghorn. Cleghorn smiled. "They've forgotten to put my juice out again. Would you be a love and fetch me some?"

Hazel put her hands in her lap to conceal the anger that would be apparent in their clenching. Cleghorn constantly asked her to do things for her—to fetch this, to take care of that, complaining about how Lacie did things and asking Hazel to "straighten that girl out," wondering at this odd way of doing things the household seemed to have fallen into. This had all probably started because Hazel had felt obliged to comply with both Cleghorn's and Burns' requests while they were being debriefed since they could not leave the debriefing sessions to run all over the house for themselves without disrupting the entire process. Now, trying to keep control of the anger bubbling up, Hazel smiled tightly at Cleghorn and said as lightly as she could, "Let me understand this: you're asking me to interrupt my lunch and my conversation with Lacie to get up from this table and go out to the kitchen and squeeze you some juice? Do I have that right, madam?" Hazel could hear the tense silence that had fallen around the table: as though they had all realized that a confrontation was in progress.

Cleghorn's gaze hardened; after about ten seconds she turned her head and looked up the table at Liz. "You see, Elizabeth? This sort of impertinence is what comes of this nonsense of communal *feedings*," she said with obvious distaste. "The service in this house is appalling."

"It's my fault," Ginger cried, shoving her chair back and rising to her feet. "I should have seen to it, but I forgot. Your juice is such a peculiar mixture that I—"

"That's irrelevant, Ginger," Hazel interrupted. "You shouldn't have your meal disrupted for such a minor matter." But Ginger fled into the kitchen, so Hazel fell silent.

"*And* she's trying to incite the others to the same impertinence. I don't understand why you allow this, Elizabeth. I—"

"For godsake, Valerie, drop it," Liz said in her weariest tone of voice. "Hazel is a secretary, not household labor. I've explained this to you before. Stop pestering her. It's you who are inciting her."

Hazel stared down at her plate. She had lost her appetite. Into the awkward silence Allison said something to Liz and the two of them resumed whatever they had been talking about before the scene had distracted them. At the head of the table, with Allison seated to her right, Liz seemed remote and distant from Hazel—as remote and distant as she had been since *their* scene the other night. Again, Hazel thought dismally, she had handled the situation in precisely the worst way she could have, by forcing this public confrontation between herself and Cleghorn—with the result that everyone sitting at the table dismissed it as having been caused by a secretary's taking affront at being asked to take on domestic tasks. She should have tried to persuade Liz to talk to Cleghorn and Burns about their adapting to this household... *Impertinent*, Hazel repeated to herself, depressed. An impertinent girl. She'd like to see Cleghorn spend some time with the Co-op women. That would open her eyes, that would change her attitude...wouldn't it?

Five minutes later Ginger returned with a tall glass of the mixed fruit drink Cleghorn favored. Cleghorn smiled at Ginger and thanked her sweetly, telling her how much she appreciated it. Ginger blushed, apparently converted into a sworn Cleghorn devotee for life. Hazel turned back to Lacie and asked her a question about growing seasons. Though she couldn't eat another bite, she would not get up and leave. She would keep her head and try to figure out why she was making a mess of her personal relations lately. Maybe, she thought, she was being unreasonable. "And to think," Hazel responded to Lacie's discussion of how well spinach grew in this climate, "I didn't even know what spinach was—except as an exotic vegetable that was mentioned in novels—until I was in my late twenties."

"Oh!" Lacie exclaimed, and giggled. "Even before the Blanket *I* knew what spinach was, because my parents worked a tenant farm— the one that's theirs now—and grew lots of it to sell. I didn't *eat* it, though, until after the Blanket. We really couldn't afford then to eat the things we were growing."

Hazel glanced across the table and saw the sneer on Cleghorn's face. What a hateful woman, she fumed. Another member of the grand sisterhood of executive women. Being around her was almost enough to turn one into a Free Zone anarchist.

# Chapter Thirty-five

Celia did not manage to take the nurse's advice to sleep, for the very thought of the looming interrogation kept her from relaxing enough to sleep. Interrogations could last for hours and hours: for as long as the interrogator chose. If she could hardly stand unaided for even a few seconds, how would she be able to stand for hours? Fear rocked her stomach, dried her throat. Repeatedly she struggled to the bucket as fresh spasms of diarrhea wracked her. What if she lost control of her bowels during the interrogation? Remembering how they had treated her when she had peed on herself during an interrogation in a previous detention, she was submerged by the familiar burning humiliation and frustrated anger the memory always elicited.

Celia did not think at all about the possible questions they might ask her: she knew already the outcome of the interrogation and reminded herself that it would be only a matter of time before Emily would get her out. That Emily would save her she did not doubt. This conviction alone made it possible for her to face another injection. For Mama, for Emily, she could hold out. It would not be forever. She must just somehow keep herself from going into filter failure, that was all that she need require of herself.

At some point the door cracked open, and a tube of food was thrown into the cell; the door shut, and Celia retrieved the tube. How much longer? she wondered. They supplied no utensils, which meant she would have to eat the food straight from the tube. She studied the label and saw that it was one of Barclay Madden's brands. Of course. Emily's father supplied the Navy with all the tubefood it consumed... Mechanically Celia opened the tube and squeezed a small amount of the mush into her mouth. Ah yes, a "breakfast" tube of oatmeal flavored with raisins, apples, and cinnamon. Saccharine and pasty with lumps, intended to simulate fruit.

When she had finished eating, Celia added the tube to the empty water bottles she had shoved into the corner, then propped herself against the cold concrete wall. Fully half the area of the cell seemed to be taken up with waste materials—plastic products and her own excrement.

It wasn't long after she had finished eating that the order came over the intercom to put on the blindfold. Her body broke into a cold sweat, as trembling, she obeyed. She heard the door open, and a male voice ordered her to move out into the corridor. Joking about her "date with the Commander," they cuffed her and pushed her roughly along the corridor. As they led her up a flight of stairs they made obscene remarks every time she stumbled. After they passed through the last of several doors she felt pavement under her bare feet and the heat of the outdoors enveloping her and realized they were taking her to another building. Without explanation they shoved her into what she knew must be the back of a van. After a short drive the van halted and they ordered her out. They took her into a building and down more stairs. By the time she reached their final destination, she was dizzy and shaking with fatigue.

When they uncuffed her and pushed her into a chair, Celia tried to compose herself by taking deep breaths and slowly exhaling them, but the effort seemed only to make her head swim. Would they allow her to sit during the interrogation? she wondered. They never had before. But then they had never blindfolded her before, either. By a strange coincidence, just as this thought crossed her mind, the blindfold was removed and her eyes assaulted by the glare of bright, highly-directional lights facing her from all sides. She blinked and held her hands to her eyes.

"Tape on," a male voice flat-commanded. "Interrogation of Celia S. Espin, June 5, 2087." Celia quivered: this procedure, too, departed from her past experiences. Never had there been an acknowledged tape or any sort of formality used. "Drop your hands from your eyes, Celia." Celia obeyed. The voice continued: "Where's your mother, Celia?"

Mama, they were after Mama. Celia gripped her fingers together and tried to keep from panicking. She had been certain that the patient her mother was rescuing had been ODS's prisoner "What are the charges against me?" she asked, fighting to keep her voice steady.

"*We* are asking the questions. *You* are answering them. To repeat: Where is your mother, Celia?"

"I have a right to legal counsel," Celia said, feeling stronger. She would stick to this point even if it got her nowhere. It gave her a reason not to answer his question. "I insist on having my attorney present before I answer any questions."

"We're not asking you to incriminate yourself," the interrogator said. "So you *must* answer. Where is she, Celia?"

"This procedure is irregular," Celia said. "You're not a grand jury, so you can't compel me to answer. I also insist on knowing who is questioning me and with what authorization."

"If your mother isn't doing anything illegal, you have no reason not to tell us where she is, Celia."

"Unless grounds are shown as to why such information is necessary, you cannot ask me to give up my right to privacy."

"*Cannot*, Celia?" the voice said with a nasty chuckle. "*Cannot?* You're a little piece of shit, Celia. And the only "right" a piece of shit has is a fast flush into the sewage treatment system. Where's your mother, slut?"

Celia kept silent. After perhaps thirty seconds her hair was grabbed from behind and her head dragged back, stretching her neck to its conceivable limits. "You were asked a question, you little piece of shit." The guard's voice snarled into her ear. "Answer the controller."

"I insist on my right to legal counsel," Celia gasped, unable to keep from whimpering with pain.

"You stupid piece of shit, you will have an attorney when—and I say *when*—we are prepared to charge you. *If* we charge you."

"I demand to have my attorney present," Celia said.

"Tell me when you last saw your mother."

"I claim the right to remain silent." Celia winced as the guard yanked on her hair. Putting his lips right against her ear, he hissed disgusting expletives at her.

"Where was your mother on the night you were apprehended?" the interrogator said.

"I claim the right to remain silent."

It was going to be a long, tedious session, to be followed by retribution. And she was so tired already. But they would not budge her in *this* session. She would hold out for as long as she had to. And then Emily...Emily would rescue her.

# Chapter Thirty-six

After Alexandra had discharged several dozen rounds during which she almost consistently hit the target (though seldom the big red Xs marking the target's "vulnerable" spots—the heart and brains), her father took off his ear mufflers and gestured her to do the same. "Not at all bad for your first time," he said. "With regular practice you'll be quite adequate a shot. But it's getting late now, and I'm expecting Wedgewood, so we'll work on semi-automatic and automatic hardware next time, and laser weapons after that."

Good. She'd given up her usual Wednesday mail run but did not wish to forfeit all her time before tea to this insanity. Playing with pistols! Considering that she—like Mama—never went anywhere without a gorilla, and considering that she could generally take care of herself in most unarmed situations, her father's insistence on these lessons with firearms struck her as a waste of time. Just because *he* had fetishes about these things didn't mean she should have to share them.

Alexandra handed Lamont the Colt and Blake the mufflers. She flexed the fingers of her right hand, for they had an odd tingle in them. Staring at them, she remembered the ring she had removed and was slipping her hand into her tunic pouch for it when she felt a distinct brush of fingers over her buttocks—a contact she perceived as intentionally offensive. She turned her head and out of the corner of her eye caught Lamont's lewd smirk at someone, probably Marlin, who was somewhere in the room with them. Anger exploded in her, unthinking and insensate, sending a flood of adrenalin pumping into her veins.

Alexandra whirled and with the full force of the momentum of that whirl delivered a high kick into Lamont's groin. Bellowing, Lamont doubled over. Still beside herself with rage, Alexandra raised her arm, chopped hard into his thick, beefy neck with the rigid side of her hand, and leaped backwards, intending to exert further force.

But Lamont lowered his head and began charging her. Instinctively she raised her leg to kick him, but he seized her foot before it connected and jerked her off balance and to the floor. What followed she perceived in jumbled confusion—her father bellowing "Take your fucking hands off her, Lamont!" and Blake's jumping Lamont from behind and encircling him with a body-hold that pinned his massive arms to his side.

Alexandra's breath came in gasps; the adrenalin had pushed her heart into the wild erratic thumping of manic acceleration. Sitting on the cork floor, panting, shaking with unreleased energy, she watched as in seeming slow motion her father moved to stand before Lamont, whose torso and arms were still clasped—perhaps even squeezed—by those thick, muscle-roped arms Blake had wrapped around him. "Until further notice," Alexandra listened to her father say, "you are confined to quarters. And you are not at liberty to discuss this with anyone but Marlin or myself. Clear?"

"Understood, sir," Lamont said stiffly.

"Then get out of here. Let him go, Blake."

Blake released his hold. Lamont brushed off his tunic sleeves and without a glance at anyone in the room turned and went out the door.

"We'll discuss this later, Marlin," Papa said. He held his hand down to Alexandra. Taking it, she levered herself to her feet. "Try some deep breathing," he advised.

Alexandra stood absolutely still with her eyes closed as she filled her lungs to capacity and exhaled very very slowly. After doing this several times, she said, "I'm okay now."

Her father took her arm and led her out of the practice range, up the stairs, and outside. Gratefully she drew in the clean fresh air, realizing just how much of a stench her shooting had made. "You do realize, I hope, that unrestrained, Lamont could kill you?" he said as they walked back to the house.

Alexandra swallowed. "I wasn't thinking of that," she said. "He got me into such a rage that I reacted without thinking at all."

"I see. That might not always be wise. You do understand that?"

"Yes," Alexandra said. "I see that now."

"So what was the provocation?"

Alexandra swallowed again. She did owe him an explanation for having attacked one of his gorillas. "He felt me up. On my buttocks," Alexandra blurted out—and felt the rage boiling up in her anew. "I could hardly believe it. I think I was going to let it pass, even though—" *Even though,* she almost said, *executive women are never to let any male get away with even accidental contact.* But Alexandra did not say this. She started again: "I turned my head to look at him and found him grinning in the most disgustingly lewd way. It was obvious the touch was deliberate!"

Her father sighed. "He'll have to go. I can't have a man whom I can't trust with you in my personal security detail. His resentment is probably monumental. So now we have to decide what to do with him."

"Do with him?" Alexandra said blankly. "That's simple: you fire him!"

"It isn't so easy, Alexandra. Let me explain a few facts of life to you, facts that may be useful in preventing you from making potentially consequential errors in the future. Lamont knows everything there is to know about my security arrangements, about this place, and, indeed, about several highly confidential Security Services matters. I *can't* simply dump him. That would be to take an egregiously stupid risk."

"Oh," Alexandra said. So one could not always be rid of difficult employees. What an unsettling thought.

"I suppose I can send him to one of my other residences," he said. "Or maybe ask Wedgewood to promote him and find a place for him in some foreign station."

"Promote him!" Alexandra cried in disgust. "For feeling me up!"

"My dear Alexandra, not everything in life works out according to an abstract scale of justice."

Alexandra fumed, but in silence. As they approached the big bed of lilies in glorious fragrant bloom she said, to change the subject, "You mentioned you were expecting Wedgewood?"

"Ahhhh," came out of him, a sound of great pleasure. "Yes. He'll be bringing me news from Goodwin. Goodwin expected the Executive to be discussing the question of my reinstatement today."

"Oh!" Alexandra exclaimed. He opened the side door and gestured her in. "I had no idea—you didn't tell me!"

He chuckled. "I wanted to spend this week as normally as possible, without that added degree of tension."

Penderel met them in the hall outside the Small Study. "Mr. Wedgewood has arrived, sir."

"Where is he?"

"In the Long Drawing Room, sir."

"Show him in here, Penderel," Papa said, and he and Alexandra went into the Small Study.

"I'll be running along," Alexandra said, hanging back by the door.

"No, I want you to stay." He gave her a critical look. "Let's be clear about this: when you're not busy with your education I'll want you to. assist me. I'm going to need you, Alexandra. I haven't got a staff left, you know. And there will be many highly confidential details that I won't be able to trust to anyone else. Further, I want you to become thoroughly informed about Security. And to pick up the nuts and bolts and even the nuances of how to run it." Her surprise must have shown in her face, for he said, "That hadn't occurred to you? I'm thinking in terms of a partnership, Alexandra…should you prove as apt as I think you will. You'll need to be able to control men like Wedgewood, you know. Thus it's essential that you—" He broke off when the door opened and Wedgewood entered. He moved to Alexandra's side. "I didn't expect you this early," he said to Wedgewood. "We've just come from the practice range." He slipped his arm around Alexandra's shoulders. "Can you believe my daughter just tackled Lamont, even though the bastard's twice her size? This woman doesn't take shit off anyone, Wedgewood."

"Lamont?" Wedgewood queried, looking slightly confused.

"She didn't like either his behavior or his attitude," Papa said. Alexandra could see he was enjoying this; it was as though he were boasting of some personal achievement to Wedgewood. "So she laid into him. Without even considering his size or skill—which she's quite familiar with. She's going to be tough, this one." His hand squeezed her shoulder, pulling her closer to him.

Wedgewood looked extremely uncomfortable, Alexandra thought—almost as uncomfortable as she felt. "I have two envelopes for you, sir. One from the Executive, the other from Goodwin."

Her father's fingers dug into her shoulder with painful force. Releasing her, he moved further into the room. "Let's have a look then, Wedgewood," he said, his voice sounding almost indifferent. He sat down in one of the chairs flanking the fireplace. Wedgewood went to the sofa, laid his attaché case on the cushion, and pressed his thumb to the lock. The case sprang open, and Wedgewood withdrew two envelopes—one purple, the other cream-colored.

Alexandra watched intently as her father opened the purple envelope first and drew out a thick sheet of purple paper. His gaze ran over it; his lips twitched. So. It pleased him. But he said nothing, merely opened the heavy cream-colored envelope and took from it a matching sheet of stationary. After reading it he looked at Alexandra and smiled broadly, and then at Wedgewood. "It's as I expected. The Executive asks me to resume the position... And Goodwin informs me that they'll give me carte blanche if I demand terms. Which is better than I'd expected." His eyes returned to Alexandra. "I think this calls for a celebration. Why don't you call Penderel, Alexandra."

Alexandra went obediently to the telephone. So they would be going back to DC, she thought. They would be leaving here. Well that was fine with her. Even if it did mean losing the Bechstein.

# Chapter Thirty-seven

"Whoooeee!" The voice shrieked. "Will you take a look at that shot of beaver!"

Weak to the point of trembling, sweat-soaked nausea, Celia tried to shut out their jeers. Concentrate on breathing, she told herself—for drawing breath, terribly difficult with her wrists bound so high above her head that she could just barely touch the floor with the tips of her toes, had become her main concern. Since they had hung her, waves of black nausea had crashed over her and plunged her into faints too many times for her to remember.

The voices were coming closer. Celia fought panic, panic that they would further violate her as she hung there, so obvious a target with her tunic hiked up past her hips. In spite of having steeled herself for it, she flinched when the hands touched her. "The Commander's finished his lunch," one of the guards said. "He's hoping you've taken his advice and done some thinking." Involuntarily Celia cried out at the painful thing done to her genitals. "You know how to think, bitch?"

When they released her she collapsed onto the floor, too weak even to stand.

They dragged her back to the interrogation room, and everything was as it had been in the earlier session. Although her voice was weaker and trembling, Celia stuck to her previous responses. After several dozen repetitions of their asking the question and her refusing to answer, the controller said, "This is your last chance, Celia. Or it's further drug therapy for you."

"I don't consent to this so-called therapy," Celia said. "I insist on having access to my own physician." The guard tugged on her arm, which he had been holding twisted behind her back, sending a new wave of pain into her shoulder.

"Take this stinking piece of shit back to her cell," the controller ordered. And the guard snapped the blindfold over her eyes and jerked her out of the chair.

As she lay in the back of the van, tears seeped from her eyes into the blindfold, tears of fear and self-pity at her physical weakness, which was worse than anything she could think of, a weakness so terrible that each wave of nausea sent her to the edge of fainting. Did the weakness come from the nausea, or the nausea from the weakness? she wondered, trying to think of something other than the animal beside her. If she could be somewhere else, could be detached from her body and what was done to it, could feel that it didn't matter, that their filth could not degrade her, she would not mind the pain so much. She tried to summon up pride for having stood up to the controller, but her courage seemed illusory now that she faced another injection, now that she was again exposed to the guards' bestiality...

As they dragged her out of the van, into the building, and down the stairs, the guards debated between themselves who would do what to her. "Hey man, you can *have* her pussy," one of them said, "'cause this one shits on herself all the time."

As he continued talking about how he would make her fellate him, Celia tried to believe that they were talking that way to humiliate her, that they would not do the things they were talking about. But in the corridor before they reached her cell they threw her to the floor and one of them smashed his fist into her vagina. The other held her nose until she opened her mouth, at which point he jammed his thumbs into the hinges of her jaw, preventing her from closing it. And then, all the time joking and comparing notes with what the guard they called "Romeo" was said to have told them about raping her, they did to her everything they had said they would do.

# Chapter Thirty-eight

After dinner they went upstairs to the Music Room even though Alexandra would not be playing that evening. They were jazzed, having drunk toast after toast to "the new Security Services" with the very special wine her father had had brought out for the occasion. Even *she* was excited—at his elation, and at the certainty that she would be leaving the island and living out in the world. It was as though a prison sentence had been lifted. Her grandparents and mother would know where she was and would come to visit her! And there would be concerts and operas and ballet and theater, and dining out, and women to talk to... Everything would be different, wonderfully different.

So good did she feel that despite the coldly appraising looks he had been giving her all evening, she almost didn't mind Wedgewood's presence. Wedgewood seemed pleased at her father's reinstatement, as though his own career depended on it. The strangeness of what her father had said about her learning to control Wedgewood made the comment linger in her mind all evening. She could not imagine doing it. He didn't seem the sort of person anyone could control. Though clearly Papa did...

Alexandra seated herself in the chair she usually took, beside the table on which the coffee tray had already been placed. Wedgewood sat in the matching chair a few feet away—because Papa always took the sofa facing the chairs, and Wedgewood knew it. "Do you care for coffee, Wedgewood?" Alexandra asked politely.

"I'm breaking out some prodigiously fine cognac tonight," her father said from somewhere behind her. "Penderel will be bringing it in shortly."

Ah yes, more celebration... When considering what to drink to celebrate, he had originally proposed Russian Vodka, but then had changed his mind, saying that she wouldn't want to drink it—though she knew the real reason was that he had recalled that he had promised her not to drink scotch or Russian Vodka for the entire rest of the year. And then he had remembered a special limited bottling of a famous cabernet from a small winery whose output was in such demand that purchasing its wine was a feat in itself. She could hear him pacing, pacing, restlessly pacing, as though he could not contain the energy of his plans and intentions. Alexandra opened a bottle of water for herself: she had drunk far too much alcohol already without adding something as potent as cognac to it. How many glasses? She had lost count. In her condition she wouldn't be able to play a scale, much less a Beethoven Sonata. But then she was prohibited from playing in front of executives outside of the family, anyway.

"I think I'd like coffee first, and then cognac," Wedgewood said, responding belatedly to her question.

Alexandra poured coffee into a cup and took it to him. She looked at her father, now standing in front of the fireplace. "And for you— Robert?" Too uncomfortably conscious of the awkwardness of avoiding it, she forced herself to use his name.

He smiled at her. "None for me. God knows I don't need the stimulation tonight!"

Penderel brought in the unopened bottle with three large snifters on a silver tray. Ceremoniously he set the cognac tray down beside the coffee tray, slipped a corkscrew from his pocket, and drew out the cork. "Shall I pour, sir?"

Papa nodded. "Oh yes, do. For all three of us."

Alexandra opened her mouth to protest, then thought better of it: why make such an issue of it? She would simply not drink it. Or if she drank any, at most a sip or two.

Penderel poured the cognac, set the bottle on the coffee tray, and carried the tray of snifters around to each of them. Then he left the room.

Alexandra cupped the snifter in her hands and admired the gleam of the glass and the golden warmth of the cognac in the room's soft gaslight. It was heartbreakingly beautiful, she thought. She wondered, though, whether it would it be so lovely by the ordinary light of LED bulbs.

Papa moved toward where she and Wedgewood sat. "I'll want all domestic heads of station at Central for a meeting on Monday afternoon." He stopped beside Alexandra's chair and perched on its arm, pressing his shoulder against the back of the chair.

"You want me to see to it the order is sent out?"

"At once. With things in a shambles, such a meeting is common sense. But I also intend to begin a new program, one the entire Executive will have to support. No more mere holding actions, no more numb reactions. It's time to go on the offensive—and not in the Pentagon's terms, either." It sounded like a declaration of war, Alexandra thought. "You'll schedule the meeting for the afternoon, because the morning, of course, must be reserved for a meeting of the directors and deputy directors." He put his hand on her shoulder, and she could hear his teeth against the snifter and the sound of him swallowing. Was he staring over her head at Wedgewood as he talked? Certainly Wedgewood seemed to be looking over her head at *him.*

Alexandra lifted the snifter to her mouth. Inhaling the fumes, she paused. And then slowly, very slowly, ventured a tiny sip. When it slid down her throat smoothly, rather than getting caught up in its burning her throat and making her choke, she noticed the taste and decided she liked it.

Wedgewood smiled very slightly, stretched his legs out before him, and set his empty snifter down on the table beside him. He wore a well-satisfied look, as though, Alexandra thought, the cognac agreed with him. "I think I can remember those items without noting them down," he said.

"Oh, and see if you can't find me a first-rate press officer. Unless Bennett has resurfaced?"

"Oh, Bennett. No, not a trace of the bitch."

"Then she's gone over to Weatherall," Papa said. And again Alexandra heard his glass clink against his teeth. And she ventured another sip herself.

"May I ask the nature of this new program?" Wedgewood said, his gleaming eyes peering bluely over Alexandra's head through the slits of his almost closed eyelids. He looked curiously feline tonight, Alexandra thought. Like a large blond cat, sleekly groomed and well muscled, relaxed but still ready to pounce.

"Of course. I think our solution is quite obvious. We need a major mobilization of public opinion—of the intensity necessary to sustain

a prolonged foreign war—against the incursions of the aliens, anarchists, and Commies that are damned close to succeeding in tearing
this country apart. Very simply, we will nullify their human rights nonsense—which is brewing more trouble than most executives seem to
realize—by getting rid of the troublemakers once and for all. The way
Frank Snelling eliminated the Crime Syndicate forty-five years ago."

Wedgewood's eyebrows pulled together. "You mean…excise
them *all?*"

Papa laughed. "No, of course not. I'm talking about selective excision, within the context of an armed propaganda campaign on a
scale we've never before undertaken. Only troublemakers and traitors
would be adversely affected, while the general population would benefit. And visibly so, too. So that anyone who might be even remotely
tempted to make trouble will of course drop the idea at once and only
the hard-core will persist. And the hard-core we can handle." His hand
moved from Alexandra's shoulder to the nape of her neck, which he
softly stroked. Shimmering sensation washed over her, sensation she
recognized with shock and embarrassment. Suddenly she found that
her glass had slipped out of her hand, onto the rug. Her father sprang
to his feet, knelt down in front of her chair, and retrieved the snifter.
"We're lucky, no breakage and not a drop spilled." Smiling, he handed
her glass back to her. Alexandra tried to compose her burning face,
but could not meet his eyes. "Oh hell," he muttered, and got to his
feet. "Will you explain the facts of life to my daughter, Wedgewood?
It seems she has illusions about that old political chestnut, 'human
rights.'" He moved to the sofa and sat down.

"With pleasure," Wedgewood said. "But first I want to notify my
pilot we need to be beating it out of here. It's getting late."

"As you like," Papa said. Wedgewood got to his feet and crossed
the room to the handset on the desk. "So their propaganda has gotten
to you," Papa said. "I can see you're upset."

Alexandra, groping for both composure and comprehension, busied herself with another sip of cognac. He seemed to think she was
upset about whatever it was he had been saying to Wedgewood. But
what was it they were talking about, he and Wedgewood? She hadn't
been paying proper attention. They'd been talking about excisions—
she had caught that much and knew she didn't want to know more.

They used the word "excision" to refer to killing: he had explained all that to her when talking about the Civil War and the Executive Transformation. But who were these troublemakers he intended to "selectively excise"? "I'm confused," she said, when it seemed he required an answer of her—though she really didn't want the clarification that she knew must follow.

He drank the remaining cognac in his glass. "I thought we'd discussed this fairly thoroughly before?" But he did not sound even mildly irritated. "As I've said time and again, what this politics of 'human rights' comes down to is the attempt of the weak to pull down the strong. Whether through being misguidedly seduced by the enemy, or whether through an identification with the weak, or through a hatred of strength. But the fact remains that the only people who are subject to the violence of the state are those who refuse to behave like civilized human beings. And what's so human about *them*, I'd like to know?"

Alexandra's head was swimming—from the alcohol, she thought, as much as from everything they were saying and…that other thing. *You're not a child now, Alexandra, don't think your sniveling is anything but weakness, weakness we can't afford…* Yes, she remembered now his talking about the weak and how dangerous it was to allow the weak any power at all. And about how fragile civilized order was, as the whole of history constantly proved… Wedgewood returned to his chair. "So, Ms. Sedgewick, you're worried about human rights?" She discerned a seemingly playful lilt of mockery in his tone, though not obvious enough to give her an excuse for taking offense.

Alexandra swallowed. She did not know any of the arguments, she only knew she couldn't understand why so much suffering was necessary—suffering of the sort she had learned about on the vid show, suffering that seemed a level of retaliation wholly out of proportion to anything those people could have done. Under pressure of their waiting for her to respond, she said, "The things that are done…they seem terribly severe. And so ugly… And this talk of killing people… These people aren't Russians, or aliens either…" She thought of that teen-aged girl who had been interviewed on one of the programs, a girl only fifteen. How could such a girl be so terrible as to deserve the things that had been done to her? How could she be such a threat to "civilized order"? Would *she* be the sort they intended to kill?

"You are, of course, too young to remember what it was like before the aliens struck," Wedgewood said, smiling at Alexandra. "Which is a pity. You don't know what a civilized world is like. At any rate, once they *did* strike, every lunatic and destroyer came out of the closet to begin their decade-long rampage of terrorism. Have you been to LA or Boston, Ms. Sedgewick?" Alexandra shook her head. "Perhaps you should take a trip to one of those places to see the extent to which these destroyers have succeeded in making life around them hell. To see what threatens the rest of the country... A good half—at a conservative estimate—of the physical properties of those cities have been destroyed. Some of the damage was inflicted by the Russians, granted, though not *that* much. These...*people*—" Wedgewood made the designation sound dubious—"have firebombed and burned and in every way imaginable sought to destroy those cities. Currently—in order to provide at least the rudiments of a semblance of orderly life for the other citizens in those cities, the vast majority of them law-abiding and patriotic—currently those two cities are under extremely tight states of siege in which every neighborhood has been sectored and partially quarantined to keep the troublemakers under control. Anyone without blue plastic must endure waits of up to two hours as they pass from one area to another. And in the meantime most areas of the cities have been devastated and have little cultural life to speak of. So now these anarchists send out their damned propaganda trying to stir up sympathy for the terrorists when they *are* punished. What about the rights of law-abiding citizens, Ms. Sedgewick?" Wedgewood's eyes seemed to accuse her of being unfair. "Surely you'll agree that they deserve to have *their* rights protected?" He stood up and shoved his hands in his pockets. "Severe? But perhaps if we'd been more 'severe' to start with things wouldn't be at the point they are at now. We need to re-instill a sense of law and order into this society, Ms. Sedgewick. Feeling sorry for the very terrorists who have created this mess is hardly a rational response." Wedgewood turned to Papa. "I have to go now, sir. I'll see you on Friday in DC."

And then they were alone, and Alexandra was filled with a heightened consciousness of her previous reaction to him that made her heart thump. Her father said, "You know from firsthand experience about how the weak can emotionally manipulate one, Alexandra.

You've had a taste of it with that girl you had here." Alexandra's face burned. "What was it you said about her making you feel guilty because you were her employer and could send her away?"

"But that was different!" Alexandra said quickly. There couldn't possibly be a parallel! "That was personal. And not as extreme, either."

"Just think about it, sweetheart. She used her weakness to make you feel sorry for her, to make you feel guilty, even though it was *she* who had been manipulating *you*."

"Only because I behaved so badly." Alexandra swallowed the last of the cognac in her glass and set the snifter down on the coffee tray.

"Bullshit. She just manipulated you further, to make you feel guilt and pity. Why should you feel bad for sending her away? After all, she was going straight into the arms of a new employer. I'm sure your mother saw to that."

"I have to go to bed," Alexandra said, anxious to escape this difficult-to-counter pressure. "I've had too much to drink."

He sighed. "And I was just going to suggest another cognac. But you're probably right. That would explain your muddle." He stood up and held out his hand. "Come, I'll walk you to your room."

Alexandra quivered. "I'm not *that* tight," she said as she rose to her feet without taking his hand. His arm went around her, and they set off for her room. Even that arm around her shoulder felt different now. Everything was changed; it was a disaster, this thing that had so inexplicably happened. How could she act normally enough to conceal it?

"You'll have a busy day tomorrow, supervising our packing. You'll have to skip your meetings with your tutors until next week, you know."

"It's almost summer anyway," Alexandra said. "Don't I get a vacation this year?"

"Hmmm, we'll see. You have to be ready for Yale in the fall, remember."

Alexandra sighed. "Couldn't I have another year before starting college?" She needed more time to figure out how to sway him away from Yale and all his plans for her. "After all, I'd be starting a year ahead of time."

"A lot of executives do," he said. "No, I think it's best for you this way. As it is you may miss some of the pleasure because of the kinds of exposure you'll be having to real life this summer. College will probably seem tame to you by comparison... Though I suppose that's not all bad."

He must be talking about himself again, Alexandra thought. That's usually what the problem was when she couldn't understand the things he was saying.

When they reached her room he smiled at her and kissed her forehead. "I'm proud of you, Alexandra. The way you tackled Lamont is all the more proof of what a fine woman you're becoming. And your poise with Wedgewood—even taking the cognac from Penderel—yes, I noticed your hesitation. I can see you'll have no problem fitting in. It will come naturally to you."

While the reason for the warm approval in his words and eyes eluded Alexandra, the fact of it overwhelmed her, even in the midst of her new frightened guilty feelings about him. She threw her arms around him and hugged him as she would either of her grandparents, and rested her head on his shoulder. She wished she could say out loud right that very moment *Papa* to him: if she could do that, then everything would be all right, for she would discover that sense of security she longed for, would feel protected from everything she did not understand. But she could not say the word; it was the one thing not allowed her by him. Silently she withdrew from him and opened the door to her suite. "Goodnight, sweetheart," he said as she went in.

She turned and smiled tremulously at him. "Goodnight, Robert," she whispered. And then she closed her door, went to the vase for parsley, and threw herself onto the bed. She had never in her life felt so confused as she did now.

# Chapter Thirty-nine

They enter in deep camouflage—this place, which is called a "military base"—their purpose the finding of clandestine places of confinement. "It'll be difficult, I know," Magyyt had said to Astrea when describing the night's excursion, "but we must not interfere, for we go only to reconnoiter. Such places fill me with horror and tempt me to destructure every atom of them, but we can't do that tonight without endangering the lives of the people being confined there. Practically speaking, we could only rescue a few—for three Marq'ssan alone cannot a liberation force make."

As the nature of this "military base" becomes apparent, Astrea is filled with something negative, powerful and strong and almost overwhelming. All about them lie deadly things, objects crying out for their own destruction—as though destruction can be the only end of destruction. Astrea communicates to Magyyt: "Why can't we simply destructure these weapons? They're no connection with the prisoners."

"If we do that, they'll know we've been here. We must merely observe this time, Astrea. You must do nothing but scan for places of confinement."

They find several, all within structures designated "barracks" except two, which are within smaller structures made of thinner materials, where the prisoners are kept below ground. As Magyyt said, these are places of horror, of as much horror as the place they had liberated in another hemisphere of the globe the night before. They think, but can't be sure, that there are seventy-eight prisoners, many of them in pain violent enough to be apparent to their scan. Like the unusual amount of destructuring they have been doing, this scan, so much more complex and difficult than any Astrea has ever done, has widened and deepened self's capacities.

"There is one thing we can do tonight," Sorben says to Magyyt and Astrea. "We can disable the three electrical apparatuses they use for torture. If we do it cleverly, they'll never suspect our interference but assume their own error in each instance."

Eagerly they cause these machines to malfunction, thereby stopping this particular torment. It isn't enough, Astrea thinks. But it is all they are allowed tonight. The thought comes to Astrea of returning here alone and destructuring every object in sight. But self can see that Magyyt is correct: doing so will not save the prisoners. The temptation leaves self, even if the anger does not.

Having accomplished what they came to do, they return to the pod and leave the place of horror. But the horror lingers on, undispelled by distance. Like the other horrors, it is something now in-formed into the deepest layers of self, inexorably linked to that powerful negative force increasingly circulating within self.

This development is not what Astrea expected, for these changes bear no relation to the standard description of first-phase responses.

# Chapter Forty

*Her dead body lies half-buried in a swamp of excrement. Mama and Emily approach; seeing her, they recoil and cry out their horror. "Could that be Celia?" Emily's voice sounds doubtful. "No," Mama says, "that's not my Celia, not that thing. That can't be my daughter."*

The image was vivid and compelling. But as she struggled to escape the tentacles of rejection and despair trailing it, Celia grew obsessed with determining whether it had been an hallucination or a dream. Had she actually dozed? Hallucinations distorted reality and could come from anywhere. But dreams, dreams often told the truth, dreams spoke from one's unconscious. Dreams one had to take seriously.

Had the drug, dose by dose accumulating in her system, lasted longer this time, or had the doctor injected her again without her having realized it? She had been barely aware of him during his last visit and even now could not tell if he had really come in here and examined her and said things to her. Perhaps he would never come again to help her between injections, perhaps her asking him while he had been swabbing her hip with alcohol whether he had taken a Hippocratic oath had made him too furious to do even the little he had done for her before... She found it difficult to concentrate and kept fighting to retrieve from memory something she knew it was important to remember. Something about the three injections... And then it would come to her that if there had been three injections, Mama and Emily must have returned from the Free Zone. But each time she grasped the point, her thoughts wandered, dwelling on what the controller had said during the last interrogation: that Emily would not be allowed to take her from them this time, that everything had been arranged to prevent it, that she would be a fool to think anyone could have her released before he, her controller, was ready to release her... And then, Celia's concentration disintegrated, dissolving into overwhelming despair and dejection, her thoughts splintering into nothing she could grasp long enough to get hold of.

When finally the door opened and they came in, Celia grew obsessed with their not having first ordered her to put on her blindfold. Why hadn't they? Did they no longer care if she saw their faces? She made these speculations with great detachment. And in fact so great was her detachment that she did not even open her eyes to see them but remained as she had been since she could last remember, lying in that one motionless position.

"Celia," the doctor's voice said sharply. "Are you awake, Celia?"

He sounded angry. But she did not answer.

She felt a touch on her wrist. Only the doctor touched her in that way. And after a while she felt his rubber-gloved fingers on her chin. "Enough is enough," he said. "Look at this. It suggests that she vomited blood. None of her responses are as one would expect. It's virtually certain she has an allergy to the drug. The response was overly violent to start with, and this time it's off the scale. For all we know she may be hemorrhaging internally. She hasn't recovered consciousness and her pulse is erratic and thready. She needs to be in supervised care. And as for the filth in this cell—the microbes that breed in feces, in case you don't realize it, engender all sorts of diseases I'm sure you'd rather not have loose, even down here." The doctor's voice seethed with anger. What he said made her remember again what she wanted to believe was a hallucination, what she kept reliving over and over again too vividly, too sharply, with too many sensory recollections for it to have been an hallucination.

"You can treat her here," the other man said. "We're not about to ruin the near completion of our efforts. The psychological aspects are as important as the physical."

"There's fecal matter in her hair, you idiot." The doctor's voice rose. "Psychological methods are one thing—"

"So they didn't do a very good job when they rinsed her head," the other said. "It's no big deal, doc. We've never seen the kind of thing you're talking about. Admit it, her jibe at you hit the mark."

"Let me put it this way. She isn't conscious. I can't examine her properly in here, so we have no idea of her state—except the obvious, that she's dehydrated and not recovering from the effects of the drug as she should have done hours ago. Does killing the prisoner help your interrogations, Jackson? Look at her, she hasn't moved since I was last in here, not even to remove her blindfold, much less to drink water or use that filthy bucket. Moreover, she's soiled herself. You expect a miracle?"

"Then we'll send the nurse in to clean her up."

"That's not adequate."

"Well that's all you're getting."

"In that case, I wash my hands of the case. I'll file a report with Crowe. From now on she's your responsibility. I'm not coming in here again for any reason."

"You think Crowe's going to let you wriggle out of this? You're crazy if you do. You gave her the injections—"

"What, so now you're worried about losing her?" the doctor jeered. "You know what you have to do, Jackson. I want her in an hygienic clinical setting. And I need to be able to do simple things like examine the blood vessels in her eyes—which under your rules I can't do. And I need to have some blood work done. And at the very least put her on an intravenous drip."

"Denied. Make do with the nurse."

"Then you're fucked, Jackson. And you'll take the hit if she goes." Celia heard their footsteps moving out of the cell and then the door closing. They thought her unconscious: which struck her as a good thing. It meant that they wouldn't interrogate her again. And maybe wouldn't give her another injection for a while, either. That was the important thing, avoiding those things without betraying Mama. Which was so hard to do now that she knew Emily would not be coming for her. A corpse lying in excrement.

Crowe, Jackson... She tried to hang onto the names, but eventually they slipped away from her, as did the conversation they had held over her corpse of a body.

# Chapter Forty-one

Groggy, grumpy, and achey, Hazel peered at the clock and saw that it was already 7:45. Liz had forgotten to call her. She heaved herself out of bed and staggered with her eyes closed through the dressing room to the bathroom.

"Darling!" Liz exclaimed. "Go back to bed. Really, I feel terribly guilty for having given you such a hard night." Not only had Hazel taken three hours to fall asleep after going to bed, but Liz had awakened twice with bad dreams; and unlike Liz, Hazel had not been able to fall back to sleep very easily.

Hazel leaned against the door frame. "Too much to do today." Her eyes were closed, and she spoke in a mumble. "I'll be okay once I have a shower and some coffee."

"I'll pour you a cup right now," Liz said quickly. "I've a fresh thermoflask right here." Her voice was unbearably bright and lively.

"After I shower." Prying open her gummy eyelids, Hazel shuffled into the bathroom.

The hot, needle-sharp spray worked wonders. It did nothing for the burning in her eyes, of course, but it did ease the muscle aches that afflicted her whenever she lost more than half a night's sleep.

Hazel was toweling herself dry when Liz brought her a big cup of coffee. "You're so conscientious, darling," Liz said. "I'm a lucky woman."

Hazel held the cup between her palms and walked back into the bedroom. She would treat herself to having the first cup in bed before she got up and dressed. As she breathed in the fragrant steam rising out of the cup, she considered Liz's change in attitude. So she was going to act as though there hadn't been nearly a week of coldness between them? It must, Hazel thought, be because of the onslaught of bad dreams. Why else would Liz suddenly gush with warmth?

Hazel sipped the coffee and eased into her waking self. Liz came into the bedroom, completely dressed. "I forgot to ask you before," Hazel said, "but what did Shirl say about the two service-techs I interviewed last week?"

Liz made a face. "Oh, I'm so sorry, I forgot to ask her. Would you talk to her yourself, darling? I'm just so damned busy—well, you *know* how swamped I am."

Hazel took another sip of coffee, then said in a tone she thought remarkably measured considering the hour of the morning and the amount of sleep she had gotten, "Don't you think you've gone overboard, Liz? All these plans and ambitions and nobody to do the work?" Instantly Liz's face shuttered with the wariness that had lately characterized the face she presented to Hazel—and only to Hazel. Hazel bit her lip and looked Liz in the eye. "I don't see the point, Liz. I really don't. I can't do the work of five, whatever you may think about my efficiency! And with these new people coming—my god, if they're anything like Cleghorn, we'll really be in a mess. Not to mention that that will make four debriefings in addition to everything else. You know, I think you'd better start requiring these renegades to bring their own help."

This last comment Hazel meant to be flippant. But to her dismay, Liz eagerly took it up. "Hazel! What a brilliant suggestion! Why didn't I think of it myself? In the future I'll stipulate that very point!"

Hazel slapped her palm on her forehead. "My god, Liz, you're incredible. Just incredible. Don't you recognize ironic humor when you hear it?"

Liz glared at her for a throbbing ten seconds of silence. "So there's no difference in you at all, is there," Liz said. "Still as petty and belligerent as you were when you first turned nasty."

What could she possibly say to such a remark? Hazel slowly shook her head. "What's happened to us, Liz?"

Liz's eyes flashed. "It's perfectly clear what's happened. You changed when you discovered my relationship with Allison."

The fact was, without Liz's continual reminders to her about it, she would probably soon forget all about Liz's sexual relationship with Allison. This intimation of jealousy had become an *idée fixe* in Liz's mind, a theory she resorted to whenever there was friction of any sort between them. Hazel swallowed the last of the coffee in her cup and climbed out of bed. "Let me put it this way," she said as calmly as she could. "Anne is leaving tomorrow. She'll spend all of today being briefed by you and Allison. That means that all the transcripts from Cleghorn and Burns' debriefings will have to be checked by me. While at the same time I have all sorts of other tasks and routines. For instance, the security decision you want me to make in consultation with Shirl, though I know ziltch about security. And numerous other things, some of them trivial, but not all. Which means that today I'll fall behind on the transcripts. And tomorrow I'll fall even farther behind…and Wednesday—do you see what I'm saying, Liz? I'm damned if I'm going to sit there listening to those fucking tapes with my eyes glued to the screen for eighteen hours a day as a matter of routine! So just what do you suggest we do?"

"I have complete faith in you, darling. It's simply not as bad as you say. You really should have slept in. If you had, you wouldn't be so negative." She patted Hazel's cheek, lightly brushed her lips over Hazel's, and left the room. Hazel stared at the door Liz closed after her in a kind of daze, until finally she roused herself to dress. The woman was incredible, absolutely incredible. What in the hell was going on with her? In the past month she had become about as accessible as a phantom locked in a mirror. A pat on the cheek, Liz? Is this a new phase in our relationship? Or a nasty piece of retaliatory ironic humor, perhaps? Whatever it was, it worried Hazel, worried her deeply, and not only because it still left her in a lurch with an overload of work.

# Chapter Forty-two

How could it be that the doctor had thought her unconscious? Not that he had even looked at her. But that the other one had accepted this judgment made no sense. Of course, she was confused and muddled. She might have misunderstood.

As for herself, she would not speak to them again, she would do nothing but wait, wait for Emily. If she moved her body in the slightest she would be forced into producing more of the filth with which they would further defile her, she would be forced into direct awareness, she would be forced into *feeling*... Lying just as she was, she felt nothing, not the fabric of the tunic where it touched her body, not the floor she lay on. Lying very still, it was possible to feel nothing, nothing at all. She was like that image of herself in the dream, lying in the pile of excrement, unmoving, dead. Only when Emily came—for the dream—no, hallucination, it had to have been an hallucination brought on by the drug—the hallucination was a lie, because Emily and Mama would know that she was alive, know that under her stillness she was still Celia, that the filth had nothing to do with her.

And yet, she had filled that bucket herself with the vilest of fluids, fluids that had streamed from her own body... Filling that bucket had been a weakness, a form of complicity if not actual collaboration in her own defilement. That such things had come from inside of her... A hot surge of bile shooting into her mouth caught Celia by surprise. But she did not open her mouth, she refused to succumb to the weakness, and the sensation of it faded, as though it had never touched her, except for the taste it left in her mouth. She would be strong, she would give them no help in anything, no words, no bodily waste, nothing at all. Let them inject her, rape her, beat her, defile her with all the most disgusting substances they could lay hands on. She would be locked inside, and they would not be able to touch her. They might be able to get in, but they couldn't force her out.

Celia's thoughts grew aimless with indifference, until finally she drifted in passive abeyance. When the sound of voices intruded into the space around her, they snared her attention without engaging her. She registered Jackson's voice, though she paid only cursory attention to it. He had brought a new doctor with him, one he addressed as "sir." This doctor refused to kneel on the floor to examine her and made Jackson have her moved somewhere down the hall to another room, where she was dumped on a table. The Velcro strip on the front of her tunic was opened, and she knew he was listening to her breathing through a stethoscope. She perceived it, but with a sort of mental knowledge that it was there, while not really *feeling* it on her skin. And then he took her blood pressure and demanded that her blindfold be removed. After arguing at length, Jackson complied. The doctor thumbed open each of Celia's eyes and shined a light in them. "What's her first name?" the doctor asked Jackson. "Celia," Jackson hissed. "Celia," the doctor called very loudly. "Answer me, Celia!" She heard the sound of plastic tearing. After about a minute the doctor said, "She's not responding at all to this stimulant. You say she was lying in exactly that position the last time you were in her cell?"

"Yeah. And the guards say she was in that position every time they looked in at her."

"Well let me take some blood from her for the lab," the doctor said.

"Can't you give her some kind of shot to bring her around, sir? We're pretty confident she'll break now."

Celia felt her arm being stretched out; a needle went into the bend in her elbow and after a while was withdrawn and her arm folded.

"Of course the real difficulty—unless Silver's concerns about possible internal damage from the drug prove to be correct—is filter failure. It's clear she hasn't had water since the injection—how many hours has it been?"

"Twenty-six," Jackson said. "She should have been in and out of interrogation by now. This is ridiculous."

"Twenty-six," the doctor repeated. "Well you see, that's very bad. You should have been forcing water down her at least twelve hours ago. And I notice her tunic isn't even damp. No fresh urine, in other words. Unless she's snowing you and has done it somewhere in her cell without your noticing?"

Jackson expressed alarm at this possibility and ordered a guard to go back to her cell and check the bucket and floor. For a moment Celia's detachment slid away from her and she felt as upset as she had felt about the dream.

"She's weeping," the doctor said abruptly. "I had my doubts before, but now I feel certain she's not unconscious."

Hands grabbed Celia's shoulders and shook her and slapped her face: she perceived this but did not *feel* it, just as she felt nothing at the sound of the words he was shouting at her.

"For chrisssake, Jackson, calm down," the doctor said irritably. "What I meant by that was that her state may not necessarily be produced solely by organic factors. Don't you find it strange that after all the fluid loss typically experienced in connection with this drug that she hasn't been compelled to take water? I said, calm down, man! Now get out of my way, goddam it, I want to check the inside of her mouth."

Jackson ceased his assault and Celia perceived her mouth being forced open and a tongue depressor thrust deep, against the back of her throat. But she did not *feel* it.

"She doesn't even have a gag reflex, Jackson. That kind of thing can't be faked. Do you understand what I'm saying, man? A gag reflex is as involuntary as blinking."

"What's the bottom line?" Jackson said sharply. "What do we have to do to get her into interrogation?"

Another voice spoke: 'I've checked her cell, sir, and I can't find anything."

"So there you have it, Jackson. You're going to have to have water forced down her and have her catheterized, at the very least. Otherwise, she'll simply die on you. *That's* your bottom line."

"Can't you give her some stronger kind of stimulant? We can't let her get away with this, doc!"

"In the first place, we don't know whether or not there's an organic problem," the doctor said. "In the second place, even if it is psychogenic, such stupors—if stupor it is—can be impervious to traumatic methods. If this woman has made—at some deep level of her psyche—the extreme decision to withdraw, even to the point of her own death, I see no possibility of successfully using trauma as a stimulus for forcing her back to full consciousness. I'll write a full report for Crowe when I've finished my examination. I'll also want a consult from a psychiatric specialist. I presume you're having her transferred to a clinical setting? I won't be able to make a firm diagnosis until I've been able to test her more thoroughly.'

"She can stay in this room," Jackson said after a long pause. "The nurse can do the things you mentioned."

"And if she goes into a crisis? I thought you understood the gravity, Jackson? Given the possibility of internal hemorrhaging, it would be foolish of you to leave her here. But when everything else is taken into account... You know, I fail to understand why you've made such a fuss over her if you're so willing to lose her entirely. I assure you, Jackson, I will be noting the strong warning I'm giving you in my report to Crowe. It will then become your responsibility."

"All right, all right, damn the bitch. Where do you want her taken sir?"

"The CNH would be best, I think," the doctor said.

"And I suppose that means I have to spare guards for her alone?"

"I'm sure you can get CNH's security people to handle that."

"Like hell I will."

"Suit yourself. At any rate, I'll phone over there and tell them you're on your way. And meet you there."

Celia heard, but the words flowed past her.

# Chapter Forty-three

Hazel came to the dinner table late. She would have preferred to have a tray in the office, work a little longer, and go to bed early. But tonight was Anne's last night. Everyone else at the table had nearly finished eating. Since Lisa had left at three for the "action" that night, she had a choice of two vacant chairs—between Cleghorn and Allison, or between Lacie and Ginger.

As she dug into the spinach soufflé, she let her mind run over the various occasions she had seen Anne that day. Each time Anne had struck her as resigned and morose. Hazel looked over at her—sitting between Allison and Liz—and noted the tension in her face and posture. Hazel glanced at Liz and found no sign of awareness of Anne's feelings. Allison, though, was patting Anne's hand and giving her her full attention. Hand-patting, cheek-patting...

It did no good to get angry. Allison probably hadn't a clue. Or Liz, either. But then Liz had professed never to take Anne's attachment to Allison seriously. And of course no one else at the table knew. They would probably all be taken in by the scene Anne and Liz would enact tomorrow, never suspecting what Liz was "up to."

"I just don't understand," Burns was saying. "To voluntarily work with terrorists is incomprehensible." Hazel remembered, now, Burns's astonishment when Liz had told her the reason Lisa would not be holding the usual afternoon debriefing session with her.

Hazel sensed Ginger stiffening and saw the knuckles of the hand holding her fork go white.

"The Marq'ssan, the Women's Patrol, and the medical team working with them are hardly terrorists," Shirl said, leaning forward to stare at Burns from where she sat at the foot of the table.

"Not terrorists!" Burns looked outraged. "Not only interfering with our legal system, but massively destroying state property as well?"

Shirl looked disgusted. "No decent human being could accept the existence of places where people are treated so inhumanely."

"Those people are criminals and deserve everything they get!" Burns turned to Liz. "I don't see why you allowed Lisa to go."

Liz paused mid-bite. "To be honest, Carol, if I were in her place, I'd probably want to go myself."

Burns looked shocked. "What on earth *for?*"

Liz smiled. "Have you any idea how much Lisa hates the Military who've been occupying San Diego for so long? After having contributed to the devastation of her own station's position there—and not at all willingly, I might add—can you blame her for wanting to do the same to Military?"

"It was hell for her!" Ginger burst out, astonishing Hazel—for Ginger never participated in these sorts of discussions. "You don't know what it's been like. First to be struggling to hold things together after the war, when Central wasn't giving the station any support to speak of, and then to be struggling against the craziness of Central after Liz left, and on top of it all to have to do so much damage to the station after she left. It's *always* been Military trying to dump on the station! Military is as much an enemy as the aliens are!"

Cleghorn leaned forward and smiled across the table at Ginger, ever so matronizing. "You're so emotional, dear. But it isn't Military that's the enemy." She looked at Liz. "You know, Elizabeth, Carol has a point. I don't think we should be undermining the principles of our own system. It will foster a disrespect for law and order."

"I can't believe you people!" Shirl shoved her chair back from the table. "I'm not about to sit here and listen to you assume that it's perfectly fine for governments to drug and torture their citizens. According to you, anyone with compassion or moral sense is a terrorist. Well, I wish now that I had gone, too. You make me feel ashamed of our species." She stood up, grabbed her plate, and left the room.

"Can you explain to me, Elizabeth, just what that girl is doing in this household?" Burns's voice sharpened unpleasantly. "I don't understand your having her in your security detail, of all things! She probably reports straight to the terrorists!"

"Give me credit for some sense," Liz said. "And now that we're alone, let me point out that having Lisa present during these actions gives us a continuing source of inside information on what those people are up to and a growing store of data on the aliens, about which we previously knew next to nothing."

Hazel considered following Shirl's example. The insanity of the discussion, the twistedness of Liz's thinking—which Liz herself considered to be "practical"—turned her stomach.

"And I'd also like to point out," Liz added, "that our previous notions of loyalty are irrelevant now. Don't imagine for an instant that people from either Security or Military are not our enemies. That's a luxury we can't afford. They're *all* our enemies now. In order to accomplish our goal we must be very clear on the need to not be seduced by old feelings of loyalty. We must be clear-headed when we decide what is to our advantage and what is not. I consider this attack on Military in San Diego vastly to our advantage. It will shake up the Pentagon even if it is, in the greater scheme of things, a relatively minor matter. Small things can cause confusion and panic—as tonight's action will do. As the San Bernardino and El Cajon actions did within Security."

Hazel stared down at the plateful of food that she had barely touched. What was she doing here, sitting at this table, listening to this craziness? Who was Liz? She no longer seemed to know the answers to either of these questions. And there beside Liz sat Anne, not eating, looking sick—as sick as she, Hazel, felt. When had everything changed, how had all this come about? Hazel sighed, picked up her plate, and carried it out into the kitchen, not caring if anyone noticed her wordless departure. Wearily she poured herself a cup of coffee and—detouring around the dining room—returned to the office and the ugliness of Burns's debriefing. If she finished that and part of Cleghorn's debriefing, her going off to Seattle to take Anne to Martha Greenglass wouldn't put her as far behind as she had feared.

# Chapter Forty-four

The pod lands just beside the ocean, not far from their final destination. Into the pod come two women, one of whom Astrea recognizes from a previous mission.

"Elena!" In turn, Gina and Luis each fold one of the women into a hug.

"But where's Celia?" asks Maureen.

The new arrivals look upset, and Luis, now frowning, takes Elena's hand. Emily, the one with an interesting field, says, "Celia's disappeared. Elena found her gone and the house totally trashed when we returned from Seattle." Emily glances at her companion. "We were afraid they might take Elena, too, so she's been staying at my house."

Gina touches Elena's cheek. "You must come back to the Free Zone with us," she says. She looks at Luis. "Tell her, Luis. Get her to be sensible."

"I have to find Celia." Elena's eyes fill with tears. "We're hoping…We're hoping she might be in one of the places you're going to tonight." She buries her head against Luis's chest. The tension among the humans is visible in their fields.

Emily puts her hand on Elena's shoulder. Astrea is struck at that moment by how the four humans' fields do not merge, by how even at this moment of great shared emotion their fields remain distinct and separate.

"ODS could have taken her somewhere clandestine, Elena," Emily is saying. "Don't get your hopes up." Emily gives Gina a look Astrea feels certain conveys significance. "I went to see Admiral Aldridge, and he claims that none of the Navy's security forces have her."

"It could be a lie," Maureen says.

"Yes. But we think it must have been ODS who dumped that woman on us. The one we brought to Whidbey last week."

Emily, Elena, Luis, and Gina strap in, and Sorben reviews the plan for the newcomers. "Remember, this won't be as easy as the other liberations. Still, all the Marq'ssan on board have been through this type of rescue: last week we liberated several clandestine prisons in Paraguay. First of all, there will be no EMP. An EMP would only put them on guard and make things harder for the prisoners when we're taking them out. Second, we will throw a temporary shield around each building in the compound, since we can't land as close to our chosen sites as we'd like, and the shields will prevent additional armed persons from coming to the assistance of their colleagues. Third, if our Paraguay experience is anything to judge by, these men will be more likely to put up a struggle than the warders we encountered in the prisons—precisely because these are clandestine places. At any rate, be prepared for difficulties. And finally, the medical team should be prepared to find the prisoners in far worse shape than those we evacuated from the official prisons. Any last-minute questions?"

The pod lifts; and because the trip is very short, it descends almost immediately. Astrea scans for those whose fields are likely to belong to guards and relays the data into the processor they use for communicating information to the humans. Magyyt and Flahn announce that they have constructed barriers around each building. Then Magyyt, Sorben, Astrea, and Dghatd leave the pod in camouflage, along with the group of men and women trained in techniques of violence that use hands and feet as weapons. Bursting with rage, Astrea thinks about how when they have finished they will destroy many of the weapons kept on this military base.

It is what self has been obsessed with since that one's first perception of the weapons when they reconnoitered here previously.

# Chapter Forty-five

"In conclusion, then, we can describe the Sonata-allegro form as the contained play of sexual difference in which the final resolution always safely returns the composer/listener/performer to the original statement, all the more strongly reinforced through the definitive resolution of the tensions created by the conflict with which it has so playfully engaged. In future lectures we will be tracing the dissolution and indeed abandonment of this playfulness during the course of the nineteenth century, a period marked by extreme distress, fear, and ambivalence regarding the question of sexual difference and sexual play, thereby undercutting the very structure of tonality, first in denying relations between tonic and dominant, and later—as continued well into the twentieth century—in subverting the power of dissonance and difference through manipulations of chromaticism and other forms of dissonance with the unconscious intention of reinforcing the authority of tonality, while, in the end, in spite of the general flight from difference, utterly destroying it. The next reading assignment will be chapters forty and forty-one in Nevelton."

Alexandra switched off the lecture just as the plane began its descent. She was halfway through a Columbia University survey of western music history correspondence course and intended to finish it before the end of the summer. She hoped that these extra courses in music history and theory would enable her to fit in studies her father deemed inessential. She knew she was probably, under her piano teacher's supervision, getting as thorough a course as any student majoring in music would. Tonight, if she got back from New York in time, she and he would attend a piano recital in which one of the sonatas analyzed in this last lecture would be performed.

She was determined to make frequent attendance at recitals and concerts her reward for all the things her father insisted she do.

An intestinal cramp attacked her just as the jet's wheels touched the ground. Given the nature of the meeting she had to attend, it would be terribly embarrassing if she had to keep getting up and running for the toilet. It was embarrassing enough that she'd have to make Blake and that aide wait while she used the toilet before getting off the plane. Though he was being careful, she could see that the aide fiercely resented having someone as young as she—and female, to boot—at least nominally in control. *He's there to give you advice, Alexandra. But he's only a professional, he has no power to negotiate. Remember that. You are my representative, not him. He's your adviser. Don't ever forget it.* How could he have done this to her? She was sixteen years old with no experience whatsoever! How could she represent him? *You already know the most important things there are to know about TNC. As for this project, you don't need to know that much. That's what the aide is for. And remember, these are only negotiations— they know they'll have to get my approval, which takes you off the hotseat, since they'll assume you'll be under orders from me. As indeed you are. I'm too busy to see to this personally, and you've already made the contact with Buchanan. This will be excellent experience, Alexandra. If you don't understand something, you make them explain it to you. And if you don't like their attitude, flex your muscles. I know you have it in you. You're a Sedgewick.*

She was a Sedgewick who unfastened her seatbelt and bolted into the lavatory without a word to the others, a Sedgewick who had to let out into the toilet all of *that*, including disgusting pieces of undigested parsley leaves. Worse, she was a Sedgewick who badly craved a good large chew although it was not yet 8:00. *Some Sedgewick, Papa.*

Emerging from the lavatory, Alexandra found the two of them standing there, not looking at one another, not talking, simply waiting. It occurred to her that the gorilla and professional probably had less in common with one another than they had with her. Biting back the apology that rose to her lips, she picked up her attaché case and led the way. The pilot stood at attention near the opened hatch. "We'll give you a call when we know our approximate time of departure," Alexandra told him, just to have something polite to say.

From the top of the stairs Alexandra spotted two cars parked nearby. As she descended, the hot humid air wrapped around her. She saw a woman getting out of the back of one the cars and squinted against the glare to get a closer look. So: Judith MacLaury herself had come to meet her. Alexandra hadn't expected such VIP treatment. Perhaps Papa had been right about the assumptions people would make about her?

"Judith, how lovely to see you," Alexandra said, holding out her hand and smiling.

Judith shook her hand and smiled back. She also studied Alexandra's face with frank speculation. The haircut, again.

"It's good to see you, Alexandra," Judith murmured. "You'll ride with me, won't you?"

"Of course." Alexandra gestured at Blake. "He'll have to ride in the front, though, if I do. You don't mind?"

"Of course not."

Alexandra gestured to the aide, and he stepped forward. "Oh, and you must meet Henry Fletcher, my aide. Fletcher, this is Judith MacLaury, Buchanan's PA."

The executive nodded at the professional but did not offer her hand. "We'd better get moving," she said. "The traffic won't be good, and since you're only here for the day..."

Alexandra directed Blake to ride next to Judith's driver and Fletcher to ride in the car that had been sent for herself. Then she got in beside Judith and, despite misgivings about how her bowels would take it, accepted a cup of coffee.

"It must be very exciting for you these days," Judith said. "Naturally I spotted you at once in the photos and vid-clips of that press conference with Stoddard in the Rose Garden. What did you think of the White House?"

"Stoddard's a real buffoon, isn't he," Alexandra said, smiling at the memory of how ridiculous that press conference had been.

Judith grinned. "Just like the actors in the soaps, you know. The public must have its dose of celebrities and glitzy lifestyles."

Alexandra sighed. "I never realized how boring press conferences were." Boring and bizarre, with everyone playing pretend and looking important.

"Well I'm sure you have many more to come, dear. You'll have to resign yourself to them." Judith took another sip of coffee. "By the way, I happened to notice the other day that Elizabeth Weatherall is a shareholder. Did you know that?"

So she was still fascinated with Elizabeth. "Yes," Alexandra said. "She owns five percent. But there's no way for her to vote, unless she can manage to give proxies to a third party. Which would then be risky for that party." Papa counted that five percent essentially his, since it was five percent that couldn't be used against him. Elizabeth had started TNC during the civil war and had invested some of Papa's funds in it. She had also taken three percent for herself. Later, Papa had given her another two percent. Several other Company people owned stock in TNC, too, and Papa considered their proxies his to dispose of. And in this particular issue concerning them today, the people in Com & Tran who owned stock in TNC would certainly throw their votes his way. Overall, Buchanan could not thwart his plan. Not that he expected Buchanan would want to do so.

"I'm surprised that she didn't liquidate at the time she went renegade," Judith said.

"Maybe she was in too big a hurry."

"Perhaps. But possibly she intends some day to reclaim her interest?"

"What happens to her dividends?"

"They're being placed in escrow. Which is a waste, for escrow accounts don't bear interest."

"Tell me something," Alexandra said, changing the subject. "I'm looking for an interior designer who specializes in hypermodern decor. My father needs his offices redone—Elizabeth bombed them when she left, you know, and then when Hill took over he rebuilt them into something my father describes as 'an abomination.' There will have to be structural changes, so it's not merely a matter of furnishings and that sort of thing."

"Hypermodern? That's a bit old-fashioned, Alexandra. But yes, I'm sure I can ask around and find someone suitable."

Good. She had no idea how to find an appropriate interior designer any more than she knew how to do all the other things he kept insisting she take care of. "My father basically wants the office to be restored to what it was. Though of course, the one thing he misses the most won't be replaceable. He had a piece of Giacometti sculpture he was very much attached to," Alexandra said.

"Well!" Judith said, pursing her lips. "Elizabeth could have removed the Giacometti to a safe place, at the very least!"

Alexandra saw Judith was teasing and forced a laugh. "It really upsets him," she said.

"I'm surprised it didn't survive. They're usually of wrought iron, aren't they?"

"This one was, but it was near the desk, where one of the bombs had been placed."

The coffee was upsetting her stomach; she should probably stop drinking it. The thought of facing a roomful of men, of doing what her father expected of her—"taking control of the situation"—grew scarier and scarier. At first it had seemed a means of escaping those horrible meetings where he and his creepiest subordinates worked out their "strategy" for getting the country "back under control." Listening to him talk about doing such things and knowing that such talk would result in thousands of people carrying out his policies had turned her stomach—and made her angry with him. Yet later, alone with him, her anger had evaporated, partly because he was different when they were alone together, partly because of her consciousness of being unable to construct any kind of opposition to his ideas that he would respect, as though nothing she said could measure up to the absolute strength of his position. And as in the past, the recession of her anger left her troubled and uncertain of her own opinions and ideas—and weakly relieved and even at moments elated that he was so pleased with her, that he held such high expectations of her as even to think of sending her to act as his representative at this high-level meeting. She knew that she must not disappoint him. In the back of her mind lurked a fear of his withdrawing into his previous attitude towards her, into coldness spiked with occasional biting contempt. She wanted to be worthy of his approval.

Alexandra withdrew her gaze from the depressing gray desolation on the other side of the window. So *this* was New York? Everywhere she looked she saw grubby tall blocks, the occasional bombed-out ruin, people in gaudy clothes lined up in long queues or scurrying along wide gray sidewalks cluttered with racks of goods and ugly signage.

She looked at Judith and tried to sound nonchalant. "Will you be present during the meetings?" If Judith were there it might not be so unbearable being surrounded by all those cold, powerful men.

Judith's gaze grew speculative. "Part of the time. I suspect I'll be in and out. Buchanan likes me to be available, but of course that always depends on the general state of affairs in the office." Judith tucked her coffee cup into a little cupboard. "By the way, I'd better warn you that apart from me, Buchanan's entire staff is made up of males. He can't abide female sub-execs. So even the secretaries and cleaning staff are all male."

"That must be awful for you," Alexandra said.

"One can get used to almost anything," Judith replied. "Anyway, my day will come. Eventually." She smiled. "And now that we've had our sociable cup of coffee, I hope you don't mind if I do some work for the little that is left of this drive?"

Alexandra smiled back. "No, of course not." She stared out the window again, this time to examine the tiny autos that never deviated from their respective lanes: this, she knew, was because they depended on the cables built into the road for their power source. She had never gotten such a close look at a mass-auto system before, for the one in DC did not work—having been sabotaged by the EMP the previous year—and of course there were no mass-auto systems in either Barbados or Maine. She should review what Papa had told her about each of the men on the DVDs he had played for her last night. Three of them had been among the original investors in TNC and had worked with Elizabeth. *They won't be surprised to be dealing with a woman, Alexandra. Most of them were used to dealing with Weatherall. Just remember that when you're sitting at the table with them. Your being a woman is no big deal for them. And your age is not a matter of public record. They have no way of knowing you're only sixteen.* Had she told Judith her age that night they had (illicitly) chatted? She didn't think so; she couldn't remember Judith's asking her—and it wasn't the sort of question it was *au fait* to ask another executive.

And of course all of them would know Fletcher. Fletcher had been an analyst for Allison Bennett and had worked on TNC projects from the very start. He even owned a few shares in TNC. When Hill had purged him, Com & Tran had snatched him up; and thanks to her father's intervention, he had returned to the Company as abruptly as he had left it. She had the feeling from his attitude when he was briefing her late yesterday afternoon that he in some way disapproved of the project proposal he was to present to the Board today. Or was it her he disapproved of? No, it was more than that, Alexandra felt certain, it was more than just her that was bothering him. She would try to see if she could figure it out.

Suddenly Alexandra noticed that they had entered a vastly transformed environment. Around them loomed enormous towers in all sizes, shapes, and configurations, pristine, glittering, superhuman. All that she could see of the sun now was its glare reflected in the glass and other dazzling materials shaping the towers. After a few minutes the car turned into the mouth of a tunnel, where the driver stopped and presented credentials to a guard stationed in a glass booth. They had to wait about half a minute for the guard to return the credentials to the driver, and then the steel barrier blocking the car's path lowered into the ground, and the car drove down the ramp into the tunnel. Lit only by blue neon lights overhead, the tunnel turned out to be one of several that formed a confusing maze. The creepiness of the lighting, the closeness of the walls, and lowness of the ceiling so bothered Alexandra that she broke into a sweat. When the car finally pulled up before what was obviously a bank of elevators, she was flooded with relief.

Judith whisked her and Fletcher into a private car, and they rocketed up one hundred fifty stories (if the numbers on the control panel were any indication of the numbers of floors in the building). They emerged into a dazzlingly bright lobby in which reflections of light bounced constantly off the gleaming white walls. The ceiling, she saw when she looked up, was glass, open to the sky and the sun above them. The sharpness of the contrast with the subterranean tunnels they had just come from sent shivers through her.

"Ms. Sedgewick, how nice to see you again," William Buchanan greeted her.

Alexandra realized that he had been hovering near the elevator, awaiting her arrival. She smiled and held out her hand. "Good morning. I think you already know Henry Fletcher?" So she wasn't to get to the bathroom before the meeting began. Unless, that is, she made a big deal of it...

"Breakfast will be very simple," Buchanan said as he walked her—without, of course, touching her—to the conference room. "Fruit, lox, bagels, and cream cheese. The lox are first-rate, though."

Oh yes, they were supposed to eat breakfast. As though she could eat a bite when under this kind of pressure! What she really wanted was parsley and water. The water she could have. But the parsley? Imagine her asking for a nice big chewy bunch of it...

The conference room—all glass and chrome and black marble floors and walls—though flooded with brilliant sunshine struck her as chilly. The seven men seated around the table rose to their feet, and Buchanan formally introduced her to each in turn and seated her on his right, with Fletcher beside her. Judith MacLaury appeared at Alexandra's elbow with a thermoflask. "Just water for now, Judith," Alexandra whispered, pulling the project file and a fresh yellow pad from her attaché case, and Judith brought her a crystal goblet and a liter bottle of water. Though the eight men busied themselves with the food, they were all waiting for her to speak.

Alexandra took a sip of water, leaned back in her chair, and drew a deep breath. "TNC, as you all know, was originally formed as a proprietary of Security Services to meet certain needs of the Executive. Until a little more than a year ago, TNC was able to meet those needs, and did so so well, in fact, that the proprietary was transformed into a public corporation more or less independent of its original arrangements and with its own agenda." Afraid her words were rushing out too fast, too nervously, Alexandra made an effort to slow her delivery. "However, everything changed when the aliens destroyed the majority of TNC's com-sats. Though TNC has several times launched replacement satellites, all have shared the same fate—namely, destruction at the hands of the aliens. Barring the discovery of *how* the aliens execute their destruction and of how to *prevent* such destruction, or of a way of disguising our com-sats as those belonging to another country or—even better—camouflaging them, the mass communications system as we have known it in this country seems doomed."

Alexandra paused and belatedly remembering she should be continually making eye-contact with these folks, glanced at the faces around the table. She saw that her saying such a thing out loud made them visibly uncomfortable. Two of the faces had gone stony and bullish, but then her father had predicted that they wouldn't want to believe it and therefore they wouldn't want to hear *anyone* (much less a young girl) saying it out loud. She sucked in another breath and continued. "It is clear, gentlemen, that the very security of this country requires our reestablishing an effective system of mass communications. My father and Edwin Goodwin, Secretary of Com & Tran, have given this matter serious thought. After due consideration and planning, they have come to the conclusion that the erection of an alternate land-based communications system is essential. They propose to combine the early communications technology of the mid-twentieth century with state-of-the-art laser technology. My aide, Fletcher, will present the details of this proposal to you. And then, afterwards, I hope we may engage in fruitful discussion." Alexandra picked up her goblet and took a large sip of water. She had delivered the spiel almost word-perfect. Even if her delivery had betrayed her nervousness, her nervousness had not sabotaged her memory, which—thanks to her piano study—was very good.

Fletcher now got to his feet and began speaking. Alexandra nibbled on fruit and covertly studied the faces of the men sitting around the table. Some of them clearly disliked the project. Others looked bored. But they would agree to it, she felt certain. What else could they do? TNC essentially belonged to the Company, even though it *was* a public corporation. And each of them knew it.

# Chapter Forty-six

When Hazel carried the pitcher of grapefruit juice into Liz's office and set it in the refrigerator, Liz did not look up from her work. Hazel returned to the outer office without saying a word herself and wondered how long Liz's stonewalling would go on. Even if she did drive Anne to Seattle this afternoon, the whole matter need not be considered settled: Anne would be delighted to move back into the household at any time. And given her attitudes about the Free Zone, it didn't seem likely she'd come to prefer to live away from the household... Or *was* such a transformation possible? Maybe Anne would surprise herself and find she enjoyed living free of executive domination.

Hazel sat down at her desk, unlocked her terminal, and logged in. The first task on Liz's list of prioritized instructions was the decoding of a sheaf of messages Margot Ganshoff had delivered. Hazel called up the program she needed to run to get the safe opened, plugged in the little barnacle, and executed the sequence of tedious routines. On finishing the sequence she pressed her thumb onto the thumbplate on her keyboard. The screen flashed the message **BARNACLE PREPARED**. Hazel then unplugged the barnacle and carried it over to the safe, reset the dip-switches, pressed her thumb against the safe's thumbplate, and plugged the barnacle into the safe's receptacle. "Password?" the idiot voice piped through the speaker. "Vivien," Hazel flat-commanded. The blue light came on, and the door of the safe slid open.

The messages this time amounted to three times as many as in the last batch Margot had brought them. Hazel thought of the number of people involved in simply moving these messages to their end destination and wondered that the system worked at all. If any of the Austrians decided they didn't like working against the US Executive, or if any of them happened to be working for one of the US's intelligence services—and such a thing was hardly a rare occurrence in foreign embassies—the entire message system could be brought down. And if any one of the women who had "come over" to Liz proved to have second thoughts, or, indeed, were doubling, the results could be fatal for the women caught sending messages, code or no code.

Hazel keyed in the correct code program, then one after another opened the envelopes, removed the flimsies, and fed each sheet individually into her terminal's intake slot. The next step in the routine was to seal the coded and decoded flimsy into a big manila envelope and shred the envelopes the messages had come in. Hazel duly fetched a large manila envelope and slid the coded flimsy in. Then she cast a speculative glance at Liz's open door. Dare she peek at the decoded flimsies? What sorts of things were these women doing for Liz? She didn't even know how many of them there were... Hazel stared down at the top sheet. *From Erica Palmer, Assistant Director of Personnel, Department of State.* The original message had contained names that only she and Liz could decode. *Concerning the suggested pattern...* Out of the corner of her eye Hazel saw Liz moving around in her office. She shoved the sheaf of flimsy into the envelope and was just sealing it when Liz passed by her desk.

"I'll be back shortly," Liz said, not stopping.

"All right," Hazel said as Liz opened the hall door and went out. Hazel fed the envelopes into the shredder, went to the hall door, and switched the lock back on. That had been a close call. What would Liz's response have been if she'd caught her reading confidential materials? Hazel carried the manila envelope into Liz's office and left it on the desk. Maybe Liz would mind, maybe she wouldn't. But that, Hazel decided, was something she would rather not discover.

# Chapter Forty-seven

Though distantly aware that her body now lay neatly arranged and tended in a hospital bed, Celia continued to visualize it as a corpse lying in a swamp of excrement. Her mother and Emily were seeking her, she felt certain. Whether they would find her—and on finding her recognize and claim her in spite of the excrement—constituted her chief preoccupation. The things done to her body she hardly noticed, for they did not interest her, and she did not *feel* them. She was beyond them all, even if corpselike and filthy. There could be no recognition on either side of the chasm that stretched endlessly between her and them. The chasm had grown so wide that not even pain, filth, or fear could tenuously bridge it. They might pretend to pull her out of the swamp of excrement, but she knew that pretence to be a mirage, a phantasm they would have her believe in, only as real as any of the hallucinations that had come to her through the drug.

When the doctor Jackson addressed as "sir" came to examine her with another doctor, their voices barely ruffled the surface of her mind.

"First question, doctor: the patients in such cases aren't conscious?"

"That's not clear, Commander. In stupors of this degree patients who recover generally say they remember nothing said or done to them, their general impression being that they were numb and insensible. You see, outside stimuli simply do not reach them. They feel neither pain nor pleasure, nor do they hear or see or smell. It is doubtful that they have much mental activity at all. Certainly EEGs made on such patients suggest only the lowest levels of brain activity."

"She can be expected to recover?"

"I can't make a prognosis without more information. Has she a history of depression? If so, the prognosis would be somewhat negative. If, on the other hand, this is a response to specific trauma, then the prognosis is optimistic."

"The trauma is something of a mystery. According to the first physician's notes, she has undergone three separate injections of Torment, which is a variant of sulfizine. I can't imagine such injections—especially since there were only three in one week—in and of themselves constituting trauma. The physician who administered the injections, however, hypothesizes an allergic reaction that intensified with each successive injection."

"I'm afraid I'm not familiar with the literature on that sort of psychological stress. My patients tend to be suffering from ailments common to people in military service."

"What sort of therapy do you recommend?"

"Drug therapy or a combination of drugs and ECT is indicated for severe depression. My preference would be for the latter."

"Electroconvulsive therapy? Hmmm. The chief question of course is the matter of how quickly we can revive her. It appears to be of some urgency."

"Really? If the matter was so urgent, why did they bother with protracted sulfizine injections when they could have used loquazene so easily in the first place?"

"I've no idea, and frankly it's not our business to speculate, though I gather there may be some strong emotional conflict involved that may have created a substantial degree of resistance. It could, however, be more complicated than that."

"I see. Well there's no telling how long she'll be like this. This condition could persist for months. It will take considerable effort to keep her alive. As you can see, we've even taken precautions against her aspirating. There's always the possibility of that in these cases."

"What I'd like for you to do now, doctor, is to write up a proposal for a course of treatment. I'll look at it and approve it as soon as you get it to me. And then you can begin. May I stress the impatience of certain people in bringing her out of it?"

"Very well, Commander."

Buried in excrement, Celia waited for her mother's voice. Only then would she struggle to stir, to call out, to be found.

# Chapter Forty-eight

Hazel hugged Anne goodbye and then, seeing the tears glazing her sad brown eyes, impulsively kissed her on the cheek and squeezed her hands. And then hugged her again. "Remember, you can come back whenever you need to," she whispered into Anne's ear. She pulled away abruptly and went with Martha to a small lounge on one of the upper floors of the Co-op Building. There they sat on the floor and drank water, and Martha invited her to help herself to the peaches in the basket she set between them. "She seems upset," Martha said.

"Yes." Hazel's throat was tight with the effort to control her emotions. "Liz can be pretty awful sometimes." Hazel tried to comfort herself with the sense that what she said was true, even if it wasn't the full truth. Anne was upset, and Liz had been awful. Wishing to get Martha off the subject, Hazel said "I love peaches," and selected a peach from the basket. When she bit into it, the sweet juice that flowed into her mouth roused her tastebuds, making her tongue tingle and her saliva flow. She thought of how little the tubefood called "peach frappé" resembled the real thing. She'd loved it as a kid, though— sweet, gooey, with only a hint of the true flavor of peaches. It had been her favorite snack food. "Are these grown here in the Free Zone? Or imported from somewhere?"

Martha gave her a shrewd look. "As you say, Hazel, Elizabeth can be pretty awful. Yet that doesn't matter to you, or not enough to leave her yourself," she said—as a question, Hazel thought. "Because your love is so strong." Was that sarcasm? But Martha did not look as though she meant it in a nasty way.

Hazel felt a blush rising in her cheeks. "That crack I made all those months ago was pretty presumptuous and self-righteous, wasn't it." She stared down at the fruit basket and sighed, and took another bite of the peach. "But I don't know any more about love. Or the power of love. It seems sometimes as though we can love only parts of a person, that the rest of her we need either to ignore or change. And sometimes it happens that we can no longer even *find* that part of a person we love, and we're left with a stranger." Hazel glanced at Martha's face, then looked into her eyes and smiled faintly.

"You're talking about yourself and Elizabeth," Martha said.

"Yes, of course." Hazel took another bite of the peach, and this time juice ran down her chin. Dabbing at her mouth and chin with a tissue, Hazel went on, "I don't know what's going to happen with Liz and me." Conscious of the serious expression in Martha's eyes, she made a face. "I probably shouldn't be talking to you about this. Liz would be furious with me if she knew. But Martha, I feel as if I'm fighting a daily battle with myself *and* with her. After all these months it seems I don't understand her at all. I'm not one of those pro-executive types, you know—I never was. And then coming here to the Free Zone reinforced and somehow clarified so many things for me. Before I met Liz I always tried to keep a distance between me and them. Executives, I mean. But now, because of my involvement with Liz, that distance is gone." Hazel smiled ruefully. "But of course if it weren't for her, I'd still be in DC working for the Justice Department."

"So you're living in a state of conflict."

"I keep thinking it's necessary," Hazel said. "I want to believe that love can make the difference in people. Making this conflict necessary. Even if she's only one of multitudes, changing even one other person is significant." Hazel felt half-ashamed of her own earnestness. "Listen to me," she mocked herself. "What an idiot I am. And of course if Liz heard me say such things… She doesn't even see that there's a problem. She sees the problem as my being difficult. Or selfish. Or idealistic…" Hazel took the last bite of the peach.

"We want to believe that people will change for love," Martha said sadly. "I don't know exactly how or why people change. But it must be possible. If we don't believe that it is, then we have no hope at all. I often wonder how the Marq'ssan can bear to be on this planet, how they can give of themselves to such monstrousness. Last night…" Martha shook her head.

"You're referring to the action in San Diego?" Hazel asked. When Martha nodded, Hazel said, "Lisa seemed upset this morning. It must have been bad?"

"Oh, Lisa," Martha said in a different tone. "You know, I doubt the Marq'ssan will have her along again. Not after last night. Did she tell you?"

Hazel wondered what she was going to do with the sticky remains of the peach. "No, what happened?"

"The vid crew was filming some guards who had been caught in acts of unspeakable brutality when Lisa flew at one of them in the most extreme, berserker rage I've ever heard of. It took three people to pull her off the man. Everyone I talked to said her rage was terrifying. And the things she screamed at him as she was dragged away! That he wasn't human, that he didn't deserve to live, that all of his kind must be wiped from the face of the earth… From what I can gather, it made the violence of the situation that much more intense and upsetting." Martha leaned forward and carefully shifted the peaches, then pulled out a small paper sack and held it out to Hazel. "Here. You can put your pit in here."

"Thanks." Hazel took the sack and disposed of the pit, then handed it back to Martha. "All she said this morning was that she had never seen or imagined such things, that the Military men in those places were animals that should be exterminated." Hazel shuddered again at the word "exterminated." Digging in her rucksack for a towelwipe, she recalled Liz's response, and her anxiety resurged—*When* I'm *in power all such places will be destroyed, no such bestiality will be tolerated.* And then Liz had made an obscene comment about Military males.

*When* I'm *in power…* What in the fuck would come of it all? Caught up in Liz's mad vertigo, would they come to spin so wildly that they'd no more be able to direct their own movement than a tornado could? How many executive women had Liz "recruited," women she said were "moles" planted throughout the Executive? Enough to do something large-scale? Enough to make toppling the Executive a real possibility? But even if they did topple the Executive, would it *matter*? Liz had callously disregarded Anne's feelings, had in fact exploited the vulnerability brought about by Anne's going renegade. And she was doing that with the others, too, and would continue doing it. Could Liz's attempts to justify herself by saying that her government would be more humane be anything more than a veil for Liz's grasping for power?

*You'll just have to learn to accept that certain things are not open to discussion. Anne's employment is between her and me and is nothing to do with you. Furthermore, although I appreciate input, the making of a decision is ultimately and exclusively my prerogative. I will not be harassed like this any longer, Hazel. You've told me your opinion, and I've given more than enough attention to it. Once and for all, drop the subject!* The image of Liz's patting her on the cheek flashed into her mind, and she felt as though her insides had been sucked out, leaving behind only pain and fear.

"What is it, Hazel?"

Hazel lifted her gaze to Martha's face; unexpectedly, her eyes filled with tears. She shook her head. "I was just realizing something," she whispered, struggling to keep her voice from breaking.

"Yes?" Martha said. "Would it help to share it?"

Hazel sniffed and drew a deep breath. "I was just realizing how bad things had gotten between me and Liz. It's wishful thinking, wanting to try to change her when we're like this. Last night..." Hazel swallowed. "You see, we've been arguing a lot lately. And last night..." She shook her head. "I can't explain. It's not that she said anything especially different, at least not different enough to strike me at the time." Hazel blinked and wiped her eyes; Martha's gaze brimmed with warmth that suffused her, making her want to grope her way to understanding her emotional upheaval. "But I can see now very clearly that nothing I can do or say will ever make a difference. She doesn't even *try* any more to understand. If she ever did. She pays lip service to the idea that I can say anything to her, that she values my opinions. But it's meaningless. Nothing ever changes except small things—when I force the issue and they don't cost her too much." Hazel's lips trembled. "But I see now that probably even those concessions are a thing of the past. I *can't* force any issue now because she won't let me reach her."

"May I make a suggestion?" Martha said softly.

Hazel knew that Martha was going to suggest that she leave Liz. Stricken at the thought, Hazel exclaimed, "I still love her!"

"My suggestion," Martha said, leaning forward, "is that you try to change your circumstances in such a way that you give yourself a better chance. Move out of that house. Stop working for Elizabeth. Then see her outside of that context. Don't you think working for her has something to do with the problem, Hazel?"

"You mean only see Liz as a lover?"

"As a friend, too, surely? Or is that a contradiction in your relationship?"

Hazel's stomach fluttered. "It sounds...I don't know. It's a gamble. She might not *want* to see me anymore." What if Liz had continued as her lover for so long only because she thought that Hazel would stop working for her otherwise?

Martha's gaze did not waver. "Hazel, think about what you just said. And then ask yourself what it is you want from your relationship with her."

Hazel grasped the water bottle with trembling fingers and drank the remaining water. "What a coward I am," she whispered.

Martha shook her head. "Don't be silly." She gathered up the empty bottles and levered herself to her feet. "I think we should go for a walk, maybe along the waterfront."

Hazel looked up at her and, accepting Martha's hand, lifted herself to her feet. "Yes," she said, "That sounds good. I just can't seem to think."

"It's amazing how conducive recreational walking is to thinking," Martha said.

As they set off, Hazel brushed aside an awareness of how her tardiness would make Liz suspicious of her having had a long tête-à-tête with Martha. Tough shit, she thought. She must not let Liz control her to that extent. Everything had gotten out of hand, out of balance. Martha, she thought, could help her to see, help her to find her way through the confusion—if, that is, she could overcome her fear, her cowardice, her desolation.

# Chapter Forty-nine

Alexandra didn't get back to the Georgetown house until after 7:30—too late for attending the concert. Though she desperately wanted to go upstairs to her suite (formerly her mother's) and get into the Jacuzzi, she went to her father's study first, to report, as she knew she must. She found him talking into a recorder, which he switched off when he saw her. "You're much later than I expected," he said. "Any problems?"

She moved to stand before his desk and hoped he wouldn't ask her to sit down. "No. It just took a long time. They discussed the proposal to death. Some of them hated the whole idea—saying it was regressive—and had a hard time making themselves vote for it."

"That's the way it usually is. But next time you can keep it from going on so long—there's a point at which you can terminate the discussion, you know."

"I don't know why they bothered discussing it at all." She put her palm flat against the surface of the desk and shifted her weight from one leg to the other. She was so tired. More tired than if she'd spent ten hours practicing the piano. "Everyone knew how the vote would come out in the end."

The right side of his mouth slid up in a half-smile. "Of course. But you must observe the formalities. If you don't, they'll feel they're being run by a dictatorship. They need the illusions that a good long bitter discussion preserves."

Alexandra did not laugh. "That's silly," she said flatly.

"You'll understand soon enough," he said. "They didn't make it awkward for you?"

She shook her head. "No. It was nothing like I thought. They were all very deferential. Especially Buchanan."

*That* pleased him. "Excellent. So. Will you be dining with me? You can give me all the gory details then."

"Yes, since it's too late for me to make the recital. And I'm too tired, anyway. But first I want a bath."

"Then I'll tell them to hold up dinner, what, fifteen minutes? Can you be ready by quarter after?"

"Yes," Alexandra said. More than tired, she felt deflated and strained to the breaking point, as though at any second she might begin laughing or crying for no reason at all.

She turned to go, but her father said, "This morning a cable came for you. And then this afternoon a basket of fruit. I told them to put them in your sitting room." "Her" sitting room: he had insisted she have all her mother's things packed up and that she appropriate her mother's sitting room and suite for herself. *Your mother will never be living in this house again.*

Curious, Alexandra went to the sitting room before going upstairs. She had received cables only four other times in her life. She stared in perplexity at the dozens of pomegranates—*only* pomegranates—filling the basket of shiny black lacquered straw. She opened the card tied to the handle of the basket. *Be careful, Persephone. There's blood in this fruit.* —*With love from Ceres.* Completely bewildered and a good deal frightened, Alexandra opened the cable. **Arriving DC Friday morning. I've reserved us Friday lunch at The Diana. F.R.** Mama *never* signed her initials to her, *never*! And what was this Persephone-Ceres stuff? As Alexandra stared from the card to the fruit, a terrible anxiety crawled along her nerves, trickling through to every part of her body. Was her mother angry at her?

"Pomegranates," her father said. Startled, Alexandra whirled. He stood on the threshold, grinning at her. "The allusion is not wasted on me. The only thing that isn't clear is where she got it from. Do you suppose she's been seeing some of those pop operas with so-called classical themes? I can see how the Hades-Persephone story would simply ravish sub-execs." His grin widened. "And women executives, too. Though it's slightly obscene of her to cast me for Hades' role, considering our biological relation."

"I don't understand," Alexandra said. His glee made her uneasy. *There's blood in this fruit.* She had never known her mother to take such a tone with her. Or to be so elliptical. She *must* be angry, to sign her initials instead of "Mama."

"After dinner you can browse the shelves in the study and look up the allusion in the reference books I have. Or check the database on your personal terminal. Is she coming to DC?"

"On Friday."

"We'll discuss this later," he said, suddenly serious. "Go have your bath now or we'll be dining at midnight."

Clutching the cable and the card in one hand and her attaché case in the other, Alexandra—holding her breath—moved past him into the hall. To her relief he did not touch her. As she trudged up the stairs she thought about how—though she did not know why—if he had touched her she would have burst into tears.

Nothing made sense. She wanted her bath; she wanted a chew of parsley. Once she had bathed she would be fine. It must simply be that she was tired.

# Chapter Fifty

When Hazel got back from the city and stopped into the kitchen to get herself a glass of iced tea, she walked in on the scene of two amazons struggling to get a massive wooden table through the narrow doorway into the lounge where Ginger and Lacie usually watched vid, and all her thoughts of her momentous waterfront conversation with Martha left her. As they tilted and shifted and rotated the table the amazons argued about whether or not they would have to unscrew the legs. Hazel said to Lacie, who stood beside Ginger, watching, "Why don't they just take it through the dining room? Surely those doorways are so much wider that they'd be easier to negotiate?"

Lacie shook her head. "Yeah, but then they'd just have to get it through the doorway on the other side, which is the same size as this doorway."

Hazel frowned. "I don't think I understand." If they were worried about doing damage in the dining room, why didn't they simply remove the breakable stuff and cover the dining room table with the heavy felt protectors that had been custom-made for it?

Now Lacie looked at her. "Whatever they do, it's going to be damned hard getting that table into the lounge."

"They're moving a table in *there*? But why? Won't it be too crowded with the furniture already in there?"

One amazon snarled a curse, and the latter admitted that her way wasn't working. Slowly they backed up, turned the table upside down, and lowered it to the floor. There was an old wad of gum stuck to the underside, pale green and bearing the imprint of an unusually long thumb.

"But we need a table in there now," Lacie said. "And this is the one they found for it."

"I still don't understand," Hazel said. "Why do we need a table in there? We only watch vid in there."

Lacie's eyebrows shot up. "Oh, you haven't heard?"

"Heard what?"

"The service-techs are to have separate eating arrangements from now on." Lacie's voice flattened into blankness of affect. "Which is why Liz had the amazons look for a suitable table. We'll all be eating in there now."

While the executives ate in the room next door? A wave of heat surged into Hazel's face. "I don't believe it," she said. "Who told you this?"

Lacie's eyes widened. "Liz told us. When they arrived with the table."

"And you, Ginger?" Hazel said hoarsely, staring hard at Ginger who, though keeping her eyes fixed on the amazons, had obviously been listening.

Ginger looked at Hazel. Nothing showed in her face, nothing whatsoever. "Liz told me a few days ago, when she talked to me about proper table service and such."

Hazel's stomach lurched. "I see. And you didn't object, of course."

Ginger's face reddened. "No, why would I have objected?"

The amazons finished unscrewing two of the table legs. Carefully they lifted the table into the air. Hazel snatched a bottle of water from the cupboard, passed through the dining room, and headed for the office. So. Now she knew: without question, she had made the right decision. The doubts she had had about leaving the household fell away from her. If Liz were willing to pull this kind of stunt it meant she didn't care in the least what she, Hazel, was thinking or feeling. Liz knew how she felt about the dining arrangements. By forcing this situation on them she was underlining the divisions of power in the household and putting all of the service-techs in an unequivocally inferior position. Hazel hesitated outside the outer office door and tried to compose herself. Her eyes stung from her deep sense of insult.

Hazel entered and without stopping at her desk went straight on to Liz's office. She knocked and opened the door. When Liz saw who it was, her face assumed a cold, wary expression. "I'm moving out," Hazel said without preamble. Liz stared at her. Something in that carefully immobile face catalyzed a wild surge of anger in Hazel, driving her to abandon her intention to avoid confrontation. "I made the arrangements this afternoon. I'm moving out a week from today. You'll have to find yourself a new slave."

Liz's eyes widened, then narrowed. "You're overreacting." Her tone of voice was as flat as the expression on her face. "I suggest you sit down and take a moment to think before launching into hysteria."

"I'm not in the least hysterical," Hazel said. "I'm angry. There's a difference."

Liz moved around her desk. "Let's keep this private, shall we?" She nudged Hazel out of the way so that she could close the door. Hazel heard the latch clicking behind her and the rustle of Liz's clothing; she felt the weight of Liz's hand dropping onto her shoulder. "Let's sit down and talk about it. I might have known you'd fly off the handle like this. I'd intended to tell you myself, but you've been so damned bad-tempered lately that I thought I'd put it off to the last minute. And then they found the table while you were in town, making that impossible." All the while she spoke Liz's hand pressured Hazel's shoulder, but to no avail: Hazel refused to budge. "Come, Hazel," Liz said. "Let's sit so that we can talk."

Hazel turned slightly and stared up at Liz. "I'm not sure we have anything to talk about now. My plan was to move out and find a job in Seattle. And—if you really wanted it—to try to work things out with you. But now..." She swallowed. "I feel..." Her eyes filled with tears, and she looked away. "It's obscene," she said, and pressed her hand against her heart, as though to stop the spike of pain piercing her breast.

"Obscene?" Liz said sharply. "What kind of nonsense do you have in your head now?"

Hazel watched Liz move to the sofa and sit. She could see the anger that held Liz's hands rigid on her thighs, that glittered in her steely blue eyes. "When I think of what you think we are," Hazel choked out. "You must think of us as having no feelings or dignity at all. As just simply there. To serve you. To be your toys when it's convenient. Nothing more than creatures to be used. To even want to see you after this—I'd be betraying myself! I should have realized all this long ago. But I let you manage me, blind me. From the start. And then it was too ugly, too devastating to face, so I had to cling to the belief that it wasn't like that. What a fool I've been!" Hazel put her arm to her eyes, to staunch and hide the tears, all the while aware of how Liz must despise her for crying.

"I don't understand a word you're saying," Liz said sharply. "Are you trying to tell me you decided before you even got home to leave me?"

Hazel lowered her arm from her eyes. "I won't live in this hellish world you're creating here! It's been getting worse and worse. I never wanted to be part of this kind of thing. I told you that a long time ago. But of course that didn't matter to you. You decided you could *handle* me, and since when does it matter what one of us wants or doesn't want for herself!" Hazel put her hands to her burning cheeks. "For some reason you decided it was me you wanted to use. Maybe I just happened along at the right time, I don't know the reason. I'm sure it's accidental. God knows with you people we're all interchangeable, but you had no compunction at all even after I told you how I felt. When I think of all those months of your pretending, merely to humor me along. Just to use me. How you must despise me for believing all your lies! It cost you nothing to lie to me, nothing at all, you've had so much practice at handling us! And what a payoff! You've used me in almost every way you've liked, all because you knew which lies to tell me." Hazel glared at Liz. "What's even richer is that you don't even pay me! I must be the most gullible and stupid service-tech you've ever had! You haven't paid me for even as much as an hour's labor since we went renegade! What is it you think, that I'm your eternally devoted slave? Is that how you think of me, Liz?"

"Why are you talking to me this way?" Liz cried. "What did that bitch tell you? You don't think I don't know who's behind all this?"

Hazel laughed shortly. "Of course you can't give me credit for seeing things myself. You consider me so feeble that I can only think and feel what I'm told to think and feel. For all you think of me, I might as well be a robot, or a child. God, how sick this is. And I've let you drug me with your lies for over a year." Hazel turned to the door and groped to open it. "There's nothing more to say, Liz. I can't stay. I can't even finish out the week as I'd planned. I'm going tonight." Hazel pulled the door open and hurtled out of Liz's office, ignoring whatever Liz was calling after her. She wanted to pack as quickly as possible—she had to get out of the house, away from Liz, away from them all.

Hazel went to the closet in Liz's bedroom and hauled out the quality suitcases Liz had given her when they went renegade and laid them out on Liz's bed. Without pausing to think, she moved back and forth between the closets and drawers in the dressing room and the bedroom, cramming her clothing and personal possessions into the suitcases. She felt like an intruder here in Liz's suite, like a stranger trespassing uninvited on another's territory. It had never really been her bedroom at all. She had always felt like a guest in the suite. But Liz had insisted she "share" the suite with her, had never agreed to her moving into a separate room. As though, Hazel thought, Liz had considered her just another possession and therefore not entitled to having her own room, her own space.

As she worked she thought about all the seemingly small incidents of the last few months that had gone to create this intolerable atmosphere, this situation in which Liz could give an order that demonstrated beyond any doubt precisely what the relationship was between the two of them, between Hazel and the other executives, and between any of the executives in the house and the service-techs, lovers or not. By that one order of Liz's she could see the entire pattern, could see what she had blinded herself to for months.

Her pain choked her, and her sense of humiliation compounded a sense of having been betrayed that she tried to suppress but could not deny. She had trusted Liz. She had let the illusion of love veil the truth, had clung to the belief that Liz loved her when clear thinking would have told her that such a love was impossible, that Liz was using her—as Liz used everybody. She had known about executives: she should have known that Liz wouldn't be different, that their relationship couldn't be different. *Who were you, Hazel, to think it could be different? You should have known. You did know. Yet you shut your eyes as tightly as you could and let her sing siren songs in your ears… Foolish Hazel, foolish foolish Hazel to have trusted an executive, to have trusted her.*

The suitcases wouldn't hold everything. Hazel debated leaving behind the things Liz had given her, but thinking of how Liz had paid her nothing for all the work she had done, she determined to take everything that was hers. She would leave some of the clothing on hangers, to be carried separately. Shifting clothing from the suitcases back onto hangers, she eventually reclaimed enough space to pack even her books.

She was closing the suitcases when Liz opened the bedroom door, entered, and closed the door. Hazel's stomach lurched: she had been hoping to get out of the house without another confrontation. Her awareness of Liz in the room with her nauseated her. She avoided looking at her as she struggled to arrange the suitcases and clothes on hangers so that she could get out of there in one trip. Liz said, "If you think you can blackmail me this time, you're sorely mistaken."

Hazel did not answer. She stacked the smallest suitcase onto the largest and draped the clothing over it and pulled the awkward one with her right hand and the single suitcase with her left. But she managed to take only three steps before the clothes began spilling off the stacked suitcases. She would have to make two trips, even if it meant more hassling from Liz. Sweating and desperate, Hazel retrieved the clothing that had fallen and rearranged the load and started again toward the door, but found Liz blocking her way. "Let me pass," she said, staring stolidly at Liz's shoulder.

"I'm out of patience with you, Hazel. I want to know exactly what that bitch said to you and what you said to her. There are certain things we're going to get straight, once and for all."

Hazel stared Liz in the eye. "Who are you to be patient with me?"

Liz closed the space between them and grabbed Hazel by the shoulders. "Apparently Cleghorn was correct when she characterized you as out of control." I'm tired of playing your games, Hazel, I'm tired of your using my love to further your own power in this household." She pressed Hazel backwards, and Hazel, fearing to lose her balance, let go of the suitcases. The top one as well as the clothing she had draped over it fell with a thump and clatter as the hangers struck the bare wood floor. "I'm not playing anymore, Hazel, do you hear me?"

"Let go of me!" Hazel lifted her hands to Liz's shoulders and tried to push her off. "I don't want any more talk, I just want to leave."

"So that you can blackmail me," Liz said, pressing her inexorably backwards, step by step. "Yes, I can see what you're up to now.

You think I'll do anything you like to keep you from turning into Greenglass's informant. Well you've gone too far this time my girl, way too far. Just how much disloyalty and manipulation do you think I'll stand for?" Her legs pressed hard against the bed, Hazel struggled to keep from falling backwards as Liz's hands bore down on her shoulders, forcing her to sit. "Now," Liz said, taking Hazel's chin and forcing her head back, "I want to know exactly what you said to Martha Greenglass today."

Because she was angry, Hazel refused to meet Liz's eyes. But her anger didn't protect her from feeling intimidated by Liz's tone and body language, which sent shockwaves of fear through her body, fear that was soon eclipsing the anger that had been fueling her for the last hour. Her legs shook with it in wild, uncontrollable tremors. *To her I'm just someone she's incidentally been sleeping with for the last year, someone she's incidentally used words of affection to, but no one really in particular, no one who matters to her...* "I won't be bullied," Hazel said hoarsely. "You've shown me you have no emotional or moral claim on me whatsoever. Nothing about me is any of your business now."

"You can't even look me in the eye," Liz said. "You've betrayed me, haven't you."

Hazel met Liz's hard, angry gaze. "Why are you doing this? You know I want to go. Or do you enjoy this kind of thing?"

"Don't play dumb with me, Hazel. I want to know exactly what you told Greenglass."

"It's none of your business, but if it will get me out of here any faster, I'll tell you. Martha offered to find a place for me to stay and to help me find a job. I took her up on the offer. I said I'd be leaving here next Wednesday, that I'd be in her office by noon."

Liz's eyes narrowed. "And of course you promised her something, didn't you. You promised to tell her everything about our operations, you promised to betray me."

Hazel's heart clenched: so *that's* what was behind Liz's bullying. "No," Hazel said, "no. I didn't promise her anything. She didn't ask me to. She *likes* me, Liz. She means well by me. She would never expect me to act as an informant against you."

"If you're telling the truth, then you've clearly failed to realize what is implicit in offers of that type," Liz said. She released Hazel's chin and turned away from the bed. "You're a fool if you think people like Greenglass will do you favors because they *like* you." Hazel stood and walked on shaky legs toward her suitcases. "We're not through talking," Liz said. Hazel picked up the handles of the largest suitcases and pulled them closer to the door.

In a blur of movement Liz knocked her off balance, making her reel sideways, falling half-over one of the suitcases, smack onto one knee. She put one hand on the floor for balance and glanced up at Liz. Her heart was pounding so violently that she began to find it difficult to breathe. Liz towered ominously over her. Childhood memories rushed over Hazel, sharpening her fear, and without even thinking about it, her body folded into its most defensive position, dropping down onto her butt with her knees drawn close to her chest, her head ducked between her knees as she braced for the first blow.

But there was no blow, and the silence beating in her ears frightened her more than the prospect of a blow. Warily she lifted her head so that she could look up at Liz. To her bewilderment, she saw Liz standing motionless, tears streaming from her eyes, staring down at her. "Look what you've done to us," Liz said. "Look what you've brought us to."

Did Liz care? Hazel wondered. But no, she must not take Liz's words and behavior to mean the things she'd like them to mean. She waited without moving, half-hoping Liz would leave the room and allow her to go without further incident.

But Liz dabbed her eyes with her handkerchief, blew her nose, and said, "Go sit on the bed, Hazel." It was an order.

She would have to leave, then, without her suitcases. Maybe she could ask Lacie to fetch them for her once she got free from Liz. It was only a matter of getting out of the room, of getting into a populated area of the house where Liz would hesitate to use violence on her. Watching Liz out of the corner of her eye, Hazel shifted slowly to her knees and then to her feet and stepped to the side of the suitcases. She turned, as though to begin moving back to the bed, then bolted for the door. But before Hazel could even touch the doorknob Liz threw what felt like the entire weight of her body against her own, slamming her into the door, knocking the breath out of her. "Damn you," Liz sobbed, "I know what you're doing. You think you can get around me by forcing us into this kind of confrontation, but you're wrong. I won't hesitate, Hazel, to do what you force me to do. I swear to you I'll do what I have to, you're mistaken to think I'm that weak!"

"I can't breathe!" Hazel gasped, fearing that the pressure of Liz's body pinning her to the door would suffocate her.

Liz's fingers dug into Hazel's upper arm, and the weight lifted off Hazel's body. "Don't try to leave this room again."

"Why won't you let me go?"

"We're going over to the bed now and talk," Liz said, tugging on Hazel's arm.

Unable to face another struggle, Hazel went without further resistance to the bed and sat where Liz told her to sit—on the side farthest from the door with her back against the headboard. When Liz sat beside her, Hazel felt overwhelmed by the sheer size of Liz's body. She leaned back against the headboard and loosely folded her hands and laid them on her knees. Her throat and tongue were crying out for water.

"Now listen to me," Liz said, her voice much smoother and cooler than it had been only seconds ago. "Let's get one thing straight, so that there will be no more games on that score. You're not leaving here. No amount of playing dumb is going to change my mind. I'm not a fool, Hazel. And I'm no Sedgewick, either. I won't let myself be destroyed simply because I'm too besotted with you to protect myself. Second, you will tell me everything you've revealed to Greenglass about my operations and this household. Third, you'll write her a letter explaining that you've changed your mind, that you've decided to try to establish a new identity elsewhere, using the plastic I set up for you when we went renegade. And then you'll follow that letter up with a phone call, to say good-bye."

In a flash Hazel saw it: only Martha's expectation that she would be going to her next Wednesday stood between her safety and freedom and Liz's being able to dispose of her with impunity.

*Dispose of her...* What was it Liz intended? Hazel looked at Liz's face for a clue to this horror, but saw only a hard mask that revealed nothing. "My god," Hazel said hoarsely, "how can this be happening? And the others? You think they'll stand by while you..." Her throat tightened to the point of choking off whatever words had been going to spill out of her. She swallowed. "I won't do it, you know. Martha will know. Martha will know you're keeping me from meeting her. If you…hurt me, whatever you do to me, she'll find out. Martha will care what happens to me, I'm not all alone, Liz, she'll make the Marq'ssan—"

"You can't manipulate me anymore." Liz's voice was harsher than Hazel could remember it ever having been. "You think I'll be soft because of my feelings for you, but you're wrong. There are more than a hundred women's lives at stake. It's a responsibility I've taken, and I won't betray them for you!" Hazel glanced at Liz's eyes and saw that they had become unrecognizably dull and remote. "Get that through your head right now, Hazel. I'll do what I have to do, no matter how much I hate it. For all your insight, that's one thing you've apparently failed to understand about executives. And it's something Sedgewick never thoroughly acquired, obviously. That's why he let Zeldin wreak so much disaster. Well I *am* thoroughly executive, Hazel, much as you hate it. I'll do everything I have to do to protect my people's lives."

"I'm not threatening anyone's life," Hazel said, unable to control the trembling in her voice. "All I want is to leave. Yet you're telling me you're capable of murdering me. I always made excuses for you, even when it came to your torturing that Navy agent. Because I couldn't face the truth: that you're without moral scruples. I'll never understand you, it's beyond me to understand someone who holds other human beings so cheaply."

"Damn you, Hazel!" Liz whispered. Her eyes were bleak, sea-green marbles. "You think if you get me torn up enough I'll be putty in your hands." She put her hands to her face. Hazel wondered if she could make it to the door by taking advantage of Liz's seeming inattention, but knew she probably wouldn't even get around the bed before Liz reached her. Liz dropped her hands, turned to face Hazel directly, and drew a deep breath. "What I don't understand is why. It hardly seems to your benefit to betray me. Your accusation about my not paying you is lame, and you know it. I'd have given you anything you asked for. As for your craving for power, you *know* how important you are to my operations, you *know* you've been my right hand, more than Allison, even. But somehow that wasn't enough. If you'd tried negotiating with me, we might not be in this mess now. Instead, you've already cut a deal with Greenglass and made the whole situation impossible for me." Liz's lips trembled. "Whatever your reasons, you've gambled on your ability to manipulate me, and you've lost. We're past the point of no return, Hazel."

The fear that had dried her mouth was swallowing her up. If Liz hurt her, how would she hold out against writing to Martha as Liz demanded? "You think everyone is like you," Hazel said. "That everyone else is as loveless and manipulating and cold as you are. Either that or stupid. Or both. You accuse me of all those things while at the same time you despise me. Do you think I doubt your cruelty? You've made it clear enough that to you I'm just another girl, I could be anyone. And since you don't care what you do to others, you'll do anything you want to me without feeling it. I've seen you with Ginger and Lacie and Anne, I know your contempt for them. You didn't hesitate to show me it. I guess you knew my ego would see to it that I thought you felt differently about me."

"That's enough, Hazel. I know what you're trying to do, it's no good." Liz leaned away from Hazel, took her handset out of her tunic pouch, and punched a number. "Lisa, is Allison there?" Hazel's heart leaped into a gallop. "No, I don't need to talk to her. Just ask her to come to my bedroom immediately..." Liz put the handset away and got up from the bed. She stood, her hands on her hips, staring down at Hazel. "I want to warn you, Hazel, that if you make a ruckus and get Lacie or Ginger upset, they'll suffer for it. And it won't help you. So if you have any decency at all, you'll leave them out of it."

Shivering, Hazel wrapped her arms around her body. How could this be happening? Just this morning she had woken in this bed, had gotten up as if it were any other morning. Granted, she had been upset because of Anne. And even when she had made the decision to move out—even then the world had felt fairly stable, despite her frustration and misery. But then she had still believed that Liz was a certain kind of human being, someone familiar and lovable (though at times wrong). Now she could find nothing familiar in this room, in Liz, in any traces of the world around her. All had become alien to her.

Allison came into the room without knocking. "What is it, Elizabeth?" she asked, glancing past Liz at Hazel before focusing on Liz's face.

"We have a crisis," Liz said in that same harsh voice. "Hazel was planning on defecting to Greenglass."

Allison's eyes darted to Hazel's face. "Hazel? But...*why?* I thought...I don't understand!"

Liz shrugged. "My mistake. I misjudged her, I misjudged our relationship. I'm sure I'll never understand why Hazel would defect any more than I ever understood why Zeldin did."

Allison swallowed loudly enough for Hazel to hear it. "What are we going to do?"

"Remember the security rooms in the under-basement?" Liz said. Hazel's stomach flopped over. She hadn't even *known* there was an under-basement. "We'll take her down there. And then we'll have to persuade her to write Greenglass a letter saying she's decided to leave the country rather than stay in the area."

"Persuade her?" Allison repeated, her voice eerily hollow. "But Elizabeth..."

"We have no choice," Liz said shortly. "If Greenglass decides we're holding her against her will, she'll wreak havoc on us. You know what she is and the kind of power she has behind her."

Allison put her hand on Liz's arm. "Why don't you just let her go, Elizabeth. For god's sake, it can't be worth it. Just think of—"

"There are too many lives at stake!" Liz's voice was ragged.

"I won't betray any of you!" Hazel cried, desperate to win Allison to her side. "I swear to you, Allison, I have no intention of telling Martha anything! I just want to leave. And since when is leaving the same as defecting?"

"My god, Liz," Allison whispered, "I don't understand what's going on here."

"What's going on is that Hazel knows almost everything there is to know about our operations and can't be trusted not to give Greenglass—or maybe even other interested parties—everything she knows. We don't have any choice, Allison. Just think of all those women in DC and what it would mean for the Executive to find out about them. Just *think* of that. And then ask yourself whether we have a choice." Liz glanced over at Hazel, and Hazel felt that already it was as though Liz weren't seeing her but rather the body of an enemy with whom she shared no personal history at all.

"Oh christ." Allison looked for a long, long moment into Liz's eyes. "I can't believe…" She bit her lip and sighed, and something happened in her face. After several seconds, she said, "All right, Elizabeth. I hope you know what you're doing. Because I sure as hell don't."

Hazel sagged back against the headboard. She listened to Liz and Allison laying their plans and determined to make it as hard for them as she could when they tried to force her out of the bedroom and down into the under-basement. If she didn't go willingly, they'd find it hard to get her through the house without attracting attention. God. What a nightmare. It would be at least a week before Martha would even begin to expect her, a week that now stretched like an eternity before her…

[ii]

Hazel drifted back to consciousness. "Hazel?" Liz's voice called.

Hazel opened her eyes, but unable to bear the light, instantly closed them again. She felt her wrist being released and realized that someone—Liz?—had been holding it. And with that realization memory flooded her: she was in the cell in the under-basement. They had been going to administer loquazene to her.

"How do you feel, Hazel?" Liz asked.

"Thirsty." The word came out in a croak. There was a bitter taste on her tongue. They hadn't let her drink water for eight hours before administering the loquazene, which was probably why her mouth felt as though it were full of glue and her lips had cracked with dryness.

"Open your eyes and sit up," Liz said. "There's water for you to drink right here." Hazel struggled to sit up; she squinted at Liz, rubbed her eyes to clear them of sleet. When she saw the glass of water in Liz's hand, she reached for it. "Can you manage it by yourself?" Liz asked as she handed Hazel the glass.

Hazel held the glass with both hands. The first drink she rolled around in her mouth before swallowing, then she downed the water in great gulps, not pausing until she had swallowed every drop in the glass. By that time her eyes had adjusted to the light. She saw Allison standing a few feet behind Liz. The loquazene interrogation had been Allison's idea. "May I have more?" Hazel asked Liz without looking at her.

Silently Liz fetched the bottle from the table and poured out another glassful. She turned to Allison. "She's all right. You can go upstairs now." Liz unlocked the door, let Allison out, and relocked it. She
returned to Hazel's cot and sat down on the edge of it. Hazel felt her
staring at her, but refused to look at her face. "I apologize, Hazel, for
accusing you of betraying me to Greenglass."

Hazel said nothing.

After a long pause, Liz said, with a nervous laugh in her voice,
"I've really botched things, haven't I. Just out of paranoia. When you
said you'd made arrangements with Greenglass...well, I thought you
were saying you'd defected to her. You do see why believing you'd defected I reacted the way I did, don't you?"

Hazel stared down at her blanket-covered knees. What was it
Liz wanted to make her believe now? "How long have I been down
here?" Hazel asked, turning the empty glass around and around in
her hands.

Liz sighed. "It's Sunday night. You've been down here half a week."

Disappointment brought tears into Hazel's eyes. She had thought
it must be close to Wednesday, that most of the week had been en-
dured. They had deprived her of sleep by keeping the lights on and
then more recently by injecting her with stimulants—all to make her
write to Martha as Liz dictated. She had thought an end was in sight,
not that she was only half-way there... Unless Liz was lying to her? It
wasn't unlikely that Liz would lie to her... She simply had no way of
knowing. *She* couldn't give *Liz* a loquazene exam.

Liz combed her fingers through her hair and rubbed the back of
her neck. Then she clasped her hands over her knee and stared at
Hazel. "What I don't understand is why you decided to leave like that.
Without even talking to me about it. Just out of the blue. We've been
so close, darling, it just doesn't make sense."

"We haven't been close for a long time," Hazel said. Her voice was
rough with hoarseness. "Anyway, why ask me about that now. Didn't
you just have your chance to ask me whatever you want to know?"

"I've treated you very badly, you have every right to be angry,"
Liz said, very low. "You can listen to the tape if you want. And then
you'll see how difficult it is to get answers under loquazene for such

complicated questions. Anyway, this is between you and me, a matter of communication, not testing. Please explain to me, Hazel."

"A conscious interrogation rather than an unconscious one," Hazel said bitterly. "I suppose you mean that if I don't answer your questions you'll make sure I go the rest of the week without sleep."

"No, Hazel, no, that's not what I meant! You're misunderstanding me. All I want is to *talk*! I want to understand what's happened to us!"

Hazel skittered off into giggles, then found it difficult to stop. "Do you have any idea what I feel like after going half a week without sleep? My head is pounding, pounding, always pounding, my eyes burn, I have muscle tics all over my body, I'm shaking with weakness, my face feels numb, my entire body aches. Right this minute I'm not even sure if I'm hallucinating or not! Maybe I'm still under the loquazene! Maybe you never injected me with that stuff! And you talk about wanting to *communicate*?"

Liz took the empty glass from Hazel and set it on the floor. "I'm sorry, I'm sorry, darling, I wasn't thinking, I didn't realize how awful you were feeling. Of course you're right, of course you need to sleep. We'll go upstairs now and you can have a Jacuzzi and go to bed. I can give you a sedative to help if you're too hyper to fall asleep by yourself." Liz stood up, went to the door, and unlocked it.

Hazel got to her feet and managed to take two steps before the room darkened and stars burst in her eyes. "Hazel!" Liz cried. Hazel felt Liz's arms around her as her vision cleared. "Are you all right, darling?" Liz asked.

"A little weak," Hazel said, already moving toward the door. She wanted to get out of the room before Liz changed her mind. The sight of the NoteMaster and the IV equipment strewn over the table gave her the creeps.

They mounted the stairs but had to stop when they reached the basement level so that Hazel could rest. Her legs felt like spaghetti, barely capable of holding her up; her body was drenched in perspiration. After about a minute Liz said, "I could carry you up the rest of the way if you don't feel up to it."

Hazel shuddered. "No. I can go on now." Slowly she stood up and this time was only slightly dizzy. Each step demanded a terrible effort, but at last she reached the top and Liz unlocked the door into the house. Hazel entered the dimly lit, carpeted hall connecting the main living room with the bedroom wing and was filled with so much relief that she realized she had actually doubted she would ever leave the underbasement alive. She stiffened as Liz took her arm, but did not demur. She was too tired, too close to the promised sleep now to expend the energy.

Liz guided her into her bedroom, turned on the light, and closed the door. "It will be a better sleep if you sit in the Jacuzzi first, darling. Unless you're really too tired?"

Hazel found it hard to decide: she *was* too tired to want to wait to sleep, but on the other hand she hadn't bathed since last Tuesday night, and her body ached all over. "Okay," she said. She was probably too jangled to fall right to sleep, anyway. It was often that way after going too long without sleep (though never had she gone *this* long).

Hazel sank down onto the bed while Liz prepared the bath. And then Liz removed her clothes and took her into the bathroom. With exaggerated solicitude, Liz got into the Jacuzzi with her and soaped and rinsed her; afterwards she helped Hazel out, toweled her dry, and slipped a fresh nightgown over her head. "I bet you feel better already," Liz said as she tucked Hazel into bed. "Do you want the sedative?"

"Yes," Hazel said, her eyes already closed. The smooth cotton sheets and clean nightshirt were heavenly. The only thing better would be sleep itself.

A few seconds later Liz gave her a tablet and water. "Sleep well, darling," she said, and brushed her lips over Hazel's forehead. To Hazel's surprise, she turned off the light and got in on the other side of the bed. Hazel lay sleepless for about fifteen minutes, dazedly wondering why Liz had brought her out of the cell. And then, at last, she dropped off, like a rock into a deep mountain lake.

[iii]

Hazel woke with a full bladder. When she opened her eyes she found Liz sitting on the other side of the room in the armchair, reading. Except for the lamp behind Liz, the rest of the room was dark. "Hello there, sleepyhead," Liz said as Hazel crawled out of bed. "Do you realize you've slept twenty straight hours?"

Hazel staggered to the bathroom. It was only while she was pee-ing that she remembered—as if it were a dream—everything that had happened. For a moment she felt so confused that she wondered if any of it *had* happened. She looked in the mirror as she washed her hands but made out very little, for the only illumination came from the nightlight in the dressing room. Twenty hours…that must mean it was Monday night, if Liz had been telling her the truth. Which left Tuesday and then Wednesday. If Liz had allowed her to sleep, surely she wouldn't… Hazel cut off the thought and summoned the energy necessary for facing her.

Liz had turned on one of the bedside lamps and was just putting her handset down when Hazel returned to the bedroom. "Allison is bringing you some food and coffee. You must be starved!"

"I was almost thinking of going back to sleep," Hazel said. She climbed back into bed and pulled up the covers.

"Oh," Liz said, sounding disappointed. "Can't you stay up for a little while? To eat…and maybe to talk?"

"Do I have a choice?" Hazel asked.

Liz stood at the foot of the bed. "Of course you have a choice, darling." Hazel watched the long tapered fingers of one hand twisting the ornate topaz ring—Liz's favorite, a gift from Vivien Whittier—on the middle finger of her left hand. "It's just that it's so important to me. To us."

For the first time, Hazel really looked at Liz's face and was startled by its strained and haggard appearance. Only one question mattered. She hesitated, afraid of what the answer might be, and then took the plunge. "Are you going to let me leave, Liz?"

Liz's face clenched in a spasm of tension that passed swiftly. "That's one of the things we need to talk about," she said.

Hazel's intestines cramped; she stared at Liz's fidgeting fingers. What could there possibly be to talk about? Either Liz would let her go or she wouldn't. And if she wouldn't… But Liz knew she'd have to deal with Martha.

After a while, Liz said, "I don't want to keep you here against your will. You don't deserve that, especially not after what I've done to you. I know now you haven't been disloyal to me."

"But?" Hazel said hoarsely.

"But?" Liz repeated. "There is no but. You can go on Wednesday, if that's what you want. The only 'but' is that I hope...I hope you'll reconsider. In spite of everything. We've had a terrible misunderstanding, darling. I want to untangle it. I can't bear the thought of losing you."

She's afraid I'll tell Martha everything, Hazel thought. She doesn't know how to keep me from leaving so she's hoping to sweet-talk me into staying.

"Obviously," Liz said, "we need to make certain changes. The payment of your salary—all of it, of everything I owe you, of course, but also making more visible the real role you play in our operations. You aren't like the other service-techs, and it's not fair that you be treated as such. There's no way you can be compared with Ginger or Lacie. And frankly, I think you're far more valuable to our operations than either Cleghorn or Burns are."

A knock sounded on the door, and Liz went to open it. Allison carried in a bed tray and arranged it over Hazel's thighs. "You look a lot better, Hazel," Allison said, smiling. "You must be famished."

Hazel poured out a cup of coffee. She was tempted to say something to Allison about how she wouldn't have looked terrible in the first place if it hadn't been for her and Liz. But her mind was working too slowly to produce an appropriate retort. She took a sip of the steaming black coffee, her first since they had locked her in that cell.

"I know you must be angry with me," Allison said, still standing beside the bed. "I'm sorry for putting you through that. But Elizabeth was so worried—"

Liz interrupted. "Not now, Allison. You can talk to Hazel tomorrow."

"Oh—but of course, Elizabeth," Allison said. Hazel heard the rustle of her gown as she went around the bed and crossed the room, and then the sound of the door opening and closing.

"Allison and I had a terrible argument about you on Wednesday night," Liz said. "She thought I was wrong to treat you that way."

Hazel took another sip of coffee. "That didn't stop her from helping you to torment me." Hazel lifted the cover off the deep soup bowl. Steam rose from it, wafting the fragrance of garlic and pancetta, black pepper and Romano cheese to Hazel's nostrils. Hazel dipped her spoon into the soup and lifted the first bite to her lips.

"She said I'd bungled the managing of dining arrangements," Liz said. "That there would have been no need for separate arrangements, that we could have just switched to having Lacie and Ginger serve and asking the amazons not to drop in—since, after all, they have their own mess arrangements in their barracks—with you and Anne—when she's here, that is—sitting at the table with us. Hazel, Allison said you were one of us. And that it was natural that you'd be hurt by my not making that clear."

Hazel put down her spoon and glared at Liz. "No. I *am* one of them. I'm not like you at all. I don't want special favors, Liz. I just want all of us to be treated like human beings. Not like, like, beasts of burden, or pets unfit to eat with you at the same table."

"My god, Hazel, what are you accusing me of?" Liz said—*indignantly*. "Is it possible you believe your own exaggerations?"

Hazel twitched open the napkin in the basket, removed a warm, crusty roll, and buttered it. "Anyway, the dining arrangements didn't have anything to do with why you locked me up and abused me." Hazel put the butter knife down and looked again at Liz. "Or maybe they did, in a way. If you'd thought of me as a human being whose feelings and well-being mattered, you wouldn't have treated me that way." Liz tried to interrupt, but Hazel plowed on, "You know, the whole time you had me trapped in this room with you when I wanted only to leave, I kept having this sense of shock at realizing that to you I was just some girl—I could have been anyone, anyone at all, I was without particularity to you—just some girl you happened to have been sleeping with for over a year, some girl you'd said and done things to purely to manage her. And that as far as you were concerned I was nobody, I didn't really exist as a person." Hazel bit into the roll.

"Hazel! It was *never* like that, never! Not even at the beginning! I can see how you might get that idea in your mind, but never *ever* have you been anything but unique to me!" Liz fetched the armchair and carried it across the room and placed it beside the bed near Hazel, and sat in it. "Please, let me tell you what I was thinking. You have to know that I've never been in love with anyone but you, darling, I've told you that time and again, you know how important you are to me! And that was the problem for me."

Liz leaned forward, to catch Hazel's eye. "When I found you all packed and ready to go, I thought at first that you were just trying to scare me into giving in about the dining arrangements. But then when you said you were going to Greenglass, I leaped to the conclusion that you must have been conniving with her all along. You see, I remembered how blind Sedgewick had been to Zeldin's manipulation of him." Liz put her hands to her cheeks and briefly closed her eyes. When she opened them and continued, her voice was unsteady. "He was so infatuated—no, obsessed—with Zeldin that he let her destroy him—and very nearly the Executive, as well. And Zeldin never loved him. She just let him believe what he wanted to believe, while she went about sabotaging innumerable Security operations. Once I got that parallel into my head, I felt certain you'd been manipulating me from the beginning. And that now you were going to destroy me if you could. Out of your hatred for executives. And god I couldn't stand the thought of allowing myself to be used that way! I was determined to do what I had to do."

Liz bit her lip. "Not that I could ever have done more than I did." She stretched out her hand and touched Hazel's knee. "Just locking you up and depriving you of sleep—I think it was Saturday afternoon when I began to realize that I might not get you to cooperate in getting Greenglass off our backs—because I just couldn't bring myself to use more direct tactics. When I finally talked to Allison about how I felt, about how I feared you had been betraying me the way Zeldin had betrayed Sedgewick, she insisted that you weren't Zeldin, that you love me, that you wouldn't betray me." Liz half-laughed, but tears stood in her eyes. "And coming from Allison—" Liz's mouth twisted. "You must have suspected that Allison is not one of your fans. She's always been a little jealous of you, darling. So for *her* to be defending *you*... When she finally suggested the loquazene exam, I jumped at it—though I was afraid, too, at what I might hear. I both hoped and feared what you'd say."

Hazel sipped from the glass of milk, then set it down and leaned back against the pillows. "I don't know what you're referring to when you talk about Zeldin and Sedgewick," she said. "But even if I did, it wouldn't make me believe you." Hazel could see what had happened: scared by the threat Martha's intervention posed, Liz had decided she needed to change tactics. To try persuasion. And the loquazene exam had probably reinforced that decision—who knew what she might have said under the influence of the drug. Maybe she'd maundered on about being hurt, maybe she'd vented her bitterness at loving someone who had only used her... After hearing such things, Liz would despise her more than she ever had. Hazel shivered as a chill swept over her; her teeth chattered. Though she wasn't in the least hungry, she swallowed another steaming bite of the *pasta e faggiole*—for warmth.

"What is it you don't believe, darling?"

Hazel returned the spoon to the bowl and folded her arms over her chest. "Stop pretending," she said, making herself stare into Liz's eyes. "How stupid do you think I am that you could think I'd fall for anything you might say to me now? After what you did to me, do you really think I'm going to believe you've ever had any real feeling for me?"

The color drained from Liz's face, even from her lips. "Darling! Don't talk to me that way! I know you're upset, but even so! It's not as though I treated you *that* badly! I *couldn't* hurt you, Hazel! Didn't you hear what I just said?"

The bed tray made Hazel feel physically trapped; she had the urge to fling it aside and flee the room and the house. But she was too afraid of triggering Liz's aggression to do more than mentally disengage. "I don't want to talk, Liz. I don't want any more of this food, either. Please just leave me alone." She leaned back against the pillows and closed her eyes.

"I'm sorry," Liz said gently. "You must still be exhausted. Maybe you *should* go back to sleep. We can talk more tomorrow." Hazel felt Liz lifting the bed tray and listened to her cross the room and go out the door. All she wanted now was to get away from Liz, to forget everything she had ever felt for her. The thought of talking again about any of this with Liz nauseated her.

Hazel sat up to turn out the light and then fell back onto the pillows. Within minutes, the privacy of the dark brought all her defenses down. She buried her head in the pillows to press back the sobs in her throat, the tears in her eyes, the horror in her belly.

# Chapter Fifty-one

As she rustled through the corridors of Security Central, Alexandra tried to guess which guards were assigned to stare at badges and which to watch people's hands. She had been fascinated since Blake had told her about that division of labor. It explained, of course, why guards never looked at one's face. But how then did they know to whom it was important to be deferential? After a little thought she realized that the guards staring at the badges would know by the security rating blazoned on each badge... As for those who watched hands, the fact that two gorillas accompanied her must immediately mark her as "important." And of course everyone else she passed *was* looking out for faces. And it was *they* who behaved somewhat, well, obsequiously.

She knew that the amount of attention she received was extraordinary, and not only by contrast to the casualness of her life before they had returned to DC. That that special aide assigned to her by the chancellor of Yale had as one of his duties seeing to all her curriculum, security, and scheduling requirements was not all *that* unusual, at least not for the daughter of a Cabinet officer. (Though he said he'd never had to arrange scheduling to suit a special commuting arrangement before—which would take some doing, including the rescheduling of certain classes.) Clearly the security requirements for potential significant hostages had to be given special attention. But the kind of attention she was getting from *executives*—that was something else.

Her mother had had quite a lot to say about it already. *This is insanity, Alexandra. It's an aberration, and it won't last. There's a certain novelty in it, and your father has somehow taken DC by storm because people are so desperate over these recent disasters... But he's ruining you. You mustn't take any of this seriously! You're a woman, and you're very young. When the summer's past it will all drift away like smoke. It's an illusion created by your father. An illusion, Alexandra...*

She might be right, Alexandra thought, but she's certainly not objective about *anything*. Her hysteria over my hair colors all her perceptions and judgments. And her hatred for Papa makes her bitter and suspicious. The fact that he now allows me to see her and Grandfather as often as I like she brushed away as a "tactical maneuver," when really it came from affection. But telling her *that* had been a mistake, for it had only brought on a diatribe about how incapable "that shark" was of affection. *He doesn't call you names, Mama. Please don't call him names. It upsets me to hear you talk about him that way.*

And then telling Mama of the decision to suspend piano lessons for a while had, for some inexplicable reason, made her cry. *It's only for a little while, Mama, until I have more time. What's the point of having lessons when I can't practice more than an hour or two a day? Lessons would only frustrate me. Please don't cry, Mama... It won't be for long. Just until things stabilize.*

Alexandra turned the ornate brass knob on the tall mahogany door and entered the "Chief's Suite." "Hello, Suzy." Alexandra smiled at the receptionist as she passed. And *all* the service-techs in the outer office said in return, "Good afternoon, Ms. Sedgewick." (She was under strict orders from her father not to let any of the service-techs in the office first-name her—under pain of their being terminated.) Alexandra flashed a smile all around and passed into Alice's office. "Hello, Alice," she said to the frosty PA her father had filched from the Deputy Director of Finance.

"Wedgewood, Stevens, and Taggart are already in there," Alice said.

"Oh," Alexandra said, wondering if her father would be irritated with her for being slightly late. "Then I'd better run," she said over her shoulder as she took off in a sprint up the hall. Pressing her thumb to the access plate on her father's door, she thought of how undignified Alice must find her. She had the feeling Alice disliked her.

The men sat at the long conference table by the window. The seat to the right of her father, marked by a sheaf of flimsy, a pen, yellow pad, and a coffee cup, had been left vacant—obviously for her. She set her attaché case on the floor beside the chair and sat. "You of course know Wedgewood and Stevens," her father interrupted himself to say to her. "But I don't think you've met Taggart." He nodded at the red-headed executive male seated beside Wedgewood, across from Stevens. Alexandra took an instant dislike to him: he gave off the same kind of vibes Wedgewood did. Her father looked at Stevens. "You can get on with your report now, Stevens."

Stevens said, "First of all, generalities." Alexandra glanced down at the sheaf of flimsy and saw on the top page the outline for a report evaluating the security status of San Diego County. "When the aliens destroyed a substantial portion of the Miramar and Point Loma bases and every nuclear vessel in the Bay last week, the Navy—and by this I include the Secretary of the Navy and Whitney himself—went into a tailspin. Morale in local Military in San Diego County is understandably low. The Navy not only has to replace its physical plant and munitions there but has the additional problem of finding an acceptable way of representing the damage and loss to its own personnel as well as to the public at large.

"Their response has been to undertake a large-scale round-up of any known troublemakers or activists on their books. Unlike ODS, Military Intelligence and Security Forces did not lose their records. I suspect that the most significant damage will be felt not at the local level per se, or even by the Navy itself, so much as by the Pentagon as a whole. I've gotten reports of widespread panic throughout Military, to the effect that it's widely believed that the aliens intend to go after the entire Military establishment, one area at a time—doing, in effect, what they did in the Pacific Northwest ten years ago. The Military in San Diego County are quite convinced that unless they can stop the aliens, San Diego County will soon be made into another Free Zone. The level of panic and paranoia at Headquarters on Coronado Island is tremendously high and rising daily.

"In the meantime, ODS is trying to pick up the pieces. But without records—for Mott destroyed everything when she went, and Central can provide data pertaining only to persons and matters of national significance—reconstruction is necessarily slow. We're operating there out of safe houses. As for the station itself...well, as you know, it's currently without a head. In my report I've recommended that the station be relocated, for Mott of course will have revealed its location to the aliens.

"The city itself has been quiet since Aldridge ordered the round-up. Our sources estimate that about 1500 people have been newly detained. Most of them are being held in the stadium, the county jail, and a few smaller clandestine locations, including Camp Elliott. So thoroughly are they taking care of terrorists and troublemakers that there's little work of that sort for our boys to do. Which means that in San Diego, at least, we can concentrate on rebuilding.

"The only center of power in the city that hasn't been damaged by the aliens' attacks has been Barclay Madden. It's beyond a shadow of a doubt that these disruptions have been to his advantage. None of his property, none of his collection forces have been touched." Stevens halted and stared at Papa for direction.

"Can we pin down a pattern in the aliens' methods of attack?" Papa asked.

"Certainly," Stevens said. "The obvious focus each of these attacks shares in common is the detention of political prisoners. I suspect this is largely for effect. Reports from stations abroad confirm this pattern in the attacks that have been taking place outside this country over the last few weeks. Second, they operate with inside knowledge. For the attacks on the Navy, the information *had* to have been inside, since all the prisoners involved were being held in clandestine locations. Our assumption is that there are women working on the inside, either doubling or aliens in disguise. In the case of the Navy's political prisoners, most of the files on their detention were not stored in the Intelligence and Security Forces' general data pool. The number of persons with access to the information they needed to *find* such prisoners is extremely limited. I gather there's a shakedown in progress now."

"But perhaps the aliens simply took a chance that they'd discover such prisoners in the course of their raids?" Papa suggested.

Stevens shook his head. "That's not at all likely, sir. In every attack the aliens *start* by going straight to the places the prisoners are being kept and releasing them *before* taking out whatever happens to be their *real* target."

"Hmmm. It should be easy enough to smoke out the doubler. Process of elimination alone would seem to make it a relatively easy shakedown." Papa tapped his pen on the table. "That's the background we have to work with. I'll get the details for myself later from the report. Now let me outline our goals and objectives as I see them and sketch out a possible strategy." He leaned back in his chair and glanced around the table. "First and most general, the mobilization of public opinion against the aliens and anarchists. Specifically, tying in the local propaganda campaign with the national one. Second and more particularly, to seize the opportunity to gain the upper hand in San Diego County over both Military and Barclay Madden. Given that Military is positively reeling already, we need a subtle local campaign to undermine public confidence in Military as a protective and stabilizing force. One possible theme: that no amount of weaponry will stand between us and the aliens, that only a unified and solid economy and body politic will protect us from their machinations. Mobilize a civic alert campaign, for citizens to be actively smoking out and exposing elements working with the aliens and the anarchists. I envisage a series of vid advertisements that will scare the shit out of such elements. Get such a campaign going, and I wouldn't be surprised if we managed to mobilize the entire city into purging itself with little help from us." He pounded the table with his fist. "The point must be pressed home that the aliens plan to demoralize the population, that these latest attacks are designed to intensify that strategy. And that furthermore, because the aliens aren't strong enough to take the entire globe, they are instead waging a war of attrition."

When his voice fell silent, Alexandra glanced up from her doodling and saw that he had stopped to drink some water before continuing. "As to Barclay Madden." His mouth twisted in a nasty smile as he nodded at Taggart. "Taggart, that will be one of your priority operations. We have solid information on the structure of Madden's organization. You'll get that information updated and then determine a pattern of excisions that will be psychologically most effective for destroying the organization. You'll probably want to include some exemplary rough stuff—not necessarily excisions—of ordinary men in the street making transactions using M-dollars or buying blackmarket goods. But the main strategy will be to systematically decimate the ranks of Madden's organization. The way Snelling eliminated every organized crime cartel earlier this century." Papa paused to pour coffee into his cup. "As for the station itself—I'm still looking for the man who can handle that kind of reconstruction job. One thing I do want taken care of immediately, though, and that's having every female employee working in or out of the La Jolla station, no matter how lowly, taken to the Colorado base for extensive evaluation. We need to determine whether Mott's left a contact behind, and we need more generally to test the remaining females' loyalty. I want the reconstructed station to be of absolutely pristine purity. Because our goal is to make that area a model of success for other stations to emulate."

After a long pause, Stevens said: "What about LA and the rest of the area, sir? The ODS office in LA has been without appropriate supervision or proper liaison with Central since the attack on the El Cajon detention facility."

Her father looked irritated at the reminder. Alexandra recalled his telling her that Stevens had been arguing for years that the station should be located in LA and not San Diego, since most of ODS's efforts were expended in LA. "It will be seen to in due course, Stevens." Alexandra tensed at the shift in his tone. "Whoever takes over the station will get the rest of the area back under control."

"My men in LA aren't doing at all badly, sir."

"Bullshit." Her father's voice took on that grating tone that Alexandra loathed. "Why otherwise would we have to go on maintaining the damned sectoring of the city? Wedgewood, how's that organization of speakers coming along? Southern California would be a good place to start that project running."

Wedgewood looked uncomfortable. "I'm having problems, sir."

"Perhaps you would be so good as to be a trifle more specific, Wedgewood." Papa's tone was sardonic.

"The project is entirely foreign in nature to what my departments are used to handling, sir. Hill terminated the entire group of PR specialists working under Bennett. So putting some kind of comprehensive package together seems a long way off. As for the speakers themselves, considering what you said about using public figures with high credibility ratings, well, it's difficult to get such a bureau organized."

"Why is that? Surely you simply have someone draw up a list of, say, two thousand names and see if you can get from a quarter to an eighth of them. Sounds pretty simple to me, Wedgewood."

"Yes, but I'm having trouble finding someone to draw up the list. As I said, sir, none of my departments—"

"For chrissake, Wedgewood," Papa interrupted. "You simply pull the names from the public opinion polls taken over the last two years! Anybody can do that!"

"Not *anybody*." Wedgewood's face, Alexandra noted with interest, was taking on a distinctly *ruddy* hue. "We need a researcher who's a public opinion specialist for that kind of thing. And then staff for contacting these people, and then there's the matter of training and—"

"Ridiculous! Are you telling me you can't organize such a thing?"

Wedgewood swallowed. "It's a matter of knowing whom to delegate this to. Bennett always organized such projects."

"Jesus Fucking Christ! That Lennox bitch deserves to be taken out—permanently." His face contorted into a grimace of fury, and everyone, Alexandra noticed, averted their gaze. Finally he took a sip of coffee. "All right." He sounded as though he were talking through his teeth. "All right. Just find Bennett and whatever of her staff you can, re-evaluate their security status, and get them the hell back to work, Wedgewood!"

The level of tension at the table made the thought of the plastic bag of crisp wet parsley tucked into her attaché case almost irresistible. But if she ducked under the table to sneak a chew he'd probably yell at her, too. And now they were arguing about whether or not Wedgewood's methods of finding Allison Bennett had been exhaustive… "What you obviously have to do is convince her mother we want her back. Since if anyone knows where she is, it's her mother." Papa scowled. "Of course that bitch may know where Weatherall is, too, but *that's* something we'd *never* get out of her. But since Bennett isn't officially wanted for treason, there's a chance we can get her back."

"All right, sir. We'll try her again," Wedgewood said expressionlessly.

"And as for finding people to put that package together," Papa said, "I'm a little surprised you don't have anyone in your department capable of it. After all, one of the functions of covert teams is the generation of effective propaganda."

"That's much cruder and more focused stuff than this general campaign," Wedgewood said.

"If your people find it so difficult, then maybe you'd better consider tapping Com & Tran for talent. Or even the other Departments.

They *all* have propaganda specialists. Such people practically grow on trees."

"Com & Tran is having its own problems," Wedgewood said. "Something to do with Goodwin's depression and his bitch's termination—Booth apparently insisted *she* go, too, since she was part of Weatherall's network."

Papa, drumming his fingers on the table, looked exceedingly exasperated. After a few seconds of glaring at Wedgewood, he turned to Alexandra. "You get along well with Goodwin. He likes you. Why don't you call his office and ask him to have a drink with you early this evening. And then see if you can't get him to come up with some people he can lend us. Or work in liaison with."

Alexandra stared at him. He wanted *her* to call up Goodwin and ask him to have a drink with her? Was he *crazy*? And then to talk about something she knew nothing about? "Do you think that's appropriate?" she asked hesitantly, wanting to refuse but afraid to do so because she didn't want him scathing at her in front of these men whose gazes were at that moment scorching her face. "I've only talked with him when I've been with you."

He smiled. "You're forgetting, Alexandra. Remember your long chat with him when I was called away to the phone during lunch last week."

But that had been to talk about his son to someone he thought sympathetic. That wasn't the same as doing business. Alexandra swallowed. "I'll do my best," she said. *No No No* she wanted to cry, she couldn't do that kind of thing.

"Make a reservation for yourself at my club. It's Goodwin's club too, you know. You make the reservation in my name and then sign in as my guest. There'll be no problem."

Beyond getting the cold shoulder from every male in the club. Could he really be that insensitive?

"Call his office now," her father said.

Why couldn't he do it himself? she fumed as she got up from the table and crossed the room to his desk. She heard her father begin speaking again and was relieved: at least they wouldn't all be listening to her making a fool of herself. She picked up the handset. "Yes,

Mr. Sedgewick?" Alice said. "It's Alexandra, Alice," Alexandra said. "Who's Edwin Goodwin's PA?"

"Nancy Abbott."

"Would you get her on the line for me, please?" She cleared her throat as she nervously waited for Alice to reach Nancy. Trapped in this situation, she craved parsley as she never had before. Crisp, clean, green, cool, wet. And currently unavailable. So near and yet so far, and all because of the presence of those damned, sycophantic males.

# Chapter Fifty-two

[i]

The middle-of-the-night hours of Hazel's last night in Liz's house fairly crawled. She had gone to bed confident that no one would stop her from leaving in the morning, but lying in the dark, tossing and turning, Hazel fell prey to fears that at the last minute Liz would do just that. Repeatedly she berated herself for not having gone that morning. It wasn't as though it would have thrown Martha off stride if she had gone a day early. But she'd wanted to avoid raising questions that she'd prefer not to answer. She didn't want to broadcast what Liz had done to her, and she knew there was a good chance that if she told Martha, everyone in the Co-op would eventually know.

The decision to stay one more day had seemed no risk at all—in the daytime. At two a.m., though, Hazel was not so sure.

Not that anyone had bothered her. Liz hadn't liked it when she'd insisted on sleeping alone, but she hadn't objected, either. On the contrary. Liz had been exerting herself to be charming, apologetic, accommodating. Liz had either been unable to go through with whatever measures she had decided to take to coerce her obedience or else had decided (on the basis of the loquazene exam?) that of the two techniques, friendly persuasion would likely be the most effective.

Repeatedly Hazel replayed the horror of the last week, each time culminating in Liz's decision halfway through a week of ill-treatment that Hazel would be less likely to respond as she wished with more of the same than if she switched tactics. And repeatedly Hazel reminded herself that Liz hadn't reckoned with her facing the fact that Liz had been cold-bloodedly using her all along. Liz, she was sure, hadn't believed she would be strong enough to stare such a shattering fact in the face. And Liz might have learned from the loquazene exam how deeply she felt, how hurt she was. The memory and her analysis played and replayed like a tape loop. Which was why as Hazel lay in the dark tossing and turning, she posed the question at the center of her anxiety: having realized how she had miscalculated, would Liz change tactics at the last minute, hoping to find some way of staving off Martha's concern and possible intervention? Hazel shivered with bone-deep cold as shadows of ideas she could not bring herself to name drifted through her mind, forming clouds of anxiety that settled over her psyche like the thickest fog, muffling and chilling her.

Hazel pulled the extra blanket up from the foot of the bed and tucked it tightly around her. Liz had become a stranger whose limits could not be fathomed, whose motives and values remained submerged below a surface that could no longer be taken as anything but a mask.

Even as Hazel grappled with such insomniac, shivery thoughts, the hall door suddenly and quietly opened, letting in a bit of illumination. A large bulk blocked the light as it moved into the room; the room returned to inky blackness as the door closed. Hazel lay frozen, her pulse so violent in her throat she could hardly breathe. The intruder crept toward the bed. "Who's there?" Hazel said.

Liz shrieked, as though startled. "It's Liz, Hazel," she said in a tremulous voice. "I didn't know if you were awake or not. Please, I'm having a terrible night. I keep waking up with awful dreams. Please, darling, please let me lie with you, just for a while."

Peering into the darkness, Hazel made out Liz standing beside the bed and realized she was smelling Liz's scent. "Go away," she said hoarsely, struggling to keep her fear under control.

"Please, Hazel. I'm afraid to go to sleep again. You know how awful it is when I have those dreams!" Liz's weight sank down onto the bed.

"Leave me alone," Hazel whispered. "Go to Allison. Or one of the others." Her arms and legs shook violently; her teeth chattered.

"For godsake, Hazel, please, I *need you*! Please, darling, please hold me!"

Liz threw herself on Hazel, laying her head on Hazel's breast, wrapping her arms around Hazel's body. Hazel felt Liz shaking, felt Liz's tears soaking through her nightgown. Here we are, both of us shaking so violently the bed is moving, Hazel thought, recognizing through her fear and distress this bizarre element of the absurd. "Get off me," Hazel said. "I know what you're doing and it won't work."

"Please, just for now, please, darling, it was so awful, you were in the dream, please don't be mean to me now, please hold me!"

"You're such a fine actor, Liz, that if you weren't an executive you would have ended up in Hollywood for sure," Hazel said.

Liz clutched Hazel's shoulders. "I'm not *acting*, for godsake. You don't think I've been making up my nightmares all these months, do you?"

"I don't know what to think," Hazel said. "I'm not even going to try to figure out what has been lies and what hasn't." Her voice dropped to a whisper. "For all I know, you might be thinking of staging an accident, to make sure I—"

"No!" Liz cried, pushing herself off Hazel. "No, how could you even *think* such a thing!" Liz's next words were swallowed by choking sobs. Hazel sat up and pulled her knees close to her chest. One part of her wanted to comfort Liz, to stop the horrible wracking noises ripping out of her throat. But another part of her listened coldly, skeptically, remembering those horrible days and nights—an eternity unmarked by any perceptible divisions of time—spent in the cell in the under-basement. After a while the sobs lessened, then turned into hiccoughs. Hazel heard Liz's gown rustle and the sound of Liz blowing her nose. "I've never lied to you, darling. I know you find it hard to forgive me for what I did to you, but my god, Hazel, that's such a far cry from— from—" Liz gulped. "From what you're talking about. And I couldn't even bear to do what little I *did* do—I was so sick I couldn't eat or sleep the whole time you were down in that cell. Believe it or not, *I* had as little sleep as you did!"

And then, Hazel thought, she has the nerve to come here tonight claiming she needs me to help her get some sleep! "I'm sure that's a lie," Hazel said fiercely. "You can sleep anytime you want to by saying your magic syllable to yourself."

"But I couldn't stand the dreams I had," Liz whispered. "They're even worse than they were. Hazel, please. I can't bear this, I just can't bear your abandoning me!"

"Let's leave everything personal out of this discussion, please. The way you always insist we do when talking about so-called non-personal things. The real point of all this is that you want to keep me here for non-personal reasons. The only use you have for so-called personal relationships is the leverage they give you for managing people like me!"

"That's *never* been true with you! I've never felt for *anyone* what I feel for you. Maybe it was wrong of me to want to bring you into my work... I don't know. I suppose I did it because it seemed that was the only way I'd be able to spend so much time with you. And god, how much I needed you, Hazel. I remember what a relief it was when you came to work for me, I remember moments when I could feel what a difference simply my awareness of your sitting in the outer office *being* there made for me!"

"Let's not muddy the issue," Hazel said angrily. "Oh no, let's keep everything clear-cut and unemotional and non-personal! Do you know what I kept thinking after that first time you injected me with a stimulant? I kept remembering the sounds that Navy spy made when you were trying to force him to talk. I kept remembering that because I knew I had to face the fact that you would do anything to me, anything at all if you thought that was the best way to get me to do what you wanted."

"But I never would have hurt you! My god, you must think I'm a monster! All the months of my loving you, that means *nothing*? I can't believe you could think that of me, I can't believe you could hate me that much!"

"Stop talking about love!" Hazel's hands clenched into fists. "I'm going to be sick if you don't!"

There was a long silence, and then Hazel heard Liz blowing her nose again. "All right," Liz whispered. "I won't be a nuisance to you. But can I ask you this: that you please let me see you after you leave here. I don't think I can bear not ever seeing you again. Please, Hazel. Even if it's just to have coffee. I—"

Hazel interrupted. "What, so you can pump me about Martha Greenglass?"

"I've never used you that way, never," Liz said quietly. "Whether you admit it to yourself or not, I've always let you know all my motives where you're concerned. I've always been honest with you. I've put my life in your hands, Hazel. You know I have. As I never would have with anyone else. Not even Allison. Because I've never felt as deeply about anyone as I do about you. I've never trusted anyone else that far. I—"

Hazel interrupted her again. "Then god help you, Liz. If the travesty of a relationship you've had with me is the best you can do, then—"

"Stop! You can't deny what we've shared! Whether you know it or not, *I* know what we had, and I know I'll never be loved as wonderfully as you—"

Incensed and shamed by this reference to her having loved and trusted someone who had used her so cynically, Hazel put her hands over her ears. "Get out!" she yelled. "Get out of here, I can't stand your lies!"

Without speaking, Liz got up from the bed, walked to the door, opened it, and went out into the hall. Only when the door had closed did Hazel—a hot spear of pain in her breast, a yawning emptiness hollowing her stomach—press her hands to her face and weep.

## [ii]

They were crossing Lake Washington on the Evergreen Point Floating Bridge when Liz said, "I know you're very angry with me, Hazel. And I understand why, too. Or I think I do. But I can't believe that anger is enough to destroy everything we've shared. It may seem that way to you now, but later... Later, when you've lost the heat of your anger, you may see that things look a little different." Though she gripped the steering wheel more tightly, Hazel looked straight ahead without once taking her eyes off the road. What I'm trying to say is, I'd like for us to keep in touch. If you had any idea how hard this is for me, how torn up I am by all this—"

Hazel interrupted. "Isn't that typical. You still think you can get to me by trying to make me worry about how *you're* feeling!"

After that, Liz was quiet for a long time. Only when they exited I-5 did she speak again. "I deserved that rebuke," she said. "But I don't feel as if I have any right just now to talk about *your* feelings. You've made that clear. Please, can't we see one another, maybe in a week or so, if only for coffee? I'm terrified you'll just disappear and I'll never see you again. I feel so...abandoned, so rejected."

Hazel drove into the Co-op's parking garage and pulled up at the gate run by the Women's Patrol; the woman waved her through, and the barrier lifted to let the van enter. Still silent, Hazel located a vacant space and parked in it. Then she handed the plastic ignition strip to Liz. This would be the last time she would ever be driving this van. "Here," Hazel said.

Liz opened her attaché case and handed Hazel a sheet of flimsy. "The transfer authorization for all the wages I owe you," she said. "And I want you to keep the van. It'll make life easier for you. God knows you've earned it."

Startled, Hazel looked at Liz's face. Any free-wheeling vehicle, even a one-seater, was beyond the means of most service-techs. But a van? A thought occurred to her: Liz must have had it fitted with a transmitter. The van would be a means of keeping track of her. "I can have the Women's Patrol go over this van," she said, watching Liz's eyes.

A flush crept into Liz's face, one of the first Hazel had ever observed. "By all means," she said. "If it will make you feel better."

"I suppose you think that if I accept it I'll eventually come back. Well I won't, Liz. I don't want it under those kinds of conditions."

"There are no conditions," Liz said. "I feel very bad about not having paid you. You were right to be upset about that. If it makes you feel better, you can think of it as reparation for all your grievances." Liz reached over and dropped the sheet of flimsy into Hazel's lap. "Before we go in, there's one last thing," she whispered. Hazel looked away from Liz's face so that she wouldn't have to watch the tears that were fast filling Liz's eyes overflow. "Could I hug you good-bye?"

Damn her, Hazel thought, slipping the ignition strip and transaction flimsy into her tunic pouch. Without answering, she left the van and headed for the elevator. Now that she could leave her luggage in the van she didn't need to drag it up to Martha's office.

"Hazel, please," Liz said, catching her up. "Just this one last thing. Please."

Hazel stopped. A note Liz's voice wrenched at her heart. Silently she opened her arms.

Liz clutched her, pressing her close. Hazel stiffened as she inhaled Liz's familiar scent. When Liz released her, she kissed Hazel's cheek. "Thank you, darling. You can't know how important it is to me."

Hazel shook her head. She said nothing, though, because she could not bear to prolong the hateful argument on how Liz really felt about her.

At the elevator they submitted to the usual inspection by the Women's Patrol's. As they stepped into the elevator Hazel said, "What is it you're seeing Martha about?"

Liz's gaze met Hazel's. "I'm going to give her some information on who is responsible for the drugging of prisoners in federal detention facilities."

"Why are you giving it to her?" Hazel asked pointblank.

Liz's eyes flickered. "You don't think I'm going to continue to confide in you, Hazel, when I know you'll tell Greenglass every word I say?"

Something in the way Liz was looking at her struck her as odd. "You don't really think I will, do you," Hazel said.

"I don't know anything about what you're thinking of doing," Liz said wearily. "All I ask is that you remember that at least a hundred lives could be put on the line by you. Sedgewick doesn't fuck around when it comes to renegades and doublers. It's a matter of *lives*, Hazel."

The elevator doors opened, sparing Hazel the need to reply, and they walked the rest of the way in silence. Hazel knocked on Martha's open door. Martha, who was seated facing the window, looked over her shoulder; she smiled warmly, and then a split second later, her eyebrows shot up. "Well, come in," she said, getting up from her desk and turning to face them. "Haven't seen you in a long time, Elizabeth. To what do I owe the honor?"

Liz smiled. "Love your enthusiasm, Martha. Two things bring me. Do you mind if we have the door closed and my jammer activated? Both items are of a markedly, ah, confidential nature."

Martha slipped her hands into her pockets. "Be my guest."

Hazel stepped further into the room so that Liz could close the door. Martha again raised her eyebrows, this time at Hazel. "I've left all my luggage in the van I have parked downstairs," Hazel said. "Which Liz has so generously given me."

The three of them sat on the floor, and Liz opened her attaché case. "Have someone go over the van for Hazel's peace of mind, would you, Martha?" she said. "And perhaps you can have it regularly inspected for her. For *my* peace of mind." Liz pulled out a sheaf of flimsy, then relocked the attaché case. "The first thing I wanted to see you about is this." She handed the flimsy to Martha. "The man responsible for ordering the drugging of prisoners in federal detention facilities is named Chase Ambrose. His father has a strong financial interest in the company supplying the drugs. Although I countermanded his order for the routine drugging, once I left Security he obviously put the old order back into effect." Liz's mouth tightened. "Ambrose ran ODS during the war. I don't know if it will change now that Sedgewick is shaking up every branch of Security. If I hear anything at all specific, I'll let you know."

Martha glanced down at the sheaf of flimsy Liz had given her. "The evidence is in here?" she asked.

"Yes. Including copies of stock certificates."

Martha's gaze locked with Liz's. "You still have contacts with these people?"

"I can't tell you that," Liz said. "If I did have contacts, knowledge of their connection with me would prove a dangerous risk to their health. Therefore the less said about whom I have contacts with the better."

"You want me to use this information?" Martha said, smiling.

Liz laughed shortly. "Obviously. If you can't use it, I'm sure the International Committee on Human Rights can."

Martha nodded slowly. "Oh, I can use it. I'm just wondering why you want me to."

Liz sketched a faint smile. "Maybe I'll need another favor from you some day."

Martha snorted. "No doubt." She glanced at Hazel, then looked back at Liz. "And the second matter?"

Liz smoothed her hair back from her face. "I'm concerned about Hazel's security. I want to stress to you how likely it is that Sedgewick has men scouring the Free Zone looking for both of us. Let me explain to you what will happen if they catch Hazel."

Hazel's stomach clenched like a fist. She had heard all this before and didn't need to hear it again.

But Liz was apparently speaking for Martha's benefit. She looked Martha in the eye as she said, "While they *might* try to use her as bait to catch me, I rather doubt it. That would be the best we could hope for. But I don't imagine Sedgewick would think that would work with me." She gnawed at her lip. "What is more likely is that they'd use the most painful and degrading means they could think of to force Hazel to tell them everything she knows about me and my operations and my location. Captured doublers and renegades are always treated that way, whether they have any information to be learned or not. It's supposed to provide an example for illustrating the consequences of treachery." Liz cleared her throat. "Further, if they capture Hazel and get information out of her, the lives of at least a hundred women—all of them working for the Executive—will be forfeit. That's the kind of information Hazel carries around inside her head."

Martha's warm brown gaze beamed reassurance at Hazel. "Hazel will be safe with us," she said.

"Goddam you, Martha Greenglass, that's not good enough," Liz said hoarsely. "You probably said that to Kay Zeldin, too, and look what happened to her!"

Martha's eyes flashed back to Liz's face. "And how much did you personally have to do with that, I wonder."

Liz's face blanched. "Kay Zeldin was arrested and shot as a traitor," she said, her voice harsh—and trembling. "The point is, she was caught. And I happen to know she was tracked most of the time she was living in the Free Zone, too. What I'm saying, Martha, is that you have got to do a hell of a lot better than that this time!"

Suddenly Hazel felt terribly vulnerable, unprotected, exposed—as she never had when living with Liz.

"Kay wouldn't let us protect her," Martha said flatly. "She refused to take the precautionary measures recommended to her, she refused all offers of bodyguards, and then she insisted on traveling to places dangerous to her. All those risks were her choice. I'm sure Hazel won't be as reckless as Kay was. You know what Kay was like. Once she determined on a course, that was it. Nobody and nothing could stop her: not even that close call she had with those SIC creeps in Edmonds!"

"Among whom was your lover," Liz said softly.

Martha's eyes narrowed. "What the hell does that have to do with anything?"

The two women seemed locked in combat, the nature of which remained elusive to Hazel. Tension crackled in the air between them. Hazel wondered uneasily if she should say something—should reassure

Liz that she would be careful, or assert her faith in Martha's ability to keep her safe.

Finally Martha broke the lengthening silence. "Let me ask you this, Elizabeth. Do you think Sedgewick and his crew would risk harming me or any other leaders in the Co-op?"

Liz frowned. "I don't know. Sedgewick isn't entirely sane, you know. It's hard to say what he might consent to have done under certain circumstances. Certainly he's not likely to order your assassination. Chase Ambrose, by the way, once concocted some bizarre scheme to assassinate you and your colleagues. Sedgewick knew he'd be stupid even to try it. But there's never any telling with Sedgewick. He's predictable in certain things—in ordering the fate of renegades, for instance—but not in others. He's been fairly consistent in his ODS policies since the Blanket. But that's not to say he might not suddenly take some new methods into his head." Frowning, she rubbed the back of her neck. "But if he does, they will probably be in the wrong direction. He's not likely to get what he calls *soft*. Does that answer your question?"

Martha shrugged. "All I'm saying is that the Executive seems not to be interested in moving openly against us. They use mainly covert means. Therefore, if we draw Hazel into our inner circle, I doubt they'd be willing to risk Marq'ssan retaliation to get her."

Liz gnawed her lip and stared hard at Martha. "If you were to get me into Security's data system as you did that other time, I'd locate every last file they have concerning their operations in the Free Zone. And give it all to you. I think that would be the best thing we could do for Hazel's safety. And you people would incidentally know everything SIC has coming down in your territory—and exactly who they have operating here."

"I'll think about it," Martha said. "I suppose you have your own reasons for wanting to get into their system."

"I'm intensely concerned about Hazel's safety," she said, very low. "It would kill me if—" Liz broke off and stared down at the rug. After a few seconds she lifted her eyes and looked at Hazel. "For godsake, Hazel, be careful. You should start practicing the defense skills I taught you. And maybe carry a weapon. I'm sure you can get somebody in the Women's Patrol to teach you to use one."

Martha made a face. "I'm not keen on people carrying weapons, Elizabeth. But if it will make Hazel feel safer——"

"No," Hazel said. "I won't carry a weapon. I can't stand the things."

Liz looked down at her hands. "All right. It was just a suggestion." She swallowed, then lifted her gaze to Hazel's face. "If you have the faintest hint that Security or Military people are onto you, please, for godsake let me know so I can help. You can always reach me through Margot Ganshoff." Liz returned the jammer to her attaché case and stood up, and Hazel and Martha followed suit. Liz directed a long, burning stare at Hazel. "If at any time you need or want anything from me, it's yours." She swallowed again and blinked. "I mean that seriously, Hazel, as a permanent standing offer."

Liz's nearly mesmeric gaze held Hazel's eyes. "Good-bye, Liz," Hazel said through the frog in her throat.

Liz turned, opened the door, and disappeared down the corridor. Hazel stared for a long while at the empty doorway.

"That sounded much more final than what you talked about a week ago," Martha said.

Hazel looked at Martha. "Too much has happened in this last week." Martha raised her eyebrows. Hazel shrugged. "I'd really rather not go into it," she said. She could not imagine ever telling anyone what Liz had done to her—or how Liz had duped and used her for more than a year.

"Of course. But if you change your mind, let me know. Sometimes it helps to talk to a third party."

"I want to put it all behind me," Hazel said, feeling strangely bleak. Today she was beginning a new life, one that she could not begin to imagine. And for the moment, at least, she had to place herself in Martha's hands. She wondered whether she weren't just trading one dependent situation for another.

Martha smiled. "Then maybe you'd like to hear some of the possibilities I've come up with for you. They're just possibilities, mind you, not limitations for choice. But I thought I could give you somewhere to start from."

No, Hazel thought as Martha closed the door to ensure their privacy. There could be no resemblance between her situation living with and working for Liz and her temporary situation with Martha. Martha didn't think or act like an executive. And that made all the difference in the world.

# Chapter Fifty-three

## [i]

Since she had time to kill, Hazel wandered aimlessly through Carkeek Park's tall, swaying poplars, both reveling in her possession of leisure and feeling at loose ends because she was so unused to having it. When she came to a vantage point overlooking the beach, she took a seat on the rustic bench provided and stared out at the gently lapping water, which at high tide covered almost the entire beach. Martha had given her the choice of accompanying her downtown or figuring out the public transport system and finding her own way to Capitol Hill, where she had arranged to meet Anne. Hazel was resolved not to allow fear of Military and Security agents rule her life. If she did, she would always be dependent on someone else to protect her. If she chose a life trapped within the confines of paranoia, what, then, would have been the point of leaving Liz's household (other than to get away from Liz)? She would be reasonably careful, for sure. But she would start, today, as she meant to go on.

Martha had presented her with a choice of living situations. She could stay with Martha, who lived on the outskirts of Carkeek Park with Dee Trent—a Woman Patroller whom Martha had asked to live with her solely to tighten security for Hazel. Dee had done all sorts of things to the house to make it as break-in-proof as it could possibly be. And Martha had given Hazel a card (which Hazel suspected had been fabricated by the Marq'ssan) that could be used to trigger a signal to Martha communicating not only her need for assistance but her location as well if for some reason she couldn't connect to the Free Net or use a handset. Of all their precautions, this device most reassured Hazel. Constantly she fingered the card, which she kept in her hip pocket.

If she chose not to stay with Martha, she could live by herself in an apartment as Anne did, or live in a collective in town, or in one of the rural communes. But Martha had explained to her that if she lived by herself or in a collective she would have to keep a low profile—including avoiding contact with known Co-op people. And Hazel wasn't sure she wanted to do that. Martha believed that if it were made plain that Hazel was closely connected with Martha herself, then neither Security nor Military would risk moving against her. But Hazel felt unsure, and listening to Martha outline the relative risks of various options, she had for a few moments wished for Liz's advice. But then she had recalled that Martha and all the other Co-op women—with the exception of Kay Zeldin—had survived years of Executive hostility—and without surface-to-air-missiles fortifying their rooftops, without a squadron of trained and armed amazons guarding them day and night, without crazy maneuvers with radios, switching cars, and all the routine subterfuge Liz insisted on. Perhaps, Hazel thought wryly, with creatures like the Marq'ssan behind one, the luxury of a carefree attitude might be possible.

Hazel checked the time and saw that it was almost 10:30. If Seattle's public transportation were anything like DC's (or post-Blanket Denver's), it might take hours to get to the Capitol Hill district. Trudging uphill, back to Martha's house, Hazel wondered if the Co-op intended to accept Liz's offer to locate the information that would tell them exactly what operations Security had going in the Free Zone. She hoped they did. If they could keep tabs on all of Security's people in the area, then she would only have to worry about Military's agents... Unless, she thought, suddenly chilled, Liz... No. Liz wouldn't have let her go if she'd intended *that*.

And yet, as she circled around the house to the back door, Hazel grew apprehensive of just that possibility. Chiding herself for being paranoid, she inserted the plastic strip into the access slot, which chimed then returned the strip, and entered. The house, so utterly silent, had a static dead feeling and smell to it—because it was so tightly sealed up, Hazel thought, or maybe because Martha wasn't much of a nest-maker—making it lifeless in the absence of living beings. Maybe it needed some plants, or a vase of flowers... Hazel changed into sandals and combed her hair, then gathered up a bottle of water, a book to read on the bus, and the street map Martha had provided her and boldly set out from the house. A bus was scheduled to pass the stop around the corner at 10:50. As she walked to the corner, she looked over her shoulder three times. She glanced at the windows of the houses she passed, but saw only a couple of cats within. Most of the yards looked carefully and creatively tended, perhaps by professional landscape designers and their crews and machinery. Suddenly the whole scene felt dream-like. Never had she in the middle of the day walked by herself in a residential neighborhood. Obviously this was the kind of neighborhood high-echelon professionals—interspersed with a few executives—lived in. But since this was Seattle—where only a few executives now lived—there might well be other service-techs than herself and Martha residing in the neighborhood.

The bus came on time. As Hazel boarded, she marveled anew at the lack of a fare to pay; the Co-op, Martha had explained, subsidized it with a surcharge on mass-auto usage collected whenever anyone paid user's fees through the Co-op's trading system (which sounded like a tax to Hazel, though Martha insisted that it wasn't). The bus was crowded, but she managed to get a seat with a clear view of the route display. During the ride, Hazel divided her attention between the other passengers, the passing scenery, and the route-display tracking their progress through the city. Martha had suggested she get off on 45th Street, since there was a bus that passed there that would take her within two blocks of where she wanted to go on Capitol Hill. There was a faster way of getting to the Rainbow Press from Martha's house, but Martha thought it best that Hazel take the least complicated route her first time using the public transport system. The other way required changing buses twice.

She had a ten-minute wait at the 45th Street transfer point before the correct bus came. She spent the time pacing up and down, covertly watching the passersby and the other people waiting for a bus. Many of those waiting, like most of the passengers on the bus, were reading newspapers. Hazel counted fifteen different newspaper boxes lined up along the curb. The headline of *The Rainbow Times* proclaimed **Bogan Boycott Ends in Victory**; *The Day's Data*'s screamed **Bogan Capitulates**; and *The Herald Daily*'s declared, **Franklin Demands Elections**. Not all of the newspapers were local, though. She could

see *The New York Times* among them—which made her shake her
head. According to Liz, the *New York Times* offered carefully selected
and watered-down versions of articles printed in the *Executive Times*
(which naturally would not be sold on the street: only executives could
purchase or subscribe to the *Executive Times*). But then all the members of the editorial board of the *New York Times* had been approved
by the Cabinet. During the war Allison had had something to do with
overseeing the editorial policies of all US newspapers...

Hazel decided to buy a *Rainbow Times*, which she knew was published by pro-Co-op people. Liz subscribed to it because, she insisted,
internal disagreements and the like could be extrapolated (one of
Allison's tasks). Hazel found the correct box, peeled the used plastic
film from the print-sensor and pressed her right thumb against the
sticky fresh film. The printer whirred and disgorged a newspaper. The
Co-op's triumph over Bogan Enterprises (of whose existence Hazel
had previously been ignorant) shared the front page with the beginning of a "roundtable" discussion among various clients and doctors
at the Whidbey Clinic (Hazel recognized Dr. Gina McCartney in the
photo shown), an announcement and analysis of a new agreement between the Consumers' Co-op and the Pierce County Food Producers'
Co-op, as well as a description of how various people in the Free Zone
would be celebrating Emma Goldman Day. Because she would be going to Sweetwater with Martha to participate in their festivities, Hazel
was amused to see Sweetwater's festivities highly touted. She noticed
a reference to an article about Emma Goldman on p. 14. All she knew
about her was what Martha had told her—that Goldman was "an
anarchist foremother" whose birthday people in the Free Zone cel-
ebrated every year. A lot of people would be taking the afternoon off,
including Martha and Anne. Hazel leafed through the paper looking
for p. 14, but then the Capitol Hill bus rolled up. She boarded it and
sat down beside a very aged-looking woman (who was also reading the
*Rainbow Times*), then located the article on Goldman, glanced at the
photo of the strange-looking anarchist, and plunged in.

By the time Hazel got off the bus she had a fair idea of why the
Co-op people liked to claim Emma Goldman as a "foremother"—and
knew, too, that just about all executives would detest such a person.
Not that some of the specific things she had defied governments for

had been all that radical, at least by modern standards, but simply because of her outspoken, defiant style—and her scorn for authority. Liz herself would agree with Goldman's call for sexual freedom (though male executives would sneer at anyone even expressing a desire for such a thing), and no one but fundamentalist lunatics would ever think the practice of birth control a bad thing (though, Hazel suddenly wondered, would Goldman be likely to equate birth limitation with the personal exercise of birth control?). But much else that Goldman had said and done would go directly against the status quo even today. Why, though, if Goldman had been such an important historical figure, hadn't she been mentioned in history books? How was it that she had never heard of the woman until she'd moved to the Free Zone?

When Hazel got off the bus she checked first the street numbers and then the address Anne had dictated to her and found that she needed to walk two blocks east. Anne had said the large Victorian house would be on the corner, surrounded by a yard full of vegetable and flower beds.

As Anne had predicted, Hazel recognized it as soon as she saw it. Unlike most of the other houses in the neighborhood, this one looked to be in superb condition—newly painted, its windows sparkling, its lawn, shrubbery, and beds neatly tended. An unobtrusive wooden sign proclaimed *The Rainbow Press*. She glanced at her watch and found she was early, but decided to go in anyway. She could always sit and read the newspaper while Anne finished her work.

So Hazel went up the front walk and climbed the few stairs to the porch where three women were sitting around a table crowded with papers and NoteMasters and coffee cups and water bottles, talking. The front door stood open. Hazel entered and found herself in a large foyer. Shelves spilling over with books lined the foyer. An old, old house—*and* books! Inveterate lover of antique shops, museums of social history, and bookstores, Anne undoubtedly adored the atmosphere. Hazel made for the wide, shallow stairs. As she ascended, she looked down over the banister at the scattering of desks through what must have originally been a spacious living room. With a shock she realized that men as well as women worked there. It had been a long time since she had last seen so many men (except in passing on the street). She had so strongly come to think of the Co-op and all its arms as being for women only that she found this male presence hard to take in.

Hazel passed the second floor landing and continued up the last flight of stairs. Glancing up and down the third floor hall, she randomly chose to go right and poked her head through the first open doorway she came to. Two men and four women were seated at a conference table. They stopped talking and stared at her, and one of the women said "May I help you?"

Hazel flushed. "I'm looking for Anne Hawthorne," she said. "She's a typesetter."

"The last room to the right at the end of the hall," the women replied.

Hazel thought about how a group of executives would have reacted if a passer-by had interrupted *them*. But they *had* left the door open. And there were no numbers or signs on any of the doors, or a receptionist downstairs, either.

Hazel paused on the threshold of the corner room to stare in amazement at the rounded, window-lined walls and the magnificent view of Lake Washington, Mt. Rainier, and a long stretch of the Central Cascades. Sunlight poured into the room from the windows and the skylights overhead, glinting and glowing on the golden oak floor, the white walls, the marble fireplace, and the vases of flowers scattered around the room. A little dazed, Hazel peered at the knot of men and women at the non-rounded end of the long room and easily spotted Anne. (Who else would be dressed so impeccably, wearing a tightly fitted, crisp cotton pants-suit and that thick silver bracelet Allison had given her last Christmas?) As Hazel stood there she saw that they were passing photo-printouts from hand to hand, debating the merits of each.

Hazel leaned against the door frame and stared out at the view for a few minutes, then went to look for a restroom, which she found just across the hall. When she came out of the restroom, she got out the newspaper and continued reading it.

After about twenty minutes, Anne's meeting broke up. Smiling, Anne went straight to Hazel and pulled her close in a long, tight hug. When she released Hazel and stepped back, Hazel saw the tears in her eyes. "All I have to do is lock my terminal and I'm through for the day. Hold on a sec." Anne slipped across the room to a desk turned to face the east windows and sat down at the terminal. After only a few seconds she got up, fitted a plastic cover over the terminal, folded up the keyboard and stowed it in a drawer in the desk, picked up her satchel and sweater, and rejoined Hazel. They linked arms and retraced Hazel's path through the building. "Can you believe we all have the afternoon off, just because it's some old revolutionary's birthday?"

"I was reading about it in the paper."

"I'll have you know I typeset that article on Emma," Anne said.

"That's what you do? Typeset the *Rainbow Times?*"

"And other things," Anne said. "I've been assigned to a book project, too. The way things work around here is a little, uh, unusual. I'll explain some of it over lunch."

"Do you have somewhere in mind we can go?"

"There's a place I've been to a couple of times that's only four blocks from here." They walked down the front steps. The porch was now jammed with people, most of them eating box lunches. "Did you notice the woman perched on the porch railing?" Anne murmured as they reached the sidewalk.

"The one with the short, messy gray hair?"

"That's Venn. She's a Co-op bigwig, and the top editor. She and one of the typesetters interviewed me for the job. At first I was pretty nervous, because Venn said that I was being hired provisionally—that after a month the other typesetters could exercise their veto power, in case they found me too difficult to work with. Pretty strange, don't you think? Of course my first thought was that it might be awful, not dealing with a particular boss. I mean, imagine if other secretaries and clericals got to decide whether or not you could stay! But it's nothing like I expected. Things are pretty relaxed, and the other typesetters seem to be easy to get along with."

Hazel stared curiously at the mostly decrepit houses they passed. Music blared from some of the open windows, and several banners featuring cartoons and caricatures of Emma Goldman hung out of the windows. "An awfully run-down neighborhood," she said.

"Yeah," Anne said. "Apparently when the Press took over that house it was a dangerously falling-down slum. But you know how people get attached to the places they live in, even when they're awful. The girls in my office say it took the Press more than a year to find places that would suit all of the tenants. Part of the problem, of course, is that there aren't that many old houses. And there's the view." Anne grinned at Hazel. "In Seattle the view is everything."

"I wonder then that they let the typesetters have one of the best rooms in the house."

Anne laughed. "I know. It's crazy. But I gather that that was Venn's idea—she said the typesetters have the most boring work of everyone in the Press. And that because of it, the view would matter more to them than to the others. She herself, she said, might as well be stuck in a basement, since her work is so involving and interesting. Anyway, it's also thought that the view refreshes us so that we're less likely to tire out."

"That's amazing. Someone like Liz would have hogged that room for herself." She snorted. "Any of them would."

"You mean executives."

"Right," Hazel said shortly.

They walked in silence for about half a minute, and then Anne said, "How is everyone?"

Hazel glanced at her. "Hasn't Allison told you?"

Hazel saw the worry in Anne's eyes. "You're the first person I've seen since I moved out, Hazel. Didn't you know that?"

Hazel swallowed at the tight control she could hear in Anne's voice. No wonder Anne was so glad to see her. She must have been feeling abandoned. "I've moved out, Anne. Liz and I had a terrible argument. We're through. For good."

"Oh!" Anne seized Hazel's arm and brought them to a dead halt. "I can't believe that, Hazel. You two are—" Her eyes searched Hazel's face, and she shook her head. "No. This is only temporary. I've never seen a relationship like yours with Liz. There's too much love there—"

"Please, don't," Hazel said quickly. "It's too painful for me to talk about. Liz was using me. She never loved me." Hazel got them moving again.

Anne's hand relinquished Hazel's arm. "I know Liz can be devious and exploitative," Anne said, "but I've been acquainted with her for a long time, and Lise has known her all her life, and Lise agrees with me that Liz is crazy about you as she's never been about anyone ever before. Why, Lise says—"

"Let's not talk about it." How could she tell Anne that Allison was doing the same thing to her that Liz had done to Hazel? Hazel's sense of Anne's fragility restrained her from adding to her already heavy burden, for she suspected that shattering the illusion of love that Allison used to "handle" Anne would crush her. Anne had left a good job—as Hazel had not, for Hazel had known when she agreed to go with Liz that she really had no choice, since staying would have inevitably led to her own doom. Further, Anne had been with Allison for years and years and years. An illusion carried on for that long must be terribly powerful. How did a person make sense of a long chunk of her life once she discovered that much of it had been formed and shaped by such an illusion? No, she must be careful with Anne.

After walking a block in silence, Anne said, "Margot Ganshoff finally got in touch with me on Tuesday. Which sort of relieved me. I was beginning to feel, well, cut off."

"Margot?" Hazel said. "Why? Is she in on this?"

Anne directed a quick look of scrutiny at her. "Didn't you know? Because I can't have a plastic account on my own behalf—since my thumbprint would immediately be spotted—I'm to have one through the Austrian government, a special account—Liz will fund the account, of course—whereby my print can't be spotted by any branch of the US government. Every government has such accounts, I gather—and the thumbprint exists only as verification of the right to use the account while being kept confidential." They reached the street Hazel's bus had run down, teeming with foot and bicycle traffic as well as the occasional mass-auto vehicle. They turned right, and Anne lowered her voice. "Of course I need an expense account for the sorts of things I'm to do. And Liz is paying me a wage, too. In addition to what I make at the Press."

"She's all heart," Hazel said sourly.

Anne frowned, but only said, "Here we are. It's a Co-op place, but it's pretty good."

Anne led Hazel through the crowded front room and down a narrow hallway, past the kitchen, and outdoors. "Do you mind if we eat out here?" Anne said.

Hazel took in the sun, the flowers flanking the courtyard, and the tables with umbrellas scattered over the brick surface of the courtyard. She grinned her delight. "Are you kidding? I can't believe anyone would *choose* to eat indoors on a day like today!"

They claimed a table near the low wall separating the courtyard from the adjacent park. "It's a little more trouble sitting out here," Anne said. "We'll have to go back inside to order and carry everything back here ourselves. Whereas inside, there's limited table service available."

Hazel accepted a menu from Anne. So people in the Free Zone liked table service...

"Can I interest you in splitting a bottle of wine?" Hazel looked up to see Anne smiling. "It *is* a holiday."

"Okay," Hazel said. "The only thing I have to do this afternoon is meet Martha Greenglass downtown at quarter to three. We're going to Whidbey Island for Sweetwater's Emma Goldman festivities."

"Ooh-lah-lah," Anne said, smirking. "So Sweetwater is taking you to their bosom? After one week of being around Co-op people, I know the significance of *that*."

"How's the pasta primavera?"

"I haven't tried it yet. I've only eaten here twice so far."

"Well I think that's what I'm going to have." Hazel looked up from the menu and smiled. "Isn't it remarkable, Anne? Here we are, both of us service-techs, eating out by ourselves, real food and even wine—for lunch!"

Anne put her menu down. "I know what you mean," she said, glancing around at the people sitting at the other tables. "Always before we could only do this kind of thing when we came with our lovers. I don't know, for some reason it adds something to the experience, being able to do it for yourself." Her brow wrinkled. "And it's not just because Liz set me up with some Co-op credit to start with—I already know that on the salary they pay me at the Press—and that's not counting the share of the Press's profits I'll be getting—I'll easily be able to afford to eat out two or three times a week. I don't understand it, either." Hazel raised her eyebrows. "That there's such a high standard of living in a place that doesn't even *believe in* The Good

Life. I mean, why is it affordable for service-techs here, but not in the rest of the country?"

"Good question," Hazel said.

Anne stood up. "Let's go order our food and get ourselves some wine and bread to get started on. I'm starving."

As Hazel followed Anne to the front of the restaurant she wondered if anyone knew the answer to Anne's question. It certainly seemed an important one—for service-techs, if not for executives.

After they ordered, they carried water, a carafe of white wine, glasses, napkins, solid, non-disposable flatware, and bread back to their table. Hazel said, "What did you mean when you referred to sharing in the Press's profits?"

Anne poured wine from the carafe into their glasses. "It's crazy how they work things at the Press." She took a sip from her glass. "In the first place, everyone that works there is supposed to have some say in what the Press prints. There are meetings to discuss prospective projects, and then once they're decided on, while the project is being carried out, the author, editor, and typesetter have meetings and discuss various aspects of the project." Anne leaned forward. "It was on Monday that Venn asked me if I'd be *interested*—that's the word she used, Hazel—*interested* in typesetting a novel. The thing is, I'd have to input the entire thing from scratch. The person who wrote it lives in Wisconsin and is basically off the grid, and so she wrote it out longhand."

"What did she mean by *interested?*" Hazel wondered. "Whether you could stand to do that kind of transcription work?"

"That's only part of it," Anne said. She took another sip of wine. "Because it will likely be a long and possibly aggravating job, the typesetter is asked to read the manuscript before agreeing to do the project. If the typesetter finds something objectionable about it, then she or he can turn down the project." Anne shook her head. "When she hired me Venn gave me this long spiel about how the Press felt that people shouldn't be forced to support or more especially help bring into existence projects they found morally or politically objectionable." Anne flashed a grin at Hazel. "These people are incredible. I typeset an article on Monday about a controversy among the public facilities workers over whether or not the Public Facilities Co-op should refuse services to the consulates of governments who've been condemned for human rights violations. It's a wonder *anything* gets done around here at all."

"So are you going to do this novel?"

Anne ripped a hunk off the golden round of bread and dipped it in olive oil. "Sure. *I* don't care about it. Though it makes me feel a little odd. Because the novel's about some feminists in Madison, Wisconsin, who belong to the Night Patrol—I gather from what Venn said that they had one there even before the Blanket. Though the story takes place at the time of the Blanket and the Civil War." She leaned forward and whispered. "Kay Zeldin makes an appearance in the story—supposedly a month before she was captured. Can you believe it? You know how crazy people are about her around here. I bet that's why the Press decided to publish the novel. Venn claims the novel would never be published in the US." Anne snorted. "She thinks a lot of books don't get published because of their political content." Anne bit into the bread.

"You could ask for a different project," Hazel said. "Maybe they really mean what they say about refusing projects you find objectionable."

Anne chewed and chewed, then finally swallowed. "I don't care *that* much. Maybe I feel a little traitorous inputting a book that glorifies traitors, but I don't want to call attention to myself, either. Liz made a big point of that when she was briefing me." The pager they had been given when they ordered went off. "I'll get it, we don't both have to go," Anne said, rising to her feet.

Hazel sat back in her chair, sipped her wine, and stared out into the park at the tall, leafy maple trees. Imagine, she thought, deciding you didn't want to work on a project because you found it morally repugnant. It *was* incredible. She could just see herself having refused to prepare that last report Liz had written for Security, outlining a plan for treachery and deceit to be exercised against Martha and other Co-op people. Liz would have thought her either demented or disloyal or both. Working on a job meant taking orders. And orders by universal practice were always meant to be obeyed, not debated. Except, it seemed, in the Free Zone.

[ii]

At the Emma Goldman celebration that evening, food, drink, talk—all of it outdoors in the balmy open air—intoxicated Hazel with its easy and amiable abundance. A steady stream of women and men stopped to chat with Martha, who repeatedly introduced Hazel to new faces as Marjorie Burroughs. Many of the people present were from the Whidbey Science Center, the Whidbey Clinic, Oak Harbor, and Coupeville, perhaps a quarter of them men. Each time one of the Sweetwater women stopped to chat Hazel and Martha were regaled with quotes from Emma Goldman's writings. Excessive quoting and the heavy use of glittersticks, Martha explained to Hazel, always formed a part of Sweetwater's celebration. All day the women spouted quotations at everyone they encountered. Of course they often duplicated one another and frequently punctuated their recitations with wisecracks and smirks. One quote in particular, "Revolution is but thought carried into action," Hazel heard at least a dozen times. As a one-liner it wasn't bad.

Hazel bit into a sweet juicy apricot and nodded at the friend Martha was introducing. The skimpily clad, elaborately tattooed woman—Ariadne—sat down with her glass of wine and held forth with a long passage of Emma's about "inner regeneration" and the "right to love and be loved." Something in Ariadne's recitation evoked an overwhelming poignancy in Hazel. When she finished, Hazel said, "I think I'd like to read some of her writings."

Ariadne's eyes lit up. "She certainly had a way with words. Apparently she was such a fantastic speaker that she could rabble-rouse crowds into precipitate action." She bit her lip. "But some things Emma didn't understand. I don't agree with every word she ever wrote or spoke. And I suppose by the end of her life she didn't either. But that's always the case with serious political thinkers, don't you agree?"

"I haven't actually thought about it," Hazel said, a little uncomfortable. She'd never read political writings much less thought about the people who produced them.

"Isn't it about time for them to be starting the music?" Martha asked. "That's always been *my* favorite part." She looked at Hazel.

"Here at Sweetwater, they usually perform a lot of songs that have been written about Emma—there've been a surprising number of them over the years. And of course since we first started celebrating Emma's birthday there've been a lot of new ones written specifically for our celebrations."

"Every year the repertoire expands," Ariadne said. "Singing, dancing, playing. Not to mention readings, of course."

"And the play tomorrow night," Martha said. That had been mentioned in the newspaper. It was to be performed at a theater in Coupeville.

"Both performances are sold out." Ariadne filched a cherry from Martha's plate and popped it into her mouth.

"Then it's a good thing we got our tickets in advance," Martha said. "Though I gather one of the professional companies is putting it on in Seattle, too."

"Ah," Ariadne drawled, spitting out the pit, "but we're more *sincere* than they are. We've got Emma in our blood."

Martha grinned. "I'll give my opinion after I've seen the performance," she said. "Not that I have anything against amateurs."

"Martha, hi," a woman's voice said. The three of them looked up at the two women looming over them.

"Happy Emma Goldman Day, Evonne," Martha said, smiling. "How are you, Elena?" she added to the other woman.

The other woman forced a smile. "Not in a very celebratory mood," she said.

"I'm glad you came anyway. Is Luis here?"

The woman shook her head. "He prefers to avoid anything in the least bit political, even when they're parties."

"Will you join us?" Martha said.

"I'm sorry, but I've already arranged to meet Susan."

"See you later then," Martha said as the two women moved off. Martha looked at Ariadne. "Thanks for refraining from quoting at her. I'm surprised she even made it here tonight."

Ariadne nodded. "Me, too."

Martha turned to Hazel. "That woman's daughter has disappeared. You may know of Celia, I think. She's the International Human Rights Committee's monitor for the Southwest US."

Hazel said, "Celia Espin? Yes, of course. And I've met her uncle—briefly. In your office, actually, do you remember?" She remembered Martha's argument with Anne, and that Luis had just been released from prison, and she reached for her sweater. It was all extremely creepy and sad.

"I may be arrested, I may be tried and thrown into jail, but I never will be silent," said an especially glittery Sweetwater woman as she sank down onto their blanket.

"How apropos, Jessel," Martha said dryly. "Meet Hazel Bell," she added.

Hazel smiled at Jessel. "You should be introducing me by my alias," she reminded Martha. "Even if it is a horrible name." Why Liz had chosen such an awful name for her was beyond Hazel.

"Right," Martha said ruefully. "Forget what I said, Jessel. Just call her Mar."

"Well that *is* a little better than Margie," Hazel said.

"Any particular reason for going by an alias?" Jessel asked curiously. "Or shouldn't I ask?"

Martha offered Jessel a sardonic smile. "Only that the SIC is after her."

Jessel's mouth rounded into an O. "Never mind," she said self-mockingly.

Ariadne slanted Hazel a curious look. "I keep hearing that someday the SIC and ODS will self-destruct. Let's drink to that." She raised her glass and clinked it against those of Martha, Hazel, and Jessel. "So Mar it is," Ariadne added after drinking. "Though your true name is so distinctive it's a shame to have to give it up." The amplified sound of a guitar rippled through the air. "Yes! It looks like they're getting ready to start the entertainment."

Hazel shifted around to face the platform and watched one of the guitar-bearing women step front center. "As we all know, Emma thought people should have a good time while engaged in the revolutionary process." She grinned. "Which is why we're going to start with the same Emma-tune we always start with, the one written by Holly Near in the 1980s. Needless to say, if anyone gets the urge to dance, we'll take that as tribute to both Emma and Holly."

The musicians got started, and as they played, several more in-strumentalists mounted the platform and joined them. The first time through Hazel didn't catch many of the words, partly because the sight of bodies springing up out of the grass to dance and leap with abandon made her more aware of the beat than the words. But she did make out "I'm dancing, Emma!" Something about the song nagged her with a sense of familiarity she couldn't put her finger on. Then, after several iterations of the refrain, it came to her: long ago she had heard an abbreviated form of this song. A different version of it had been among Aunt Dawn's collection of what she called "Women's Music" on CDs that she would play (when both Mom and Dad were out of the house, of course) before the Blanket had spoiled the enter-tainment center.

After a couple iterations of the song, the musicians detoured into variations of the tune. A young man Hazel didn't know drew Martha into the dance. Smiling, Ariadne leaned her dark fuzzy head close, and Hazel felt its softness brushing against her cheek. "Feel like dancing?" she said into Hazel's ear.

Dancing was something Hazel had never done much of—and never to this kind of rhythm, so different from modern music. But the beat was so strong that she was already moving her body to it. So she smiled at Ariadne, and together they leaped up from the blanket and, holding hands, joined the others "dancing at [their] revolution."

# Chapter Fifty-four

As dark falls over the ocean, Astrea lands the pod on the beach and with no trouble at all finds the way into the woman's house. She is sitting at a desk, facing the open window. "Emily," Astrea calls softly.

The woman whirls to point a weapon at Astrea. She looks puzzled for a moment, then says, "Astrea?"

"Yes. Why do you point a weapon at me, Emily?"

Emily lays the weapon down on the desk. "I'm nervous these days," she says.

"Have you found your friend? I talked to her mother today, and she seemed to think you hadn't."

Emily looks pained. "Not yet. It's very hard this time. I'm wracking my brains trying to figure out what to do next. I've tried everyone I can think of. No one will admit they have her or know where she is." She sighs. "How is Elena?"

"She's terribly sad." So sad, in fact, that being in the same room with her had made Astrea sad, too. Astrea remembers the scene on the pod at the end of that long horrible night, the scene of Emily and Elena weeping in one another's arms, and of many others weeping quietly by themselves. "I want to help, Emily. If you can think of places where she might be, I'll take you to them in camouflage. We can search for her together."

Emily's face changes, her eyes widen and grow a darker, more intense brown. "You'll help me? By yourself?"

"I'll be sufficient," Astrea says. "But I'll need you to tell me places to look. We'll start tonight. And if we don't find her tonight, we'll try other nights, for as long as you can think of places for us to look."

"Thank you, thank you so much!"

Astrea shapes a smile on self's human face and extends a hand. "Tell me where we should go first."

Emily guides self to yet another place filled with the instruments of war. Astrea scans every structure but finds only armaments and personnel. They go next to another military place—and there, scanning, Astrea finds prisoners. In camouflage they move through the structures, searching through the dozens of prisoners. "So many," Emily says. "There are so many! I never guessed!" Once they come upon a scene of pain and misery. "The screams hardly sound human," Emily whispers.

The terrible anger flares up, suffusing Astrea's soma, making it harder and harder to go on without intervening. "We must not do anything, for we're only on reconnaissance," Astrea whispers to Emily, trying to talk to self the way Magyyt and Sorben had that other night of reconnaissance. But the anger grows, and repeated epithets and words beat a tattoo in Astrea's consciousness, stirring hatred and fear of creatures who would do such things, feeding a fierce desire to instantly stop such creatures once and for all. The others have insisted that the Boldeni were like that, that humans are not unique in their cruelty to and exploitation of other selves, and that extermination only contaminates the selves that engage in such destruction of life. Astrea finds that hard to believe.

When they return to the pod after having looked at every prisoner on the base, Astrea scans below for a long time. And then, too angry to stop, this Marq'ssan destructures everything that can be destroyed without harming living creatures. Somehow Astrea holds back from killing those that cause the most loathsome of feelings, con-fining the rage that threatens to consume self in a conflagration like none self has yet known. It is difficult to remember why self must not kill them, difficult to think of them as creatures that must be allowed to live.

When the destructuring is finished, Astrea goes on to the next place Emily names. Emily of course knows nothing of the destructuring. Imagining what Sorben and Magyyt might say about it, Astrea decides to tell no one. It will be self's secret.

# Chapter Fifty-five

Alexandra sat down at the piano for the first time in three days. Instead of starting with the usual scales and technical exercises, she opened the concerto score to the second movement and began playing the transcription of the orchestral introduction, imagining the muted strings and lilting winds as she played. When she came to the piano's entrance, the fingers of her right hand squeezed out a lyrical pianissimo, each note of the first two phrases' falling lines clear and distinct yet in their fluidity melting into the others. In the third phrase, the first in which the line rises and the tension begins to build, she let the poignancy she always felt when playing these notes pour out of her until the orchestra—played of course by herself—took the line and finished it.

Alexandra lost herself in the movement's power. But as the tension mounted in the long series of trills straining upward in increasing intensity, she grew aware of her father standing behind her. She tried to shake off the awareness, but he put his hands on her shoulders, and his touch sent waves of sensation rippling through her body. Finally, finally, the intensity of the trills culminated, carrying her into the piano's first statement of the theme with which the orchestra had opened the movement.

She played on until she reached the final low B that would drop to B-flat in an abrupt transition to the third movement, when her father said, his voice barely audible, "Don't go on to the next movement."

Alexandra took her hands from the keys. She swallowed hard, feeling suddenly out of control of herself, her feelings, her senses. "I've never heard it played quite like that," he said. "I've always found that movement a little boring, something one had to get through in order to hear the rondo."

"I think it's very powerful," Alexandra said evenly. "Even though it's so simple and delicate."

His fingers tightened. "Yes. I can feel that in your playing. I enjoyed it immensely."

Alexandra raised her hand to the score and closed it and tried to think of what she would play next.

"We're early," he said. "Come down to the study with me so that I can brief you a little on this evening's concerns."

"You think that's necessary?"

"Of course. Why else would I ask Warner to hostess the dinner?"

Alexandra attempted to hurry out of the room ahead of him, but he caught her up and took her arm. "Let's see how you look," he said. She stood quite still with eyes averted while he inspected her appearance. "Almost perfect," he said. "Except that you need something interesting in the way of jewelry. Something rich and vivid, to complement your coloring." That was one way of putting it, Alexandra thought. But then she had *his* complexion, not Mama's delicate, transparent perfection.

As they descended the staircase she tried to think of what she could say—without either offending or enlightening him—to get him to not touch her at all. To have this response to a man was in itself horrible, and most definitely non-executive; but when that man happened to be her father, it passed the stage of being horrible and became nothing short of monstrous. Insanity, Alexandra told herself, a degrading, perverse sickness. I look at him and find him repulsive on sight. I think about what kind of person he is—did he really order that man Taggart to *kill* people?—and I feel nauseated. But somehow none of that seems to matter when he touches me. It's the worst kind of bestiality conceivable, that I could think and know and see one thing and *feel* something totally contrary to my perceptions and judgments. How can this be? Am I insane?

"Have a sherry with me?" he asked as she sat down in one of the pair of massive chairs flanking the fireplace.

She shook her head. "I'd better not. Not if I'm going to be drinking wine at dinner."

He slanted a penetrating look at her. "Good idea. We'll be having sherry before dinner with the guests anyway. I'll wait, too." He settled himself in the other chair. "Let's run over the guest list. First, Heinrich Goetler, Austria's Ambassador to the United States. Ludwig Muller—officially the Austrian embassy's cultural attaché, but in reality their top intelligence man in the US. And then of course there's Crannock. And the Undersecretary of State for European Affairs, Basil Sanderson. And last but not least, Baldridge, a Company man Hill pulled because Weatherall had brought him along, but whom I've reinstated." His eyes glinted, and she knew he was enjoying the lesson. "Take a guess at the reason for this particular assemblage."

"Does it have something to do with Austria's involvement in the human rights issue with the aliens and anarchists?"

"Very good," her father approved. "That's one aspect of our problem with Austria, certainly. Their cozy relations with the anarchists generally, and the specific fact that a representative of the Austrian government was present at the time the aliens and terrorists raided the Federal Detention Facility in El Cajon. There's another connection, however, that I don't think you're aware of." His eyes narrowed. "Apparently they've made some kind of alliance with Weatherall."

"What!" Alexandra studied his face. "But how? And why? Why would they be allied with her?" Alexandra's pulse raced: so Elizabeth hadn't simply run away! She was *doing* something! Which, Alexandra realized, was what her father had been saying for months... "*Why* is perhaps the most important question of all," he said slowly, rubbing two fingers over his chin. "As for *how*, at the very least they're channeling messages to her."

"You're going to try to make them tell you where she is?" Alexandra asked somewhat breathlessly. It would be *terrible* if he found out where Elizabeth was.

"Fat chance they'd tell me voluntarily. But they might be interested in communicating certain things to me. Their reasons for dealing with her in the first place, for instance. If, that is, there's something they hope to get out of us in return."

"You mean they may be helping her so that you'll do something for them that they want very much, simply to induce them to stop helping her?"

He grinned. "You see. All it takes is a thorough reading of Machiavelli, and even someone your age can catch on to modern diplomacy in no time." His grin faded. "But we'll see if we can't put a little pressure on. Austria is small beer, after all. And they heavily depend on us for their security, as anyone looking at a map of Europe must realize."

"If that's true, then why would they risk our abandoning them?"

He gave her a sharp look, as though her even raising such a question rendered her suspicious. "They know we're unlikely to do that," he said. "Doing so would put the security of Western Europe on the line."

"Then how are you going to pressure them?" Alexandra asked.

"There are other sources of leverage."

That was about as vague as you could get, Alexandra thought. "But they seem to have us over a barrel?"

"That's a damned stupid thing to say." He frowned at her. "How can so small a government have *us* over a barrel? It makes as much sense as talking about a mouse having a tiger over a barrel."

"But if the security of Western Europe depends on their cooperation with us—" Alexandra began.

"Look, Alexandra," he said impatiently. "Military factors are just that: factors. They don't determine everything. To refer you back to Machiavelli, military power is there to be used for making certain diplomatic moves possible. Military power is a threat, a factor in strategy, and in most cases should be nothing more. The fact that those idiots raided Cameroon is not to be taken as a model for sound diplomacy. Although if we're clever, we can now, of course, *use* the fact of those raids to further manipulate and intimidate Austria."

Alexandra didn't understand any of it. "Is there anything…you expect of me?" she asked, worried he might make some new demand completely beyond her.

"Pay attention and look intelligent. Oh, and see if you can engage Crannock in particular. His presence is more a matter of propriety than anything else. He can only get in the way of Baldridge, Sanderson, and my own efforts. Not, you understand, that anything will be worked out at this sort of gathering. But some things may be communicated and possibly set into motion." Again he rubbed his chin with two fingers. "My main reason for having you there is to accustom you to these sorts of affairs, to further educate you. After it's all over we'll discuss what did and didn't happen."

A knock sounded, and the door opened and Alice Warner came in. Even in evening clothes she looked frighteningly severe. "Any special instructions, Mr. Sedgewick?"

"You've had them show you both the dining room and the drawing room?"

"Yes. Sherry in the drawing room before dinner?"

"Right. As for after dinner, I'll decide on that based on how things are going at the time."

Alice swished out. Alexandra envied her composure and wished her father would let her take such a normal, inconspicuous role herself, instead of leaving her role-less among a group of powerful males. As hostess she wouldn't have been noticed—which was probably, she reflected, precisely why her father had insisted that Alice assume that role at this dinner.

[ii]

So they'd had sherry, and then dinner, and then port, and then dessert followed by coffee, and now, at eleven o'clock and still seated around the dining room table, they were drinking cognac—everyone except Alice, of course.

But finally they'd gotten around to the subject of the aliens, and the ambassador waxed enthusiastic over all the benefits of "working with" the aliens and the North American Free Zone, including their considerable assistance with cleaning up nuclear plants that had been impacted by the Blanket as well as other ecological disasters that had been around for decades. "The aliens have a technology superior to ours that can be used for constructive purposes. Why pass up such benefits? You will note, Mr. Sedgewick, that we've suffered no ill-effects from our association with them. Our social and political structures have not toppled, we have not been overrun by anarchists or communists, and, of course, none of our industries have been destroyed. They haven't touched *our* chemical plants."

"They're drawing you into their net," Papa said. "Slowly they are pulling you into dependency. It's an old game, Your Excellency. But eventually there will be a price to pay. Suppose they insist you open up a Free Zone in Austria? What then?"

"They do not dictate to us, my friend," the ambassador said. "They don't even have a say in who is to represent Austria in our dealings with them."

"But what is it that Austria is required to do in return for so much bounty?" Baldridge said. "Or are we expected to believe that the same aliens who destroyed the world as we once knew it are Fairy Godmothers simply crying out to shower the benefits of their superior technology on the human species?"

"We trade with the North American Free Zone, not with the aliens themselves." The ambassador's tone was rather short.

"And you give sanctuary to the terrorists favored by the aliens," Papa said, his voice smooth and cool as the chilled cream of spinach soup they'd drunk earlier in the evening.

"As well as make speeches against the US before the United Nations," Baldridge added.

"No need to continue, Baldridge," Papa said. "The point has, I think, been sufficiently made that Austria is not being the best of, ah, friends with one of the very best friends she has in the world."

Alexandra tilted her glass against her lips and as it clicked against her teeth realized there was no cognac left in it. How had she drunk it so fast without noticing? As she set the glass down she caught Alice's eye on her. Flushing, she glanced up the table at her father. Alice seemed to disapprove of her as much as her mother did. The ambassador had said something that her father didn't like, she could see it in the way he had twisted his lips. She'd have to try to glean from the conversation exactly what he'd said: it must be important.

"And apart from the obvious dangers to us of sharing intelligence with a government who is dealing openly and directly with our enemies is the added complication of your developing connection with a renegade from the SIC, the person who tops Security's most wanted list," Papa was saying. What was it she had missed? She glanced at Muller and observed him shaking his head very slightly at the ambassador, who sat diagonally across the table from him.

"Is this an official complaint, Mr. Sedgewick?" the ambassador suavely queried.

"What Robert is saying——" Crannock said, but Papa cut him off.

"It's quite unnecessary for you to interpret my words to the ambassador, Walter. What I am saying, Your Excellency, is that trafficking with my government's enemies is hazardous to the health of our general and specific relations. How do you expect the SIC to share intelligence with your people when you've given us distinct reasons not to trust them? Weatherall, especially, is a case in point. I can't imagine what your excuse for dealing with her can possibly be."

Muller and Goetler exchanged a look. A service-tech came into the room and went around the table replenishing everyone's cognac snifter. Alice must have gotten a signal from Papa, Alexandra thought. When the service-tech left the room, Goetler, swirling the cognac around and around in his glass, said almost casually, "Security Services might do well to consider making peace with Weatherall. She's no enemy to the executive system, Mr. Sedgewick. And she has a fast-growing following."

Papa snorted. "Women renegades, no doubt."

The ambassador shook his head. "Not only women, not anymore. You're underestimating her, my friend."

Papa turned to Muller. "She's probably more of a threat—at least an immediate threat—than the aliens. Do you want women running your system? That's the one thing she has in common with the anarchists and aliens. They all want power in the hands of females."

Alexandra took a large gulp of cognac. If they were going to start talking about women she might as well crawl under the table right now. She hated it when he talked about women. Any second now he'd start saying crude and obscene things... She would prefer to hear more about what Elizabeth was up to. It still seemed mind-boggling that the Austrian government would risk alienating the US to help her.

[iii]

As they walked through the grass in the dark Alexandra noticed that hardly any stars came out at night in DC. She stumbled, but her father held her steady. "You're drunk, Persephone," he said.

"Yes," she said sadly, "I know. You can tell?"

"If nothing else, your flush gives you away. Why do you think I kept us all at the table instead of moving back into the drawing room?"

"Oh. Are you angry with me?"

"You were quiet, Persephone. In your shoes Daniel would have shot his mouth off, or otherwise embarrassed me. I should have realized the full gambit from sherry to wine to port to cognac would be too much for you. You held up fairly well until the cognac. No, of course I'm not angry with you. What was it Crannock said to you, anyway?"

"Oh him. He wanted to tell me about how diabolical the aliens are."

"Diabolical? Was that the word he used?"

"Yes. Diabolical. That they disguise themselves as humans but they're really horrible, demon-like reptiles planning to rule the world and use humans as slave labor and food."

A low laugh rumbled in his throat. "Oh, that's wonderful. Crannock is as loony as Devito was."

"What *do* the aliens want?"

"They want first of all for us to fall into anarchy. As for their ultimate purpose, who knows? I don't see that as important. What matters is holding onto our civilization. Clearly that's key. They need for our civilization to fall before they can accomplish their ends. It's why we need to organize the massive campaigns for preserving civil order that I'm initiating."

"Where are the gorillas?" Alexandra asked, suddenly concerned that they might be shot while wandering around the grounds of the house. "Do they know we're walking out here?"

"Gorillas?" he queried. "What in the hell are you talking about?"

"Oh," Alexandra said, realizing she'd used a women's term. "I mean the security detail," she mumbled, abashed at her slip.

"You call them gorillas?" He sounded half-amused, half-incredulous.

She decided she would be clever by letting him think it was her personal idiosyncratic term. "Well they're so hulking big and loutish," she said. "They especially look like gorillas when they're working out."

"Better not let them hear you, Persephone."

But of course the gorillas knew what the women called them. It was only the executive males who didn't know. Alexandra sighed. "I want to ask you something," she said.

"Then ask me."

He would probably say no. But she would ask anyway. "Mama's going to Norway in two weeks. To see the sun all night." That wasn't exactly right, but it was something to do with the arctic circle and the summer solstice. "Can I go with her? It would only be for a week."

"She's going to Norway? For that?" He snorted. "What will her crowd of parasites think of next? No, my dear, you may not go. No doubt slumming, too—there's very little of Norway I can imagine your mother finding of interest."

"I haven't had my week with her this summer."

"You can see her whenever you like right here in DC," he said. "Everything's different now when it comes to your security, you know. You can't go gallivanting off into unknown situations as if you were just anybody. Look at Goodwin—he's a basket case. And he wasn't particularly close to his son, either. I doubt if he was as close to him as I am to you."

"Let's sit down in the grass for a while," Alexandra said. "I like the smell of the roses here." The grass was dry and pleasantly cool. The breeze made the muggy air just bearable, Alexandra thought, lying flat on her back. For a few seconds she felt dizzy, but the dizziness passed. Yes, she was drunk. She knew Alice found her disgusting. But *he* wasn't angry. "The ambassador wasn't afraid of you," she said, searching for the Big Dipper in the sky.

"No, he was angry. And arrogant as hell. Did you notice his telling me that there was nothing I could do to make Austria uncomfortable enough to drop their liaisons with the aliens, anarchists, and Weatherall?"

"I didn't understand very much of the things he said about NATO and Europe," Alexandra admitted.

His hand clasped hers on the grass between them. "Why remark on his not being afraid of me, Persephone?"

He shouldn't call me Persephone, Alexandra thought. "Almost everyone's afraid of you," she said. "Even Crannock."

He snorted. "Crannock is an idiot." Finding the Big Dipper, she soon traced out the Little Dipper. But where was Orion? After a long silence he said, "Do you count yourself among the 'almost everyone,' Persephone?"

Apprehension coiled in her belly. Alexandra disengaged her hand from his. After a long pause she asked, "Why do you think the Austrians are helping Weatherall?"

His fingers lightly clasped her wrist, and his thumb moved over and over that small area of skin on the inside, sending shimmering waves of sensation up her arms, into her breast, down into her groin. "But you're not afraid of me, Persephone, are you."

"I think you like for everyone to be afraid of you," Alexandra whispered.

"Let's not talk about 'everyone.' Let's stick to ourselves. You're not at all afraid of me, are you. Because you know I love you."

Alexandra thought of suggesting they go in now. "You like for people to be afraid. For me, too," she said softly, and felt her body quiver at her audacity.

"You're exaggerating," he said after a few seconds. "You don't like the ways I can make you uncomfortable when you do or say things you shouldn't. But you mustn't confuse that kind of apprehension with fear. It's important that you know that I'd never harm you. You do know that, don't you?"

"But," Alexandra said, struggling to find the words that would say some of what she was feeling, "You told me about what you did to that woman, Kay, you told me that to frighten me, didn't you. You said you loved her, but you hurt her anyway."

"Good god, sweetheart, I didn't tell you about Kay to *frighten* you." He rolled onto his side and lifted his head and moved it closer to hers, perhaps to try to make out her face in the dark. "I wanted you to know about her because she was one of the most important people in my life. Why should telling you about her intimidate you? I had nothing to do with her death—she brought that on herself when she went renegade. As for hurting her—there's a world of difference between hurt and harm, Persephone. She and I both hurt one another a great deal. But that's not the same as doing harm. Believe me, I would have prevented her death if I could. But it wasn't possible."

So what was he saying, Alexandra wondered. That short of worrying about that person killing oneself one did not feel fear of another? He leaned closer to her. At the touch of his fingers on her face, powerful waves of sexual sensation swept over her. His dark rich scent, so utterly different from any she had known, filled her nostrils.

"I think you feel as close to me as I feel to you," he said softly.

One part of her wanted to jump up and run away into the house and up the stairs to her room where she could lock herself in, away from him, where these feelings would be only phantoms in her head and nothing to do with this real flesh and blood person lying so close beside her. Another part of her longed for...something more. In spite of her fear, and in spite of her excruciating shame, this wanting part of her seemed to immobilize her, kept her lying still in the grass, savoring and hating the sensations that had spread over her entire body.

She lifted her hand to his face. She felt first smoothness, and then a roughness under her fingers which, she realized, was the part of the face men who did not have the beard gene treated had to shave. It repulsed her a little, but not enough to cut through the thick sensual fog enveloping her. Her fingers found his lips and, when he kissed them, pressed past them to his teeth. At the sudden contact between her fingers and his tongue a spear of sensation streaked from her breast to vulva.

"This is madness, Persephone. You don't know what you're doing."

But she brought her other hand up to his neck and felt his earring, and the shape of his ear, and his hairline as she stroked his neck and then let her hand slip down over the silk, to press him closer to her.

"Alexandra. You've had too much to drink. Tomorrow you'll regret this."

"*You're* always touching *me*," she said when he moved away from her.

"You're too old to be playing these kinds of games with me." His voice sounded cold and distant. "You're a grown woman. You should know what you're doing."

"I was forgetting," she said, "that you can't feel anything."

His voice was abrupt. "It's not that simple." He sat up. "Come, let's go in." He stood up and waited for her to get to her feet. Swaying under an attack of vertigo, she grabbed onto him. "Steady does it," he said. They started walking. "You'll want to drink lots of water and take a big dose of B-complex before going to bed. That way you won't feel quite so terrible between the time you wake up and the time you take your morning-after." But she hardly paid attention to what he was saying, for almost all her attention was concentrated on his arm circling her shoulders as they walked, laboriously, back to the house.

[iv]

Alexandra first woke at around five—with a heaving stomach and raging headache. She took the morning-after her father had left on the nightstand and stumbled into the bathroom to strip off her evening clothes (which she had gone to sleep in) and shower. Then she crawled back between the sheets, drank a half-liter bottle of water, and drifted in and out of sleep, intermittently falling into heavy dreams, only to wake and review over and over the scene in the grass.

She burned with the shame of having revealed her sickness to him. He must despise her now. She kept remembering the words he had used to talk about Clarice. That would be how he would be thinking of her, too, from now on. It was her uncontrolled female sexuality—shameful because she *hadn't* controlled it. She was living confirmation that everything the males said about unfixed females was true. What could be lower than lusting after her own father? And why *did* she, anyway? He was fifty years older than she, and male—his body could only be disgusting, she knew that—and unapologetically brutal. She must be perverted, or sick. If Mama knew she'd never speak to her again.

At 10:30 Alexandra still lay in bed—the drawn draperies preserving the room's dark silence—thinking of how she could never get up and go out into the rest of the house, wishing she could run away to Barbados. At the knock on the door she cursed her nakedness under the sheet and was trying to decide whether or not to tell the service-tech to wait while she went to get a gown when the door opened and her father walked in. She groaned and pulled the sheet up to her neck, only just managing not to pull it over her head. "How're you feeling?" he said, closing the door and coming over to the bed.

"As if I'd like to disappear." Alexandra stared at the hyper-modern painting of Beethoven hanging on the far wall.

He sat down on the edge of the bed, and Alexandra shifted toward the middle. "I meant your hangover," he said.

"The morning-after helped." She drew a deep breath. "Please don't tell Mama."

"Tell her what? That you drank too much and got a hangover?"

Alexandra swallowed. "You know what I mean."

"I imagine she'd be the last person I'd be likely to tell, don't you?"

"I don't know," Alexandra said. "You always want to blame her for everything bad you find in me."

"Yes, I thought you'd be embarrassed. That's really the worst of it, you know."

She darted a glance at him: he didn't have one of his nastier looks on his face. "It must be nice to be——" She barely caught herself from saying "fixed."

"You mustn't take this too seriously," he said. "People often have anomalous experiences when they're drunk. They don't mean anything. The best thing you can do is put it behind you and be glad it happened with me rather than with someone else."

She saw after a few seconds that he didn't take any of it seriously, that he assumed she had just been feeling the drink and had settled on him because he happened to be there. In other words, he dismissed it all as the temporary aberration of a child. Instead of relieving her, the realization angered and chagrined her. He could think of her as the same because her behavior was simply a manifestation of immature drunkenness, because she was too young and inexperienced. "Send me back to Barbados!" she said—and realized that she might not necessarily like life at her Grandmother's now.

"Don't make such a big deal of this. These things happen."

Alexandra made herself look into his eyes. "You don't understand anything." She hated his patronizing attitude. "I've been feeling this way since before we left Maine! I'm sick, don't you see? You *have* to send me away. There's something wrong with me."

He held out his hand to her. "First, give me your hand." Alexandra swallowed; hesitantly she moved her right hand from where it clutched the sheet at her neck and placed it in his outstretched palm. His fingers closed around hers. "Second, calm yourself. There's no reason whatsoever for getting hysterical. What we need to do is to talk calmly, clearly, and openly—for ambiguities can be very dangerous, Alexandra."

The last thing she wanted was to put any of what she was feeling into words, whether to him or to herself. Once put into words, anything could happen. Anyway, she didn't really *trust* him with her words.

"Do you agree with me, that we need to be open and honest with one another?"

"I'm so ashamed," Alexandra whispered. "Don't you see it would be best if you just sent me away?"

He shook his head. "That's the last thing I'll do. Apart from your welfare—which I can't see as being well-served by my abandoning you to a pair of irresponsible parasitic women—there's the not insignificant fact that you've become an important part of my life." He smiled. "Look at me, Alexandra: you've changed my life. You've turned me around. It's your doing, you know. Do you know why I'm wearing these clothes?" For the first time Alexandra noticed that he was wearing thin white muslin trousers and a matching short-sleeved tunic. She shook her head. "I've been out already this morning—if, you can imagine it—playing that ridiculous game, golf, with Whitney, Crannock, Goodwin, and Booth." He shook his head. "If you'd told me a year ago I'd get up at the crack of dawn to play golf with those men, I'd have laughed my head off. But here I am, as fully involved in the world as I've ever been. Because of you, Alexandra. Because of our love. So don't talk nonsense about my sending you away."

Alexandra wondered if that could be true. She'd been assuming that his depression was gone because he was wanted back in the Executive. Was she really more to him than a pawn to push around? *Would* it make him feel bad if she weren't there? Half the time he treated her like a child... He talked about love, but it was hard to believe. She stared at their clasped hands. "If that's true..." She bit her lip. "Then I'm sorry. But I don't see how I can bear staying here. I know it's going to get worse. At first it wasn't bad. But...it's getting harder. And last night... Somehow last night changed everything. I can't explain. But it has." She met his gaze. "If I go away, then I'll eventually stop feeling this way." She swallowed. "I can't even look at myself in the mirror. Please don't make me stay with you."

"In fact, what you're upset about is not your feelings and our relationship so much as guilt at coming up against a taboo. Right?"

"It's sick, and it's wrong," Alexandra stated.

"There's no such thing as sick and wrong when it comes to sexuality. These things are all a matter of social convention, Alexandra. This taboo, although it's nearly universal, exists within the context of concrete social structures and conveniences. As far as I'm concerned, as long as sexual behavior remains a private matter between individuals, there's no need to feel guilt. It's only when it becomes a matter of social importance that guilt enters into the picture. If you think about it that way, you'll see that if this remains strictly between us there's no need for talking about right and wrong."

"You're saying that people should feel guilty only when they're caught doing something wrong?" Alexandra asked.

"No, no, that's not what I'm saying. First of all, you have to get rid of this idea that it's wrong. Think of it this way: a lot of people still think that sexual relations between women is wrong. But you don't feel that way, do you." Alexandra shook her head. "That's because you've grown up in an atmosphere that considers such relations natural. But historically that hasn't always been the case. And among many people in American society at large it still isn't the case." Alexandra knew this was true; she had felt Nicole's disapproval, for instance, of her sexual relations with Clarice. "And incest between consenting adults falls into the same category. As do other sexual practices outside the accepted societal norm. So you see, it is a matter of which practices you've been raised to consider right and wrong. What I was saying about discovery is that there needn't be shame unless one is directly exposed to the condemnation of society. That as long as one keeps these things decently private, it's nothing to do with anyone but the people directly—and privately—involved." He smiled. "I came to understand this quite early. You see, before my surgery, my sexual practices weren't exactly, ah, the norm. I realized that as long as I kept my sexual life private and kept it from impinging on my public life, what I did could in no way be felt by myself to be socially—and thus morally—reprehensible. Morality is a matter of social relations. Where social relations are not involved, one need not suffer such socially inflicted disorders as shame and guilt."

How could saying these things make one stop feeling ashamed? Alexandra wondered.

"Does this help you at all?" he asked after a long silence.

Alexandra tried to withdraw her hand from his. "I don't see how it has anything to do with my problem. I mean, it would be like my having a mad passion for a heterosexual female. The only thing I could do would be to avoid her." Everyone knew that. The first thing one did when looking at a girl was to note whether or not she was heterosexual, precisely to avoid the problem of desiring someone entirely unavailable and unresponsive. One looked at girls differently, depending on their sexual identification.

"I said we should speak clearly and openly, Persephone." Alexandra winced at his use of that all-too-ironic name. "You're thinking that the reason I stopped you last night is because I'm disgusted by the very idea?"

Alexandra felt the blush return to her cheeks. "Not only is it sick, but you're desexualized. I told you I know how stupid this whole thing is. I know the feelings can only be one-way."

"Not at all. The reason I stopped you last night is because you were drunk. In something this serious between us it's essential that both of us know what we're doing. I'm not unwilling to add a sexual dimension to our relationship. And by the way, though I don't have strong genital sensations, that isn't to say that I've no sexual feelings whatever, or that I can't take a certain sort of pleasure in sexual activities."

Alexandra looked at him in sudden fear. "You mean—?" She could not say it. "But I don't know… I don't think we… I mean, we can't just…"

"I see," he said rather dryly. "It's a very different thing when we talk so cold-bloodedly about it. Last night if I hadn't stopped you, you would have been faced with a *fait accompli* when you'd sobered up. And thus wouldn't have a sense of responsibility." He shook his head. "I'm not going to assume sole responsibility for this, Alexandra. It's your decision. I'll accept whatever you decide. But I want no misunderstanding between us about my pressuring you into something you didn't understand or didn't want. Considering that I'm your father and thus in a position of authority over you, every precaution has to be taken against even subtle forms of pressure." He smiled at her. "As I said last night, I love you, and don't want to harm you. I'd like to be as close to you as you'll allow me." His eyes grew somber. "I think you understand very well that if we did add a sexual dimension to our relationship, our feelings for one another would grow much more intense. Intense sexuality is always a frightening prospect, Persephone. You're right to sense that and react with caution." He paused, and Alexandra knew he wanted her to say something, but she had no idea of what to say. Words at this point seemed too dangerous, too significant. "Tell me what you're thinking and feeling," he urged when she remained silent.

"I'm upset," Alexandra heard herself saying. "I want to go away." Her eyes filled with tears. She wanted Grandmother, she wanted to be safe in Grandmother's house where she wouldn't have to think of any of this terrible stuff, where she would be away from him. "Please send me away," she begged.

"You're not a child, Alexandra. I've already told you I'm not going to do that. It's not an option. You'll have to choose among the options you have at hand. You're old enough to know that you can't always run away from things because they're difficult or unpalatable."

"It's not fair to make me stay!"

"Don't talk to me about fair," he said, his voice suddenly cold. "Circumstances are circumstances. There is no such thing as fair. You want me to make it easy for you so that you don't have to take responsibility for your own decisions. All your life you've had your decisions dictated to you. That's been your mother's doing. You could either accept them or rebel against them, but they were never your decisions and you didn't have to consider them anything more than a given you could either react passively to or take a scornful attitude toward. That's the way most people are, Alexandra. Taking responsibility is what distinguishes the best executives from the rest of the world. It's time for you to begin to do that." He released her hand, took a folded handkerchief from his pocket, and passed it to her. "I realize you think I'm being terribly hard on you, but later on you'll understand what I'm saying and see that I'm right."

Alexandra blew her nose into his handkerchief. "I'm so confused."

"Yes, of course you are. You need to do some thinking. You haven't really thought about any of this, have you." She shook her head. "No, of course not," he murmured. "Well now you will. When you're ready to talk about this again, we'll talk. You know you can ask me anything, don't you?"

No, Alexandra thought, I don't know that at all. But she nodded, since the question was rhetorical.

"Good." He got up from the bed. "I'll be working in the study for the rest of the morning. After lunch I'll probably go in to the office. We're still on for the dance concert tonight?"

Alexandra nodded again, still unable to speak.

"Good. I'll see you at lunch then, if not sooner." He bent and kissed her on the nose. "Don't make yourself miserable, Persephone. Nothing is that terrible, you know." He turned and left the room.

Alexandra pressed her face into the pillow. If only she *could* run away. She felt as though she were drowning and he had just refused to let her climb into the only lifeboat. And she thought she knew why, too: he was pleased about this; for some reason he was pleased that she had sexual feelings for him. Whatever he said about it being her decision, he *wanted* her to "add a sexual dimension" to their relationship. Somehow she knew this, even though none of it had been stated. Not only was he holding all the cards and cheating, but he wouldn't let her fold her hand and leave the game, either. He called these things circumstances, but they were circumstances he controlled. *He* wasn't being fair, for all he claimed all of this was her responsibility. But then *he* never played fair at all.

Of course, anyone could have told her that, anyone at all.

# Chapter Fifty-six

Astrea gives up: an hour's meditation has done little to help self understand the previous night's actions. But as if that weren't enough, when self emerges from the meditation chamber, it is to find Sorben and Magyyt in the corridor, waiting.

"We've come to see how your explorations are going," Sorben says.

"I'm learning a great deal." Astrea speaks truthfully, even as self struggles to maintain equilibrium.

"But working so on your own when you are new to human culture, you must have a lot of questions," Magyyt says, implying a willingness to explain or interpret Astrea's new experiences. "Where have you gone, what have you seen since we saw you last week?"

Astrea's field contracts involuntarily until self realizes and relaxes it. "Some of the time I've been going out with Emily Madden, helping her search for her missing friend."

Magyyt and Sorben exchange a long look. But in fact, Astrea observes, their fields are almost touching. Sorben says, "It must be difficult. You're so unused to humans. Have you visited the people Leleynl works with? Or spent much time in the Free Zones? Or met any of our many human contacts scattered around the planet? You need to see the possibilities, to see the positive, Astrea, lest the negative—which is so pervasive among humans—destroys your ability to stay among them."

"You're probably right," Astrea admits. "But I feel so strongly the pain of this woman's friend and mother and uncle that I must do what I can to help them."

"We can't solve the humans' problems," Magyyt replies. "Not even all of us together. Those of us who've stayed on here have chosen the methods best suited to each self. Who, after all, is to say what methods are most helpful to the humans? But before each of us began working actively, we spent years learning this world and its people. Not everything is comprehensible at once, Astrea."

"You think my efforts misplaced," Astrea says aridly. That one surmises that Sorben and Magyyt routinely see terrible things happen without attempting to do anything to stop them. Self might not understand all there is to know about humans, but self can understand which of them are beyond hope in the depths of their bestiality. Ending the life of another is wrong, clearly: but by not interfering in many of the situations self has observed on this planet one faced responsibility for not preventing other deaths. The humans are so depraved that the intricacies of Marq'ssan morality and philosophy are of no use in helping the humans to change. Whatever the heinousness of self's error, Astrea knows that to watch and do nothing would leave self equally if not more wrong for the many more lives that would inevitably be lost.

But it would be a mistake even to attempt to discuss this with Sorben and Magyyt. They have been on earth for so long that they have become calloused to brutality and bestiality. No one would ever link what happened to those humans with Astrea—or even with Marq'ssan in general. The men's hearts simply stopped beating. Humans will never know or even guess why. No one *could* know unless self confessed. And to confess would be in some way to consent to the horror of this planet. And that, self will never do.

# Chapter Fifty-seven

"He's alone and expecting you," Alice said. And Alexandra flinched at the frigidity in her voice.

Slowly she walked up the hall. By the time she reached the door of her father's office her mouth had dried, her cheeks were burning, her limbs and vulva aching, and her heart pounding painfully hard. Did her physical response stem from anxiety or desire? In truth, she could no longer tell the two constellations of sensations apart.

After a few seconds' hesitation, she pressed her thumb to the access plate. The door slid open, and she went in. For a moment she stood on the threshold, preventing the door from closing and locking; she stared at her father, sitting behind his desk, reading flimsies. The silence in the room seemed loud in her ears. Finally she approached the desk. "I got your message," she said.

He looked at her and removed his glasses. "So there you are. Did you enjoy lunching with your mother?" His eyes still held that look both speculative and knowing that had been there since Sunday.

Alexandra tensed. Obviously he meant it ironically. "How could I?" she asked bitterly. With her mother, now, she could only be false.

His smile was nasty. "You're right. Lunch with Raines would be a punishment too much for even a saint to bear."

"That's not what I meant!" Alexandra flashed out. "And you know it!"

He sighed. "Sit down, Alexandra, and for godsake lighten up. It was just a joke."

She took the chair before the desk and folded her hands in her lap. She had been avoiding him as best she could, though he behaved—*almost*—as though nothing had happened. But if his behavior hadn't significantly changed, in subtle ways his attitude had, as reflected by the expressions that came into his eyes when they were alone. Every time she saw him she wished afresh she hadn't exposed herself to him.

She felt ashamed and vulnerable. Knowledge of her secret seemed to have given him a terrible moral advantage over her, an advantage they were both acutely aware of.

"So far," he said, "I've received only the minutes of the TNC board meeting you managed a couple of weeks back. There's been nothing at all stirring from any of the parties who are supposed to report directly to this office. This project, I think, may be extremely important, at least judging by the sorts of propaganda Weatherall seems to be cranking out." At Alexandra's start of surprise, he snorted. "She's promising that if she is allowed to 'reorganize the Executive'—her words, by the way—she'll be able to arrange for an agreement with the aliens to leave our satellites alone."

He tossed his pen down in disgust. "Damn the bitch. And the Austrians and Dutch are lending her credibility, too." He drank from his coffee cup. "I've got to present the executive world with an alternative, for she's touched on a damned sensitive spot. She always understood just how important the com and vid networks were, of course. And if she *is* dealing with the aliens, then obviously she'll have vast advantages to offer over what *this* Executive can do or offer to do."

Why wouldn't the Executive agree to deal with the aliens? Alexandra wondered for the hundredth time. If Elizabeth and these other governments didn't fear the contact, why should the Executive? Elizabeth wasn't naive or irresponsible.

"I want you to get this project moving."

Alexandra gaped at him. "Me?"

"Because of Hill's purge, things are so fucking disorganized that I'm having to spend all my energy trying to repair Security's most basic organizational structures. You can feel your way through it. I don't expect miracles. But I want you to study the project file and try to learn everything you can about the parties involved. TNC is presumably overseeing most of the contractors. Fletcher has a list of them. Then there's Com & Tran's people, and ours, too. Fletcher's included in the project file a detailed flow-chart of all the component parts of the project and the parties responsible for each aspect. You'll need to make site visits to check on the parties involved, no matter who is designated as controlling them—checking out what they're doing, showing interest, and forcing them to toe deadlines—deadlines you can work out with Fletcher. That's the only way to make projects like these go at a reasonable speed. I've told Fletcher he can increase the budget for overtime and so on. You needn't be concerned with the financial end of it, since I've spared some of our best finance men to the project. What's needed is a little pressure." He smiled. "We can see what kind of a management style you're going to develop. You needn't be abrasive, you know. But they'll try to get around you. Your challenge will be to hold firm and make them commit themselves to meeting the project's demands."

Alexandra stared at him. She was just a kid. She hadn't even been to college yet! "If it's so important," she said, "then it shouldn't be left to me. No one's going to pay any attention to me."

"Don't start that again." He picked up his pen, and Alexandra stared at his broad, thick-fingered hands and the black hair that grew over them almost like fur. "Anyway, if you can't handle it, you can't handle it. Think of it this way—you'll do a better job than Fletcher. There's no sense my assigning this kind of executive job to a professional—and at this moment I seem to have only professionals available for this project. No one will pay Fletcher the slightest attention. He's a nonentity. And believe me, no one will think that of you. They'll try to get around you, but that's something you can learn to deal with."

"When will I be doing this?" Alexandra asked, knowing it would be useless to refuse.

He smiled, perhaps at her capitulation. "You can start Monday when we get back from California. I'll tell Warner to make an appointment for you with Fletcher. You can have the office next door. And by the way, when will they be remodeling this place, anyway?"

"During the month of August," Alexandra said. "What you just said about California...does that 'we' include me?"

He put down his pen and leaned back in his chair. "Yes, of course. We're going to pay a visit to the San Jose station. We'll stay for the weekend in the house at the winery. I'm intending to visit one or two domestic stations every week. In this case, I'm timing my visit to coincide with Wedgewood's initiation of the San Jose station personnel in our armed propaganda campaign. His trainers will be working with the local ODS men for close to a week. Wedgewood will be there part of the time. I thought it a good idea to give the boys a pep talk myself before Wedgewood started their training. In the past I've found that such personal efforts always boost morale enormously."

Things were bad enough without thinking about his horrible "armed propaganda" campaign. "Can't I stay in DC?" she asked, thinking of how horrible it would be to have to listen to his "pep talk"—which she'd heard three times already—and of how awful it would be to have to tour a station and meet more creeps.

He stared at her for a long time before answering. "I think it will do us good to get away. We can spend a little time in San Francisco; you'll like that, I know. And then it will be pleasant to stay at that house, it's so wonderfully quiet and peaceful."

He wanted her to have to be alone with him; she *knew* that was what he was really saying. "You won't let me go with Mama," she said, "because of security considerations. Can't I visit Grandmother in Barbados for a couple of weeks? That can't be so difficult a security situation, can it?"

He spoke into the handset on his desk. "Until further notice don't disturb me for anything short of a priority-one emergency, Warner." He put down the handset and looked at her. "If we're going to talk about private matters, then precautions must be taken. We don't want her walking in on this conversation, do we."

Alexandra did not reply. She had had no notion that asking not to go to California with him would lead to any of that other stuff.

He stood up and moved around the desk. "Let's go sit over there." He gestured to the furniture on the other side of the room.

"Can't I have just two weeks away?" Alexandra said, not looking at him. Maybe in two weeks she could pull herself together.

*Imagine two weeks away from him, free of that constant intense awareness of him. Imagine two weeks to re-find yourself, to free yourself...*

"Come," he said, moving toward her. Afraid he would touch her, Alexandra sprang to her feet and crossed the room and sank down into one of the ghastly engulfing chairs Hill's decorator had favored. Her father sat opposite her. "Don't think I haven't noticed you've been avoiding me. You're going to have to come to terms with your problem, Persephone."

"I *hate* your calling me that," Alexandra said desperately. "You make everything a mockery." She glared at him. "You put it all on me, you're saying it's my problem alone. Even though you won't let me go away. And even though it's your touching that starting everything."

His eyes narrowed. "I've never once touched you in a sexually suggestive way, Alexandra. And if you're honest you'll admit it."

"Men aren't supposed to touch us at all! *Any* touch is wrong!"

"That's the lamest thing you've said yet. And your persistence in using words like 'wrong' only further muddies the issue."

Tears pricked her eyes. "You say you love me. But if you really cared for me you wouldn't make me suffer like this. You'd send me away."

"Oh no you don't, my dear. I once sacrificed a great deal for love, and suffered terribly for it, more terribly than you can imagine. You talk so glibly about suffering, but you haven't the faintest idea of what suffering is. I'm not about to make that same mistake twice."

God. He was talking about *her* again! "How can you even want me around when I'm like this?"

He smiled. "Love, they say, is blind."

She glared at him.

"No, no, I'm *not* making fun of you. But the fact is, I do want you around, and I do love you, even when you're feeling sorry for yourself and being difficult. You're a strong person, Alexandra, and smart as a whip. You'll eventually find a way to come to terms with this situation, and then you'll wonder what all this fuss was about."

He always talked to her as if she were a *child*. "I hate you, you fucking *bastard!*" She snatched up the small glass sculpture on the table beside her chair and flung it at the tall brass floor lamp a foot or so to the right of his chair. When it struck the pole, it broke into pieces, one of which came within inches of her father's head.

He glanced at her, then knelt on the rug and retrieved the four largest pieces. Alexandra put her hand to her mouth; her entire body was shaking. He carried the pieces of glass over to his desk, then stood there, just looking at her. When he finally spoke, his voice was dry and weary. "It's hardly surprising that your feelings toward me are ambivalent. I seem to have a penchant for inspiring ambivalence in those I love. But however great your ambivalence, Alexandra, I strongly urge you to keep such thoughts to yourself. Like most people, I tend not to respond very well to such announcements."

Alexandra's eyes filled with tears. He *was* a bastard, but she was horrible, too. Violent. Like *him*. She cleared her throat. "May I go now?" Her voice came out high-pitched and trembling. Her heart, she noticed, was still racing.

"Yes, Alexandra, you may go. And tell Warner I'm again accessible."

Alexandra fled his office and wished she could flee herself, too.

# Chapter Fifty-eight

Hazel loved the view from Martha's deck. In the foreground below stretched the poplars and cedars and firs of Carkeek Park; in the distance lay Puget Sound, glistening blue under the fair evening sky, framed by the snow-capped Olympics at the edge of the horizon. "What a wonderful place this is to live," Hazel said as she took a piece of black cod between her chopsticks.

Martha fairly glowed. "For years I told myself I had to live exactly as I'd been living during the first years of the Free Zone—austerely, in Laura's house, which was collectively run. Even though I didn't lead the kind of life conducive to collective living. I mean, I was always disrupting the household's schedule. Looking back, I'm surprised they never asked me to leave. Finally, I convinced myself that I needn't feel guilty about living more or less alone." Martha laughed. "Though since I have a lot of visitors, the fact is that I'm seldom *alone* in this house." She popped a piece of fish into her mouth.

"With the kind of work you do I'd think you'd want some time and space to yourself," Hazel said between bites. "This negotiation you're facilitating for those two cooperatives or collectives or whatever they are sounds like it could be mighty aggravating."

Martha took a swallow of beer. "The problem is that everyone has different politics, different priorities. Some cooperatives work on a consensus basis, others on a democratic basis. Those that operate on one system often give differential treatment to those who operate on another. So that when single cooperatives then join larger cooperatives—for instance, a food co-op joining the collective made up of a lot of co-ops—there are built-in frictions from the start just based on whether or not the model used is consensus or majority rules. Everything—and I mean *everything*—has to be discussed. And then when new members come in they often want to change the rules the original members formulated. And then of course there are arguments about who to do business with and who not to do business with, and so on and so forth." Martha smiled wryly. "Fortunately this tends to be less my problem than Laura and her people's. I mainly deal with extra-Zone trade. Which is not to say that political issues aren't troublesome in extra-Zone trade. On the contrary. But often things are more clear-cut—except when dealing with cooperatives and collectives of the other Free Zones."

"It sounds terribly complicated," Hazel said. "I guess you have to have an easy-going nature to do that kind of work."

Martha shrugged. "I just try to separate the individuals I deal with from the policies they're pushing. Sometimes that's hard. As in the rare instances that I find it necessary to deal with multinational corporations."

Hazel ate a bite of rice and vegetables. Liz rated Martha as extremely adroit at the negotiating table. "Do you suppose the Executive will ever decide to negotiate with the Free Zone?" she asked, curious about Martha's opinion on such prospects.

"I wouldn't bet on it," Martha said. "From everything the executive-controlled press says, it looks as though an even more reactionary bunch than the last crew have taken over the Executive. I'm beginning to think that they'll stand any amount of pressure we and the Marq'ssan put on them as long as they don't seem to be making concessions." Martha gave Hazel a long, thoughtful look. "We've been considering Elizabeth's offer, you know."

Hazel snatched up her glass and gulped down several swallows of beer to give herself a few seconds before replying. She still hadn't worked out what to tell Martha and what to keep to herself. There was Anne's situation to consider, for one thing. Even though what Anne was doing made her uncomfortable, Hazel did not feel prepared to expose her. Nor did Hazel want to endanger the lives of the women in Liz's household—including Liz herself—or the lives of the women doubling for Liz. Comprehending the implications of information was something Hazel had never before attempted to do—at least not on this scale. "Which offer?" she asked Martha. "The information on the drugging, or getting Liz access to Security's system?"

When Martha finished chewing a bite of fish, she said, "Oh, we'll use the stuff she's already given us—once we verify its accuracy."

Martha paused to drink. "But the actual proposition she made—that's something else. Obviously we'd like to know what those bastards are up to here in the Free Zone. But in arranging access for her we'd be doing her a gigantic favor. We know damned well she's not going to confine herself to serving our interests. It would help if we had some idea of the reason for her attacks on the Executive. At first we assumed revenge to be her motive. But it's obvious there's more." Martha's gaze met Hazel's. "And then of course there was her reference to a hundred women's lives on the line in Washington."

Hazel licked her lips and swallowed. "Well, Martha, I might as well tell you. It's hard to believe, I know, but what Liz is after is nothing more than the downfall of the current Cabinet. She says she wants to 'reform' the Executive—after first taking it over. That's what she's after."

Martha stared at her. "You're not serious."

Hazel laughed nervously. "She's got a network of women working for her in DC. She intends to undermine the Executive on the one hand while campaigning to get the support of executive society at large on the other—by arguing that the current Executive's methods are counter-productive. She would like to transform the Executive into a model of government. Peace and tranquility for all. The Good Life restored. And, she says, direct dealings with the Marq'ssan."

Martha looked skeptical. "It's hard to believe. And what about the Free Zone?"

This was where it got tricky. Hazel took another bite of fish between her chopsticks. "She wants to get along with the Marq'ssan, Martha. And she says she's opposed to the repressive policies Sedgewick has been using. At this point she considers the Free Zone a necessary evil."

"Until she gets into power," Martha said dryly. "At which point she'd undoubtedly do her damnedest to get the Free Zone back under the Executive's thumb."

"I don't know. She swears she's opposed to using violence against citizens. That civil rights are essential for the kind of society she wants to reconstruct."

"Hmmmph."

A loud meow pierced the air. Hazel rose half out of her chair to lean over the railing. A calico cat sat on the ground below with her neck thrown back, staring up. Looking her straight in the eye, it me-owed again. "I think she wants our fish," Hazel said.

Martha grinned. "That cat loves seafood so much that I've seen her scavenging dead fish on the beach." A third meow was almost painfully loud. "Damn! No question, she's going to be down there making her racket as long as we're out here. Sad to say, if we give her a bite or two she'll just demand more." They ate for a minute or so without talking. "Oh, by the way," Martha said, smiling slyly, for a fleeting moment looking a bit feline herself. "Ariadne says she's com-ing tomorrow to visit for a couple of days." The fourth meow had a distinctly pathetic tone, as though the cat knew that her imperious attitude was getting her nowhere. Martha's smile widened. "She likes you a lot, Hazel."

Hazel avoided Martha's gaze. "She's your friend. She's probably coming to visit you," she said.

"Maybe, but I doubt it. I could tell she was disappointed that you decided not to spend some time at Sweetwater."

"I'm not... I don't think I..." Hazel bit her lip. She decided to be blunt. "I don't want another lover right away."

"Ariadne mainly goes in for flings—apart from her long-term re-lationships within Sweetwater, that is."

"Well, I still don't think..." Hazel was not willing to explain how sexually dead she was feeling.

"And the second message," Martha said, resting her chopsticks diagonally across her empty plate, "was from Margot Ganshoff. She would like you to dine with her tomorrow night. She asks would you please call the consulate tomorrow and tell her yes or no.

"Shit," Hazel muttered. "Margot Ganshoff is one of the last peo-ple I want to have dinner with."

"I know what you mean. I spent a few months last year evading her advances myself."

"I suppose she thinks it's open season on me now," Hazel said glumly.

Martha poured more beer into their glasses. "What is it with these executive women?" she wondered. "I assume Margot's typical? Not that I've had much experience with them. But I have this feeling about them..." She frowned off into the distance.

Hazel took a long swallow of beer. "In the first place, as I recently found out, executive women are not supposed to have sexual relationships with one another. Did you know that, Martha?"

Martha stared at her. "You're kidding!"

"No, I'm dead serious. They are absolutely forbidden it—unless they don't care about being accepted by other executive women."

"But why?"

"Good question. I asked Liz about it once, but she wouldn't answer. I suspect that was because it must have something to do with their attitude toward sex and their sexual partners—something she didn't want me to know about."

Martha picked up her glass. "That's really weird."

Hazel noticed that the cat had stopped her racket and gone away. "I don't believe they think service-techs are human. In the sense, I mean, of their ever being able to feel anything for us, or empathize with us." She swallowed hard and blinked against the tears prickling her eyes. "That doesn't stop them from finding sexual gratification with us. But clearly they think of these sexual relationships as giving them the means of exploiting us." Hazel half-laughed; she kept her eyes focused on the water stretching out to the mountain-edged horizon. "Surely you've noticed that women in love will really put themselves out for their lovers. And as long as there's the illusion of love in return, some of us will go pretty damned far without even questioning it. And god what actors they are, they know exactly how to foster the illusion, they know all the correct responses. They've got it down to a science. But I'm damned sure they think the effort is worth it—since they get loyal slaves in return for all that acting."

"Hazel, are you all right?"

Unable to speak, Hazel nodded, then wiped her eyes with her sleeve.

"Maybe they're not all that way," Martha said. "Margot and Elizabeth, yes, but surely not *all* of them?"

Hazel looked at Martha. "Yes, all of them!" she choked out.

Martha took Hazel's hand. "Maybe you're right, I don't know much about these things. But I think it's Elizabeth you're upset about."

Hazel sniffed and cleared her throat. "I hate her for what she's done to me!" she cried. "The way she used me—not just that, Martha, but that I held nothing back! I *trusted* her!" A fresh wave of tears gushed from Hazel's eyes as the pain in her chest expanded.

"I could swear that woman loves you," Martha said. "Even last week when she came with you, the vibes I was getting from her—just think of how concerned she is about your safety, Hazel! Surely that means she feels *something* for you!"

Hazel shook her head. "No, no, no! I'm not so stupid that I don't know what *that* was all about. You heard her, she's scared shitless Sedgewick's crew gets hold of me. Because of what I know. Just the fact that I know where that house is—that's enough to make my safety critical! And then everything else—if they caught me it would ruin all of Liz's plans and incidentally place her and others in danger."

"That may be," Martha said, "but I still think she's in love with you. God knows every time I've seen the two of you together I've felt the strength of her attraction to you. *That* part wasn't one-way, Hazel."

"Oh, Martha, what you were feeling was her fear that you'd subvert me." Hazel tried to smile. "I used to think she was jealous, but then I realized that she was just worried you'd open my eyes. She's *never* felt anything for me—except sexual voracity, of course, and even that I now have to wonder about."

"Then that was her loss," Martha said, squeezing Hazel's hand.

"I'm sorry. I didn't mean to be such a burden on you. I didn't realize—"

"No, no, I think it's good that you're finally talking about it. This kind of pain—" Martha's eyebrows knit. "It's hard to face. It's not only loss of your loved one, but a blow to your self-esteem, too. Because you feel so put-down by your lover using you, you feel so shattered when you've trusted her with the most precious parts of yourself only to find yourself scorned and betrayed."

"Yes," Hazel said, "that's exactly it. Here I am crying, and I have the feeling Liz has been sneering at me, laughing up her sleeve at me for over a year now."

"I don't think she's laughing now, Hazel."

Hazel brushed her hair back from her face. "Maybe not. She's probably too pissed-off at my foiling her machinations."

"I don't believe it's entirely possible for two people to have a relationship in which one person is intensely engaged with the other without at all touching the other, no matter how manipulative and using the other intends the relationship to be." Martha's compelling brown gaze comforted Hazel with its warmth. "Look at it this way, Hazel: Elizabeth has been used to all the little things you've been doing for her and her ego, she's been enjoying for over a year all the affection and warmth you continually lavished on her. She's going to miss that and therefore miss you. Whether she loves you or not."

Hazel laughed shortly. "There's always more where I came from. Liz has only to lift her finger to fill my place. I've seen the effect she has on other women."

"Hmmmph." Martha released Hazel's hand and picked up her glass. "*I* never felt the pull. I guess she's just not my type. Too physically beautiful, too overpowering, I suppose."

Hazel reached for her own glass. "That's only because she never turned it on for you. She can be irresistible when she wants to."

"I wonder. Maybe you just think so because you yourself were so attracted to her."

"Damn." Hazel scowled into her beer. "I don't really want to talk about her."

"Okay." Martha smiled. "Then how about a walk on the beach?"

"Give me a few minutes to wash my face," Hazel said. She finished the last of the beer in her glass and carried their dishes into the kitchen. Some things Martha understood so well. And that she did comforted Hazel. Martha reminded her of Puget Sound—strong, deep, cool, and clear, always catching and reflecting the light and warmth around her.

Around Martha, the world became a different place.

# Chapter Fifty-nine

What could be more boring than spending the morning listening to her father review the San Jose station's current projects with Dawson and the officers involved in them? Sitting at the table beside her father, paying little attention to anything they were talking about, Alexandra watched the faces of the men who came and went as ordered. More amusing, Dawson's female service-tech came frequently into the room (for Dawson had been left without a PA when Hill had purged Dawson's previous PA) and set up a flirtation with Alexandra. The girl had a long, narrow body, dancing and warm rather than sly or sad brown eyes, light brown skin, and thick curly black hair. She bore not the slightest resemblance to Clarice.

Still, as the morning wore on, Alexandra's restlessness made it nearly impossible for her to sit quietly. By the time Dawson announced lunch, Alexandra was on the edge of screaming or falling into fits of uncontrollable wildness. She thrust her chair back and sprang to her feet, impatient for the slow-moving males to get themselves away from the conference table. Her father gave her a look that seemed to warn against rambunctiousness. She refused to acknowledge the warning. The tension from the previous day's scene in his office still crackled between them, constantly thrusting Alexandra toward the brink of defiance. She had come close to refusing to fly out with him that morning but had at the last minute shrunk from openly challenging him. When it came down to it, she couldn't face the price angering him would exact. She wasn't that far gone—yet.

Dawson led them to the rear of the building and outside to a shady terrace. Alexandra was delighted to see that Denise would be serving. As she passed her, Alexandra brushed her fingers over the girl's hip, then glanced back over her shoulder at her. Denise smiled and widened her eyes suggestively. Alexandra sat at the table and laid her napkin in her lap with a pleasant sense of anticipation.

She drank two glasses of wine with the meal, hardly noticing what she ate, for she fixed her attention on Denise to the exclusion of all else. They constantly exchanged covert looks and indulged fleeting touches as the girl moved around the table while the two males discussed the problem of Hill's purge and the general question of the reliability of executive women. Her father assured Dawson that if he located his previous PA and sent her to Central for a loquazene evaluation, he could have her back—provided, of course, that she proved reliable.

After Denise served them coffee, Dawson dismissed the girl. Alexandra plunged into flatness. After toying with her coffee spoon, she excused herself from the table and went back inside. She used the rest-room, then—trying to ignore Blake's inexorable, dogged attendance—set off in search of Denise. Stuck in this intolerable situation, she might as well take what amusement she could get.

Alexandra found the girl in Dawson's outer office, typing. She frowned at Blake. "Wait outside in the corridor, will you? There's nobody in here but me and her." Blake's eyes swept the room as though checking for as yet unnoticed terrorists. Only after he had thoroughly satisfied himself that her safety would not be compromised did he step outside the room and close the door behind him.

Denise at once got up from her stool, moved to within a foot of Alexandra, and smiled up into her face. Alexandra's heart pounded very fast and hard as she gazed down into eyes swimming with light and excitement. She touched her fingers to the nape of the girl's neck; trembling, she bent to kiss her. The girl melted into her, pressing her breasts and hips against her, tangling her tongue with Alexandra's. Alexandra's body exploded with heat and desire. They rubbed against one another, and Alexandra's fingers explored Denise's neck, ear, and throat, drinking in the textures of her skin and the shape of her bones. "Can you meet me tonight?" Alexandra said, breathless with intensity, astonished that an assignation could be made so easily with someone just met.

"Yes...whenever you want," Denise whispered.

Alexandra whispered back. "I'll figure out the details before we leave here this afternoon. Do you know where there's an executive women's club in the area? That would be our best bet."

"Yes, I know where it is." Denise giggled. "I've been there often."

Alexandra pressed her lips to Denise's for one last taste. She knew she should go but found it difficult to tear herself away. All she could think of was making love to this girl right on the spot—until she heard the door open. She sprang backwards, away from Denise, and mechanically smoothed her hair. She could feel her father's anger in the very stance of his body as he stood holding the door open. "We've been waiting for you," he said in his most cutting, rasping voice.

Alexandra, flushing, walked past him into the corridor. Blake stood impassive, as though unaware of any drama that might be unfolding. Her father took her arm in a less than gentle grip and hurried her along the hall toward Dawson and the retinue so pointedly waiting for them. Alexandra recalled that her father's "pep talk" was scheduled for after lunch. She fantasized creeping out of the pep talk (who would notice? They'd all be so hyped up with blood-and-guts rhetoric that nothing she could do would attract the slightest notice) and going back to Denise. But she knew that if she did, her father would be so furious he'd keep her from meeting Denise later.

"I'd like a few minutes of privacy with my daughter, Dawson," he said when they joined the group of waiting males.

Dawson glanced at the nearest closed door and nodded. "You can use this room, sir." He opened the door to reveal a conference room.

Her father propelled Alexandra into the room. He closed the door, then released her arm and faced her with blazing eyes. "Do you remember our talk in the car going to Lucia last spring?" he said.

Alexandra shuddered. "Yes," she said quickly. "I remember."

"If that is so, will you please be so good as to tell me what the *fuck* kind of excuse you think you have for your outrageous conduct today?"

Alexandra turned away to think, but he grabbed her arm and shoved her against the wall, which in turn made her body rev up the way it did when she worked out. "My conduct hasn't been outrageous," she flashed back at him—and at once felt his fingers dig even deeper into her flesh.

"Your *flagrant* display of your so-called sexual interest in that sub-exec cunt is an unequivocal violation of the propriety I went to great pains to instruct you about. *If* your interest in her is genuine, then you clearly lack a proper control over your sexuality, for your *mind*, my dear daughter, should have been on the matters at hand being discussed by the executives present." His face had gone a dark, angry red. "Instead you not only ogled and pawed that girl, you actually followed her out of the room! In any woman executive such mindless behavior would be deplorable, but in *you*, considering your situation and position, it is inexcusable. Therefore, until further notice, I forbid you to so much as *look* at much less *touch* any sub-exec we happen to come into contact with. Is that clear?"

"You've got no right to forbid me such a thing!" Alexandra shot back at him. "It's none of your business how I spend my leisure!"

He looked as though he were just barely restraining himself from further violence. But suddenly his other hand grabbed hold of her hair and yanked. "Let me put it this way," he said through his teeth. "If I find you violating my prohibition, I'll punish you. Is that clear?"

Alexandra closed her eyes as sickening waves of fear crashed over her. "Yes," she said quietly. "Understood."

He let go of both her hair and arm and drew a couple of breaths, presumably to calm himself. "Another warning," he said, considerably cooler. "Don't try playing these kinds of games with me. I'm not some sub-exec cunt you can fuck with. I know what you're doing and I won't have it."

Alexandra put her hand to her throat. "I don't know what you mean."

He snorted. "The hell you don't. I'm perfectly aware you hoped to provoke me." His stare was cold. "Don't try to manipulate me again." His gaze inspected her. "Straighten your hair. The entire station is waiting for us."

Alexandra smoothed her shaking hands over her hair and down her tunic. "May I tell the girl I can't meet her tonight?"

"No. I'm sure she'll figure it out for herself." He went to the door, opened it, and waited. She followed, her steps leaden. Numbly she realized that he had taken one more thing from her, one more of the things that might make life bearable to her. And now she would have to listen to him psyching his creeps up to beating and even killing "terrorists and anarchists." Clearly, he wanted everyone in the world to be as miserable as he was.

She hated him.

# Chapter Sixty

Hazel said, "I think I *have* decided. I think I want to attend the UW, starting in September. And in the meantime see if I can pick up what I'd need to know in order to do some work for the Co-op part-time while going to school." Hazel had her doubts about whether she *could* do the kind of work Martha seemed to be talking about. But if she found it beyond her, or didn't like it, she would have time to look for a part-time clerical job before school started. Such a job would probably have to be outside the co-op system, for almost none of the collectives or co-ops hired people to do specifically clerical work, except for specialized areas like accounting, typesetting, and software-adaptation.

"I have a feeling you might be good at facilitation," Martha said. "I've seen you in action, you know, working for Elizabeth Weatherall."

"The Human Rights Committee can always use organized, articulate people," Beatrice said.

"Yes, but not everybody can stand to concentrate on human rights," Ariadne said. She stretched her legs full-length and crossed them at the ankles. Hazel stared with admiration at the tattooed branch of bougainvillea twining around her right ankle and calf. "You have plenty of time to experiment before September, Hazel. The trick is to stop thinking of yourself as a secretary."

Beatrice laughed. "Can you guess, Hazel, that Ariadne was a secretary before she joined Sweetwater twenty years ago?"

Ariadne shot Beatrice an indignant look. "You didn't have to put it in *years*, Bea."

"Listen to the woman." Martha grinned. "Longevity treatments must be going to our heads—if it's coming down to our trying to conceal our ages."

Everyone—Ariadne most joyously—laughed. "Actually, though, I'm giving some of them up." Color stained her cheeks. "I've decided to get pregnant. We're going to have children at Sweetwater."

"Ariadne!" Martha cried. "That's wonderful!"

Ariadne's smile was shy. "Actually, we already do have children at Sweetwater—two of them—since our latest additions brought children with them. They've changed the atmosphere in all sorts of little ways, and that got us to considering the whole issue. I don't know *why*, but somehow we never really thought about it before, not even when that John Doyle thing got going. Anyway, besides me, Heddy and Pat are also planning on getting pregnant. So that there won't be such a massively big ratio between adults and children."

Martha grinned. "There will still be a lot of adults per kid."

"Which will be good," Beatrice said. "Sorben had some interesting things to say about child-raising on Marqeuei. Apparently their current system involves several adults nurturing each child. Although the biological parents are usually the primary nurturers, the others play an important role in the child's development." She sighed with pleasure, and her gray eyes shone so brightly in her worn, wrinkled face that they looked almost silver.

"Have you decided about the sex of the children?"

Beatrice answered. "Of course, we discussed that extensively—as you would naturally expect. We're going to take whatever comes. It's important that boys be raised differently than they've been, you know. So we shouldn't shrink from the possibility of having boys."

"It must have been a hard decision, Ari," Hazel said softly, "to decide to give up all future longevity treatments."

Ari shook her head. "But we've made a special arrangement—that's the beauty of it: we've convinced the Health Collective that since there are so many of us who will be acting as parents to these children, we can arrange to take a reduction of treatments spread out among ourselves. They came up with a complicated formula for figuring it out. It seems they're quite flexible in adapting their structures to nonstandard social arrangements."

"One of the original arguments against the quid-pro-quo-linking of the two was the likelihood of such sacrifice eroding the parent-child relationship," Martha said. "Giving up who knows how many years of one's life must inevitably cause at least unconscious resentment in the parents and a terrible sense of obligation and burden in the child."

Hazel recalled how constantly her parents had impressed upon her the many material sacrifices they had had to make to have her. "My theory about why people have kids," she said, soberly chipping in, "has to do with their expectation of getting a lot of status for being allowed to, since only a small minority of those who apply are granted permission. And of course parents are inevitably disappointed. God knows *mine* were. When I think about what it would have been like if they'd given up years of their lives for me, I have to shudder."

"Yes," Beatrice said, "but as it stands now in the Free Zone, only people who are willing to give up longevity treatments would even consider it. There's no status to reap from giving *that* up. So that would weed out all those types to start with."

"Still," Ariadne said, "this whole thing feels pretty screwed up. I don't think the health collectives' solution *is* a solution. At least not a long-term solution. Though the arrangement they made with us is a step in the right direction—*I* think."

Martha said, "Every time I've taken part in discussions on this subject I've gotten the feeling that most of the reasons people have for wanting kids are, when looked at carefully, terrible reasons. Passing on their genes, having the status of having been selected to reproduce, or simply for reasons having to do with power in various forms. No wonder it's such a touchy issue."

Ariadne gave Martha a troubled look. "And you think our reasons are political, too?"

"I don't know, Ari. I suspect that your motives are very complicated and mixed."

"What I'm most aware of is that we will be bringing new persons into our world," Ariadne said slowly. "I know there will be a lot of love involved. But I can see you could convincingly argue that we can just continue bringing new people—adults, or other people's children— into Sweetwater, since our reasons need to be scrutinized." She sighed. "I have to admit that part of our discussion has included expressions of the desire to help bring a new generation—with new perceptions, new attitudes, new forms of socialization—into the world. Which is, ultimately, a political motive. And I suppose that's also the reason we decided that boy-children would be welcome in Sweetwater. Is such a motive wrong, Martha?"

"That's not all of it," Beatrice said. "There's also a desire on the part of some of us to experience parenting. Not everything is so straightforwardly political. Any more than anything else is."

Martha set her glass down on the floor. "But everything is. Even making love. Ultimately. It's more a matter of not doing things for primarily instrumental reasons."

"Yes, that is the point, isn't it?" Beatrice said. "We don't choose to have sex in order to accomplish a political end. While at the same time we know that the political is embedded in everything we do or say and is therefore not avoidable and so we must be aware of it in our relations with other people. Because we want to avoid manipulating or being manipulated. And therefore sometimes we don't do certain personal things because of their political implications. Looked at from that point of view, it becomes more a matter of one's approach to parenting rather than the unavoidable facts implicit in it." Beatrice picked up her glass and started to drink, then, hesitating, looked at Martha. "Believe me, Martha, we've been over this ground."

Martha's smile was slight, obviously a matter of politeness. "Of course. And I know that if you've had Sorben in on some of the discussions, you must be thinking carefully about it."

"I'm checking into the Birth Center tomorrow," Ariadne said.

"How does it work?" Hazel asked. How did people bring about pregnancy—especially women without male sexual partners?

"First they change my DNA. Then, if everything goes as it should, I'll begin menstrual cycles." She made a face. "That's one of the tricky parts—sometimes bodies don't respond properly and have to be tinkered with in order to stimulate the reproductive cycle into functioning. Anyway, once I've re-established my reproductive cycle—which may take months—then I'll have some of my eggs removed—providing they're functional, which, given my age, they might not be—and have one of them fertilized with sperm. From an anonymous donor. After which the fertilized egg will be implanted in my uterus. And then, voilà! I'm pregnant."

"That's a lot of ifs, Ari."

Ari looked at Martha. "True. But if I do have functional eggs, they can tinker my body into working. That's really the question. There's a twenty-five percent chance my eggs won't be good. So the odds are more or less in my favor."

It was certainly a long drawn out process before pregnancy even began—and it seemed that all the trouble went to the woman. It was a wonder, Hazel thought, that women ever wanted to go through with it, whether they lost longevity treatments or not. And this is what her own mother had gone through to have her? While working full-time as a robotics-tech? But it might have been easier for them, since they probably bypassed some of the bother by fertilizing the egg during sexual intercourse...

A wave of revulsion swept Hazel. She got to her feet and asked the others if they wanted more wine, then went out to the kitchen to fetch it. Human existence, she decided, was downright bizarre. It was a wonder the species had lasted as long as it had.

# Chapter Sixty-one

## [i]

Alexandra lay on a chaise lounge in the walled-in terrace outside her bedroom. No more crying, she resolved, exhausted by her last paroxysm of tears. What she needed was to be strong and mature, to deal with her situation realistically, to face the facts.

The fact was that she couldn't bear his being so angry at her. That fact took precedent over all the other facts. An evening of biting remarks tore her up more now than it ever had. A few months ago she had been able to sit with her anger bottled up and use all the patience and coping techniques Grandmother had spent years teaching her. But she had been detached from him then. And she always knew that she would be going upstairs to the piano, or to her bath, or to a letter to or from Mama, or to a book—or, sometimes, to Clarice. But there was no escaping *this*. He knew her better now, he knew some of her most vulnerable points—because she had trusted him. And then there was the contrast: he'd been so easy with her, so warm and approving. Having tasted his affection, his contempt pained her all the more acutely. It felt so good when things were going well between them, when he saw her as an adult and someone he respected.

But of course the worst of it was his knowing her secret and knowing just how much like him she was. She felt him making assumptions about her, assumptions she didn't understand but the very intuition of which hurt. He knew her the way know one else did.

What she hated most was how everything had changed. Accusing her of playing games would not have occurred to him even a week ago. But now he thought differently about her. Certain of his remarks kept coming back to her, stinging her afresh each time she remembered them. And his crudity had grown freer and more explicit; she felt certain he unleashed it on her because she had exposed herself to him. Whether he used it when talking about her or another female, it stung like an insult to her, an affront to her very being. She suspected he understood this, too, and intended it. The way he flung the word *cunt* at her suggested that he did.

What could she do? It felt as though he were closing in on her, confining her more and more, stripping from her every source of relief from the pressures he forced on her. If he continued angry, the pressure would become unbearable and his contempt would destroy her. She was cut off forever and ever from Mama. Her music seemed to be sliding away from her day by day. And her most fundamental identification no longer held up, for she had betrayed her identity as an executive woman in almost every way possible. She doubted she could even look Elizabeth in the eye were she to meet her now. The fact was, he was all she had. The only identification possible to her now was as his daughter, his protégée.

All the things Mama and Elizabeth and Grandmother had said to her about being an executive woman were so far out of her reach that they might as well have been a fairy tale made up to tell small executive girls to comfort them for being second-rate, in second-place. "Don't be envious of Daniel," Grandmother had often said. "Daniel will be deprived of some of the best things that you'll have the privilege of enjoying when you're an adult." Where was her piano study now? Her wonderful time in college? Her life of travel with Mama? *Oh Alexandra, we'll have such a wonderful life together when you're a grown woman. We'll go everywhere, see everything, we'll have a fantastic time!* They had hardly even told her about *him*, had hardly mentioned his existence, for he surely would have no bearing on *her* life. Boys went to their fathers, girls to their mothers. Her father would provide her with a trust fund, and she would see him perhaps once a year (but maybe not, since this particular father was so busy with Important Things), and he would help arrange her maternity contract...

She'd always wondered about her absentee father, especially when she'd gotten old enough to realize how important he really was. She had a few vague memories of him, but she wasn't even sure they were real memories, for Mama had often described life before the Blanket in the Georgetown house to her and put images into her head. Mama had said he was the perfect father—well-connected, wealthy, and someone one hardly saw. One's relations with male relatives were always best when infrequent, for then the disagreeable things never had a chance to develop. Alexandra should try to hold out for a girl-only maternity contract, for then she'd have the greatest amount of freedom in child-raising. The males tended to interfere with the raising of boys. Again and again Mama had repeated this advice and had also said how much more rewarding it was raising girls, since boys in the end always hated you for being female...

Alexandra went inside to bathe her eyes. She couldn't get around it; it was staring her in the face, blocking all movement. Because of what she had started last Saturday night, because of what she had revealed to him last Sunday morning, everything had changed. She could not expect to keep his love—if he did, in fact, love her as he claimed—she could not expect to keep in his good graces as long as she resisted becoming his lover. It didn't matter that she thought it shameful or that she feared it so terribly: because she had told him of her attraction to him he had significantly redrawn the map of their relations, and now apparently—for that was the only way she could explain to herself why he seemed so furious with her—considered her resistance to a sexual relationship with him a resistance to intimacy with him in general. She felt him crowding in on her, determined to tear down every barrier he could discover as an affront and obstacle to his needs and desires. He claimed it to be a matter of her desires— that it was all *her* problem. But she sensed he had some desire here, too, desire frightening because of her inability to fathom it.

She dried her face with a towel and combed her hair. She imagined what tomorrow would be like—when they were to go to San Francisco. Originally she was to have had the morning to herself while he toured the Bay Area via chopper with Dawson and the top ODS officer briefing him. And then they were to have lunched alone together, with a "surprise expedition" he had arranged to follow. But in his current mood it was conceivable he would force her to tour with him and perhaps even extend the tour into the afternoon, just to punish her. And then she would face another long disagreeable evening full of more nastiness, more lecturing, more humiliation...

She couldn't face another day of constant cold contempt. She just *couldn't*. She leaned against the bathroom wall and closed her eyes.

She didn't want to be at war with him. Not just because she didn't have the stomach for it. But because if she had to live with him, she needed him to love and respect her. She would just have to make her peace with him. She would have to smother her anger and fear; she would have to find a way to live with her shame. Perhaps if she held onto her anger, kept it hidden away from him, small, hard, compact, she could still keep a part of herself safe and untouched. He would be nice to her again, and then she would be able to breathe, and he'd loosen the reins as he had before. He would love her again, maybe even enough to let her do the things she needed to do, to let her go. One year at Yale needn't be the end of her piano study if she could only return to her proper life. It wasn't too late. She could still recover if she could make him see how important it was to her—and if she could make him *really* love her. And maybe she could. Maybe she could make him love her so that he'd want her to have the kind of life she really, really wanted.

Alexandra looked at herself in the mirror, carefully avoiding the reflection of her eyes.

She would go to him now.

At the very thought, her heart galloped, and her knees shook. She mustn't be weak, she must do it. Now. He would be pleased with her if she went to him now, and then everything would be as it had been. Alexandra put her hands to her cheeks and drew a deep breath. Go, she told herself. Go do it, *now*. Don't think about it anymore. Just do it, do it.

She moved across the bedroom as though she were sleepwalking. She opened the hall door. Where were the gorillas? she wondered. It was essential that no one ever suspect or even speculate. She stood motionless and listened. She could hear at least two of them in the den, playing cards. Some of the others would be outside. But none were hanging out in the hall: which meant this house must be regarded as a super-safe place. Barefoot, she crept down the hall to the thick redwood door at the very end. She stood before it for a long time, trying to nerve herself to go in. She swallowed hard and put her hand on the ornate brass knob. She would not knock, for she didn't want to attract the gorillas' attention. She turned the knob and pushed the door open.

The room was dark except for the circle of light shed by the reading lamp attached to the elaborate mahogany headboard. He stared at her as she stepped inside and carefully closed the door. She tried to smile, but her face felt too stiff and frozen to move. She willed herself to walk over to the bed. One step on the redwood floor, and then another, and then she was walking on the rug, and it was as though she were watching herself approaching the bed. He had been reading some kind of report, she saw. He took off his glasses and laid them and the sheaf of flimsy on the nightstand. She stood just inches from the bed and looked at last at his face. What was she doing here? It wasn't too late to stop. He'd know, and maybe say something awful, but she *could* still leave.

"You have something to say to me?"

Alexandra started; she realized she had no idea how long she had been standing there. Something to say to him? she numbly repeated to herself. Words. With him it was always *words*. Her distress intensified. Fear, she thought, seeing herself standing beside the bed, this is fear. He always insisted that things be put into words. She tried to clear her throat but could not seem to get rid of the frog that was sticking in it, distorting her voice (which was hers but also *not* hers). "You said last Sunday when we talked," she began, but found herself lacking the words necessary to continue. She swallowed, pulled in a deep breath, and tried again. "What I mean is," she whispered, staring at the collar of his nightshirt, "I want to make love with you." Her words sounded so hollow, so false. Was it true? *Did* she want to make love with him? She could not conceive of feeling this afraid of making love with a woman.

"That's really very charming," he said, "but don't you think you owe me an apology for your behavior today?"

Alexandra's gaze flew to his face. That too? But her father's eyes were watching her with grave reserve. It's too late now, she thought. She had to go through with it, with whatever he made necessary. "I'm sorry," she said tremulously. "I'm sorry I behaved so badly. Please don't be angry with me anymore." Her voice sounded childish in her own ears, and that increased her sense of humiliation.

He opened his arms wide. "Come," he said, still watching her with that intensely serious, detached gaze. Alexandra perched on the edge of the bed, facing him, and wondered what came next. She knew next to nothing about normal male sexuality, much less about that of fixed males. "Let's lie down together," he said, very low. She stretched out beside him, careful to keep her body from touching his, and tentatively put her hand on his night-shirted chest. "You're trembling, Persephone."

"I don't even know what you look like. Naked, I mean," she said awkwardly. She had never seen a naked male body in the flesh.

"It doesn't matter," he said. His fingers moved over her face. "I'll make you feel so good you won't think about a thing."

"But what about you?" she asked anxiously, unable to imagine what would give pleasure to a fixed male.

He raised himself on his elbow and bent his head to kiss her. His mouth was hard and cool. This was so different. She experienced again the evocation of the cave, yes, but of a cave that seemed to be made of him—of his body, of his mouth, of his hands, of his tongue, surrounding her with dark warmth, instead of one they built and shared together. The cave felt surprisingly physically solid, but left her feeling more subject to withdrawal and being abandoned and left shivering and alone in the cold light. Yet even when he took his mouth from hers to slip off her gown and caress her breasts and belly she still felt him surrounding her all over. His arms were so thick, his body so *large*.

Alexandra opened her eyes and put her hands on his nightshirt to remove it, but he said, "No, no, leave everything to me this time. You're the inexperienced one." His gaze lifted, and she saw a fierce gleam in his eyes, as though they burned dark-colored flames. "It's much better when one of us has control, so that the other can completely lose control. You'll see. Just let yourself go, let me take care of everything. I promise you I'll make you feel more than you've ever felt." That hard, serious thing in his face frightened her, so she closed her eyes and slid her arms around him and hung onto the familiar sensations of pleasure as protection against so much strangeness.

## [ii]

Alexandra woke a half-hour before the girl was due to bring her coffee. Almost at once she remembered, and the world turned inside out. It really happened, it's not a dream, she thought and rolled over onto her stomach and buried her face in the pillow. She didn't even have the excuse of having been drunk, for she'd only had two glasses of wine with dinner. She had gone in there and done those things calculatedly and knowingly. How *could* she have? She must be completely depraved, inhumanly perverse. And to have felt those things… Yet she hadn't enjoyed it. But that must be a lie she was telling herself, for how could she have *felt* those things and still imagine she'd hated it? First being so afraid, and then humiliated… The things he had said to her…it meant he thought of *her* that way now. The way he thought of girls like Clarice. It made everything worse instead of better, knowing now that there was always that contempt lurking behind every word he said to her, every look he gave her. Knowing such things about herself and knowing he knew, too: how could she live with it? It would be better if she were dead.

When she heard the door open she did not roll over but instead put her arm over her face so that the girl wouldn't see she'd been crying. She heard the drapes being drawn, and then footsteps approaching the bed and the coffee tray being set down on the bedside table. But instead of hearing the footsteps going out, she felt the bed shift as it took the weight of another body. It wasn't the girl, she realized. She knew his smell: it was *him.*

"Are you awake, Persephone?" he said, and she felt his fingers on her neck. She rolled out of his reach, still holding her arm over her eyes. She wanted to tell him to go away, but it seemed to her that she couldn't, because of last night. "It's a beautiful day," he went on. "As soon as you drink your coffee and get dressed we can go for a walk— we can take a look at the vines and maybe go up to the olive grove. It's a walk I haven't done for years, though a long time ago I used to do it every morning I stayed in this house."

After a long pause Alexandra managed a dry, "Okay." She didn't move her arm from her eyes. She tried to think of how to ask him to leave.

"But why are you way over there, Persephone? Come kiss me good morning."

"No!" she burst out before she knew what she was saying.

"Oh fuck," he said half under his breath. Then, in his normal tone of voice he said, "Look at me, Alexandra."

Alexandra rolled onto her side, putting her back to him. "If you go away I'll get dressed," she said, her voice not quite steady.

"I think we need to talk first. Don't you?"

"No! You *always* want to talk. If you want me to get dressed and walk with you, I will. Only go away and give me fifteen minutes to myself."

"We *do* need to talk," he said. "It's obvious you're upset. I thought we went through all that last night. You promised me you would drop all this nonsense about incest being shameful."

"Please can't we leave it?" Alexandra pleaded. "I promise you that I won't bore or annoy you with crying or anything like that, if you'll just give me a few minutes by myself. Is that a lot to ask?"

"It's not a matter of my being bored or annoyed, Persephone. I can—"

"Stop calling me that!" she shrieked. "Do you think I'm so stupid that I don't understand?"

"Things are getting rather thick...Alexandra. And your putting your back to me doesn't help matters. I've told you before that ambiguities are dangerous. Therefore we *must* be open with one another. Now roll over and look at me. I'm not leaving this room until I'm satisfied we understand one another."

Given his tone of voice, she knew he would stay until he made her go through another of their "talks." Of all things, she didn't want to expose herself to him further. Every time they "talked" he learned more about her that he would subsequently manage to use against her. He already knew more than she could bear. She drew a deep breath and sat up and leaned back against the headboard. Effortlully, she moved her eyes to stare at the side of his face. "Would you pour me a cup of coffee, please?"

He poured coffee from the thermoflask into the cup and handed it to her. She saw that he wore the same outfit he had worn last Sunday to golf in. "Why have you been crying?" he asked. "I thought I'd surprise you and that you'd be happy to see me. Instead I find you miserable."

Alexandra gulped the steaming coffee. "I'm sorry for fussing," she said as matter-of-factly as she could. "I'll be fine, I promise. I won't spoil the walk." She gulped more coffee.

"Stop evading me," he said quietly. "It's insulting to me to imply that I don't care how you're feeling. I do care, Alexandra."

"You can see now that we don't need to talk," she said quickly. "I was just being silly." She briefly met his gaze—to prove to him there was no problem—then stared down into her coffee cup.

"What did you mean when you said you weren't so stupid as to not understand about my calling you *Persephone*?"

Why wouldn't he let it *drop*?

Alexandra slid out of bed and went to the closet. What had happened to the San Francisco trip? Had he postponed or canceled it? She would need something light if they were to be walking outdoors. Too bad she didn't have her tennis clothes here. She'd have to wear the thin silk and hope it wouldn't be *too* hot this early in the day. "I can be dressed in five minutes," she said as she draped the tunic and trousers over her arm. She started for the bathroom.

But he got up from the bed and stepped in front of her and put his hands on her shoulders. "I'm very close to getting annoyed with you, Alexandra." She registered a warning in his voice. "Put those things down and come over here and sit down with me and talk."

He *was* annoyed, Alexandra thought angrily. He *liked* his horrible "talks." He *liked* making her feel bad. Trembling from his touch, she wrenched herself away from him and went to the foot of the bed and sat. He followed and sat beside her. "Ambivalence is one thing, but this is something else, isn't it. Now explain what you meant when you objected to my calling you *Persephone*."

Alexandra swallowed back the idiot tears that again threatened. "You know very well what I meant. It's a game to you, isn't it. To see how bad you can make me feel. That's what you like, making others feel awful. Somehow it makes you feel good."

He held her wrist. "What kind of a tangle have you got in your head, Alexandra? You're going to have to explain this to me. And I'm not asking to make you feel bad. You're completely wrong when you say I want to make you feel bad. I would have thought I'd made that obvious last night." He turned her face toward his, and his gaze scoured her face. "Now tell me why it makes you feel bad when I call you *Persephone*."

Alexandra flushed. "At first I thought you were doing it to make fun of Mama. But since everything happened last weekend, I know it's me, too." She felt her lips tremble, and she rushed on. "And then last night, when you said all those horrible things to me, and called me those names, I knew it was the same as when you call me that. Because you think of me now the way you think of girls like Clarice."

His breath hissed in. "Listen to me. You have to learn how to separate what we do when we have sex from everything else. All those things we say and do are in play, and they have nothing to do with anything else. Dirty talk is a normal part of lovemaking, sweetheart. It's not supposed to make you feel *bad*!"

"A normal part of lovemaking?" Alexandra said. "But girls don't talk to one that way. And I wouldn't talk to them that way, either."

"I have no way of knowing what is normal in sexual relations between women," he said dryly. "But I might point out that you aren't very experienced and so *you* probably don't know, either."

Alexandra swallowed. "But then why did you make me say your name all the time? You didn't want *me* to say those things to *you*."

His hand stroked hers. "But I was in control last night. When you are in control, then you can call me anything you please. I can assure you I'll like it." He chuckled. "And do anything you like to me, too, and have me call you whatever you like. But we haven't gotten to that point yet, have we. You're very new to all this, Per—ah, I almost forgot. You see, I want to call you that, it feels very affectionate to me to do so, because it's a name just between us. There's no connection with anything you need to feel ashamed of. I don't use it to ridicule you—or your mother. Though maybe the first time I used it I was feeling amused at her. But that quickly faded. I do hope you aren't going to forbid me to call you that. Because I like it immensely." He put his arm around her shoulder and pulled her close to him.

He was right, she didn't really know what was normal between women. She was so inexperienced that she had jumped to conclusions about what was normal in lovemaking.

"What other awful thoughts are you having? I want you to tell me. So that I can make you see that everything is good between us; so that

I can make you feel how much I love you. I woke up this morning and felt so happy, Alexandra. I jumped out of bed and got down to work almost immediately, until it got late enough so that I could decently come wake you up."

Relief flooded over her. It had been the right thing to do—he was happy with her again, and had forgiven her. Effusive with warmth and gratitude, she flung her arms around him and pressed her face into his shoulder. "You make me feel so silly," she said.

"Good." He squeezed her, then held her away from him. "Now tell me. Am I allowed to call you Persephone, or do you forbid me?"

Alexandra looked at his teasing face, but saw that he was serious. She smiled sheepishly. "Now that I understand, it's all right with me, if you want to call me that."

He kissed the tip of her nose. "Good. Then why don't you get dressed so we can have our walk. I'll tell them to make us an enormous breakfast for when we get back. Okay?"

Alexandra nodded, and they got up from the bed, she to dress, and he to give orders about breakfast. The sun pouring into the room made the ornate nineteenth-century furniture look warm and rich instead of stodgy and overbearing. It *was* a beautiful day, and the wind-ruffled silvery green olive grove would be heavenly. He still loved her after all, maybe even more than he had before. She *had* done the right thing.

# Chapter Sixty-two

This is the life, Hazel said to herself, looking up from the book she had borrowed from Martha. She still wasn't used to not being on duty 24/7 as Liz's assistant. Contemplating the mix of pleasure and anxiety her freedom brought her, she considered possible solutions as she lazed in the sun and breathed in the fresh scents of Puget Sound (a good deal less ripe here in the Waterfront Park than on Carkeek's beach). She needed a goal or organizing principle for structuring her new life, she decided. And then laughed wryly at herself for what it said about her personality. Still, she knew that the insight was sound. So she formed the resolve of sampling all of Seattle's many parks before the summer was out. Not exactly a grand ambition, and certainly one she wouldn't mention to just anyone. But it would give her a plan for getting her over the psychological hump of transition.

Sitting in the grass, reading Kay Zeldin's account of the events of eleven years past, she found herself repeatedly looking up from the book and gazing at the world around her with a sense of unreality. The particular chapter she was reading, describing and analyzing the relationship between the women on the national delegations and their respective governments, sent chills chasing up and down her spine. Zeldin's descriptions were vivid enough in themselves, but Hazel's personal acquaintance with a few of the principals involved intensified their effect. She knew Sedgewick's office; she knew Sedgewick himself. And—of course—she knew Liz.

Hazel stared out at the water. If Liz were to read this chapter, she mused, she would be forced to understand the nature of what her own position must always be where the Executive was concerned. Though Zeldin had not been an executive, she had had the ear of the Executive. But what had that, really, signified? Early in the period of negotiations on s'sbeyl, Ursula Hodges, one of Australia's delegates, had been killed during an interrogation that had taken place after she

had returned to her government full of enthusiasm for the possibilities opened up by the Marq'ssan. And Zeldin herself had been forced
to watch a Sweetwater woman being tortured (Susan Sweetwater, to
be specific)—as a warning.

Hazel recalled Liz's shock at Sedgewick and Booth's "cracking
down" on her after she had begun negotiating with the Free Zone.
How could she not have known the limits of her power? A new understanding of the conditions of power had obviously been among the
major insights Zeldin had drawn from her experience trying to work
for the Executive. In an earlier chapter Zeldin had written:

> The system itself places severe restraints on the creative pos-
> sibilities of power. I was given tremendous power by Sedgewick
> over the ruling Security forces in Seattle, which would have
> allowed me to carry out any number of arbitrary arrests or as-
> saults or unit-to-unit searches. In short, I was given free rein
> to exercise any degree of repression I deemed appropriate.
> I had no power whatsoever, however, to prevent arrests or,
> indeed, what we now call The Capitol Hill Massacre in which
> hundreds of lives were lost. This deployment of power is en-
> tirely typical of the executive system. This negative, inevitably
> abusive conception of power lies at the heart of the bankruptcy
> of every system of government in existence. Creativity, threat-
> ening the status quo because it is a source of change, simply
> cannot be tolerated by governments. Thus the power exercised
> by governments is almost always negative. The main differ-
> ence between governments is the extent to which restraints are
> placed on abuses—and therefore on the power of those in posi-
> tions of authority.

Everything Hazel had seen of Liz's operations, everything she
had seen of Security's policies and methods, confirmed Zeldin's words.
Her experiences had been different, less dramatic, but illustrative all
the same of the very things Zeldin had been talking about. And the
more she read the more she understood her own experiences. The
strange thing was that she had begun to feel a deep longing to talk to
Zeldin. Only Zeldin, Hazel thought, would have been able to explain
to her about Liz and the other executive women in the household;
only Zeldin would have been able to put her own chaotic tentative

insights into a semblance of coherence... But they had killed Zeldin. According to the second preface of the book, they had killed Zeldin at a time when Liz by her own admission and Anne's reckoning had been in control of Security Services. The irony stuck in her heart, twisting, turning, sending hot spears of pain through her every time she forgot and began to imagine talking to the woman who had written such a book.

"Hazel?"

This soft summons startled Hazel out of Zeldin's discussion of the impact seeing a woman being tortured had had on her second round of negotiations on board *s'sbeyl*.

"Liz!" She craned her neck to stare up at the powerful, towering figure. She had forgotten the sheer size of the woman, exaggerated now by her standing directly over her. "What do you want?" she said, trying not to panic. This was, after all, a public place. Surely Liz wouldn't try anything out here in the open where there were witnesses who could finger her?

Liz knelt in the grass. "I'm sorry," she said, "but I had to see you. I couldn't stand to stay away any longer."

"I don't want to talk to you."

"Please." Liz implored with her eyes. "Please don't hate me, Hazel. I'm so miserable without you. These last weeks have been hell for me."

"I don't hate you, Liz. I think I feel sorry for you."

Liz's eyes widened. "What do you mean?"

She looked genuinely afraid. What, Hazel wondered, could Liz possibly *think* she meant? "I had serious doubts before, but now that I'm reading this I know for certain you're being a fool to think you can work through the Executive." Hazel held up Zeldin's book. "You're deluding yourself. You're wasting your time. The executive system is nothing but sterility."

"So you're taken in by her lies, too," Liz said bitterly.

"I recognize the truth when I read it," Hazel said. "Everything that I've seen and experienced working for you makes me believe what she says in this book. And if I can understand, you with your education and experience should certainly be able to, too. Maybe, Liz, you should read this book yourself."

Liz dug her fingers into the grass. "What you don't seem to understand, darling, is that I will make things change. In a much wider and more effective way than these Co-op crackpots could ever dream of. Anarchy is no solution. Zeldin created a power vacuum in 2076 when she destroyed the Executive. You saw what happened. Well when *I* destroy *this* Executive, I'll *be* there to fill the vacuum, to put this country on the road to health and productivity."

It was hopeless trying to argue with Liz. "You know what really gets me as I read this book?" Hazel said.

Liz watched her warily. "No darling, I don't."

"That I can't talk to her. To Kay Zeldin, I mean. I can tell from reading her words that she would be wonderful to talk to. I have this terrible sense of loss." Hazel stared down at the grass and brushed her fingertips over the points of the strong green blades. Her throat closed with a sudden tightness. She looked at Liz. "It must have been you who ordered her death."

Liz's eyes widened with horror. "No, Hazel. No! Not me. Sedgewick was responsible. You can't blame me for that." She looked out at the water. "But you're right. You probably would have liked talking to her. She was remarkable. Though it's hard to say in what way, precisely. I felt bereft at her death, myself." Her gaze returned to Hazel's face. "But in some way her death was inevitable once she betrayed Sedgewick." Frowning, she gnawed at her lip. "My god, the woman was one of the most flagrantly destructive traitors this country has ever seen, Hazel. *I* couldn't have stopped her execution, you know. Only Sedgewick could have. And he chose not to."

"You see?" Hazel said. "What kind of power is that? That's exactly what Zeldin was talking about in her book."

"Please. You don't understand what you're talking about, darling." Liz sighed. "Let's not talk anymore about such things. I came to see you for personal reasons. Because I miss you so desperately." Liz stretched out her hand to touch Hazel's, then withdrew it. "Tell me how you've been."

Hazel looked into Liz's eyes: "This last month has been the best of my life."

Liz flinched.

"That's not what you hoped to hear?" Hazel said. "I suppose you were hoping I'd say *I've* been miserable?"

Liz's mouth twisted. "I don't want you to be miserable. But the *best*, Hazel? I don't believe that." She gnawed more at her lip, which was so unlike her that Hazel couldn't stop watching her do it. "Unless getting away from me makes you that happy?"

Hazel hesitated before answering, wanting neither to give Liz hope—if that's what this was about—nor be cruel (but how could anything she say hurt Liz?). "It's the life I'm leading here," she said.

"You're in love with her?"

"With Martha?" Hazel asked, surprised. "No, of course not."

"Then there's someone else?"

"Oh Liz, is that what you think it takes to make life good for me? You're wrong, you know. In any case, getting involved with someone new is not something I'm likely to do for a while."

"Then you still care? There's something still there?"

"That's none of your business!"

Silence. Liz tore up a handful of grass and cast it violently away from her. "I wonder if I'll ever understand what's happened between us," she said. "I've been over and over everything I can think of and I can't see where I went wrong."

"That's how you think of it?" Hazel said. "As where you went wrong? Don't you understand, Liz, I've seen through it. I can't be managed now!" Hazel's gaze fell onto the book. "What was she like, Liz?"

"What?"

"What was Kay Zeldin like."

"Lord, Hazel, why do you have to keep dragging her into this conversation?"

"You knew her." A seagull landed a few yards from where they sat and scrutinized them as though suspecting they had food they were concealing.

"Yes, I knew her," Liz said. She paused. When, after a moment, she went on, there was a tightness in her voice that hadn't been there before. "What I can tell you won't satisfy you. She was brilliant. I think she understood more of what was going on around her—I mean the things lying beneath the surface of words, the *implications* of things—than anyone I've ever known. Her mind was always working, even at the worst of times. Of everything about her, that still impresses the hell out of me. Perhaps it was this aspect of her that gave her so much power—or no, not power, exactly." The seagull flapped noisily and soared out over the water. "Strength, maybe, I suppose that's the best word I can come up with. Even backed into a corner that woman emanated strength. It was almost frightening at the same time that it was, well, exhilarating..." Liz's gaze returned to Hazel's face. "If I hadn't captured her, everything would be different today." She laughed a little. "And the Free Zone—who knows? The Free Zone might have taken over the rest of the country by now. But her Achilles heel was her attachment to her husband and her desire to find him. It made her rash."

"*You* captured her? You personally?"

Liz's face clenched. "Oh god, I did say that, didn't I." She sighed. "Yes, Hazel, I captured her myself. In Boulder. We were both attending the same concert. We were both late returning to our seats. The orchestra had just sounded the first chord of Beethoven's Seventh when we met on the stairs. She ran; I pursued. And of course I caught her. You know how fast I am." When Hazel said nothing, Liz went on, "I suppose you're going to tell Greenglass that. I should have denied it, but I've never lied to you, and it's hard to start now."

Hazel tried to imagine Liz chasing the woman the holograph in the Co-op Building had been modeled on. She said, "Since you were in control then, I suppose it doesn't really matter that you personally were the one to abduct her." Liz's face relaxed a little. "What happened next, after you caught her?"

Liz looked away. "Let's not go into the gory details."

"Was she tortured, Liz?"

Liz's gaze moved sharply back to Hazel's face. "No! That at least you can give me credit for. She had to die, yes. But I stopped them from going through the usual procedures for captured renegades."

"Why did you run after her and capture her? Why didn't you just pretend you hadn't seen her?"

Liz's eyes blazed at her. "For godsake, Hazel! Enough! I won't discuss this any further!"

"You were the one who came here wanting to talk to me," Hazel said. "And by the way, how did you know where to find me?"

"I decided it would be better to approach you in the open," Liz said slowly, "because I thought you might not let me into the house." She pressed her lips together for a few seconds, then added, "Of course I can find you when I want to. I always have someone keeping an eye on you—" Hazel opened her mouth to voice her outrage—"because," she continued hastily, "I am so worried about your safety. That's the only reason, you know. I wouldn't *spy* on you, darling. I just need to know you're safe."

"I don't care what your reasons are! Call your spies off me!"

"You hadn't even noticed, had you," Liz said.

"That doesn't mean I don't mind having my privacy violated!"

"If you didn't notice the amazons you sure as hell wouldn't notice anybody Sedgewick would put onto you. For godsake, Hazel, think!" Liz laid her hand on Hazel's thigh just above the knee. "I've told them to be discreet, not to bother you. You must let me do this." Liz's fingers moved lightly over the fabric covering Hazel's leg.

Hazel grabbed the book and her bag and scrambled to her feet. Liz sprang up, too, and put her hand on Hazel's arm. "Don't touch me." Hazel glared up into Liz's face, angry at the wash of sexual sensation Liz had triggered just by touching her.

"I'll go now," Liz said. "I can see you want me to." She half-smiled. "Maybe we can talk again another time."

"If you harass me, Liz—"

"I promise I won't bother you, darling. You needn't worry about that." Without warning she ducked her head and brushed her lips over Hazel's forehead. "Good-bye, love," she said before Hazel had time to react and strode off, down the path that paralleled the edge of the water, large, confident, executive, her short fluffy blonde hair gleaming in the noontime sun.

Hazel stared after her, disturbed by the scent of Liz in her nostrils and the sense of Liz's hard yet pliant body evoked from memory, bemused at the fragments of Kay Zeldin she had offered. Unable for the moment to return to the book, she ambled along the path and stared out at the water. "Damn that woman," she said aloud as she perched on a rock at the edge of the water. Glancing down at the book, she caught sight of the picture on the back of the book jacket and found herself wondering how Kay Zeldin would have handled the situation.

Some of the things Liz had said about Kay came into her mind, and she sighed. Maybe Liz herself would have been a different person if she had let Kay go. But they would never know that now.

# Chapter Sixty-three

Aware of her father's gaze, Alexandra stretched her mouth into an effortful smile as she went to her grandfather and hugged him. He kissed her cheek; then, as he held her back from him, his warm brown eyes, all loving approval, roved her face. "My little rosebud has blossomed," he said. Alexandra flushed, thinking for the first time in her life how absurd his pet name for her was. "Look at you, you're so tall! And grown up," he added, sighing.

The irony was almost too much to bear. Urbanely, her father thrust himself into their "reunion." "Will you have a drink, Varley?"

Alexandra hoped her grandfather would refuse. The less she saw of her mother and grandparents around her father, the better. But "Thanks, Robert," her grandfather said. "I seem to recall that you keep a decent scotch."

Smiling faintly, her father pulled a bottle out of the liquor cabinet, poured a good-sized shot into a heavy-bottomed crystal glass, and handed it to Grandfather. "And you, Alexandra?" he said, turning to her. "Will you join me in a sherry?"

Alexandra glimpsed the look of surprise that flitted over her grandfather's face. "No thank you," she said hastily.

They all sat down, the men in the massive chairs by the fireplace and Alexandra alone on the sofa. Carefully she crossed her legs and smoothed the frothy green silk over her knee.

"Are you going to be in DC for long?" her father asked.

Grandfather shook his head. "No, I'm afraid not. At this time of year Washington is the last place I'd want to be. The stench combined with the heat is an unbeatable combination." He turned his head toward Alexandra and smiled. "I was rather hoping I could induce Alexandra to go north with me, to that little summer place I've got up in the mountains in Montana."

She glanced at her father and then away, for his face had set into an impassive mask revealing nothing. "I don't think I should, Grandfather," Alexandra said haltingly. "I've been working on a project for Security. I have an obligation to carry it through."

His bushy dark eyebrows rose about an inch. "I had no idea you were working for Security. Felice never mentioned it."

"Well, actually," Alexandra said, "I haven't told Mama about it." She licked her lips. "There didn't seem to be a good reason for telling her. And since it's a Security project..."

Grandfather stared down into his glass. "I see."

Alexandra looked at her father and found him studying her. Flushing, she looked back at her grandfather. "It does sound lovely though," she said wistfully, feeling guilty for letting him down.

He knocked back the rest of his drink. "Well, shall we be going? Our reservation is for seven-thirty."

Alexandra jumped to her feet like a jack-in-the-box. "Yes, of course," she said breathlessly, anxious to get him out of there. She went to him and linked arms with him. Her father took Grandfather's glass and carried it over to the liquor cabinet. Somehow they got out of the study, with Alexandra saying goodbye several times to her father and the men shaking hands and mentioning the possibility of "getting together" sometime before Grandfather "went north."

"I hope you don't mind my trailing an escort everywhere," Alexandra said when they reached the foyer and she saw Blake waiting. "He has to ride in the front, I'm afraid. That's the rule."

Grandfather snorted. "In my opinion that's a little excessive." Blake opened the front door, and they went out. "The only times I ever had 'escorts' were in extreme periods of crisis. During the civil war, and during the Transformation."

"I've been studying the Executive Transformation," Alexandra said, pleased at having found a safe topic. Grandfather's driver held open the back door of the car. Alexandra slid over the seat to the far window. She would ask him about his experience of the Transformation and then she'd ask him how his trip to Japan had gone. If she were lucky, the two topics would just about get them through dinner.

# Chapter Sixty-four

While Martha took charge of reheating the rice and dal, Hazel set out the raita, hot lime pickle, and chapati and opened two bottles of the case of home-brew some people from Port Townsend had recently brought Martha. "So basically what I'll be doing is arranging and co-ordinating between various groups for the projects the Committee has in progress. They seem to think my previous work experience fits me for such a job, though I did warn them that I was only a secretary." Hazel finished buttering the chapati, wrapped them in a towel, and put them in the microwave. "God it's hot," she complained. "Do you think it'll ever rain again?"

Martha laughed. "You may have noticed that while they com-plain, most people are enjoying themselves swimming and boating and kayaking."

They sat—as they usually did—on the balcony to eat. "I had a hard time putting down Kay Zeldin's book," Hazel said. "It's abso-lutely riveting."

"Yeah, she certainly knew how to write," Martha said.

"What was she like, Martha? *You* knew her. There's something in her writing…it's hard to describe, but I keep feeling as I read that I'm getting glimpses of her mind, of the very essence of her being."

Martha took a long pull on her beer before answering. "I have to admit I had mixed feelings about her. It was only when I heard the news about her capture and execution that I realized how much she meant to me, personally." Martha ate a bite of dal. "You see, I first thought of her as the Executive's mouthpiece. Because of the role she took right after the Blanket. I hated her for collaborating with them. She was so damned articulate! The first I saw her was on vid, when she cleverly shifted the mood of most of the delegates after Leleynl gave the Marq'ssan's major address." Martha ate another bite. "Did you happen to see any of that?"

Hazel tried to remember, and then her memory of those days, of where she was at the time the Blanket struck, of the vid technology that had literally rained down from the sky, came flooding back—the four of them at home, trapped there together because of the curfew, and Dad furious and taking it out on Aunt Dawn—threatening to denounce Aunt Dawn as a feminist to ODS (in spite of the obvious fact that ODS would hardly consider Aunt Dawn worth bothering over)…"Now that I think about it," Hazel said slowly, "I do remember a little. I *do* remember Kay. I remember my father taking pride in the Executive's having sent someone who 'had her head screwed on straight,' as he put it. Somehow I never made the connection."

Martha said, "I can see why. Anyway, that was my first impression. And then when I began attending meetings on *s'sbeyl* myself, I disliked her even more. She was so damned slick. We were all thrown into an uproar when Kay cleverly managed to work out a vid concession for the Executive."

"I read that chapter this afternoon. It's hard to believe that the Free Women agreed to such a thing."

"Yeah." Martha sighed. "To this day I'm convinced no one else could have managed to get them to do it. I don't know how she did it. It's not as though the Free Women at that meeting were stupid. On the contrary. Jo Josepha was there. But apparently Kay was able to so forcefully manage the others' perceptions that they lost sight of the larger picture." Martha ate another bite of dal. "The first time I met her was after she'd abducted Elizabeth and Sedgewick. The Marq'ssan introduced her to me as someone who was responsible for having saved my life." Martha half-laughed. "Naturally this injected more than a little ambivalence into my feelings about her."

"How did she save your life?"

"Kay helped the Marq'ssan rescue me from ODS's clutches. You see, I was a little stupid in the way I went about trying to politicize my neighbors. I showed them a light Sorben had given me when she, I, and some others broke into the ODS Building looking for documents proving there was a planned national campaign for raping women." Martha paused to take a swallow of beer. "Anyway, one of the neighbors at the meeting informed on me, and ODS burst into my apartment and dragged me off to detention. Put me in solitary—in a room without light, sound, or heat. God it was cold. I didn't even have a chance to grab my coat when they took me. I got crazy pretty fast. Had no idea how long I was there. Now and then they opened the door and threw in a bottle of water, so I wouldn't go into filter failure, I suppose. According to Kay, Sedgewick intended to have me brought to Washington so that they could interrogate me there. He intended *her* to be a part of the interrogation team. They hoped to find out about 'the terrorists'—as the Executive called the Marq'ssan—through me."

Hazel shivered. "God, Martha, how horrible. So Kay saved you from that."

"Yes, she passed on everything she learned to the Marq'ssan, and Sorben came and took me out of detention." She set down her glass and picked up her fork. "So when I learned that Kay had been instrumental in saving me from *that*—well, I started to feel pretty mixed-up about her. Especially since Sorben and Magyyt insisted that Kay was trustworthy and wanted to work with us—and that we needed her."

They ate a few more bites in silence. Hazel tried to imagine what it must have been like for Kay and Martha to meet. "And she was a professional, too," Hazel said after a while. "That must have added to the way you felt about her."

Martha laughed. "Damn straight it did. A professor who had once belonged to the Security Intelligence Cadre and had been working for Sedgewick? But Kay was so apologetic for that background—working for the SIC, I mean. She never told us why she originally quit it. She did say that when Sedgewick showed up in Seattle right after the Marq'ssan zapped us with the Blanket she had no doubts about going back to work for him—that she felt an emergency of that magnitude demanded that she put aside any scruples she might have working for the SIC." Martha took another swallow of beer. "I guess when she first told us that, I thought she was just trying to excuse herself. All I could see was that she had been one of them and had worked against us on *s'sbeyl*, even if she did eventually come to her senses. I think it was reading her book that made me start to think differently about her." Martha smiled ruefully. "Even when she handled the executives for us when we were working out the details for the Withdrawal, I couldn't acknowledge how courageous it was of her to show herself openly to those people. Only later did I realize just how much executive hatred she had become the focus of. She was a symbol to them, I think, of The Enemy. The Enemy that first burrows from within and then attacks from without."

"And how did the Marq'ssan feel about her?"

"Ah," Martha said. "It took me a long time to realize that Kay somehow understood more of what the Marq'ssan were trying to teach us than any of *us* did. I of course considered myself far in advance of her—after all, I'd been a declared anarchist for years! But after a while I was forced to admit that she understood a lot that I didn't. Sometimes during a meeting she'd say one sentence and by that one sentence turn everything upside down and inside out." Martha put her empty bowl on the floor beside her chair. "Goddess knows the whole fiasco with Louise and the Night Patrol would probably not have occurred if Kay had been around. She would have made us confront the problem and deal with it."

"Liz said to me that if Kay had lived, the Free Zone may well have taken over most of the country by now," Hazel said, curious about what Martha would think of such a theory.

"Taken over?" Martha sounded grumpy. "What the hell is *that* supposed to mean? The problem with Elizabeth always has been that she doesn't have the faintest idea about how we think. She's always applying executive concepts to us. As though we are a government, as though we are power-hungry."

"Liz thinks you've got an executive inside you," Hazel said softly, knowing full well that she was pushing one of Martha's buttons. "That's how she explains your ability to handle responsibility as well as the success of the Free Zone. Because you're at heart an executive."

Martha snorted. "Wonderful. That's just wonderful." She glared at Hazel. "I bet she'd think I should take it as a compliment, too."

Hazel grinned.

"Yeah, well, being at heart an executive is the last thing I'd want to be," Martha said. "Christ. Leave it to Elizabeth."

"Well you see," Hazel said, "she has to find some explanation for why the Free Zone isn't devastated by anarchy."

"So she just refuses to believe we have an anarchy."

"Right. You're all just executives in disguise."

"I think I need another beer." Martha pushed her chair back from the table an stood up. "What about you?"

Hazel handed Martha her glass. "Please. And I promise not to repeat any more of Liz's provocative remarks tonight." She laughed at the expression lingering on Martha's face.

Martha managed to smile. "It *is* a little hard to take," she said. "It makes me want to scream. Do you suppose Elizabeth will ever see what's right in front of her face?"

Hazel shook her head. "No, Martha, I don't. Remember how people pretended that the Marq'ssan were terrorists because they couldn't face the truth? Some people probably still can't take it in. In some ways, the truth about the Free Zone is like that. It's impossible that there are aliens from outer space using their superior technology to force us to change. Therefore they're only terrorists who are producing special effects to fool us. Likewise, it's impossible that anarchy can work; therefore there is no anarchy. I bet there are people living in the Free Zone—apart from Liz and her household, I mean—who play pretend in both those ways. They live in another world than we do, Martha."

Martha carried their glasses inside.

Liz's household was in another world, Hazel thought. In Liz's household service-techs were of a different species, below executives. At least that's how it worked out if you ignored what they said and paid close attention to the things they did. Executives in one dining room, service-techs in the other. No, Liz would never see the Free Zone for what it was. Not given the way she shaped reality in her own household. For all her superior education and access to information, Liz was functionally blind. Not Martha, not Hazel, not a single living being would ever get Liz to see what lay undisguised before her very eyes.

# Chapter Sixty-five

"So we're on tomorrow for lunch and the Phillips afterwards?" Grandfather asked as they approached the front door.

"I'll be at Security Central in the morning," Alexandra said. "Shall I meet you somewhere?" Blake had gotten the door open and stood holding it for her.

"I'll pick you up there. Is one o'clock all right?"

"It's fine," Alexandra said. "Goodnight, Grandfather."

He leaned close and pecked her on the cheek. "Goodnight, dear."

Alexandra went straight to the kitchen for parsley. Then, munching a fat mouthful, she moved on to the study. Her father, seated at his desk, was scribbling on a memo pad as he talked into the phone. "Yes, yes, Ed, I assure you I'll put the word out at once. Now that we know about this connection, I'll find us a crack negotiator and start working on these new people who are apparently involved. It's bad losing Morgan, of course, but for Mark this altered situation may turn out to be more promising... Yes, yes, leave it to me. Considering the power of the very image of aliens and anarchists teaming up together, it should be a piece of cake. But for your part, Ed, you've got to get moving on this campaign. Though you've had almost two months already, you seem to have done nothing—" He looked over at Alexandra and made a wry face at her. She sat down on the sofa and chomped her way through the rest of the parsley. "Yes, Ed, all right... Yes, yes, I'll get on to Stevens as soon as we hang up... That's right... Yes, I'll be getting back to you. Don't sweat this one, I have a feeling that if we act swiftly enough this will prove the break we've been looking for, however catastrophic things may appear to be."

When he hung up he called Rollins, whom Alexandra knew to be on the Night Desk at headquarters, and ordered that they find Stevens and have him call him at his private personal number stat. Then he came and sat beside Alexandra on the sofa. "So how was it?" he asked as he put his arm around her.

Alexandra turned her face to him and initiated a deep kiss. They stopped only when the phone buzzed. She leaned her head back against the sofa and—with her eyes still closed—listened to him move away from her and flip open his handset. "Sedgewick," he said, then went on almost immediately, "I've just gotten a call from Ed Goodwin who tells me the Mujeres Libres group have contacted him and announced they have killed two of Simon's hostages—Joshua Morgan, one of ours, and one of the Navy's men. They say that unless we call off our excisions against Mujeres Libres they'll kill Mark Goodwin next. I want you to get the word out stat to halt all excisions of anyone even remotely connected with that group. And then I want you to initiate a search for a first-rate hostage negotiator with a proven record. I suggest you try the big city municipal police forces. Get a short list to me by seven tomorrow morning, and then I'll choose one. We've got to move on this, Stevens. I don't want to lose Mark Goodwin. Clear? Good. Then get started on this now." He put the handset down and returned to the sofa.

Alexandra opened her eyes. "What is happening?"

He took her hand and laced their fingers together. "Simon's group—the ones who are holding the hostages, including Goodwin's son—have apparently joined forces with Mujeres Libres, a militant feminist group operating in LA. Yesterday we excised two of their cadre. Though we haven't gotten verification of the deaths yet, there's no reason to doubt that they really did kill Morgan and the naval intelligence officer as they claim. It's critical that I extricate Mark Goodwin from this—you know how Ed is taking it. And I've more or less assured him that I would." His mouth tightened. "Apart from my fellow feeling for his predicament, there's also the point that I will have his absolute eternal loyalty if I get him back his son. I need Goodwin, and Com & Tran. And Mark Goodwin is one of ours. According to what Weatherall always said, Goodwin was the brains of that Free Zone CAT. We owe him, Alexandra."

Alexandra stared down at their intertwined fingers. Violence begets more violence, she thought. How could he have expected the terrorists not to respond to the slaughter of their members with further violence? "You see," she said hesitantly. "Killing is a mistake. They'll just get more out of control."

He shook his head. "You're too inexperienced to make that kind of generalization. As a matter of fact, though the terrorists' first response may be to escalate their level of violence, at a certain point they'll find their resources exhausted, and they'll have to cope with the psychological strain of the threat of these excisions on their members. Also, since we're being extremely careful—we're not talking about slaughter here, Persephone, but selective partial surgery—the leadership of these groups will be decimated to the point that they'll lose their organizational cohesion as well as their sense of direction. All those who aren't diehards will simply melt away. There's nothing uncontrolled about this project."

*This project.* What a way to talk about murder.

He put his right arm around her; his left hand played with her fingers and the rings on them. Now tell me how it went with Varley."

Alexandra shrugged. "Okay, I guess. He told me a lot about his experience of the Executive Transformation. Did you know that Mama was born around that time? He said Grandmother is fifteen years younger than he is."

"Your Grandmother is my age almost exactly," he said. "Did he say anything about your not going away with him?"

"Not much," Alexandra said carefully. "He said he was troubled that I've gotten myself so involved with Security when I'm too young to understand what I'm doing. And that he thought it a shame that someone my age should feel she couldn't take a vacation, and that I needed to relax before starting school. That it would be hard on me, since I've never sat in a classroom before."

"Nonsense," he murmured. "And what did you say?"

She stroked the fur-like hair on his knuckles. "Oh, I said that it was just this one project, and that I was learning a lot."

"You can go if you like. I wouldn't be angry at you for it."

Alexandra turned her head to look at him. "I don't want to leave you. I don't think I could stand being away from you for a whole week." It would be like being stripped naked and tossed out into the snow. She would be always wanting him and thinking about him, while at the same time be afraid Grandfather would know, would somehow intuit it from her face or voice or words.

"Are you happy?" he asked, very low.

Alexandra shifted so that she could press her head against his chest. Both his arms went around her, and she could feel his love surrounding her. That wonderful feeling surged inside her, filling her with the ecstasy that she thought must be close to adoration. "I never knew it was possible to feel this way. To be this close to another person. To feel all this love. Sometimes I feel as though I'm going to burst!"

His arms tightened around her. "Me too, Persephone. I never thought I could be happy again. But you make me happy." She felt his lips in her hair and lifted her face to kiss him again. If she could, she thought, she would crawl inside his body and press herself close to his internal organs. Because he himself was the cave, he was the cave of warmth and love.

# Chapter Sixty-six

Astrea was in Brazil with Magyyt when Emily signaled her wish for a rendezvous. Certain that Emily must have found Celia, Astrea grew excited—and then anxious when other reasons for the summons offered themselves as likely. Self has not experienced this much emotional volatility since childhood. Now, landing just after dark on the beach, Astrea finds Emily waiting on the terrace and hurries to her. "Have you found her?"

Emily nods. Even in the dark Astrea can see that her eyes are shining. "I bribed one of the officers who hang around my father. She's in the naval hospital on Coronado Island."

They had scoured Coronado Island but had never thought of the hospital.

"From what my contact was able to learn, it seems she's in some kind of coma."

"Don't worry." Astrea, hearing the desolation in Emily's voice, strives to reassure her. "There's always Leleynl. Leleynl knows how to heal humans."

"But we must take her to Whidbey first," Emily says anxiously.

Astrea finds Emily's hand and grips it. "Where her people are."

"Yes. And where they know at least something about how to heal people who've been damaged by torture." Emily pauses, then continues, "I've packed up a big load of stuff to take to Whidbey because I don't know whether I can risk coming back here after we've gotten Celia to safety. I've arranged for someone to go in the car to the airport tonight and take a plane out—to give my watchdogs the impression that I'm leaving town so that they won't get suspicious when I don't leave this house for so many days."

So they load the pod with all the things Emily has packed up. Then Emily goes upstairs to say goodbye to the woman who *will* be flying out—whom she'll hopefully be meeting in Seattle.

Astrea lands the pod on the roof of the military hospital. Since they know nothing of the hospital, they flit in camouflage from room to room and floor to floor, searching for Celia. They find her, finally, behind a door guarded by a uniformed man holding a long evil-looking weapon in his arms. Astrea throws a false image around him to prevent his seeing the door opening, and they go in.

Celia is lying in a bed on her side, at the mercy of a tangle of tubes and wires. Her body is still and her face waxen. Only when Astrea scans is it clear that she is breathing.

As Emily takes Celia's hand and whispers her name, Astrea de-structures an area of the outer wall and fabricates a mini-shuttle. The fabrication exhausts self, though not to the point of depletion. "Emily," Astrea says.

Emily turns and sees what Astrea has done. "How did you *do* that?"

"We can roll her bed inside the shuttle," Astrea says.

"But that means disconnecting everything from the sockets," Emily says. "And she might need the tech she's hooked up to to keep her alive."

Astrea scans Celia more thoroughly and concludes that Celia will not die if cut off from the power source. Self says, "It's all right. You can disconnect the bed from the power source."

Emily looks anxious, but unplugs the two thick cables from Celia's bed. While Emily rolls the bed into the shuttle, Astrea scans the guard outside. What if he hears and comes in before they've gotten away? In a fierce surge of emotion, self is engulfed by the conviction that he and all his like must cease to exist. It is easy; it takes almost no energy to stop his heart. He will never torture or kill or hold another person prisoner again. And now they needn't worry that he will interfere with the evacuation.

They take the shuttle to the pod, and the pod lifts them high above the atmosphere. "To the Free Zone," Astrea cries, exhilarated as never before. Emily, holding Celia's hand, croons her name and kisses her hand and smoothes her fingers over Celia's brow.

According to the others, Leleynl's way brings results in the very slow long-term. But this kind of result, Astrea finds, *feels* better.

# Chapter Sixty-seven

## [i]

In the grayness, sounds came into focus as voices, voices Celia belatedly recognized. She could not seem to open her eyes; she tried and tried but they seemed to be glued shut. Or maybe even sewn shut? Could that have been done to her? Panicking, she made a sound in her throat.

"Celia! Celia, can you hear me?" It was the voice she had been waiting to hear. "If you can hear me, honey, open your eyes or make some other sign." Celia struggled. Effortfully, she pried her eyes open. Blurred figures wavered before her. I'm hallucinating, Celia thought. They had given her another dose of that drug and she was hallucinating. She had only imagined her mother's voice. Again. Weeping, she let her eyelids fall shut again.

"Celia, it's all right, honey, you're safe." Celia *felt* a warm hand taking hers, a hand that *felt* like her mother's. "You're on Whidbey Island, Celia. Luis is here, and Emily, and Gina, and me. You're safe, honey, you're with those who love you."

"Hallucination," Celia tried to say, but she heard the word come out mangled beyond recognition.

"Open your eyes, Celia. Please. You're safe now with your Mama," the voice of love urged.

She wanted to see Mama, even if she were just an hallucination. This time when she got her eyes open, she held them open. And when she blinked, some of the blur cleared away. "Mama?" she said, staring into her mother's face, and this time the word came out right.

Mama was crying. "You'll be all right now, Cee. You'll be fine."

"I need to wash," Celia said. "They made me all dirty."

"Welcome back, Cee." Celia raised her hands to her eyes and rubbed them, then blinked several times more. Emily, she saw, was standing beside Mama.

"We've been worried sick about you," Luis said, and Celia saw that he stood on Mama's other side.

"Not hallucinating?" Celia asked, looking from face to face. "You're really there?" Surprised, she registered the absence of pain: "I don't feel the drug…" She focused on Emily. "You found me. I knew you would, though they said you couldn't this time. I knew you would find me, whatever they said."

"It took us a long time, Cee," Emily said.

Celia pushed herself up into a sitting position. Her arms trembled from the strain, and a wave of lightheadedness washed over her, darkening her vision, then quickly receded.

"Careful of all the tubes, Cee," her mother said. "Among other things you've got a Foley catheter in you."

"How long?" Celia said, urgently needing to know the date. They looked puzzled. "How long has it been? What is the date?"

"It's July twenty-third, Cee," Emily said.

Celia closed her eyes, the better to fight her disorientation and confusion, the better to grasp the abrupt shift in reality. Filth, she thought. All that time lying in her own dirt in that place of filth. But now she could be clean. She opened her eyes again. "I've got to have a shower."

They gave her a glass of water to drink while Elena and Luis disconnected all the wires and tubes. Her legs were barely able to hold her up, but Emily helped her to the bathroom. Leaning against the wall, clutching the safety rail, she felt the hot, needle-hard shower and knew it was real, knew the nightmare was over, even if everything seemed cottony and strange and elusive.

She, Emily, Elena, and Luis had all come out of it alive. They had survived and were safe. It was hard to take in; it was hard to understand. *Safe.* They were all of them safe.

[ii]

Celia stared out the open window at the flat expanse of fields stretching under the hot wide sky to the horizon. Without turning around, she said, "Susan tells me this used to be a Navy base. Before the Marq'ssan demolished all their weaponry in the Free Zone."

"Yes, that's so," Gina agreed. "Tell me, Celia, are you angry at me for bringing up the subject, or at your mother for telling me?"

Celia's hands clenched into fists. Aware of Gina waiting—and probably staring at her back, examining every line and movement of her body—she shoved her hands into her pockets to hide her fists and turned away from the window. Gina still sat seemingly relaxed, in the armchair facing the one Celia had vacated, with her legs propped in the same position on the coffee table. Celia envied her her relaxation. She felt as though the entire musculature of her own body had turned to stone. "You think I'm angry with myself, I suppose," she said.

"That's a possibility, too." Even Gina's voice sounded relaxed. But then talking to *patients* who'd survived torture was her *job*. It wasn't *her* feelings that were being poked with a stick. "And then there's yet another possibility."

Celia gave Gina a mocking look. "Which goes without saying. Of course I'm angry at those bastards! *I* know why I have this problem, Gina. But that doesn't make a damned bit of difference! *I* know it's all psychological, that my skin and hair and scalp are hygienically clean, that if samples were taken and put under a microscope there'd be nothing there but innocent tissue—" Celia broke off and bit her lip.

"Innocent tissue?" Gina echoed. "That's an interesting expression."

"You know what I mean." Celia fumed. "And don't think you have to point out the significance of that slip, either. I'm perfectly aware of every aspect of the problem. I should be, I've been living with it for a month, and I'm not stupid!"

"As I said earlier, we can do something about it if you like." Gina recrossed her legs. "In fact, we have a variety of options to choose from. But it might be a good idea to talk about the more general problem before dealing with the very concrete problem of keeping you from damaging your skin and scalp. You see, there's more involved here than a simple obsessional response. Even if you stop feeling and smelling feces and urine in your hair and on your face and in your nostrils, you won't have gotten to the root of the problem. Which means you'll still feel bad, Celia, still find it impossible to get a decent night's sleep."

Celia glared at Gina and shoved her fists into her pockets. "Don't you think I know that?" she shouted. "I'm the one having nightmares, not you!" Celia turned and stared out the window again and felt the silence in the room behind her feeding her irritation. Why couldn't Gina simply get on with this hypnosis or self-hypnosis or whatever the thing was, to help her to stop smelling and feeling the filth, to stop her from gagging every time she smelled her own urine and feces as she expelled them from her body? As for the nightmares, they'd gradually go away, that's what everyone else said. "In time," Susan said. "In time it's possible to sleep the entire night through with only occasional bad nights. In time you'll lose a lot of your fear—though you may always be afraid of men in a group..." Susan had been there; Gina had not.

"What about the other time, Celia?" Gina finally broke the silence. "What did you feel after that previous time?"

Celia's stomach heaved. She turned to face Gina. "Why bring that up now? That's all past. And anyway, it wasn't as bad. I hardly remember that now." The sickness in her stomach was bad enough to make her lightheaded and coat her skin with a cold sweat.

"You never talked to anyone about it, did you," Gina said. "I wonder why. Surely you could trust your mother and Emily? Couldn't you?"

"It was past. I had to get on with more important things than feeling sorry for myself," Celia said. Her voice rose, to drown out the buzzing in her ears. "Why dwell on something that only upset me? When people needed me?" Celia stood rock still as her vision dimmed and the buzz in her ears got louder.

"Are you all right, Celia?" Celia felt Gina's arm around her shoulder. "I think you should sit down, don't you?" Firmly she guided Celia to the chair, and Celia collapsed into it and clutched the arms. "Can I get you a glass of water?"

Gina's voice barely penetrated the din. But the lightheadedness began to pass off, and the buzzing receded. "I'm all right," Celia said. Her vision cleared. "But a glass of water would be good, thanks."

Gina brought her the water, and Celia sipped it slowly. When Celia finished it and leaned forward and put the glass down on the coffee table, Gina removed it and carried it outside Celia's line of vision.

When Gina was again seated across from Celia, she resumed where they'd left off. "Let me see if I understand this," she said. "Are you saying that once this obsession of trying to cleanse yourself is dealt with, you intend to try to ignore everything you're feeling? Do I have that right?"

Celia fingered the shell in her tunic pocket that Emily had brought her, the shell she had picked up on Emily's beach more than a year ago, the shell that was one of the few possessions remaining from her past life. Her fingers traced the slight whorls marking its smooth polished surface; if she closed her eyes while fingering the shell she could sometimes remember the sound of the ocean and now and then could visualize Emily's beach as the sun glinted off the placid green waves rolling shoreward. She looked into Gina's face. "There's not a damned thing that can be done about my anger, Gina. If that's what you're talking about. There's no way I can touch those bastards, at least not right now. Maybe we can get Jackson and Crowe and Silver, I don't know. But facts are facts. And I have to learn to live with them."

"Hmmm." Gina recrossed her legs. "But I think you're angry at others, besides. And at yourself—for surely what you've done to your face is strong self-punishment, however you look at it. You're angry at your mother and Emily for abandoning you, and at the rest of the world for letting this happen. You're angry at me, Celia. Because I was safe here on Whidbey Island while you were in hell, because like a lot of the rest of the world I was living as though everything were perfectly normal. And here I sit talking to you, I who am someone who can go to sleep and stay asleep without much trouble. Prying and poking away at you. Of course you're angry at me, Celia." Celia looked again at Gina and briefly met her gaze. "Maybe you should tell me so yourself," she added.

"But it's irrational. *I* know it's not your fault I was tortured."

Gina said, "Maybe you should still tell me so yourself."

Celia bit her lip. "As for Emily and my mother, it's ridiculous to say I blame them for abandoning me. When all the time they were doing everything they could to find me. And I knew it, even at the worst of times. It was what kept me going."

"Oh really?" Gina said. "I seem to recall your writing in your statement that the main subject area of the interrogations was your mother's whereabouts. Maybe part of you feels you suffered on her account?"

Celia exploded. "We both know they would have treated me that way no matter what! My mother's whereabouts was a pretext! That's how torture works! I've read the literature, Gina!"

"You keep talking about things at the rational intellectual level. Several times in this session you've referred to what's in 'the literature.' But deep feelings don't always conform with what one intellectually knows."

"Can't we just get on with the hypnosis?"

"If you insist."

"I do insist," Celia said. "Even as we sit here I'm imagining I can smell it and that you can smell it too and are dying to get away from me because of it."

"Okay," Gina said. "It would be best if you stretched out on the couch or the floor. You need to be relaxed."

Relaxed, Celia thought as she got up from the chair. Relaxed was something she couldn't feel without tranquilizers. Every time she tried going off the tranqs she felt like she was about to jump out of her skin... Relaxed: a luxury, something for people like Gina, who could use the word so casually. Celia lay down on the couch and settled a cushion behind her head. Maybe this hypnosis would work. It was worth a try. It damned sure was a hell of a lot more constructive than all this endless *talking*.

# Chapter Sixty-eight

"Hazel," Jan said softly from the threshold. Hazel looked up and smiled at the woman who was the closest to a secretary the Co-op got. "They've broken through."

"Incredible!"

"Weatherall apparently has a stunning knack for such things."

"She's the one who broke through?" Hazel said as she logged off and locked her terminal.

"Oh yes," Jan said—as though to say *who else?*

They walked down together to the office two floors below where efforts at breaking into Security Services' electronic data system were concentrated. "There are three of them there," Jan said.

"Three of Liz's group?"

"Oh no, there are *five* of *them* altogether. What I meant was, there are three executives. All there together in that room." She slid Hazel a wry look. "I've never seen so many executives together at once."

More interesting would be to know what Liz was making of the Marq'ssan, Hazel thought. "Then you've been lucky," Hazel said dryly. "I wish I could say the same thing."

Jan offered her an uncomfortable laugh but did not pursue it.

The office, one of the windowless inside-corridor rooms largely vacant except when out-of-towners needed office space before, during, and after Steering Committee meetings, was crammed to the gills with women, most of them sitting with their eyes glued to their terminals. Hazel nodded at Shirl, who stood by the door as though on guard, and Shirl nodded back. "How've you been, Hazel?" she said.

"Really fine," Hazel said, smiling meaningly into Shirl's eyes. "And you?"

"Not bad. Things are pretty much the same as they always are out there."

Hazel nodded coolly and moved into the room. Glancing around she located first Liz, then Martha, and finally Sorben. Liz, she saw, had brought her laptop. Hazel knew for a fact that Liz's laptop had an enormous capacity for data storage. She wondered if she should inform Martha of this in case Martha had not already figured it out for herself. Hazel took the chair beside Martha, who was staring at a monitor that was replicating everything showing on Liz's screen.

"What I'm doing now," Liz said, "is penetrating the Special Operations section, which will probably be one of the two main locations for the files we want." The master directory list of code names began scrolling down the screen. "The trick now will be to figure their system of operation and subject naming. For example, we'll need to figure out what code name they've assigned, say, to Hazel. I'm going to start on the assumption that they haven't jettisoned their general coding protocols, such that they've probably continued deriving code names for operations and subjects in the Free Zone from science fiction."

Martha said, "You've got to be kidding!"

Liz looked amused. "It all started with references to the Free Zone as the Twilight Zone. And then the fact that the Marq'ssan were involved made it all too irresistible to come up with code names like Operation Galactica, and so on."

Hazel shivered. Operation Galactica had been the code name for the plan for tricking and ambushing Martha and other Free Zone leaders. A click of Liz's mouse brought up a new display showing hundreds of words that were apparently code names. "So," Liz said, "they haven't bothered to do more than tend to their outer defenses. Can you believe it, they haven't changed any of the internal codings? They just assumed I'd never make it into the system! We're in luck, women." The scrolling halted, the screen convulsed, and a new set of names began scrolling down the screen. "Yes, see? What does Andromeda sound like to you? It sounds like a Free Zone operation to me. Let's take a peek, shall we?" The screen emptied, and in three-inch characters the word Andromeda flashed for perhaps half a second before giving way to what was obviously the top of a document.

*Proposal for Operation ANDROMEDA,* 7/10/2086 Over-Controller: ESSEX Local Controller: SHASTA Purpose: Recovery of renegades DELPHINIUM and YELLOW PRIMROSE (hereafter

DEL and YPR), location 80-20 likely T.Z. Local Personnel: Already in place—SHASTA; imported: INGLAS, CONNESS, RAINIER, SOUTHESK.

There followed figures for an operating budget and instructions for collecting information from five areas of the Zone that would allow them to narrow the scope of their search.

"So, Hazel." Hazel looked up and found Liz smiling at her. "They've given us flower names. Which is what security has always done for renegades. I could give you odds I'm Delphinium and you're Yellow Primrose."

"That's a lot of money they're willing to spend on finding us," Hazel said.

"And this is only one operation. Note, the over-controller named is Wedgewood." Liz turned back to her terminal. "As for Shasta, that's someone who at the time I left was working in Eureka. I forgot about him because he was working under the control of the San Jose station and not under the Edmonds CAT. Which must be why they decided they could shift him north—since none of the Edmonds people would know and nothing would be showing in the records Simon got her hands on."

Martha said, "You're saying there are agents stationed all over the Free Zone?"

"There was Shasta in Eureka, Galan in Bellingham—under control of the Vancouver BC station, and Velino in Spokane and Knittelfeld in Yakima, both of whom operated out of the Boise station."

"My god," Martha said. "How many *stations* do you have on this continent?"

"A hell of a lot more now than we had before the Blanket. But if you don't mind, I suggest we see where this project went and what its current status is." The screen scrolled rapidly through documents, most of them reports to Essex.

"Before the Blanket you had hundreds of ODS offices around the country," Martha said. "Literally hundreds."

"So," Liz said, stopping the scrolling. "Look, here they report a sighting of us at the gallery Margot Ganshoff and I often used for contact. After which they staked the place out, and their local agent, Asimov, eventually spotted me. Hmmm. I'll have to let Margot know.

But fortunately we lost them." Liz turned to Hazel. "You see, darling, it pays to take all the precautions each and every time." She looked back at the screen. "That was their first solid confirmation of our presence here. I imagine after that they closed down a lot of other operations and put everything they had here."

"Is Asimov the name of a person living and working in Seattle?" Shoshana asked, speaking for the first time since Hazel had entered the room.

"Asimov is a cryptonym for a locally recruited agent," Liz said. "All agents recruited in Seattle are given as their cryptonyms the names of science fiction writers."

"Is there any way we can find out Asimov's real name?"

"Of course," Liz said. "I'll tap the cryptonym index once we've pulled everything from this section of the system. The cryptonym index is in another—deeper—section."

"What's Sedgewick's code name?" Martha asked.

"Windsor," Liz said absently as the screen resumed rapid scrolling.

"And yours?"

"In order to save time, we should probably enter a command for searching and making a file-dump of all documents cross-referenced under the various code names we've already encountered. We can do that while I continue to collect more and more code names."

"I wonder why Elizabeth isn't answering my question," Martha said.

"Her code name was Tudor," Hazel said.

Martha snorted. "Now that takes the cake. Though delusions of monarchy shouldn't surprise me, I suppose. I wonder Sedgewick didn't choose to call himself Napoleon while he was at it."

"My code name wasn't *always* Tudor," Liz said in a perceptibly sharp voice. "I only adopted that after Zeldin put Sedgewick out of commission."

"You people are incredible," Martha said.

"Allison, will you do a search through the file-dump for other appropriate operational code names, please?"

Allison input commands into her terminal and stared at the scrolling screen. Occasionally she called out a name. "Operation Sirius…

Operation Corona... Operation Black Hole...Operation Sagittarius... Operation Omega Centauri... Operation Sunspot..."

Hazel felt a touch on her shoulder and looked up to find Lisa standing behind her. "Will you take a break with me, Hazel?" she asked, her voice so low Hazel had to strain to hear what she said.

Hazel studied Lisa's face, then decided *what the hell*. She might as well see what Lisa wanted. It certainly wasn't to pass the time of day with her, a service-tech.

As they trudged up the stairs Lisa said, "I see you've taken to wearing Free Zone clothing."

"It's wonderfully comfortable." Hazel almost added that she had stopped shaving her legs, too, but decided such a comment would be excessively provocative.

She led Lisa to a lounge on the other side of the building where they sat on the floor and drank water. "There's sure to be stuff in there on me," Lisa said. "I can hardly wait until we figure out what new code name they've slapped on me."

"I'm surprised they didn't call Liz Forget-me-not," Hazel said, grinning. "Delphinium is remarkably lacking in rancor, don't you think?"

Lisa frowned. "What's going on with you two? Elizabeth won't tell me. I think Allison knows, but she won't talk either."

"If Liz won't tell you what makes you think I will?" Hazel wondered whether Liz hadn't told Lisa for fear she might turn against her. Or no, Hazel thought, how could Lisa turn against Liz? Lisa had burned all her bridges behind her. There was nowhere else for Lisa to go. Every other alternative had been closed off. Liz had Lisa where she wanted her. "Anyway, you might as well not even try to persuade me to come back. I know what she's up to, I know her motives, I know her down to the bottom of her icy cold heart."

Lisa sighed. "For godsake, Hazel, the woman's a wreck. Do you have any idea how hurt she is? Don't you care?"

"She put you up to this, didn't she."

"If she knew I was talking to you about this she'd be furious," Lisa said, looking straight into Hazel's eyes. "She's testy enough as it is. She just about bit my head off when I asked her why you left. I haven't dared to bring it up since then. I thought she'd get back to normal after a week or two, but she's as bad as she was the day you left. She's

driving all of us batty. She reduced Ginger to tears twice last week."
Lisa sighed. "It's hard to believe you two have separated. I could have
sworn this was it for Elizabeth. I mean, she's been a changed woman."
Lisa took a sip of water and looked speculatively at Hazel. "Did you
know her before you got involved with her, Hazel?"

Hazel's fingers dug into the plastic pleats of the bottle. "No. I got to
know her because she picked me up and decided to string me along."

"That's a peculiar way to put it." Lisa frowned. "Well, you probably have no idea what her sexual style was before you got involved
with her. Let me put it this way: I've never met or heard of anyone as
promiscuous as she. If it weren't for the responsibilities of her job she
probably would have gone through a dozen different sexual partners a
day." Hazel snorted. "I'm not kidding, Hazel. I've seen her when she's
been on vacation. In a single night that woman could go through four
or five girls. That's what she was like. Then I come up here and find
her very close to monogamous. Which isn't her nature, dear." Lisa
gave Hazel a sardonic look. "And not only that, but I find her bringing you in on everything and agreeing to make fundamental changes
in the way the household is run, all because she wants to please you."
Lisa bit her lip. "And then you tell me something about her icy cold
heart? Obviously she wants you back. What is it, won't she give in on
some particular point?"

Hazel's heart beat so hard she could hear it thudding in her ears.
"I won't go back for any reason."

Hazel's words hung in the air for about half a minute. Softly, Lisa
said, "She's a proud woman, Hazel. If there's something she's failing
to say, I'm sure it's not for lack of feeling. Give her another chance,
dear. Please. Don't let this thing, whatever it is, come between you.
That kind of love and devotion doesn't grow on trees, you know."

"What bullshit." Hazel's throat grew tight with the threat of tears.
"As far as Liz is concerned love is the delusion that makes service-techs
do what executives want them to do."

"Hazel!" Lisa looked shocked. "How can you say that? That woman is in serious pain!"

"Well *I'm* not," Hazel said angrily. "Which is something you ne-
glected even to consider. But then *my* feelings don't count. Otherwise
you would have *first* asked me if I was in pain from having left her be-

fore laying this crap on me about *her* pain. But then you people never do think about *our* feelings, do you."

Lisa stared at her. "If you're that happy to be free of Elizabeth," she said after a while, "then I guess I made a mistake. I just assumed..." She shrugged. "I guess you had *all* of us fooled. Even me. And Allison. You seemed to exude love from your very pores. I see now that I made a mistake." She got to her feet. "Do me a favor and don't mention to Elizabeth that I talked to you about this. I can see why she'd be angry with me if she knew. It would only rub salt in the wound." Without waiting for Hazel to respond, Lisa left the lounge.

Hazel sat for a few minutes longer, finishing the water, thinking. Or trying to think. Her head was filled with a babble of dizzying contradictions she wished she could shut out. "Damn Lisa," she said out loud as she got to her feet. She's confused me, who knows why... Liz could have put her up to this, or maybe Lisa was different from Liz and Allison and Margot and all those others, maybe Lisa had failed to understand, maybe Lisa was as much under the delusion as any of the service-tech lovers of her peers.

Hazel deposited the empty bottles and cups in the appropriate bins. By now the group might have gotten to more current operations. Soon they might know if Security had learned yet that Hazel had taken to living in the open, away from Liz. Hazel shivered. She needed to know, but it gave her the creeps thinking of those people writing reports about her, giving her a name. *Yellow Primrose.* Incredible. Absolutely incredible. But that was Security for you.

# Chapter Sixty-nine

Celia took a bite of the pasta. *Yuck.* It was limp and slimy. "Sorry, Emily," she said, making a face. "It's been so many years since I've cooked that everything I touch I seem to screw up." And Emily, Celia thought, was used to the best.

"Don't worry about it, Cee. I'll concentrate on tasting the pesto, which is really quite wonderful."

"It's Sweetwater's pesto," Celia said. "Susan brought me a big jar of the stuff this afternoon. When the basil and spinach and garlic crops come in they make it in enormous quantities. Apparently whatever they don't sell at the local farmer's market they freeze for the winter." Celia took a big gulp of water. Limp pasta, even with brilliant pesto, was revolting. So typical of everything in her life these days. "So how are things going in Seattle?"

Her fork almost to her lips, Emily looked at Celia and raised her eyebrows. "You mean with Martin and Jean and the rest of Mytilene?"

"Yes. It must be difficult for them, being uprooted without notice. They had no reason to expect *they'd* have to run." But they couldn't have stayed. Military police would be snatching up and interrogating anyone Emily had had anything to do with since she had begun her simpatico activities. And no question, Martin's cartoons would not bear the kind of examination they'd have gotten under the circumstances.

Emily finished chewing and swallowed. "Except for Martin, they've also lost the clientele they've established over the years, and now since I can't afford to support them financially, they as well as I have to find a way to earn a living." Emily dabbed her mouth with her napkin. "Sometimes I think of contacting my father—to see if he'd be willing to help me. But..." Emily put her napkin back in her lap, then stared down at her plate and wrapped another bite of fettuccine around the tines of her fork.

Celia gave up all pretense of eating. "I don't know much about your relationship with your father," she said. "But surely he wouldn't turn you in? Isn't it possible he might help you in some limited way?" But how would someone like she, Celia, understand how a man like Barclay Madden would react to his daughter's having gone renegade? She knew very little about how male executives felt about their families.

Emily put her fork down and looked across the table at Celia. "Oh, I'm sure he'd agree to help me—for a price." Celia could hear that there was more, so she waited for Emily to go on. Emily took a drink of water before continuing. "I think he'd insist I come back. That he would refuse to transfer more funds into my plastic account. And that he'd stipulate that I agree to a loquazene examination by Aldridge and his crew—with certain guarantees given to him for my safety." She laughed bitterly. "Some of them might want to put me in prison, but they wouldn't, you know, not if my father took a hand in it. Which I imagine he would. I can't see him losing his heir so easily. So he'd make a deal with Aldridge that I be available for certain limited in-terrogation—I can just see Daddy's men in the room, watching—and then I'd be released to Daddy's custody." Emily's mouth twisted. "And of course I'd have to promise Daddy to 'behave.'" Her eyes glinted. "You get the picture, Cee?"

"Oh yes. And I could see how they'd figure that once they'd got-ten all the names you knew out of you no simpatico would go within a mile of you. And probably your father wouldn't allow you to come and go without supervision." All those trips to the Free Zone, when Emily had simply informed her office to make shift while she was away, all her subterfuge with her cars and drivers and drop-places and fancy electronic technology that protected her privacy and security—all that would be forfeit, and Emily would have no choice but to play their game or no game at all.

Emily sighed. "But really, Cee, it's best not to think of that. I've left all that behind, and I have fewer regrets than you might imag-ine." A smile broke over her face, like the sun bursting through the clouds. "Almost all of the people I really care for are here with me, and that's what matters. And we're all alive, Cee, and we're all free. One hundred percent survival rate of all those I love. I feel pretty lucky, you know."

Celia noticed the smudges her fingerprints and pesto-smeared lips had made on her water glass. She itched to wipe the glass clean. Celia said very low, "I hope I'm worth it. Because I know damned well that if it hadn't been for me, you and the others would still be in San Diego."

Emily's smile widened and warmed. "As I said, I'm lucky. You don't know how happy I am just to be sitting across the table from you, sharing a meal."

Celia took the napkin from her lap, dipped it in her water glass, and wiped the outside of it, beginning with the bottom and working up to the rim. "I'm going to be fine now," she said. "Gina taught me to hypnotize myself today and helped me set up a mechanism for stopping this." She touched her still painful face. "The lotion you gave me is first-rate. And now it will have a chance to really work. Because I *won't* be scrubbing my face with alcohol anymore."

"Oh, Cee, that's great news! Maybe we should have had wine with this meal!"

Celia laughed. "You hardly ever drink wine," she said. The glass now looked pristine, so Celia replaced her napkin in her lap and set the glass back on the table. But glancing at it, she saw that she had left new fingerprints. What she needed to do, she told herself, was avoid looking at it. And so she did.

"This is such progress I think we should celebrate," Emily said. "Before you know it, you're going to be clamoring to leave this island paradise and come live with us in Seattle."

A wave of nausea washed over Celia. She couldn't imagine living in a city, exposed to all those...people. "Maybe so," she said carefully. "At any rate, today I told Gina that I didn't need any more sessions with her."

Emily looked surprised. "Oh? Are you sure, Cee? I mean..."

Celia's hands fisted in her lap. "I can talk to Susan and some of the others. They understand much more than Gina ever could. Gina hasn't been there, Emily. She keeps twisting everything. It's infuriating." Emily said nothing, only continued to watch Celia's face. "Damn it, Em, I know what she's doing. She thinks I should put *everything* down in the deposition for the Human Rights Committee. And I just don't think it's necessary. The sulfizine was bad enough. Torture is torture. I don't see why I have to bring all the obscene stuff into it. They don't need that. There's enough in the sulfizine treatments to suffice for showing their culpability. I don't see why I should make a spectacle of myself just to make my case more emotionally loaded."

"It's your decision, Cee. As it is, we can be fairly certain those doctors will be facing serious ostracism by their peers once your deposition gets out. And that's very important. I really don't see how Gina can argue with that."

Celia pushed her plate away and rested her elbows on the table. "God, I'm suddenly very tired, Em." She smiled wearily at the other's serious face. "How long will you be staying?"

Emily smiled back. "Oh, a couple of days. And then I have to get back. I've pretty well decided to work with the International Human Rights Committee—and with an eye toward finding clients for Mytilene work. Though as long as I'm limited to staying in the Free Zone, I suppose I won't be able to do much. But we'll see. I'm pleased about doing this work, you know. It's a vast improvement over working for Daddy, and I take satisfaction in knowing I can handle certain situations and tasks that my executive training gives me an inside track on. There aren't many executives available for the work."

Celia drank the rest of the water in her glass. Once more she polished the glass with her napkin. What she needed, she thought, were lungfuls of clean, fresh air—outdoors, away from food and plates and glasses and other smudgeable objects. "Before I get completely dragged out, why don't we drive over to the beach and get in a walk, Em. There's dessert, but maybe it would be better to have it when we get back."

Emily agreed; she, too, seemed to have lost her appetite somewhere along the way. Snatching up sweaters, they hopped into the two-seater Emily had driven from Seattle and headed for Deception Pass. The sunsets there were sometimes even better than the ones they'd watched from Emily's deck.

# Chapter Seventy

Magyyt calling. But there can be no other answer than yes, of course that one chooses to go.

Astrea wonders: have they been talking about self? But perhaps Magyyt has a specific reason for calling, a reason having nothing at all to do with self's choice to work apart from the other Marq'ssan on this planet. Astrea doesn't know Magyyt well enough to speculate with any certainty.

Astrea lands on Mt. Baker as instructed, near a pod that has not been camouflaged. Magyyt, Tyln, and Sorben are already there, perching in the sunlight on smooth, gray boulders that are at their surface radiating heat but are substantially cold within. The lightness of self's enlarged body on this planet seems even more pronounced up here where the blue vault of sky stretches endlessly, making self feel less immediately bound to the ground. Astrea walks through a patch of snow. *Three of them.* Why three of them? And why do they call now?

That one perches on a rock near Magyyt, whom self prefers of the three. Thick black flies swarm and light on self's face and arms. Unlike many of this planet's insects, these are neither charming nor interesting. Before speaking to the others, Astrea scans the flies and produces a body-scent to repel them. Then self listens to what the others are saying in Immeni.

"If this massive campaign of murder is a response to our liberation of those prisons, we *must* reconsider continuing such a tack," Tyln is arguing. "We surely can't stop them from killing. Unless you think we should further damage their economy?" From Tyln's tone of voice it is clear that that one believes it important *not* to damage the dominant economy.

"But so far this has been a response of the US government only," Sorben points out. "None of the other governments have stepped up the level of their violence after the liberation of their prisons. It's possible that the US's response is less to do with the liberations than with a general change in policy more or less independent of those actions."

"Sedgewick's organization has a long history of such campaigns. The only difference this time is that it's directed against those being labeled subversive." Magyyt seems to agree with Sorben.

"Maybe what we need to do, then, is find a way to discredit Sedgewick's organization," Tyln says.

Sorben's field ripples. "Discredit it? With whom? In whose eyes would discrediting that organization matter?"

Magyyt turns to Astrea. "And your opinion, Astrea?"

Astrea feels the force of their combined attention and effortfully keeps self's field from contracting in protective response. "My opinion is that the individuals directing the violence should be dealt with."

"Oh?" Tyln says in one of Boldeni's most sarcastic inflections "And how would you 'deal' with them?"

Astrea replies in Boldeni also: "By destroying all their personal economic power. Such things seem to matter greatly among humans. And by destroying the physical systems around them that support their power. It would be easy enough to do. And would divert their energies to trying to protect their most basic economic interests."

"Do you hear that?" Tyln says. "This one not only thinks such negative methods are a solution, but considers *individuals* responsible for the mess on earth!" Tyln's human gaze bores into Astrea's. "Surely you realize that there are always more where they came from, that it is the entire structure of their thinking that needs to be addressed, that getting one individual out of the way will only lead to another's taking that one's place? Are you familiar with what happened when shortly after the outset of our open engagement here we helped Kay Zeldin isolate Sedgewick? Though he and his organization were severely damaged by this, not only did they eventually recover, but others stepped into the vacuum. They shifted to lower technologies and more local authority structures, but in almost every case an authority structure was quickly established and enforced. It is this habit of and dependence upon the authority structure we have been working to change, Astrea. Not the individuals controlling such structures."

Preaching, preaching, as though self needs to be told such simple things. "I know all that," Astrea retorts. "But you were talking about a specific problem, the specific problem of that organization killing people in retaliation. *If* retaliation it is. They might very well have started the killing anyway. They're frustrated enough by the problems they're having with their technology as well as their problems controlling the cities since their economy still hasn't recovered from the traumas of the last decade. Which *you* started," Astrea points out, irritated at their failure to admit the extent to which Marq'ssan have been tinkering with human civilization.

"Suppose we took out the chief individuals," Magyyt says. "Then what?"

"If when you first opened everything up," Astrea says, glad to be delivering an opinion that has developed over weeks of observation, "you had insisted on placing responsible people at the head of the governments you were dealing with—and I've met some responsible people here, I know that they exist—if you'd done *that*," Astrea insists, "then you could have worked on educating humans in a more effective way. These small Free Zones are not adequate. They're perceived only as thorns in the flesh of the governments, and as they stand now if you left earth many of the people in the Free Zones would be murdered and the Zones themselves taken over again by the governments that previously ruled them. All that could have been avoided. It would have been easiest to do at the beginning. Especially considering the number of Marq'ssan involved at the outset of the intervention."

Growing more and more excited, Astrea finds self's field expanding and strengthening almost to the edge of Magyyt's. "But it could still be done—with this one government at the very least. I don't understand why you don't do it. We have the power to bring them to their knees and agree to whatever we stipulate!"

Magyyt, pulling in that self's field, edges away. "You alarm and grieve me," that one says in an Omauo that wraps painfully around Astrea's viscera. "Your way of talking strikes the most unpleasant resonance with memories I carry from years long past in Bolddan," that one laments, now in Immeni. "I, Astrea, was of Bol. I was among those who treated with arrogance all other ambients. I was among those who believed the Boldeni ambience the only correct, progressive, *civilized* way for Marq'ssan."

For a few seconds Magyyt shows Astrea that Marq'ssan's natural form. "You see the markings of ambient, Astrea?" Magyyt says as that one's field realigns to human form. "At one time those markings were a matter of unconscious pride to me. *Unconscious*, Astrea. I hardly knew it even mattered to me. All of it submerged within self. That's how deeply *that* arrogance can run. I sense the same arrogance in you. You talk of destroying, destroying, destroying. Is it you, Astrea, who has been destructuring at US military installations?"

"You can't accuse me of being in any way Bolddan," Astrea raps out in harsh, staccato Boldeni. "I abhor all that, I always have, like all Marq'ssan born since those evil days. We aren't touched with that, we've never been contaminated—as you *have*, Magyyt. *You* may be obsessed with that past, but it's not *mine!*"

"Is it possible you don't see the danger inherent in this intervention situation? The danger for Marq'ssan?" Sorben says. "There's a relevant analogy to the old Bolddan dominance, Astrea. And your arrogance proves the point! We must not take the attitude that human ambients—and I suggest for a moment we think in such projective terms—we must be careful that we don't consider Marq'ssan ambients superior to human ambients!"

"But we *are* superior!" Astrea cries. "We *are!* Their savagery and barbarism are evident! They murder and slaughter and torture without hesitation! How can we possibly consider them our equals?"

"Think about what you're saying!" Tyln says. "Superior! Where do you get such a word? Only from Boldeni! The concept doesn't exist in any other Marq'ssan language! Doesn't that tell you something, Astrea? That you couldn't even *say* such a thing in any other Marq'ssan language?"

"Can you deny that murder and torture is barbaric?"

"There is much among humans that is 'barbaric'—as you call it, Astrea," Magyyt says, "and murder and torture are merely the most visibly objectionable signs of this systematic oppression pervading human institutions. Nevertheless, to set ourselves up as dominant over them would be only to fall into the trap of their system. If we talk about superiority, then we too must think of ourselves as barbaric. For there's then only one thing that can happen, and that's the establishment of our ambient over theirs, and perhaps even the adoption of their tactics. For it's always been so-called superiority that has led to murder and other less visible forms of oppression, Astrea."

*Murder.* That is what they would call what self has done, Astrea realizes. They would call self a murderer. They would claim self is like *them.* "I see what you're saying, Magyyt," Astrea says after a while, "but I would not eradicate their cultures. That is not what I seek. In that way there's no comparison with old Bolddan. Rather I would help them to find their way. Stronger measures are required than the ones you have been taking. How can we help them if we're always worrying about being as barbarous as they?"

"I loathe your talk about barbarism," Sorben says. "It reminds me more than anything else of the old struggle."

"But *that* word exists in Immeni as well as Boldeni. And it's a word that's appropriate. How else describe such moral heinousness?" They fall into a long silence. So, Astrea thinks, they can't answer me. They know as well as I do that human cultures are mired in barbarism.

"There is one thing that I think needs to be recalled in this conversation," Magyyt finally says. "We must always keep in mind that we are doing this for ourselves, not for them. That whatever we do is for the sake of our own selves. That was a lesson it took a long, long time to learn. And until it was learned the Bolddan struggle could not be resolved. We are not intervening to save them from themselves, Astrea. We are intervening for our own sake. And we must always be sensitive to the danger of internalizing their values and attitudes as we struggle. Which is why we can't separate ourselves from the things they do. If we think of ourselves as above them, as saving them for altruistic reasons, then we are lost. We always understood that as the principle danger from the intervention. Perhaps you didn't realize this. Remember, altruism is another Boldeni concept. It's a false concept, one that plays into the superior-inferior structure. Whatever we do, we must first take care that we ourselves are not damaged. Exercising the vast power you advocate would place us in terrible danger. Imagine our returning to Marqeuei and deciding we didn't like things we saw there. Marq'ssan do not have a perfect society, Astrea. It's even *likely*—especially since we've been away so long—that that could happen. If we ever imagined for a second that it is possible to think in terms of superior-inferior, we could very easily relapse into violence against and oppression of others. It is never possible to act upon others and not in turn be affected. Whatever happens to those around one—especially the more they are similar to one's self—the more greatly one is affected. No one is isolated enough not to inevitably respond to the harm one has done. No one."

"I resent your preaching at me!" Astrea faces them almost as if they are enemies. "There's no need to teach me what I learned early in my admittedly young life. But let me point out that when we stand by and allow immense harm to be done to others, we are ourselves doing harm by allowing it and must obviously suffer morally in consequence." Astrea looks from Magyyt to Sorben to Tyln and back to Magyyt. "After all, that was the reason it was decided not merely to quarantine Earth, isn't it. Precisely because we would still be affected by what we knew of the existence of humans."

"A quarantine was never seriously considered," Magyyt says.

Astrea sneers. "Maybe not when you were last on Marqeuei, but lately it's been a very popular idea. And may yet happen!"

"I asked you a question before, Astrea, and you didn't answer," Magyyt says after a pause. "Let me repeat it for you. Is it you who have been destructuring military structures?" Magyyt's human eyes stare hard at Astrea's human face. "We've been wondering, Astrea, for humans are incapable of destructuring things themselves. And it is rare for a Marq'ssan to do such things without mentioning it to others."

"Are you accusing me of something, Magyyt?" Astrea draws self's field in tightly and moves further away from the others.

"Does it bother you that we want to know?" Sorben says.

"I don't know why it would," Tyln murmurs. "Why should a Marq'ssan want to hide self's activities from others?"

"Yes!" Astrea does not confess, but announces her responsibility, her *initiative*. "Yes, it is I who have been destructuring weapons of death and instruments of torture. All these things *should* be destructured. If you had been doing that all along these people would not be able to carry out their savagery."

Magyyt sighs. "You see, we're back to the same problem. Astrea, how can it be that you don't understand that these things, while important, are not the key to the problem? The demolishing of structures of authority, the teaching of responsibility, the de-legitimation

of violence so thoroughly linked to authority in the very ways children are raised and the ways deviants are treated are the things we
most need to accomplish! Destructuring physical objects can help, but
how much better if the humans themselves choose not to have such
objects! Can't you enfold this complexity, Astrea? Your de-finitization
of this one manifestation falls into the trap of accepting a structure by
which an origin is determined and doggedly pursued to the exclusion
of all else! Perhaps you need to try thinking about human structures
exclusively in Immeni and Omauo, if only for a short time in order to
show you the limitations of your conceptualization."

"Why aren't you *doing* anything? Talking about conceptual limitations does nothing to change the mess we see all around us here!"

They fall silent for half a minute. Then Sorben says, softly,
"Perhaps we should show you some changes in progress, Astrea.
You've seen such a limited sampling of human life. And you've seen
very little of the humans we've been personally working with."

"The changes Leleynl l Absq san Phrglu has wrought," Magyyt
adds, "are perhaps the most significant. Because Leleynl has chosen
not to consider the global situation at large, has chosen not to concern self with governments. Leleynl has worked with individuals for
a long, long time."

"Let's visit Leleynl now," Sorben proposes.

Astrea feels trapped; self thinks of the sorts of things said about
Leleynl, even back on Marqeuei, for Leleynl is old and circulates immense *bahlamm*, as Astrea remembers feeling that one time self had
met that one. "Another time," Astrea says.

"Why not now?" Magyyt says. "What is so important for you to do
that you can't visit Leleynl l Absq for a few hours?"

Astrea can't think of any viable reason for refusing. "All right! So
I'll go with you! Though I'll say now that while Leleynl's accomplish-
ments with individuals may be impressive, there is no evidence that
such individual changes affect the whole."

"We'll discuss the question of that later," Sorben says. "And
Leleynl will probably have plenty to say on the subject anyway. As
you'll see."

Glumly Astrea boards the pod and sets course for a location on the
continent of Africa in an area called Zambia, an area that is not a Free

Zone, yet is a place where, according to Magyyt, changes have been slowly occurring. Astrea reserves judgment. If it isn't in a Free Zone, then savagery will be the rule. In which case a few humans opposing barbarism won't amount to much.

# Chapter Seventy-one

Hazel looked up and saw Liz standing on the threshold in the pool of sunlight flooding in from the windows behind Hazel.

"Do you have a few minutes? I want to talk to you about our analysis of the documents we took from Security's system."

The flowery lavender silk seemed to swirl around Liz, veiling the hardness of her toughly muscled body; her eyes, aquamarine today, were bright, though her face was otherwise subdued. Hazel's body tensed. In the absence of that icy mass of anger that had blocked all her senses where Liz was concerned, Hazel now suffered a renewed awareness of her sexual attraction to her. "Sure, I have a few minutes," she said. "What's the upshot? Do they know I've moved out of the household?"

Liz stepped inside, closed the door, and took the chair on the other side of the desk. "Not yet," Liz said. "But it's very odd." She frowned. "I think—and Shoshana agrees with me—that there's someone in the Co-op—working right in this building, probably—who is reporting to them. Because there's a mention of Marjorie Burroughs in their reports on Greenglass. You see," Liz said, "they have someone who reports regularly on Greenglass and other important Co-op people. It's been reported that Marjorie Burroughs has moved in with Greenglass and that Marjorie Burroughs is working on the International Human Rights Committee." Liz's forehead creased. "It's a curious thing. They had someone regularly on the look-out for your comings and goings here, and they do mention you—as Yellow Primrose, of course—coming into this building. And sometimes they catch you coming out, and tail you, and then lose you. But somehow they haven't made the connection between you and Marjorie Burroughs."

"How do you know it's Marjorie Burroughs?" Hazel asked, confused. "I mean, if they always use cryptonyms—"

"No, darling," Liz said, "they only use cryptonyms for certain people. They wouldn't bother giving Co-op people cryptonyms unless they're working for Security. The reason they give *us* cryptonyms is because we're renegades. And therefore there are reasons why they'd want to take secrecy precautions."

"Oh. So they *have* seen me coming and going from here. What about Lisa? She's been in and out quite a lot."

"Yes," Liz said, "they've spotted her four times."

"I'm surprised they haven't just grabbed us."

"They wouldn't do that. Not unless they get desperate. In the first place, it would be risky trying to pull off in this vicinity. After all, the Women's Patrol are right here. Second, I'm sure they're hoping that one of these times they can tail us to headquarters. That's what they're really after. To get all of us at once." Liz bit her lip. "All that's spelled out, by the way, in some of the operations documents. But who knows how long they'll go on following such a policy. They may eventually decide it's not worth it."

Hazel smoothed her fingers over the long space bar near the bottom of her keyboard. "So what do you think? What's the general picture?"

Liz leaned forward. "Well one thing is positive, and that's that we'll be able to identify most of the people operating in the Free Zone. Shoshana assures me they'll deal with them..." Liz frowned. "I'm not sure I trust the Co-op people to handle Security operatives. But I'm willing to let them take their shot first. Otherwise..." Liz's gaze met Hazel's. "Otherwise we will deal with them as we see fit." Hazel's swallowed "It's our survival, Hazel. Yours and mine," Liz said, holding Hazel's gaze. "As for this possible mole in the Co-op—it won't be that easy to work out, since her cryptonym is kept secret even from Central. That's how much care they're taking to protect it." Liz half-smiled. "Which figures. I remember how hard we worked to establish a mole when I was running things."

"And now you have Anne," Hazel said quietly.

After about five long seconds Liz said, "Anne isn't a mole, Hazel. She's not spying on the Co-op. She's recruiting people for Allison's project. There's a big difference."

"I don't agree," Hazel said. Liz said nothing. "How much are they on to what you're up to, Liz?"

Around and around and around Liz twisted the plain gold band she wore on her right index finger. "They know a lot. But then I expected they would. I've been deliberately dropping clues all over the place." She looked up at Hazel. "But they don't know *where* we are. And they don't know exactly the nature of our connection with the Austrians." She swallowed. "One of their projects—one that has been in progress for the last three months—is to abduct you and use you to get me. Apparently that Navy agent heard enough between us to draw certain conclusions about your importance to me." Liz lowered her gaze. "Sedgewick initiated this operation after interviewing the agent—whom Security only recently had access to. I gather Military refused to let Security get near him until Sedgewick, freshly reinstated, threw his weight around."

The dryness of Hazel's mouth prompted her to go to the cupboard and get out a bottle of water. "Would you like some, Liz?" she asked, showing her the bottle.

"Yes, please." Hazel got out another bottle and two glasses. She felt Liz's somber eyes watching—no, *assessing* her. "I hope you're planning to be very careful about every exit you make from this building," she said as Hazel set the bottles and glasses on the desk. "And that you're careful about maintaining your Marjorie Burroughs alias."

"I'm extremely careful, Liz. There are ways out of this building that I was only recently told about. Ways not many people working in it know about."

Liz poured water into her glass. "Remember, we don't know how much this mole may know," she said. "Even if she doesn't connect Hazel Bell with Marjorie Burroughs, she may still be fairly high up in the hierarchy."

Hierarchy? Hazel wondered. *What* hierarchy?

"And I should also point out that it may only be a matter of time before she sees a photo of Hazel Bell and then that'll be that. They'll stake out Greenglass's house and know they can take you whenever they want. Since you're so free with the kinds of solitary activities you like to pursue."

"Ah, but your amazons will always be there, right, Liz?" Hazel's tone was flippant, but she had to clutch her glass to steady her suddenly trembling fingers.

"Not always, Hazel. They lose you once you get into this building. And then usually pick you up at home. But you can't count on their being able to necessarily deal with anything a Security CAT can mobilize. The amazons are relatively inexperienced. I've tried to give them thorough instruction on the sorts of maneuvers operatives would be likely to try pulling if they see an opportunity for taking you. But they don't have the hard experience that would make me feel sure I can rely on them."

"We don't have any other choice," Hazel said flatly.

"That's not true." Liz stared intently across the desk at Hazel.

"I won't move back, Liz, not even for protection. I've made a new life for myself, I've gone too far now to go back to all that."

"I promise you, Hazel, it wouldn't be the way it was," Liz said urgently, earnestly. "Even though I know I've lost you, I haven't been able to keep from daydreaming about what it could be like if you came back. Everything would be different, I promise."

"There's no chance of my going back. You have to accept that."

Liz set down her glass. "I do accept it, Hazel. It's just that sometimes I wish a little more actively than at other times."

Hazel gulped the rest of the water in her glass. There was nothing she could say without either being cruel or giving Liz an opening. And she did not entirely trust herself now to deal with the latter. If Liz were to embrace her...

Liz said into the silence, "I have this feeling, Hazel, that you're not as angry with me as you were."

The subtle caress that had slipped into her voice worked on Hazel's body. Hazel looked warily into Liz's eyes. "I think I'm seeing things more clearly than I did," she said. "But I haven't changed my mind about breaking with you."

"But perhaps you forgive me for what I did to you?"

Hazel swallowed. Liz must be referring to the imprisonment and drugging in the basement. "I suppose so. I still think it was wrong, but I don't believe now that you found it easy to do."

"If that's so, can't we—"

Hazel interrupted. "No. What a terrible thing for you, Liz. That you can't manage to live consistently. That you're so enslaved to that perverse reality I used to think you left behind when we went renegade. I can't live in your reality, Liz. It's as basic as that."

"My *reality*." Liz said. "I don't understand what it is you think you're saying, Hazel. You've made it pretty clear that you like Greenglass and her ways. I suppose that's what you mean. That and your distaste for executive values and mores, which you've made painfully obvious. You're saying it's a matter of conflicting preferences for lifestyles that's keeping us apart?"

"Nothing so petty, Liz."

Liz's eyes flickered. "My god, I can see it in your face, darling. You do still love me, don't you. But that somehow doesn't matter—enough."

"You made it clear that our love was ultimately secondary to your ambitions," Hazel said. "You used me, Liz. I might have been wrong about your motives for being my lover, but still you used me. As you would if I went back to you. Because that's how you operate. You don't know any other way. In fact, I don't know if you could love anyone without constantly managing her. I bet you even manage Allison, don't you."

"You're so wrong about this," Liz said, but apparently without hope of changing Hazel's mind. She picked up her attaché case, rested it on her knees, and fiddled with the handle. "So you're going to work for the Human Rights Committee? You've decided on that for certain?"

"And attend classes at the University," Hazel said, a little defensively. "I know at my age it's ridiculous, but I always wanted to go to college. I did go for half a year to the community college in Denver, but the Blanket changed everything. I was the only one in the family who could get work at first..."

"I know so little about your past, darling," Liz said. "I see now I never noticed how little you ever said about it."

Hazel laughed shortly. "It's not very interesting, Liz. And I'm sure it would be a little too grubby for executive ears."

Liz's cheeks flamed. "That isn't fair of you."

Hazel swallowed. "No. You're right, I'm sorry, that wasn't fair. You've always been tactful about such things." She sighed. "You'd better let me get back to work, Liz." Hazel held herself under a tight rein to keep from rising from her chair. She must stay on this side of the desk. Liz would try to push it if she gave her the slightest chance.

Liz stood. "I want to keep in touch with you about our security problem," she said.

Hazel nodded. "All right. See you."

Liz smiled slightly, then turned, opened the door, and went out into the corridor. Hazel's breath rushed out, and she realized she had been holding it. As she listened to the swish and rustle of Liz's silk fade, she acknowledged the ache of loss. How odd, she thought, that after so long I'm going through a sort of grief at separation. And how unexpected. She stared with blurred vision at the chair Liz had sat in, at the bottle and the glass Liz had drunk from. She was being silly, Hazel told herself. When it was her decision to leave, when she could throw herself into Liz's arms any time she chose, when the only obstacle between them was her own will to stay apart.

Hazel swiveled around in her chair and stared out at the sky, at the windows of the rose-glass building three blocks away, at the glimpse of Capitol Hill and the Cascades visible from her window. She made herself think of what it would be like if she returned to Liz. And then she turned from the window and went back to compiling the list of things she needed to do to prepare for the meeting of North American monitors scheduled for the first week in October.

# Chapter Seventy-two

"Of all of us, Lee knew her best," Beatrice said. In the fading light spilling down on them through the high windows that faced north, Beatrice's workshop looked its usual comfortable quotidian self in spite of the shock making Celia's bowels writhe. Beatrice, she supposed, would be considered an artisan rather than an artist. But Celia found Beatrice's artistry far more to her taste than that of any of Emily's Mytilene crowd and her workshop a place of both comfort and beauty. At the moment, though, its comfort and beauty felt strangely unreal. Here they were sitting on a rug Beatrice had woven, propped up against cushions Beatrice had also made, drinking wine and chatting, while at the very same time that other world continued on, conterminous, like a parallel universe.

Celia had met Jo Josepha only twice, but she retained a vivid memory of her. Not only had Jo appealed to Celia because of certain values they shared, but she had stood out from all the women who attended those meetings. Jo had locked horns with Martha Greenglass's group even though almost everyone else had either stayed neutral or lined up behind Greenglass. She had not seemed tired at all though she had been struggling for longer than anyone Celia had ever met—before the Blanket, even. She had been a practical woman, working as others of diverse political and philosophical persuasions did within the Boston Collective, something Celia could not imagine ever happening in LA or San Diego. Apart from the difficulty of organizing people of different politics, one always had the sense that organizing within one single entity would give ODS a more direct target and perhaps a nearly justifiable reason to go after them—for organizations were more of a threat to the system than the same number of individuals working separately, and perhaps were susceptible to manipulation... Celia no longer felt certain of the rights and wrongs of political involvement... Could she still describe herself as "neutral"? If she had lived in Boston, wouldn't she have joined them? It might have seemed necessary to her, as it had to Jo Josepha...

"Kelly and the others were ambivalent about leaving," Sorben said. "But they feel there's little they can do right now in Boston. Only militants using violence against the government are choosing to stay."

"It sounds as though ODS has gone on rampage," Beatrice said. "I can't remember things ever being this extreme. Shooting people down in the street and leaving them there...not to mention the mass disappearances and the bodies being found in vacant lots..." Beatrice wrapped her arms around herself. "What in the hell is going on, Sorben?"

*Shot down in the street*—Jo Josepha's end. Celia remembered her grin as she had handed her a cup of coffee in that monastery in Ecuador. *You're either very foolish or very brave.* Jo had said that to her, Celia. While clearly underplaying the danger of her own situation.

Celia asked, "Are you sure they were ODS?" Damn, her voice was tremoring. They were all looking at her. And then looking away. With the kindest intentions, of course.

Sorben wasn't looking away, though. "There are strong indications it was ODS, Celia. No other groups have taken to acting openly in the streets like that. Even in what they call the Gray Zones."

"What on earth are Gray Zones?" Beatrice asked.

"They're areas fenced off from contact with the rest of the city," Sorben said. "ODS justifies doing this in Boston and LA by claiming that this is the only way violent subversives can be contained. Unlike most other areas of the city, it's much more difficult getting in and—especially—out of Gray Zones."

"They sound like big prisons."

"You might put it that way. At any rate, a large number of the women in the Boston Collective lived in one of these Gray Zones. We expected an initial response of stepped-up retaliation, but I'm surprised ODS started openly shooting people in the streets in one of those areas, since the Gray Zones are the areas most likely to take the part of the victims and react violently."

"Bastards," Celia muttered.

"Some kind of response is needed," Emily said. "Response to this escalation, I mean. I wish we could get the population of the United States to see exactly what the reality of their political structures are.

As it is, Sedgewick and Whitney and whoever else is orchestrating the slaughter will get away with it politically, since all they have to do is go on foisting the same tired old mythology onto the public, who since they've always bought it will unthinkingly go on buying it." Her mouth twisted with angry disgust, and Celia had to wonder if it was "the public" she was really disgusted with. "But what else can we expect, when they believe all that nonsense about elected officials? When I think of how the person on the street thinks that Wayne Stoddard is running this country... It makes me feel everything is hopeless. Because if they can buy that big a lie, they'll buy anything."

"It's not that we haven't tried our damnedest to discredit the mythology," Beatrice said. "But somehow the executives have this credibility that we just can't seem to crack. It doesn't matter how many times people see them caught in lies—somehow it all washes off."

"It's more comfortable for most people to believe the lie," Sorben said. "And even if they don't believe the lie, until there's massive discomfort, a government's credibility doesn't actually matter unless a genuine participatory democracy is in place."

"And even when there's massive discomfort they can often find scapegoats," Beatrice said. "They're still claiming everything is the Marq'ssan's fault. Just as they claimed Kay Zeldin was responsible for starting the Civil War."

I should stop drinking wine, Celia thought. I'm going to need to take a pill tonight. There's no doubt about it. The way my body's shaking, if I don't knock myself out I'll be waking up screaming, all night long. Celia watched Beatrice light a half dozen of the scented candles Sweetwater made and sold all over the Free Zone. Beatrice was so serene, even in anger. And Susan had said that even she had had some bad times, before Sweetwater, that she had been raped, forty years ago. According to Susan, Beatrice remembered very little about the experience, except that it had happened. But of course not remembering didn't mean not being scarred. Sometimes when Beatrice's gray eyes looked into Celia's it felt as though a golden elixir exuded from Beatrice, surrounding and seeping into Celia by osmosis, and then she would be warmed and feel strong and good and would know she would make a sound decision about what to do next. She would feel all this in spite of the irritation she sometimes felt toward Beatrice—irritation at Beatrice's lack of understanding about the law and the ethical principles now so lacking in the world...

"I'm not discouraged," Sorben was saying. "In spite of this recent escalation of violence, I think we *are* seeing change. It's a slow thing, you know. There's no way it can happen over night. It certainly didn't on Marqeuei."

"Maybe the escalation is inspired by fear?" Beatrice said—in a doubtful tone of voice.

"Perhaps," Sorben said. "It's hard to know the reasons policies take shape and are carried out. It's seldom so simple as one particular cause. I imagine they are quite frightened by our liberation of their prisons. It was a reminder that their control is not absolute."

Emily said, "The Marq'ssan are beyond them. They don't even know how to think about you, much less attempt to control you. As far as I know, most executives don't talk much about Marq'ssan. As though to deny you are there."

"And then the Marq'ssan make them acknowledge their presence by doing something like liberating a prison," Beatrice said, grinning.

"Thereby challenging the executive construction of reality," Emily concluded.

"While in the meantime people are dying," Celia said, half under her breath. They all must have heard her, she thought, judging by the expressions on their faces. How dare she rain on their parade: she knew that's what they were all thinking. "Things weren't this bad before the Blanket," she said defiantly, though not looking at Sorben.

"That's a matter of opinion," Beatrice said into the tense silence.

"But that's a long discussion we should save for another night," Sorben said to Celia. "There's a lot that I could tell you about things before the Blanket. I was an observer on this planet for years. But I can't stay long tonight, so it's best that we wait till another time to talk about it." She smiled. "That's assuming you'd like to talk about it?"

"Of course." Since when did a lawyer back down from a discussion on the premise that she would lose the debate? She, Celia, was not like the Sweetwater women or Martha Greenglass or any of those types. Not that she meant to put down service-techs, but her understanding was well-grounded in a thorough education and training that left people like Greenglass and Beatrice handicapped in conversation.

"Someone told me," Celia thought to say, "that Marq'ssan don't consider gender to be important, that you choose to appear as women to us for political reasons. Is that true?" Sorben nodded. "Then what true gender as a Marq'ssan are you?" Celia asked.

Sorben laughed. "Amazing. I've just realized that no one has ever asked me that question before! Okay, Celia, I'll tell you, though I assure you it makes no difference whatsoever. Biologically I am male—that is, I don't naturally produce eggs, but am naturally able to fertilize them. Although if I wished, I *could* produce eggs, since we are able to change our bodies as we wish."

"You don't feel odd dealing only with women then?" Celia asked curiously.

Sorben laughed again. "To tell you the truth, Celia, I never have quite understood about gender differences, except in an abstract way that I suppose you might describe as political. For me, assuming a human body is far stranger than assuming a *female* body." Her grin faded. "There's another biological difference that used to seem highly significant to me. And that's a difference determined by what we Marq'ssan call ambient. One's ambient—which, after a long history of deliberate genetic engineering—was visibly marked on one's body and determined where one lived and the languages one spoke and the sorts of relations one had with those of other ambients. There are altogether seventy-eight ambients on Marqeuei. We still include our ambient in our names. A remnant of our past, and one we've heavily debated over the years." Sorben sighed. "But that's another night's discussion, too." She nodded at Beatrice. "Beatrice can tell you some of it."

Beatrice raised her eyebrows. "Frankly, I don't understand much of what Sorben and Magyyt have told me. It's too different from anything I've ever heard of."

"It's morphologically similar to relations on your world," Sorben said. "But I must go now." She rose to her feet. "I imagine that once Kelly gets some rest she'll want to work on a media project in response to the Boston situation. You'll get her connected up with the appropriate people, Beatrice?"

Beatrice also stood. "Of course. Though I think she already knows some of them."

"And let me know if you need technical assistance," Sorben added.

Beatrice and Sorben left the barn together, leaving Celia and Emily alone. Emily shifted so that she directly faced Celia. "Jo Josepha was the lawyer you told me about?" she said softly.

"Yes," Celia said, her voice uncomfortably husky. "God she was frustrated. She'd been underground for more than ten years. Caught between militants on the one hand and pacifist anarchists on the other. Did she know that was how it would end?" Celia wondered, then shook her head. "No. Of course not. No one ever really believes it will end that way. It's not something thinkable." Celia clasped her hands tightly together. "But she was living so dangerously. I mean, for her the situation was cut and dried, the way it wasn't for me or my mother or Luis—or you, Em. She knew that if she were caught, they'd—" Celia broke off, unable to put any of it into words. ODS had been after Jo for years. That said it all. Emily nodded. "It's hard for me to imagine, now, how she could have stuck it out. When all she had to do was to ask the Marq'ssan to evacuate her. But she was committed."

Emily's gaze held steady. "Don't think that means, Cee, that everyone should be that way. I'm not at all sure that that was the best thing for Jo to have done. Maybe she would have accomplished more if she'd left."

Celia swallowed. "It's easier to think that. Though she did say she hadn't been able to practice law for years." Celia's eyes filled with tears. "I'm so confused," she whispered. "On the one hand I can barely hold myself together even in a place as safe and sheltered as this. On the other hand I keep feeling I should go back, underground. Because there will be fewer and fewer people with legal expertise available to help. And because the way things are going, no one will want to serve as monitor."

"No, Cee, you first have to take care of yourself." Emily scooted across the rug. She put her arm around Celia's shoulders. "You can't be useful until you're healed."

"I am healed," Celia said, furious at the tears she could not seem to stop.

"No, Cee, I wish that were true, but it's not. And you know it too. You need to love yourself, Cee. Only then can you make the kind of judgments you seem compelled to make."

"Oh god, I wish I could go *away* from myself!" Sobbing, Celia let Emily put her arms around her. "I hate being me," Celia gasped, "I wish I could start over! Because here I am, free, and all I do is wallow in it, dreaming terrible things and always so afraid."

When Celia quieted, Emily, stroking Celia's hair, said, "You were strong enough to survive, Cee, you were brave enough to keep on though you knew what they might do to you. And you have so much you can do ahead of you. Only you have to give yourself a chance now. Your strength makes *me* feel like a weakling, Cee. It was you and your mother and Luis who showed me the way, who made me realize I had to take even the limited chances I took. You don't have to get killed to prove your usefulness or strength, you know."

Celia blew her nose. She felt drained, empty, exhausted. "Imagine," Celia said. "I wake up out of a nightmare into this paradise where I'm safe and people are so kind to me—and I'm miserable."

"Nightmares hang around for a time, deep inside us," Emily said. "They're horrible because they touch us in the deepest places of our psyches. There's no such thing as a trivial nightmare. No matter how paradisial our surroundings when we escape from them."

Celia looked at Emily with surprise. "What you say...makes sense to me, Em." Something so simple seemed somehow to say so much.

"The only problem is that getting out of the tentacles of the nightmare's traces is sometimes a hard thing to do, Cee. It's hard work. And takes a strong stomach. That's where strength and bravery will be most needed." Now Emily's eyes filled with tears. "I wish you didn't have to be so alone to do it, Cee. Because it's your own strength and determination and bravery that will heal you. But we're with you, Cee. We love you. *I* love you."

Celia embraced Emily, pressing herself close to this woman she felt so deeply about. She might not be able to make sense of the insanity of the world, but at least she had Emily.

# Chapter Seventy-three

In darkness, Hazel groped her way through the deactivation of the alarm and heaved open one of the balcony's plate-glass doors and stepped out into the night. She stood a long time at the railing listening to the wind rustling through the trees. The claws of fear gripped her for a few seconds as she thought of how there might be someone below, watching the house—watching for her. But she stared up at the sharp thin sickle of moon suspended above the trees, waiting... Motionless, she breathed in the fragrance of geraniums and—closing her eyes—felt the breeze brushing the silk of her gown against her legs. She pressed her hands against her breasts. The surge of sexual feeling, of tingling, trembling desire had taken her by surprise. After everything that had happened, still her body responded to the caress in Liz's voice.

Hazel opened her eyes and stared out at the whispering trees, out at the dark branches she could barely distinguish against the night sky.

Desire for Liz, yes. But not enough to give up...all this. To give up the feelings blooming inside her even as she stood here wanting to make love to Liz—no. Impossible. She had discovered other seductions that drew her further and further from Liz's world. The seduction of being a part of those lengthy—interminable, some of the older women called them—discussions. Discussions fascinating for their excursions into realms of what-if: *what if we try such-and-such*...or, *what if we do that*...realms of what-if that were not idle talk, but preparation for action. The Co-op women were creating reality as they went, not succumbing to larger forces as Liz, for all her power, did and had always done... Liz supposedly would make her an honorary executive if only she would return to the household. To *choose* to be an executive? Unthinkable. No, Liz, no. I choose this reality, I shall *create* reality, not submit to the reality that rules you. Nor can I think of crossing back and forth between these two parallel universes existing at one and the same time. Not even that, Liz. Not even for love. Come to my universe if you like, but don't think I'll ever return to yours.

Hazel lifted her arms, stretched them wide and high as though embracing the night extending out all around her. "I choose!" she sang out, ecstatic. "I choose! I choose this life!" She threw her head back and laughed and felt the wind wrapping her gown around her body as a great gust swept through the trees. And the silver sharp sickle of moon hanging above the trees glittered, waiting...

*Seattle*
*October 1985–February 1986*
*revised November 1996*

Coming Summer '08

# *Stretto*

## *Book Five of the Marq'ssan Cycle*

**Don't miss the Grand Finale of the Marq'ssan Cycle!**

The final volume of the Marq'ssan Cycle opens in January 2096. Now stable and thriving, the Pacific Northwest Free Zone has become a base for change across the continent. In the United States, the career-line women led by Elizabeth Weatherall now hold positions of importance in the Executive and are attempting to enact a reformist, liberal agenda. Security operative Ann Hawthorne, recalled from the Free Zone to headquarters in DC, finds that her difficulty adjusting to life in the executive system is more than the "culture shock" she first assumes it to be. Hazel Bell, who under the guise of holding "self-help seminars" exports subversive ideas in her frequent trips to the US, heads a large team of activists negotiating change with Elizabeth Weatherall and the Executive. Alexandra Sedgewick, under deadly siege by Weatherall, searches for the transcript Weatherall is desperate to suppress. And Emily Madden, under Astrea's tutelage, learns to "see" the world as the Marq'ssan do.

# About the Author

L. Timmel Duchamp is the author of *Love's Body, Dancing in Time*, a collection of short fiction; *The Grand Conversation: Essays; The Red Rose Rages (Bleeding)*, a short novel; and *Alanya to Alanya, Renegade*, and *Tsunami*, the first three novels of the five-volume Marq'ssan Cycle. She is also the editor of *Talking Back: Epistolary Fantasies* and *The WisCon Chronicles, Vol. 1*. She has been a finalist for the Nebula and Sturgeon awards and short-listed several times for the James Tiptree, Jr., Award, and will be a Guest of Honor at WisCon 32 in May 2008. Her stories have appeared in a variety of venues, including *Asimov's SF* and the *Full Spectrum, Leviathan, ParaSpheres*, and *Bending the Landscape* anthology series; and her critical essays have appeared in *The American Book Review, The New York Review of Science Fiction, Extrapolation, Foundation*, and *Lady Churchill's Rosebud Wristlet*. A selection of her stories and essays can be found on her website: http://ltimmel.home.mindspring.com. She lives in Seattle.

Coming from Aqueduct in 2008

# Centuries Ago and Very Fast

## by Rebecca Ore

*When I first met him running on the moors, I thought he was gypsy or part Paki with his otter body and the broad head that ended in an almost pointed chin, but he said he was European, old stock, some French in the bloodlines. His left little finger ended just below where the nail would have been...*

A gay immortal born in the Paleolithic who jumps time at will, Vel has hunted mammoths, played with reindeer tripping on hallucinogenic mushrooms, negotiated with each successive wave of invaders to keep his family and its land intact, lived as the minor god of a spring, witnessed the hanging of "mollies" in seventeenth-century London as well as the Stonewall riots in twentieth-century New York City. He's had more lovers than he can remember and is sometimes tempted to flirt with death. *Centuries Ago and Very Fast* offers fascinating, often erotic glimpses of the life of a man who has just about seen it all.

*England, that has such beautiful men in it, wasn't even an island when Vel was born, and Vel was born in drowned country between here and there...*